Tyrants, Dictators And Kings

Part I Libertas

Book 7

Of The Warrior Series

By

Sandra J Yearman

Seraphim Publishing LLC

We Will Bring Light To All The Dark Places

Registered trademark-Sandra J Yearman

Seraphim Publishing
438 Water St
Cambridge, WI 53523
sandrajyearman@gmail.com

Library of Congress Catalog Number: 2015900908

ISBN: 978-0-9890263-5-2

First Edition

About The Author

Sandra J Yearman is a native of Wisconsin, where she currently resides. She graduated from the University of Wisconsin with a Bachelor of Arts degree in Journalism. Sandra was a member of the United States Army Reserves for over twenty years. She retired from the Dane County Sheriff's Office in Madison Wisconsin as a sergeant.

Sandra is a cancer survivor. And it is on this journey that she says she found her voice and began to write. She established Seraphim Publishing LLC in 2008. Sandra has spent decades supporting and working with rescued domestic animals.

Books written by Sandra:

<u>Novels</u>

Brother Kings
The Scroll And The Sword
Song Of The Second Son
The Faces Of The Damned
A Single Lion Roars
Stand Before The Children
Tyrants, Dictators And Kings

Poetry

This Book

Is Dedicated To All

People Who Desire To

Be Free.

Contents

7

Chapter I
The Gift

"We came as soon as we heard," Bekka said as she entered Gabriel's house. "Hannah these are my parents Sam and Ella, they didn't want me to make the trip alone."

"You are more than welcomed here, please come in," Hannah said. "We are all still so in shock. Lila was so young and healthy, she had no problems with her pregnancy then…" Hannah paused as she tried to compose herself. "Honestly I am not really sure what did happen."

"Where is everyone?" Bekka asked as tears continued to stream down her face. "It's so quiet."

"Elan, Cassandra, Melinda and Vivian took all of the children on a walk to try and cheer them up. Please come into the dining room and I will fix you something," Hannah said and led Bekka's family from the front foyer. "Maxwell and Emeral are with Luca making funeral arrangements. The baby lived but Luca won't even look at her. Vitomas and Annabelle have been taking care of Emma because they are still nursing babies."

As Hannah walked into the kitchen, Ella said. "Hannah you look like you haven't slept in days, I will help you." Moments after Hannah and Ella disappeared behind the kitchen door a dog could be heard barking then the voices of children started to fill the house.

"Bekka," Nicholas yelled. "Christopher, Bekka is here." Nicholas ran to Bekka and hugged her. Christopher ran into the dining room and the other children stood back as Christopher ran to Bekka. She lifted him onto her lap and hugged Christopher tightly as they both cried.

"Hello I am Sam, I'm Bekka's father," Sam said as he held his hand out to Vivian.

"I'm Vivian, Raphael's wife."

"We are sorry," Cassandra said and hugged Sam. "We should have introduced you; Sam is Ella here too?"

"She's in the kitchen with Hannah."

"Where's mother?" Vivian asked as Hannah and Ella walked out of the kitchen carrying trays of food and coffee.

"She took your brothers into the city. They are buying groceries and some other things," Hannah replied wearily.

After Elan, Melinda and Cassandra hugged both Sam and Ella, Elan asked Hannah, "Have you given them rooms yet?"

"No, Elan would you please take care of that?" Hannah asked as she poured coffee. Bekka was still holding Christopher so Cassandra and Elan motioned for Ella and Sam to come with them.

As soon as the four were walking up the stairs to the bedroom chambers, Cassandra said. "Hannah is a wonderful physician and she has been so filled with guilt because she couldn't save Lila that she hasn't been able to eat or sleep. It's all just so sad."

Elan opened the door to a small parlor. "There are three bedrooms in here and a balcony," he said. "We do have other empty chambers if you don't like this."

"This is beautiful," Ella said. "This home is incredible."

"We keep adding onto it because the family is growing," Cassandra said. Then she thought she should explain. "I should have said the team but really we have all become one huge family."

"That's exactly what Bekka has said also," Sam said. "And speaking of family, I know more people are coming from the Ice Caves for the funeral."

"Good," Elan said. "Luca wanted to delay the funeral so the rest of the team could come back for it. It will probably be a few more days before everyone gets here."

"We are really glad you came," Cassandra said. "Bekka and Christopher have a special bond and he really needs her right now."

"Well, we just fell in love with that boy when he came to visit," Ella said. "The poor little thing has seen so much tragedy in his life."

When Cassandra, Elan, Ella and Sam returned to the dining room, Bekka and Luca were hugging and crying. Sam picked up Christopher and hugged the boy as he and Ella walked towards their old friends Emeral and Maxwell. "We are glad you came," Emeral said as tears ran down her face. "We have all just fallen apart."

"Lakin and others will be arriving tomorrow or the next day," Sam said to Maxwell. "While we are here let us know what we can do."

"I just can't stop crying," Natasha said as she soared in the air in Calen's arms. "How could something like this happen?"

"Honey we will never know," Calen said sadly. "I can't even imagine what Luca is going through."

"You really should have left me at my castle," Erebus said as he had said many times before. Dack was carrying Erebus as Gabriel's team was returning home for Lila's funeral.

"Considering it was full of demons when we got there that wouldn't have been smart and you know it," Dack said then his voice softened. "I know you lost your wife not too long ago; if it's too difficult for you to stay at the house I am sure you can stay at the castle."

Erebus did not speak for several moments. "For such a young man you are pretty perceptive," Erebus said with a sad smile.

"Duncan it is about time that you called to us," Miranda scolded as she and Daniel appeared in Duncan's home.

"I know," Duncan said sadly. "But I thought we would find them. Tell me are my sons alive?"

"Yes but not for long," Daniel warned. "Hecate is going to try and run the trials."

"Never has a demon with status and power lower than an Old One attempted such a feat. She knows little of what she is doing which puts many more in danger besides George and Ivan."

"Tell me what must I do to save my boys?" Duncan asked fearfully. "Must I kill Sampson?"

"If you kill Sampson now, Hecate would kill your other sons just for revenge," Daniel said. "Duncan we need you to tell us exactly what you want the heavens to do."

"I want you to help me save George and Ivan and to stop Sampson's transformation. I know I should have prayed for help sooner."

Over the next two days Christopher spent all of his time with Bekka. Daily most of the women at the house would go to the castle at different times to visit baby Emma, who was a healthy baby girl.

"We owe you so much," Emeral said as she and Ella were visiting Raul and Vitomas who took primary care of Emma."

"It's the least we can do," Vitomas said. "She really is a good baby."

"Luca is living out my worst nightmare," Raul said seriously. "Every time Vitomas gives birth I am terrified I am going to lose her. Honesty we can't do enough to help. But I am surprised that Luca still hasn't come to see the baby."

"Maxwell and I plan to talk to him," Emeral said as she held her granddaughter. "I am not trying to make excuses but we are all just so in shock. Ella and Sam have been so much help because it's like the rest of us can't think any more."

"I don't think one person in that house has had a night's sleep since Lila died," Ella said softly. "I am just so glad that Sam and I came and could be of help."

Adrone ran into the house as Hannah, Vivian and Iris were preparing the midday meal. "Raphael is home," Adrone yelled then ran back outside.

11

Vivian quickly ran out of the house and was followed by the rest of the family. It was only Raphael, Koby and Dagon who were in the yard. Koby was shocked to see Bekka and her parents walk out of the house and he quickly walked up to them and hugged them all.

"Where is Luca?" Dagon asked.

"He doesn't come out of his chambers much these days," Hannah said. "You should go to him."

"I don't know why," Vivian said as she hugged and kissed Raphael. "Now that I see you I can't stop crying. Her death was horrible Raphael." Then Vivian stepped back. "You should go with Koby and Dagon, Luca needs to see you."

"Raphael are others coming?" asked Hannah.

"The rest of our group is staying at the castle. They said they didn't want to intrude but to let them know if we need help. Isn't Gabriel's group back?"

"No," Hannah replied. "I will be so glad when he gets home."

Dagon was the first to enter Luca's chambers and found Luca lying on his bed. The room was dark because the drapes were closed. Luca was so lost in his pain that he didn't realize Dagon was in the room until Koby and Raphael entered also. Dagon pulled the drapes open so sunlight could fill the room. Koby poured four glasses of whiskey and all of the men sat on Luca's bed.

"I'm glad you came," Luca said in a whisper then took a sip of his whiskey.

"We don't really know a lot about what happened," Raphael said. "Would it help if you told us?"

Luca started to speak then stopped so he could compose himself. "I'll try but we may need more whiskey," he said as tears filled his eyes.

It was late afternoon when Gabriel's group entered the house. As Sam and Ella watched the tearful reunion they were surprised to see a man wearing a sorcerers' robe walk into the dining room; but neither of them said anything. After the greetings and introductions most of Gabriel's group went to Luca's chambers to visit him.

"Erebus, Gabriel said you might feel more comfortable staying at the castle but know you are welcomed here also," Hannah said.

"Thank you Hannah, that is kind," Erebus replied.

"At least stay for dinner," said Hannah.

"Thank you I will, it smells very good," Erebus said then he turned to Sam and Ella. "I can read the looks on your faces. Yes I am a sorcerer but Gabriel won't let me stay in my castle because a group of demons attacked us as soon as we arrived."

"What!" Hannah said. "Gabriel didn't say anything about that. Did they know you were coming?"

"Apparently, we believe Hecate to be behind the attack."

"Were any of our people hurt?" Hannah asked with concern.

"Just minor wounds. Fortunately I had put a protection spell on my home so we got advanced notice that I had intruders or we would have been walking into an ambush."

Lila's funeral was held the following morning. Luca's spirit had left him and his body was simply moving. The Sanuri preformed the service which was attended by literally hundreds of people. After Lila was lowered into the ground Luca kept standing at the site as the guests went to the castle for a midday meal.

"Come on son," Maxwell said as he and Calen gently pulled Luca away from the grave which was in the royal cemetery.

Luca felt numb as he walked through the crowd at the castle and spoke with people. Emeral overheard Luca's remarks to Lakin about baby Emma and Emeral knew it was time that she spoke with her son.

Emeral took Luca's arm and walked him into a small room off from the Great Hall. She shut the door then walked up to Luca and hugged him tightly. "My dear son you have this all wrong. That sweet little baby did not kill Lila. That baby is a gift to you from Lila. Only The Great Ruler knows why Lila died when she did and for all we know Lila could have had something wrong with her for a long time."

"But she really didn't leave you because part of her is in Emma and Emma will watch over you and take care of you like Lila would have. After seeing the way that Lila died I suspect she knew something was wrong for a long time but she held on so she could give you the most precious gift that she could. I know you are confused and angry but don't take it out on that child. She needs you."

Luca's body started to tremble as he held onto his mother and cried. Emeral cried too and after a few minutes she said, "Come, I am going to introduce you to your daughter." They returned to the Great Hall and walked up to Raul and Vitomas. "It's time," is all Emeral said and the four walked to the west wing of the castle where two nurses were watching Raul's and Vitomas' children.

"I'll get her," Vitomas said as Raul, Luca and Emeral sat down in the parlor. Within moments Vitomas placed Emma in her father's arms. Emma was dressed in pink and wrapped in a pink blanket. "She's a beautiful baby," Vitomas said. "She looks like Lila with those big green eyes and reddish blonde hair."

Luca stared at Emma in awe for moments before he said in almost a whisper, "Emeral I think you are right." The tears were flowing down Emeral's cheeks as Luca looked at Vitomas and Raul. "Emeral said that she thinks Lila knew something was wrong for a long time but she hung on so she could give me Emma as a gift." Both Raul and Vitomas started to cry.

Chapter II
The Voices of Children

George and Ivan had been kept in total darkness since their capture. They had been captured separately and neither knew where they were or that they both were captives. Hecate ordered this treatment, not so much as a torture but she knew what dangerous warriors they were and she did not want to give them any advantages.

Hecate had been spending less time with her lover Orbus and more time with her husband Sampson as her pregnancy progressed. Demons carried their young for eighteen months, twice as long as humans. Because the baby was half human, Hecate had no idea when she would deliver the baby. While she enjoyed being pregnant she was daily amazed at how quickly her stomach was growing; something she would not have expected with a human baby.

Hecate had no plans of ending her romantic or business relationship with Orbus; but she found herself consumed with what demons called 'the nesting faze' of her pregnancy. Hecate's pregnancy was tempering her ambitions and her taste for blood. Hecate was more interested now in providing for her baby and helping Sampson to complete his trials.

Hecate had decided to oversee the trials herself because she could not get any of the Old Ones to help her. They refused because they were focused on the wars in the hell regions. And because of Hecates' history of turning against her benefactors; no one trusted her. Not that demons ever trusted, it was not in their nature but Hecate had ruined her reputation among the Old Ones.

The problem that Hecate did not share with Sampson was that it was well known that the trials should never be interrupted in any way. Because the being who was undergoing the trials was also undergoing constant transformation of both body and soul. To save Sampson, Hecate had interrupted the trials once; to do so again could have dire consequences for Sampson so Hecate knew she must prepare herself for the task. And that is where her three dark Rualas earned their value to her; because she sent them to the ends of the world to find the things she needed.

15

That fateful evening when Hecate saved Nada, Bruno and Morgan from the Hutas, she made them surrender their souls to her. But as any savvy business woman, Hecate also paid them well. The Rualas were paid for each mission and they received bonuses for every act that was above and beyond what she asked. Hecate was pleased at what enthusiastic workers the Rualas became. It benefited her greatly to have them working for her because she needed to keep her attention on Sampson.

Sampson the strong and vital Venator was suffering from an array of side effects caused by Hecate interrupting his trials. She never admitted to Sampson that she did not understand most of his side effects because she did not want to scare him more than he already was. Nor did Hecate understand why his side effects kept changing. Sampson was in constant pain causing Hecate to often drug him to give him relief.

Hecate could not send her Rualas to the underworlds but people often create their own hell worlds within worlds and to these dangerous and undesirable places she sent the Rualas. Hecate needed information on how to conduct the trials and how to heal Sampson. She was desperate and would try any spell or concoction she heard of. Not only did these things not heal Sampson but some made his symptoms worse. She began to wonder if another more powerful being was preventing Sampson from healing.

"Sanuri how good to see you," Hannah said as she moved so he could enter her house. "What an unexpected surprise. Are you here to see anyone in particular?"

"Actually I would like to speak with as many of you as possible. Maxwell told me that no matter how busy everyone is, your family always gathers for meals. Which is why I am imposing just before your midday meal."

"Sanuri a visit from you is never an imposition. And I insist that you stay and eat with us. My only question is do you want to talk with us over the meal or meet in Gabriel's study?"

"Perhaps the study would be better; away from little ears."

Hannah led the Sanuri into Gabriel's study where most of the men in the house had gathered to discuss the mission.

"The Sanuri would like to meet with all of us, well except the children," Hannah said. "I will gather the others."

"Please have a seat," Gabriel said to the Sanuri. "We are always honored by your visits. Would you like some coffee?"

"You know me so well; yes I would love some."

Behind Gabriel's desk was a large table with trays containing coffee and sweet cakes. As Gabriel poured the Sanuri some coffee, Jasper ran into the room to greet the new visitor. The Sanuri laughed and petted the dog as Jasper licked his face.

Then the dog stopped jumping around and sat and quietly looked at the Sanuri who in turn was staring at the dog. All the men in the room now focused on the Sanuri and Jasper. When Natasha and Hannah entered the study, Natasha started to call to Jasper but Raphael put his hand up for her to be quiet.

All of the adults on the team, except for Melinda were seated in the study before the Sanuri and Jasper broke their intense gaze. "You were talking with him weren't you?" Gabriel asked in amazement.

"Yes and I will tell you in a moment but aren't we missing some people?" the Sanuri asked as he looked around the crowded room.

"Bekka and her parents did not come because they aren't part of the team," Koby said. "Would you like me to get them?"

"Yes, please and I will wait until you return before I share with everyone what Jasper said."

"Well, if we have a few minutes I am going to bring in more coffee and sweet cakes," Natasha said and quickly left the room.

Natasha walked back into the study moments before Sam, Ella and Bekka entered with Koby. "Sam would you close the door please?" the Sanuri asked as he stood up in front of the group. "First of all I wanted to meet with you for a variety of reasons. Hannah I can smell food cooking, if this meeting goes too long we can finish it after the meal, so tell me when to stop."

"When I first entered your home I asked The Great Ruler to heal all of you from the horror and the guilt you feel because of Lila's death. I do not know why such a young and seemingly healthy woman died but you know how Lila lived. She would want all of you to love each other and baby Emma."

As the Sanuri spoke crying could be heard within the room. "Lila loved you all very much and being part of this large and crazy family brought her great happiness. I don't know if she can see you now but if she can I know her heart would break at the pain you are all in."

"It's Christopher that I worry about," Bekka said. "He has seen so much death in his life."

"Bekka stop and think about what you just said," the Sanuri said warmly. "Everyone in this home, including the children have seen more than their share of death. But it is the love that all of you share that will help you to heal. Christopher will heal also, but he is not the only child impacted by Lila's death."

The Sanuri paused, "Just a few moments ago I had a very interesting conversation with Jasper." Everyone in the room smiled when the Sanuri said these words. "Now mind you I am a bit prejudice but I believe that animals are truly one of the most wonderful gifts from The Great Ruler. Your loyal dog had a horrible home which he ran away from, only to nearly starve to death in the forest. That was until the morning he heard the voices of children. Jasper is filled with gratitude for the life he has now and he loves all of you very much. He sees the sadness in you and it breaks his heart."

"He told me that Lila would take him for walks and several times she collapsed. Jasper would stay with her to protect her but she never told any of you what happened. Jasper too loved Lila and he didn't understand why so many times she would stop along their walks and sit down and cry."

"But why wouldn't she tell me?" Hannah cried. "I could have helped her."

"Hannah I can't tell you exactly but I don't think you could have helped her and Lila realized that. She did not want to distress any of you. But I have been told that she prayed many times to live long enough to deliver Emma."

The Sanuri now turned to Luca. "I know initially you blamed Emma for Lila's death. That is not what happened. If you want to honor Lila, love Emma and Christopher with all of your heart." Everyone in the room was crying although they did not realize they were also healing.

"Jasper told me some other things also," the Sanuri continued. "He sees the goodness in all of you yet he asked me how much you can see. Animals have many gifts, they can see Angels and demons when humans can't. He has seen Angel's in the children's playroom and sometimes walking in the house. But that first morning when he found you he saw demons in the forest and they were following you. Apparently some of you take the children into the forest every week for training. Jasper follows so he can watch for demons."

Every man and woman in the room was shocked at what the Sanuri was saying. "Has he seen demons during the training sessions?" Gabriel asked.

"He says he only saw them the first time."

"How will we know if he sees them again?" asked Thor.

The Sanuri now looked at Jasper who was lying at his feet. "He will look at them and growl. I don't need to tell you that only the most powerful demons can keep their forms from you. If that happens just call out to the Angels."

"But now I must change the subject. I will be leaving for Ryed tomorrow; in fact The Lion was specific as to the time I should leave. Nada, Morgan and Bruno have sold their souls to Hecate and are doing her bidding. Both of Duncan's sons disappeared a few days ago but Duncan did not ask the Angel's in until last night. I will be staying with the Clan of Gesmal for a while."

"We will go with you," Thor said and jumped out of his chair.

"No they want all of you to continue with your mission as planned but I am sure we will be working together at times."

"We were making changes to some of the plans when you arrived," Gabriel said. "Lakin and some of the other Rualas who came for the funeral will be accompanying both my group and Raphael's group now."

19

"Calen and Natasha are going to remain here and help take care of the family and Koby is trying to decide if he wants to stay back since Bekka's baby is due in a matter of weeks."

Gabriel now looked at Bekka, Sam and Ella. "You would be more than welcomed to stay until the baby is born. Your presence here has been a blessing to us all. You have helped our family when we were incapacitated with grief."

Emeral turned and looked at Ella and Sam. "You should stay for a while," she said. "Gabriel is right."

"We will discuss it," Sam said with a warm smile.

"Are there any other changes?" the Sanuri asked.

"No," Raphael replied.

"I think the changes you have made will be good for everyone," the Sanuri said. "The Lion wants you to wait at least a week before you leave again."

"Did he say why?" Raphael asked.

"No and I didn't ask him." The Sanuri now turned and stared at Misha and Diana who were sitting with Vivian and Thor in the front of the room. "Since I walked into this room I keep seeing the same scene. Misha and Diana I see the two of you climbing up a very dark and bleak mountain and each of you is holding a small boy with blonde hair. I cannot tell if the boys are humans or Rualas."

"We've been talking about starting a family and Diana has picked two names for sons," Misha replied.

"I don't really understand what I am seeing but I don't think that is it."

Chapter III
Unforgiven

The following morning Sudfad's family and guests had just taken their seats at the dining room table while Marie was carrying in trays of food. "I have just one more tray and I will be right back," she said and left the room.

"So what time will you be leaving?" Sudfad asked the Sanuri.

"Stop! You cannot go in there," Marie yelled.

"He will see me," bellowed a man angrily.

"Guards!" screamed Marie. "My Lord!"

Raul, Simon, Archetenus and Sudfad jumped up from the table as a man in a ranger's cloak burst into the dining room. Marie was running behind the man and two soldiers quickly caught up with the intruder and grabbed each of his arms. The mysterious figure appeared to be a large man. His riding boots were well worn as were his leather pants. A green and brown cloak covered his shirt while the hood concealed his head.

Once the man entered the dining room he stood silent and motionless as he faced Sudfad. The soldiers started to pull the man from the room. "We are sorry My Lord," uttered one of the soldiers.

"Wait," ordered Sudfad, who was still standing at the table. "What is the meaning of this sir?" Sudfad asked the intruder.

"My mother was Nadia of the Kozach Tribe," said the angry voice.

Sudfad's face turned white and he paused for a moment before speaking again. "A man shows his face," Sudfad said sternly. "Remove the hood." Since the man's arms were restrained one of the soldiers pulled the hood down exposing the man's head. Renya gasped and put her hands to her face. The entire room was silent as the angry young man boldly stared into the eyes of each of the adults at the table. When the intruder and Raul met eyes they both stared at each other with horror.

"Raul, you could be twins," gasped Vitomas.

21

Raul and the man continued to stare at each other in silence until little Ariel held out her arms and said "Papa" to the intruder. The man looked at Ariel, then for the first time he seemed to notice all of the small children and babies in the room. As the man looked at them a great sadness consumed him and his anger appeared to leave his body.

"Son, what is your name?" Sudfad asked softly.

"Michael, my name is Michael," the man said as he turned and looked at Sudfad.

"That will be all," Sudfad said as he dismissed the soldiers. "Marie, would you bring a plate for Michael?" Sudfad motioned for Michael to take a seat at the table. Everyone else sat in stunned silence.

"Tell me of your mother," Sudfad requested.

"She died this spring and on her deathbed she finally told me who my father was," Michael spat.

"Son, you have to believe that I didn't know," Sudfad said with sincerity.

"But you never came back," Michael said emotionally.

"She told me not to," Sudfad said, then he turned to his left and placed his hand on top of Renya's hand. "Honey do you remember me telling you about Nadia?" Renya nodded but did not speak.

"Please everyone continue eating," implored Sudfad. "When I was a very young man, I talked my adopted father, King Alexandras into building military outposts in various locations of the kingdom so we could better protect our people. He agreed with my ideas and had me oversee the construction at the sites. When I was at Fort Nir I met a beautiful young girl named Nadia. We fell in love and I asked her to return with me to Salar. She told me that since birth she had been promised to another and she would not dishonor her family. She told me to leave and never to return to her. My heart was broken and I returned to Salar."

"I swear by all I believe is holy I had no knowledge of a child. Six months later my father sent me to Lentz on business and I saw an extraordinarily beautiful girl full of fire and passion who was trying to break a wild stallion. I married her and she became the love of my life and the mother of my children." As Sudfad spoke he grasped Renya's hand. When Sudfad finished talking, Renya turned to Michael and reaching out her arm she grasped his hand. Renya looked deeply into Michael's eyes and with her normal courage and grace she began to speak.

"Michael I can certainly understand why your heart is filled with anger. But you must know that your father is a wonderful man and a great father. If we would have known of your existence, we would have brought you home long before now."

Michael looked into Renya's eyes without speaking. Tears started to fill his eyes and flow down his cheeks. Suddenly he looked embarrassed and glanced towards the other men to see if they saw him crying. Marie was standing next to the table and she too had tears in her eyes.

"Marie, please show Michael to his chambers," Renya said so Michael would not be embarrassed because he was crying in front of the family. "He can have the rooms next to the Sanuri." Then looking back at Michael, Renya said in a soothing tone, "I am sure you could use a hot bath and some rest."

Michael stood up and turned to follow Marie when Sudfad said, "I will have the soldiers bring your things in."

Without turning Michael replied, "I am wearing all I own." and walked out of the room.

The Sanuri had been watching Michael intently since his appearance in the dining room. After a few moments the Sanuri said, "Now, we have Seven Sons." Everyone at the table turned and looked at the Sanuri but no one spoke. The entire family appeared to be stunned until Vitomas broke the silence.

"Raul, he has nothing, could I give him some of your clothes so he at least has something clean to change into?"

"Of course," said Raul and kissed Vitomas' hand.

23

Vitomas left the dining room and hurried to the west wing. She felt like crying although she did not understand why. She chose an outfit and hurried to Michael's chambers, as she did not want to disturb him once he started his bath. Vitomas knocked on the door. "Michael it is Vitomas I have some clothes for you."

When Michael opened the door he was not wearing a shirt. "These belong to Raul but they are clean until we can get you some new things," Vitomas said. "Michael who did that to you?" Vitomas was staring at the numerous scars that covered Michael's broad chest and muscular arms."

"Thank you," Michael said as he gently took the clothes from Vitomas' hands and closed the door.

When Vitomas returned to the dining room, Raul stood up when he saw the look on her face. "Vitomas are you alright? Did he do something to you?"

"No, no Honey it is nothing like that," said Vitomas as she took her seat at the table. "When Michael opened the door he wasn't wearing a shirt. Raul his entire body is covered with horrible scars. He looks like he has been whipped."

Michael did not return to the dining room for breakfast nor did he leave his chambers. Shortly before lunch, Sudfad knocked on the door to Michael's chambers. Michael opened the door without speaking. "Son, I don't even know where to begin," Sudfad said. Michael motioned for Sudfad to enter the room and take a seat.

"You are part of this family now Michael. I realized that I didn't introduce you to anyone this morning and I apologize for that. I guess I was so stunned that I forgot my manners. Son, we have a lifetime to catch up on. I hope you plan to live here in the castle with us. I don't want to lose you again." Michael stared at Sudfad with disbelief as he listened to his words. Sudfad stood up and walked to the door. "Lunch will be served in half an hour, plan to join us in the same room we were in this morning."

After Sudfad left Michael collapsed in a chair. He had hated his real father all of his life for leaving him and his mother with that monster. Michael's stepfather was a cruel and vicious man.

Michael bore the brunt of his stepfather's rage simply because Michael was not his blood son. When Michael found out that his father was the King of Wetpr, a man of wealth and means who could have saved him anytime, he lost control. Every mile that he traveled towards Salar, Michael thought about ways of killing Sudfad. Michael expected to do battle with Sudfad's family and he expected to lose his own life. But Michael never expected the reception that he received.

Michael had long ago learned to bury his feelings and expectations as the pain was too great. Now he felt overwhelmed and as if his emotions were running wild and he had no control over them. Michael slowly looked around the beautiful rooms he was to live in and tears filled his eyes. Never before had he a bed to sleep in.

"It is uncanny," Vitomas said as she and Annabelle were putting the children in their seats around the small table in the dining room. "If Michael didn't have curly hair and that small scar on his cheek, he and Raul would be identical."

"I felt so sorry for him. I can't even imagine how he feels," said Annabelle. "Did you see him cry when Renya was talking to him?"

"Girls," Marie said loudly as she walked into the room with a stack of dishes. Vitomas and Annabelle were the only two adults in the room; when they looked up Marie motioned that someone was behind her. In a few moments they saw Michael stand in the doorway. He looked uncomfortable and unsure if he should enter. Vitomas and Annabelle both walked up to him.

"We met earlier, I am Vitomas. I am Raul's wife. Raul is the son who looks exactly like you. And this is Annabelle she is married to Simon, he is tall and blonde and another one of your brothers." Each woman took one of Michael's arms and walked him over to the children's table.

"Now we are really going to confuse you by introducing you to all of our children," Annabelle said. "Don't worry we won't expect you to remember all of their names." Annabelle pointed to each child as she said their name then Annabelle said, "Children this is your Uncle Michael."

Michael swung his head around and stared at Annabelle when she said this. Michael, Vitomas and Annabelle all had their backs to the dining room door and did not realize the rest of the family were gathering in the hallway watching them.

Little Samuel reached his arms up for Michael to take him. Michael bent down and picked the child up. No sooner had he done this when Arianna extended her arms to Michael. "Can you hold two?" Annabelle asked.

"Sure," he said with an uncomfortable smile.

Annabelle put Arianna in Michael's other arm. "As you can see most of our children look like their fathers," she said then laughed.

"Oh I don't know, I think she looks just like you," Michael said as he nodded towards Ariel.

"She belongs to Vitomas," said Annabelle. And they all laughed.

"He is smiling," whispered Renya as she and Sudfad stood in the doorway watching.

"Those two girls could charm the devil himself," said Marie with a grin and turned and walked towards the kitchen. Raul and Simon grinned at her comment.

"Michael, Annabelle and I thought we might take you shopping this afternoon; that is unless you would rather have one of the men take you," said Vitomas.

"Oh no, no we can go," said Michael.

"Good," said Annabelle, "We will leave an hour after lunch. We have to put the babies down for their naps first."

"When Raul and Simon brought us here we had been prisoners of King Roch and we didn't have any belongings either. They took us shopping and bought us everything we could need or want. Annabelle and I had never even been in a nice store before, we felt so embarrassed," Vitomas explained.

"You were prisoners?" Michael asked in disbelief.

"We can tell you about it this afternoon," Annabelle said as she turned and saw the family watching them.

"What is everyone standing in the hallway for?" asked Petra as he walked up to the dining room.

"Why, we were waiting for you," replied Sudfad as the family entered the dining room.

"Since I failed to make introductions this morning, everyone, we will do them now before we are seated," said Sudfad. "Michael this is my beautiful wife Renya." Michael was still holding the two children so he just smiled at Renya. "And this is Raul."

Annabelle interrupted. "Let me take her so you can shake hands with your brothers." Annabelle said as she took Arianna out of his arms.

Sudfad continued, "Simon, and Petra. We have one more adopted son named Matthew but he lives in Lentz and we can tell you about him later. These are Annabelle's parents Alexander and Laurel." All the men had been shaking hands with Michael, but Laurel hugged him tightly. "These are friends who are staying with us," Sudfad continued. "This is Archetenus and his wife Delilah and their twins Ava and Benjamin. And this is the Sanuri."

"The Sanuri, is that your name?" asked Michael.

"It is rather more my title," said the Sanuri as he shook Michael's hand.

"What does it mean?" Michael asked.

"In the old language it means wise teacher."

That evening, Raul was lying in bed reading, waiting for Vitomas to join him. "Emma went right to sleep but Miranda was wide awake for a long time," Vitomas said as she slid under the covers and cuddled against Raul. Vitomas kissed his cheek. "Honey there are some things I wanted to tell you when we were alone." Raul put his book on the side table and turned and looked at Vitomas.

"Today when Annabelle and I took Michael shopping, it was so sad. It was like he was afraid to choose anything to wear. And finally he told us he has never had new clothes before." Raul did not say anything.

Vitomas continued, "He was very nice and once we got him to open up a little he was funny. But when we got home, Annabelle and I helped Michael carry his things to his chambers. She and I just started putting his clothes away. I was hanging up his shirts, when I heard Annabelle ask him if he was alright. I turned and saw Michael just standing in the middle of the room looking lost. Annabelle asked him if there was something wrong with his chambers and Raul," Vitomas got tears in her eyes.

"Michael said he wasn't used to all of this. He told us he has never had a bed to sleep in before." Raul put his arms around Vitomas and kissed her on the forehead.

"Honey, I can't imagine how difficult this must be for you and Simon. But Michael is your brother and I think he really needs us. He doesn't say much but I think he has had a horrible life. Raul think about it, what if your roles were reversed; how would you want this family to treat you?"

Raul hugged Vitomas tightly saying, "I don't think I can ever tell you how much I love you. You know Honey you are making me a better person."

"Raul you are a wonderful person; it is like the entire family is feeling some sort of pain since Michael showed up. But no one can change the past."

"What are you doing out here so early," Simon asked. Simon was standing at one of the horse corrals on the royal grounds.

"I thought I would pick out a horse for Michael," Raul replied.

"That is why I am here too."

"Let me guess, did Annabelle have a talk with you last night?" Raul asked with a grin.

"Yes," said Simon. "And I felt guilty all night."

"What do you think about that chestnut stallion?" Raul asked as he and Simon walked around the largest corral. The rays of the sun were just appearing and both men carried lanterns.

"I don't know; I kind of like that black stallion at the far end."

"I suppose we could ask him to pick out his own horse," Raul said.

"From what the girls said, I don't think he would."

"The black stallion it is then," Raul said. "Now let's find him a good saddle."

Almost half of an hour later Raul and Simon joined the rest of the family for breakfast.

"Where have you two been?" asked Annabelle.

"We were picking out a horse for Michael," Simon said. Michael turned and stared at Simon with disbelief. Both Annabelle and Vitomas smiled proudly.

"We are all in the military," Raul said looking at Michael. "So is Archetenus; we thought you might like to join us this morning while we instruct the troops."

"Thank you I would," Michael said. "What are you teaching them?"

"This morning it is hand to hand combat." Raul said. "Have you ever been in the military?"

"No," Michael replied. "But I grew up fighting."

"Excellent," said Archetenus, who could see how uncomfortable Michael appeared.

"So Michael did the girls let you pick out any clothing you liked or did they dress you the way they thought you should be dressed?" Simon asked with a broad grin.

"Oh and look who is talking," said Annabelle as she put her hands on her hips. "Michael don't listen to him. Whenever he and Raul pick out dresses for us they are so tight we can barely move."

"I don't' think I ever noticed that," Raul said and laughed.

"From what some of the people in town were telling me, it sounds like you did a pretty good job teaching your wives how to fight," Michael said as he looked at Simon.

"We took Michael to the Green Dragon Inn, so he could have some of Myla's wonderful desserts," said Annabelle. "And some of the people were telling him about the time Roch's men tried to kidnap us."

Michael looked at Sudfad and said, "They introduced me as your son."

"Well you are Michael," Sudfad said. Then he saw the look on Michael's face. "Did you think I would be mad?"

"Yes."

"Michael I didn't abandon you or disown you; I didn't know you existed," Sudfad said softly. "You are my son and part of this family now."

Michael didn't speak for a few moments then he said apologetically, "The girls are so kind, but they really bought me much more than I need."

"Nonsense son, you are a prince now; and honestly you have no idea of all the responsibilities you just inherited," Sudfad said.

"We got him everything but dress clothes because we didn't know if he was going to be fitted for a uniform," explained Vitomas. Then she looked at Michael. "For ceremonies all the men wear the military uniform."

"And we took him to the jewelers to get fitted for a family ring," Annabelle said sheepishly. Both Sudfad and Renya smiled.

"Good," replied Sudfad. "We will have to add Michael's birth stone to our rings." Renya took off her ring and handed it to Michael.

"The girls designed these. There is a birth stone for every member of the family," explained Renya as Michael examined the ring.

"And with all these grandbabies we all may end up wearing two rings," Renya said smiling.

Michael was looking at the golden emblems of a sword and a scroll on the side of the ring. "I understand a sword but what is the meaning of the scroll?"

"You truly have inherited responsibilities that you could have never imagined," said the Sanuri. "I was supposed to leave for Ryed yesterday but I postponed the trip for two days so Sudfad and I can explain some of these responsibilities to you. Michael, this situation is overwhelming for all of you and Sudfad's family is trying to make you feel welcomed. Perhaps you could tell them a little about your life."

"I am not sure I should talk about it in front of the children," Michael said in almost a whisper.

"They are young, I do not think they will understand," the Sanuri said.

Suddenly Vitomas and Annabelle started to laugh loudly as Marie set a huge chocolate cake in front of Michael. "The girls told me you had never tasted chocolate cake until yesterday, so this one is just for you," Marie said and smiled as she looked at the other sons. "Now don't you worry I made more."

"Thank you Marie," said Michael who was visibly touched by the gesture.

"Michael you know why your mother sent Sudfad away," said the Sanuri. "Why don't you tell us about your stepfather?"

"How do you know these things?" Michael asked as he looked at the Sanuri.

"He is not like other men," said Sudfad. "But he can explain that later."

"I can guarantee you will not like some of what I am about to say," said Michael. "As you know mother was from the Kozach Tribe. The warlord who now leads that tribe in my stepfather. Mother told you she would marry him because she didn't want to dishonor her family. But in truth she married him to prevent her clan from being murdered."

"My stepfather's name is Karzman; he is a cruel dictator of his people." Michael turned to Vitomas and Annabelle. "So much of what you told me yesterday sounded familiar. Our childhoods were not all that different." Vitomas grasped Raul's hand as they listened to Michael speak.

"Karzman is a huge man with red hair and a red beard. I was their first born and obviously did not look like either him or mother. When mother finally told me about you," Michael said as he looked at Sudfad. "She said she never told Karzman about you for fear he would kill you." Renya gently rubbed Sudfad's arm as Michael spoke.

"Karzman knew mother had been unfaithful to him and he spent the rest of her life making her pay for that. He used to beat and torture both of us, until I got big enough to protect her. He is a demon," Michael said the words with disgust. "I have three step sisters and Karzman has raped all of them. I also have two step brothers who follow in their father's footsteps."

"Michael how did you get all those scars?" Vitomas asked softly.

"When I was a child, he would tether me to a stake in the ground and whip me."

Laurel was visibly crying as was Delilah. Tears were running down Marie's cheeks as Michael spoke. Renya placed her hand on Michael's arm and said, "Michael you are home now."

Michael got tears in his eyes. "Sudfad, I grew up hating you because you never came back and saved us from that monster. As I got older I wanted to kill you and those were the thoughts that I had when I came to your home. I never expected you to claim me as your son. And I never expected to become part of your family. I know I have not spoken much since I arrived and that is because my heart has been filled with anger for so long. I think it was the anger that kept me alive and now that the anger is gone, I don't really know what to say or do."

The entire room was silent for several moments before Sudfad spoke, "Son I am so sorry. If I would have known I would have come for you and Nadia. She had such a loving and gentle nature it breaks my heart to hear how Karzman treated all of you. I am thankful that you came here and I understand why you would want to kill me."

32

"But as Renya said you are home now and I only hope I can make some of this up to you. A son should not bear the punishment for the sins of his father."

There was an awkward silence in the room until Petra spoke. "Michael do you go to school?" Petra asked. Everyone at the table smiled at Petra's question, since Michael was a grown man.

"I have never had any schooling," Michael replied.

"Papa can he come to classes with me and Kyra?" Petra asked enthusiastically. "Oh please Papa." Petra looked at Michael and said in a low voice, "Mr. Vandrew is really grumpy."

Sudfad looked at Michael, "Would you like an education?"

Without hesitation Michael said, "Yes."

"Currently Petra and his friend Kyra have private teachers but I am in the midst of building a large Learning Center on the property. We can start you with private teachers and when you are ready for the university you can attend the one I am building or both Raul and Simon attended Cicero College which is about an hour north of here."

"Come to school with me," said Petra as he was nodding his head rapidly.

"Why don't I go to a couple of your classes and see what they are like." Michael said with a broad smile on his face.

Both Sudfad and the Sanuri thought it would be best if Michael spent some time with his brothers before they talked to him about his responsibilities. Raul, Simon, Michael and Archetenus returned to the castle just before the evening meal was served. When they walked through the front door Marie was standing in the foyer. "Look at you boys," she scolded with a grin. "You would think you were kids again. I don't want to be in that dining room when your mother sees you."

"Where is she?" asked Simon smiling.

"Why, she is in the dining room with the rest of the family waiting for you; you boys better go in there." Marie turned and walked towards the kitchen laughing.

The four young men walked into the dining room and took their regular seats. Renya stood up putting her hands on her hips and stamping her foot. "Boys what is the meaning of this? You tell me right now what you did."

Annabelle and Vitomas stared at the men; all of them were covered with dirt and had bruises and cuts on their faces, arms and hands.

"I'm waiting," said Renya who was visibly angry.

All four men were trying not to laugh when Raul finally spoke, "Michael came to training today. We were teaching hand to hand combat and some of Matthew's fighting style. Michael said his stepfather used to make him cage fight and he showed us a few moves that he learned. That's all."

"Why are you all injured?" Renya asked.

"Because we all tried the moves on each other," Simon said with a grin. "And you sure can tell Michael is one of us because when he hits you it feels like a horse kicked you."

"Are you boys ever going to outgrow this behavior?" Renya demanded. All four of the men were grinning but no one answered. Renya turned and looked at Sudfad and saw that he was grinning also. "Oh, I suppose you think this is funny. Sometimes I think you wish you could join them," Renya said angrily.

"Sometimes I do," Sudfad said with a laugh.

Renya sat down with a huff. Marie was waiting until the yelling was over before she brought the food into the dining room. As she placed the platters and bowls on the table she was trying not to grin. No one spoke for several minutes. Then Annabelle asked, "What is cage fighting?"

"It's when you put combatants in a ring or cage and they all fight until there is only one left alive," Archetenus explained.

34

"Sometimes its men fighting men and sometimes they are fighting creatures."

"It's like the Gefrey Games that Roch used to hold," Vitomas said. "Roch used to make me watch those games and they were horrible. Michael how old were you when he made you do that?"

"The first time I was eleven," Michael said without emotion. "I think he really thought I would die. But when I won he kept putting me in the cage and betting money on me. Karzman made a lot of money off my fighting."

"Did you fight men or beasts?" Annabelle asked. "Archetenus fought often in the Gefrey Games, he became a hero."

"He told me." Michael said. "He is a great fighter. I too fought both men and beasts."

"That is awful, Michael," Renya said sadly. "How old were you when you stopped?"

"I was seventeen," Michael answered with a distant look in his eyes. He paused for a few moments then continued. "I was working in the fields when my little stepsister Nina ran to me screaming and crying. She said that Karzman was killing mother. I ran to the house and mother was lying on the floor with him on top of her. Karzman was punching her in the face and there was blood everywhere," Michael was looking at Sudfad as he spoke, then he turned his gaze to the rest of the family.

"Mother was about the size of Vitomas (who was the smallest woman in the room) and Karzman is about Simon's size. It turns out Karzman was raping one of my stepsisters and mother tried to stop him. I beat him until he was unconscious and then I kept beating him. Mother begged me not to kill him; not because she wanted him around but because she was afraid of what would happen to me. I left home that night, I kept asking mother to come with me but she wouldn't. She stayed with that monster."

"What did you do after that?" asked Annabelle.

"At first I tried to stay in the area so I could be close if mother needed me. I worked all sorts of odd jobs. Then mother begged me to leave because she was afraid that Karzman would have me killed. So I traveled for a few years and got work where I could."

35

"Mother and my sisters would leave messages for me with the priests at the monastery in Philiste. I was working in the diamond mines in Lentz when a priest from the monastery in Tufold told me he had gotten a message that my mother was dying. I returned home to see her. She was in bed dying with my sisters around her and Karzman and his sons were nowhere to be found. That is when she finally told me about Sudfad. After she died I came here."

Chapter IV
Seventh Son

During the first two days of Michael's presence in the castle, he was kept occupied with this brothers and sisters-in-law while Sudfad sent letters to the ruling families of Lentz and to Sorren. Sudfad did not have any of his sons attend meetings on these two days so Gabriel and the others could discuss the addition of the Seventh Son to their mission plans. While Sudfad was truly grateful to discover he had another son, he as well as his entire family were still somewhat in shock by the revelation. But Sudfad knew it was probably not a coincidence that Michael appeared when he did.

The evening of the second night Sudfad and the Sanuri met with Michael in Sudfad's study. For the first few hours it was just the three men talking but later Raul and Simon were invited to join them. Michael was a practical man and could not wrap his mind around the things that Sudfad and the Sanuri were telling him. It was not that Michael thought they were trying to deceive him; it was that the concepts seemed preposterous to him. But as the night wore on Michael began to understand his destiny.

The five men talked all night; their meeting ended when Marie knocked on the door to tell them breakfast was served. "All of you look awful," Renya said as these men joined the rest of the family around the dining room table. "I hope you plan to get some sleep?"

"Not this morning," Sudfad said to Renya then he turned to Michael. "Every morning after breakfast I have a meeting with my leaders to discuss the business of the kingdom and the missions. Michael starting this morning I expect you to attend these meetings. I know all of this is overwhelming you but after you speak with Gabriel and Raphael you will have a better understanding of the urgency of some of this. In fact, I would like you to spend some time with those men before they leave."

"He should probably spend some time with Archetenus and Jared too," Raul said.

"I was thinking the same thing," said Archetenus.

"First things first," said Renya. "What was Michael's answer?"

Sudfad smiled proudly, "He is my son, he said yes."

"To both roles, the Keepers of the Scrolls and the prophesy?" Renya asked.

"Yes, although we still have much to explain to him," the Sanuri said. "And I am afraid that task will fall on all of you because I must leave for Ryed this morning."

Renya now turned to Michael, "First I want to tell you that I am proud of you." Tears came to Michael's eyes as Renya said these words for it was the very first time he had ever heard them. "And secondly, I have refrained from introducing you to any of our friends because I didn't want someone to slip-up and talk about your roles until the Sanuri spoke with you. I hope you didn't think we were hiding your presence here?"

Michael looked surprised, "No, I have felt just the opposite. As I said before I never expected to become part of your family and after just a few days everyone is acting as if I have been here forever."

"That's because you fit in with us so well," Simon said. "Which I find remarkable since your life has been so different from ours."

"Now Michael I want you to be honest with me because I don't want to overwhelm you but I would like to have a celebration to introduce you to our kingdom. But I want you to tell me when you are ready," Renya said with a big smile.

"I don't think that is a good idea now," the Sanuri warned. "He is the Seventh Son and the terrorists will realize that when they see him. I think small celebrations would be appropriate for a while. None of us believe it is a coincidence that Michael joins us on the eve of such important missions, although we have not spoken to the Angels about that yet."

"I understand," Renya said then she turned to Archetenus. "Do you think Zoya would be up for coming to the castle say in two nights from now?"

"Jared said she is doing all of the chores in the house like nothing happened, I would say yes."

"What happened?" asked Michael.

38

"She just had a baby," Delilah said. "Many of us have had babies in the last few months, it's kind of an epidemic," she said with a smile.

"Michael do you feel up to a gathering of our team members and friends in a couple of days?" Renya asked.

"Sure, do I need to wear anything special because I haven't gotten my dress uniform yet?"

"No," Renya replied. "Does that mean you will be joining our military?"

"Yes," Raul replied. "Which brings up a point that we need to work on a schedule for him; for his studies and his training."

"I don't need to remind you that while Gabriel and Raphael are leading two teams, they are not The Seven Sons and it is highly likely the three of you boys and Matthew will need to assist on this mission," the Sanuri said.

"Son, I don't mean to embarrass you," Sudfad said. "I know you weren't allowed to go to school but can you read and write?"

"Yes, mother taught me," Michael said. "She also taught me to read and write in the old language of her clan."

"What language is that?" the Sanuri asked.

"Cerfic."

"I have never heard of that language," Renya said.

"It is very old," said Michael.

"Michael I hope you understand that the only reason I asked was so we could determine where to start with your studies," Sudfad explained.

"I understand and honestly I am a fighting man. From what I have heard about these missions they sound interesting and important so other things can wait."

"A man of my heart," Archetenus said.

The meeting in Sudfad's study had barely begun when there was a knock on the door. Renya entered with Emeral and Hannah. "I am sorry to interrupt," Renya said. "I just want to introduce Michael to my friends. Michael stood up and walked over to the women. "Michael this is Emeral, she is the wife of Maxwell and the mother of many of the men in this room. She also has led our soldiers in battle." Michael extended his hand but Emeral hugged him instead.

"Careful Michael, Mother adopts almost everyone she meets," Calen joked.

"You are just the mirror image of Sudfad and Raul," Emeral said with amazement. Then she turned to Sudfad. "How could his stepfather not know Michael is your son? Hasn't he ever seen you?" Everyone in the room now stared at Emeral.

"That is a very interesting point," the Sanuri said. "There might be more to all of this; let me see what I can find out."

"And this is Hannah, she is the Court Physician and Gabriel's wife," Renya explained. "She is also an active member of Gabriel's team besides having small children."

As Hannah hugged Michael, Gabriel said, "Tomorrow Michael will be spending the entire day with us."

"Good," Emeral said. "Plan to stay for dinner we will fix something special."

"What time will you be coming over?" Hannah asked.

Michael looked at Gabriel who said, "I would imagine right after the meeting."

"Good, I will make sure everyone is around to meet you," Hannah said, then she turned to Gabriel. "If you plan to be spending most of that time in your study I will make some treats."

Gabriel smiled, "Michael our wives feed us well."

After the women left the study the Sanuri turned to Michael.

"Michael that look on your face is anything wrong?"

"No."

"Why don't you tell the others what you were thinking," the Sanuri suggested.

"Can you read minds?" Michael asked in amazement.

"At times," the Sanuri said. "But I bring this up because all of you only have a short time to understand each other before the next battle."

Michael paused and when he spoke it was the Sanuri who he looked at. "Karzman would tether me to a stake or keep me in a cage when I was a boy and..." Michael paused again. "And here you all act so proud to have me in your family."

"We are," Raul said loudly.

During the meeting that King Mathas held every morning, a small group of Enrops flew through the window which the King always left open for them. The ancient birds handed envelopes to Mathas, Fahron and Claudius.

"I see that other envelope has Sorren's name on it," Claudius said to the Enrops. "We expect him here soon. You can leave the envelope and rest and eat."

Mathas and Fahron had both started to read their letters while Claudius spoke with the Enrops. "Matthew please bring the rest of the family in here now." Mathas requested in a serious tone.

"What is wrong?" Matthew asked with concern.

"It's not that anything is wrong," Fahron said. "The Seventh Son is at Sudfad's castle, it is who he is that Mathas must explain."

"Sorren, your timing is perfect," Claudius said as Matthew led Rosa, Angelina, Sorren and Shara into the study.

"Two days ago an intruder was stopped as he charged into Sudfad's dining room," Mathas explained.

"The man wore a hood over his head and well, when the hood was removed a young man who is identical to Sudfad and Raul stood before them."

"What? I don't understand," Rosa said.

Before Sudfad met Renya he had been stationed in northern Wetpr where he met and fell in love with a woman named Nadia. Sudfad asked Nadia to marry him but she was pledged to another and had been since birth; Nadia said she would not dishonor her family. But it turns out she was actually saving her family from being murdered. Nadia had a son with Sudfad." Rosa gasped loudly. "Nadia never told Sudfad about the boy and didn't tell Michael, that's the boy's name, who his father was until she died."

"Michael's stepfather is Karzman the ruthless war lord of the Kozach Tribe. Karman tortured Michael and Nadia, he raped his own daughters and the list goes on."

"Karzman sounds like Roch," Mathew said.

"I was thinking the same thing," Stephan added.

"Sudfad says that Michael was filled with anger that Sudfad never came to save him and Nadia and that anger is about the only thing that kept the boy alive. He stormed into the castle with the intent of killing Sudfad and dying in the attack. But you know Renya, she welcomed the boy into the family and apparently had him crying within moments of his arrival. The Sanuri said that Michael is the Seventh Son."

"Sudfad must feel so guilty," Angelina said. "I mean for not saving Michael and Nadia, not conceiving a son."

"We know what you meant," Fahron said and handed her his letter. "Apparently all the letters are the same."

"You know this is not a coincidence that Michael arrives just before these missions," Sorren said.

"Not to change the subject but does Sudfad say how Luca is doing?" Thaos asked. "Nikki thinks we should visit him and while I feel the same way, I am not sure about traveling with the babies."

"Sudfad didn't write anything about Luca," Claudius said as he handed his letter to Thaos. "But I imagine Sudfad himself is in shock over Michael's appearance."

"Ingr said she wanted to visit Luca too," Stephan said. "Maybe we should go." Stephan turned to Matthew. "Want to come along?"

Before Matthew could answer, Sorren said. "The Seventh Son is here, I would certainly like to meet him and I am sure others of you would also. Let's send Sudfad a letter telling him we are coming for a visit."

"It will have to be soon," Claudius said, "Because they will be leaving for that mission."

"Is Michael going on the mission?" Rosa asked.

"I wouldn't be surprised," Mathas replied.

"I'll watch the kingdom, the rest of you go," Fahron said. "You should probably leave today or tomorrow."

"Fahron, tell Chaez to come with us," Thaos said. "That way we can introduce him to everyone and still get some training in." Fahron smiled.

Mathis sent letters to Sudfad and Gabriel immediately after the meeting and by noon a caravan of carriages and soldiers were leaving Lentz. When Sorren returned to his village with the news, Thomas and Sasha decided to return to Wetpr to visit Luca. Thomas invited Hugo and Greta to come with them and to stay with his parents. This invitation thrilled Hugo and Greta who immediately packed their belongings. Sorren also invited Batina's family to join them. Edgar and Cora, too were thrilled and joined the caravan.

Shortly after the caravan started its journey eastward, Chaez rode up to Thaos, Stephan and Matthew, all of whom were riding side by side. "I want to thank you for bringing me along," Chaez said. "And I have a question for you. I'm thinking that perhaps I should stay in Wetpr because I won't really know anyone and I won't have any other responsibilities besides training. I am thinking I can devote more time that way. What do you think?"

"Honestly Chaez I think that is a really good idea," Stephan said. "It certainly isn't that you can't learn, it's that you have so much to learn in such a short time."

"I agree," Matthew said. "Raul and Simon do training with their soldiers almost every morning and a lot of it is exactly the things you need to learn. I will ask them to include you. And you know Renya and Sudfad will let you stay at the castle until the barracks are ready."

"Thanks, I appreciate that," Chaez said. "Before I left I told my parents what I was thinking. They both approve and gave me, actually a lot of money to pay for my training. Do you know if I give it to Sudfad or Gabriel and Raphael?"

"Can't answer that kid," Thaos said. "You might be the first paying customer at that Learning Center, so they may not even know yet. You should ask Claudius and Sorren they are on the board of advisors."

"Thanks," Chaez said and rode forward to catch up with Claudius.

"I hope he makes it," Matthew said. "It will kill him if he doesn't."

"He must want it bad," Stephan said. "Cuz that kid is black and blue from training and still comes back for more."

The Sanuri left for Ryed immediately after the morning meeting. Archetenus and Jared stayed at the castle and told Michael about their pasts and their experiences as they deliberately changed their destinies. Jared and Archetenus could not tell their stories without explaining a great deal about the Insidiae and the Grand Masters. Michael was fascinated with what the men were telling him.

Both Archetenus and Jared liked Michael, like them he was a mountain of a man who grew up fighting for his life. These three men soon discovered they shared many traits including the loneliness of their lives prior to becoming involved with Sudfad and the others.

"Can't imagine how hard this must all be for you," Jared said.

44

"But believe me when I tell you coming here is the best thing you could have done. And when Zoya's feeling a little better, I want you to come out for dinner. My place ain't much compared to Gabriel's home or this place," Jared said referring to the castle. "But it is a second chance for me and I am grabbing on with both hands. I suggest you do the same thing."

Michael loved children and in the very short time he had been at the castle he bonded with his nieces and nephews who adored him. When Michael, Jared and Archetenus entered the dining room for lunch little Alexander, Anthony, little Sudfad and Samuel all swarmed the men and wanted to wrestle. "After lunch, I promise," Michael said with a laugh.

"Well, this is a surprise," Jared said when he saw Zoya sitting at the table with their baby. "Did you drive here?"

"No Laurel and Alexander came out for a visit and invited me in," Zoya said as Jared walked around the table and kissed her.

"We will drive her back in the boca," Alexander said.

"Michael come over and meet my wife and son," Jared said with pride. Zoya had already been told about Michael. "I can't believe how much you look like Sudfad and Raul," she said as Michael walked towards them. Michael extended his hand to shake with Zoya. She took his hand but did not let go.

"Is something the matter?" Michael asked uneasily as Zoya stared at him.

"My wife is a seer," Jared explained. "The spirits didn't talk to her the entire time she was pregnant. She must be back in business."

"Michael, as Jared said spirits talk to me and I know that scares people. But most of the time they have good things to say. I know your mother's name is Nadia and that is who is speaking. She is so happy that you are here. She is making me feel warm to show me how happy she is. And now she feels so badly that she didn't tell you about Sudfad earlier. She said she should have known he would claim you and give you a home but for some reason she was afraid." Michael stared at Zoya in shock.

"Nadia says she can see things so differently now and she knows you are destined to become a great warrior. She says she fears for your life because she knows Karzman wants to kill you but she hopes that someday you can go back and help your sisters escape because now that you both are gone..." Zoya paused.

By now all the members of Sudfad's family were in the dining room and staring at Zoya. "Someone just interrupted your mother," Zoya paused again. "They aren't telling me who they are but they are showing me bloody altars. I just saw the name Fiona. Fiona is warning Nadia about talking to me. Now they are gone."

"Fiona is my mother's mother," Michael stammered.

"What about the altars?" Sudfad asked. "Does your tribe worship demons?"

"Not that I know of," Michael said. "Although in some ways that wouldn't surprise me. But why would Fiona warn Mother?"

"Fiona said everyone is being watched and Nadia must be careful what she says," Zoya explained.

"How can a spirit be in danger?" Simon asked. "Or did she mean that Nadia could get Michael hurt?"

"I don't know," Zoya said. "But I would imagine that really powerful demons can be threats to anyone."

"Son, Zoya is very accurate in what she sees and hears. She has warned us about attacks and provided us with a great deal of information. The Sanuri said she is a gift to us. I too had difficulty believing at first," Sudfad said.

"No, it's not that," Michael said contemplatively. "As she talked it was like; I'm not really sure how to explain it. You know when you wake in the morning and you can vaguely remember a dream from the night before. I suddenly felt like there was something I need to remember."

That night Gabriel's team sat in stunned silence as Gabriel told them about Michael for the first time.

"How come you didn't tell us about him before?" Natasha asked.

"Because Sudfad asked us not to," Gabriel replied. "He wanted the Sanuri to talk to him first. And I understand considering this isn't just a lost son but Michael is also a Keeper of the Scrolls as well as The Seventh Son of prophesy."

"Well I felt sorry for him," Emeral said. "He just looks lost. Renya said the clothing he was wearing were literally rags and he rode a horse that was so old she is about to die. He has never slept in a bed before and he has never eaten chocolate cake before so I am making my special desert for dinner tomorrow." Everyone at the table grinned at this remark.

"Apparently Michael came here with the intent of killing Sudfad and dying during the attack," Maxwell explained. "But Renya told the boy that he was home now and if they would have known of his existence before they would have brought both Michael and Nadia home."

"Sudfad said you could see the anger drain from Michael and he started to cry. He was embarrassed that they saw him crying so Renya had Marie set Michael up in chambers on the first floor. Vitomas got some of Raul's clothing for him and took it to his chambers. When Michael answered the door he wasn't wearing a shirt and Vitomas said his body was covered with scars."

"Now, Emeral brought up an interesting point this morning," Raphael said. "Michael is a little bigger than Raul with curly hair and a small scar on his cheek but other than these things they are absolutely identical. Emeral questioned how Karzman could not know Sudfad was Michael's father and perhaps that is why he tortured the boy so."

"Maybe Karzman never saw Sudfad," Melinda said.

"The King's picture is engraved on all of the coins," Calen said and I am sure on other things.

"I just feel so sorry for him," Diana said. "Isn't there something we can do to help him?"

"Honestly I think just being his friend," Gabriel said. "It sounds like he has been treated like an animal most of his life."

47

"He was so touched that Renya wanted to introduce her friends to him. You all do know that the meeting we are having with him tomorrow is not private. All of you can join us but most of what we are saying will be review."

"You said he is a good fighter," Vivian said. "Perhaps some of us could tell him about our clan; that would be a way to get to know him."

"Actually we were planning on asking you to speak with him," Raphael said. "The only other thing that we really know about him is that he loves children. Raul's and Simons boys just hang on him."

"Children don't judge," Emeral said. "Part of that could be that Michael feels more comfortable with the children."

"Who is this boy you are talking about?" Nicholas asked as all of the children sitting at the small table were listening to the conversation.

"Sudfad just found out he has another son," Hannah replied. "His name is Michael."

"How come he didn't know he had a son?" Adrone asked.

"Well..." Hannah started to say then paused as she thought about her words.

"You know that Koby is the daddy of my baby," Bekka said to the children. "And you know that I left and went home. Well, Michael's mother did the same thing but she didn't tell Sudfad she had a baby in her."

"Did she come back?" Joey asked.

"No," Bekka replied.

"Why not?" Joey asked again.

"Because a really bad man said he would kill her family if she did," Vivian said.

"Bekka are you going to leave again?" Nicholas asked.

Bekka looked at both of her parents and Sam spoke.

48

"We have decided to stay here until after the baby is born," Sam explained. "It will be easier for Koby to see the baby and honestly we are enjoying being here and helping out." Sam didn't want to say that part of the reason they were staying was to help Christopher through his grief.

Koby was sitting next to Bekka and put his arm around her and kissed her. "I am very glad to hear this," he said.

"I think we all are," said Emeral.

"What Father didn't say was that neither of my older sisters have children and they want to be grandparents," Bekka said with a warm smile. "And of course they just inherited that table of grandchildren over there." Bekka nodded towards the children's table.

"That's how we felt when we came here too," Joshua said. "It will be good that you are staying especially since most of us will be leaving soon."

"Luca once I have the baby I will be nursing so we can bring Emma home if you would like," Bekka said to her friend. Luca was still paralyzed by his grief which was another reason Bekka and her parents wanted to stay.

"Thank you, I appreciate that," Luca said then looked at Gabriel. "I think I will start attending the meetings again, if nothing else just to get my mind on something else."

"I think that is wise son," Maxwell said.

Without Luca's knowledge both Calen and Natasha told Gabriel they would be staying home instead of going on the mission. Everyone in the family was worried about Luca and Christopher in particular but the impact of Lila's death weighed heavily upon them all.

There was an uncomfortable silence after Maxwell's comment so Raphael turned to Hannah. "Although Michael was never allowed to go to school, his mother taught him to read and write in two languages. One of the languages neither Gabriel nor I have ever heard of. If you wouldn't mind I would like to see if he could translate some of your father's papers."

"Of course," Hannah said. "What is the language?"

"Cerfic, he says it is the language of his mother's clan."

"I have heard of that," Joshua said with surprise. "It is a very old language barely used anymore. It used to be spoken frequently in Ryed, I don't know about other kingdoms. What clan did Michael's mother belong to?"

"I don't believe he said," Raphael replied. "We can ask him tomorrow. So you say it was a common language?"

"Yes but it was a language of the masses not the wealthy. It is not a language of money which is probably why it died out."

"Well, that makes me hopeful that perhaps some of those manuscripts are written in Cerfic," Gabriel said. "I wonder what Michael is doing tonight?"

"Oh, Gabriel you don't want to bother him," Hannah scolded.

"Honey time is against us here."

"I'll go to the castle now and ask him if he wants to come over and help with translations," Calen said.

"I'll go with you so I can visit Emma," Luca said. "Christopher do you want to come?"

Twenty minutes later Calen and Michael walked in the front door of Gabriel's house. Michael couldn't stop smiling. "That was the most incredible thing," he repeated several times.

"His first flight," Calen said with a grin as the family came to greet them. Calen looked at Gabriel, "I didn't tell him everything that Joshua said about that language."

"First introductions," Gabriel said. "Michael this morning we were telling you that there used to be seven of us as the main body of the team. Well, everyone is getting married and our team has turned into one huge, crazy family. Trust me no one expects you to remember everyone's names after tonight but you should know that besides the Rualas we have members from two other warrior tribes here."

50

"The Sanuri said that this collaboration between good people, standing up to darkness is a sign that the Prophesy of The Seven Sons is unfolding."

It was apparent to most of Gabriel's team that Michael was a little uncomfortable with the attention he was receiving. After the introductions and a tour of the house which included the children's playroom and fort, Gabriel, Raphael, Joshua, Vivian and Michael shut themselves in Gabriel's study to try and translate manuscripts. Within moments Hannah brought a tray of snacks into the room. "I have eaten more food in the last few days than I have in weeks," Michael said with a grin and filled his plate.

Gabriel handed out drinks as Raphael handed out stacks of manuscripts. "Between Raphael, Joshua, Vivian and me we can speak a number of ancient languages but we are baffled by some of these texts. Since none of us recognize the Cerfic language we are really hoping that is the language some of these manuscripts are written in," Gabriel explained. "Joshua told us that Cerfic was a common language spoken by the masses in Ryed, he didn't know about other kingdoms."

"Michael where was your mother's clan from?" Joshua asked.

"Northern Wetpr, well I take that back. They have lived in Wetpr for centuries but they were originally from Stordt I believe. I was told they moved because of the constant wars."

"A couple hundred years ago King Sharonne greatly expanded the borders of the Kingdom of Stordt and some of the lands he conquered belong to Ryed," Raphael explained. "It could be possible that your ancestors are originally from Ryed."

"Was Karzman from your mother's clan?" Vivian asked.

"No, when he was young he led a group of men through Wetpr and from the sounds of it they killed and burned everyone and everything they came in contact with. I never heard where he came from, he just referred to it as Tameric but I have never seen that word on a map or heard anyone else say it. I was told he fought with my mother's clan and said he would spare them if they gave him Nadia. My mother said he asked for her by name which surprised her clan since they were unfamiliar with Karzman's men."

51

"Did she ever ask Karzman about it?" Vivian asked.

"My mother was terrified of him, she only spoke to him when she had to. My first day here Annabelle and Vitomas were trying to put me at ease. They took me shopping and told me of their pasts and how they came to the castle. I know you are familiar with King Roch, so I am telling you this to help you understand. Many of the stories they told me; well, they could have been talking about Karzman."

"So when Karzman demanded Nadia did she know Sudfad?" asked Gabriel.

"They were courting. Mother said she lied to Sudfad to get him to leave because she was terrified that Karzman would kill him."

"So she wasn't promised to Karzman from birth?" Raphael asked.

"No, mother said Karzman gave her clan forty-eight hours to make a decision and during that time mother sent Sudfad away."

"Michael, there is just so very much to tell you about what we are involved with," Gabriel said. "But I am sure that the Sanuri told you that the demons and dark lords have spent centuries speculating as to who The Seven Sons of prophesy would be so they could kill their family lines. I am becoming suspicious of Karzman and his motivation for marrying your mother," Gabriel said. "I would like to talk to you more about this subject."

"Perhaps I should tell you about what happened today," Michael said. "I spent the morning with Jared and Archetenus and they taught me a lot. When we entered the dining room for the midday meal, Jared's wife was visiting and as soon as she saw me she said my mother was talking to her."

"I have heard of seers but never met one before so I really wasn't sure what was happening. She told me that mother was very happy that I was with Sudfad and now regrets she did not tell me he was my father sooner. Zoya said someone interrupted mother and showed her, that's Zoya, images of bloody altars. Then Fiona, my mothers' mother warned Nadia about talking to anyone and the spirits left."

"I am assuming that someone in the castle explained that Zoya is not a charlatan?" Gabriel asked. "Believe me we all were skeptics but Zoya's visions have literally saved our lives. Did Zoya hear the warning?"

"Fiona said something like it was dangerous because so many eyes were watching. I am sure you can ask her the exact words."

"Interesting," Gabriel said. "Michael I just remembered you were up all last night so I don't want to keep you long. Maybe you could just look over a few manuscripts and give us some guidance as to the language."

"Actually I am fine now, I was really tired earlier this afternoon, but you are right this whiskey may hit me."

"Michael the two scrolls on top of that stack could possibly have information for our mission, if you wouldn't mind looking at them first," Raphael said then turned to the others in the room. "Now that we know that Cerfic was spoken in Ryed perhaps we could get some information from the priests at Rubar. I am sure they are hiding things from the Teivel Clan."

Michael was carefully unfolding a scroll because the leather was so fragile. "This writing is so old that some of the words are faded and pieces of the leather have fallen away but this first scroll is written in Cerfic," Michael said. "Do you want me to write the words down?"

"Thank you Miranda," Vivian said loudly.

"Who is Miranda?" asked Michael.

"Apparently our guardian Angel," Raphael explained. "Michael after the horrible life you have led this may be difficult for you to understand but all of us in this room are realizing your presence here is a gift to us. As Gabriel said there is just so much to tell you, eventually you will understand what we mean."

"No one has ever said anything like that to me before," Michael said with a note of sadness in his voice. "Ever since I came here it is like I am living a dream, everything is so different."

Chapter V
Forces in Motion

"Michael you're still here?" Cassandra gasped as Michael, Gabriel, Raphael, Joshua and Vivian joined the rest of the team at the breakfast table the following morning. "Didn't any of you sleep?"

"No they were up all night," Hannah said with disapproval as she was pouring coffee into cups.

"We made a lot of headway last night," Gabriel said as he kissed Hannah on the cheek. One of the scrolls was written in Cerfic. To save us all time, Michael translated the words and read them out loud as Vivian wrote them down." Hannah gave Gabriel a pensive look. "This scroll was written a long time before your father was born." Gabriel knew that Hannah was worried that information about her father would be revealed in the manuscripts they were studying.

"We believe the author of the scroll was a shaman or healer of a tribe in Ryed. Over the centuries Stordt was expanded because the kings conquered neighboring lands. Ryed is considerably smaller now than it was centuries ago. We were studying maps and believe that the area this healer describes is now land that the City of Nora is built on. Which could explain how Arthur obtained the scroll; he owned mines and other businesses," Raphael explained.

"The author of the scroll doesn't give us the name of the village, unless those words already faded away because the scroll is very old and in poor shape. It sounds like his village was made up of hunters and farmers not warriors. The author gave very long descriptions of the beauty of the land and the beauty of his people which we found curious until Michael got further into the manuscript."

"The lives of the villagers changed dramatically after two young people stayed with them. The people claimed to be brother and sister and were both young adults. The healer says that shortly after these people entered his village people started to suffer from all sorts of maladies, including madness."

Raphael continued, "The healer said he tried everything he knew but he could not help the many patients who were being brought to him daily. He says the people who did not get sick changed and became violent and agitated. He said there was constant fighting among his people and some of the fights ended with murder."

"Then one day these strangers who the healer refers to as the children of Ahriman told the villagers they could save everyone if they but bowed down and worshiped them. Many people did and apparently were instantly healed. Those who didn't were slaughtered on altars which apparently was the fate of the healer. His final words were 'they are coming for me.'"

"So that is how Emeric and Banaka increased their power," Gabriel said. "Like the demons their power must increase from the souls that fear and worship them."

"That is fascinating," Maxwell said. "Are other manuscripts written in Cerfic also?"

"Yes," Gabriel said. "Michael has already started to translate a second one."

"Michael you haven't sleep in two days," Hannah scolded. "I want you to get some sleep right after the morning meeting." Michael looked at Hannah and grinned.

"I know she sounded like your wife there," Calen said with a grin. "But she is the Royal Physician."

"Actually I feel fine," Michael said. "I know I should be exhausted but I am not."

"Miranda," Vivian said without further explanation. Vivian felt strongly that Miranda was responsible for Michael's sudden appearance and the help he could provide. "I need to get some sleep but he is fine."

"Besides today is my day to spend with your team and I am becoming fascinated with the more I hear," Michael continued. He did not tell them that he was extremely happy that he could translate the scroll for them because the act made him feel of value to the team.

"Then we will do this," Hannah said as others grinned. "We have many unused rooms in this house. If you get tired, get some sleep."

"Yes Hannah," Michael replied with a grin.

"We sleep in the playroom sometimes," Nicholas said. "You can sleep in there."

"And I would imagine he could get a lot of sleep in there," Calen joked.

Vivian looked across the table at Diana and Thor. "Father and I were going to teach Michael about Venatores and our clan but I think we both need some sleep. Will you do that?"

"Of course," Thor said then he turned to Micha. "Do you want to join us or are you going to spend the day with Bianca?"

"She is coming over, we both can join you."

"I was going to ask Batina to teach Michael about the Nordes Tribe, perhaps Bianca can help her," Gabriel said.

Batina was proud to get an assignment from Gabriel, "I would be honored, just tell me when," Batina said.

"Well, we will all be going to the meeting, then Michael probably wants to change his clothes and we can return," Gabriel said.

"If we have time can I set up some targets so I can show him how we train?" Batina asked.

"That's a great idea," said Dack. "We should set up the field for the Bozie game and we can all play and train."

"We'll help you," Dagon said to Batina.

"Why don't some of you come with me for a while," Bekka said. "I wanted to take the children into Salar and buy ice cream." All of the children's faces broke into smiles at this statement.

"Why don't I drive that small boca and the children can ride," Iris suggested.

"I'll go with you," Natasha said.

"So will we," Elan said of him and Cassandra.

"Melinda do you want to help Thor and me get things ready to show Michael?" Diana asked sweetly.

"What do we have to get ready?" Thor asked. Diana looked disapprovingly at Thor then rolled her eyes which caused him to break into laughter. "Melinda and I are talking again if that is what you were trying to accomplish here." Then Thor turned to Melinda and asked, "Would you like to join us?"

"I don't know, I should probably go with the children."

"You don't have to," Natasha said. "We can watch them."

"Alright," Melinda said and smiled at Thor.

Thor looked across the table at Michael, "Michael I have to warn you my sister is the matchmaker around here."

Michael looked at Diana and grinned. He felt very comfortable and accepted among this group of strangers; something that surprised him very much. He was accepted by Sudfad's family and they treated him well but there was still so much tension in them all and unresolved feelings. But here Michael felt more relaxed; like there were no expectations of him. Gabriel's team seemed to simply accept Michael for who he was and they showed him great gratitude for his help.

"Michael," Vivian said. "I know you just got here and things must be crazy for you but you seem to have a talent for languages as my father has. I have always admired that in father. Raphael and Gabriel both studied ancient languages when they were students at the monastery and I will be taking some of those same courses soon. Perhaps you would like to join me."

"You are going to a monastery?" Michael asked with surprise.

"She will eventually be going to Cicero College," Raphael said. "But as you know Sudfad is building a Learning Center here. We have a Patronus headquarters near the college and many of our priests have volunteered to teach at the Learning Center."

"As you can see Vivian is carrying our first child and she has been very sick a great deal so one of the priests, Padre Markle has offered to tutor her and anyone else in the house who is interested."

"I am so very excited," Vivian said. "He is coming Saturday for my first lesson if you want to join us?"

"Is this knowledge something that is useful to your missions?" Michael asked.

"More than you can imagine," Gabriel replied as he could see the interest in Michael's eyes.

"I will come and see what it is like; what time should I be here?" Michael asked.

"Right after the midday meal," Vivian said.

"Now that it looks like our family will be here for a while," Joshua said. "Perhaps I should sit in on those classes also."

"Father that would be wonderful," Vivian said happily. Then she looked at Michael, "Father is amazing, he learns languages so quickly it is a gift."

"Will Padre Markle be tutoring you after we return from Ryed?" Thor asked.

"I hope so," Vivian said. "I don't think I can travel back and forth to the college with a new born baby."

Thor looked at Diana and said, "It would be wise for us to take those studies too."

"I was just thinking the same thing," Diana said. "Is there a limit on how many students can attend?"

"At the monastery our classes are quite large," Raphael said then he looked at Gabriel. "This interest really pleases me. Perhaps we should set up a small classroom here."

"I agree," Gabriel said. "Raphael, Hannah and I all very much believe in education and it pleases us greatly to hear you are interested in learning."

"Gabriel, the carpenters are almost completed with the work in the nursery and playroom, we could have them work on a classroom next," Emeral suggested.

"After breakfast we will decide what we need," Gabriel said.

Joshua looked at Paul and Adrone, "You two need to pay off your mother's ring. I think painting the nursery and playroom would be a good start."

"They get to paint!" Christopher said enthusiastically. "Can we help?" This was the first time Christopher sounded excited about anything since Lila died.

"Of course," Emeral said as the rest of the adults grinned. "In fact I just had a wonderful idea. We will paint the walls a light color then when that paint dries you can paint pictures on it."

All of the small boys looked at each other excitedly. "Gee Grandma," Nicholas said and the adults broke into laughter.

"I don't know how she does it," Natasha said. "Emeral always knows what to say."

"Raphael, Cassandra and I were considering postponing our studies because we just adopted Cicely and with all of you leaving for those long missions. Does Padre Markle teach any of the courses we will need?" Elan asked.

Raphael smiled and looked at Hannah. "Why don't you write down what courses they need and I will find priests who teach them." Then Raphael turned back to Elan. "Our priests are very well educated and honestly some of them are rather bored at the headquarters. I am sure I can find someone with the knowledge you need."

"They need to study many sciences," Hannah said. "Which means we need to buy certain things for the classroom in addition to the right books. I will start on that right away. Elan and Cassandra this too makes me happy."

"Gabriel, Hannah and Raphael offered to pay for educations for any of us who are interested," Bekka explained to her parents. "And Sudfad will write letters to get everyone into the university."

"That is a very generous offer," Sam said. "Elan, what are you and Cassandra studying?"

"We want to become physicians," Elan said with a proud smile. "Hannah is already allowing us to help her."

"That is admirable," Sam said with sincerity. "Bekka you weren't interested?"

"I had other things on my mind," Bekka replied with a smile.

"Of course," Sam replied thoughtfully.

"Ratri and Batina I don't know how much time you plan to be with us," Gabriel said. "But that offer applies to all of our team members. If either of you want to attend college just tell me or Raphael."

"Why, I never thought about such a thing," Batina said. "We are honored at your offer."

"There isn't a time limit on the offer," Raphael said. "So think about it."

During Sudfad's morning meeting it was decided that Michael would postpone some of his other training so he could spend more time with Gabriel's team. Gabriel and Raphael hopped that Michael would be able to translate more manuscripts before the teams had to leave for the missions. Sudfad was also happy that Michael had expressed interest in studying ancient languages.

This was the first meeting that Luca had attended since Lila died. While many felt that his presence was a good sign, Luca was quiet through the entire meeting.

"I am sorry to interrupt," Renya said as she entered the study. "But we just received a letter from Mathas and another from Sorren and they concern everyone here."

"Many people from Lentz are coming here to see Luca and to meet Michael. Apparently once they made the decision to come they left within hours because they did not want to detain Gabriel's team from leaving for the missions. Joshua, Thomas and Sasha are coming as well as Sasha's parents. Batina's parents are also coming. Raphael, Chaez is coming to meet everyone and hopefully train."

"Sorren sent his letter after they had started the journey here," Renya continued. "Fahron gave Chaez a very large sum of money to pay for training and schooling but Chaez is unsure who he should give the money to." Renya handed Sorren's letter to Raphael and Mathas' letter to Sudfad. "I had invited all of you over tonight for a small celebration but I think we should wait and have a larger celebration tomorrow night when the people from Lentz get here. Would that be a problem for anyone?"

"Actually that works out well because some of us stayed up all night working," Gabriel said. "I need to tell Hannah that we will have more guests."

"May I see the letter?" Luca asked. "Renya did you tell them the details so I don't have to keep repeating it?" The sadness in Luca's voice touched everyone in the room.

"Emeral and I sent them a letter explaining everything," Renya said sweetly. "So you shouldn't have to answer a lot of questions. Luca you and Lila touched many people; your friends want to show their respects and to be there for you. If you don't feel ready to face a large group yet, tell us." Luca got tears in his eyes as Renya spoke.

"I can't believe we agreed to do this," Bruno complained as he, Morgan and Nada flew into a dark cavern inside a mountain that was part of the Rosu Mountain Range. The Rosu Mountain Range ran parallel to the Safer Mountain Range and extended from the east coast of Opots to the Waste Lands of Manod forming the southern boundary of the continent. This particular mountain was in the Kingdom of Marba, home of the Hutas and directly behind the castle that was once owned by the demon Sporos.

"Did you see how everything is dead for miles around that castle?" Nada asked. "What do you think caused that?"

"That castle belonged to Sporos," Bruno said. "You know the friend of the Sanuri's who was a priest then became a demon. Morgan and I joined the fight at that castle and it was a hell of a fight. But it's the stench of this place that I can't stand, it makes my eyes water."

"What the hell!" Morgan yelled. "Stop, the cavern just turned into a small tunnel. We are going to have to walk."

"This is gonna be bad if we run into Hutas," Bruno said.

"You have been complaining since we started this mission," Morgan whispered. "Stop, do you smell that?"

The three Rualas were walking through a passageway that was so narrow they had to walk single file. They were walking in darkness. "Oh my god!" Nada said and started to cover her mouth and nose but vomited on the ground."

"Thanks, you got some on me," Bruno said in an angry whisper.

"Will you two shut up," Morgan whispered. "I hear something."

All three of the Rualas stood motionless and listened. "Is that chanting?" Nada asked in a whisper of the faint sound they were hearing.

"I don't think Hutas chant," Bruno whispered and the three slowly moved forward. As they walked the putrid smells became stronger and the chanting louder. Ten minutes later they could see the reflection of a fire dancing on the stone walls of the passageway and moments later they entered a large cave.

"What is your purpose here?" asked a haggard old woman who was sitting near a fire. There were five fires in the cave and all of them had kettles on them. The contents within the kettles was giving off the putrid smell that was making all three Rualas nauseous.

"Hecate sent us," Morgan said. "Are you Risha?"

"Yes, come closer, my eyes aren't so good anymore."

All three of the Rualas felt uneasy as if they might be walking into a trap. They slowly walked closer to the old woman. "I never thought I would see the day when Rualas would be the minions of a demon," Risha said sarcastically. "Do you have the money?"

"You're pretty haughty for a witch," Morgan said with indignation as he handed Risha three large pouches of gold.

"And the witch who controls the domain you are in. You would be wise to think about that," Risha said as she opened the pouches and dropped the contents on the ground. "Hecate sent me more than I asked for," Risha said approvingly. "I assume she told you to return immediately to her, if you delay the potion will lose its potency."

"Is that what's cooking in the pots?" Bruno asked.

"I am a dealer in potions," Risha replied. "It is a better profession than being a traitor to my people." As Risha spoke she picked up a small pouch that was lying next to her leg and handed it to Morgan.

"So what is your issue with us?" Morgan asked defensively. He considered witches beneath him and didn't like being judged by one.

"Even witches have standards," the old woman said and grinned; revealing a mouth that contained only a few teeth. "Be gone now." The three Rualas stared at the old woman for a few moments since they all wanted to strike her but they thought better of it and turned and left the cave.

"You did well," Orbus said as he walked out of the shadows towards Risha.

"You pay well," Risha replied with a grin. "You will get your money's worth."

Michael was surprised that he was not exhausted, so after Sudfad's meeting he returned to Gabriel's house with other members of the team. Gabriel immediately called a small meeting to tell everyone that they would have company on the following day and a celebration the following night.

With this news all of the women in the house went into a tizzy as they prepared for their guests. Michael laughed when he saw the commotion the news caused. Iris was ecstatic that Thomas and his new family were coming to stay and immediately ran upstairs to prepare rooms. Batina on the other hand felt awkward that her family was coming on a surprise visit until Gabriel and Hannah calmed her.

Some of the women went shopping while others started to prepare food for their guests. Adrone and Paul helped Dagon, Sam, Koby, Dack and Joao clean out the playroom and nursery and start painting the walls, at Emeral's request.

"It's always crazy here, that is what I like," Micha said as he, Bianca, Thor and Diana met with Michael to explain the training of Venatores and the customs of their tribe.

"Besides understanding the roles that we play," Thor explained. "If you come with us on our mission we will be working with our village; that's why Gabriel wants you to know these things."

"You mean the mission you have coming up?" asked Michael.

"Yes, but Gabriel's team has worked with our village before," Diana said. "Thor and I were hunting in the north so we can't tell you about that battle but you should ask the others. The ground opened up exposing the hell regions."

"She's telling you the truth," Micha said when he saw the look on Michael's face. "I was there and will tell you about it but first we have to cover the things that Gabriel told us."

"Gabriel hasn't said anything about me coming on this mission," Michael said.

"If you want to come just ask Gabriel; he will tell you if he doesn't think you are ready," Thor said.

Hecate drugged Sampson and left for her home planet of Sidus to look for her lover Orbus. Within moments of her departure, Duncan heard Daniel's voice. "Hecate and the Rualas are gone, Sampson has been given drugs and is sleeping in their chambers."

Duncan led a group of Venatores who had been waiting outside of Hecate's lair for the opportunity to rescue Ivan and George. Daniel had already told Duncan of the routes he must take to find his sons. Both Venatores were kept in separate areas that were on opposite sides of Hecate's lair. Lit torches were affixed to the stone walls which greatly aided Duncan and his men.

The stench of demon filled their nostrils as the Venatores walked deeper within the earth. Even though Duncan had been told that Daniel would warn him when Hecate returned, Duncan was anxious to get his sons out of the caverns.

The tunnels and caverns which Hecate had built around her lair were not expansive and there were many turns and blind spots in the tunnels. In less than twenty minutes Duncan found the first cavern; he grabbed a torch from the wall of the tunnel and entered. The light of the fire blinded George who was chained to the wall by both his wrists and ankles.

"George, it's your father," Duncan said as he visibly searched the area for traps. Duncan did not see anything he considered a trap and told some of his men to move forward. The shackles restraining George were not secured with a key but a bolt apparatus. Within moments the Venatores had the shackles off from George but he was too weak to stand on his own. While one group of Venatores took George out of the caverns, Duncan led the rest in search of Ivan.

Ivan was found in a cavern similar to the one that held George. Ivan was covered with bruises and unconscious. "This is too easy," Duncan said as his men unshackled Ivan and started to carry him out of the caverns. What Duncan did not realize is that the Angels were not the only beings watching him and his warriors. Orbus had been spying on Hecate's lair since she first told him where it was. Orbus wasn't physically at the lair but he had an ancient orb which allowed him to view into other worlds. Orbus had smiled when he saw Duncan and the Venatores hiding outside of Hecate's lair.

Orbus was jealous by nature and now that he had Hecate back he did not want to lose her again. Orbus knew that if Hecate discovered he killed Sampson she would leave him. So Orbus had been plotting ways to kill Hecate's human husband that could not be associated with him.

Orbus did not want Sampson to complete his trials because that would make Sampson a more formidable opponent. Shortly after Orbus discovered the Venatores outside of Hecate's lair he summoned her to meet him on Sidus. The moment Hecate left her lair Orbus performed a spell that disabled the security measures Hecate had put into place around her home.

Daniel and Miranda were watching all of this. The Angels understood that Orbus was not a current danger to Duncan and his warriors so the Angels did not interfere. That is until Duncan turned towards Hecate's chambers with the intention of killing his son.

"Duncan leave him," Daniel warned. "There are other forces in motion that endanger Sampson, forces that will keep Hecate's eyes off from your village and Gabriel's team." Reluctantly Duncan left the lair and returned to his village. Ivan regained consciousness on the journey and was given food and water as George had been. Ivan received his wounds at the hands of the three Rualas. Both George and Ivan said they never saw Hecate or Sampson during their imprisonment.

There was great rejoicing when the rescue team returned to the village with both of the chief's sons alive. Immediately every member of the village started preparations for a feast. Duncan's wife Liza could not stop crying and hugged and kissed her sons again and again. Duncan did not tell Liza that he was stopped from killing Sampson and he was not sure that he ever would. Duncan felt that the painful decision to kill his own son should be his burden to bear.

Orbus did not understand why Duncan turned back from Hecate's bedroom chambers but after some thought he determined Duncan could not kill his own son. Orbus immediately reestablished Hecate's security measures. He did it in such a way that the essence of Tritor, a powerful demon of Sidus was left in place of the essence of Orbus. Tritor too, was a former lover of Hecate's who had never lost his lust for the seductress. Hecate would believe that Tritor tried to interfere with Sampson's trials.

Orbus was unfazed by the fact that Hecate was pregnant with Sampson's baby. In fact, Orbus planned to use the pregnancy to his advantage.

Hecate was not the kind of woman to be controlled but she could be distracted. Orbus knew how badly Hecate had always wanted a child and he saw how her pregnancy seemed to be tempering her. While Orbus doubted the child would keep Hecate out of the demon wars he thought it would keep her out of the beds of other men.

As soon as Michael returned to the castle that evening he walked into Sudfad's study. "So how did your day go?" Sudfad asked.

"I really like them," Michael said as Sudfad handed him a glass of whiskey. "I learned about the Nordes Tribe and the Clan of Gesmal today. I will say I was impressed although it seems strange to me to think of women warriors."

"Well I certainly hope you didn't say that," Sudfad said with a laugh. "The girls on that team would have challenged you to a fight."

"I started to realize that," Michael said with a grin. "I spent most of the day with Gabriel and Raphael and they not only told me about the mission they are planning but prior missions. They also told me more about the Angels and the Prophesy of The Seven Sons. While I will admit some of this is difficult for me to understand, everyone on the team believes I was sent here at exactly this time because of the mission."

"They are not alone in that thinking," Sudfad said as he leaned back in his chair and looked at his son.

"So you believe that too?"

"Our entire family believes that."

"Then I think I should tell Gabriel that I want to go on the mission. I wanted to talk to you first."

"I won't lie to you son. The Angels told us a little about your tortured life. And while you seem to be handling the changes and the realization about your destiny just fine, well, do you think you are ready for a mission?"

"Like I said there is a part of all of this that sounds just crazy to me but, I can't really explain it. I think I am supposed to go on that mission."

"Then tell that to Gabriel tomorrow."

The caravan from Lentz did not arrive in Wetpr until the early evening of the following day. King Mathas sent Enrops in advance to tell both Sudfad's and Gabriel's households that the caravan would initially stop at Sudfad's castle. Everyone from Gabriel's home including the dog Jasper were at Sudfad's castle when the visitor's from Lentz arrived.

As always the reunions were joyous with lots of hugs and kisses. Michael stood back and watched the scene before him. In a few moments Luca joined Michael. "While I appreciate them coming I am dreading this," Luca said in a low voice. After a few minutes Sudfad called Michael forward and introduced his son to all of the guests. To Michael's surprise the reception towards him was warm also. Women were hugging and kissing Michael and men were shaking his hand and acting as if he had always been part of the family.

The reception that Michael received touched him greatly although he tried not to show it. But there was something else; something that was pulling at his heart strings, something that was making Michael feel both good and sad. After all of the introductions were completed, Michael realized what was causing him to have such conflicting emotions. He had never seen a family like this before, they were all so genuinely happy to see each other that Michael could feel the love in the room. And for a brief moment Michael flashed back to his life with Karzman and the anger took hold again.

Ingr was the first guest to see Luca in the back of the room, she handed baby Sicily to Ryan and walked over to Luca. Ingr did not speak, she put her arms around Luca and they both cried. "He is just so crippled by Lila's death," Emeral said to Bella and Rosa as they watched Luca and Ingr. Luca and Ingr caught the attention of many but no one approached them until they stopped crying and hugging. Then it was Nikki who was trying to be strong for Luca but found herself crying also.

Renya and Emeral knew that Luca did not want to be the center of attention so they directed the guests into the Great Hall for refreshments. "Bekka, Bekka." Christopher's voice rang loudly as he and Amy walked through the group. Bekka was introducing her parents to Sorren and Shara when Christopher found her. "Amy this is my good friend Bekka," Christopher said excitedly.

"Bekka this is my girlfriend Amy and look what she gave me. It's a warrior bracelet." Christopher held out his arm and showed Bekka a braided leather band with beads that was tied to his wrist."

Sorren smiled and winked at Bekka and her family. "Our little warriors earn those in training," Sorren said then he turned to Christopher. "Amy must like you if she gave you hers."

"Amy I have heard a lot about you," Bekka said. Both Christopher and Amy smiled.

"Sam, Ella look," Christopher said and proudly showed them his wrist. "Amy these are Bekka's parents." Christopher turned back to Ella and Sam and said again, "This is Amy."

"Amy it is very nice to meet you," Ella said. "And that is a nice gift you gave Christopher."

"I know," Christopher said. "I have to show it to Batina." Christopher grabbed Amy's hand and they ran through the crowd.

"They are so cute," Shara cooed.

"It's good that she came," Sam said. "That's the first time Christopher has acted like his old self since Lila died."

"Another baby," Stephan called out jokingly as Jared and Zoya entered the Great Hall with baby William.

"It's been kind of an explosion of babies around here," Thaos said to Michael. Thaos liked to study people; it was a well-honed skill he developed that had kept him alive. While Michael somewhat intrigued Thaos, Michael also reminded Thaos of his old friend Derick although Thaos wasn't sure why. "I don't have to watch any babies tonight all the women have them, want to have a drink?"

69

"Sure," Michael said with a slight smile. "I have to admit I feel a little out of place."

"I can understand," Thaos said as he took a bottle of whiskey and two glasses from one of the tables. "I wasn't born into this family. In fact I was a hired fighter; I got involved with them and changed my life. Best thing I ever did."

"You sound like Jared."

"Understand I am not bragging when I tell you this I am stating fact," Thaos said as he filled the glasses with whiskey. "Archetenus, Jared and me were about as bad as you can get. Well, that might not be true some of the fellas we've chased down and fought with this group are pretty damn bad, but some of them were demons too." Thaos laughed. "And look at us now happy lives, beautiful wives and beautiful babies. I'll tell you I never thought I would live long enough to have a life like this."

Michael watched Thaos carefully as he talked. "Why do I have a feeling there is a reason you are telling me this? Did Renya ask you to talk to me?"

"No one asked me to talk to you. Your shirt isn't all buttoned and from what I can see your chest looks like mine. So I would imagine your back does too. Those damn horsewhips can wrap right around you if a fella knows how to use them right. I'll bet if we started talking we would find out our pasts had a lot in common; which means our futures can too. Hang around, give these people a chance before you take off."

Michael stopped drinking his whiskey and stared at Thaos. "How did you know?"

"I've seen that look before, hell I've had that look before. Just give it a chance before you make any decisions you might regret later."

Michael looked around and when he spoke his voice was lowered. "I came here to kill Sudfad. I thought I would die too and I didn't damn well care. Next thing I know I am part of the family; don't get me wrong because everyone has been so good to me. But when the Sanuri talked to me he told me I was Sudfad's oldest son which means I am next in line for the throne, me!"

"Thaos most of my childhood I was kept in a cage. I don't know how to be a king and I don't think I want to know."

"I am sure they will prepare you but you do know that Raul and Simon have prepared their lives to be King; if you don't want that role just tell them. I doubt if there would be any hard feelings. Did Raul tell you how he met Vitomas?"

"She told me some."

"I've met other kings besides Sudfad and Mathas, in fact I've been hired by a few. Sudfad and Mathas act more like normal folk than most royalty and that is how they raised their sons. Raul wanted to be treated like a regular person and he didn't want the responsibility of the throne, so he just took off. Traveled for a couple of years, lived off the land."

"He met Vitomas during his travels. Apparently once Raul and Simon fell in love they both settled down and accepted their responsibilities. Now I am not saying that is the same with you; what I am saying is that Raul would probably understand some of your thoughts. Besides I think everyone is more concerned with you being one of The Seven Sons than the next King."

"And that's another thing. I know people aren't lying to me but boy this is all so hard to swallow."

"I said those same damn words when I first got here but I can tell you it is all fact. And because you haven't been here long, I'll bet you haven't even heard half the stories. If you're a fighting man these are some of the best damn battles you will ever see. And your father and brothers are real warriors they don't sit on their butts like a lot of rich folk and expect others to do their fighting. In fact Renya is as tough and well trained as any of the men. Emeral is too; those are two older women you don't want to get into the ring with," Thaos said with a grin.

"Are you speaking the truth?" Michael asked with a big grin.

"Just ask to hear a few stories," Thaos said. "Better yet ask one or both of them to a competition. If the Sanuri talked to you then you know that you are a Keeper of the Scrolls too. That was all one big secret until about a year ago. I have heard stories about demons waiting for Sudfad to leave the castle to inspect the forts, then they attacked."

"And it was Renya who led the troops and defended the castle. You've probably heard that most of us in Lentz are married to women warriors, well I'll tell ya they all admire Renya and want to be like her."

"I've never even heard of women warriors until I came here," Michael said with a big grin. Yesterday I met Gabriel's team and, well, let's just say my eyes were opened."

"I'll bet they were," Thaos said and laughed. "The Nordes Tribe and the Clan of Gesmal really train their warriors much better than most armies train their soldiers. But take a word of advice, its hard being married to a woman warrior. Not because of anything they do, but while most of us in this room have fought alongside of our wives, well its' different. You said when you came here you expected to die and you didn't care and that is how I was most of my life. The last really big battle I was in, Nikki was pregnant and really sick and fighting too. I was so worried about her it was hard for me to keep my focus."

Chapter VI
Destinies

Sorren walked to the front of the Great Hall and yelled, "Can I have everyone's attention." As the people in the room became quiet Sorren continued. "Bianca, Darla and Jasmine will you please come up here?" The three young warriors walked hesitantly to the front of the room. "I was at King Mathas' castle when the group of people you see here decided to come to Wetpr; we left within hours of making the decision. I returned to the village and invited all of your families."

Sorren continued, "Darla your father was delivering a calf, Bianca your father and brothers were hunting and Jasmine your father was working in the fields. These families decided to accept the invitation but they were going to leave a few hours after we did. They are all traveling together and I expect they will arrive tonight. They wanted to see you off before the mission." All three young women looked excited; then Jasmine turned and looked at Sudfad and Renya who were standing to her right. "Is it alright if they stay here?"

"Of course," Renya said with a smile. "Sorren sent us a message on the day they left Lentz, we have chambers prepared."

"Thank you," Jasmine said.

"Is Edward here?" Sorren called out.

"Yes," Edward answered and laughed.

"Don't be surprised if Toni comes with them." Sorren said with a grin.

"Edward you have so many women chasing you one of these nights there is going to be a cat fight," Jared joked and everyone in the room laughed.

"Thanks for letting me know," Edward said. "I asked someone to come to this celebration, I will cancel that now."

"Bring her too," Archetenus said loudly. "It could be entertaining."

Nikki walked up to Thaos and Michael who were still standing by themselves and talking. "You both look so serious," Nikki said and smiled. "Michael this is the newest member of our family James Duran." Nikki introduced the baby she was holding.

"Thaos he looks just like you," Michael said.

"Both of our sons do," Nikki said with pride. "Thaos so many people have thanked us for bringing Amy here because Christopher is doing so much better."

"We just adopted a seven year old girl and she and Christopher are in love," Thaos said. "He even asked me for permission to marry her when they grow up."

"Everyone thinks they are so cute except for Thaos," Nikki said. "He acts like they are going to run away and get married."

"I will tell you it's the strangest thing how protective you get once you have children," Thaos said then grinned. "Guess I remember what I was like when I was single."

"Thaos, Christopher is six years old," Nikki scolded.

"I'll leave you two," Michael said. "I am going to take your advice, we will see how this goes over."

As Michael walked away Nikki asked, "What did he mean?"

"I'll tell you later," Thaos said and watched Michael walk up to Sudfad.

"Sudfad can I speak with you, Raul and Simon in private?" Michael asked seriously. "I am sorry to take you away from the celebration."

"Nonsense, the boys are over there," Sudfad said and nodded to a table. "I'll get them and we can meet in my study."

Michael walked straight to the study and waited for the others. "Is something wrong?" Simon asked when he saw the look on Michael's face.

"I have to talk to the three of you about something and, well, you might get pretty mad," Michael said as Sudfad, Raul and Simon sat down. "You know why I came here and you know I never expected to become part of your family." Michael hesitated before he continued.

"That first night that I talked with the Sanuri he told me something that frankly scared the hell out of me. I guess I should have realized it but I never thought about it. Sudfad I didn't even think about being your eldest son and the heir to the throne. All of you have been so good to me but honestly I don't want to be a king."

"Thaos told me that Raul and Simon have prepared for the role their entire lives," Michael continued then looked directly at Sudfad. "They should have that position they earned it. I would still like to be part of this family and keep my other responsibilities."

"Son, you will always be part of this family," Sudfad said. "And I believe we just learned a great deal about you. I will be honest the family has talked about preparing you for the throne; you certainly aren't ready now but that doesn't mean you won't be someday."

"Even if I knew how to be a king I don't think I would want it. Sudfad most of my childhood I was kept in a cage what do I know about running a kingdom and being responsible for all those people? Besides it should go to Raul or Simon."

"First of all, no one is mad at you," Simon said. "But I am curious why Thaos was involved in this."

"It was the damndest thing. I had been thinking about leaving just so I wouldn't have to be king. Thaos walks up to me and said he recognized my look. He told me to stay and give a new life a chance and to tell you how I felt."

"Well I am certainly glad that he talked to you Michael," Sudfad said. "I just found you and I don't want to lose you again. You don't have to be king but there is still a great deal you have to learn about the position because my sons fill it from time to time."

"Well I am alright with that. I am a hard worker, I don't want to shirk my duties; I just don't want to sit on the throne."

"Most men would want that power and wealth," Raul said skeptically.

"I've already found what I always wanted and I am content and happy and this is the first time in my life I could ever say that," Michael said emotionally.

"Perhaps now would be a good time to tell him about Stordt," Simon suggested.

"Well, then I am going to pour us all some whiskey," Sudfad said.

Sudfad told Michael about his childhood with Roch and explained how his parents sent him away to protect him from Roch's insanity. Sudfad explained how Roch murdered his parents and how the King and Queen of Wetpr, who were his uncle and aunt adopted him. Sudfad explained the reign of terror that Roch brought upon the people of Stordt. Then Sudfad took the three wills that his father had written and handed them to Michael. "I never knew these existed until a little over a year ago. Look at the dates, Father wrote these before he was murdered; he must have suspected something would happen to him."

After Michael read the wills he asked, "Isn't Roch dead?"

"Yes and the two men who claimed the throne after Roch are dead also. We are told that a demon named Zieman now controls Stordt," Raul said. "That demon also put bounties on the heads of every member of Gabriel's team because he was afraid the team would uncover some plot the demon is working on. By rights our family should have that throne too."

"What are you going to do?" asked Michael.

"Stordt is a kingdom filled with demonic men," Simon said. "Our wives fought with us for days because they did not want us to take that throne and put our families at risk. We did not believe Annabelle and Vitomas but after spending some time in Stordt we now understand."

76

"And to answer your question we haven't decided what to do yet. We feel our roles as The Seven Sons and Keepers of the Scrolls take priority over expanding our territory now."

By the time Sudfad and his sons returned to the celebration the last of the visitors from the Nordes Tribe had arrived. "Is this what it is always like?" Michael asked Sudfad.

"What do you mean?"

"Everyone is so happy."

Raul and Simon were standing next to Sudfad and Michael. "We need to introduce you around," Raul said and slapped Michael on the back.

The four men returned to the celebration.

It was another two days before Morgan, Bruno and Nada returned to Hecate's lair with her potion. When they entered Hecate's chambers they were surprised at the condition that Sampson was in. He was lying on the sofa and his body was covered with long dark hair; Sampson's face was contorted and he smelled like a demon.

"Did he already change?" Nada asked as Morgan handed Hecate the pouch containing the small vial of potion.

"No, he keeps changing back and forth," Hecate explained. "This is what he looked like when he was going through his trials in Baal's realm. I had to pull him out because those damn humans and Rualas almost killed him."

"They were in hell?" Bruno asked.

"Yes, the Angels led them in and protected them."

"What humans are you talking about?" Morgan asked.

"You should know; so many of your people work with them," Hecate said sarcastically.

"Do you mean Gabriel's team?" Morgan asked.

"And the others, the kings of Wetpr and Lentz, the chief of the Nordes Tribe and those Venatores; oh and I almost forgot the Sanuri. I will kill them all, they will regret laughing at me!" Hecate's voice keep raising as she spoke until she was almost yelling.

"And you're saying that Angels were with them?" Bruno asked.

"That's what I said, why?"

"We didn't think we would be going against Angels," Morgan said.

"Are you afraid?" Hecate asked sarcastically.

"No," Bruno said although he did not believe his own words.

"Good," Hecate said. "Now bring me the prisoners."

"Together?" Morgan asked.

"Yes, they haven't had anything to eat or drink since you captured them, they won't be able to fight you."

The three Rualas entered the cavern where George had been imprisoned first. "What the hell!" Bruno said as they observed the empty shackles hanging from the stone wall. The cavern was small so it only took minutes for the three to search it. They quickly ran to the second cavern that no longer held Ivan.

"I really don't want to tell her this," Bruno said, referring to Hecate.

"Well, just how the hell did they escape is what I would like to know," Morgan said. "Hecate said she has spells on this place. They had to have had help, who could get in here?"

"Another demon maybe," Nada said.

"Or an Angel," Bruno added. "I really don't like this."

"Come on we've got to tell her," Morgan said and the three Rualas returned to Hecate's chambers.

"Hecate both Venatores are gone, we searched the chambers and there isn't any footprints or signs of intruders. You know they couldn't escape without help. Who is powerful enough to get past your spells?" Morgan asked.

"What!" shrieked Hecate and ran out of her chambers to the caverns. The Rualas followed her. Hecate was shaking, she was so filled with rage as she looked into both caverns.

Morgan was deliberately trying to keep Hecate's rage focused away from him, Nada and Bruno. "It's as if they just disappeared. Are there demons more powerful than you that would try and stop Sampson's trials?"

"Why did you ask that?" Hecate said suspiciously.

"Because humans can't just disappear without help. So we figured it was another demon or an Angel," Morgan replied. "And you told us you had this place protected, so it had to be someone stronger than you to release them."

Hecate was so filled with rage that it took her several minutes to calm down. "What you are saying makes sense and I do have enemies. You must go now, I have inquiries to make."

"Do we get paid?" Bruno asked.

"Of course; come to the chambers."

"Won't that potion help Sampson?" Nada asked.

"It should help him get his strength and form back but he still needs to meet the requirements of the original trials."

"Do you want us to go back to that village and see if they returned?" Morgan asked.

"Yes, don't do anything just tell me," Hecate said.

After Hecate paid the Rualas she waited for them to leave her lair before she gave Sampson more of a sedative. Hecate inspected the vial of potion then locked it in a chest on the floor. She grabbed some candles and went to her unholy altar.

"Get rid of her," Hecate yelled as she materialized in Orbus' bedroom. Orbus was lying in bed next to a Zehno demon.

"Hecate our relationship is not exclusive, don't just drop in like this," Orbus said calmly. "She's not leaving."

Hecate stared angrily at him for a few moments, then she calmed herself. "I need to talk to you, it is business. When should I return?"

"Come back at noon," Orbus replied and Hecate vanished as quickly as she had arrived. He knew Hecate well, she always wanted what she couldn't have then when she got it she would get bored. Orbus was not going to make the same mistakes this time with Hecate; he planned to keep her on her toes.

The visitors from Lentz had originally planned to stay for three days but as a group they decided to stay longer. Raphael and Gabriel spent a great deal of time with Chaez which included lengthy visits with members of Sudfad's family. On the morning of the fourth day, Raphael and Vivian took Chaez to the Patronus Headquarters at Cicero while Gabriel met with Raul, Simon, Sudfad and Michael in Sudfad's study.

"I will try not to take up a lot of your time," Gabriel said. "But I need to tie up loose ends before I leave. You have all had a chance to speak with Chaez; do any of you have concerns that he has the same evil in him as his brother?"

Since it was Simon's wife who was victimized by Timothy, Sudfad's family was letting Simon take the lead on this issue. "No, he's a good kid but he is a kid. Are you sure he has what it takes to be a Patronus priest?"

Before Gabriel could answer Raul said, "I agree with Matthew in that I could see Chaez as a regular priest."

"He has led a pampered lifestyle until he made the decision to join our ranks. He is working very hard to change his life," Gabriel explained. "Chaez was horrified at the monster that his brother had become and he saw the effects on his family. Chaez seems sincere about wanting to stand up to such darkness."

"But, he has to come a long way in his fighting abilities to make it through our training. Would you allow him to join your military training exercises while my team is gone? Chaez feels that if he can stay here he will have no responsibilities that will distract him from training."

"Of course," Simon said. "But you know he is going to need more than that."

"And that was going to be my second question," said Gabriel.

"We can work with him and we can assign some of our men to spend time with him," Simon said. "And since the barracks aren't completed he can live here."

"Thank you and now for the second matter," Gabriel continued. "Raphael and I told Fahron what Chaez's education would cost and Fahron sent five times that amount. Chaez said Fahron wants us to use the extra money to help students who can't afford to pay for the education, which is most generous but..." Gabriel paused.

"But what if the kid washes out," Raul said.

"Then we make sure that he doesn't," Sudfad said. "Everyone seems to have the mindset that Chaez will fail. I found the boy to be responsible and very driven. So many people curl up and hide from the face of evil; I commend the boy for wanting to take a stand. We have the finest military in all of Opots; there isn't a reason we can't train him to become a mighty warrior."

"I don't understand the real problem here," Michael said. "Don't you teach fighting in your training?"

"Yes, but traditionally many men apply for the positions but only the very best are chosen so the students start competing with each other from day one. Many priests spend years preparing for the challenges to become a Patronus priest. We did tell Chaez and Fahron that Chaez can apply at another time if he isn't ready yet."

"Well what does the kid need to know?" asked Michael.

"He needs to be able to fight like us," Simon said. "At least to complete the training."

"But especially the first month, the weaker students are weeded out," Gabriel said. "Many people from Lentz have been working with Chaez and he has progressed a great deal but he was never even in a fight before he started training."

"We have a week before we leave for Ryed," Michael said. "Let me work with the kid for a while. Fighting is the one thing I really know."

"Good," Gabriel said with a broad smile. "Raphael and Vivian took him to the Cicero Headquarters they plan to return for the midday meal. My take on Chaez is that he is self-conscious of his naivety of fighting and he is trying to please all of us. He needs to get that fire in his belly, maybe you can help him with that."

When Hecate returned to Orbus' chambers she was still visibly angry. He smiled when he saw the look on her face. "If I didn't know better I would think you were jealous," Orbus said.

Hecate walked up to Orbus and kissed him passionately on the lips. "Perhaps I was or perhaps I wasn't," she said suggestively. "But that is not the reason I am here. Someone broke into my lair and helped Sampson's brothers to escape. I need help to find out who would do this."

Orbus poured Hecate a glass of wine and sat down next to her on the sofa. "What makes you think the Venatores needed help escaping?" he asked.

"They were shackled to the walls, injured and weak. I hadn't given them food or water."

"Did you weaken them because you don't believe Sampson is strong enough to fight them?"

Hecate was initially angered by this question but then answered, "Yes, he is in great pain and I keep him sedated most of the time."

"Was he in your lair when the Venatores escaped?"

"Yes, but he was sedated."

"Was he injured?"

"No," Hecate replied suspiciously.

"Well that should give you some indication of who broke in; don't you think the Venatores would have killed Sampson for his crimes?"

"Orbus, you are right. And those humans I hate would have done the same thing. I have been so angry I haven't thought this through. My Rualas believe that something more powerful than me, either a demon or Angel must have helped my prisoners because they thwarted my security spells."

"Without knowing any more than what you just told me I would agree with the Rualas. Don't you think the Angels would have destroyed Sampson?"

"I don't know they may have taken mercy on him because he is in such bad shape."

"He is in that shape because of the Angels."

Hecate stared at Orbus then asked with concern, "Do you think I am like this because I am pregnant?"

"I don't follow you."

"Orbus you know me, I am shrewd and meticulous; little confuses me. But both you and the Rualas see things that I should have; it's like I am not thinking right."

"Perhaps you are just so worried about your husband that it is effecting you?"

"I can't imagine that; no I think it is something else."

"Like what?"

"I don't know. I wonder if someone has put a spell on me and is trying to diffuse my power."

"Perhaps but perhaps you just don't make wise decisions when you are emotional."

"How can you say that?" Hecate snapped angrily.

"You went after Gabriel's team and those other humans for revenge. You have lost every battle with them and incurred the wrath of many Old Ones from your actions. Think about it Hecate, when was the last time you lost a battle?"

The blood drained from Hecate's face as she thought about Orbus' words. He continued, "Hecate you have wondered why I have been hesitant about jumping into the wars; part of that is you. You never listen to anyone, you jump into things without thinking things through and you have made some very poor decisions. I am not saying this to make you angry; you asked me and I am telling you the truth."

"But I have always been like this," Hecate said defensively.

"Have you?"

"You think I have changed?"

"I have noticed many changes in you since we have reunited."

"Like what?" Hecate asked sincerely.

"You have always been passionate and spontaneous and I love that in you. But now it's like you are driven by anger and hatred and I think these emotions are weakening you."

"Sanuri it is so good to see you," Chief Duncan said as the Sanuri dismounted from his boca in the center of the Village of Gesmal. "To what do we owe this visit?"

"Well, I am not really sure," the Sanuri said as he extended his hand to Duncan. "The Angels told me to come here. I suspect it has to do with those three Ruala criminals who are spying on your village."

"Now?" Duncan asked as he looked around.

"Yes, tell me are Ivan and George alright?"

"They are recuperating in the house; Hecate had taken them prisoners. It was those Rualas who actually grabbed the boys."

"Let's go inside so I can see them and you can tell me what happened," the Sanuri suggested.

Both George and Ivan were sleeping in their rooms when the Sanuri looked in on them. He placed his hand on the forehead of each of the sleeping men before he left their rooms. In the meantime Duncan's wife was setting food and drink on the table for their guest.

As the Sanuri ate, Duncan explained about the kidnappings and the search for his sons. Duncan told of his conversation with the Angels and the morning they rescued Ivan and George. When Duncan's wife left the room Duncan leaned forward and told the Sanuri about his intention to kill Sampson and Daniel's message which stopped him.

"I find that message interesting and believe that has something to do with my presence here," the Sanuri said as he filled his cup with coffee. "As I said Duncan, I was told to come here and stay with your people; I was told nothing more. But as I entered your village I had a vision of those three Rualas spying on all of you. Have either George or Ivan been out of this house since you brought them home?"

"No, they have remained in bed."

"For now, keep their drapes closed so no one can see in. I am guessing that the Rualas are trying to figure out where your boys are. As you can imagine they will try to abduct them again but also Hecate is now highly paranoid and is trying to figure out who helped them escape. This will distract her for a while."

"Sanuri you will stay with us," Duncan said. "When Liza returns I will have her prepare a room for you."

"Thank you, it is probably the wisest thing for me to stay close to your family. After I finish my coffee I am going to tend to my horses then take a look around. Do the Half-Mans still visit?"

"Yes, most of my people cannot speak their tongue so the Enrops translate. We give them baskets of food twice a week and they give us information. Ever since they spoke with Miranda and Daniel the Half-Mans seem to feel they must be our protectors."

85

"Perhaps the Angels told them that," the Sanuri said.

"We are a village of Venatores," Duncan said with pride.

"And they represent nature; there is no reason you can't take care of each other. Now Duncan I am going to share some information with you that you will tell no other until I tell you the time is right. In a few days Gabriel's team will leave Wetpr for Ryed. They are working two missions because the Teivel Clan has infiltrated Sudfad's military. As they did research for this mission they learned how the Teivel Clan rules this kingdom with its darkness. In the coming weeks there may be a war in this kingdom, you need to be aware."

"Are they going to overthrow the Teivel's?"

"They will try if they can get the backing of the people of this kingdom. The Angels told them of a group of freedom fighters who they must contact for assistance."

"Our swords stand ready if they need them," Duncan said with pride.

"While Gabriel could use them, at this point we may not want to remove your warriors from this village, in fact we may want to tell them to stop hunting so you have all of your Venatores here."

Chapter VII
Gabriel's Tribe

While the families of Darla, Jasmine and Bianca stayed at Sudfad's castle with the majority of guests from Lentz, Batina's family and Sasha's family stayed at Gabriel's home. Edgar and Cora as well as Hugo and Greta were not only honored by the invitation but also by the accommodations. Hugo and Greta stayed in the chambers of Joshua's family, along with Thomas and Sasha. Edgar and Cora stayed in the chambers of Ratri and Batina. Neither of these couples brought their other children since their visits were a surprise and they felt they did not want to impose more than they were.

The guests only added to the excited energy that usually permeated the household. Both Greta and Cora insisted on helping with meals and other duties when they weren't shopping or being entertained. Everyone understood that Gabriel and Raphael were making final preparations for their mission and wanted to help. Hugo and Edgar examined equipment, cleaned weapons and helped pack gear. The days were filled with activity and seemed to fly by for the families.

"So Batina, you and Ratri haven't told us if you plan to make your home here in Wetpr," Edgar said on the morning of the day before the guests were to return to Lentz. "This is certainly a beautiful home that Gabriel has given you."

"We haven't decided," Ratri said. "We are still in shock that Gabriel gave us these chambers. If we stay here that would mean we would become permanent members of the team. We just haven't made any decisions yet."

"Gabriel said that even if we decided to live someplace else that these chambers would be our home when we were in Wetpr," Batina said. "Everyone here is fun and so kind but I still feel like an outsider. I'm just not used to all of this."

Edgar and Cora looked at each other and smiled. "You two have a lot of decisions to make but you don't have to make them right away. We have already been writing with Ratri's parents and you two will always have a home in their house as well as ours."

"Cora and I think you have an opportunity here that you shouldn't take lightly. In your place I don't believe I would want to give up this home or the chance to work on Gabriel's team."

"So you wouldn't be mad if we stayed here?" Batina asked.

"No and we thought that might be a concern which is why I brought the subject up," said Edgar. "Wetpr is only a three day ride and I am sure much shorter if Ratri flies you. Bring Joseph and Clair here when they come for the wedding ceremony; I am sure they will say the same things."

"Well, that makes us both feel better," Ratri said. "Batina and I feel like all of you have done so much for us that we don't want to hurt anyone's feelings. We will probably stay here for a while at least until we make some permanent decisions. Know that you are always welcomed to visit. Gabriel offered us larger chambers if we wanted them. Which I am thinking we should take so there will be more room for the entire families."

"Really?" Batina asked. "Do you think we should?"

"They offered and it would be nice to have your brothers and sisters come or both our families come at the same time."

"Well, Cora and I have truly enjoyed this visit and will come again. Sorren and Shara love coming here and we understand why. Now, we didn't want to talk business while we were here but Joseph and Clair plan to come in two weeks for a visit and the women have a small list of wedding questions for you two," Edger said with a laugh and winked at Ratri.

"Chaez don't worry about hurting me," Michael said as he and Chaez were training near one of the barns on the castle grounds. "The object is to hurt me." Chaez punched Michael in the stomach and Michael didn't flinch.

"Alright stop for a minute," Michael said. "Chaez I told you about my life and how anger was really the only thing that kept me alive. Well, I know you have anger in you and lots of it. You have to stop pretending it isn't there and use it."

"I want you to think about the pain that Timothy caused your parents. I want you to imagine that I am Timothy and you are stopping him from hurting Tabeth. Imagine yourself in that shed, he's going to kill your sister how will you stop him? That's why you are doing this isn't it so you can stop monsters like him?"

Chaez's face lost its color as Michael was talking. Tears started to well up in Chaez's eyes. He didn't move, he just looked at Michael for several moments. Michael knew this was the final test and if Chaez did not respond to this he would never make it as a fighter.

Two, three minutes passed and Chaez just stared at Michael. "Chaez maybe this isn't..." Michael did not finish his sentence because Chaez let out a scream of rage and pain. He flew at Michael, punching, kicking and gouging and all of the time crying. At first Michael just blocked the punches and kicks, then Michael started to fight back and Chaez did not stop his attack.

Michael punched Chaez so hard that he fell onto his back, Chaez jumped to his feet and attacked Michael again and again. After twenty minutes they stopped. Both tired and bleeding. They sat on the ground and Michael held Chaez as he cried.

"Boys!" Renya yelled loudly as Michael and Chaez entered the Great Hall for lunch. "Are you alright?"

Now everyone in the room turned and looked at the two men who were covered in dirt, blood and bruises. Michael slapped Chaez on the back and said proudly, "He found his fire." Chaez did not speak but smiled although it was difficult for many to realize that since his lips were swollen and his right eye was swollen shut. Sorren let out a war cry and everyone laughed and smiled.

"I'm going to have Hannah come over after lunch and look at both of you," Renya said in a scolding manner. Michael looked at Chaez and winked.

Since this was the last day that the guests from Lentz would be in Wetpr, Gabriel's team was hosting an outdoor feast with games.

The games were scheduled to start after the midday meal and the feast would be served in the evening. Sudfad's family and their guests, as well as Archetenus, Delilah, Jared and Zoya were invited. Renya changed her mind about calling Hannah to the castle and instead made Michael and Chaez go to Gabriel's house after they ate lunch.

"What on earth!" Emeral said when Michael and Chaez walked in the backdoor carrying baskets of food.

Michael laughed before he said anything. "Renya wants Hannah to look us over and since we were coming Marie sent some food for the feast. Is Gabriel here?"

Emeral opened the kitchen door and called for Gabriel and Raphael then she handed Chaez a raw steak.

"What is this for?" Chaez asked.

"Put it over that eye," Emeral said with a grin.

Both Gabriel and Raphael started laughing when they entered the kitchen and saw Michael and Chaez.

"He's ready," Michael said.

"Did Chaez give you those wounds?" Raphael asked in amazement.

"He sure did," Michael said with a proud smile. "He was bottling up his anger instead of using it. He's doing this because he wants to beat the hell out of Timothy and others like him. Once he realized that, we pretended I was Timothy. He will need to keep practicing so he can control his anger but he's learned a lot."

Gabriel smiled with approval. "Chaez honestly we have been afraid you wouldn't make the training. But if you can fight Michael like that, I'm not worried anymore."

"Grandma, Grandma," Nicholas yelled as he flew through the kitchen door. "We need you in the playroom."

"Nicholas what is the matter?" Emeral asked fearfully.

"It's Bekka," Nicholas said as he was running back to the playroom, in lead of the adults.

"No need to panic," Bekka said as she was sitting on the floor surrounded by children with Jasper licking her face. "I think the baby is coming."

Michael immediately picked Bekka up, "Where do you want her?" He asked Emeral.

"I'll show you. Gabriel, Raphael get the others. Chaez will you stay here with the children for a few minutes?" Emeral directed.

"I could probably walk," Bekka said as she was embarrassed that Michael was carrying her.

"That's alright," Michael said as he followed Emeral up the stairs to the second floor of the house.

By the time Michael set Bekka on top of her bed, other family members started to rush into the room. Within minutes Bekka's bedroom was filled with people.

"How long have you been having contractions?" Hannah asked.

"Since last night."

"What!" Koby almost yelled. "Why didn't you say anything?"

"Because I knew it would be a long time before the baby came. Koby, my parents are in Salar shopping with Joshua and Iris."

"We'll find them," Joao said as he and Dack ran out of the room.

"Everyone, please go back to the games, there is no need for everyone to sit up here," Bekka said as she gritted her teeth.

"She's right," Hannah said. "And I need to examine Bekka so all of you should leave now."

"I'll start making some tonics," Vivian said and started to leave the room. Then she saw the fearful look on Luca's face. "Luca come with me," Vivian said and gently took his hand.

"Can I help deliver the baby?" Cassandra asked.

91

"Of course," Hannah replied.

"I don't want to," Elan said. "Because Bekka is like my sister."

"I'm glad to hear you say that Elan," Bekka said and laughed then she turned to Melinda. "Check on Christopher and the other children I think they got scared because Lila died giving birth."

"Don't worry about the children, we will all watch over them," Greta said then she and Cora left the bedroom.

Natasha walked in with an armload of towels and clean bedding. "I've got hot water on the stove," she announced.

"Please everyone leave," Hannah said.

"Koby you can come back later," Emeral said and took her son's arm.

"Koby you better start figuring out some names," Bekka said and tried to laugh.

"Names," Koby said nervously as Emeral ushered him into the hallway. "We still haven't decided on names."

"Have Diana help you," Misha said with a grin as he could see how nervous Koby was.

"Come on Koby," Diana said and took his hand. "I'll get some paper and you can tell me what names you have been considering."

"The feast should still go on," Emeral said to the family members who were standing in the hallway. "Natasha does Bekka have anything here for the baby? Perhaps we should get her a few things."

"I'll go with you," Batina said to Natasha and the two women left for Salar.

"Do you want me to tell Sudfad and the others not to come?" Michael asked.

"No, just tell them Bekka is having a baby so some of us may not be at the feast. They can still come and enjoy themselves," Emeral said.

Shortly before the feast was to be served, Natasha walked outside and announced to the crowd, "Bekka had a baby boy and he looks just like Koby, if anyone wants to come inside. Family filled the hallway outside of Bekka's chambers as friends waited their turns. As soon as all of Gabriel's team was inside of the chambers Koby carried the baby out. "Meet Ian Maxwell Luca," Koby said with a beaming smile. "Ian is Sam's middle name and you know the rest." Koby handed the baby to Emeral who turned and said.

"Luca you should hold your namesake first."

Luca pushed through the front of the crowd and looked at the baby. "You named him after me too?" Luca asked in awe as Emeral put the baby into his arms. "How is Bekka?" Luca asked as he continued to stare at his nephew.

"I'm fine," Bekka called out from the bedroom. "And I am starving."

"Iris is getting you a tray," Emeral said loudly and smiled as Luca handed the baby to Maxwell.

"You two couldn't look any prouder," Gabriel said to Sam and Ella.

"Our first grandchild," Ella said. "I am so happy I could burst."

The festivities at Gabriel's home lasted late into the night as bonfires were built. "We should have hired some musicians," Hannah said. "I didn't even think about it."

"Chaez brought his guitar," Michael announced. "But he can't sing cuz his face is too swollen. And actually so are his hands."

"Dack can play," Joao yelled out.

As Chaez got his guitar, Joao set up a chair for Dack in front of one of the bonfires. "Sorren plays too," Shara called out.

93

"Good," Dack said. "Because I mostly know Ruala songs. And this first one is for baby Ian."

"We haven't done this in ages," Renya said happily as everyone crowded around Dack and sang along.

The following morning breakfast was bittersweet at both the house of Gabriel and the castle of Sudfad. The guests from Lentz planned to leave right after the morning meal. Thomas and Sasha planned to return to the Village of Tyger with Hugo and Greta. While Thomas expected his mother to take it badly he didn't expect the reactions he received from his brothers. Both Paul and Adrone were crying at the breakfast table and Micha was visibly upset.

Batina too was saddened that her parents were leaving because she didn't know when she would see them again. Gabriel looked at the long faces sitting around the tables, then he stood up and announced, "We need to have a toast. Hannah, Natasha will you get the glasses?"

"I'll get the wine," Raphael said and left the room.

"Perfect timing," Gabriel said as Koby helped Bekka into the dining room. She was holding Ian.

"Bekka should you be out of bed?" Ella gasped.

"I just can't stand being up in that room away from everyone," Bekka said and handed the baby to her mother.

"She was going to walk down here herself," Koby said as he held out a chair for Bekka.

"What is this?" Bekka asked as Natasha set an empty wine glass in front of her.

"We are having a toast," Gabriel replied as he and Raphael were opening bottles of wine.

As Hannah, Gabriel and Raphael were pouring wine, Vivian and Natasha walked out of the kitchen with small trays of glasses of cherry juice. "The children can toast too," Vivian said and the children excitedly took their glasses.

94

"Don't drink until Gabriel tells you," Natasha said and laughed.

"To baby Ian, it is always a blessing when a baby is born," Gabriel said as he held up his glass. "And to new friends and family, may our bonds never be broken."

As the adults took a sip of their wine, Christopher yelled, "Now Gabriel?"

Everyone laughed. "Yes Christopher, now," Gabriel replied. And the children drank their juice.

"I would like to say something," Joshua said and stood up at the table. "While life here is so very different from our lives in our village; my eyes have been opened a great deal. Over the last few days I have spent a great deal of time with Maxwell, Sam, Hugo and Edgar and while we all come from very different worlds we are so very similar. I will admit I did not expect that. And Gabriel and Hannah, I don't know how you do it but the moment someone walks through that door they become part of the family; and we all feel it."

"I agree," Hugo said and stood up. "Sorren has told us so much about all of you, yet Greta and I did not expect to feel the way that we do. Everyone in this room feels as family to us." Hugo laughed. "You do know that if this family keeps growing you will have a tribe."

"To Gabriel's Tribe," Maxwell said and raised his glass of wine.

After the toast, Gabriel said, "Last night so many people said how much they enjoyed singing along with Dack and Sorren that Hannah and I realized we need to buy a few instruments. Dack after breakfast I will give you some money so you can buy a couple of guitars." Dack and Joao looked at each other and got big smiles on their faces. "Does anyone else play an instrument?" Gabriel asked.

"Batina plays the flute," Edgar said with a look of pride.

"Father!" Batina said and blushed.

"Daughter you play well, don't be shy."

95

"Then we add a flute to the list anyone else?" Gabriel asked. "Hannah plays the piano but obviously that can't be moved outside for celebrations."

After a moment of silence, Sam said, "Bekka."

"I can play the fiddle although it has been some time."

"Dack you are in charge of buying these instruments," Gabriel said and returned to his seat.

"Batina come shopping with us," Dack said then turned to Bekka. "Can you tell me what you want?"

"I can come with you," Sam said.

"Perhaps those of you who know how to play can teach the children," Hannah suggested.

"I would like to learn how to play the guitar," Diana said. "That was really fun last night."

"Dack, we'll come with you too," Misha said.

"Well, this is absolutely wonderful," Emeral said. "There is nothing like music for the soul."

"Why didn't you tell me this before?" Vitomas asked Raul as they took a morning ride after their guests left. "Does Annabelle know?"

"Simon and I weren't sure if Michael would change his mind. You have to admit it is hard to believe that someone would give up the throne."

Vitomas stopped her horse and turned and looked at Raul. "Listen to yourself; remember when we first met? You didn't want the responsibilities of the throne so you left home."

"You're right," Raul said and chuckled. "But I also wanted adventure."

"Did Michael say why he didn't want it?"

"He said he wasn't prepared, which is true. But he also said that he has found everything he ever wanted and he is content and happy."

"Raul you grew up with in a loving family. You always had food and you didn't have to live in fear. For those of us who didn't grow up like that; what we have now is a dream come true. I have no doubt that Michael is telling you the truth because that is exactly how Annabelle and I feel. While you and Simon seem to accept Michael you still don't trust him. Perhaps you should talk to him more and I mean really talk Raul, not about horses and fighting. You might change your mind on some things."

"Gabriel can I talk to you for a moment?" Ratri asked after all of the guests were gone and the household was settling down. Batina was in Salar shopping for instruments with Dack, Joao, Sam, Misha, Diana and Thor.

"Of course, let's go to my study."

After Gabriel closed the door, Ratri sat down and started talking. "You know that Batina and I only knew each other a week before we married and we were so focused on this mission that we really didn't make any plans for our future. Our parents are taking care of all the wedding preparations for us and we feel we owe them a great deal. What I am trying to say is we were afraid our families would be angry if we stayed in Wetpr for longer than this next mission. But we talked with Edgar and Cora and decided we would like to become permanent members of your team, if the offer is still there."

"I am glad to hear you say this," Gabriel said as he leaned back in his chair. "Honestly I expected you to tell me you were going to leave after this mission. Batina seemed pretty upset this morning about her family leaving."

"As Edgar pointed out Wetpr is a reasonable distance from their village."

"And it would only be three days for us to fly to the Ice Caves from here. I will tell you that Batina and I are still honestly in shock that you made us the offer and gave us the chambers."

"I don't know why. Ratri you have volunteered for many of our missions. You work well with everyone and you are a good man to have around. While I don't know Batina well, she did impress us when she stood up to Nada and her boyfriends to save Christopher. We knew she was well trained but Ratri you know that you never really know how someone will react under pressure. I believe you will agree with me that Batina has a lot to learn but she has the heart and mind of a warrior the rest will come with time." Ratri did not speak but nodded.

Gabriel continued, "Our team is growing because everyone is having families but at the same time because of the families not all members are available for every mission. Most of us would prefer that our wives did not work on missions while they are pregnant and as you can see we are kind of exploding around here," Gabriel said with a grin. "Vivian did work on a dangerous mission when she was fist pregnant but she has been so horribly sick all of the time that she realized she had to stop for a while. So while it seems like there are a lot of us we are shorthanded."

"Batina and I aren't planning a family for a while, we have to get to know each other first," Ratri said with a grin. "So we should be available for whatever you need. Just so you know, I have already been talking with Batina about expectations. She's a hard worker and will pull her share."

"Good, I'm glad to hear that. Now since you've had your first visit from family, would you like to move to larger chambers?"

"Yes, thank you, I believe we would. But they don't have to be anything fancy."

"I'll get Calen and Natasha they are kind of in charge of the housing."

Chapter VIII
Commitment

"Morgan the way you keep kissing up to Hecate someone would think you are trying to be her favorite," Bruno said and winked at Nada who grinned.

"Believe me I am doing it for us. I really don't trust her and as angry as she gets I don't want her turning on us. If she thinks we are invaluable she will keep us around longer."

"I don't think we have a choice in that matter, we sold our souls and unless I am stupid I don't believe there is a way we can get them back," said Bruno. "Believe me I have been thinking about it."

"You mean we have to work for her forever?" Nada asked with amazement.

"She owns us," Morgan said. "And while I don't totally understand how it works; it gives her control over us."

"Well, I'm not sure I like that," Nada said angrily.

"Hell, it's a little late to think about that now," Bruno said with a laugh.

"Well then how does this really benefit us other than she pays us well?" Nada asked.

"I don't believe Hecate planned this to benefit us," Morgan said. "If nothing else she is shrewd. She came to us when we really couldn't say no."

"Well maybe we can test it?" Nada suggested.

"What are you talking about?" Bruno asked with irritation.

"I mean we really don't know what our boundaries are, maybe we should find out."

"And get killed?" Morgan asked. "I think we need to plan this very carefully."

The morning that Gabriel's team planned to leave Wetpr for Ryed there was a terrible storm; so they were forced to wait until the skies cleared. In the preceding week many more Ruala warriors had joined the mission to the relief of all. With the additional warriors, Koby decided to stay at the house for a couple of weeks with the intention of joining the team later.

Calen and Natasha stayed back to help take care of Luca, Christopher and baby Emma besides the other duties. Luca suggested that going on the mission might help him but the entire household voted him down. Elan and Cassandra stayed behind with their newly adopted children.

Sam and Ella promised Gabriel they would stay at the house and help with things until the team returned from Ryed. Gabriel and Raphael changed some of the assignments after they received more Ruala volunteers. As soon as the storm dispersed, Gabriel, Lakin, Diana, Misha, Thor, Joshua, Micha, Bianca, Ratri, Batina, Erebus and Michael left for Ryed with forty Ruala warriors.

Raul, Simon and Matthew were to await word if they were needed on the missions. Since the team that Gabriel was leading was being flown by Ruala warriors they planned to fly over the Kingdom of Stordt, stop in Nora then enter Ryed.

Gabriel was carrying papers from King Sudfad for both High Priest Rueben at the Patronus Headquarters in Nora and Generals Colter and Orlan at Fort Nora. The papers contained information about the missions. Once in Ryed, Gabriel planned to stop at the Village of Gesmal to speak with the Sanuri before they proceeded northward.

The following morning after Gabriel's group left Salar, Sudfad held a smaller meeting. Raphael, Calen, Luca, Maxwell, Edward, Archetenus and Jared were in attendance besides Raul and Simon.

"Father I believe I should speak first," Raul said and stood up in front of the group. "All night I had dreams where I heard Miranda's voice. She told me it was unwise for Simon, Matthew and me to remain behind on these missions."

"She said that terrorists spies have seen Michael and fear he is another son of the prophesy. Teivel has received this information and will lay in wait for Raphael and Edward as soon as he hears of the inspections. She said to let Raphael and Edward proceed as planned but Simon, Matthew and I should follow them but not make our presence known at the forts scheduled for inspection."

"Send a message to Matthew at once," Sudfad said. "Raphael and Edward are scheduled to leave in a week, have him be here before that. Maxwell and Archetenus you two are now acting commanding generals; I want Raul and Simon to brief you on your duties before they leave. Jared, I know you were going to sit this one out because of the baby but we might need your help at some point."

"Actually that is why I have been coming to the meetings. Zoya recovered quickly and William sleeps pretty much through the nights, so I am not needed as much as I had expected."

"Well know you can always bring your family here," Sudfad said. "In fact if you do get involved with this mission it might not be a bad idea to move Zoya and William here for a while."

"Appreciate that," Jared said.

"You lucky bastard," Archetenus joked to Jared. "Our two babies are up all night. As soon as one goes to sleep the other wakes up. I'm considering hiring some nurses so me and Delilah can get a little sleep."

"Archetenus if you are serious about that statement," Sudfad said. "Talk to Marie. All of our nurses are her family members and we have been very pleased with them."

"We can fix up some chambers for them to stay in too," Raul added.

"Thanks I will do that," Archetenus said. "Especially with the promotion I will need to be alert."

"That is what I was thinking too," Sudfad said.

Hecate had spent the previous two days in her lair thinking about everything that Orbus said to her during their last encounter. Every time that Sampson awoke, she gave him more sedatives, not as much for his comfort as she wanted to be alone to think.

While Orbus' words angered her, Hecate realized there was a great deal of truth in what he said. Orbus had known Hecate for hundreds of years as both a lover and an adversary. He had seen all sides of her and now he was telling her she was not focused and that her hatred and anger were weakening her.

Orbus thought these were the reasons she had lost every recent battle against the humans. Then to add insult to injury he told Hecate that if she could not win against humans she would never win a battle in the demon wars. Orbus was no longer supporting her quest to rule a hell domain.

Hecate had tried to blame her lack of focus on her pregnancy until Orbus reminded her that she was losing battles before she conceived. Hecate now wondered if carrying a child that was half human was weakening her. Then she wondered if Sampson was weakening her. As Hecate sat on her sofa trying to decide if she wanted to go into her bedroom and murder Sampson, the three Rualas flew into her lair.

"I did not summon you," Hecate said curtly.

"We have news you will want to hear, then we will leave," Morgan said with obvious irritation. "The Sanuri is in the Village of Gesmal."

"When did he arrive?" Hecate asked with interest.

"We just saw him," Nada said. What Nada, Bruno and Morgan did not realize was that the Sanuri had been in the village for days but the Angels were blocking his image from them. The Sanuri also did not realize this.

"He walked directly into Chief Duncan's home," Bruno said. "And we still have not seen Sampson's brothers. We peaked into their bedroom windows but did not find them."

"You have done well," Hecate said. "Let me reward you."

"I have a better idea," Morgan said gruffly. "I assume you procured us because you believed we would be assets. We are intelligent, well trained warriors stop treating us like fools."

Hecate stared at all three Rualas before speaking; the Rualas were prepared to go to battle with the demon. "I see," Hecate said slowly. "Pour yourselves some drinks." Hecate nodded towards a table that contained glasses and bottles of whiskey and wine. The Rualas did not move immediately because they thought Hecate was trying to trick them. "This is no trick, actually I want to ask you some questions. So please have a seat."

"Morgan you are correct in your thinking and the three of you have proven yourselves well. Now what I am about to say may surprise you. First Nada, I know you have many children; when you carried them did you ever find yourself unfocused?"

Nada was shocked at Hecate's question. "All of the time but I had so many children that I was just plain overwhelmed."

"I have not been myself lately and recently a close friend made me realize that. I am hoping it is because of the baby I carry. I have many more projects besides helping Sampson through his trials and I may need your assistance in other areas, of course I will pay you well."

"So what exactly are you saying?" Bruno asked.

"You noticed things after our prisoners escaped that I did not. Things I would normally have noticed. I do not know if my current condition will get worse before the baby comes and I have many enemies from, well let's just say that I have many enemies. I still have not determined who assisted the prisoners with their escape or how they did it."

"For the time being I would like the three of you to be in charge of the security matters of my lair. While you do not have the powers to go against a demon, you are observant and smart. I will need you to keep me informed of even the littlest things you discover. And I will double your pay in this matter."

"Hecate I am going to speak to you as a woman not a demon," Nada said boldly. "Is this your first child?"

"Yes and it is half human so I don't know if that makes a difference."

"I don't care how powerful you are normally; once you start going into labor and right after you have the baby you aren't going to be in any condition to fight other demons. Now Morgan, Bruno and me can take care of humans but as you said we can't fight demons so you need to plan for this. Are you planning on having the baby here?"

"I'm not sure yet," Hecate said hesitantly. Hecate had always been such a powerful force that she could not conceive that she would have moments of weakness.

"The reason I am asking is I think even demons would know this which means they might try to attack when you are vulnerable. Someone already got through your defenses once. Will Sampson be a full demon by then?"

"I don't know," Hecate said. "I'm not even sure how long I will carry the baby because it is part human." Hecate was silent for a few moments. "Perhaps you should leave now, I have some business to tend to."

"I know you are mad at me Vitomas but I can't very well say no," Raul said.

"I'm not mad at you, I am just mad. We just had another baby and now you have to go on a mission again."

"I hate being away from you and the children but I can't say no to the Angels; you do understand that don't you?"

"Of course I do, it's just that we miss you so much. And these missions are so dangerous."

"Simon and I were talking and we are thinking we should hire another nurse, since we won't be here to help out. Archetenus is talking to Marie now, to see if he can hire one of her sisters to help with their babies. Neither he or Delilah have gotten any sleep since the twins were born."

"That's up to you and Simon. But you should know that Emeral and Cassandra came by while you were in the meeting and they took Emma back to their house. Bekka has offered to nurse both of the babies."

"This baby isn't going to have any shortage of mothers," Emeral said as she held Emma. Koby, Luca and Cassandra were moving Emma's things into the chambers that Bekka shared with her parents.

"I really appreciate this," Luca said.

"She should be home with us," said Bekka. "And my parents offered to help get up at night, especially if both babies are awake."

"I was thinking about that," Koby said. "Maybe I should move in here for a while to help out."

Ella and Emeral looked at each other and smiled. "These chambers are small and already getting crowded," Emeral said. "I think we should move all of you to larger chambers."

"We could," Bekka said as she looked at her parents. "But Koby can sleep in my room too."

"I tell you what," Sam said. "Why don't you and Koby figure that out? It really doesn't matter to your mother and me." Sam, Ella and Emeral were all hoping that Koby and Bekka would renew their relationship and were happy to see how close the young couple became after Ian was born. Koby adored his son and never wanted to put him down.

"You two are so funny," Cassandra said with a grin. "You were both so terrified to have one baby now you are taking care of two."

"Now I wonder why I was so scared," Bekka said. "Somehow this all seems really natural."

"Well I am glad to hear you say that," Emeral said. "Koby you don't seem so frightened anymore either."

"I think I stopped being scared the moment I held Ian," Koby said. "I never would have expected to feel so attached to him."

"Well since Elan and I haven't had a baby yet, we want baby time with both Emma and Ian," Cassandra said with a grin.

"Here take him now," Bekka said as she handed Ian to Cassandra. "Koby and I should talk about living arrangements."

"Well before you do that why don't we all go and look at that other chambers?" Emeral suggested. "As fast as our family here is growing, Calen is designing some more chambers for the house. He said we are going to have to take out the gardens on the east side of the house to do more construction."

"I don't know if we have had a day yet that there wasn't men working on the house," Luca said jokingly. "The carpenters love us."

The group walked down the long hallway and Luca opened a door that led into a large, sunny parlor. "Why, this is absolutely beautiful," Ella gushed as they looked at what Calen referred to as family chambers. "This is a home."

"The chambers you are in now are basically for guests," Luca explained. "The larger chambers are living quarters. You are going to be here for several months and now with the two babies you might be a lot more comfortable in here."

"The reason I suggested this," Emeral said is because there is a small nursery off the master bedroom. You can barely fit the two baby beds in Bekka's room now."

"So this is empty?" Sam asked as he admired the chambers. "It wasn't built for anyone?"

"Each of the boys gets a chambers like this when they have a family," Emeral said. "And as fast as people have been getting married, Calen planned ahead. So to answer your question it is empty."

"Now that I see this, I think we should take it," Koby said as he walked out of one of the bedrooms. "If Sam and Ella take that farthest bedroom they might actually get some sleep at night."

"Then Bekka and I will stay in the master bedroom with the babies."

Emeral looked at Ella and Sam and winked. "Well, let's get the others to help move your things," Emeral said happily.

Hecate had to search three taverns on Sidus before she found Orbus. "A little early in the day to be in a tavern isn't it?" Hecate asked with irritation when she found him gambling.

"You are really cranky since you got pregnant my dear. It never mattered to you before," Orbus said with a smile and kissed Hecate on the forehead.

"Can we talk for a couple of minutes, then I will leave you alone?" she asked.

As Orbus stood up from the card table one of the demons asked, "Your baby Orbus?"

"Unfortunately no," Orbus said and took Hecate's hand and led her to a table at the far end of the tavern.

"Orbus although you really made me mad I thought about all of the things you said and I realized you were right. Then my Rualas walked in and one of them told me off because of the way I have been treating them. I couldn't argue because I haven't been myself, so I offered them a drink and more money to take charge of the security of my place. While I didn't like the way Morgan talked to me they are good and well worth the money."

"Hecate you've always liked men who would stand up to you no matter what species they were," Orbus said with a grin.

"You know me so well," Hecate said. "But I asked Nada some questions about pregnancy and she told me something that really concerned me and that is why I am here. I haven't given any thought to what it will be like actually delivering the baby. Nada said that while I am having the baby and for some time afterwards I won't be in any shape to fight and they can't protect me from other demons. Nada said that my enemies will know when I am vulnerable and probably attack. And I don't know if Sampson will be a full demon by then. He can't defend me and the baby."

107

"Hecate are you really telling me you are just thinking about this now?" Orbus scolded. "This is exactly what I have been talking about. You are so distracted you aren't paying any attention to what is important. I'm beginning to think you should pay those Rualas to babysit you and I am not joking."

"Orbus will you protect me and the baby for a couple of days?" Hecate asked. "I will pay you well."

He sat back in his chair and smiled. "Hecate you have never asked me to take care of you before. Let me just savor the moment. Of course I will but I don't know how to deliver a baby."

"I don't expect that. I need to find a place and to hire someone. Even I can't believe I didn't plan for this. Humans only carry babies for nine months and look how big I am; I have no idea when I will give birth."

"You will have the baby at my home and stay with me. There's some places near here where we can find a midwife. Let's go now and find out what we need to prepare," Orbus said. "And I am not taking your money."

"Thank you so much," Hecate said sincerely. "Now probably isn't the time that I should tell you I was thinking about killing Sampson. He may never be right."

Orbus grinned. "You think that is going to make me sad? Hell, I will do it for you."

"I can't believe you changed him," Bekka said to Koby as she was putting Emma to bed.

Koby was sitting up in bed waiting for her, this was their first night together since they had broken off their relationship. "Seems like we always had babies in the house growing up," Koby said. "Both with my real parents then with Emeral and Maxwell. I know a lot about taking care of children."

"Well you still surprise me," Bekka said and slid under the covers next to Koby, who immediately hugged and kissed her. "This feels nice," she said and kissed him again.

"Bekka, I've really missed you, I am so sorry for what I did."

"What we both did," Bekka said and started to cry. "Koby I shouldn't have left. I realized that before but especially since we are back here. I really feel like this is my home."

"Bekka I am glad to hear you say that. Please stay. We will figure this all out."

"But what about my parents?"

"They should stay too, honestly don't they seem really happy here?"

Bekka wiped the tears from her cheeks and stared at Koby for a moment as she thought about his words. "I thought they were just happy because I was having a baby but I think you are right."

"Remember how Emeral and Maxwell told us they felt useless in the Ice Caves, all the children were gone and there were no battles to fight. They both love it here because they feel needed and they are. Can you even imagine it here without them now? I'm not so sure that Ella and Sam don't feel the same way. They haven't stopped moving since they got here. If they aren't with the children they are helping around the house. Now that Emeral said a garden has to be moved, Sam's going to do it so the plants aren't destroyed."

"You know I didn't think about any of that," Bekka said somewhat with surprise. "I guess I have been so focused on our issues. My parents love children and neither of my two older sisters have any. When I went home I told them the stories behind all of the children here and I think my parents fell in love with them even before meeting the children. Koby you might really be right. I should talk to them."

"We can talk to them together," Koby said. "Married or not we are a family now; but we should also talk to Gabriel and Hannah, it is their house."

"Of course," Bekka said then paused. "No, you are right, I didn't mean to exclude you. And you are right too, that we are a family now. Koby I have been so scared and overwhelmed that I feel now like I am coming out of a fog; I know that may sound crazy. All I could think of before was running away from everything and now I couldn't imagine running away from Ian."

"I wasn't much better," Koby admitted. "And now I look at our son and at you and I realize I could never leave either of you. Bekka I love you and I want to marry you but I realize it may be too soon for us to have this talk."

Bekka didn't answer she was looking deeply in Koby's face. Koby leaned down and kissed her on the lips. As their passions started to surge the cry of a baby pierced the night. Both Bekka and Koby started to laugh and got out of bed.

Hecate did not return to her lair that night she stayed with Orbus on Sidus. Orbus had exactly what he wanted and he was trying to figure out how to keep it. Hecate had come to him and wanted him to take care of her and the baby. While Orbus had been devising plans to get Hecate to come back to him, Nada's few words had more impact than Orbus' schemes. As Orbus lay in bed holding Hecate he thought he would have to reward Nada someday.

"Demons!" Bruno yelled as a warning to Morgan and Nada who were patrolling the exterior of Hecate's lair. But the warning came too late. The three Rualas were quickly surrounded by beasts they had never before seen. Although the three Rualas tried to fight their efforts were futile as the demons quickly restrained them. A larger demon which looked different from the rest suddenly materialized before the group and walked up to the three Rualas who were struggling against their captors. This demon walked in front of Morgan, Bruno then Nada and stared at each of them.

"Take her," the demon ordered and instantly Nada and the two demons that held her vanished.

"What the hell!" Bruno yelled.

The demon giving orders now walked closer to Morgan and Bruno, he dwarfed both of the Rualas. "Our orders were not to kill you, unless you forced us. Please force us." He said with a sneer. Both Morgan and Bruno stopped struggling. "As I thought," the demon said condescendingly. "Tell your owner that if she wants her husband back, Visterle has some work for her."

"Who is Visterle and how will Hecate contact him?" Morgan asked.

"Hecate knows and well, if she doesn't she will need to find out," the demon replied.

"What about Nada?" Bruno asked.

The demon sneered again. "Visterle is bored," he said and the demons disappeared. Morgan and Bruno quickly ran into the lair which appeared untouched except for the fact that Sampson was missing.

The following morning, Sam and Ella walked into the dining room of Gabriel's home, each carrying an infant. "Maxwell where is Emeral?" Sam asked with a huge smile.

"In the kitchen," Maxwell said. "And you certainly are all smiles."

"Our children would like to talk to the two of you," Sam said. "They are in the hallway."

Maxwell quickly walked into the kitchen, took Emeral's hand and sped her out of the room. "Maxwell what is going on?" Emeral asked.

"We will find out in just a moment," Maxwell said and led his wife to the hallway outside of the dining room. By the time that Maxwell, Emeral, Koby and Bekka returned to the dining room the team was sitting down to breakfast.

"Why is everyone smiling?" Natasha asked suspiciously.

"Raphael would you marry Bekka and me today?" Koby asked.

"I would be proud to," Raphael said and stood up, walked over to Koby and shook his hand, then hugged Bekka. The rest of the team got out of their chairs and congratulated the young couple.

"They wanted to get married right after breakfast," Emeral said. "But I told them we have to do a few preparations."

"We want something small and simple," Koby said.

"And later we will have a big celebration when everyone is here."

Dagon looked at Bekka's hand then asked sarcastically, "Brother did you consider buying her a ring?" Everyone in the room laughed.

"That's on our list for today," Koby said. "Neither of us have had any sleep because both babies were up all night. Since we already have Ian we want to make it official now and have more of a celebration later."

"We want to get married in one of the gardens like Vivian and Raphael did," Bekka said.

"This is just wonderful," Hannah gushed. "I am so happy."

"Why don't you have the wedding early evening," Natasha suggested. "That will give us time to prepare a few things."

"Where the hell have you been?" Morgan yelled when Hecate returned to her lair. She was surprised to find Morgan and Bruno in her chambers.

"You will not talk to me that way," Hecate said indignantly.

"Demons took Sampson and Nada," Morgan said angrily. "Hecate if we are to work for you we have to have some way to contact you."

"What!" Hecate said and quickly looked in her bedroom. Hecate searched the room for any sign of the intruders then returned to Morgan and Bruno. "Tell me everything that happened."

"We were patrolling outside when dozens of demons suddenly materialized around us," Bruno explained. "We tried fighting but they got us pretty damn fast. Then this other demon appears and he doesn't look like the one's holding us. He tells some of his men to take Nada then he gives us a message for you. He said if you want Sampson back Visterle has some work for you. Morgan asked who Visterle was and how you could find him and the guy says if you don't know you will have to find out." Hecate did not speak, she walked over to a table and poured three glasses of whiskey.

"They said they took Nada because Visterle is bored," Morgan said. "Who the hell is Visterle and how do we get Nada and Sampson back?"

"Before I answer that question; I have one of my own," Hecate said as she handed Morgan and Bruno each a drink. "Did those demons enter my chambers or did you take Sampson to them?"

"We didn't touch Sampson," Morgan said gruffly. "As soon as they left we ran in here and found him gone. Then we called to you and tried to figure out how to contact you."

Hecate walked over to one of the several large chests that sat on the floor of her lair, she took some items from the chest and handed them to Morgan and Bruno. Both Rualas were each holding a leather necklace with a gold medallion. Hecate's face was carved on each medallion. Put the palm of your hands on top of the medallion and call my name, no matter where I am I will hear you. As you know five Old Ones were imprisoned in The Abyss and demons from many worlds are fighting over their territories. Moloch was one of these Old Ones and Visterle was his main lieutenant."

"So why does he want Nada?" Bruno asked.

"I am sure for the same reason you two did; for sex," Hecate replied. "Before those five Old Ones were imprisoned I was, shall I say, at odds with a few of them. I had nothing to do with them losing their battles with the Angel's but I certainly wasn't sad to see them fall."

"While all of this is disturbing what you don't understand is that my lair has been hidden from the eyes of other demons. I am sure that the demons you described were underlings which mean's one of the Old Ones was responsible for making them suddenly appear and disappear. While I am strong enough to do these things I cannot move an army. After I spoke with you last, I changed the protection spells on my lair."

Hecate took a gulp of her whiskey. "I should have been alerted if anyone tried to enter here. I was not and my protection spells were not strong enough to keep the intruders out. I am sure this is a trap but why didn't they just kill Sampson then me?" Hecate asked more to herself than to Morgan and Bruno.

"I am also sure it is a trap," Morgan said. "But why didn't they kill us and how do we get Nada back?"

"You are still useful to many," Hecate said. "Never before has any demon owned a Ruala and as for Nada. You can't go where she will be taken. Only another demon can. I will have to think about this. Now tell me everything again, even the smallest details. First describe the demons."

Nada lost consciousness as she was transported between worlds. She was groggy and disoriented when she awoke in a room which was lit by hundreds of candles. Nada jumped up as her memories returned. It was then that she realized she was shackled to the headboard of a huge bed. She strained at the shackles but was not strong enough to break them. A trained warrior, Nada now carefully looked around the room for weapons and clues as to her whereabouts.

Nada gasped when she saw a silver tray sitting on a table near the bed. A variety of cutting instruments were neatly lined up on the tray. The walls of the room were covered with thick dark red drapes. The bedding matched the drapes. There was some furniture in the room, pieces one would expect to see in a bedroom chambers. The bed itself was of incredible proportions which made Nada wonder what kind of a creature it belonged to.

Chapter IX
Unisons

"Misha," Diana said as they were flying towards Ryed. "Ever since the Sanuri told me about those visions he was having of us with two small boys it's been bothering me."

"What do you mean?"

"Well, like you at first I thought he meant those would be our children someday. But you know the mountains he described sound like the ones Gabriel and some of the others saw when they were in hell dimensions."

"I was thinking the same thing but I didn't want to worry you."

"Misha, we are partners you have to stop keeping things from me," Diana scolded. "You certainly wouldn't like it if I kept things from you."

"You're right," Misha said and kissed Diana on top of her head. "So you are worried we will have to go into a hell dimension?"

"No, I had a dream last night where I saw the same things that the Sanuri described. At first I thought I had the dream because I have been thinking about what he said. But even this morning, I feel haunted because there was something familiar about those boys and I have a really bad feeling."

"Well, I don't know a lot about dreams and visions but we will be in your village tomorrow you can ask the Sanuri or when we take a break talk to Lakin, he has powers that the rest of us don't."

"Misha in the dream I couldn't tell if the little boys were humans or Rualas because of the way we were carrying them. But they both had hair like Christopher and well, I thought they looked like you. Misha I am going to ask you something that will probably make you really mad but I mean it sincerely. I know that you and your brothers have all dated a lot of women before settling down. Is it possible some of you have children you don't know about? Or children you do know about and haven't claimed?"

115

"You are really serious aren't you? There's more that you aren't telling me, what is it?"

"In my dream we were running from something and we were both really scared, not for ourselves but for the little boys. And when I said they felt familiar, they did but they also felt like family."

"Within the hour of Morgan and Bruno telling Hecate about the abductions she was back on Sidus.

"Orbus I have to admit I am really concerned," Hecate said after she told him about the abductions. "The Old Ones attacked my home. Have you ever heard of such a thing? And especially now that I am about ready to have a baby."

"Well Visterle isn't an Old One unless he just conquered a realm and I think we would have heard about that. So who is he working for now? And why would they want you to work for them? You know I warned you about making so many enemies among the Old Ones. There is always retribution even if it takes a while." Orbus had nothing to do with the abductions and was genuinely concerned for Hecate's welfare.

"The Rualas think it's a trap for me and I agree with them," Hecate said. "I was thinking about putting Sampson out of his misery. I am just going to let Visterle have him."

Orbus grinned at Hecate's admission. "Hecate you know I have always been in love with you. Come back to me permanently and I will take care of you and the baby."

"First of all that would put you in danger and secondly are you saying you would raise the child of another?"

"Hecate you know I too am powerful and have many resources. And as for the child. I have always wanted to have a family with you. You were the one that never wanted a permanent relationship. But if you come back to me, it is for good this time so think about your answer. Your rage driven actions are the reasons you are in this situation. And especially now that you don't seem to be thinking clearly; I will protect you but you need to let me handle things."

"What do you mean?"

"Instead of defying everyone and acting like the lone warrior you need to keep a low profile now, especially with the baby."

"You mean hide?"

"That would be part of it. Hecate you have always wanted a child. Take some time from the politics and enjoy your baby. We can make plans and when you reemerge you will be stronger and more focused. We have known each other for hundreds of years you know you can trust me."

Nada had no idea where she was or how long she had been there. She remembered the demons attacking Hecate's lair and little more. The sight of the bedroom was not consistent with Nada's ideas of a hell region so she was hopeful that she was still in Nunc.

Several hours passed as Nada tried to free herself from her restraints. "Your efforts are useless but I like the fight in you," a voice said. Nada quickly looked around the room without seeing anyone.

"If you like to see a fight then release me," Nada yelled. All she heard was laughter, then silence.

"Who are you and where am I?" Nada demanded as the fear was rising within her.

"Nada where do you think you deserve to be?" the voice asked.

"Am I in hell?" Nada asked in a whisper. And again she heard laughter.

"So you think you deserve to be in hell? You know there are many others who feel the same way about you and your boyfriends." Nada was quiet as she was trying to figure out how this voice knew these things. "There are many kinds of hell, some are perpetuated by true demons and others are created by humans. But I will say you, Morgan and Bruno garnered a great deal of attention. Never before had Rualas created hell in their worlds. And you were exposed by that tiny little Venator, who will probably kill you someday."

"How do you know these things? Who are you?" Nada asked fearfully. Suddenly a dark fog appeared at the end of the bed. She tried frantically to escape. The voice laughed and continued to laugh as the fog started to take form. Nada stared with wonder as she saw different faces flashing before her in the fog. "I know you," she gasped as one of the faces started to become clearer and take on more context. "You were at King Sudfad's castle. The image of a human man now sneered at Nada. "I even talked to you," she said in disbelief.

"I don't know why you are acting so shocked demons walk among mankind all of the time. Hell the humans call to us."

"I know you can't really be a human so who the hell are you?"

"My name is Visterle," the man said as he sat down on the edge of the bed near Nada.

"Are you a demon?" Nada demanded although she was scared of the answer.

"You know I am."

"What do you want with me?"

"I thought we could have some fun. What's the matter Nada, cat got your tongue?"

"Please, let me go."

"Nada how many times have your victims said that to you?"

"Where am I?"

"A place where your friends can't come and rescue you and your mistress isn't coming after you."

"You mean Hecate?"

"She's how I found you. I was watching her and behold she was watching you."

Nada did not want the demon to know how scared she was. She mustered her strength and demanded, "What is your price to let me go?"

"Oh you are going to pay," Visterle said and his form started to change again. Nada screamed hysterically as a new face appeared.

As the afternoon seemed to fly by, Hannah and Natasha cooked a feast for the celebration of Koby's and Bekka's wedding. Vivian and Cassandra were in charge of setting up the garden for the ceremony. Emeral, Iris and Ella were helping Koby shop as Bekka stayed at the house with the two infants. The others helped where ever they were needed which mostly amounted to moving furniture and running errands. Sam was helping his daughter with the babies.

"Bekka, the reason your mother and I didn't answer you and Koby this morning is that, while we like the idea, we will feel better once you talk with Gabriel."

"Koby is going to talk to Hannah and Raphael since we don't know how long Gabriel will be gone," Bekka said. "Do you really think Gabriel is going to mind? You and Mother have been a lot of help around here and remember there are two more babies coming. Everyone is against hiring outsiders to help with things because of all the terrorists and the attacks on the children. With you here they don't have to hire anyone. We are going to have four tiny babies here besides all of the other children soon."

"And you know that everyone who is having a baby normally works on the missions," Bekka continued to try and persuade her father into staying in Wetpr. "Gabriel is already worried about Hannah because she is involved in so many different things for the King and the orphanage besides taking care of this house and the children."

Sam laughed at his daughter's persistence. "If your mother and I stay we want to pull our share, like the others. Joshua told me he had to order Gabriel and Raphael to put him and Iris to work; which made Joshua mad when he found out how much help they needed."

"Just taking care of a place this size and feeding everyone is a task besides everything else. No, if we stay it won't be as guests."

"Hannah, Natasha you have to come out front," Cassandra said as she peeked her head into the kitchen. As the three women walked out the front door Cassandra continued. "Maxwell had Alexander make a huge doll house for our girls."

"Oh my god!" Natasha said as she and Hannah approached a small boca that held the dollhouse. "Look the house looks just like ours."

"Oh Maxwell this is so wonderful," Hannah said and kissed Maxwell on the cheek. "The girls will love this."

"Oh, there is a lot more," Dagon said as he took two large sacks out of the boca. "Alexander made furniture and Iris and Laurel made dolls, and doll clothes."

"I don't know why I am so excited about this," Natasha said as she took one of the bags from Dagon.

"Vivian and Melinda are taking the children for a walk so we can set this up," Joao said. "They just left out the back."

"Look at these things," Natasha gushed as she started to set dolls and doll furniture on the ground.

"I hope the children enjoy those things as much as you do," Calen said with a grin. "I just cleared a path in the house so we can carry it in without hitting anything. I hope we still have this when Lily is old enough to play with it."

"Everything that Alexander makes is so well made," Maxwell said. "And besides these children aren't as hard on things as you boys were."

"Yeah, we did break everything," Luca said as he grabbed one corner of the dollhouse.

"I'm glad we expanded the playroom or there wouldn't be room for both the fort and the house inside," Maxwell said as the group rearranged the playroom.

"Elan is getting Bekka and Sam," Cassandra said and joined Hannah and Natasha as they were setting up the furniture and dolls.

"I just can't believe these things," Natasha said. "Calen they made little rugs and curtains and everything. We might be playing with this more than the children."

"I was just thinking that," Calen said and winked at Luca.

Bekka, Sam and Elan got to the playroom just as all the children were returning from their walk.

"Wow!" Christopher yelled when he saw the huge playhouse.

Christopher, Adrone, Nicholas, Joey and Paul all ran to the doll house and looked inside. Vivian and Melinda set Cerey and Cicely down in front of the house and the little girls screamed with joy.

"This isn't just for the girls is it?" Paul asked.

"It's a gift from Maxwell, you will have to ask him," Hannah said.

"The girls play in your fort it is only fair that they let you play with their house," Maxwell said with a huge smile.

"Thanks Grandpa," Nicholas said and all of the children ran to Maxwell and hugged him. Adrone and Paul now thought of Maxwell and Emeral as their grandparents also.

Bekka looked at Sam and said, "See what you would be missing out on."

"Orbus you know I am not the type to be put into a cage," Hecate said.

"We have been talking about this for hours, Hecate. I am not trying to put you in a cage; I am trying to protect you and the baby from your own impulsive actions besides your enemies. Tell me one time in all the years we have known each other that you felt like I was trying to put you in a cage," Orbus said with frustration.

"Orbus you are right, I just have never depended on anyone else before; it will take some time to get used to."

"So then you agree to everything?"

"Yes."

"Then we leave for Orantho tonight, I have a home on that planet and I have worked for Samael, he is as strong as Ahriman was and will protect us," Orbus explained. "You have to cut ties with those Rualas because everyone knows you own them. I don't care if you kill them or set them free, just get rid of them."

"I gave them medallions so they can call me," Hecate said with concern.

"Does Visterle have that now?" Orbus yelled.

"No I gave them to Morgan and Bruno after the abductions."

"Well, you are going to have to get those back."

"What about my treasures, I have caves of riches stowed away."

"If you are being watched, others are probably aware of your hiding places."

"No, I haven't been to some of them in a long time. We might need some of that money for bribes."

"You stay here," Orbus said. "Decide what you want to take from your lair. I will be back with a crew that I often hire. We will get all of your things."

"I am going to Nunc with you."

"Yes, but we aren't spending a lot of time there. We will just be grabbing things and leaving," Orbus said and walked out the door.

To the surprise of Koby and Bekka, the Royal Family came to the small garden wedding as did Archetenus and Delilah and Jared and Zoya. Emeral and Ella had bought Bekka a simple light blue silk dress that was fitting for a garden wedding.

Koby surprised Bekka not only with extravagant wedding rings but also a light blue sapphire necklace and earrings to wear with her dress. Luca and Cassandra stood up for the young couple. And although the wedding was simple many thought it was elegant.

After the wedding the family and guests entered the dining room for a toast before the meal. All of the children thanked Alexander, Laurel and Iris for the dollhouse and proudly showed their new toys to all of the guests. While everyone was being entertained by the children, Vitomas, Annabelle and Natasha had Joao and Dack set up tables in the parlor and filled the tables with gifts.

"There are just so many little babies here," Ella remarked. "This is so much fun."

"Guess you aren't going to have a honeymoon for a while," Calen joked as Ian started to cry.

"I wish Gabriel was here," Hannah said sadly. "He would be so happy about all of this."

"We should be at the Village of Gesmal by mid-morning," Gabriel said to his group as they sat around the evening campfire. "Remember Hecate is probably watching us as well as other demons and who knows if Nada, Morgan and Bruno are actually working for her. So be on the lookout for anything out of the ordinary.

"Erebus," Thor said. "While I commend you for not hiding who you are, in those robes you are walking around with a target on your back. If you changed clothing would the demons still recognize you?"

Before Erebus could answer Diana spoke, "Several of us have been thinking the same thing. Could you use your magic to change your appearance?"

"Are you afraid I will get you hurt?" Erebus asked with a smile.

"You are part of the team and we don't want you to get hurt," Misha said.

Erebus was quite taken back and touched by Misha's statement. "I thought you thought of me as the enemy," Erebus said sincerely.

"That was before we got to know you," Diana said with a grin. "You kind of grow on people."

Gabriel smiled as he watched the look on Erebus' face. "You know they are right," Gabriel said. "I have extra clothes with me if you want to change. And actually you might be more help if you could slip in and out of places without being recognized."

"You know Hecate has demons watching for you," Misha said. "And that statement included my mother, Morgan and Bruno."

"If you are going to change I would recommend doing it before we reach the village because we know for sure Hecate is spying on the Venatores," Gabriel said.

To everyone's surprise Erebus took some clothing from Gabriel and walked into the woods to change. When he returned to the fire everyone grinned. "That hair and beard looked better with your robes," Thor said with a grin.

"I could cut your hair," Diana said excitedly. "I am pretty good at it; I cut Thor's hair."

"Yeah and I still have both ears," Thor joked.

Erebus, himself, couldn't believe he was letting Diana cut his hair and beard. When Diana was done, she handed Erebus a small mirror and everyone clapped as he looked at his new appearance. "You just look like a regular father now," Thor said. "Seriously you will be safer this way."

Gabriel passed around a bottle of whiskey and a bottle of wine. "To Erebus," Gabriel toasted.

Erebus laughed. "I don't even recognize myself. I think I look a lot younger."

"You do," Diana said. "You look very nice."

As Diana was about to sit down next to Misha, he said. "Maybe you should talk to Lakin now about your dream." Misha didn't want to tell Diana that her dream bothered him also.

"You can come with me," Diana said and the two walked over to Lakin. Diana told Lakin everything she had previously told Misha. When she was done talking Lakin put the palms of his hands on either side of her head and stared into her eyes, which drew the attention of the rest of the group. Lakin closed his eyes and started to emit a sound similar to humming. Now everyone in the group started to gather around Lakin, Misha and Diana.

Lakin stopped humming and asked Diana, "Did you feel anything while I was doing that?"

"I just felt tingly," Diana said with a grin.

"I asked for permission to see your vision," Lakin explained. "And that is what it was, not a dream. You are right to be concerned because it does appear that you and Misha are in a hell dimension. And as for the boys I don't recognize them but I had the same feelings that you did. There is a reason that is being shown to you but I cannot tell you what it is. And as for your question about the fathers of the children I can't tell. But I believe this is connected to this mission and should be shared with the others."

Diana now realized that everyone was gathered around them. "Before we left Salar, the Sanuri said he had seen visions of Misha and me with two small blonde haired boys and we were climbing a stark mountain. Last night I had the same dream but I somehow knew that we were running from something and that Misha and I were really scared for the children."

"I felt like the children were familiar enough to be family and I thought they looked like Misha's family, I mean his adopted family. Misha and his brothers had a lot of girlfriends so I wondered if these little boys were maybe sons that Misha or his brothers didn't know about."

"That is all I saw too," Lakin said. "But for the Sanuri to have more than one vision of this and now Diana, I believe it to be important."

"I agree," Gabriel said then he turned to Misha. "Is it possible these children are related?"

"Of course anything is possible but you know all of us; if we knew we had children we would claim them."

"If anyone has paper and a pen I can draw what I saw," Diana said. "Then maybe one of you can recognize it."

"I have some," Batina said and ran back to her pouch.

"What concerns me is that they are in a hell dimension," Gabriel said as Diana was drawing.

"We asked the Sanuri if the boys could be Diana's and my sons in the future and the Sanuri said he didn't think so," Misha said.

It took Diana almost twenty minutes to complete the drawing, she handed it first to Lakin. "You draw well, that is exactly what I saw." Gabriel and Misha looked at the drawing together then handed it to the others. Joshua was one of the last people to look at the drawing.

"Something about this is very familiar," Joshua said thoughtfully as he stared at the drawing.

"Do you recognize the children?" Diana asked.

"No, it's like I have seen this entire picture before but with different faces."

Orbus, Hecate and a crew of twenty demon's emptied all of Hecate's caves containing treasure except for one, Hecate wanted to leave it in case she needed it on Nunc. The demons that made up the crew were not powerful enough to transport themselves through dimensions but Orbus and Hecate had the power to transport the group. Load after load of treasure was transported to Orbus' home on the surface of the planet of Orantho. This planet was the largest in the Astrum Solar System and the farthest from the three suns. Orantho also had more hell dimensions than any other planet in that solar system.

It was almost dawn when Hecate, Orbus and the crew materialized in Hecate's lair.

She showed the hired demons the items she wanted moved, then Hecate and Orbus walked outside of the lair. Morgan and Bruno were watching the lair from the trees and flew down to the ground when they saw Hecate.

"I have taken a new husband," Hecate told the Rualas. She deliberately did not tell them Orbus' name. "And I am moving to a place that I cannot take you. I have two options to either kill you or free you. You have served me well, so I will free you. But should I return to this world I may call upon you. I will need my medallions back."

"So does this mean you no longer own our souls?" Bruno asked as he handed Hecate the medallion.

"That is exactly what it means. You are free men. Go to the cave where I always leave your payment and you will find enough to keep you happy for a very long time."

"What about Nada?" Morgan asked after he handed his medallion to Hecate.

"There are thousands of hell dimensions. I don't know which one she is in or even if she is in a hell dimension. I will see what I can do but I would not hold out hope that you will ever see your friend again."

Before Morgan or Bruno could reply, Orbus and Hecate disappeared. "Do you feel any different?" Bruno asked.

"No, and I am not sure if that is good or bad," Morgan replied. "I don't like leaving Nada and I don't believe that Hecate will try to find her."

"Well I am not going to search a thousand hell dimensions to find her, there's a lot other girls in this world," Bruno said. "Let's see if Hecate was telling us the truth about our payment."

"You know the way Nada is," Morgan said and laughed. "She might like being screwed by a demon."

"You don't seem to get as much pleasure out of receiving pain as you do by inflicting it," Visterle said sarcastically to Nada and laughed. "But as you know this is for my pleasure."

Nada was unshackled and lying on top of Visterle's bed. She was naked and faint from pain and was bleeding from dozens of wounds. She did not speak as she heard Visterle mumbling in a strange language. Suddenly Nada realized she felt different. He laughed as Nada looked at her arms and legs. "You healed me?" Nada asked incredulously. "Why?"

"That was just the foreplay my dear," Visterle said and Nada felt like she was being consumed by his presence.

Chapter X
Manipulations

"How can this be?" Chief Duncan asked.

"I don't know any more than I told you," the Sanuri said.

"This is what the Angel must have been talking about when he stopped me from killing Sampson," Duncan said. "Please, let's go in the kitchen and tell the rest of the family.'

Liza, George and Ivan were sitting at the kitchen table when Duncan and the Sanuri entered the room. Liza immediately stood up and started to fix two plates of breakfast food.

"This morning, just before I woke I had a vision," the Sanuri explained as he sat down at the table. "I also heard the voice of the Angel Daniel. The vision was rather fragmented and I did not recognize the worlds I was shown. Hecate and the Rualas have left this area, I think Hecate is taking refuge in another world. She has released her holds on the three Rualas but they have been split up. I was shown a picture of the three surrounded by demons, then the demons took Nada."

"And Sampson?" Liza asked.

"As you know Hecate pulled him out of Baal's domain before the trials were completed. And our army attacked him as holiness surged through their swords. Holiness is deadly to demons. From what I saw it appears that Hecate has been trying to heal Sampson and has been keeping him sedated because of the pain. The image I saw does not look like the son you knew Liza. That son was lost to you long ago," the Sanuri explained.

"Is he still alive?" asked George.

"That I don't know. It appears that the same demons that took Nada took Sampson. At this point I have no idea of where they are or what has happened to them."

Duncan had been staring at the Sanuri as he spoke. "When you first told me this I thought only of the safety of my family and people. But now I see it with new eyes. The Rualas worked for Hecate."

"Other demons attacked her home, took her husband and one of her slaves. That is why Hecate has left. But why take Sampson and not kill him?"

"Hecate is an incredibly powerful demon, I would presume someone is holding Sampson hostage because they want something from her; what, I cannot tell you."

"Do you think she will pay the ransom?" Ivan asked.

"Hecate is a ruthless demon, I have no idea what she would do."

"You can eat, the food is not poisoned," Visterle said as he returned to the bedroom chambers where Nada was imprisoned. "Believe me I don't want to kill you."

"Why not?" Nada asked angrily as she grabbed a piece of bread from the tray next to the bed.

"You are my new pet, I plan to keep you around for a while," Visterle had been walking towards the bed and now sat down next to Nada.

"I am no one's pet," Nada said indignantly.

"You certainly acted like it yesterday and all last night," Visterle said with a salacious grin.

Nada looked at the demon defiantly. "Why do you keep changing form, can't figure out what you like?"

"Because I can and your fear pleases me. Tell me my pet which form do you find most pleasing?"

Nada stared at Visterle as she was trying to determine his trick. "If I tell you will you present that form or make sure that I never see it?"

Visterle laughed loudly. "I like your attitude, most captives would be crying for mercy. I will present it."

"The human one," Nada said as she ate a piece of fruit from her tray.

"But of course," he said and laughed again.

As he started to transform again, Nada said angrily, "I hate that slimy one. Do you have a true form?" Nada knew she needed to understand her captor if she had any hopes of escape.

"Yes, you have seen it and it terrified you, now is this better?" Visterle kept grinning as he was truly enjoying his cat and mouse game with Nada.

"Yes, you actually look handsome. That is the same form I saw in Wetpr who were you supposed to be?"

"Who did I look like?"

"In this form you are built like a warrior but that day you wore the clothing of a nobleman."

"I must have made an impression for you to remember that." Nada did not respond. "I was in the crowd watching Hecate. The crowd was made up of warriors and noblemen."

"I can't believe no one recognized you."

"You didn't."

"Didn't Hecate?"

"If she did it doesn't matter but she seemed focused on other things. Last night she released her hold on your soul and that of your friends."

"I don't understand what that means?"

"You are no longer her slave which is good since you belong to me now. And your friends are free."

"I don't belong to you and how do you know these things?"

"Every time you or any other person calls to darkness it is as if you open a door to all forms of darkness. And when you sell your soul you have given us the keys. You have been letting us in since your husband died. Hecate was focused on you because she was reading your life, every dirty little detail."

Nada stared at Visterle afraid that he was telling the truth. "Hecate and I both saw the same things, the darkness in you is delicious and your beauty is like the topping of a cake. I have plans for you my pet."

Visterle's words were frightening Nada and she tried not to show it. She knew Visterle knew he was scaring her. "Do you want to know what my plans are?"

"I'm not sure," she said and started to cry.

"Are you crying because I can see all of your deeds or are you crying because you are scared of the future?"

"I don't know, probably both," Nada said sadly as she suddenly felt completely hopeless. "Are you telling me the truth?"

"While you have no reason to trust me, I have not lied to you about anything, at least not yet," Visterle said and laughed. "You do know that Morgan and Bruno lied to you all of the time."

"I don't believe that," Nada said defiantly. "Besides how would you know?"

"They gave us the keys also. You think they are coming to rescue you but they are not." Nada did not respond to Visterle's comment so he continued. "Are you done eating?"

"Yes."

"Well my pet today we are going to play a new game." Visterle stood up and held his hand out to her; he was still in human form. "Well come on," he said as Nada looked at him.

"I don't have any clothes."

Visterle laughed loudly, "A modest demon?"

"I'm not a demon," Nada said as she wrapped the sheet around her and stood up.

"Your soul is darker than many who serve me; come." Visterle took Nada's hand and led her through a doorway. It was the first time she had been allowed outside of the bedroom chamber.

Nada studied everything with the eyes of a warrior; looking for avenues of escape. They walked down a beautiful hallway.

"This doesn't look like hell to me," Nada said as she thought they might be inside of a palace.

"You have no idea what hell looks like, it transforms appearances like I do. Here," Visterle said and opened a door that led into a beautiful parlor. He continued to hold Nada's hand and led her through the parlor to an equally beautiful bedroom. "The closet is filled with clothes and there is a bathing room through that door." Visterle nodded at a door as he spoke. "I will return in an hour and you will show me what it is like to make love between humans and Rualas. You will take the lead on this."

"And if I don't?"

"Do you want to return to the other room?"

Nada was quiet for a moment. "Keep the form you have now," she said reluctantly.

Visterle continued to laugh as he walked out of the chambers.

Gabriel and his group arrived in the Village of Gesmal mid-morning. Gabriel had been sending messages to both Duncan and the Sanuri so the villagers expected their guests. Although it was early in the day, a feast was prepared. Everyone in the village came up to Joshua, Micha, Thor and Diana and hugged them.

"Now it is my turn to show you off," Diana said to Misha, then she proudly introduced her husband to her clan. All of the Rualas in this group had been in the Village of Gesmal when they rescued the prisoners from Ogg. The villagers welcomed them warmly. Ratri was introducing Batina to the Venatores as Micha introduced Bianca.

Gabriel could tell that both Erebus and Michael felt out of place. "Come with me," Gabriel said and the men walked towards the Sanuri and Duncan.

"My how you have changed," the Sanuri said warmly when he saw Erebus' new appearance.

"Believe it or not the children feared for my safety," Erebus said. "So I obliged them."

"And I believe it was a wise move," the Sanuri said. "This is Chief Duncan of the Clan of Gesmal and this is Erebus, he is a sorcerer who has a castle not far from here. He is helping us in this mission."

"A sorcerer," Duncan said in disbelief. "I don't understand."

"While we have many obvious differences we have many enemies in common. The same people who Gabriel and Sudfad hunt killed my wife. I assure you I am not a threat to you or your people. Although my presence here may be dangerous since Hecate is hunting me."

"And Chief Duncan this is Michael the eldest son of King Sudfad."

"It is an honor," Duncan said.

"Here, Renya and Sudfad sent you some gifts," Michael said and handed several packages to Duncan."

"We have much to tell you," the Sanuri said and looked at Duncan to see if he would invite Erebus into his home.

"Please come inside," Duncan said and led the men to his house.

"So where do you want to go?" Bruno asked Morgan after they awoke in the cave that contained their treasures.

"I was thinking that Port Friada would be worth seeing, but I am not sure I want to leave our loot here."

"Nora is closer and they almost worship Rualas there; it might be a great place to meet some girls," Bruno said.

"Alright, but I want to do a better job of hiding all of this."

Visterle smiled when he returned to the chambers and found Nada prepared for him.

She had curled her hair and was wearing fragrance. "I wasn't sure what you wanted me to wear," Nada said nervously.

"I like what you chose," Visterle said as he looked admiringly at the red lace negligee Nada was wearing. "You have made love to many men, why do you seem so nervous?"

"Well last night wasn't exactly pleasant," Nada retorted.

"As I said, today we play a new game. Today you make love to me and if I like it, we can play this game more often."

Nada slowly walked up to Visterle, she stretched upwards and put her arms around his neck and kissed him on the lips. Nada's mind was running wild as she tried to block out all of the images and focus on passion. Visterle responded to her kisses and within a few moments Nada was unbuttoning his clothes.

"I find this all very interesting," Gabriel said after the Sanuri explained his vision from earlier in the morning. "It's like our way has been cleared so we can concentrate on the Teivels."

"I am about to tell you something that I did not tell my wife," Duncan said. "The Angels helped us rescue George and Ivan; when they were safe I reentered the lair to kill Sampson. I heard the voice of the Angel Daniel, he told me to stop and that things were in motion that would take Hecate's eyes off from our village."

"But we still don't know if Sampson is a threat?" Gabriel asked.

"In my vision he was greatly incapacitated," the Sanuri explained. "That is all of the information that we have now."

"Duncan if it is alright I would like my team to spend the night here then tomorrow we will leave for Erebus' castle," Gabriel said.

"Of course, you are always welcomed here."

"I believe I will make that journey with you in case there is another welcoming committee waiting for you," the Sanuri said. "Then I will return here until you need me again."

Raphael and Edward inspected the facilities at Fort Salar as practice for their inspections on the mission. The inspection was a surprise to the soldiers. Both Raul and Simon assisted Raphael and Edward and taught them the procedures. Since Raphael and Edward commanded Fort Salar they already knew the fort would pass the annual inspection but they followed protocol in case there were any terrorists in Salar. To do an annual inspection on only one fort would raise suspicions and it was Fort Polta they wanted to gain access to.

The following morning, Raphael, Edward, Dagon, Dack, Joao, Darla and Jasmine left on the mission. Over three hundred soldiers accompanied them; many of these men were actually Patronus priests wearing the uniforms of the Wetprian Army. They traveled northwest towards Fort Nir, which was located in the central interior of the kingdom.

Nada had been Visterle's captive for three days although it seemed much longer to her. She tried to keep track of time by making a small mark on the inside of the closet door for each new day. Visterle allowed Nada to stay in the nice chambers as long as she pleased him. Her first night of torture was so horrifying that Nada did not want to repeat it and tried to please her demon master. She was not a fool and realized how Visterle was manipulating her and it angered her daily that his manipulations were working.

Other than her first night, Visterle had not really hurt Nada. He brought her beautiful things and expected her to wear them. She did not want for food or drink and her chambers were luxurious. But so far she had not been allowed outside of her chambers except for the night in the torture room. But what Nada was the most appreciative of was that Visterle maintained a human form for her. That first night her physical pain was not as terrifying as staring into the eyes of hell.

Visterle spent every night with Nada and portions of each day. While she was still too frightened to ask him what his plans were for her, she did wonder what he would do when he tired of her. Nada still had no idea where she was. She had seen no one besides Visterle.

The things Nada needed would simply appear in her chambers. she never heard the sounds of others and although she had windows in her chambers she believed the views to be facades. When Nada looked out of the windows of her prison she would see a scenic view of pastures and hills. But there was never any sign of life, not even an insect. She never saw the wind blowing or rain coming down. The scene would be light then it would be dark for night.

It amazed Nada that Visterle seemed to go to lengths to provide her with a comfortable setting. At the same time she was terrified of what he was hiding. Nada did not believe she was in a tranquil world with this demon. She knew she must be in his hell dimension and Nada was not sure she was ready to learn more.

Gabriel's group was now traveling slower because the Sanuri was driving his boca from the Village of Gesmal to the castle of Erebus. Gabriel anticipated a two to three day journey, unless they were attacked. The first evening of this leg of the journey, the group was telling Michael and Lakin about their previous experience going to Erebus' castle.

"If it was Hecate who set the trap for us," Gabriel said. "She will do it again. She probably put bounties on us so any variety of mercenaries may try to attack."

"While I sense that Hecate has been somewhat weakened," the Sanuri explained. "That would have no effect on bounties and energies she already had in motion."

"Erebus, I am not really sure how your black magics work but don't you get some insight into Hecate's actions?" Gabriel asked.

"While I can, by making contact with anyone in the underworlds I am exposing my position. Any really powerful demon or sorcerer would be able to trace the energies that I send out," Erebus explained. "Normally I would not care but I don't want to jeopardize your mission."

"So there isn't anything you can do to protect yourself?" Diana asked.

"Oh, I can protect myself and I will but as soon as I use the magics it will be like waving a red flag before the hell dimensions and yelling here we are."

"I am glad that you explained that to us," Gabriel said. "You knew all of this didn't you?" Gabriel now asked the Sanuri.

"While he doesn't admit it, Erebus is fond of all of you and wants to protect you. In his world he is more powerful than some of you may believe."

"Diana why don't you show the Sanuri your picture," Gabriel suggested.

"I had a dream and saw this. At first I thought I had the dream because I was remembering your visions," Diana said as she handed the drawing to the Sanuri. "But I knew that we were running away from something and we were scared for those little boys we are holding. And I felt really familiar to the boys like they could be family. Don't you think they kind of look like Misha or his brothers?"

"That is the same image that I was shown. Normally I receive a vision once, I saw that twice and now you have been shown it. This is important but at this point I cannot tell you why."

"Sanuri I am convinced that I have seen that same image with different faces," Joshua said. "It is haunting me. I think I saw it in a book."

"You have been studying a lot of books at my house," Gabriel said.

"I am racking my brain to remember where; it is like the answer is right before me but I can't see it."

"I brought some of the books we were studying," Gabriel said and walked over to his pack.

"I'll help you look," said Diana.

"I think we all will," Thor added and walked to Gabriel.

"I always have a collection of books in the boca," the Sanuri said. "I have a feeling we should be searching them also."

138

The first day of Raphael's and Edward's journey was uneventful. That evening as they made camp both generals felt uneasy as if something was not right. They doubled the perimeter guards and had sergeants constantly walking around the perimeter checking on their men.

"It's not like we are being watched, it's something else," Edward whispered to Raphael as they sat near a fire reviewing their maps.

"Honestly I thought I might be imagining it until you said something," Raphael said. "There are probably demons around us that we can't see."

"I know that dark lords use ravens as their eyes. Is it possible that Teivel uses some other creature? Because we haven't seen any ravens?"

"It would be smart if he did, they must know we are aware of ravens," Raphael said. "I will be back in just a moment." Raphael walked a small distance into the forest and said in a whisper, "If an Angel is sending us a warning please explain." There was no response. Raphael thought for a moment then smiled. "Should I be asking to speak with an Angel?"

"You are learning," Miranda said as she appeared before him. While Raphael had been in her presence many times he always felt weak and in awe of Miranda.

"Teivel has spies at every fort and he has been alerted about the inspection. While he is not worried about the fort passing the annual inspection he is a highly paranoid man and suspicious of everything. You are being watched but not in the manner you believe. Teivel has an orb similar in appearance to the one that Jared brought back from hell. But Teivel's orb is not a gift from The Great Ruler. You will need to obtain that orb before you can help Gabriel and his group in Ryed."

"So my men are safe from attack tonight?"

"Yes, the danger will increase the closer you get to Fort Polta."

"Since there are spies at every fort, one, do we have spies among us and two, do we need to clean out every fort?"

"Of course you have spies among you; you should come to expect that. But if you kill them, Teivel will become suspicious. Hangered and Janson are your spies. As for the forts; these spies are minions who will be exposed and weakened when you sever their connection with the Teivel Clan."

"Tell me of this orb that Teivel possesses," Raphael said. "Can he hear us talking?"

"You and I no and neither can he hear your conversations with other humans or Rualas. But if you speak personally with his spies or other demons or dark lords he will hear. So I would use that to your advantage. And while he can see some of what you do he cannot see everything."

"Then they know we have the Rualas and the girls with us," Raphael said. "That defeats us using Darla and Jasmine to gather information."

Miranda smiled. "Raphael think this through. Those Nordes warriors have brought many disguises and your two spies are men not demons. Hangered and Janson have no special powers; don't you think they would be flattered by the attentions of two beautiful young girls? Darla and Jasmine can distract them as well as obtain information and all of you will be close by to protect them if they need it. But Raphael know that Darla and Jasmine are better trained warriors than those soldiers."

"If I have a meeting with my team will Teivel see us?"

"Not with the storm that is brewing," Miranda said. "Have your meeting." With these words the Angel disappeared.

Raphael quickly returned to Edward. Dagon, Joao. Dack, Darla and Jasmine were sitting around the fire talking.

"How did you know I was going to call a meeting?" Raphael asked.

"We didn't," Dagon replied. "We are just visiting."

"I was just speaking with Miranda," Raphael said and quickly explained their conversation. Everyone in the group was now speaking in whispers.

"I am not really surprised at this," Edward said. "At least we aren't going to be attacked tonight." Edward paused and looked at Darla and Jasmine. "So are you willing to spy on the spies?"

Both women smiled. "This is going to be fun," Darla said. "But you will have to point them out to us."

"It might be better if we do," Dagon said. "We don't want them to think they have the attention of the generals. And Jasmine you are going to tell me I sound like your big brother again but don't take any chances and tell us even the smallest detail because it could be important."

"When our team was smaller," Raphael explained. "Natasha was the only woman and Gabriel made her have a word or mannerism to warn us that she needed help. Because we can always fight but we don't always want to expose our mission."

"What would she do?" asked Jasmine.

"She is clever," Dagon said with a smile. "Remember she would not dress as a warrior for these roles, so sometimes she would drop a hankie or pull out a scarf and blot her neck and face as if she was hot. If she was in a restaurant she would order white wine and raise her glass; that was always a sign for us to get her out of there."

"You can really do anything that would not draw attention as long as you plan ahead and tell the rest of us," Raphael said.

"Well, since we are dressed as warriors we shouldn't change that while we travel," Jasmine said as she looked at Darla. "We don't carry hankies or scarves and," Jasmine paused. "We do have different colors of beads and feathers for our hair."

"But we might not see that far away," Joao said. And for a few moments all of men looked at what Darla and Jasmine were wearing to figure out a signal.

"I have it," Raphael said. "Vivian and Hannah often wear their hair in ponytails."

"And from what I have seen you two always wear your hair down. If we find you some bandanas you can nonchalantly put your hair in a ponytail and that will be our signal that you are in trouble."

"I have bandanas," Dack said. They are both red so we will be able to see them."

"Now remember it might take us a little bit to get to you," Edward said. "You are both smart girls if you feel like something isn't right give us the signal right away. We don't want you fighting with those soldiers unless you really have to because that will tip Teivel off."

"And we will take a lesson from Dack's relationships to set this up," Joao said with a grin. "Everyone has seen us spending time together. One of you get in an argument with Dack and decide you want to get away from us for a while."

"Why me?" Dack asked and laughed.

"Because that is all you and Valerie did," Jasmine said as everyone laughed. "We thought you just fought so you could make up."

"Making up was fun," Dack said with a mischievous grin. "So then are one of you going to make up with me?"

"In your dreams," Jasmine said and ruffled Dack's hair.

While a storm did not form over Raphael, Edward and their soldiers an incredible storm developed in northwestern Wetpr. Torrential rains and great winds battered the area. One of the walls surrounding Fort Polta was struck by lightning and caught fire. The fire raged despite the heavy rains. Trees were up rooted. A tree fell through the roof of the lavish house of General Cedrick T. Kretcher which stood within the walls of the fort. The River Neior which was east of the fort flooded its banks in the heavy rain.

Lightning struck the fort a second time, the office of General Kretcher burst into flames destroying everything inside. Fort Polta was situated in a heavily forested area. Trees toppled over blocking the front gate of the fort and crushing areas of the great wall that surrounded the compound.

Kretcher cursed as the blinding rain poured inside of his house, destroying his belongings. He was so focused on his home that he did not realize the extent of the damage that the fort was suffering. When one of the lieutenants briefed Kretcher about his office the General flew into a rage. Soldiers ran chaotically trying to put out the fires that were spreading throughout the fort.

"How can these fires build in such rain?" Kretcher yelled out loud. "There is more to this!"

Kretcher was actually Cedrick Teivel, the leader of the Teivel Clan. A dangerous and explosive man, he was consumed with paranoia. Many of the soldiers at Fort Polta who did not realize that Teivel was a dark lord whispered that their general was insane. While Kretcher lived within a world of shadows, his fearful delusions created enemies that did not exist. It never entered Teivel's mind that Angels might be behind the devastating storm. Kretcher had closely been monitoring the demon wars and at times added to the chaos by supporting certain agendas.

Kretcher immediately thought the attack on the fort was a warning from a powerful demon or dark lord. He ran back into his home to find his orb. Areas of his house were flooding. The fallen tree only damaged the roof but the weight of the water entering the house collapsed the second floor of the home. Kretcher could barely walk through the first floor because of the debris. Water was up to his knees and rising. Kretcher heard a thunderous roar and ran out of the house as the first floor collapsed into the cellar.

Hangered and Janson were drifters who enlisted in the military of Wetpr basically for food, lodging and a steady paycheck. They were both originally from Zorta and had no allegiance to Wetpr or to King Sudfad. These two men had known each other since childhood. Hangered was the leader and Janson the follower; a relationship that suited both men. Neither man was particularly bright although they had both attended grade school. Hangered had more common sense than Janson who was obsessively superstitious.

Hangered was a large man with an almost square head. He had reddish-blonde hair that was short and curly. He had powerful arms from years of hard work and he always felt the need to protect Janson who was considerably smaller and slight of frame. Janson had short black straight hair which he wore parted on the side. Both men had worked perimeter guard the night before and now sat groggily around their campfire drinking their morning coffee. Hangered was the first to hear women's voices and looked around.

"Wha cha lookin for?" asked Janson.

"I think those girls are around here, be quiet."

"You are such an ass sometimes," Jasmine said loudly as Dack, Joao, Darla and Jasmine walked just east of the campsite belonging to Hangered and Janson.

"Well you never listen," yelled Dack.

"You Rualas think you know everything, I'm really getting sick of your attitude," Jasmine said loudly. "Who made you boss anyways?"

"Boss? You're the one who is always telling everyone what to do," Joao said to Jasmine.

"Joao you just leave her alone, you're as bad as Dack," Darla said and deliberately tripped over Jason's saddle that was lying on the ground.

"Let me help you," Jason said and quickly stood up and offered a hand to Darla.

"Thanks for the help," Darla said sarcastically to Joao, who was trying not to grin. Then Darla turned to Jason and said, "Thank you," with a big smile.

"She's already flirting and in front of us," Dack said angrily.

"Just go away, we are sick of you," Jasmine said. "I mean it."

"Fine!" Dack yelled and the two young Rualas walked away trying hard not to laugh.

"You girls want some coffee?" asked Hangered.

"Thanks," Jasmine said and sat down near the campfire. "Sorry you had to hear that."

"Are they your boyfriends?" Hangered asked as he poured two cups of coffee.

"That's just it they aren't, we all work on Gabriel's team together. And those two act like they own us," Jasmine said with frustration. "We are Nordes warriors and have been training our entire lives and those two act like we are stupid and helpless."

"Well you don't sound stupid to me," Hangered said.

Darla was sitting next to Janson and asked, "Why do you have strings tied on all of your fingers?"

"To keep demons and witches away," Janson said sincerely.

"Does it work?" asked Darla.

"It must cuz I don't never see none," Janson replied.

"Is there something special about those strings, like are they blessed or something?" Jasmine asked.

"No just strings."

Jasmine was going to ask another question but decided it was pointless so she turned to Hangered. "I'm Jasmine and this is Darla what are your names?"

"They call me Hangered and he's Janson."

"It's nice to meet you," Darla said sweetly. "We don't really know any of the soldiers."

"So tell us about yourselves," Jasmine said. "How long have you been soldiers, where are you from?"

Jasmine's request opened a floodgate; both Hangered and Janson were flattered that these two beautiful women wanted to know about them. The two men kept interrupting each other as they proceeded to tell every detail of their lives.

After twenty minutes one of the sergeants walked by and barked, "Pack up, we're leaving."

"Well, we should go," Jasmine said.

"You can always come back for a visit," Janson said shyly.

"We might just do that," Jasmine said with a flirtatious smile. "You're really nice."

Jasmine and Darla returned to the campsite they shared with the Rualas. Raphael was waiting at the campsite for the women to return. "Well?" Raphael asked.

"It worked," Darla said. "But they really aren't what I expected."

"What do you mean?" asked Raphael.

"They are really nice and well, kind of stupid," Jasmine said which made Dack, Joao and Dagon laugh.

"Seriously they don't seem dangerous at all. In fact I feel a little sorry for them, they seem kind of lonely," Darla said. "They grew up together in Zorta, went to grade school and left Zorta to find their fortune but it sounds like they failed at everything they tried so they joined the military so they could eat and have a place to sleep."

"Janson, he's the smaller one, has strings tied on all of his fingers to keep demons and witches away," Jasmine said. "They can't know they are working for a dark lord."

"It is a possibility they are both just good actors," Raphael said.

"If they are acting they are really good," Darla said.

"They invited us back," Jasmine said. "Besides information is there anything else we should be looking for?"

"Don't go through their things," Raphael warned. "If this is all an act they will be watching you as much as you are watching them. Just keep talking to them for now. Sounds like you did a good job."

Chapter XI
Revelations

The evening of the second day of the journey from the Village of Gesmal to the castle of Erebus, Diana asked Batina and Bianca to take a walk with her before dinner. They stopped in a small clearing in the forest not far from their campsite. "I know you don't know me very well," Diana said. "And I am not good about being discrete. So I will just come out and tell you that some of the guys asked me to talk to both of you."

"Have we done something wrong?" Bianca asked with concern.

"No it's just that neither of you talk, I mean except to your fellas. And you seem so intimidated of everyone that you kind of stay in the shadows. They need to get to know you because we all depend on each other in these missions. I was like you my first couple of missions and every time Gabriel would tell me to participate and say what was on my mind. Then on one mission I was the only one who knew how to track demons and I realized I did have things to offer the team. The two of you wouldn't be here if you didn't have things to offer."

"Why did the others ask you to talk to us instead of Ratri or Micha?" Bianca asked.

"All I know is you are acting so intimidated by everyone that some of the guys are getting scared to talk to you because they think they will make the situation worse. And what you need to understand is the three of us are going to be gathering information, which means we are going to have to talk to a lot of strangers and have to fit in wherever we are. I think some of the guys are starting to worry you won't be able to do that. Everyone knows you can fight it's the other tasks they are wondering about."

"Before we got here, Ratri told me the same things," Batina said. "I am not a shy person but I am still acting shy around my husband and well, I am so worried I won't measure up."

"If you want to keep going on the same missions with Ratri you are going to have to get over that," Diana said. "You took on Nada and her boyfriends without blinking because you wanted to save Christopher. You've already impressed everyone."

"I wasn't this shy when I was with the other group," Bianca said. "I think part of my problem is I am realizing that I really care about Micha and I don't want to look bad in front of him or his father."

"If you do your assignments well you won't look bad," Diana said. "But for now just start talking to people. Every night we all sit around the fire and talk and neither of you say a word. Tell a story, tease someone, ask questions. Thor told me he was going to tease you the other night, Bianca but he stopped because he was afraid you might cry."

"Cry! Why would he think I would cry?"

"Maybe because he doesn't know you well enough. So tell us about your lives or tribe. I know," Diana said with enthusiasm. "Is there a game or something just from your tribe that you can teach us? You do know that most of us don't know that much about your tribe."

"We could teach everyone Triolie," Batina said. "But it is a gambling game, do you think Gabriel would mind?"

"I think Gabriel would be very happy to see you interact with the other members of our team. You know I told you how intimidated I was at first. One night some of them asked me to explain the stones on my lamsman and we talked for hours, they were all really interested in the ways of my clan," Diana explained. "And they all love to eat; do you have any recipes of your tribe?"

"Of course," Batina said. "It's just that everyone always compliments your cooking so I didn't want to offer."

"Alright, why don't you two cook dinner tonight then teach everyone that gambling game afterwards? And it wouldn't hurt if you told us a little about your tribe. Do you agree to that?"

"Yes and we are sorry," Bianca said.

"You have nothing to be sorry for. I will be honest I would like to get to know you better too."

"Let us see what we can find for herbs or berries and we will be right back," Batina said.

"We'll take care of everything," Diana said loudly as a ruse to Gabriel when she returned to the campsite and found him and the Sanuri working around the fire. Diana walked closer to Gabriel and said in a low voice, "It was exactly as you thought."

"Where are they?" Gabriel asked.

"Gathering plants and berries, they are fixing you a Nordes meal tonight," Diana said with a smile. "And they are going to teach us a game."

"You did well," the Sanuri said warmly. "Perhaps Gabriel and I will do some research before dinner."

"Sanuri can I talk to you a moment?" Diana asked.

"Certainly," the Sanuri replied and walked away from the fire. Diana followed him and when they were alone she started to speak then saw how the Sanuri was smiling at her.

"Do you already know what I am going to ask?"

"I might. Does Misha know you are pregnant?"

"I don't know how you do that," Diana said with awe. "No one knows because I wasn't going to be kicked off this mission and thankfully I am not sick like Vivian. But that it why I am concerned about those visions of the little boys. Are you sure they aren't our children, you know mine and Misha's?"

"I can't give you that answer, at least not yet. But I do think it is only fair that you tell Misha and Gabriel. They aren't going to send you home. And while Misha always acts strong he is still healing from everything with Nada. As if her past actions weren't bad enough her current ones bring him great shame. I think that if he was focusing on being a father it would help him greatly."

"Well, if I tell them I will have to tell Thor and you know him; he will tell everyone."

"We are all family here, would it really hurt for them to know?"

"If they want to send me home I will refuse to go," Diana said with defiance.

"Diana we all know you are greatly needed on this mission. I believe the Angels sent you and Thor to us to help with this mission and I am not the only one who believes that."

"Alright," Diana said then she stomped her foot and said, "Darn I hope this doesn't ruin everything."

Earlier in the evening most of the men divided into hunting groups and left the area. Only Gabriel, Erebus and the Sanuri had remained at the campsite. Almost thirty minutes after Diana left Bianca and Batina they returned to the camp. These women always carried empty pouches on their belts. They had filled some of the pouches with berries, wild onions and herbs. Both Batina and Bianca were laughing and more at ease.

"I unpacked the pans and provisions," Diana said. "Let me know what you need me to do."

"You cook every meal we don't need your help unless you want to learn some of the recipes," Bianca said. "The people of our tribe like to eat too and we found some good things. We're going to make a griddle cake and cover it with a sauce we will make from the berries; that will be desert. And we found blue flowers. We put the petals in the biscuits and they taste really good."

"Teach me," Diana said and the three women gathered around the fire.

"Erebus you are welcome to join us," the Sanuri said as he saw Erebus sitting alone and reading.

Erebus walked up to Gabriel and the Sanuri who were sitting behind the boca with a stack of books. "I didn't want to say anything last night because I didn't want to scare Diana. But I too think I have seen a similar picture as you have had in your visions. And my literature is vastly different from what all of you read," Erebus said solemnly.

"I think it was wise that you didn't say anything, you will find out later what I am talking about," the Sanuri said and returned to his reading.

"Something sure smells good," Joshua said as his hunting party returned loaded with meat.

"Thor is Misha with you?" Diana called out.

"No."

"Batina and Bianca are fixing dinner tonight, the food of their tribe," Diana announced.

"Well, this will be a treat," Joshua said.

Bianca stood up, "Joshua, Micha can I speak with you for a moment in private?" Bianca started to walk away from the campsite before either man said a word.

"Is everything alright?" Micha asked with concern.

"Not really," Bianca said. "Diana talked to Batina and me and made us realize that we have been acting so intimidated of everyone that we really haven't become part of the team. I am not a shy person but part of the reason I am acting like this is because of you two."

"I don't understand," Micha said as Joshua smiled.

"When I was on the other team I really missed you Micha and I realized how much I care about you. And now that I am on your team I just keep worrying that I am going to do something to look bad in both of your eyes."

"You have nothing to worry about Bianca," Joshua said and kissed her on the cheek. "I am going to leave the two of you alone."

"Your father didn't have to leave," Bianca said.

"Yes he did," Micha said and took Bianca's hand. "The same thing happened to me while we were separated. Bianca I know we have a million things to discuss but that can come later, will you marry me?"

"Misha will you come with me?" Diana said as she ran up to Misha as he and Lakin landed at the campsite.

"Diana is something wrong?" Misha asked when he saw the look on her face.

"Just come with me."

Diana and Misha walked a little ways from the camp. "Diana what is the matter?"

"This isn't how I planned to tell you," she said seriously. "The reason I have been so worried about those visions of us is because we are going to have a baby. And before you even start to yell; I refuse to go home."

"Are you positive, how far along are you?"

"Well the Sanuri confirmed it and I think I am about three months; I am not going home."

Misha picked Diana up and twirled her around then kissed her on the lips. "Thor," Misha yelled. "Thor get your ass over here." Thor ran to Misha and Diana but before he could speak Misha said, "Thor you are going to be an uncle."

"Really?" Thor asked with a big smile and hugged Diana.

"I'm not going home," Diana said adamantly.

"Does Gabriel know?" Misha asked.

"I wouldn't tell him before you, silly."

Misha took Diana's hand and the three walked back into camp. "Gabriel, everyone, Diana and I are going to have a baby."

"I'm not going home," Diana said loudly. "Gabriel, I refuse to go home."

"Honey you are staying here with me," Misha said happily as members of the group walked up to congratulate them.

"Besides Misha and I have to watch out for you," Thor said and hugged his sister again.

"What is going on?" Micha asked as he and Bianca returned to camp.

"Diana is pregnant," Joshua said with a happiness that lit up his eyes. Micha and Bianca looked at each other. "Why don't you tell us your news also?"

"How did you know?" Bianca asked.

"I know my son."

"What is your news?" asked Diana.

"Bianca and I are getting married; of course I have to ask her father first."

"Well I would say we certainly have a great deal to celebrate," the Sanuri said. "I might be able to find a few bottles of wine in my boca."

"I don't know if all of you know that Thor and Diana have always been part of our family. I feel like I just gained a daughter and a grandbaby," Joshua said proudly.

That night Gabriel's group feasted and celebrated. Enrops were sent to the Village of Gesmal, to the Nordes Tribe and to Gabriel's home with news of the baby and the marriage.

"Erebus you can always do research," Diana said. "Come over and join us for this game."

Erebus was fond of Diana. She was exactly the person he would have wanted a daughter to be. He, like the Sanuri, had a feeling of foreboding about the visions of Misha and Diana. Now that they all realized that Diana was pregnant, Erebus felt the visions were a warning, but of what he didn't know. He was reviewing spells that might help him find out if Diana and Misha were in danger; but Erebus didn't know if preforming the spells themselves would put everyone in more danger.

"No come here and sit with us," Diana said happily to Erebus and moved closer to Misha.

"Before we teach you this game," Batina said as she and Bianca stood before the group. "We want to apologize. While Bianca and I are confident in our skills as warriors, we have been feeling in awe of all of you. We don't have the experience you do and that has intimidated us because we want so badly to do well. Diana made us realize that we haven't become part of the team because we have been letting our insecurities take control and we are sorry for that."

153

"And in our ignorance Bianca and I assumed all of you were knowledgeable about our tribe. So starting tonight we will share with you our lives in the Nordes Tribe."

Ratri and Micha looked proudly at their wives as the women spoke. "The game that we will teach you is called Triolie and it is one of the few games of our tribe that doesn't require the skill of a warrior. But it can get you into a lot of trouble," Bianca said and laughed. "It involves dice and you can either bet money or some other valuables or take a drink of whiskey whenever you lose your bet."

"I don't want everyone hung-over for the journey," Gabriel said with a grin. "We should be at Erebus' castle tomorrow and there may be another battle."

"That's what we thought," Batina said so we are going to hand out chips and all of you can decide what you want to bet whether it is chores or money or anything else."

"I am playing," Lakin said and moved closer to the fire. "I love to gamble."

Both Raphael and Edward realize they were no longer plagued with the feeling of uneasiness they had experienced before Raphael spoke with Miranda. Neither general was aware of the storm that had crippled Fort Polta. The fort had not only been severely damaged by the winds, rain, falling trees and fires but the morning following the storm flood waters from the River Neior destroyed anything that had survived the storm.

Little stood between Fort Polta and the River Neior; by time the fast moving water hit the fort it was a churning mass of trees, boulders and other debris. While the fort was decimated, no lives were lost. General Kretcher sent riders to the other forts and to King Sudfad with news of the destruction.

Kretcher realized how vulnerable his men were and immediately sent soldiers into the large port City of Polta to buy supplies. The City of Polta was almost a two day ride northwest of the fort. The city was built on the shores of the Sea of Talmont which was the western border of the Continent of Opots.

Kretcher divided his soldiers between work crews on the fort and patrols that were to help the local people who may have suffered the same fate as the fort. Kretcher himself sorted through the debris of his home and office. He did not want the other soldiers to find remnants of his unholy altars or tools of his black magic. Nothing had survived the forces of nature.

Much of the fort had been washed away by the flood waters. Kretcher realized some of his things may have survived but have been deposited elsewhere. Two days later as Kretcher prepared to leave the fort to hunt for his missing property, some of his patrols started to return. Kretcher's rage and paranoia took on new proportions when the soldiers reported that the fort appeared to be the only thing damaged in the storm.

That night Kretcher sent a long letter to members of his clan in Ryed. The letter included lists of items he needed brought to him at once. Like all dark lords, Kretcher sent the letter by ravens. Shortly after leaving Kretcher the small flock of ravens was attacked and killed by a large flock of Enrops that grabbed the letter and flew to Raphael and Edward.

Jasmine and Darla spent considerably more time with Hangered and Janson. Both Nordes warriors realized this was their first clandestine mission and they lacked experience but the more the women talked with Hangered and Janson the more they believed these soldiers were simple men who had been tricked.

As for Hangered and Janson, they were elated to have Jasmine and Darla pay so much attention to them. These two men were not warriors and in actuality there were no other titles they could claim. Neither Hangered nor Janson had the social graces or wit that would endear them to others. The truth was that no one ever paid attention to these men which was one reason they were so close.

"The more I get to know them the more I feel sorry for them," Darla said to Raphael and Edward the morning of their third day out of Salar. "Honestly I think Jasmine and I are the only friends they have. They haven't even tried anything with us; they just seem so happy to have someone to talk to."

"I agree with Darla," Jasmine said. "Maybe someone else should talk to them just to make sure we aren't missing something. I mean we can keep them distracted, but I don't know how they would send out messages. The camp is surrounded with Enrops and well, they told us they went to grade school but Janson asked Darla to help him with a letter to his mother. I helped Hangered write a letter to his folks and those two can barely read and write. If the Angels wouldn't have given you their names I would think your information is wrong."

"I'll have a couple of the Patronus priests befriend them," Raphael said. "If everyone from the team approaches them it will look suspicious."

"Perhaps those two were chosen because they are so innocent and gullible and they don't realize what they have gotten themselves into," Edward suggested. "And maybe they will be contacted in the future for information. I think Jasmine and Darla should continue befriending them and have the priests perhaps take a different angle."

"You mean have the priests pretend to bribe them?" Dagon asked.

"Yes or they could mention that they were approached for information," Edward said. "I'm starting to feel sorry for these guys just listening to the girls talk about them. It could be that Hangered and Janson are really in trouble and don't even realize it."

Erebus did not receive any warnings of intruders in his castle as the group approached his home. "Stop here," the Sanuri said to the group, then he sent Enrops ahead to look for any signs of danger. Within the hour the birds returned.

"We didn't see anything suspicious besides the dead trees around the castle," one of the Enrops reported to the group.

"Yeah, what caused that?" Thor asked. "We saw the same thing near the lands of the Teivels."

The Sanuri looked at Erebus, who was sitting next to him on the front seat of the boca. "Evil causes that," Erebus replied.

"Erebus are you really that evil?" Diana asked with a smile. "Because you sure don't seem like it."

Erebus laughed, "Well, I am not sure if that was a complement or an insult. I guess the best I can tell you is that I was that evil."

"I think you are beginning to realize how powerful The Prophesy of The Seven Sons is," the Sanuri said. "And why the dark forces have been trying to stop it from unfolding. While you have all become friends and family look at the eclectic group that has come together to stop the demons and dark lords."

"Different tribes and species are coming together. Kings, noblemen, warriors, mothers and fathers, ex-criminals, holy men and our evil or not sorcerer," the Sanuri added with a smile. "And look at how you have all transformed since you banned together; perhaps that too is part of the miracle of the prophesy."

Chapter XII
Sidus

"I'm not sure I feel better that no traps were set up," Gabriel said as his group inspected Erebus' castle. "It just means that Hecate will try something else."

"Who cleaned this place?" Misha asked.

"We got rid of the bodies," Gabriel reminded Misha.

"I know but it was still a mess," Misha replied.

"I have that married couple take care of this place. Arlene cooks and cleans and Theodore is a handy man," Erebus said.

"I'm not sure it is a good idea to have them come around while we are here," said Gabriel. "If nothing else for their safety."

"We can do the cooking," Batina said. "And anything else that needs to be done."

"Erebus can you tell your staff to take a holiday?" the Sanuri asked. "It would be the best thing."

"Since they didn't know I was coming home they shouldn't be back until tomorrow morning," Erebus said. "I can tell them then unless you think I should go to their house tonight?"

"No that might raise suspicions," the Sanuri said. "Tomorrow is fine. They just can't see the Rualas."

"There are plenty of rooms take any ones you want," Erebus said to his guests. "I have a large library you can use but there are some books you shouldn't read, I will put them away. Girls, if you want to do the cooking there are chickens in the back and a large garden."

"How can the garden grow when the trees died?" asked Diana.

"It took me a while but I found a way to protect the garden," Erebus replied. "There is also a smoke house in back and a cellar with canned goods. I will be honest I don't know exactly what Arlene stocks."

"Thanks we will take a look around," Diana said. "I am sure everyone is hungry."

"Wait," Gabriel said to Batina, Bianca and Diana. "Erebus are their spells on anything that would harm the girls?"

"Not anymore," Erebus answered with a grin. "I took them off as we approached."

"Diana if you are going to fix lunch I will set up a room for us," Misha said then yelled, "Come on Thor you might as well stay with us. Has anyone else noticed that Thor can't stop smiling since he found out he is going to be an uncle?"

Thor laughed loudly, "I know I am so happy you would think I was going to be a father."

"Well, you know you are going to be babysitting a lot," Diana joked.

"I better be," Thor said as he and Misha left the room.

Erebus laughed and said, "I really enjoy them. But I am worried about those visions."

"I think we all are," said Gabriel.

The first messages from Salar were delivered to Gabriel's group that evening. "Tell your birds it is safe for them to eat from the garden," Erebus said and started to walk out of the room but changed his mind and walked up to Gabriel and the Sanuri who were sitting at the dining room table. "Sophie had all of her things sent here while we were in Taperia. It has been difficult for me to go through her things so there are many chests and cases that I have not opened. You are welcomed to look at them. You might find something useful."

"That is very generous of you," the Sanuri said. "But I think both Gabriel and I would feel better if you joined us. Perhaps after dinner we can look at some of the things?"

"That is fine," Erebus replied. "I am going to be in the library hiding books." He laughed loudly at his own statement.

Gabriel smiled as he read a letter from Hannah. "Koby and Bekka got married. Everyone will be pleased to hear that. And they brought Emma home so Bekka can nurse her." Gabriel paused. "Sanuri, Lila always seemed so healthy and full of life, do you know what killed her?"

"Have you never wondered why Lila and Christopher don't look anything alike?" the Sanuri asked.

"I noticed but nothing more."

"Lila's real mother died giving birth to her as did her grandmother giving birth to Lila's mother. Christopher is the son of Lila's father and stepmother. Lila never wanted to say anything because she and Luca wanted a baby so badly. She made her choice and knew the risks."

"I don't know if that information would make Luca feel better or worse," Gabriel said. "Do you think I should tell him?"

"Why don't you tell Emeral and Maxwell and let them tell Luca when they think he is ready."

Raphael and Edward decided to make an early camp so some of the men could go hunting. "Why aren't you two with your new boyfriends?" Edward asked Jasmine and Darla as they walked into the area that Edward was setting up as a campsite.

"We found Hangered and Jason but they were talking to a couple of soldiers so we left; we figured it was the priests," Jasmine said.

"I hope you got a good description of the soldiers in case they weren't priests."

Jasmine and Darla looked at each other. "We'll be back," Darla said as they quickly left the area. Edward laughed.

"Read this," Raphael said as he walked up to Edward and handed him a letter. "It's from Kretcher."

"What!" Edward said and grabbed the letter. "Well, I'll be damned," Edward said after he read the letter. "I was wondering why Miranda told you a storm was brewing."

"I thought she meant symbolically. Kretcher is going to have his hands full which means he won't be paying as much attention to us."

"It's like the Angels cleared the way for us," Raphael said with a smile. "Where is everyone?"

"Still hunting, except for the girls. They saw Hangered and Janson talking to a couple of soldiers and assumed they were Patronus priests. I told them to get good descriptions in case they weren't."

"I've been concerned about taking the girls into the forts, just because there are thousands of men at each post. How do you think they would react if I suggested they share lodging with Dack, Joao and Dagon?"

"They all seem like good friends, I am sure they would see the wisdom in it. Bring it up tonight."

"You can go in now," the midwife said to Orbus who entered the bedroom and smiled as he saw Hecate holding her baby.

"It's a boy," Hecate said with a warm smile. "Would you like to hold him?"

Orbus took the baby and sat down in a chair next to Hecate's bed. "Hecate, he doesn't look like he has any human in him. Are you sure he's Sampson's son?"

"Orbus I was pregnant before you and I got back together. He's not your son," Hecate said gently.

"You are my wife now; I want to adopt the boy."

"Orbus why would you want to do such a thing?"

"Hecate you know I have always wanted to have a family with you and this little guy helped bring us back together."

"I think that is very generous of you but..." Hecate hesitated.

"Don't tell me you are thinking of finding Sampson now," Orbus said sternly.

161

"No, I was wondering if you would resent the boy because he was fathered by another."

"No, we will raise him as ours. Have you decided on a name?"

"No, actually I hadn't given it any thought."

"Let's name him Otu, after my father," Orbus said with pride.

"Any word from Hecate?" Visterle asked one of his lieutenants.

"Nothing," the lieutenant replied as they looked through the bars of a cell where Sampson was lying on a bed.

"I didn't expect her to come after the girl but I did think she would want her husband back," Visterle said.

"What is wrong with him?" the lieutenant asked. "He keeps changing form and sounds like he is in a lot of pain."

"Hecate pulled him out of Baal's domain before he completed his trials."

"Why the hell would she do that, she knows the consequences."

"I heard an army of humans and Rualas entered the domain and attacked him. They were being protected by Angels."

"I heard that story to but I didn't believe it."

"Well, I think you are looking at the proof," Visterle said with a sneer. "The bastard does look bad."

Visterle left the dungeons and returned to Nada's chambers. He laughed when he caught her trying to unlock a window. "Don't stop because of me, you can't get out but it will amuse me to watch you."

Nada glared at him. "Why are you back so soon, you just left?"

"Don't you like having me around?" Visterle asked with a grin as he poured himself a glass of whiskey.

"I hate to admit it but I am getting used to you," she said. "And that in itself scares me."

"You are starting to like me," he said and sat down in a large overstuffed chair. "You just won't admit it to yourself."

"Do all demons have such egos?" Nada asked with a grin.

"Probably my pet. Now why don't you come here and sit on my lap; I have some questions for you."

"What kind of questions?" Nada asked as she sat down on Visterle's lap. She kissed the demon then said with a coy smile, "If I answer your questions will you answer some of mine?"

"I'll think about it," he said. "Did you know that my men took Hecate's husband when they took you?"

"No, they took Sampson. Are they giving him his medication?"

"What medication?"

"Hecate was giving him all kinds of things, some to ease his pain, some to help him keep his form and then she was experimenting with potions to help him transform into a demon."

"You seem to know an awful lot about this," Visterle said with surprise.

"When Hecate was gone I would have to give Sampson his medications. Most of the jobs she gave us were to get things for him. Then we would protect him while she was gone."

"Was she gone a lot?"

"Almost every night and she would come back smelling of sex," Nada said with a laugh.

"Do you know where she went or who she was seeing?"

"No, she never told us. She was actually pretty nice to us although we didn't trust her."

Visterle laughed loudly. "I don't think I have ever heard anyone say that Hecate was nice."

"Oh, she would get mad but mostly she sent us on errands. She paid us well and gave us extra whenever we did a good job or extra work for her."

"I always heard she paid well; I wonder if she is softening up because she is having a baby."

"She told us she was having a hard time focusing and asked me if that was because of pregnancy. Visterle did you break into her lair and steal Sampson's brothers?"

"I don't know what you are talking about, tell me."

"Baal said that Sampson had to kill his two brothers to complete the trials. We captured them and someone broke in and rescued them. Whoever did it must be more powerful than Hecate because her protection spells didn't work."

"Interesting," Visterle said. "I wonder who else is after her."

"Hecate said she had a lot of enemies are you one of them?"

"Technically no."

"Then why did you take Sampson?"

"You ask a lot of questions."

"You have me locked in a prison. Who am I going to tell?"

"Enough about Hecate and Sampson what were your other questions?"

"Where am I and I don't know anything about you besides your name?"

"We're on Sidus."

"I don't know what that means."

"Sidus is a different planet than the one you were on."

"We are in a different world? I thought we were in some hell place underground."

"There are all kinds of hell worlds. On Sidus all of the humans were conquered centuries ago so the hell domains are above ground. And why do you want to know about me?"

Nada gave Visterle a quizzical look. "Because you are my lover now."

"Is that what we are?" Visterle asked as he stared into Nada's eyes.

"Well, what would you call it?"

"You actually mean what you are saying, don't you?"

"Yes," Nada said hesitantly. "What is wrong? Did I make you mad?" Nada's eyes widened then she asked angrily, "Are you married!"

Visterle roared with laughter. "I don't believe you. You're a captive of a powerful demon and you're worried that I am married. Nada what would you do if you got out that window?"

"I don't know. You tell me I am on another planet. I might just look around. I don't like feeling like I am in a cage. And you haven't answered any of my questions," she said with irritation.

"I'm not mad and I'm not married but I am surprised. I thought it would take longer."

"What are you talking about?"

"I thought it would take longer for you to become attached to me."

"Was that your plans for me?" Nada asked and smiled. "But I never said I was attached to you."

"You lie. Didn't anyone ever tell you that you can't lie to a demon? Well this is going to change the game. Do you want to get out of your cage and see some of Sidus?"

"Yes! Are you serious?"

"Sidus is very different from the World of Nunc. There are cities and businesses like on your world but they are frequented by all manner of creatures from different worlds. I expect you to act as my companion; if you do not it will be the last time you leave your cage. Do you understand me?"

"Yes, actually I am excited."

"Stand up," Visterle said. As soon as Nada got off his lap, he walked over to her closet and started to pull out dresses. "Wear this one," Visterle said and handed Nada a black silk dress and black shoes. I will be right back, I am going to get you some jewelry."

"Jewelry are we going someplace fancy? It is hard for me to imagine wearing jewelry in hell."

"You have no idea who I am or the world you are in. I'll be back soon."

Visterle returned a short time later carrying a small chest which he set on a table in the bedroom chambers. "Are you ready yet or are you trying to get out a window?"

"I'm ready but you are going to have to help me with the back of the dress," Nada said as she walked out of the bathing room.

"You look beautiful," Visterle said and started to fasten the buttons on her dress.

"What is that?" Nada asked referring to the chest.

"I am going to start you out with that and if you are good you will get more."

"This is all so confusing," Nada said sincerely. "I didn't expect any of this."

"Open it," Visterle said after he buttoned Nada's dress.

Nada gasped and was speechless when she opened the chest which was overflowing with beautiful jewelry. She looked at Visterle then back at the jewels then back at Visterle. "Is this real?" He laughed but did not answer. "Help me pick out something to wear."

Visterle knew what was in the chest since he had just filled it with jewels. He sorted through the jewelry which was heaped together and handed Nada rings, earrings and bracelets. Then he held up a large diamond necklace. "Turn around and hold up your hair."

"Visterle why are you doing this?"

"Doing what?"

"It is so irritating that you don't answer my questions."

"Perhaps I am not sure you are ready for the answers."

"Now you are scaring me. You're not going to sell me are you?"

"I hadn't thought about it," Visterle said. "Turn around." He smiled. "Perfect." He stared at Nada for a few moments as if he was deep in thought. "The world I am going to show you tonight is different from what you imagined. But what you imagine and fear exists here also. I had not planned on introducing you this early and I am not sure you are ready."

"What are you going to show me," Nada asked fearfully, remembering her first night as a captive.

"It is not what you are thinking. I told you I had plans for you when I stole you and you have been too afraid to hear what they are. Tonight I will be introducing you as my queen and I expect you to act like one."

"Your queen!" Nada gasped. "You stole me to be your queen? Who are you?"

"I am a demon who is proud and does not like to be embarrassed. If you make me regret taking you out tonight you will spend the night in the playroom." Visterle always referred to his torture chambers as the playroom.

"I'm not going to embarrass you. I am looking forward to this but I am in shock. I thought you stole me to punish me for my crimes. I thought every night was going to be like my first night here that is why I have been so confused."

Visterle smiled and held out his arm, "Well my pet; let's have some fun. Nada took his arm and expected to walk out of the bedroom but in an instant they were standing in a crowded tavern. The voices and the music were loud. The tavern was smoky and had a strange sweet smell. Nada was intrigued; the tavern was filled with dozens of different types of creatures. She was not sure if they were all demons or not. The creatures were drinking, gambling and dancing. Nada looked at Visterle and smiled.

Although Michael liked all of the members of Gabriel's group he felt a little out of place because the group tended to divide up into couples. Lakin carried Michael the first day the group left Salar and by the end of that day the two had become friends. Michael was fascinated with Lakin's stories about his people and prior missions. Over the days, Michael opened up to Lakin more than he had anyone else since arriving in Salar.

Lakin too, was curious about Michael, this Seventh Son of prophesy who had grown up being victimized by demons. Lakin saw something in Michael that no one else had besides the Sanuri. The energy field that surrounded Michael was no lighter or darker than any of the other Seven Sons but it seemed electrically charged. Neither the Sanuri nor Lakin had seen this before and did not understand its meaning. Michael appeared to be an easygoing and calm man yet the energy around him was like a storm. Both Lakin and the Sanuri felt this deserved watching.

Nada thought it was daytime and was surprised at how busy the tavern was. Visterle knew most of the creatures in the tavern. Nada found it curious that the creatures recognized him since he still maintained a human form. Visterle seemed to enjoy showing Nada off and she enjoyed every moment of the attention. Not wanting to incur his wrath Nada played the perfect companion. She was friendly, affectionate to Visterle in public and deferred most questions asked of her to him.

Nada's curiosity overtook her fear and she enjoyed the strange patrons of the tavern. She saw no other humans or Rualas; the various creatures she met all spoke, danced and drank.

Nada did wonder how she could understand what everyone was saying but she didn't want to ask Visterle any questions until they returned to her chambers.

The Patronus priests who had disguised themselves as soldiers and spoken with Hangered and Janson, met with Raphael and Edward that evening. The priests had similar impressions of the two terrorists as Jasmine and Darla.

"They are either really stupid or really cunning," Padre Sornce said. "We tried being discrete at first but they kept staring at us like we were speaking a different language. Finally Finn comes out and asks them if anyone offered them money to spy and they both looked shocked. Finn told them the reason we were asking was because we were approached and wondered who else had been."

"Honestly Raphael if they aren't incredible actors something is really wrong here," Padre Finn said. "Is it possible that something was planted on them that they are not aware of? Raphael this is going to sound cruel but I have had dogs smarter than those two. Janson is definitely the weaker of the two and follows Hangered's lead on everything. But they both seem like they would blindly follow anyone's orders."

"So it is possible that the terrorists picked two innocent, vulnerable men to do their dirty work for them," Edward said. "That disgusts me. I mean have some balls will ya."

"I'm going to talk to Miranda before we do anything else with these two," Raphael said. "In the meantime have Jasmine and Darla continue to watch them."

Raphael walked a small distance into the forest. "Miranda, Daniel I know you are listening. I need clarification. Are Hangered and Janson innocents who we must protect?"

"You have seen another face of darkness, Raphael; it does not fight with honor," Miranda said. "This is a lesson you must never forget because the lives of many will depend on your decisions."

"I want to speak with those men but will I be letting Teivel know we are on to him?"

"I believe he is still trying to find his orb in the refuse from the storm," Daniel said.

"And thank you again for helping us," said Raphael.

"The key to finding the information you seek Raphael is that your priests asked Hangered and Jason if they had been approached by strangers," Miranda explained.

"Someone they knew," Raphael said. "That may mean more of our soldiers are spies."

"Or something that appeared like someone they knew," Miranda said. "It is what those men carry with them that you should be concerned with." In that instant Miranda and Daniel disappeared.

Raphael returned to Edward, Padre Finn and Padre Sornce. "You are right in your assessments but they carry something that I need to find. Is their camp close to others?"

"Not real close, they don't seem to have any friends," Padre Sornce replied.

"I don't want to make a spectacle out of them but we need to search their things and talk with them," Raphael said.

"If you are concerned about other soldiers seeing you, we will show you a less direct way to get to their camp."

Nada and Visterle spent the entire day in the one tavern because they started gambling. Both had been drinking all day and by evening their passions were taking control. They were already tearing each other's clothes off as soon as they materialized in Nada's bedroom chambers.

"I will be your queen," Nada whispered into Visterle's ear.

"My pet that will require more than you realize now but I am glad that you are submitting so soon."

"Generals," Hangered said in astonishment. He and Janson stood up so quickly that Janson kicked over his cup of coffee.

"At ease," Edward ordered.

Hangered's eyes widened when he saw Padre Finn and Padre Sornce with the generals.

"The reason we are here," Raphael explained. "Is that we received information that the two of you were given something that is dangerous to both you and the rest of the troops."

"Sir we already told Finn and Sornce that the only strangers we have talked to in weeks is Darla and Jasmine," Hangered said nervously.

"Did anyone you know give you something maybe before we left Salar?" Raphael asked.

"Sir you can search our things, we don't have much," Hangered said.

"It might be very innocent looking," said Edward.

Hangered and Janson looked at each other with confusion then Hangered spoke, "Well Lieutenant Tarp gave Janson that book; but we really don't read much."

"Have you opened it?" Raphael asked.

"No, do you want me to get it?" asked Janson.

"Just tell me where it is," Raphael said.

"In that saddlebag that Darla is leaning against."

Darla quickly stood up and reached for the saddlebag. "No, let me get it," Raphael said.

"There's only the one book in there," Jason said. "I was just gonna show Darla and Jasmine cuz they are helping us with our readin and writin."

Raphael dumped the contents of the saddlebag on the ground. Only a few items fell out, including a black leather-bound book. Raphael heard Miranda's voice in his head, "Don't open it, throw it into the fire and tell everyone to stand back."

171

"Stand back everyone," Raphael ordered and threw the book into the flames. Immediately screams from hell resounded through all the campsites. Images of Talmuth, red demon snakes and other monsters appeared to be trying to jump out of the flames.

"What are those?" Janson asked fearfully.

"Demons," Edward said.

"Demons," Janson screamed. "I was karin demons?"

"Did Tarp give you anything else?" asked Edward.

"No," seriously look through our things," Hangered said. His eyes were wide with fear. Raphael searched the meager belongings of the two soldiers. "General are we in trouble?" Hangered asked.

"No but I want you to tell me or General Edward if anyone else gives you anything."

"We sure will," Janson said.

"Jasmine, Darla you can borrow some of my books if you want to help them with their reading," Raphael offered.

"Is that why you girls talk to us cuz of that book?" Janson asked.

"At first it was," Jasmine said. "But we like you and will be your friends. And hopefully by time this mission is done you can write letters to your families."

Chapter XIII
Symbols

Because Nada was conforming to Visterle's demands he started to take her out of her prison every day, which thrilled Nada. Visterle was cunning and knew that word would eventually reach Hecate that he possessed her Ruala. Visterle theorized that Hecate would figure out that he also had Sampson and that would force her to negotiate with him.

Never before had a demon had a Ruala warrior as a mate and Nada possessed exceptional beauty. She was admired and watched by most of the creatures on Sidus which fed Visterle's dark ego. He wanted Nada to represent his status and power so he showered her with fine clothing and jewels.

But Visterle was not the only one to get satisfaction from the arrangement. Nada was working hard to get Visterle to trust her because she realized that might be her only way to escape him. But her ego was also being fed by the attention she was receiving. And although Visterle was her capture, except for the first night he treated her better than any boyfriend; the exception being her late husband Adwell.

While Visterle and Nada both played their parts and had their agendas they soon started to enjoy each other's company especially on their outings. And their passions grew as they fed each other's darkness.

The day after Gabriel's team settled into Erebus' castle, Gabriel, Joshua, Micha, Diana and Thor set out on foot for the monastery at Rubar. Lakin, Misha and twelve other Rualas watched over those on the ground. Since many of the local people were the eyes and ears for the Libertas, Gabriel wanted to be seen in their lands. The Venatores wore their traditional clothing which identified them to the peasants. The Rualas were to stay out of sight unless Gabriel and the others needed them. Gabriel estimated it would take them three days to make the journey on foot.

There were two small villages that were both east of the castle of Erebus.

Michael, Bianca and Batina were to dress in clothing that the local people wore and spend time in these villages trying to obtain information. Erebus allowed them to ride his horses and Ratri was in charge of this aspect of the mission.

Both Batina and Bianca carried weapons but they were concealed. Michael was not to socialize with the two women but to keep an eye on them. Batina and Bianca argued that people would be more willing to talk to them if they were alone. The Village of Benjem was directly east of the castle and the Village of Marlas was southeast of the castle and south of Benjem.

Ratri, Michael, Bianca and Batina understood that strangers would be obvious in these small communities, so they did not hope to gain information right away. The first two days Michael, Bianca and Batina rode into Benjem and tried to learn the layout of the village. The women were friendly and spoke with people but did not try to obtain information. Michael drank in several taverns and talked to some of the men who frequented them. Ten Ruala warriors led by Ratri discretely watched over the group.

The rest of the Ruala warriors remained at Erebus' castle with the Sanuri. If he made a public appearance outside of the castle he would soon draw the attention of the Teivel Clan and every other dark lord and demon in the kingdom. It was too early in the mission for the Sanuri to make his presence known.

"Thor what are you doing?" Diana asked loudly as her brother grabbed her arm to help her cross a small stream.

"I'm just taking care of my little sister," Thor replied with a grin.

"You're worse than Misha, I don't need help. If I wasn't pregnant you would probably push me into the water," Diana said and laughed.

"Indulge him," Joshua said with a smile. "We are all going to be watching out for you.

"I knew I shouldn't have told anyone..." Diana said but stopped before completing her sentence as a bird quickly flew out of a small thicket.

Joshua held his hand up and the group of Venatores split up and circled the thicket. Two Tarus demons had been watching them and now charged at Micha and Joshua who were the closest to the thicket the demons were hiding in. Tarus demons are large and powerful, often measuring at ten feet tall. While they walk on two legs they have the heads, necks and shoulders of an ox.

"Right," Joshua yelled to tell his son which demon he would be attacking. Micha and Joshua each threw a knife that landed into an eye of one of the demons. While both of the demons roared with pain, they did not stop their charge at the Venatores.

As Micha and Joshua released their second knives, Thor and Diana ran up behind the demons and with swords drawn they severed the leg muscles of the demons at their knees. Both of the demons were now blinded and crippled. Joshua gave the order and Thor and Micha each cut off the head of one of the demons.

A round of applause came from the Rualas and Gabriel. "I am impressed," Gabriel said. "I have never really seen Venatores in action before. You killed those demons in seconds."

"It's not often we work as a group," Joshua said with pride.

"We didn't find anything on them of importance but they both bore this tattoo," Micha said as he handed Joshua a piece of skin he had cut off from one of the demons.

"Thor cut off the other one," Joshua ordered. "Where we are going we might need these."

"I haven't seen this symbol before," Joshua said as he showed the skin to Gabriel and the Rualas. The tattoos were drawn with black ink and both were identical. There were four dots with a sword under each dot. The first three swords pointed down and the last sword pointed up.

"Has anyone seen this design before?" Gabriel asked as he passed the two skins around the group.

"Is this common for demons to wear tattoos here?" Lakin asked.

"Yes, because Ryed is home to so many gangs," Thor said.

"Diana and I killed plenty of demons with tattoos but none like these." Gabriel put the pieces of skin into a pouch and the group continue their journey.

Raphael led his troops to the castle of Gabriel's family which was within miles of the monastery at Philiste. After Gabriel realized that he and his family were going to make their home in Salar, he turned his castle over to the Patronus which were headquartered in the monastery. The personal belongings of Gabriel, Raphael and Natasha had been packed and were stored in two of the chambers.

"This brings back memories," Raphael said to Edward as they led their men through the gates surrounding the castle. Raphael smiled when he saw their welcoming group.

High Priest Nicholas was the senior leader of the Patronus organization and the senior high priest at the monastery at Philiste. A large and muscular man with short gray hair and the presence of perpetual youth.

"We got your message," Nicholas said as he waited for Raphael to dismount. The men hugged as other priests walked up to Raphael and Edward.

"Edward, this is High Priest Nicholas, who I have told you about and my good friends, High Priest Uriel, High Priest Gregory, High Priest Caleb, Padre Edgar and Padre Joram; and this is General Edward."

As Edward was shaking hands with the priests Nicholas said to Raphael, "I will have your troops taken to the barracks."

"We have some members of the team with us which includes two young women," Raphael said. "I would like them to stay inside of the castle."

"Of course," Nicholas said and motioned to some of his men to come forward while still talking to Raphael. "We have a fine meal prepared for your arrival please come inside."

"Would you like company?" Erebus asked when he found the Sanuri sitting on the large, decorated porch and reading.

"Of course," the Sanuri said and watched the sorcerer as he sat down in a rocking chair. "Erebus, when you were almost killed and I read your mind to find out what happened, I saw many other things also. You knew you were being watched by the Insidiae and you deliberately made your presence known at the castle of Sudfad. You let the Insidiae know you were aiding their enemy and you thought you would die in the battles that would follow." Erebus did not speak but listened to the Sanuri. "Do you still feel so suicidal?" the Sanuri asked.

"I was honest about everything you said with both Sudfad and Gabriel," Erebus replied. "I guess I haven't thought about it much lately but I don't know if anything has really changed. Why do you ask?"

"Because you are changing whether you realize it or not. You had no emotions besides the anger that was driving your revenge. While that is still an issue, it does not seem to be your only emotion anymore."

"I will admit that I like Sudfad and Renya and the members of Gabriel's team but I don't think that has dissipated my need for revenge."

"No but your new friendships are opening doors inside of you which have been sealed for far too long."

"Sanuri I don't plan on changing," Erebus said and laughed.

"Whether you planned it or not you are."

That evening Visterle and Nada were taking a break from gambling in one of the taverns on Sidus. Visterle was sitting on a stool and Nada was standing between his legs. The two had been kissing for some time when a loud voice rose about the normal noise of the tavern.

"Visterle want to sell that Ruala?"

Nada could feel Visterle's body stiffen. "Get behind me," he whispered into her ear.

"But I can help."

"Do as I tell you," Visterle said sternly.

Visterle looked at the group of demons standing before him and smiled. One demon was standing in front of the others and he was the one doing the talking. The other patrons in the tavern moved away from the group.

"Are you asking or are you someone else's mouthpiece?" Visterle asked as he stood up and started to transform from his human appearance.

"The demon in the forefront grinned and said tauntingly, "I was asking for me but I am sure my friends would like some of her too."

"Fairoot she's not for sale and even if she was you could never afford her. You're not respected enough for all of your boys there to follow you so I assume your boss is paying for this." Fairoot was angered by Visterle's remark which was made worse by the laughter of some of Fairoot's followers. "So what do you really want?"

"The boss is waiting for an answer but apparently you are too busy with your new toy to get back to him," Fairoot said challengingly.

"Tell Salzar that I will talk to him when I am ready and I don't discuss business with underlings."

"Well maybe you need some prompting," Fairoot said with a sneer and threw a knife at Visterle while the entire pack of demons charged him. Nada grabbed a knife out of a sheath being worn by a creature sitting at the bar watching the fight. But when she turned back towards Visterle and his attackers she didn't understand what was happening. It was as if the attackers were surrounded with a dark cloud. Nada could not distinguish Visterle's form in the brawl within the cloud.

One of the tavern patrons decided to take advantage of the distraction and grabbed Nada's arm. She quickly turned and stabbed the creature in the stomach then slit his throat and pushed him away. Nada grabbed a second knife from the body of her dying attacker and readied herself for more attacks which came within seconds. The creatures coming towards Nada did not look like the demons Visterle was fighting. Nada figured these creatures would not have the courage to go against Visterle so they were taking advantage of the situation.

Three creatures charged Nada, who flew into the air and kicked the creature closest to her in the head. The second creature was tall and was reaching for her when she stabbed him in the eye then slit his throat. The third creature grabbed her ankle and was pulling her downward, the first creature now grabbed Nada's other leg.

Nada repeatedly stabbed both creatures as they pulled her to the floor but she did could not get any kill strikes. Suddenly the creatures screamed in pain and let go of her. She looked up and saw Visterle in his true horrific form. "Nada come to me," Visterle ordered. As soon as Nada was at his side the two creatures that had been attacking her burst into flames.

"Is there anyone else who would like to join in?" Visterle asked in a loud and challenging voice. When no one responded Visterle grabbed Nada and they materialized in her chambers moments later. Visterle took on the form of a human again and Nada saw that he was bleeding from many wounds.

"Can I treat your wounds as if you were human?" Nada asked quickly as she helped Visterle to sit in a chair.

"No."

"Visterle tell me what to do; how do I stop your bleeding?"

Within moments items started to materialize on a table near the chair. "Pour the potion into the wounds and cover them with the leaves."

"Drink this," she said and handed Visterle a large glass of whiskey as she started to work on his wounds. "How do I get the leaves to stay on?"

"They will," he said.

Nada was so focused on Visterle's wounds that she didn't notice how he was watching her. "What happened to all of those demons you were fighting?" she asked.

"I sent them back to Salzar. My business with him is not finished."

"Well, it might be for a while; you have a lot of wounds," Nada said as she removed Visterle's shirt. "Whatever this potion is it really stinks." He laughed but did not say anything for several minutes. "If you are going to pass out I need to get you to the bed." Visterle did not reply. "Visterle are you going to pass out?" Nada asked as she was working on the wounds on his back.

"I'm fine."

"The hell you are," she said. "You're going to need to conjure up another bottle of that potion." As soon as Nada finished treating the wounds to Visterle's back she realized there was blood soaking through his pants. "Ok, the pants come off now." Visterle stood up and unfastened his belt as Nada pulled his trousers down. "Would your blood be red if you weren't in a human form?"

"No, it would be black."

"Guess I should have guessed that," Nada said. "When I am done with this last wound is there something I can give you?" A small bottle appeared on the table. "You need stiches," Nada commented.

"What you are doing will heal them."

"Will that stuff in the little bottle make you pass out?"

"It might," Visterle replied.

"Then let's get you in the bed first," Nada said and tried to pull Visterle out of the chair. "You know you need to help me don't you?" she asked with frustration. Nada looked up and saw the way Visterle was watching her and she got angry.

"Visterle if this is another one of your stupid tests I am going to stab you myself, now get out of that chair." He laughed and stood up and Nada helped him to their bed. "You are always playing so damn many games I never know what is real with you," she scolded. "You make me so damn mad sometimes."

Nada covered Visterle with blankets and ran to the table and grabbed the small bottle of potion. "Just hand it to me," he said and drank the bottle down.

"Before you fall asleep, are we safe here or is Salzar going to send more demons after you? Because you need to tell me how to stop them."

"We're safe, now come, lay down with me."

Rualas guarded Gabriel's group since they could see farther and took turns sitting at the fire with the other members of the team. "I am hoping to be at the monastery by tomorrow afternoon," Gabriel said. "I am thinking about having all of you stay outside while I go in and look for High Priest Othnial."

"And how long should we give you before we come looking for you?" Lakin asked.

"I think you should take Thor and Diana with you since we think they know one of the brothers," Joshua said. "If nothing else the priest maybe more inclined to believe you if you are with Venatores because the Teivels do not rule us."

"I agree with Joshua," Lakin said. "Have Joshua and Micha stand outside of the monastery so any of the Libertas can see them and the rest of us will be hiding."

"It's a plan," Gabriel replied.

After dinner that night, Raphael and Edward entered the rooms where the possessions of Gabriel, Natasha and Raphael had been stored.

"Shouldn't there be more than this?" Edward asked as they were searching through boxes.

"We already had a lot of things shipped to the house," Raphael said. "And the rest of this stuff will need to go but for now we need those books on the list and I am looking for my mother's jewelry."

"Did Natasha actually play with dolls?" Edward asked with a grin as he pulled a ragdoll out of one of the boxes.

"Not usually," Raphael said with a smile. "That is why that doll is in such good shape. We should bring it along; Natasha probably wants Lily to have it."

Edward laughed out loud. "If this box didn't belong to Natasha I wouldn't believe this. There is a bullwhip underneath that doll. Do you think she would mind if I used it?"

"Go ahead, I'm sure that is not the only one you will find."

"She has a diary in here and a letter to her parents," Edward said. "I'm going to bring these things back to her."

After a few minutes of silence Raphael announced, "I found my mother's things." Edward noticed the emotion in Raphael's voice. "My parents were very poor; but I want Vivian to have mothers' things."

"Vivian will love them just because they are from you," Edward said. "I've never gotten the idea that she had much store for money. In fact I have noticed that about most of the wives of the team members. I don't mean to get personal but is that something all of you look for?"

"Not intentionally," Raphael said. "But I think many of our wives have similar characteristics. None of them are superficial. They are all warriors of sorts with generous hearts. Look at Natasha and Diana; I really think they are a great deal alike, although I have never said it to Misha or Calen. It's like both brothers married the same girl."

"Not to change the subject but maybe you should take a look at this," Edward said as he was looking into a large chest. Raphael walked over to the chest and to his horror saw the dead body of a man wearing the robe of a Patronus priest. "He hasn't been dead that long," Edward commented.

"Look through the other chests, I am going to get High Priest Nicholas," Raphael said and left the chambers.

"Bad news," Edward said when Raphael and Nicholas returned a few minutes later.

"You found more bodies?" Raphael asked.

"Two and both of these look a lot worse than the first one did."

"What do you mean," Nicholas said as he approached the chests.

"I can't be sure but it looks like someone threw acid in their faces, maybe to blind them before an attack," Edward replied and moved so the two high priests could get a closer look at the bodies. "I don't think any of these priests have been dead more than a day or two," Edward said. "I didn't want to move them until you got here."

"Did you search all of the chests?" Raphael asked.

"Yes and I just started to search the room when you walked in," Edward replied.

"Both of you stay here," High Priest Nicholas said gravely. "I'm going to get some of the men."

"Wait, get the members of my team too," Raphael said. "And have them bring paper and pen."

"Why?" Nicholas asked with amazement.

"I want to study these bodies," Raphael said. "I wouldn't be surprised if some of these cuts aren't ritualistic."

Almost five minutes later, Dagon, Dack, Joao, Jasmine and Darla entered the chambers. "Nicholas said to tell you he is doing a headcount of his men and searching the castle," Dagon said as they all walked towards Raphael.

"Can any of you draw well?" Raphael asked.

"Joao is really good," said Dack.

183

"I can draw a little," said Jasmine.

"I suspect some of these injuries are ritualistic and perhaps so is the way the bodies are set in the chests," Raphael explained. "I want you to draw the priests how they look now and again after we remove them from the chests. I want the rest of you to help Edward search these rooms. All of these things belong to Gabriel, Natasha and me, we hadn't had them shipped to Salar yet."

"What did they take out of these chests to make room for the bodies?" Dagon asked.

"Good question," Edward said. "There weren't any piles of things on the floor."

"So far all we know is that the bodies appeared to have been killed before we got here," Raphael said then kneeled down and prayed over each murdered priest.

"Visterle wake up," Nada said as she shook him. "Visterle someone is at the door."

He looked at her groggily. "What?"

"I said someone is knocking at the door; do you want me to get it?"

"No, you stay here," Visterle said and got out of bed.

"What the hell happened to you?" asked one of Visterle's lieutenants named Zortus.

"Salzar sent some of his boys after me," Visterle replied with annoyance. "What is it?"

"Hecate's husband, I don't even know how to explain it. You have to see it for yourself."

"Zortus this better be serious because I am in no mood for playing games."

"Boss, I'm not sure if Hecate is doing something to him to help him escape or what."

"Nada stay in bed I will be right back," Visterle said over his shoulder and followed Zortus down to the dungeons. The four demons that were watching Sampson now moved so Visterle could get closer to the bars of the cell. Visterle stared at the image before him. Sampson appeared to be unconscious but he was floating several feet above his bed and surrounded by a red cloud.

"That cloud was dark blue when I left to get you," Zortus said.

"Tell me everything," Visterle snapped.

"The guy was screaming like he always is because he is in pain," one of the guards said. "Then he stopped and it got real quiet, like a strange quiet and we come in here and see him floating. Only at first there wasn't a cloud around him but there were lightning strikes like someone was opening a portal."

"Hecate is not strong enough to breach my perimeter," Visterle said. "One of the Old Ones is doing this, but I thought they all turned against her."

"Maybe they aren't trying to help the guy," another guard commented. "He looks like he is dead."

"Zortus go back to my chambers and get Nada. She was taking care of Sampson while Hecate was screwing around with other demons. I have some questions," Visterle said then he looked at Sampson and started to mumble. Immediately lightning bolts started to shoot around the cell. The cloud around Sampson now looked like black smoke. Visterle mumbled again and Sampson's body continued to float but now it was also thrashing around.

"I didn't have time to get dressed," Nada said when Visterle saw she was only wearing a robe.

"That's fine. Tell me when you gave Sampson any of those potions did you ever see anything like this?" Visterle asked.

"That's Sampson? He looks so different. Are you sure that is him?"

"Nada what are you talking about he looks the same as when we grabbed him."

185

"No, can't you see his legs are changing shape as we look. And his ears didn't look like that before."

"It's a pfison screen," Visterle said and with a wave of the demon's hand the cloud disappeared and Sampson crashed onto the bed. Now Visterle and the guards could see what Nada had seen.

"I don't understand," said Nada.

"Someone put a screen up so we couldn't see Sampson transforming," Visterle said as he stared at Sampson.

"But why could I see it?" Nada asked.

"Because those screens are sensitive and have to be created to block specific creatures," Visterle explained. "I wonder if whoever was doing that believes Sampson is going to turn into a powerful demon." Visterle turned back to Nada. "Tell me about the potions."

"Most of them were in small dark bottles. There was never anything written on the bottles but the caps had different designs."

"What were they?"

"I don't know what they are called but I could draw them for you."

"Get her something to draw on," Visterle said to one of the guards.

"There was one bottle that Hecate sent us to Marba to get from an old witch in the mountains. Visterle, I don't know what Hecate gave him when I wasn't there. When she was preparing to leave she would hand me certain bottles and tell me how much to give him. I think some of them were sedatives."

The demon guard returned with a sort of slate with a writing instrument that Nada did not recognize. As Nada drew the symbols she had seen on the bottle caps Visterle started to mumble. Suddenly there was the sound of an explosion and a scream. "What happened?" she asked.

186

"I found who created the pfison screen," Visterle said with a sneer. Then he looked at his lieutenant and said something in a language that Nada could not understand. Zortus turned and left the dungeons.

"The last picture is the potion we got from the witch but I don't know if Hecate ever gave that to him. All of the others were potions I gave to Sampson."

"And you are positive these are the symbols?"

"Yes, I am not lying to you," Nada said with irritation.

"The reason I ask is because there are more to these symbols than you realize," Visterle said. "Were there symbols in the room or on the bed that he was in?"

"Yes," Nada said as she took the slate from Visterle and started to draw. "I wrote next to them where I saw them," Nada said as she returned the slate to him.

Visterle was quiet as he seemed to be studying the drawings. After a few moments he smiled. "You did well my pet. It is time for you to return to your chambers, I have business to take care of."

"Visterle, you are in no shape, your wounds haven't healed," Nada scolded.

Visterle looked at her as if he was angry and she wondered if she shouldn't have said those things in front of his men. "I'm sorry," Nada said, fearing Visterle's wrath.

"My pet you are sounding more like a wife every day," Visterle said and took Nada's arm. Within seconds they materialized in the bedroom chambers.

"Are you mad at me?" Nada asked.

"No but keep in mind our audience when you talk."

"Do you want me to look at your wounds again before you leave?"

"No," Visterle said and pulled Nada close to him. "You have been full of surprises tonight, pleasant surprises. You could have run away from me while I was in battle but you fought at my side. When I was weak and injured you could have attacked me but you took care of me and genuinely seemed concerned. You are no longer my captive, I am taking you as my wife Nada." Visterle kissed her passionately on the lips.

Nada was shocked at Visterle's words. "Does that mean the same thing here as where I come from?" She asked seriously because she feared she would have to go through trials like Sampson. Visterle laughed and disappeared.

The bodies of the three dead priests had been removed from the chests and placed on top of clean sheets that were spread out on the floor. Raphael carefully cleaned the blood from the bodies of the priests exposing similar markings cut into each of the victims.

"What do they represent?" Edward asked as he and the others looked at the markings. Cut into the chests of each priest were four dots with a sword underneath each of them. The first three swords were facing down and the fourth sword faced upward.

"I have no idea," Raphael said. "Joao make sure you draw all of the marks on these bodies in case they all are some types of symbols."

"I may have found something," Dagon announced as he had been searching the chambers. "You're going to have to come here." As members of the team gathered around, Dagon pointed out muddy footprints in a closet. "They are facing the door like they were hiding."

"The mud isn't fresh," Edward said as he knelt down to examine it. "So they were hiding in here before we came."

"But, why would people be coming in here if it is just a storage area for you and Gabriel?" Dack asked.

"They must be looking for something," Raphael said. "And if they didn't find it." Raphael paused. "I need to send messages to the house and to Gabriel."

After Visterle left the dungeons, the guards returned to their card game. They never saw the smoke that started to rise from Sampson's body nor did any of the guards hear the malicious laughter filling Sampson's cell. Sampson's body writhed with pain. The laughter became louder and louder until the guards who were several hallways away heard it and left their game to find the source.

Sampson's spasmodic movements became more and more violent until he threw himself from the bed to the floor of his cell. The impact of hitting the cold stone floor woke the beast from hell. Sampson did not know where he was as he looked around his surroundings and growled.

Sampson did not know who he was as he tried to collect the erratic thoughts and images that were bombarding his mind. Sampson did not remember Hecate although her name kept flashing in his mind's eye. Visterle's words played over and over in Sampson's head, 'Nada took care of Sampson while Hecate was screwing around with other demons.'

Chapter XIV
The Battle Begins

The first two days that Michael, Bianca and Batina worked in the Village of Benjem were uneventful for all three. They found the people surprisingly friendly but learned little else. This morning the three were already on the road heading towards the Village of Marlas when the sun peaked through the night sky. All of the land between Erebus' castle and these two villages was worked up as farm fields. A few trees dotted the landscape but little more. Small farmhouses stood but acres apart. While the images seemed scenic and tranquil, secrets were hidden everywhere.

Since there were few trees in this area the Rualas were exposed while following their teammates; which is why they now started the journeys before sunrise and returned to the castle after sunset. Batina, Bianca and Michael were all feeling more comfortable in their clandestine roles and this morning they broke up the boredom of the journey by talking about their experiences in Benjem.

Suddenly they heard the squawk of a yellow jay which was the signal from the Rualas flying overhead that something was wrong. The three warriors became quiet and listened to their surroundings. Within seconds they heard it, muffled screams. "Which way is that coming from?" Michael yelled up to the Rualas.

"I see flames, southeast," one of the Ruala warriors yelled. Batina, Michael and Bianca left the dirt road and followed the Rualas through corn fields. It took a few minutes before the three riders could see the flames that were now shooting high into the sky. Although Michael, Batina and Bianca were riding as fast as they could, the Rualas beat them to the farmhouse which was fully engulfed in flames. The fire was too intense for anyone to enter the building. The Rualas were searching the ground for prints and searching by air for survivors when the three riders arrived.

"This way," a Ruala yelled and headed towards a field of high alferto grass. Whatever was moving through the high grasses of grain was heavy and trampling the plants.

Michael saw three Rualas dive towards the ground and he shot ahead of the female warriors. Loud bellows were heard in the crisp morning air then a woman's scream. Three Rualas were fighting with eight demons when Michael caught up with them. Without dismounting Michael pulled out his sword and cut the head off from the demon closest to him.

A Nordes war cry rang out behind Michael as he ran his sword through the back of another demon. Bianca jumped onto the back of a demon that was holding a woman, Bianca slit the demon's throat then jumped off its back. As Bianca leaned down to help the woman another demon charged at her. That was when she realized they had run into an ambush.

Few Ruala arrows shot through the air because of the fear of hitting the hostages or team members. Batina chased a demon that was running with a child thrown over his shoulder. She leaned from her horse and stabbed the demon in the kidneys. He bellowed and turned. For a moment Batina paused as she looked into the eyes of pure evil. Her horse reared as the demon grabbed for her. The demon turned and ran. Batina rode ahead of the demon and turned, cutting him off from his path, then she jumped off her horse and faced him.

The demon dropped the child and charged Batina. Her first knife landed between the eyes of the monster. Her second knife severed its windpipe. The demon fell to its knees but did not die. Batina thrust her sword through its heart. When she was sure the demon was dead she pulled her knives out of him and grabbed the crying child and quickly mounted her horse, heading back towards the battle.

Michael was rolling on the ground punching and gouging a demon when Ratri ran his sword through the demon's back. Batina handed the little boy to a woman who was standing in the middle of the chaos and crying. The woman grasped the little boy and hugged him tightly. "They still have my daughter, they still have my daughter," the woman screamed.

"We heard her," Ratri yelled as he and another Ruala started to search the area. Michael thrust his sword through the heart of a demon that he had just thrown to the ground. As Michael was withdrawing his sword he heard Ratri yell.

Looking around Michael saw four demons that were battling the Rualas and Bianca and Batina. Michael jumped onto his horse and rode in the direction of Ratri who was diving towards the ground.

Ratri flew over a demon, kicking it in the head with such force that the demon released the young woman he was carrying. "Run," Ratri yelled to the woman who looked at the two Rualas who were landing.

The woman ran back to the demon that had dropped her. She grabbed an axe that was on the demon's belt and impaled it into his skull. The woman pulled the axe out of the demon and grabbed a knife from its belt. She ran towards Ratri who was battling two demons when another Nordes war cry rang out.

Michael jumped from his horse and grabbed the neck of a demon who was on top of Trace, one of the Ruala warriors. Michael snapped the monster's neck and tossed its body off from the Ruala warrior who was bleeding with a shoulder wound. "I'm alright," Trace yelled as another demon charged towards them. Michael turned and thrust his sword into the stomach of the demon then pulled the sword out and with a powerful swing, Michael cut the demon's head off.

The rescued young woman ran up behind one of the demons fighting with Ratri. She jumped onto the demon's back and slit its throat. Batina dismounted and stood back to back with Ratri as they fought four more demons. "Join us," Batina yelled to the young woman who did a forward roll between two demons and fought with Ratri and Batina.

Michael stood over Trace, protecting the injured Ruala as other demons charged towards them. Michael was a powerful man, whose blows were knocking the huge demons off their feet. Within moments other Rualas joined the battle that soon came to an end. "Trace is hurt," Michael yelled. The group gathered around Trace as Satter, another Ruala warrior was packing crystals into Trace's wounds.

"The crystals are turning black, there must be demon poison in him." Satter yelled. "We need to get him back to the Sanuri right away. Satter picked Trace up and started for the castle, two other Rualas followed.

"The Sanuri?" the young woman asked.

"You know him?" asked Ratri.

"I have heard of him," the woman replied as she looked at her rescuers. "I don't recognize your tribe," the woman said to Batina." But the others must be Ruala." As the woman spoke she looked into the air and saw her mother and brother flying towards them in the arms of two Ruala warriors. The woman smiled and ran towards her family.

After Michael examined the bodies of the demons he walked up to the family. "How is it a farm girl can fight like you do?" Michael asked. The mother and her children looked at Michael but no one answered his question. "Do you know what kind of demons those were or why they attacked you? Still the family stood in silence.

"These warriors risked their lives to help you at least you could tell us your names," Ratri said.

The young woman boldly stood in front of her mother and brother, facing Ratri and Michael. "My name is Rachel, this is my mother Zelda and my little brother Zack. My father is dead inside of that burning house."

"Is there any place we can take you and your family?" Ratri asked kindly. "Do you have family near?"

Rachel turned and looked at her mother who whispered something to her daughter. "We would appreciate it if you would take us to Marlas," Rachael said.

Ratri looked at Batina and nodded so Batina walked closer to the family. "My name is Batina and that is Bianca we are warriors with the Nordes Tribe from Lentz. The warrior you fought with is my husband Ratri and this is Prince Michael from the Kingdom of Wetpr. We are here with the Sanuri and others as we are hoping to find the freedom fighters so you can tell no one that you saw us. Bianca, Michael and I will give you a ride into the village, please do not tell anyone you have seen the Rualas."

Rachel stared suspiciously at the members of Gabriel's team. "How have you heard of the freedom fighters?"

Batina looked at Ratri who said, "You can tell her." It was apparent to all that Rachel felt more comfortable talking to Batina than to the men.

"We have heard that there are people courageous enough to stand up to the Teivel Clan. Among our group are Venatores from the Clan of Gesmal."

"Why would any of you care what happens here?" Rachel asked.

"Because the Teivels are bringing their evil into other kingdoms," Michael said in a less confrontational tone then he had previously used. "They have sent assassins after members of our families and we are here to stop them."

"You think a hand full of people who don't know these lands can stop the Teivels?" Rachel asked challengingly. Everyone in the group smiled at her question.

"First you have no idea who we are," Ratri said with pride. "And secondly that is why we want to join forces with the freedom fighters."

"And just how do you plan to do that?" Rachel asked.

"Part of our group should be arriving at the monastery in Rubar today," Michael said to see Rachel's reaction and he was not disappointed. She almost gasped as he spoke the words.

"We know your people live in terror and are victimized by the war lords and dark lords," Batina said kindly. "You have no reason to believe us but we are telling you the truth. Rachel you fight like a warrior if you can help us we would greatly appreciate it."

Rachel opened her mouth to speak when Zelda yelled, "Rachel no, they will come after us again."

"Is that why the demons attacked you?" Michael asked.

"How can I know for sure that you speak the truth?" asked Rachel.

"Would meeting the Sanuri convince you?" Ratri asked.

194

Rachel looked at Ratri then searched the faces of all who stood before her. Rachel turned and looked at her mother and little brother. "I need to take care of them," Rachel said to Ratri.

"We can bring all of you with us," Batina suggested. "The castle is huge."

"Castle," Rachel gasped. "The only castles around here are owned by sorcerers; now I know that you lie."

"One sorcerer that you speak of is dead and the other is also an enemy of the Teivels. He has joined us," Ratri said.

"And you believe this?" Rachel challenged.

"For all that Erebus is he loved his wife who was murdered by associates of Teivels; he will get no rest until he has his revenge. And trust me," Ratri said with a grin. "He isn't what you would expect."

"What do you mean?" Rachel asked suspiciously.

"Well, when he isn't wearing his robes he reminds me of my grandfather," Bianca said with a smile. "We are not your enemy, but we understand how scared you must be."

"I am scared for my family," Rachel said with anger.

"Just come with us and meet the Sanuri," Ratri suggested. "You don't have to stay at the castle. We will take you to whatever village you want."

Rachel looked back at her mother and brother who were watching her fearfully. Then she looked at Batina. "Alright but if you hurt them I will kill you."

"I would expect nothing else," Batina said. "Do you want to ride for fly?"

Rachel, Zelda and Zach all chose to ride and it was obvious to everyone that Zelda was mad at Rachel for her decisions. Rachel rode with Batina, Zelda rode with Bianca and Zach rode with Michael. Although Zach did not talk he tightly leaned against Michael.

Both Zach and Rachel looked like their mother, who herself was still a young woman for having a teenage daughter. All three had dark hair, large brown eyes and olive skin. Both Rachel and Zelda were beautiful women. But it was obvious that Rachel led the family.

Michael and Ratri both found it unusual that no one in this family was crying although Rachel had said her father was dead inside of the burning house. While Michael suspected Rachel was a member of the freedom fighters he did not trust her.

Rachel and her family all became fearful when they saw Erebus' castle. "It's alright," Batina assured Rachel as they rode through the gate of the stone wall that surrounded the castle. Ratri and the other Rualas did not wait for the riders to dismount; they ran inside of the castle to check on Trace. The Sanuri walked outside as he could see that their visitors were afraid to come inside. When Zelda saw the Sanuri she bowed and told her children to do the same.

"Zelda, please stand up," the Sanuri said warmly. "You do not bow before me."

"You know my name. It is true what they said," Zelda stammered. "I was afraid you were spies for the Teivels."

"Just the opposite," Erebus said as he walked up behind the Sanuri.

"This is Erebus the sorcerer you are all so afraid of," Batina said with a smile. "This is Zelda, Rachel and Zack."

"You are afraid of me?" Erebus asked with curiosity.

"You're a sorcerer," Zelda said.

"Yes but I am no threat to you. Please come in." Zelda's family hesitated.

"Maybe Rachel isn't a freedom fighter," Michael said sarcastically. "She's afraid of a lot." Rachel turned and gave Michael an angry look that caused him to laugh loudly.

196

"Come on mother," Rachel said and they all walked inside of the castle.

"How is Trace?" Michael asked the Sanuri.

"He will be fine. Satter and the others told us what happened."

"We told Rachel and her family why we were here," Michael said as he looked at Rachel. "She fights like a trained soldier, we suspect she could help us connect with the freedom fighters. But, understandably they do not trust us so we brought them here to meet you."

"Are you hungry?" Erebus asked Zach. The eight year old boy nodded. "Why don't we all go into the kitchen and you can talk in there."

Batina and Bianca poured coffee and put a large morning cake on the table as the Sanuri spoke. "We are here to stop the madness and to help your people but we cannot do it without the help of the people themselves. Which is why we want to speak with the brothers to see if they will help us."

"How do you know so much? None of you are from around here?" Rachel asked suspiciously.

"I will tell you but you will not believe me," the Sanuri said and took a sip of his coffee. "You do know that I work on behalf of The Great Ruler. I am not alone and when we need guidance He sends us Angels. We were already looking into the Teivel Clan because of the terrorism they are sponsoring in other kingdoms. It was the Angels who told us about the plight of your people here. You do not have to believe me nor do you have to help us. Just understand that for the first time in a very long time your people have hope on the horizon."

"This is the Sanuri," Zelda said to Rachel. "If he says Angels told him, he is telling the truth."

"We fight people and demons like the Teivel Clan so we have accumulated many enemies. Some of those enemies have put bounties on our families and friends," Ratri explained as he sat down at the table.

197

"That is how we learned about the Teivels. We will fight them with or without the help of your people. But with your help we may be able to return your kingdom to the people instead of the dark lords and demons."

"Rachel we have been honest with you and exposed our mission and location," Michael said. "Now show us good faith and tell us what really happened to your father."

"Tell them Rachel, or I will," Zelda said.

"He was taken as people in Ryed often are. Demons and soldiers who work for the regime break into our homes and take our families. He was taken almost five months ago," Rachel explained.

"Why was he taken?" the Sanuri asked.

"Because he worked with the freedom fighters," Zelda replied. "As does my only daughter. We believe that is why those demons came for us today."

"Erebus, I should have asked you but I told Zelda that they could stay here for a few days," Batina said. "I am sorry that I over stepped my bounds."

"Nonsense, there is plenty of room here," said Erebus.

"Where do you think your father is?" Michael asked.

"If he is still alive perhaps in the dungeons of the Teivels," Rachel said. "I went to the City of Teivel right after they took him but I couldn't find out any information about him. I was planning to return but I cannot leave my mother and brother without protection."

"That is quite a journey to travel in such dangerous lands," the Sanuri said.

"All land in Ryed is dangerous," Rachel replied. "I am filled with shame that I have not returned sooner."

"Then come with us," Batina said. "Zelda and Zack can stay here and you can travel north with us."

"You help us gather information and we will help you find your father," Michael said.

"Mother will you stay here?" Rachel asked.

Zelda looked at the Sanuri then at Erebus, both men smiled and nodded. "Yes but be careful my daughter," Zelda said in almost a whisper.

No one at the Philiste Headquarters of the Patronus had sleep the previous night. The revelation that three of their members had been brutally murdered shook this organization to its very core. Never before had anyone successfully breached the security of a Patronus headquarters although many terrorists had tried. But to know that someone walked the halls of the headquarters, murdered priests and escaped was beyond the comprehension of many of the priests.

"We searched every inch of this building and the grounds, not once but three times," High Priest Nicholas said with frustration. "Nothing, the only clues were the muddy footprints and the symbols carved into the bodies." Nicholas was addressing the entire headquarters. It was mid-morning and most of his men still had not eaten or taken a break of any kind. "There must be something that we are missing!"

Raphael had been standing in the doorway of the large room listening to High Priest Nicholas. Everyone in that meeting room was stunned by horror and grief. Raphael left the meeting and walked out into one of the gardens and prayed. "Forgive me but I don't even know who to call to. Please bless the souls of my friends who were murdered and protect us all. If you can give us any insight into this heinous attack I would appreciate the help."

Raphael thought that perhaps Miranda would speak with him, he was surprised when The Lion materialized. "We all are overwhelmed, I know I should have called to you sooner. Please help us and tell me what I must do?" asked Raphael.

"Those priests were not killed here, their bodies were brought back here to cripple you with the horror. Who is strong enough to carry three bodies and yet walk unnoticed throughout your complex?" The Lion asked.

199

"It is one of us?"

"He is not but he has been posing as one of you for so long that he is accepted in the group."

"Tell me who he is?"

"He is gone, he ran after his crimes. His name is on no roster because he never really belonged here. You will find him when you reach Fort Polta."

"Teivel was behind this?"

"Teivel and other members of the Insidiae are like a cancer that slowly grows until it consumes the body. And the body never realized it was under attack until it is too late. I have already told Sudfad to send Raul, Simon and Matthew to assist you. They will meet up with you at Fort Stanus; wait for them there." With these words The Lion disappeared.

Gabriel's group arrived at the monastery in Rubar mid-afternoon. They watched the monastery and the surrounding area for a while before Gabriel, Joshua, Thor, Micha and Diana walked into the monastery. Gabriel was in the lead looking for High Priest Othnial while the Venatores were watching the entrances to the huge building. Within moments of entering the main building of the monastery a priest approached Gabriel.

"I am High Priest Gabriel and I bring a letter for High Priest Othnial from the Sanuri may I speak with him?"

"Of course, I will take you to him. I am Padre Nebat." When Gabriel shook hands with the priest both men stared into each other's eyes and realized they both were hiding something. Gabriel thought that the priest was either a freedom fighter or one of Teivel's men. "Are the Venatores with you?" Padre Nebat asked.

"Yes," Gabriel replied and watched the priest's face closely.

"They look as if they are preparing for a fight," Padre Nebat said.

"We have many enemies in this kingdom, please may I speak with High Priest Othnial?"

The priest turned and Gabriel followed him down a long corridor, they turned left and walked down a second corridor before they stopped before two double doors. Padre Nebat opened the doors and Gabriel saw a man sitting behind a desk. "High Priest Othnial, High Priest Gabriel is here to see you. He says he has a letter from the Sanuri."

High Priest Othnial smiled and walked towards Gabriel with his hand extended. "I have heard of you, what does a member of the Patronus want in Ryed?"

Gabriel glanced at Padre Nebat who was still standing in the room. "I thought only the Patronus had priests who carried themselves as warriors. Perhaps you should read this letter before I say anything else."

"You may leave," High Priest Othnial said to Padre Nebat. "He is who he says."

"There are four Venatores with him," Padre Nebat commented.

"Two of them have a friend among you," Gabriel said as he was watching for a reaction from Padre Nebat. "They are members of my team."

"A priest has a team?" Padre Nebat asked suspiciously. "What is the Patronus?"

"We are an army of warrior priests."

"And what does this army fight?" Padre Nebat asked.

"Demons, dark lords, Grand Masters, the list goes on." Gabriel said as he stared at Nebat. "Tell me Padre will I be battling against you or standing with you?"

As Gabriel and Padre Nebat talked High Priest Othnial read the letter from the Sanuri. Now Othnial looked at Padre Nebat and said, "Dominic close the door and both of you take a seat."

"Well, that answers my question," Gabriel said.

201

"In the future a real priest would leave when his High Priest told him to do so."

Othnial returned to his desk and Gabriel and Dominic sat in large leather chairs that were set very near to the front of the desk. "Gabriel this letter is very interesting, you may be exactly what I have been praying for," Othnial said. "Do you know of Dominic?"

"Yes, and two of the Venatores with me saved Asher from a pack of demons some months ago. They are here to prove that we come in good faith."

"Dominic, Gabriel is legendary among priests. He leads covert missions against enemies as ours," Othnial explained then he turned to Gabriel. "Do you want to explain the rest?"

"There are aspects of my other missions which I cannot reveal but because we are very successful many of the demons are now hunting my team. While we work for the church we also work on behalf of King Sudfad of Wetpr. He and his family are basically active members and because of that their family is targeted and threatened."

"The Insidiae have tried to kill three of King Sudfad's sons among other atrocities. While investigating the people behind these attacks we realized there was a powerful dark lord acting as the commanding general of Fort Polta in western Wetpr. His name is Cedrick Teivel Kretcher."

Gabriel continued, "As we investigated him we learned about his clan and the reign of terror they have set upon the people of this kingdom. In our investigations we have also learned about the Libertas. Without going into a lot of detail now, my team in Ryed is going to keep the eyes of the clan distracted while High Priest Raphael and others eradicate the clans' presence from Wetpr. We will do this with or without your help. My proposition for you to consider is; do you want to take back your kingdom? We can go farther than being a mere distraction but that we cannot do without your help."

Both Dominic and Othnial stared at Gabriel in disbelief so he continued speaking. "If we combine forces and defeat the Teivels it will be up to you to determine who sits in the seats of power."

202

"We will have nothing to do with that. We all have homes and families and will leave Ryed as soon as our mission is completed. But bear in mind, the people here have been terrorized by cruel dictators for life times; they know nothing else and will be susceptible to that type of regime again."

"We heard stories about an army that stayed with the Clan of Gesmal," Dominic said skeptically. "They attacked Ogg and rescued the prisoners and they fought demons that attacked the village. Is that true?"

"That was one of our missions. A demon paid the creatures of Ogg to kill our families. They kidnapped two of our wives and as we searched for them we learned of the prisoners in Ogg."

"How could humans do such things?" Dominic asked.

"Because we had the help of the heavens," Gabriel replied. "The Sanuri is here in Ryed, but he is not making his presence known yet. My team here is small but powerful. If you decide that you do not want to fight the Teivels that is your decision but I would appreciate any information you can give us to help in our mission because it has already started."

Chapter XV
The Teivel Clan

That same afternoon Rachel talked to the members of Gabriel's team which were staying at Erebus' castle. Bianca took notes as Rachel talked about the horrors the Teivel Clan had inflicted upon the people of Ryed. Night raids were a common occurrence throughout the kingdom. Groups of demons or the soldiers of Teivel would raid farms and villages, throw hoods over the heads of people and remove them from their homes. Usually these people were never seen again. Rachel explained that it seemed the victims of these attacks were chosen at random. It was a tactic to keep the populace submissive through fear.

Unlike some dictators the Teivels did not publically execute their prisoners nor did they display the bodies for public view. The secrecy and uncertainly that the Teivels cultivated crippled their people more than the certainty of knowing that a loved one was dead. The Teivels fed paranoia to keep their people off-guard so they wouldn't congregate against their rulers.

The Teivels had ruled the Kingdom of Ryed for centuries. The clan had allowed kings to sit on the throne but these kings were nothing more than puppets for the Teivels. The current King, Nehmota and Queen Vasart had not been seen for some time and many feared they were dead. Nehmota and Vasart had two sons Prince Vincent and Prince Barid. It was rumored that the Royal Couple had their sons secretly transported from Ryed and hidden in another kingdom. Because of this rumor many feared their king and queen had been punished by the clan.

Monsters and demons walked freely in Ryed, it was the humans who held no power. Rachel explained how over the centuries groups of citizens would try to revolt against the Teivels but the uprisings were always easily squashed. Many believed the Teivels had spies that watched for any signs of conspiracy against the government and attacked the participants before a full scale uprising could form.

As Rachel was explaining life in Ryed to the Sanuri and others, Gabriel, Joshua, Thor, Micha and Diana were being led through passages under the monastery at Rubar.

Dominic and High Priest Othnial were taking Gabriel's group to meet other members of the Libertas.

"We are deep within the earth," Othnial explained. Our predecessors built a maze of tunnels and chambers to hide people from the monsters of this kingdom. I keep them well maintained so we don't have any cave-ins."

"I am glad to hear that," Thor said sarcastically. "I'm really not much for caves and such."

"Do the freedom fighters live down here?" Diana asked. "That must be a horrible existence."

"It's better than the alternative," Dominic said solemnly.

"We had missions in Stordt. We killed King Roch but when he was in power no citizen of Stordt could leave that kingdom without a note from the king," Gabriel explained. "How do the Teivels keep your citizens in Ryed?"

"Fear," High Priest Othnial said with a sigh. "The people put up their own walls and fences with their fear. You offer to change our kingdom, I don't know if the kind of fear that is ingrained in our people will ever be healed. I pray for their healing and I pray for help but I too am losing hope."

"The Great Ruler has heard your prayers," Gabriel said warmly. "It was Angels who told us about your plight and sent us here."

"You are an answer to a prayer?" Dominic asked sarcastically. "That doesn't renew my faith in religion."

"Dominic," Diana scolded. "You just wait. I didn't believe them either when they talked about Angels. Have faith."

"That's easy to say," Dominic said.

"The prisoners of Ogg lost all faith and hope," Joshua said. "Their lives have been changed forever. The Angels helped Gabriel's team and the armies that joined them. Our village became a huge hospital for the prisoners. And the Angels walked among us and healed everyone. As difficult as it may be to believe what we say; we are telling the truth."

"Are you saying you have actually talked with Angels?" Othnial asked.

"Yes. In a way you might say we work for them," Gabriel replied.

"How do people breathe down here?" Diana asked as the air was becoming thick and dank.

"We got used to it after a while," Dominic said.

"Gabriel can't we take them back to the castle?" Diana asked. "At least get them out of this. The Rualas could fly them so no one would see."

"How many of you are down here?" asked Gabriel.

"Just eight," Dominic replied. "What is she talking about?"

"The Teivels have many enemies, some of whom have joined our mission," Gabriel explained. "We are staying at a castle here." Gabriel did not say anything else as they entered a cavern that contained tables, chairs and makeshift beds. Every man in the cavern jumped up and grabbed a weapon as Gabriel's group entered.

"Put down your weapons," Dominic said. "And pull up a chair because you are never going to believe what these people are going to tell you."

"I know you," Asher said with a smile and walked past his brother to shake hands with Thor and Diana. "Dominic, Fennel these are the two Venatores I told you about, the ones who saved my life. You are married now?" Asher asked Diana with a smile when he saw the rings on her hand.

"And pregnant," Thor said proudly.

"My husband is one of the Ruala warriors who is here," Diana explained.

"Rualas, here, in Ryed?" Asher asked. "Why?"

"That is what High Priest Gabriel will explain," Othnial said.

206

The bodies of the three Patronus priests were buried behind the castle that was Gabriel's family's home. After Raphael relayed the words of The Lion, the Patronus were crippled no more. High Priest Nicholas increased the security measures at both the monastery and the castle. The fire burned within the priests, they now realized they were at war; several hundred volunteered to join Raphael's mission.

Raphael sent messages to the other Patronus headquarters to warn them of possible terrorist attacks. The deaths of the priests were included in Raphael's daily messages to King Sudfad, Gabriel and Vivian. The inspection of Fort Nir was performed the day after the burials. Raphael and Edward brought more troops along on the actual inspection than they had originally planned. In addition to the normal inspection procedures, Raphael's men thoroughly searched the fort for unholy altars or any other sign of demonic activity.

Commanding General Simmons was initially surprised at the way the inspection was being conducted. But at the end of the day Raphael and Edward met with Simmons and told him about the terrorist attacks in Salar and against the Patronus priests. Simmons was a man of integrity; he would never allow demonic activity at his fort. After Raphael and Edward were convinced that is was safe they told Simmons about their mission. He immediately dispatched one thousand troops to join Raphael and Edward.

After The Lion had met with Sudfad and told him to send more troops to join Raphael and Edward, Sudfad immediately sent a message to Matthew. It took a day and a half for the message to be delivered by Enrop. It took Matthew and the two thousand troops he was leading three days to travel to Salar.

On this morning three of The Seven Sons and six thousand troops left Salar for Fort Stanus. They left before receiving Raphael's message about the murdered priests.

Everyone remaining in the household at Gabriel's home sent gifts or baked goods along with Raul and Simon.

Both Hannah and Vivian were greatly relieved that more troops were being sent on the mission. King Mathas was prepared to send more troops if necessary and Chief Sorren also offered to send warriors. Sudfad was concerned that a large group of mixed warriors and soldiers would alert the Teivels that they were going to be attacked so he had the soldiers from Lentz dress in Wetprian uniforms and had Sorren's warriors on standby.

Additional flocks of Enrops seemed to appear out of the heavens. These giant birds patrolled Salar, the Village of Gesmal, all of the Patronus headquarters and the soldiers and warriors working on the mission. "What is this?" Erebus asked the Sanuri as they walked into the garden behind the castle and saw the sky was black with Enrops.

"Additional help," the Sanuri replied. "Something must have happened."

Zack ran out into the garden, "Mother says that breakfast is ready you should come in."

The two men followed the boy into the kitchen. "Something smells really good Zelda," Erebus said.

"Since you are allowing us to stay here and protecting my family I will be doing the cooking and cleaning; it is the least I can do," Zelda said with determination. "Batina told us that you told your staff to take a holiday, which is wise because you don't know who you can trust in this kingdom." The Sanuri looked at Erebus and winked at Zelda's comment.

Within moments of everyone sitting at the breakfast table, an Enrop flew into the kitchen and handed a note to the Sanuri. "We are going to have more company Erebus, I hope that is alright," the Sanuri said as he read the note.

"Of course. It's nice having everyone here, usually it is just me."

"Who is coming?" Michael asked.

"Gabriel and the others met with some of the members of the Libertas and are bringing eight of them back here."

"Really?" Rachel asked with concern. "It is very dangerous for them to be seen."

"There are enough Ruala warriors to fly them all back here," Satter said. "I wonder if that is why all of those Enrops showed up."

"I think something else happened," the Sanuri said. "That's not a flock that's an army, we must be heading towards a battle."

Sampson was disoriented and in pain. Although he did not know where he was; he understood he was imprisoned. A voice inside of Sampson's head kept telling him to pretend to be unconscious and to listen to the guards. The same voice told Sampson many things. Things that filled Sampson with anger, things that filled him with the desire for revenge.

Sampson's thoughts and memories were fragmented. He did not understand if the voice he heard in his head was his own thoughts or the voice of another. Sampson lay on his cot trying to remember what led up to him being put into a cell. He struggled trying to regain his memories. The one thing that was consistent was a single word that kept appearing in his mind's eye, the word HECATE.

Visterle materialized in Nada's bedroom chambers. She was still asleep so he removed his clothing and crawled under the covers next to Nada, who immediately sat up in bed. She stared at Visterle who had retaken a human form. Nada looked as if she was going to cry which confused him but the look quickly passed and she punched him in the shoulder.

"Visterle you've been gone almost four days. Four days!" Nada repeated as her voice became louder. "You just left me here alone. I didn't know if you were dead or never coming back. As powerful as you are can't you conjure up a damn note to let me know you're alright? Don't you laugh at me or I will hit you again." Nada tried to punch Visterle but he blocked it then put his arms around her and pulled her close to him.

"You missed me," Visterle said with a big grin.

"No I didn't," Nada replied and scowled at him.

"You are the worst liar. So what did you do while I was gone?"

"What did I do?" Nada repeated angrily. "What could I do, I sat here and thought about you. And wondered if you had died of your wounds or left me."

"You mean you didn't realize the door was unlocked?"

"Unlocked are you serious?" Nada asked and jumped out of bed and ran into the parlor of her chambers. She opened the unlocked door and looked both ways down the hallway. Then she returned to the bedroom. "Was that unlocked the entire time?" Nada demanded.

"I guess you stopped trying to escape," Visterle said and laughed.

Nada jumped onto the bed. "Damn you Visterle and your damn games. What would have happened if I would have walked out that door?"

"You would have walked around the castle but the guards were told not to let you go outside."

"We're in a castle? Is it yours?"

"Yes it is," Visterle said and grabbed Nada's arm and pulled her across the bed so she was closer to him. "Nada I want you to listen closely to me. There are times that I will have to leave. You are my queen now and I plan to give you more and more freedoms but you have to earn them. You have done well. You may walk freely within the castle except for the dungeons. You do understand that if you violate these privileges there will be consequences."

Nada smiled and put her arms around Visterle's neck and kissed him. "Are you home for a while now?"

"Yes."

"Good and next time send a note," Nada said and giggled as she pulled off her nightgown.

Michael was getting bored sitting in Erebus' castle waiting for Gabriel and the other's to return. "I can't stand sitting around," Michael announced after breakfast. "I'm going into Benjem and nose around."

"We'll come with you," Batina said. "There should at least be news about Rachel's house being attacked."

"People don't speak freely about the attacks," Zelda said. "They will say little in front of you because you are strangers. They will think you are spies for the Teivels."

"I'll go with you," Rachel said. "We should go to the market, people come in from the farms on market day."

"You're welcome to come but is that wise?" Michael asked. "Is it safe for you to be seen?"

"Our home was closer to Marlas; people in Benjem might not know the demons came for us."

"Of course we will accompany you," Ratri said. "In case there are problems."

"Rachel, I will give you some money and buy some clothes and things for you, Zelda and Zack," Erebus said.

"We can't take money from you," Zelda said as she was shocked at Erebus' words.

"I have the money and all of you need at the very least a change of clothes."

"I will pay you back," Zelda said.

"You already are. You just keep cooking like this," Erebus said with a smile and left the kitchen table. When he returned he tossed two small pouches of gold coins to Rachel. "Get some candy for Zack too."

"And you were afraid to come inside the castle," Michael said teasingly to Rachel who was looking inside of the pouches.

"Erebus thank you," Rachel said. "You must know that everyone believes that all of the sorcerers and witches work for the Teivels. Isn't that why you all come to Ryed?"

"All I can tell you is that I am not aware of anyone who works for the Teivels," Erebus replied. "But, I'm not a social person and I don't go out much."

"I believe you have become much more social over the last few months," the Sanuri said. "It's hard not to when you are staying at Sudfad's castle."

Erebus' face reflected his surprise at hearing the Sanuri's words. After a few moments Erebus said, "I hadn't thought about it but I believe you are right. I did enjoy my stay there." Then Erebus looked at Zelda and the others. "I fell in love with a wonderful woman when I was young. Her brother betrayed us both and devised a scheme that separated us. Later I went to the Kingdom of Stordt to help a friend and found my lost love. Neither of us had ever married. And it was while I was in Stordt that Sophie and I learned what her brother had done to us." Erebus paused.

"Sophie and I married and without going into more details; men who are associated with the Teivel's killed her. Gabriel and his team were the only ones who tried to help us, even knowing I was a sorcerer. I joined this mission because I wanted revenge and then I wanted to die. I was injured in a battle and King Sudfad and Queen Renya took me into their home and treated me as family. Now mind you they work for The Great Ruler. Their castle is always filled with people and children; it was a very pleasant experience."

No one in the room spoke so the Sanuri said, "Erebus has made many friends in Wetpr. Some of the team members were so worried about him, they asked Erebus to change his manner of clothing and to cut his hair and beard."

"Erebus you really look so much better this way," Bianca said with a smile. "This look seems to suit who you are better."

"I'm not sure about that," Erebus said with a laugh.

"Erebus, I think you have changed more than you realize," Ratri said. "There is nothing wrong with being happier."

Gabriel's group resumed their journey to Erebus' castle before sunrise. They were all anxious to get the members of the Libertas to a safe location, unseen. Dominic and his fellow freedom fighters were exhilarated not only to be flying but to be in the fresh air and to feel the warmth of the sun again.

The evening before, Gabriel's group sat captivated as the Libertas told of their existence in the dark Kingdom of Ryed. More than once Gabriel said the stories were very similar to that of King Roch and his terror hold on the Kingdom of Stordt. Every member of the Libertas who was traveling with Gabriel's group had lost their families and friends to the dictatorship of the Teivels. Most were lost during the nightly terror raids, the rest died in battle. The members of this small group of freedom fighters had become a family themselves, for they had no one else.

"I still have a bad feeling about leaving High Priest Othnial behind," Dominic yelled over to Gabriel as the two men were being flown side by side.

"I didn't like it either," Gabriel replied. "But he was right, if he were to disappear a lot of questions would be asked. Perhaps we can get him after all of you are safely hidden."

"I don't believe we will ever be safe in Ryed," Dominic said seriously.

"You know that Joshua was serious about his offer for all of you to stay with their clan," Gabriel said. "They are good people and fierce warriors."

"We would just be bringing Teivel's armies upon them," Dominic replied.

"We are raised to slay monsters," Diana yelled as she was listening to Dominic and Gabriel talk.

"Yes but how many thousands of monsters can you fight at a time?" Dominic asked seriously.

"You might be surprised," Misha yelled over. Then Misha returned his attention to Diana.

213

"I already sent Emeral and Maxwell a letter telling them you are pregnant and asking them to prepare a nursery in case this mission goes on for months. So if you want anything in particular for the nursery you should let Emeral know."

"I don't really know much about things like that," Diana said and laughed. "But I am sure that Iris will help her. I'll bet that Emeral is just so happy with all of these babies coming. If we have a girl we should name it after her, does Emeral have another middle name besides Lily?"

"No, but after you put me and Thor in charge of choosing the girl names I spoke with Maxwell and he said Emeral had a list of names that she really liked if they would have had more daughters. I thought perhaps we could use one of those names."

"Have you seen the list?"

"No."

"Did you already tell Maxwell the boy's names I picked out?"

"Yes, was it supposed to be a surprise?"

"No, that is fine. Was he happy?"

"Yes, very much so. Of course I told him when we went home for Lila's funeral so we didn't know you were pregnant."

"In your next letter ask Emeral for her list."

"I will do that tonight."

"We have some time yet," Diana said and laughed again. "You and Thor are so funny; I have never seen either of you this happy before."

"That reminds me, if we do have twins, Thor is going to move into one of the extra bedrooms in our chambers to help out."

"Whose idea was that?" Diana asked happily.

"Both of ours. We are getting along really well now."

"I noticed that and it makes me happy."

214

After the mysterious storm that damaged much of Fort Polta, Cedric Teivel started to leave his post and return to Ryed on a frequent basis. Teivel was not a man who believed in coincidences. The storm that destroyed his home, office and all of his personal belongings did not disrupt any area other than the fort. He knew he had been attacked, he just did not know who his attacker was and that gnawed at him every day. Teivel had more resources in Ryed to help him discover the identity of this mysterious adversary.

When Teivel was assuming his disguise as Commanding General Cedric Kretcher at Fort Polta, he tried not to draw attention to himself or to his fort. Teivel did not want King Sudfad to discover that he was replacing the soldiers with members of the Insidiae and criminals for hire. But his role as Kretcher was in direct contrast to Teivel's normally flamboyant personality.

Like many dark lords, Teivel turned to dark magics for power and for greed. Teivel was consumed with his quest for power. He wanted ultimate control of everything and he wanted everyone to know that he was the one in control.

Teivel would tire of his role as General Kretcher because he had little patience for the mundane. When he would return to his home in Ryed he often held huge feasts and celebrations. Teivel took the prisoners from the dungeons and forced them to fight in the Gefrey Games for the amusement of his guests.

It was at one such game that Teivel came up with an idea to show the people of Opots his power and his glory. Teivel decided to host the first Gefrey Games that would be open to all the peoples of Opots. The games would be held in the City of Teivel and would be a spectacular event.

The more that Teivel considered this idea the more it fed his ego. "Finally the kingdoms will know my superiority; finally the kingdoms will fear me," Teivel thought as he sat in the war room of his castle in Ryed.

Like many fear driven tyrants, Teivel sought to control the minds of the people of his kingdom. He would send his men out among the people of Ryed with decrees or false rumors to instill fear. And the people of Ryed were very fearful; a fear that crippled, a fear that blinded and a fear that ignited the passions of the freedom fighters.

Chapter XVI
Dreams

As the family sat down for breakfast in the house of Gabriel, Iris turned to Vivian. "Honey you look so good are you finally feeling better?"

"It's kind of amazing," Vivian said happily. "I have been so sick since I got pregnant and this morning I feel great. I hope I stay this way."

"Well, I was really sick with every one of you that I carried," Iris said. "Unfortunately you may take after me."

"Not to change the subject," Bekka said. "But do you plan to continue your morning training sessions?" This question was directed to Vivian, Natasha and Hannah.

"I hope so," Hannah said. "I am learning so much and its fun."

"But I think Elan is getting sick of training with us girls," Natasha said and laughed.

"Oh, he enjoys it," Cassandra said. "He talks about it a great deal."

"Well, Koby and I talked and when Ian and Emma are a little older I want to join you," Bekka said. "I need to get back in shape."

"They only train for one or two hours in the morning," Emeral said. "You should be able to join them soon. I will help watch the babies."

There was a lull in the conversation at the table for a few moments then Vivian said seriously. "I want to tell all of you something. Last night I kept having the same dream over and over but it was more like a voice I was hearing than a normal dream. It was about Berta."

"We know she was killed by a demon but we never found out why or what role she played with Shanksaw. The voice kept telling me to go back to that house and investigate."

217

"Although the voice didn't say it, I kept feeling like we missed something really important. Then this morning I wake up and I am well for the first time in many months. I don't think that is a coincidence."

"Hannah and I will go with you," Natasha said excitedly. "This may be fun."

"Well, you girls certainly aren't going into that house by yourselves," Calen said. "I was there when we found the body and it was a gruesome sight. We did look around but didn't find anything that appeared that Berta worshipped demons."

"You are welcome to come with us," Vivian said. "None of you got to know Berta like Diana and I did. Neither of us believe Berta was a bad person. I would like to find out what happened to her; I mean for all we know she got killed because of us."

Calen turned to Luca and said, "Why don't you join us, it will get your mind off from things." Calen was referring to Lila's death which was still crippling Luca.

"Actually this does sound interesting, I think I will," Luca said. His statement pleased everyone at the table.

"You know with Sam and me and Iris and Emeral here," Ella said. "We can watch the house and the children, go and do what you need to do."

"I can tell that you want to join them," Cassandra said to Elan when she saw the look on his face. "Go, we will be fine."

"I would like to go, this sounds interesting," Elan said. "Koby do you want to join us?"

"I think at least one of us should stay here," Koby said. "If this turns out to be something maybe I will join you later."

Vivian was not the only member of Gabriel's team to have been plagued with dreams the previous night. Diana had been thrashing around so violently that Misha was afraid that something demonic was attacking her in her sleep.

No sooner would Misha wake Diana than she would fall back into a deep and troubled sleep. When Diana did fully wake up, she slid from beneath her blankets and started to prepare breakfast for the group.

"You look awful," Thor said to Diana as he poured himself some coffee. "Are you feeling alright?"

"No, I need to talk to the Sanuri," as Diana spoke she started to cry. "Thor I had that vision again last night. Over and over I saw the same image but this time I heard voices but I couldn't understand the language."

"What were the voices like?" Thor asked as he sat down near his sister.

"It was all so strange. It wasn't like the voices were talking directly to me or even to the images I was seeing. It was like I was listening to some kind of meeting. Mostly different men were talking but sometimes there was chanting."

"Diana you know we are all worried about those visions, especially now that everyone knows you are pregnant. As soon as Lakin wakes up I think you should tell him. Did you tell Misha?"

"Not yet. I must have been making noise because he kept trying to wake me up; but it was like I couldn't leave the vision."

"I am going to start holding morning meetings which I expect Gabriel will continue when that group joins us," the Sanuri said to the people staying at Erebus' castle. "Last night Michael talked to me about their experiences in Marlas; but since it was late many of you were already sleeping. Michael would you tell the rest of the group your information?" The meeting was being held in the large kitchen; which had become the gathering place for everyone staying at the castle.

"Perhaps Zach should go outside and play," Michael suggested as he stood up and faced everyone.

"I am not sure I want him outside alone," Zelda said. "I will go with him and Rachel can tell me the information later."

"Going into the village with Rachel was very different from what we had experienced before. People trust her and while they still gave the rest of us suspicious looks; they did talk in front of us," Michael explained. "Rachel did not reveal our mission but did tell the villagers that they could trust us. Rachel why don't you hand out those maps you were working on."

"According to the villagers there has been a great increase in the nightly raids against citizens. Since Rachel knows this area she drew maps and indicated the homes that had been attacked and when the attacks occurred. Rachel why don't you explain your maps," Michael continued.

Rachel handed the last of her maps to the Rualas warriors in the back of the kitchen and walked in front of the group. "Understand those of us who live in Ryed are accustomed to the terror raids. It is simply a part of our existence. Those of us who stand against the Teivels understand this is a means they use to cripple our people. And since this means is so effective they don't have to raid the villages and farms every night. Sometimes they go weeks or months without a raid."

"But as you can see from the maps, in the last few weeks there have been nightly raids with more than one target; which is also unusual. As you can see I drew lines to connect the locations of the raids but I did not see any clear pattern. We have always believed the raids are random. If someone sees something different please tell us."

"Rachel, has this increase in raids ever happened before?" the Sanuri asked.

"We have seen this before when the Teivels are concerned about uprisings. But even then we never see such an increase."

Now Ratri stood up. "I am sure all of you are thinking the same as us that Gabriel's group has been compromised. But we did not get any information to support our fears."

"It could be possible that another group is planning an uprising," the Sanuri said. "But I don't believe in coincidences. Do you think it would be beneficial for your group to return to Marlas or do you want to take Rachel to Benjem?"

"I doubt if we will get any more information form the villagers at Marlas, at least not this soon," Rachel said.

"The sun is already up which means that the Rualas will be exposed," the Sanuri said. "Plan on traveling to Benjem tomorrow morning. Now that being said; we are expecting Gabriel's group back this afternoon and he may want a change of plans."

Ratri stood up again and addressed the group. "I was with the group of Rualas who flew out of the demonic fog to get supplies for the wounded that were being cared for at the Village of Gesmal. We went to a small port town called Benfax. The villagers were telling us that more and more ships were arriving at their town because the Teivels extort money from the ships when they go to Rubar. It sounded like the sailors bring a lot of news to that village. It is farther from here than Benjem and Marlas but it might be worth our while to go there."

"I think that is an excellent idea," the Sanuri said. "But as you spoke I was overwhelmed with a feeling that we should all stay at the castle until Gabriel's group gets here."

Neither Misha nor Diana mentioned her nightmares to Gabriel's group as they ate breakfast. But as soon as the meal was over Misha took Diana's hand and walked up to Lakin. Thor saw the three walk away from the group and decided to join them.

"Lakin, Diana and I have not spoken about what happened to her last night but I don't think she was having normal nightmares. I almost woke you up to see if a demon was attacking her," Misha said then turned to Diana. "You need to tell us what happened. Do you remember?"

"I have never experienced anything like that before," Diana said. "I just keep seeing that same vison of me and Misha with the two little boys over and over. But I kept hearing voices. I don't think the voices were talking to me and Misha; I felt like I was listening to some kind of meeting but I couldn't understand the language they were speaking."

"Diana said it was men talking and sometimes they would chant," Thor said.

221

"Misha kept trying to wake me up but it was like I couldn't leave the vision although I don't understand that at all. Lakin can you look into my mind and find out why I am seeing these things?"

"First tell me did you notice any changes to the visions you were seeing? Really think, anything even small might be important."

Diana closed her eyes and remained quiet for several moments as she tried to recall the visons of the previous night. "You're right," Diana said and opened her eyes. "In these visons the children were crying and Misha and I were trying to keep them quiet because we knew there were enemies close." Diana closed her eyes again. "Misha the boys are twins but I can't tell if they are Ruala or human because of the way we are holding them. You said there were twins in your family. This is starting to really scare me."

"I think this is starting to scare all of us," Lakin said as he walked up to Diana and placed the palms of his hands on either side of her head. Lakin started to softly chant. Thor moved closer to Misha and Diana as he watched Lakin.

By now the rest of Gabriel's group realized that Lakin, Misha, Diana and Thor were missing. Within moments Gabriel and Joshua joined Lakin, Diana, Misha and Thor. One by one other members of the group joined them; everyone stood in silence and listened to Lakin chant.

After many minutes, Lakin opened his eyes and looked at the group that now surrounded them. "Last night Diana keep seeing that same vision over and over and this time she heard men's voices although she could not understand the language." Lakin looked down at Diana and asked, "Did you experience anything while I was doing that?"

"No. But what did you see?"

"I saw what you saw but I couldn't hear the voices. But I felt that you were seeing these things because Dominic and the others are with us. Diana you need to show them the drawing you did."

"I'll be right back," Diana said and left the group.

222

"I don't understand what you were doing?" said Dominic.

"I am a healer of my tribe," Lakin replied. "And the Sanuri has also taught me many ways of healing people that are not of this world. I prayed that Diana's visions would be revealed to me so I could help her. I saw the same images as she will show you in just a moment and this time I felt both Misha's and Diana's fear for the safety of the children they were carrying."

All of the freedom fighters were standing together as a group. Diana walked up to Dominic and handed him the drawing. "What scares me is that looks like a hell world and those boys are twins. I am pregnant and there are twins on both sides of our family," Diana said as she watched Dominic's face. "You have seen that before, haven't you?"

Dominic handed the drawing to Asher. "Teivel has that same drawing painted on the insides of his prisons but the faces are not you and Misha."

"Do you know why or what the picture means?" asked Misha.

"No. But in Teivel's paintings the people look like they are from ancient times because of the way they are dressed. It too is a man and woman carrying two small children. Other than your faces everything else is the same."

Immediately after breakfast, Vivian, Hannah, Natasha, Calen, Luca and Elan left for Berta's house. Although the men wanted to fly with the women, Vivian felt they should drive the small boca in case they would be bringing things from Berta's house to examine.

"I know you told us about this," Hannah said as the group walked into Berta's house. "But the hair on the back of my neck is rising."

"We got what was left of her body out of here to bury," Calen said. "But we didn't clean the place up."

"I don't think she had any other family besides her husband," Vivian said as she was reading the bloody writing on the walls. "So hopefully no one else has been in here."

223

"That voice didn't tell you where we should start looking did it?" Luca said as he looked at the cluttered parlor and kitchen.

"No," Vivian replied. "Berta worked all of the time, I don't think she had much time to take care of her house. I am going to start in the bedroom."

Calen, Luca and Elan decided to search the second floor hoping that it wasn't as cluttered as the first floor. But to their disappointment the second floor was in worse condition. Vivian yelled to the men, "Berta was a really smart woman if she wanted to hide something, it is probably in a clever place."

Hannah and Natasha searched the kitchen. "Doesn't it seem like she has an awful lot of crocks of dried goods and spices for just two people living here?" Natasha asked as she looked at the three huge cupboards lined with rows upon rows of crocks.

"I was thinking the same thing," Hannah said. "I'll start putting containers on the table and you start emptying the crocks."

"Most of this just looks like regular cooking ingredients," Natasha said as she emptied the first shelf of crocks. "But I don't really know what all can be used for spells."

"This is actually a cute house if it wasn't so messy," Hannah said as she was searching the pantry.

Calen walked to the top of the stairs and yelled down to the women, "Vivian you and Diana said that Berta couldn't read but there is a huge bookshelf up here. We are going to start on that."

"I wonder if her husband could read," Natasha said after she heard Calen yelling.

"I am beginning to wonder if more people lived here than Berta and her husband. There must be three sets of dishes in this pantry besides all of the food," Hannah said. "Do you think it is possible that some of Shanksaw's men were staying here?"

"At this point I think anything is possible," Natasha said. "I don't feel the presence of a demon but something seems really wrong about this place."

224

Since the Sanuri wanted all of the warriors to stay at Erebus' castle until Gabriel's group returned, Zelda, Batina and Bianca were cooking a huge feast.

Rachel, Ratri and Michael worked on maps. Diana and Thor had previously drawn detailed maps of the areas they had hunted in. Now Rachel was drawing detailed maps of other sections of Ryed.

Erebus took the Sanuri to the room where all of Sophie's belongings were stored. Erebus had not opened any of the chests or carrying cases; now the two men carefully searched each item.

The remaining Ruala warriors searched the areas for signs of demons. An army of Enrops still flew around the castle. The birds said The Lion had sent them but they didn't know the reason. Since it was unusual for the Angels to send such a large number of Enrops, the Rualas prepared for an attack.

It was late afternoon when Gabriel's group arrived at the castle. The Sanuri suspected that Dominic and his men would be leery of entering a sorcerer's castle so he was the first to greet the group in the front courtyard.

Gabriel saw the look on Dominic's face when he saw the Sanuri. "Didn't you believe me?" Gabriel asked with a grin.

"So much of what you said was unbelievable; I didn't know what to think."

"The women have prepared a feast and told me the food is ready," the Sanuri said with a smile. "We can make introductions in the dining room."

The eight freedom fighters were dressed in little more than rags. They all stopped and stared at the food on the dining room table. "It has been a long time since any of us have eaten such a meal," Fennel said with sadness in his voice.

"Please take seats," Erebus said. "The women have worked hard on this meal."

"Erebus are you alright?" Diana asked because Erebus looked as if he had been crying.

225

"Yes, the Sanuri and I have been searching through Sophie's belongings. This was something I could not do before."

"While we have a great deal of business to discuss," the Sanuri said. "I believe we should use this meal as a chance to get to know each other. Then we will have a meeting afterwards."

"For someone who says he is not social, I can't believe the size of this banquet room," Thor said to Erebus with a grin.

"It's from the previous owners. In fact this is the first time I have sat in here. I will admit it is nice to have all these guests." Now Erebus looked at Dominic. "I can see the suspicion on your faces. Perhaps I should introduce myself first and tell you why I am involved."

"You're just in time for dinner," Emeral said as Calen, Natasha, Hannah, Vivian, Luca and Elan entered the house.

"I am sorry we were gone so long," Hannah said and started to walk quickly towards the kitchen.

"Hannah everything is prepared. Ella, Iris and I work quite well together," Emeral said with a smile. "Now I am curious if you found anything."

"First of all when we walked into the house we felt like we were back in Misha's old chambers. The house is a mess which is why it is taking us so long. We didn't finish," Calen said.

"Certainly you are kidding," said Emeral.

"I wish he was," Luca said. "But we are all suspecting that more people than Berta and her husband were living there."

"Did she have children?" Emeral asked.

"She never mentioned any," Vivian said as she started taking items out of a bag. "We don't have any proof yet but we suspect that some of Shanksaw's men were there."

"We didn't feel the presence of demons but we all felt like something was very wrong," Natasha said.

"We found a few things that we need to examine but like Calen said; it will take us a while to search everything."

"Are you planning on going back tomorrow?" asked Emeral.

"Actually we were planning on going back for a while after dinner," Calen said then he grinned. "Do you want to come along Mother and share the fun?"

"I believe I will. Now why don't you show me what you found."

"Berta said she couldn't read but there was a huge bookcase in one of the rooms, with hundreds of books," Vivian explained. "Elan found two books that look like they were written in some kind of code and another book that appears to be a ledger. I found a pouch of papers underneath the floorboards of her bedroom and Natasha found keys hidden in a crock of flour. But for all of the time that we spent there we only got a small start."

"Luca and Hannah talked to Berta's neighbors and although they didn't get any information they both felt the people were acting scared," Calen said.

"Although I was only with Berta for a short time, I just feel like she was a victim in all of this," Emeral said. "And it's been bothering me that Vivian suggested that Berta may have been killed because of us. If you don't mind I would like to help you figure all this out."

The Sanuri was pleased that some of the tensions were easing as this eclectic group of warriors enjoyed their feast and started to introduce themselves. The Sanuri knew what these people would face and to succeed they had to learn to trust and to work with each other.

Since the banquet room was so large, the Sanuri also held the meeting in that room after the meal. The meeting lasted late into the night.

"Everyone looks exhausted," Gabriel said. "I believe we should resume this meeting in the morning. We still have to prepare rooms for Dominic and his men."

227

"I agree," the Sanuri said. "And the rooms are already prepared. Diana if you don't mind I would like to look into your mind after the meeting."

"I was going to ask you to," Diana said. "Last night really scared me. If I wasn't pregnant I wouldn't be so worried about those visons.

"Can some of us stay?" Gabriel asked.

"That is up to Diana," said the Sanuri.

"You can all stay for all I care. I just want to know what all this means."

To Diana's surprise everyone in the room remained seated except for Zelda who took Zack out of the room. Both Misha and Thor walked up to the Sanuri with Diana. The Sanuri placed the palms of his hands on either side of Diana's head and stared into her eyes. The room remained silent.

After many minutes the Sanuri let go of Diana's head and said, "Perhaps I should speak with the three of you alone first."

"Now you are scaring me," Diana said. "Please just tell us."

"Misha, Thor do you want me to tell you in front of the others?" the Sanuri asked.

"We don't know what you are going to say," Thor said. "I don't care."

"Does this have anything to do with Nada?" Misha asked.

"Yes and that is why I am asking."

"Go ahead," Misha said angrily.

"First I want to tell you that the vision you are seeing is very complicated because it brings information about several things. Demons are not causing you to have the visions, in fact just the opposite. The heavens are expanding your mind to help us and to warn you. First I have to tell you that when I get messages from the heavens they are often complicated but perhaps that is because my mind is limited."

228

"The good news is those are your sons you are carrying."

"So I am pregnant with twins?" Diana asked excitedly.

"Yes. Now for the rest; Nada was taken captive by a very powerful demon. He worked for Molach and is now trying to take over that hell domain since Molach is imprisoned in The Abyss. This demon has now made Nada his queen and while she still has the status of a captive that will change. The visions are a warning that Nada will come after you but I can't tell you any more than that for now."

"The reason you have been given this information in that particular scene is important for this mission. Misha your face and Diana's face were inserted into an ancient image as a clue to us. While I do not have all of the information yet, the reason that image is used by the Teivel Clan is because it is significant to the Grand Masters; a significance we need to learn."

Now the Sanuri addressed the entire group. "The Teivel Clan is not led by Cedrick Teivel as many believe but by two Grand Masters who are brother and sister. Their original names are Emeric and Banaka but they have now taken the names of Valdus and Oriah. Teivel was their father's name. It is important that we find out the meaning behind that image."

"What about the voices Diana heard?" Misha asked.

The Sanuri smiled. "That was actually the heavens helping us again. Those men were speaking in the ancient language of Cerfic and fortunately for us Michael can translate that language."

"But I can't remember the exact words," Diana said.

"Pray to have the words revealed to you; I do believe you will be shown," the Sanuri said.

"Should I do this now?" Diana said.

"That is up to you and Michael," the Sanuri replied.

Diana looked at Misha then across the room at Michael. I would like to do this now unless either of you don't want to."

"Fine with me," Michael said.

229

"Wait," Misha said as Diana turned towards Michael. "While I can believe my mother becoming the wife of a demon; why did he take her?"

"He is trying to trap Hecate because of her treason against Molach. The same demon also took Sampson. But Nada is a very beautiful woman and that also played a part."

"What is the name of this demon?" Misha asked.

"Visterle."

Chapter XVII
Clues

For days Sampson lay in his cell listening to the voice in his head which was telling him to pay careful attention to the guards, their words and their routines. A couple of times a day a guard would slide a tray of food under his cell door but Sampson rarely ate. The voice told him to pretend that he was sleeping.

Sampson realized he was being held as a prisoner but he could not remember his life before waking up in this cell. Sampson was filled with rage but he did not understand why. He simply obeyed the voice in his head, the voice of his master, the voice of the demon Ael.

Ael was one of the Old Ones who came to Nunc with the second group of thirteen powerful demons. Many of the Old Ones who had been recently defeated and imprisoned in The Abyss were from this particular group of demons. While demons do not form friendships in the human sense of the word, Moloch, Ipos, Raum, Bentra and Zede were colleagues of Ael. And Ael blamed Hecate for their demise.

Of course Ael was not the only demon who blamed Hecate for the fall of these powerful demons. Unknown to Hecate or Orbus several bounties had been placed on her. While Hecate made enemies among the Old Ones because she followed her own agendas and did not work with them; she was not the traitor she was being accused of.

Emeric and Banaka were spreading many false rumors in the underworlds about Hecate. These two scheming Grand Masters were trying to cause conflicts among the demons of Nunc so they would be distracted when the demons from other worlds attacked.

Raphael, Edward and their troops spent several additional days in Philiste to attend the funerals of the murdered Patronus priests and to assist with the investigations into their deaths. On the night before Raphael planned to lead his troops southwest towards Fort Stanus Joao, Dack, Dagon, Jasmine and Darla paid him a late night visit.

"We know it is late but we have something to show you," Dagon said as Raphael opened the door to his room.

"Of course, come in. Is this something that Edward should hear also?" Raphael asked.

"Yes," Dagon said.

"Why don't one of you get him while I light some candles," Raphael said and walked over to the hearth in his room.

"Sorry to wake you," Dagon said to Edward when Dack and Edward entered Raphael's room.

"I was awake. I haven't had a good night's sleep since we found those priests," Edward said as he joined the group that was gathered round the hearth.

"We're all staying in the same room," Dagon explained. "And tonight Joao asked us all to look at the pictures he had drawn of the bodies. He said he felt like he was missing something that was right before his eyes. Joao do you want to tell the rest?"

"I have been overwhelmed with this feeling that we missed something in the room where we found the bodies. I have been looking at the drawings but I didn't say anything until tonight. It turns out all five of us have been having the same feelings. So we brought out all of the drawings and scrutinized them as a group. It was Darla who first saw something." As Joao spoke he walked over to Raphael and Edward with a handful of drawings.

"We've been wondering where the things are that were removed from the chests to make room for the bodies. We all assumed that those chests belonged to Gabriel and you. But look at these pictures. I saw the caked mud on the bottom of the chests and even drew it without really thinking about it," Joao continued. So we all went back into that room and picked the chests up. Everyone one of them was caked with mud on the bottom."

"Wouldn't someone notice a man walking around with a large chest?" Edward asked.

"That's what we thought too," Joao said. "So we started looking through those chambers for a secret entrance. While we were in there Padre Edgar walks in to see what we are doing."

"He asks us how we got into the chambers because they are supposed to be locked. We told him the doors were unlocked and asked him who had the keys. Padre Edgar said the keys were hung on a hook in High Priest Nicholas' office. But while Padre Edgar is talking to us he examines the door lock and found a small ball of wax that prevented the door from locking."

"The door wasn't locked the day you and I went in there," Raphael said to Edward. "I really didn't think that was suspicious."

"So anyone could enter those rooms without getting a key," Joao said.

"But as large as those chests were, there had to have been more than one man carrying them," Dagon said. "That is why we woke you. One large man could carry a body over his shoulder but those chests are heavy. There were more intruders in here than we thought."

"Is he dead?" Nada asked when Visterle brought her to Sampson's cell.

"No, but he has transformed into a demon. Which means one of the Old Ones is behind this because Hecate isn't powerful enough to change him," Visterle said.

"Are you sure because Hecate was going to try to put him through the trials herself. That's why we captured his brothers."

Visterle was studying Sampson as Nada spoke. He knew that Sampson was listening although he pretended to be unconscious. "And Hecate told you this?" Visterle asked.

"Yes, that is why she was sending us all over to get the things she needed to perform the trials."

"Why do you think she hasn't come for her husband?" Visterle asked as he watched Sampson.

"Does she know where you are?"

"She can find out."

"Well you know she was really pregnant and since the baby is half human she didn't know when it would come."

"So the baby is Sampson's?"

"That's what she told us," Nada said as she too could see Sampson moving.

"You are sure the baby doesn't belong to her demon lover?" Visterle asked then laughed as Sampson jumped off from his cot and slammed his body against the door of his cell. Sampson was making noises but not speaking.

"He looks like an animal. Can't he talk?" Nada asked as she looked into Sampson's eyes.

"Whoever is behind his transformation did not do him any favors. They turned him into the lowest level of demon; so he is a puppet for whoever owns him now."

"I don't understand," Nada said.

"Think of a trained dog."

"Can't you tell who owns him?" Visterle did not answer Nada's question. "Will Hecate be able to change him back?"

"I think the question is will Hecate still want him." Visterle asked as Sampson slammed himself against the cell bars again. Visterle realized that Sampson could understand what was being said even if he couldn't speak.

Visterle took Nada's arm and the two materialized in their bedroom chambers. "You did that to see how he would respond, didn't you?" Nada asked.

"I know he has been pretending to sleep but I didn't know if he could understand what was being said."

"Do you think Hecate will come for him?"

"Would you?"

"Why would someone do that to Sampson?"

"Hecate has a lot of enemies. If they think she loves her husband that would be a blow to her."

"Is that why you took him?"

"You are asking too many questions. Why don't you change and we will do a little gambling," Visterle said.

Raphael went to the chambers of High Priest Nicholas and explained the findings of his team.

"This is worse than I thought," Nicholas said solemnly. "Who would suspect terrorists walking in our quarters?" Nicholas paused. "Are you still planning on leaving in the morning?"

"Yes, unless you would like us to stay and help."

"We have been operating on the assumption that we had one intruder who has left the area," Nicholas said. "With the possibility of more intruders your travel plans may be compromised. I think it would be wise to stay a little longer and not announce your travel plans far in advance. Also, three hundred priest have requested to join you. It breaks my heart to say this but we should make sure they are really our men."

Over the next two days, Vivian, Emeral, Natasha, Hannah, Calen, Luca and Elan continued to search Berta's house. But after three days of searching this team had not finished the house or searched the barn and shed that were on the property. Because the extreme amount of clutter in the house was impeding the search; on the second morning Emeral searched and cleaned one of the bedrooms so the rest of the family could move Berta's belongings into that room as they cleared other rooms.

"Berta was so clean and organized at work that I can't believe this is her house," Vivian kept repeating with disgust.

"At least we haven't found any unholy altars or demonic things yet," Natasha said as she opened up a cupboard that was filled with linens. Natasha was piling the towels and folded sheets on the floor when she saw several items stained with blood.

"I may have sound something," Natasha called out as she separated the blood stained linens from the clean linens.

Hannah and Emeral were searching the first floor of the house with Natasha and now turned their attention to the blood stained linens. Hannah and Emeral were unfolding the linens as Natasha brought them out of the cupboard.

"These stains aren't fresh," Hannah said. "These sheets have been laundered. But that is a great deal of blood. There must have been more than one wounded person here."

"The more we search the more I think some of Shanksaw's men were staying here," Natasha said as she finished emptying the cupboard.

After the women searched the linens and the empty cupboard they moved the cupboard away from the wall. "Why, there is a book hanging from a hook back here," Emeral said as she pushed the cupboard farther from the wall so she could reach the book.

"What is it?" asked Natasha.

"I'm not really sure yet," Emeral said as she looked at the pages. "I think this is the code to those ledgers." Emeral turned a few more pages. "There's lists of names with locations written next to them," Emeral continued. "Some of these names are the alias' that Shanksaw said he used; I wonder if they all are."

Both Natasha and Hannah were now standing near Emeral so they could also look at the book. "Look at these; they look like family trees," Emeral said as she flipped through the last ten pages of the book.

"Wait! Go back a page," Natasha said. "These names don't belong to families, these are demons and the hierarchy of their organizations. Vivian and Diana were right, there is a demon named Cronn and he is a lieutenant for the demon Zieman, who sits on the throne in Stordt. I think we hit the jackpot," Natasha said with a big smile.

"Boys, Vivian come down here," Emeral called. Finding such an important book, energized the search efforts of the group, who worked late into the day.

Just as they were preparing to return home for dinner, Calen called out that he had found a box hidden under some floor boards. The group now gathered in the room that Calen was in. The box was filled with papers, which Calen was handing out to the group.

"The papers I have appear to be a family history," Hannah said as she was quickly reading them. "Why would they hide papers like this?"

"Vivian you said that Gus had a brother named Harold, who Berta married," Luca said. "But here it looks like Gus had three older brothers, Harold, Theodore and Percy. I wonder if Theodore or Percy is really Shanksaw, if so that would explain a lot."

"It's getting late," Emeral said. "We need to get home; we will have to study these papers later."

Raphael and High Priest Nicholas stayed up until dawn talking and reviewing the names of the priests who had requested to join Raphael's team. Raphael and Nicholas planned to sleep a few hours then to meet with each of the three hundred priests separately to determine if there were any imposters in the group.

After Raphael returned to his room, High Priest Nicholas met with twelve of his most trusted priests and told them about the information that Raphael's team had uncovered. These priests were to interview their comrades to determine if anyone had seen men carrying large chests into the castle.

As soon as Raphael returned to his room he woke Edward, Dagon, Joao, Dack, Darla and Jasmine and told them about their change of plans.

Many of the members of Gabriel's group also sat up until dawn. Most of these individuals were watching Diana and Michael. Diana had followed the Sanuri's directions and prayed to have the words in her visions revealed to her. To Diana's surprise she actually saw the words in her mind's eye. She spelled each word for Michael who wrote them down.

Misha and Thor sat with Diana but they were collaborating on a long letter to Emeral and Maxwell. Misha wrote down everything the Sanuri had told them, after Misha described Diana's visions. Thor wrote that he would be moving into the same chambers with Misha and Diana to help with the babies. Thor told Emeral to have his belongings moved if they needed to use his room before the team returned from Ryed.

While both Misha and Thor were ecstatic that Diana was pregnant with twin boys; the warning about Nada terrified them both. Thor did not tell Emeral and Maxwell but the warning about Nada was another reason he wanted to move into the same chambers with Misha and Diana. Misha had previously told Maxwell the names that Diana had picked out but not Emeral. Now Misha wrote that the names would be Maximus Bartholomew Joshua for one son and Thor Adwell Gabriel for the second son. They planned to tell the team the names during breakfast.

Gabriel, Lakin, Joshua, Ratri, and the Sanuri met for several hours. When they realized that Dominic, Fennel and Asher were still up they asked them to join their meeting.

"We need to set the table for breakfast so some of you are going to have to move," Bianca said with a laugh. Most of the group were still in the banquet room with Diana and Michael.

"Michael, I'm not seeing any more words," Diana said. "I am going to help with breakfast."

To the surprise of the women, several of the Ruala warriors helped them set the table and bring the platters of food out. "Michael just walked into the meeting with the Sanuri and the others," Rachel said as she entered the kitchen. "I don't know if we should wait on breakfast now."

"I'll go ask," Diana said but as soon as she left the kitchen all of the men from the meeting were entering the banquet room. As everyone was sitting down, Misha, Thor and Erebus poured glasses of wine for the group.

Misha proudly stood in front of the group and said, "Before we return to business Diana and I would like to tell you the names we have chosen for our sons. Maximus Bartholomew Joshua and Thor Adwell Gabriel." Both Joshua and Gabriel smiled proudly.

"For those of you who do not know," Misha continued. "Diana and Thor were recently adopted by the same family that adopted me. Maximus is after our adopted father; Bartholomew is Diana's and Thor's father, Adwell was my birth father and you know Joshua and Gabriel."

Everyone applauded. Erebus said the toast, "To Misha, Diana and their babies; may they have long, happy and safe lives."

Gabriel stood and said the second toast, "To family may our bonds never be broken." Everyone including the freedom fighters repeated the toast. "That was a nice way to start off the day," Gabriel said as he took his seat.

"Did Michael finish the translation?" Micha asked. "Because I think we are all really curious to hear it."

The Sanuri stood up. "Understand that while this was a gift to us it is also confusing. Diana was hearing part of a meeting but we don't know when this meeting took place or who the participants were; so we may have some research to do yet. Michael do you want to read it out loud?"

Michael stood up and addressed the group. "From Diana's understanding there were five different male voices that she heard. And the men seemed to be arguing. The only name that was spoken was Viktor. He was warning the other men about the strangers who were bringing a great plague upon the people of Ryed."

"Before you continue," Dominic said. "The Teivels have destroyed most of our written history so what we do have is passed down through the generations verbally. There is a story about a powerful priest named Viktor who tried to stop the Teivels from taking control of our people. The story says he died a horrible death but it doesn't say who killed him."

"Well, that makes more sense," Gabriel said.

"One of the voices is telling Viktor of all the wealth and power these strangers have promised to those who would bow before them," Michael continued. "Viktor is telling the men to think about the price they will have to pay for their power and wealth. One of the men is trying to sway Viktor by telling him they will build him a temple and people will worship him."

"Then another man says that the people will follow Viktor and if he doesn't agree to join the strangers many innocent people will be killed."

"While this sounds like the birth of the Insidiae in this kingdom; we really don't understand the message for us," Gabriel said. "Is there anyone here who can give us some insight?"

"If anyone would have old manuscripts it would be High Priest Othnial," Fennel said. "As Dominic said our stories are passed down from generations and who knows how accurate they are."

"We were talking about High Priest Othnial in our meeting. He stayed behind so as not to raise suspicions but we all fear for his safety. Rachel has been making maps of the locations attacked during night raids and the number of attacks has greatly increased lately. Rachel said this often happens when the Teivels believe there will be an uprising. This afternoon some of us will be returning to Rubar to get Othnial," Gabriel said.

"I should go with you," Dominic said. "I know that monastery like the back of my hand."

"I am not sure that is wise," Gabriel said. "Your safety as well as that of your men is very important to your people."

"Dominic is right," Asher said. "That monastery is a maze and that is because High Priest Othnial had it redesigned to confuse intruders. One of us should go with you."

Gabriel looked at the Sanuri who nodded. "Very well everyone get some sleep after breakfast and we will leave after the midday meal," Gabriel said then he turned to Dominic. "Dominic after breakfast I would like Batina and Bianca to meet with you and your men. I am going to purchase new clothes for you and have my sister forge papers for you. Please give Batina and Bianca your clothing sizes and any alias names that you want to use. We can't expose you by going to a tailor so some of my people will buy your things."

"I am very good at sewing," Zelda said. "Although all of my things were destroyed in the fire. But if the girls get me some needles, threads and scissors I can tailor the clothing."

"Excellent because I want every one of them to have a nice suit. The Teivels won't be looking for noblemen." Gabriel said then turned to Michael. "That goes for you too."

"Perhaps I should ride into the village with them," Zelda said. "But I want Zach to stay here."

"Plan on leaving before sunrise tomorrow morning so the Rualas are not seen. Also we should buy more weapons," said Gabriel.

"That may not be necessary," Erebus said. "The prior owners of this castle died and many of their things are still here. I have a weapons room, although I don't use it."

"Ratri you are in charge of making sure everyone has sufficient weapons. If you need money let me know," Gabriel said.

"What if we don't really know what size we wear?" Seth asked. Seth was a cousin to Dominic, Fennel and Asher.

"I will measure you," Zelda said.

"Michael I will give you enough money to purchase several sets of clothing for everyone. How you want to get that accomplished is up to you."

"Until recently I was never in a store so I will let Zelda and the girls help with that," Michael said.

"Aren't you a prince?" Rachel asked.

"It's a long story. But I just recently found my birth father. I was a prisoner most of my life." While many people stared at Michael, no one said anything.

Erebus broke the silence. "Ladies if there is any food or anything you believe we need; let me know and I will give you the money."

"You know none of us feel comfortable with you buying us clothes," Dominic said.

"You will be playing parts and you have to be dressed for it," Gabriel said. "Honestly you all look like you have been on the run for some time. Just think of the clothing as disguises."

"Now you can choose alias names or let my sister come up with some but once the names are picked you will have to become familiar with them so you will respond appropriately when that name is called."

"It might not be a bad idea to have Natasha send some of those fake beards and things along," Misha said.

"Batina write down the hair coloring of each man so Natasha can match some things up," Gabriel said.

"Gabriel's team specializes in covert missions," the Sanuri explained when he saw the amazed looks on the faces of the people from Ryed.

Chapter XVIII
Rualas

"We should have moved here long ago," Tina said as she and Charles sat on their balcony at the Endleson Hotel in Nora enjoying their morning coffee. "I feel like a queen."

"I agree dear," Charles said as he studied a map that he had spread out on the table on their balcony. "This morning we are going to look at land west of the city. Just to be on the safe side I would like to stay as far away from Fort Nora as possible."

"Charles do you really think those generals would recognize us and tell Sudfad?" Tina snapped.

Charles looked up from his map and stared angrily at Tina. His voice was harsh and stern as he spoke. "Tina you lost us a fortune and disgraced us by your reactionary moves. We agreed that I would handle things here in Nora. I don't know what has happened to you over the years. You used to be so shrewd and calculating and I loved that in you. Now you blow-up at every little thing without thinking anything through. Pull yourself together. I will be taking the lead on this Nora venture."

Tina stared angrily at her husband but did not speak so Charles continued, "The people here practically worship King Sudfad remember that. Don't you think they would serve us up on a platter if they knew the King had banned us from his kingdom? Now play nice and keep your big mouth shut!"

"Do you have to leave so soon again?" Nada asked as she was giving Visterle a backrub in their bedroom chambers.

"I have work to do my pet," Visterle said then rolled over on his back and pulled Nada on top of him. "I like it that you will miss me."

"Well it's not just that I miss you but I get so bored. Can't you give me something to do? I don't like sitting around."

"Are you serious?" Visterle asked with a grin.

"Yes," Nada said with emphasis. "You know I am not stupid there are a lot of things I can do."

"I've never said you were stupid. What are you thinking about?"

"I don't really care; I just want something to keep busy. Would you like just sitting in this room waiting for me to come home?"

"You can walk around the castle." Visterle said then laughed at the disapproving look Nada gave him.

"I am serious Visterle."

"I don't want you outside of the castle without me."

"After that bar fight I am fine with that but I go crazy when you are gone."

"Do you want to decorate the castle?"

"I could but it's already beautiful and I was hoping for something more interesting. I am really good at drawing, do you need any maps made; hell I would even clean weapons just to keep busy."

Visterle laughed loudly, "Let me think about this."

"Now this is the life," Bruno said as the three girls who spent the night with Bruno and Morgan left their room in the Endleson Hotel. "An endless supply of women and they treat us like kings."

"While I agree; I have a bad feeling. Been having it for days and it's just getting stronger."

"What the hell are you talking about? We've got more money than we ever dreamed of and women are throwing themselves at us. We've never had it this good. You sound like an old lady."

"Can't explain it. It's like the hair on the back of my neck is standing on end and I don't have a clue why."

Visterle's demeanor became more serious. "Nada I have a question for you and I want you to really think about the answer before you say anything. Would you betray Morgan and Bruno?"

Nada looked shocked at the question, then she scowled. "Is this another one of your tests to see if I am loyal to you?"

"Just answer the question. You were with those two for a great deal of your life. And don't lie because you are so bad at it."

"Honestly I don't know. And I don't know if I really understand your question. Are you asking me if I would choose them over you?"

"No but I would like to hear the answer to that question also." Nada pulled away from Visterle so she could study his face. His questions were making her nervous and suspicious. "Tell me the truth and don't worry about me getting mad."

"Why do I feel like you are setting me up for something?"

"I'm not but you apparently want to help me so I am asking these questions."

"Honestly I don't know if I could betray them, I guess I never thought about it. I don't want to see them dead, so I hope you aren't thinking about killing them," Nada said. "And as for your second question. I was terrified of you at first. But you treat me better than any man I have ever been with besides Adwell. And when you were gone last time and I didn't know if you had died of your wounds; well I realized how much I care for you. If I had to choose I would stay with you."

"I believe you are telling me the truth," Visterle said as he stared in Nada's eyes. "If I took you back to Nunc would you try to escape?"

"No, besides where would I go. While I would like to accompany you Visterle. You are making me nervous. Are you considering using me in some way to hurt Morgan and Bruno?"

"I have been having your friends watched to see if they have any contact with Hecate. I want to know what was said when they last saw her. And I was thinking about taking you back to her lair so you can tell me if anything is changed?"

245

"What do you mean? Doesn't she still live there?"

"No, her essence is no longer on that world. Hecate is powerful, but not powerful enough to hide from me without the help of an Old One. I am trying to pick up her trail."

"Do you think whoever turned Sampson into a monster is protecting Hecate?"

"No, just the opposite. Sampson showed such rage when you and I spoke her name that I believe whoever is controlling Sampson is going to use him against Hecate. And the more I think about that idea I like it."

"Can't you just read Morgan's and Bruno's minds? I mean it sure seems like you can read mine."

Visterle laughed again. "That's not how it works but I am glad you feel like that."

"Visterle, if you can read my mind you know I am serious. I am bonded to you now. But you have to understand that Morgan and Bruno are really my only two friends and I don't want to be responsible for their deaths. I don't know how demons feel about friends but for Rualas and humans it is a strong bond."

"My pet I am not thinking about killing your friends. Actually they might be very useful to me which is why I spared them when I sent my men to get you and Sampson. Hecate was brilliant in her idea to own the three of you. But I will tell you this only once; I am proud and jealous and I will not tolerate you betraying me in any manner. Do you understand?"

"Visterle, I won't betray you; I promise."

"An Enrop delivered a message addressed to both of us," Gabriel said as he walked up to the Sanuri who was mediating in a garden."

"What does it say?" the Sanuri asked.

"I thought we could read it together," Gabriel said and opened the envelope. "Well this is interesting."

"This if from Sudfad, he says that one of the Ruala death squads found Morgan and Bruno in Nora. They are living in the Endleson Hotel. Soto, the leader of the death squad, understandably doesn't want to endanger citizens by forcing a confrontation in public. But, while Soto and his men have been watching Morgan and Bruno they discovered that a group of demons have also been spying on the two Rualas."

"Since this is an unusual situation, both Sudfad and Manu agreed to have Soto and his men watch both the demons and the Rualas until they can figure out what is going on. Generals Colter and Orlan have been notified and directed to work with Soto and his men."

"Does the letter say what Morgan and Bruno have been doing?"

"Spending a great deal of money, drinking and picking up women."

"Hecate must have released her hold on them," the Sanuri said. "There is most likely two reasons the demons are watching them. The first being someone is after Hecate and hoping that those two Rualas will lead them to her. And the second is that those Rualas are valuable assets for the demons. Those demons may want to abduct Morgan and Bruno and are waiting for the right opportunity."

"On another matter; Erebus would like us to help him continue searching Sophie's things."

Morgan and Bruno were eating lunch in the dining room of the Endleson Hotel when they both started to laugh. "Well looky here," Bruno said and smirked as Charles and Tina stood in the doorway of the dining room and stared at Morgan and Bruno with horror.

"Join us," Morgan said loudly.

Charles and Tina looked at each other and walked towards Morgan and Bruno with trepidation. "This must be a reunion of outcasts," Bruno said as Charles and Tina sat down at their table.

"Keep your voice down," Tina snapped. "We are trying to start a new life here."

"Charles how you have stayed with this bitch so long is beyond me," Morgan said as he stared at Tina.

"I have wondered the same thing," Charles said. Tina spun around and stared at Charles which caused Morgan and Bruno to laugh loudly.

"So what have you heard about us?" Charles asked.

"That you pissed off a lot of people, were publically reprimanded and suddenly disappeared." Morgan said.

"How did you hear that?" Tina asked. "I mean who would tell you?"

"News travels fast and why did you say it like that," Bruno asked.

"You don't know?" Charles asked seriously.

"Know what?" asked Morgan.

"Haven't you met any other Rualas here?" Tina asked.

"Spit it out; what is going on?" Morgan demanded.

Charles leaned close to Morgan and Bruno and spoke in almost a whisper. King Manu and the Grand Council heard about your crime spree and they have sent death squads after you. That is why we were so shocked to see you sitting here boldly. All the Rualas know about it so if any of them have seen you they probably sent word to the Ice Caves."

"Are you shitting me!" Bruno said loudly.

"They were afraid your actions would cause a war between the humans and Rualas," Charles said.

"Now I know why I have been feeling like we are being watched," Morgan said as he looked around the dining room uneasily. "I don't think they will attack us while we are surrounded by humans. I have to think about this." Then Morgan stared at Tina and Charles and asked, "Are you living at the hotel?"

"For now, we are taking up the offer for free land and plan to build a home. We aren't fighters like you two; we don't want to get involved with all of this."

"No but you can get information for us," Morgan said. "Sounds like you talk to a lot of people."

"And why would we help you?" Tina asked in a condescending tone.

Bruno looked at Morgan and grinned, "Don't you think King Sudfad's people would be interested in learning Tina and Charles are here?"

"What do you need us to do?" Charles asked grimly.

"Did you draw suspicion by buying so much clothing?" Gabriel asked Michael and Ratri when their group returned from Benjem late that afternoon.

"There was only one General Store but we all split up and bought things," Michael said. "But folks didn't seem real interested with us. Here we grabbed one of these for you." Michael handed Gabriel a written notice. "We were told Teivel's men started posting these this morning and people suspect that is why there have been so many raids."

"I don't understand the correlation," Gabriel said.

"Teivel puts his prisoners in the ring to be slaughtered," Ratri said.

"What are you talking about?" the Sanuri asked as he joined the three men.

"Teivel is announcing Gefrey Games which will be opened to contestants from all of the kingdoms. Do you think this is some kind of trick?" Gabriel asked as he handed the notice to the Sanuri.

"Oh, I think there is more to this but I believe it is a power play by Teivel. The Angels caused a storm that decimated Fort Polta and Teivel's home; while nothing else in the area was harmed. This was done to turn Teivel's eyes from all of our teams."

249

"I have been told that Teivel borders on insanity and I am sure he is highly paranoid. He knows he was attacked by someone but he doesn't know who. He wants to intimidate his enemies. I am sure these games will be grand events that we should use to our advantage."

Raphael and High Priest Nicholas did not find any imposters among the three hundred Patronus priests who requested to join Raphael's group. Raphael and Edward kept their departure time and date secret for three days; then they woke their troops and left for Nir in the middle of the night.

Without any unplanned delays it would take Raphael's army over a week to reach Fort Stanus where they were to join Raul, Simon, Matthew and their troops.

Raphael had requested additional Enrops to join them and they doubled their scouts and perimeter guards. But even with the additional security measures, both Raphael and Edward felt they were being watched.

"I don't know why you wanted Charles and Tina to help us," Bruno complained. "They are worthless and I am feeling like a trapped rat just sitting in this hotel."

"They are better than nothing and I am convinced we haven't been attacked because the squads don't want to endanger the humans," Morgan said. "I don't like sitting around either but if we kill one death squad there will just be others. I don't want to spend the rest of my life looking over my shoulder and I haven't thought of a good plan yet."

"I never thought I would say it but I wish Hecate was here," Bruno said with disgust.

"I've been thinking the same thing. Do you think that if we went back to her lair we could find something to use to call her?"

"If the death squads are watching Morgan and Bruno they will see us," Tina said fearfully.

"Tina just shut the hell up. You must have said that two hundred times in the last few days. I know that. I am trying to figure out a way we can turn Morgan and Bruno in without exposing our identities."

"I've been thinking the same thing," Tina said. "If we send an Enrop to the Ice Caves we will be exposed. But what if we wrote a note and paid someone to deliver it to Fort Nora?"

"I have thought about that also but that still puts us in a precarious position. I would like to protect us as much as possible."

That evening Morgan and Bruno were in their hotel room drinking whiskey and working on plans to escape Nora. "What the hell!" yelled Bruno as he grabbed the hilt of his sword.

"Morgan, Bruno don't fight," Nada screamed, then in a calmer voice she said. "Listen to what he has to say."

An army of demons literally packed the hotel room with Visterle and Nada standing in the middle. Demons had immediately grabbed Morgan and Bruno, who stopped resisting when they saw Nada.

"Nada are you alright?" Morgan asked as he was shocked to see her.

"Yes, I am married now and my husband may be the only one who can save your lives."

Visterle was in human form and smiled at Nada's words. "There are Ruala death squads in and around the city. I assume they have just been watching you because they saw my men spying on you. I can save your lives but I want you to swear allegiance to me like you did to Hecate. I will be your protector," Visterle said.

"Why would you do that?" Morgan asked.

"Because I want you to work for me just like you worked for Hecate."

"Would you pay us?" Bruno asked.

251

Visterle laughed loudly. "I like your priorities. Of course I will pay you."

"Nada is this a trick?" asked Morgan.

"No, it really isn't. I was scared when they first took me but I have a really good life now." Both Morgan and Bruno stared at Nada as they tried to read her face.

"Alright," Morgan said. "You have a deal."

"There is just one thing," Visterle said. "I know your past relationships with Nada. She is my wife now. If you even think about rekindling anything with her; you will wish I let the death squads kill you."

Chapter XIX
Masters

"The demons disappeared," Soto yelled to the members of the death squad he was leading. The Ruala and Shettee warriors now charged towards the Endleson Hotel. When Visterle transported his small army, Morgan, Bruno and Nada from Nora, Visterle also transported the demons who had been assigned to spy on the two Rualas.

People in the hotel stared with amazement as the warriors ran inside of the hotel and up the grand staircase. Soto already knew the number of the room that Morgan and Bruno had been staying in. But when Soto reached the door it was locked. He kicked the door twice before it opened. "It reeks of demon in here," Soto yelled with frustration as his men started to search the room.

"There's no sign of a fight," one of the Ruala warriors said. "They must have been outnumbered."

"My bet is that they went willingly," Soto said with disgust.

Morgan and Bruno looked around with surprise when they materialized inside of Hecate's lair.

"It's really empty in here," Nada said.

"Nada look around and tell me what is missing, while I talk with your friends," Visterle said without looking at her. Now Visterle addressed Morgan and Bruno. "I want you to tell me everything about the last time you saw Hecate."

"After your demons took Nada, Bruno and I ran in here to check on Sampson. Of course he was gone so we kept yelling for Hecate because we didn't know where she was or how to contact her," Morgan explained. "She shows up here a few days later, smelling of sex. I yelled at her for not giving us a way to contact her and she didn't even get mad. She handed Bruno and me two medallions with her image on them and told us to hold the medallions and call her name."

"Do you still have those?" Visterle asked.

"No and I am getting to that part," Morgan said. "We gave her your message and told her everything that had happened. I know she is powerful but Hecate looked scared. She said she had some business to take care of and wanted us to guard her lair. About a day and a half later she shows up here with a guy who she says is her new husband."

"Hecate tells us she is leaving Nunc and that she can either free us or kill us. She freed us but said if she returned she might want us to work for her again. She asked for the medallions back."

"Is her new husband a human or a demon?" Visterle asked.

"A demon," Morgan said. "But she didn't tell us his name or anything. We can tell you what he looked like."

"Have Nada draw him but he probably wasn't showing you his real face. Did you come in here after they left?"

Neither Morgan nor Bruno spoke for a moment then Bruno said. "No. The way Hecate would pay us is money and jewels would just materialize in a cave near here. She told us to check the cave for our final payment and that is what we did."

"Visterle there is a lot missing from here," Nada said. "Furniture and huge chests she might have had help."

"I am sure she did," he said then he nodded to one of his men and the demons started to search the lair.

"Do we have to leave our treasure behind?" Bruno asked.

"No but I want to go to that cave," Visterle said. "I am trying to pick up Hecate's trail."

"Miranda and Daniel would you please join us?" King Sudfad called out as he was starting the morning meeting. Maxwell, Calen, Luca, Koby, Archetenus and Jared were in attendance.

"It was wise of you to call to us," Daniel said as the two Angels materialized in Sudfad's study. "Before you ask any questions explain Gabriel's letter."

"I am handing out a notice that I received from Teivel," Sudfad explained. "As you read that I will explain this letter. As you know the Sanuri is with Gabriel's group and they had previously told us that there has been a great increase in the number of terror raids in that kingdom. Apparently Teivel throws his prisoners in the arena to be slaughtered at his Gefrey Games and the citizens of Ryed believe that is why there have been more abductions."

"Both Gabriel and the Sanuri believe these games will be the perfect distraction and a means to get our men into that kingdom without raising suspicions. Gabriel would like to have a number of our men enter the games as contestants. He has also sent letters to Mathas, Sorren, Manu and Neputa."

"Teivel is offering big prizes to the winners," Archetenus said. "So why is he really doing this?"

"Teivel knows that only Fort Polta and his home were destroyed in that storm. He is a paranoid man and wants to show the world how powerful and rich he is," Miranda explained. "Also, although Teivel maintains a low presence as General Kretcher that is certainly not his true personality. Teivel has a great need for attention, to say he is flamboyant is an understatement."

"Do you agree these games are the distraction we need?" Sudfad asked.

"Yes," Daniel said. "But they are also a gift. We told you before that Teivel's prisoners are kept in a variety of locations. They will all be moved to the arena for these games."

"Then we should send men to be contestants as well as spectators," Sudfad said.

"So you are going to free the people of Ryed?" Miranda asked. "Because if everything is not in place your men will be killed."

"Miranda what would you have us do?" Archetenus said before Sudfad could answer the question.

"Archetenus you are the only one in this room who has fought in the Gefrey Games. Why don't you explain how they are run," Miranda said.

"I have fought in other games besides Roch's. Usually they are held in a huge arena that is filled with seats. Every game I have fought in; the arena was surrounded with soldiers. The contestants are either forced to participate or they pay a small fee to participate. You don't know who or what you will be fighting until you are in the ring. You might be fighting more than one person, animals or monsters. And the fights are to the death."

"On the ground level of the arena where the combatant is standing; there are usually nothing but doors, but they look like cell doors. So you don't know which door your opponent will be released from. The prisoners will be kept in cells close to those doors. If we are going to save those people we need to get our men down there first or the guards will kill the prisoners."

"Do you know anyone else who has fought in those games?" Daniel asked.

"Thaos and Michael," Archetenus said. "Miranda from the way you are smiling I know what you are thinking."

"A human has never said that to me before," Miranda said and her smile widened.

"I should go to Ryed and help Gabriel and I would like to. But we just had the babies and Delilah needs so much help," Archetenus said.

"You named the babies after Angels, do you think we would not watch over them?" Miranda asked Archetenus then she turned to Sudfad. "You would be wise to release Archetenus from his duties and have him handpick men and women who he believes could fight in these games."

"Women," Sudfad repeated with surprise.

"You want a distraction," Daniel said. "There are many who have never seen women warriors. They could be the biggest distraction you have."

"Also Miranda and I will visit Mathas' meeting this morning and suggest that Thaos takes the same role as Archetenus. You have six weeks before the games; that is not much time to prepare to overthrow a dictatorship."

"Archetenus you know we will take care of your family," Sudfad said. Then Sudfad looked at Calen, Luca and Koby. But before Sudfad could speak Daniel said.

"Sudfad you would be wise to send Calen and Natasha to Ryed. Few of the people with either Gabriel or Raphael have an understanding of covert operations. The freedom fighters are marked men; they will need disguises. Have Natasha take everything she can find."

As Daniel spoke, Miranda walked up to Luca. "It is time you healed my child," Miranda said and kissed Luca on the forehead. "Lila's heart would break to see how crippled you have been by her death. She would want you to start living your life again and to be a good father to Emma and Christopher. You will never forget her but your spirit has returned." The tears ran down Luca's face as Miranda spoke.

"Sudfad, perhaps you should have Luca temporarily replace Archetenus," Daniel said.

"Zoya's going to be so mad but I am going too," Jared said. "Sudfad can I move my family inside of the castle?"

"Of course."

"They should move into our chambers with Delilah," Archetenus said.

"Archetenus I know Natasha will want to fight and I don't want her to," Calen said.

"Calen when I look at you it is as if you have bound yourself with rope. A rope made up of your fears for your family. It is time that you freed yourself," Miranda said and kissed Calen on the forehead. Tears filled Calen's eyes and in that instant the Angels were gone.

Raphael waited until his army made camp for the night before he shared the contents of the letter he had received from Gabriel with this team.

"Six weeks before the games," Dagon said. "Are we going to spend most of that time at Fort Stanus? Because if Teivel is watching us I think that will look suspicious. Besides that is a lot of down time, maybe some of us can help Gabriel's group until we are ready for our part."

As Dagon was talking a small flock of Enrops landed in the campsite. "These letters are from Wetpr," one of the giant birds announced. "We are to tell you to read the one from the King right away."

Raphael read Sudfad's letter which contained all of the information from the morning meeting with Miranda and Daniel. The team listened quietly to Raphael's words but as soon as he finished Jasmine asked, "Can Darla and I fight in those games? The Angels said women warriors would be a distraction."

"While you are well trained, I am not sure you are ready for something like this," Edward said. "I have been to these games; I think you need more battle experience."

"Well can you teach us what we will need? It sounds like we will have down time?" asked Jasmine.

Before Edward could answer Dagon said. "I agree with Edward but if Archetenus, Thaos and Michael are all going to be working out of Erebus' castle. Perhaps we can take the girls there for training."

"I like that idea," Raphael said. "Tonight I will send notes to Gabriel, Sudfad and Archetenus. But I want you girls to keep something in mind. We may not know all the reasons that Teivel is sponsoring these games. It would not surprise me if they were fixed so stay alert and be careful."

"What do you mean?" asked Darla.

"Oh, there are a number of ways that someone can cheat at those games and you both are beautiful young women so there may be private agendas," Edward said. "Don't expect anyone to fight honorably."

"Joao you look like you want to say something," Raphael said.

"First I am moving so they don't punch me," Joao said with a grin and moved away from Jasmine and Darla which caused everyone to laugh.

"If the games are fixed like you are suggesting, those of our teams that compete may be in the most danger of anyone. Of course it is up to you Raphael, but if you decide you can spare us maybe Dack and Dagon and I can watch over Jasmine, Darla and the others. I mean we could pull them out of the ring if necessary."

"It is a good thing that you moved," Jasmine said with a grin.

"That is a good suggestion," Raphael said. "But let me discuss it with Gabriel and the Sanuri before I make a decision, since you are the only Rualas with our group." Then Raphael smiled. "I'll bet when I open this letter from Vivian she will be mad that she can't fight in the games."

"You did well today my pet," Visterle said as he and Nada materialized in their bedroom chambers. "I may take you with me again."

"Really, oh I would like that," Nada said with enthusiasm. "And thanks for not killing Morgan and Bruno. They will work well for you."

"They are assets but that could change anytime. One of the reasons I may take you with me more often is so I am not leaving you in the castle with them."

"Visterle I told you that you have nothing to be jealous about," Nada said angrily. "And if it is going to bother you that much why don't you have them stay someplace else."

"If I do they may not last long; this is a world of demons."

"So what are you going to do?" asked Nada.

"I already have some jobs for them, I just want to make sure they understand who their master is first."

Chapter XX
Eyes in the Darkness

The next few days were a constant barrage of messages sent between Raphael's group, Gabriel's group, King Sudfad, King Mathas, Chief Sorren and King Manu.

On the morning of the third day after the meeting between King Sudfad's leaders and the Angels Miranda and Daniel Archetenus led one hundred men to Ryed. The soldiers all dressed in civilian clothing. They had two large bocas filled with supplies but both bocas had false bottoms built in. Over two thousand weapons filled the bottom of each boca. These weapons were to be given to the people of Ryed who would help with the uprising.

Also in these bocas, were cases of empty crocks and the chemicals needed to make explosives and smoke. Hannah wrote several copies of the instructions and gave them to Archetenus. Thaos, Stephan and Sorren led another group of fighters from the Kingdom of Lentz. Although they left their homeland on the same morning, they would be traveling three days behind Archetenus' and his men.

Archetenus crossed the border into the Kingdom of Stordt with his group intact; they did not divide up into smaller groups. Archetenus showed the notice that Teivel had issued about the Gefrey Games to the border guards. When the guards saw the treasures that would be awarded as prizes they asked Archetenus for a copy of the notice and did not hinder his group. As soon as Archetenus was out of sight of the Taperian soldiers he sent Enrops to Thaos telling him how to handle the border guards.

Calen was flying with Natasha; they rejoined Archetenus' group after they passed the border guards. Since Calen was flying and would not be searched by border guards, he was carrying a small fortune in gold coins as well as items to make disguises for the freedom fighters. Archetenus drove his men hard because they all wanted to get to Ryed as soon as possible.

It had been decided that King Manu would send Ruala warriors to both Fort Stanus to join Raphael's group and to Erebus' castle to join Gabriel's group. Dagon, Joao, Dack, Jasmine and Darla left Raphael's group to join Gabriel.

As fortune would have it, Teivel's men also gave notices to Ruala warriors who were in Nora. These warriors were actually members of the death squads sent after Morgan and Bruno. But officially inviting the Rualas to participate in the games added a new dimension to Gabriel's plans.

Michael was in charge of preparing the warriors at Erebus' castle for the Gefrey Games. Batina, Bianca and Rachel were also going to fight. Diana begged to be allowed to fight in the games but Gabriel wanted all of the Venatores to lead the groups that would rescue the prisoners because he felt the prisoners would be more likely to trust the Venatores.

One of Dominic's men had spent some time in one of the cells of the arena and now provided Gabriel with a description of the arena. Noah, was in his early thirties with large brown eyes and black hair. Anger filled his voice as he described his time as a prisoner of the Teivel regime. Dominic, Fennel and Asher started to send out secret messages to their supporters. The messages did not include any of the information of Gabriel's plans. The messages consisted of one word: *Soon*.

The Sanuri and Gabriel were pleased when Erebus volunteered to be of assistance; a choice which would change his life. Michael was both humbled and made proud when the Sanuri told him; that the experiences that Michael suffered for so many years would help to save many lives and possibly to free a kingdom. And Rachel and Zelda held out hope that they would find Rachel's father alive in the prisons within the arena.

Visterle told Nada that he would be gone for a few days but he never left his castle. He wanted to spy on Nada and her two former lovers. Since Nada kept asking Visterle to give her work to keep her occupied in his absence, he told Nada to write down every detail she could remember from her time with Hecate. Visterle knew that only demons as powerful or more powerful than him could mask Hecate's trail; he was looking for clues.

Visterle was pleased that Nada never left her chambers the first day or night that he was spying on her.

Nada did not consider the fact that Visterle would spy on her; she was keeping herself occupied with her new assignment.

The night of the second day, Visterle was feeling relieved that Nada made no efforts to contact Morgan and Bruno and neither of the men attempted to contact her.

On this night Visterle decided to teach his new Rualas who was their master. Morgan and Bruno were both awakened by groups of demons grabbing them. The two Rualas were separated and each chained in a separate room. Both men had fought with their attackers and now screamed and cursed as they were imprisoned.

Morgan and Bruno had lost track of time while they were chained in their dark cells. Many hours later, Visterle materialized in Morgan's cell. The torches on the walls now gave off light as flames ignited and shot up to the ceiling of the cell. As Morgan looked upon Visterle with loathing, Morgan's chains fell off. Morgan charged Visterle, who now changed to his original form. Morgan's screams were heard throughout the dungeons.

On the night of the third day that Visterle was spying on Nada he returned to their bedroom chambers. She was sitting up in bed working on her assignment when Visterle materialized near the bed. Nada squealed with delight and jumped out of the bed to kiss him.

"You're home," Nada said happily as they embraced.

"Actually I never left."

Visterle's words did not sink in as Nada kept kissing him. "I don't understand what you mean," she said.

"I wanted to see if I could trust you and you have done well."

Nada pulled away from him and took a couple of steps backwards. "Visterle what are you talking about?"

"You were lovers with Morgan and Bruno for years. I wanted to see what you would do when you didn't think I was here."

"You were spying on me! Visterle you make me so damn mad sometimes. As powerful as you are can't you tell when I am telling you the truth. Nada's anger rose within her as she yelled. She jumped towards Visterle and attempted to punch him in the face but he grabbed both of Nada's arms and restrained them behind her back.

Visterle was laughing at Nada's attack, "I love your spirit he said and attempted to kiss her but Nada pulled away. "So you are mad at me my pet?"

"Yes I am," Nada said angrily. "How would you like it if I did something like that to you?"

"Actually I would expect it; you are so trusting."

Nada stopped struggling and stared at Visterle because something in the tone of his voice made the hair rise on the back of her neck. "Visterle did you do something to Morgan and Bruno?"

"They now understand who their master is." Visterle was still holding Nada tightly against him as he spoke. Her face turned white at Visterle's words.

"Visterle what did you do? You didn't kill my friends did you?"

"They are fine now; like you were after I taught you."

Nada stared searchingly into Visterle's eyes then tears started to run down her face. "Nada are you crying because I hurt your boyfriends?" She did not answer but kept staring at him. "Nada do you still care for them?" Visterle asked angrily.

"I'm not crying because of them, I am crying because of you," Nada said and tried to pull away from Visterle. "Let go of me."

"Not until you tell me what you mean."

Nada was crying so hard now that it was difficult for her to talk. "I know you are a demon but you are so good to me that sometimes I forget. I was so proud of you for saving their lives and now...I think I just realized that..."

"That what Nada?"

"That I am in love with a monster."

"You're in love with me?" Visterle asked in a sarcastic tone.

"Oh now make fun of me," Nada said angrily as she continued to cry.

"I'm not making fun of you, my pet. I am trying to determine if you are telling me the truth."

"I don't love you; I hate you," she yelled and cried harder. Visterle laughed and hugged Nada.

"First of all my pet, I am a monster and I have never lied to you about that and secondly," Visterle paused. "I am trying to think how to explain this. "Demons are very different from other species, love is not a part of our vocabulary. You act shocked that I am jealous and suspicious; those words are in our vocabulary. You should have suspected this but you are so trusting of me."

"So Visterle what are you really saying to me?"

"My dear, I have been around since the beginning and I have never had anyone tell me that they loved me before."

Nada stared at Visterle as she was trying to read him before she spoke. "I can't be the first women you have had. I find this confusing."

"Nada you certainly aren't my first woman or my first wife. But prior to you, my relationships have been with other demons."

"Don't demons love each other?"

"We develop strong bonds but do not love in the sense that you understand."

"So you could never love me?" Nada asked in a fearful whisper.

"Nada, I can tell this is hurting you and I am not trying to hurt you but I don't believe I am even capable of having that emotion. I can tell you that I am very fond of you and that I want you; and that may be as close as I can get."

264

Nada's vulnerability and admission that she loved Visterle spurred his passions to new heights. While Nada complied with Visterle's lust, the reality of her situation was taking on new meaning for her.

Dagon, Joao, Dack, Jasmine and Darla happily reunited with Gabriel's group at the castle of Erebus. These five team members added an additional day to their trip because they flew to the City of Teivel to view the arena where the Gefrey Games would be held.

"Excellent!" Gabriel said proudly when Joao and Jasmine handed him the drawings they made of the arena and the immediate surrounding area.

"We didn't want to take up any more time," Dagon said. "But some of us should return to draw out the entire city. There is a great deal of construction going on which we are assuming is for the games but it could definitely change the layout that anyone here remembers."

"Dagon, you are in charge of identifying the artists among us and making sure the drawings are completed. I am sure you will want to wait until the time is a closer to the games to put your group in place. I am proud of what all of you have done," Gabriel said.

"Mother said to bring you in because dinner is ready," Rachel said as she walked up to the group which was standing in the front courtyard of Erebus' castle. Jasmine and Darla both laughed when they saw the looks on the faces of Dagon, Joao and Dack when they saw Rachel. Gabriel too grinned at the three young men.

"This is Rachel," Gabriel said. "I have written to you about her and her family. This is Dagon, Jasmine, Dack, Joao and Darla."

"Please forgive our brothers here," Jasmine said with a mischievous grin. "Don't let them scare you off because they look like they just fell in love. They are all great guys and powerful warriors." Rachel blushed and was obviously embarrassed by Jasmine's words.

Gabriel continued to grin at the group of young people, "Let's go in and finish introductions then we will have a meeting after dinner. We are expecting Archetenus and his group something tomorrow."

Archetenus, Jared and their small army had stopped at the Village of Gesmal on their way to Erebus' castle. Not only did Archetenus bring gifts and letters for the villagers but he carried sensitive papers from King Sudfad for Chief Duncan.

Following the Sanuri's advice, Chief Duncan had ordered all of his Venatores to remain in the village and not to hunt demons. The Sanuri had been receiving visions; but they were fragmented scenes of Sampson in his demon form.

The visions repeatedly showed Sampson unleashed as a beast from hell. Although the Sanuri did not see who Sampson's victims were in his visions; the Sanuri feared for the safety of the villagers. And a voice inside of the Sanuri's mind kept telling him that Sampson was not the only threat to these brave warriors who had sworn their allegiance to The Great Ruler.

"I don't know why I felt bad about leaving that village," Jared said as he and Archetenus ate their dinner near their campfire. "I know they are fierce warriors but, guess I am not sure how to explain it."

"Like you were leaving sheep surrounded by a pack of wolves," Archetenus said. "I know I have been having the same feeling. I got real bonded with those people on the Ogg mission. In fact I called out to Miranda to see if she wanted us to leave them; but I haven't heard from her. And that in itself makes me uneasy because she usually answers.

Archetenus continued, "I know I am sounding paranoid, but the fact that this trip has been so easy gives me a bad feeling too. Either the Angels are clearing the way for us or something is setting us up."

One hundred Ruala warriors who were waiting to join Raphael's group at Fort Stanus, flew out and joined Raphael and Edward after Dagon and the other members of the team left for Ryed. Although Raphael and Edward were only two days travel away from Fort Stanus, a prevailing feeling of uneasiness plagued all of the warriors.

Raul, Simon, Matthew and the armies they led planned to arrive at Fort Stanus a day prior to Raphael's group. Immediately upon their arrival at the fort, the three princes intended to meet with Commanding General Craven and brief him about their missions.

Craven was a longtime friend and stanch supporter of King Sudfad. The King had assigned almost three times as many soldiers to Fort Stanus than were stationed at any other fort. Craven knew that Sudfad was preparing for a battle and he hoped the princes were bringing him the information he needed.

Craven had watched Raul and Simon grow into men and felt like an uncle to the princes. Because of his bond to the Royal Family, Craven took extra measures to ensure the security of his fort. All of the commanding generals at the various forts had heard the stories about spies in their military and unholy altars found in military buildings. Craven in particular was a man of integrity and not only had more frequent inspections done on his post but he personally interviewed each of his officers.

Now on the eve of the arrival of the princes; Craven had his most trusted officers inspecting the fort and the soldiers. Craven was not a paranoid man but he too felt a strong sense of uneasiness.

After Thaos, Stephan and Sorren left Lentz with their army, they stopped in Salar to meet with Sudfad. Claudius wanted to go with his sons and Sorren but Mathas wanted Claudius to lead the additional troops that would most likely be needed once the battles began. As usual Angelina, Ingr and Nikki wanted to go with their husbands but between babies at home and babies on the way they stayed in Lentz.

Chaez was temporarily living in Sudfad's castle while he trained to join the Patronus priests.

Although Chaez realized he still had much to learn he was proud of what he had accomplished and was feeling considerably more confident in his abilities. When the soldiers from Lentz arrived in Salar, Chaez begged Thaos and Stephan to take him with them to Ryed. Against his better judgment Thaos agreed but told Chaez he would not be allowed to fight in the Gefrey Games. It was decided that Chaez would help Gabriel's team once they reached Ryed.

Thaos, Stephan and Sorren led a group of seventy-five of the best soldiers and Nordes warriors in Lentz to the Gefrey Games. King Sudfad provided this group with two large bocas of supplies, as he had done with Archetenus' group. And these two bocas also had false bottoms built in them that held several thousand weapons.

Sudfad also gave Thaos, Stephan and Sorren large quantities of gold coins to pay for the entrance fees into the games for their warriors and any other expenses they might incur.

When the group from Lentz reached the border between the Kingdoms of Stordt and Wetpr they showed the border guards the notice of the Gefrey Games, as Archetenus had advised. Not only did the guards allow the group from Lentz to cross the border without problems but they told Stephan of the many groups of both men and demons that had crossed their border heading for the games. As soon as they were out of sight of the guards, Sorren sent notes to Gabriel, Sudfad and Mathas with this new information.

Chapter XXI
Fears

Archetenus and this men arrived at the castle of Erebus several hours sooner than expected. They arrived mid-morning with an army of Enrops flying overhead.

"The birds just showed up," Jared said to Gabriel as he met them in the front courtyard. "Don't suppose that is a good sign."

Other members of Gabriel's group were now coming out of the castle to greet their comrades. As soon as Calen and Natasha landed, she flew into Gabriel's arms and hugged him tightly. "We have gifts and letters," Natasha said after she kissed her brother two more times.

"We will show your men where they can put the horses," Joshua said as he and Micha greeted Archetenus and Jared.

"The Sanuri wants everyone staying inside of the castle," Gabriel said. "We suspect there are spies in the area. Come in."

"Wait, did Sudfad tell you he was sending weapons with us?" Archetenus asked.

"Yes but he didn't tell us how in case the message was intercepted," Gabriel said.

"Well, let us show you," Archetenus said and walked to the back of one boca while Jared walked to the back of the second boca. Both men were now surrounded with warriors. Archetenus and Jared started pulling bags and kegs of supplies out of the bocas and handing them to the others, who were stacking the supplies on the ground.

"It's pretty damn clever," Jared said. "You'd never guess there was a latch here." Both men opened hidden doors in the false bottoms of the bocas then stood back for the others to see the cache of weapons.

"How many men can we arm?" Fennel asked as be pulled a sword out and examined the blade.

"Between these two bocas, there are almost five thousand swords, knives and daggers. Thaos' group stopped in Salar and got two bocas just like this."

"This is unbelievable," Dominic said with emotion in his voice.

"Have ya figured out how ya going to get the weapons to the people?" Jared asked.

"Dominic and his men will have to disperse them," the Sanuri said as he and Erebus now joined the group. "The people here have been brutalized for so long that they will not trust strangers. And I apologize for being late. Erebus has been gracious enough to allow me to look at Sophie's belongings and we just found some things of interest."

"Where is everyone else?" Archetenus asked.

"Michael is preparing them for the games, they are behind the castle," the Sanuri said.

"Let me get some men to put away these supplies and weapons and Jared and me will join Michael," Archetenus said.

As the men were talking, Thor, Misha and Diana walked up to the group. "We can show them where the supplies go," Thor said.

"We heard congratulations are in order," Jared said as he and Archetenus both extended their hands to Misha.

"I can't fight in the games now," Diana said with a pout. Jared smiled and winked at Misha.

"Take it from me and hire a nurse right away," Archetenus said. "As soon as one baby goes to sleep the other one wakes up."

"Thor is moving in with us," Diana said with a grin. "He's going to be our nurse."

"That's me," Thor said then laughed. "By the way, the girls are fixing a feast for you but it's not done yet," Thor said and put his arm around his little sister.

Gabriel wanted to have a mission meeting right after Archetenus' group arrived but the Sanuri thought it better that the groups get to know each other first. Once Archetenus' group had settled in and all of the supplies and weapons had been brought into the castle, everyone joined the warriors who were training for the Gefrey Games.

Using the drawings provided by Joao and Jasmine, Michael had set up a makeshift replica of the floor of the arena. "This is pretty damn good," Archetenus said as he looked at the training field.

Michael handed Archetenus and Jared the drawings the arena. "Dagon has a small group of artists in the city now doing a lot more drawings," Michael explained. "Apparently Teivel has a lot of construction going on for the games and it is changing the look of the city."

Michael now looked at his students which included Dominic's men. "This is Archetenus and Jared. They are both professional fighters and Archetenus ruled the Gefrey Games in Stordt. In a few days another group will arrive and a man called Thaos is the third of us who has fought in these games and lived to talk about it. Now that we are getting more teachers we can break you down into smaller groups to make the training more realistic."

"In Stordt," Archetenus said. "The arena was so large that often more than one battle was going on at a time; which meant you had to be aware of flying weapons and animals or monsters that weren't your intended competition. We are going to make this training as real as possible because we want all of you to live to tell about it. Corse we don't have no monsters or animals to train with."

"Can't Erebus conjure some up?" Thor yelled.

Now the crowd turned and looked at Erebus. "I have the ability but once I start performing spells, others in the dark worlds will be able to find our location. Let me discuss this with Gabriel and the Sanuri."

As Raul, Simon and Matthew met with Commanding General Craven in his office, Enrops started to land on the windowsills.

At first it was one and two birds but soon the sills on all four of the small windows to the General's office were filled with birds. All three of the princes realized this was unusual behavior for their winged friends. Raul was just about to hand King Sudfad's papers to Craven, which contained information about the mission, when one of the birds grabbed the papers from Raul.

Both Simon and Matthew drew their swords as Raul grabbed General Craven. "He's not the real general," one of the birds said. "He is a demon."

"I figured as much when you grabbed the papers," Raul said as he now pressed a dagger tightly against the demon's throat. "What have you done with Craven?" Raul demanded.

"Are there other demons?" Matthew asked one of the Enrops in the room.

"He is the only one we saw," the bird replied. "But there was a flock of Ravens which we killed."

The demon stared into Raul's eyes and laughed condescendingly. Suddenly smoke started to rise from the area where Raul's dagger was touching the beast. The demon started to struggle and scream with pain as holiness surged through his body. Raul pressed the dagger tighter against the demon's skin and he started to convulse. "Tell me where Craven is?" Raul yelled. "And I will spare you."

"Why would you?" asked the demon as he was clenching his teeth in pain.

"Because he is important to me," Raul said. "Now tell me."

"In the cellar of his house," the demon said as his black blood was slowly oozing down his neck. Simon quickly ran out of the office and yelled for soldiers to follow him to the General's house.

"Is he alive?" Raul asked angrily.

"He might be. You said you would spare me."

"I need to find out if you are telling the truth." As Raul spoke with the demon, Matthew slowly moved closer to them.

272

"Who sent you?" Raul demanded.

The demon tried to talk but the holiness that consumed the blade of the dagger was burning his throat. Raul could see that the demon was in distress and slightly pulled the dagger back. "Who sent you?" Raul repeated.

Simon quickly ran into the office. "We have him and he is still alive," Simon said as he angrily ran up to Raul and pushed his dagger into the throat of the demon. The demon started to smoke and burst into flames.

"You weren't really going to spare him were you?" Matthew asked.

"Of course not," Raul said as the stench of the burning demon was making his eyes water. "But I had hoped to get more information."

"We may already have some," Simon said. "Follow me. I had Craven moved to the physician's office but I want you to look at his house. That bastard drew symbols on the walls with Craven's blood."

"Miranda, Daniel we know you are here because of Raul's dagger," Matthew called out as they walked towards the General's house. "Is this writing those demonic curses?"

"You're learning," Miranda's voice was heard in only the ears of the princes. "But these are not curses, you can enter." As soon as Matthew, Raul and Simon entered the house, Miranda and Daniel appeared to them. "Craven will live. He refused to die at the hands of a demon and called out to The Great Ruler."

"Then why wasn't he released?" Simon asked angrily.

"My child, you know the man who you grew up with," Miranda said. "As soon as he heard the demon chanting and praying to his masters, Craven realized he could learn a great deal. So he pretended to be unconscious and memorized the words of the demon."

"The demon spoke in our language?" Raul asked.

273

Daniel smiled. "Craven did not pray to be released; he prayed to defeat the darkness and he was given the gift of understanding the words of the demon. You would be wise to copy every word and send letters to the Sanuri, Gabriel and Sudfad. While some of what the demon said sounds like a puzzle, it is a puzzle which will unfold before you in the future.

"Are there other demons here?" asked Matthew.

"No," Daniel replied. "And the demon you destroyed was strong enough that he could not be killed by one human. Which is why we touched your blade, Raul. But you are three of The Seven Sons. Together you now have the power to destroy such demons."

"Are our powers growing?" Simon asked.

"The prophesy is unfolding," Daniel said and the two Angels disappeared.

"The hair on the back of my neck is standing on end," Edward said to Raphael, who was riding next to him. The two men were leading their troops to Fort Stanus.

"I know," Raphael said. "I have been feeling the same way all morning." Raphael again looked up at the Ruala warriors and the Enrops that were flying overhead, for any indication of trouble. "Something isn't right."

"Maybe Teivel is watching us through his crystal ball again," Edward said in a half joking manner.

Suddenly small plumes of white smoke materialized in several areas of the ground that surrounded the troops. The smoke appeared, then disappeared, then appeared again with more frequency. Raphael stopped the troops. "Smoke is appearing all around you," one of the Ruala warriors yelled down to Raphael and Edward.

"Miranda," Raphael yelled. "Daniel, what am I leading my men into?"

"A better question would be to ask what you should do," Miranda's voice was heard by Raphael only.

"Keep your troops moving in a straight line, do not deviate from your course. We will handle the rest."

Raphael turned and yelled in a commanding voice. "We move forward, do not deviate from our course. The Angels are with us."

No sooner had Raphael said these words than a horse reared up and screamed with fright as the earth fell away next to him. The rider managed to control his horse that wanted to run. The troops proceeded forward as the earth groaned and cracked around them.

"Are the doors to hell opening again?" Edward asked.

"The Angels said to keep moving and they would take care of the rest," Raphael said. "They didn't tell me what was happening."

Raphael's horse started to stumble as the ground underneath its hoofs became soft and dissolving. "Raphael now is the time for you to be a beacon of faith for your men," Miranda's voice whispered into his ears.

Raphael kept moving forward but yelled over his shoulder. "Do not let the fear that grips your hearts take control. The Angels are watching over us. They have never let us down before. We move forward."

Raphael's message was repeated down the ranks as the soldiers and Patronus priests continued their march. Silently many of the Ruala warriors were watching to see if the troops on the ground needed to be rescued from the earth that was starting to take the form of quicksand.

"Edward do you know any songs?" Raphael asked as he could feel the fears of his men.

"Yes but I am not sure they are the kind that priests sing," Edward said with a laugh.

"We have to get their minds off from their fears, sing whatever you want."

Edward's robust voice bellowed out, "I knew a girl from Calix..."

The leaders of the men riding behind Edward and Raphael understood what Edward was doing and started to sing along. Voice after voice raised in song and the troops marched through the fields filled with traps of black magics.

Per the instructions of the Angels, Raul, Simon and Matthew copied down the words and symbols the demon had written on the walls of the cellar in Craven's house. As the three princes were climbing the ladder to exit the cellar, Matthew was the last in line and as he grabbed the last of the ignited torches from the wall he said loudly, "It's all disappearing, the writing and symbols."

Simon and Raul stopped their climb up the ladder and looked at the room. "Miranda, Daniel are you doing that or are there more demons here?"

"We have cleansed the house; Craven may move back in if he so chooses," Miranda's voice said.

When the three princes arrived at the physician's office they were more than surprised to see Craven sitting at the physician's desk and writing the words the demon had spoken.

"You looked like you were dying when we brought you in here," Simon said. "What happened?"

"I am fine," Craven growled. "The only thing that bastard really hurt was my pride. Now you boys grab a cup of coffee and sit down, we have things to discuss," Craven said to the princes.

"Theodore, I'm going to have to take over your office for a little while," Craven said to the physician.

"It's the damndest thing I ever saw," Theodore the Physician said to the three princes. You saw what he looked like. I leave the room for a moment to get hot water and towels and this is what I found when I returned." The princes smiled. "Theodore now looked at Craven. "Since I don't have any other patients, I'll get you some clean clothes. The men shouldn't see their commander running around here half naked."

"Wait it might not be safe to go into my house," said Craven.

"The Angels cleansed it," Raul said and grinned when he saw the shocked look on the physician's face. "They said you could move back in if you wanted."

"Angels, demons and I don't know what all," Theodore huffed. "I am a man of science; I don't understand any of this." Theodore marched out of his office and closed the door behind him.

"Now before you boys say anything, let me talk first," Craven said. Then he looked at Matthew. "I am assuming you are Matthew."

"Yes," Matthew said and extended his hand to shake with Craven.

"You boys know how close I am to Sudfad; why he is the brother I never had. But I will be honest. You know I believe in The Great Ruler but it has been difficult to understand and accept all the things that Sudfad has told me. Now I am not calling him a liar."

"Oh we understand," Raul as he refilled everyone's cups with coffee.

"Well as soon as I went to bed last night I started having nightmares and in them I saw that damn demon but I didn't understand what it all meant. Then I heard a voice; now you have talked to Angels so hopefully you won't think I am crazy. But the voice said that I would be attacked before morning. The voice said the Angels were with me but I had choices to make. I could fight my attacker or I could go along with the situation and discover important information; of course I would have to trust that they would protect me."

"Well damn as soon as the voice stops talking I see that damn demon standing over me. I recognized him from my nightmares. So I, so I prayed to The Great Ruler to watch over me and I put up a half-hearted fight with the demon and let him think he had bested me. Well the bastard drags me down to the cellar and hangs me by my wrists. Then he cuts me and uses my blood in his damn, I don't know what to call it, ceremony. The demon had his back to me as he is writing on the walls and I heard that voice in my head that said listen and remember."

"Now mind you that demon was talking in some strange language but all of a sudden I could understand what he was saying so I dropped my head and pretended I was unconscious and I tried to memorize every word. He repeated a lot of words and phrases so I am writing down how many times I heard him say these things. I'm not done yet so give me a few minutes before I forget."

"The Rualas and the freedom fighters are in battle," an Enrop squawked as it flew to the warriors who were training at Erebus's castle. The Ruala warriors took to the air, many of them grabbing their human comrades.

It was apparent to Misha, Archetenus, Michael and the others who were following the Enrop that Ratri, Dominic and their men had been ambushed. As the responding warriors descended to the ground they saw that members of their team were literally surrounded by an army of demons. The Ruala's dropped the humans they were carrying and returned to the air to attack the demons from above.

Various war cries rang out in the morning air as the demons realized they were now fighting on multiple fronts. Thor stayed close to Diana as they attacked demons as a team.

"Get her out of here," Ratri yelled to another Ruala as they could both see that Batina's arm and side were covered in blood.

"No, I am not leaving you," Batina yelled and plunged her sword into the stomach of a demon. The battle was bloody but ended quickly after the reinforcements from Erebus' castle arrived.

"Keep a couple alive for the Sanuri," Lakin yelled as he packed crystals into the wound of a Ruala warrior.

"Lakin," Ratri yelled as he now brought an unconscious Batina to the powerful healer. Joshua, Micha, Diana and Thor helped care for the wounded as others tied up two prisoners and walked among the demons to make sure they were dead.

Chapter XXII
Paranoia

As Raphael and Edward led their troops through the traps that were laid before them by the demons, screams from hell could be heard but no demons were seen. Edward sung louder to drown out the hellish sounds and his troops followed him. The singing helped to bond the men and to calm their fears. The troops traveled in such a manner for over an hour before they saw a change in their surroundings.

The hellish screams stopped. The cracking and groaning of the ground ceased and the earth returned to its normal consistency. "Now it's too quiet," Edward said to Raphael as they both looked around uneasily.

"Miranda, Daniel," Raphael called out.

"Just keep moving," Daniel said. "You really are alright."

"I heard his voice this time," Edward said with amazement.

"I think we all did," yelled down one of the Ruala warriors that was flying directly over the commanders.

"Edward do you feel that?" Raphael asked in a low voice.

"You mean that the air suddenly feels thick and smells different?"

"Yes," Raphael said. "Know any more songs?"

"Pull the arrows out of those bodies," Archetenus yelled. "We don't want anyone to know the Rualas are here."

"This one has a strange medallion on," Dack yelled out as he pulled the necklace from the neck of the dead demon.

"These are the same kind of demons that attacked Rachel's family," Michael said to Jared as they were both searching the bodies of demons.

"Lakin the crystals are turning black," Ratri said in horror as he watched Lakin pack crystals in the wound on Batina's left side.

"I know and she's not the only one. We need to get all of the wounded back to the Sanuri," Lakin yelled as he finished bandaging Batina's side. Ratri picked up Batina and quickly ascended into the air. His heart was pounding wildly. Ratri was crying and praying.

"Think we should burn these bodies?" Jared asked. "There master is gonna know something ain't right. Don't want them suspecting us."

"There are a lot of rival demon gangs in this area," Dominic explained. "And most of the farmers don't have the means to kill an army of demons."

"We can always help things along," Asher said with a grin as he pulled a medallion from his shirt pocket. "The leaders of the gangs wear these. This belongs to a different gang and I am leaving it among the bodies."

"I like how you think," Archetenus said with a laugh. Within minutes every warrior was being transported from the battlefield and back to Erebus' castle.

"I don't understand what that means," Simon said as he was reading the demonic phrases that Craven had written down.

"The Sanuri is at Erebus' castle," Raul said as he was making a copy of the phrases Craven had written. "Between the two of them I would think they could figure some of this out."

"Hand me some paper and I will help you," Matthew said.

"I can't believe those cuts are healing," Theodore said loudly as he helped General Craven put on his uniform jacket. "All of this is so unbelievable."

"Are you going to stay in that house?" Simon asked.

"I'm not letting no damn demon scare me out of my home. In fact I planned to have you boys as my house guests. That is unless you would rather stay in one of the other buildings?"

"Your home is fine," Raul said then he glanced at Theodore.

"While we are making copies perhaps you should read the papers Father sent."

"Stay here," Theodore said. "I don't have any patients anyways."

"Good," Raul said and looked at Craven. "We killed the demon in your office and it really stinks now."

Archetenus, Michael and Jared were among the last of the warriors to leave the battlefield. When they entered the castle they saw a makeshift hospital in one of the large parlors. The Sanuri was walking among the wounded and placing his hands on them.

Gabriel walked up to the three men and said, "It's not that the wounds are so bad but they all have demon poison in them."

"I wonder if we should expect that at the games," Archetenus said as he quickly moved so Natasha could get past him with an armload of towels.

"I was thinking the same thing," Gabriel said. "After the wounded are cared for I am calling a meeting to better understand what happened."

"What do you mean?" Jared asked.

"Fennel said it is very unusual to see an entire army of demons sent out to do the terror raids. And apparently the group you killed works for Teivel. There has to be a reason they were so close to the castle."

It had been several days since Tina and Charles discovered that Morgan and Bruno were missing. Tina and Charles were in the dining room when they saw the members of the death squads running into the hotel and up the stairs. Of course Tina and Charles assumed the death squads were going to capture Morgan and Bruno and were surprised when the Ruala warriors walked out of the hotel without their prisoners.

Soto, the leader of one of the death squads stayed at the front desk and spoke with the manager as the other Ruala warriors left the building. Soto explained the situation and tried to pay for the door he had kicked in but the manager would not take his money.

Soto explained how dangerous Morgan and Bruno were and if the two Rualas returned; Soto told the manager to contact the commanders at Fort Nora.

Both Tina and Charles were beside themselves with curiosity as they watched Soto. So distracted where they that it was not until Soto left the building that Charles realized Soto had looked directly at them.

Tina and Charles returned to their chambers in the hotel shortly after Soto left the building. But they stopped at the room that Morgan and Bruno had shared first. Charles searched the room for any riches that Bruno and Morgan may have left behind. They found little and what was in the room stunk of demon.

Charles and Tina left their chambers little over the next few days as they were fearful that Sudfad's soldiers would come for them. Charles got some maps and the two tried to determine other areas they might want to live. It wasn't that Charles and Tina were afraid to move to another city; their problem was that they had no money. The people of Nora were providing everything to the two Rualas free of charge and Charles and Tina were taking advantage of everything they could. They knew they would not be so lucky in another city.

"We need to get our hands on some money," Tina repeated for the third time as she paced in front of the small table that Charles was sitting at in their chambers.

"This from the woman who has never done a day's work in her life," Charles said sarcastically. "Tell me dear do you plan to get a job?"

"Charles this is serious," Tina snapped.

"And so am I. Are you suggesting we steal the money we need?"

"Steal isn't really the word I would use," Tina said as she looked shrewdly at her husband.

The Sanuri eradicated the demon poison from the wounded at Erebus' castle. None of them had life threatening injuries; the poison was their biggest threat. After lunch was eaten, Gabriel held a meeting in the large parlor so that the wounded warriors could also be a part of it.

"I'll go first," Dominic said and stood up. "But first I feel we should not delay our original plans of getting High Priest Othnial out of Rubar. I feel like we have abandoned him."

"I am responsible for that change of plans," the Sanuri said. "While I understand your devotion to him; Othnial is safe and protected. He can be of more use to us at the monastery right now." Dominic did not want to question the Sanuri but Dominic's fears for Othnial's safety were overwhelming him. "Dominic I can see the pain in your heart but you must know that I speak the truth. We will not forsake your friend."

Dominic was quiet for a few moments. "He is more than a friend. He is the best man I know and he has practically been a father to us since our parents were murdered. Fennel, Asher and I owe our lives to High Priest Othnial; it is difficult to leave him behind."

"He is a shrewd and faithful man whose heart has been ignited with hope since Gabriel spoke with him. Othnial will be just fine," the Sanuri said. "And speaking of that first conversation between Othnial, you and Gabriel; I have been told that we really are here as an answer to Othnial's prayers. Do not think The Great Ruler will abandon him."

Dominic became choked up and composed himself before speaking again. "As all of you know, Ratri's team has been transporting my men to the areas where we can leave messages and weapons for the people who support us. We have an elaborate security system that has not been compromised; at least not yet. To see such a large army of demons is highly unusual. I am wondering if Teivel suspects something. Sanuri were you able to get any information from those two demons we took prisoner?"

"First for those of you who didn't know, Lakin ordered his men to take the demons to a cave that Rachel had previously told us about. We did not want them here in case a powerful demon could track them," the Sanuri explained. "I looked into the minds of both beasts and saw what we have already suspected. That they are gathering victims for the games. But that was not the reason that army was near here."

"A few weeks ago the Angels orchestrated a storm of incredible proportions that literally attacked Fort Polta and destroyed all that Teivel owned there. When Teivel discovered that nothing but the fort and his home and office had been destroyed he realized he had been attacked but he did not think it was from the heavens. Teivel has been trying to manipulate matters in the demon wars and thought a powerful demon was attacking him."

"Apparently last night a similar storm struck his castle here in Ryed. Teivel was in his castle at the time. From what I saw in the minds of the demons, considerable damage was done to the castle. Teivel has sent armies of demons out to find information about who is attacking him. The demons came upon you accidently."

"But wouldn't Teivel be able to find that information with his magics?" Erebus asked.

"I saw an image that many of the instruments that Teivel needs to perform spells were destroyed. Now if his powers were weakened, that I cannot answer," the Sanuri said. "I also saw something else which was interesting. I saw images of your King and Queen but I could not tell if these were images of the past or the present. I understand they have not been seen in public for a very long time."

Fennel stood up and spoke, "King Nehmota and Queen Vasart were loved by their people although everyone knew that Teivel held the real power here. It was rumored that the King and Queen smuggled their two young sons out of the kingdom to protect the children. Shortly after this rumor surfaced the King and Queen disappeared. Everyone believes that Teivel had them murdered."

"Two young sons," Diana said loudly as she stood up and looked at the Sanuri. "Could they be the children we see in those visons? You said the visions had multiple meanings."

"Diana the images you saw have been painted on the walls of the dungeons for centuries," Asher said.

"But the Sanuri always says the heavens have more than one meaning for the information they give us. Now think about it. The images are a man and a woman trying to save two small boys from demons. Fennel isn't that basically what you just said?" Thor laughed as everyone in the group now looked at the Sanuri.

"Joshua I believe your daughter here may be on to something," the Sanuri said and smiled warmly. "Of course I don't know that as fact yet. Also there was something that disturbed me about the images I saw of Nehmota and Vasart. I am not sure they aren't imposters."

"But why would Teivel have impostors?" Fennel asked. "He doesn't really need the King and Queen."

"Teivel is a manipulative and power driven man who has been waiting for his time to shine, so to speak," the Sanuri explained. "I suspect he has many reasons for hosting the Gefrey Games, besides that he wants recognition by all kingdoms. It might be politically advantageous for people to think that Ryed still has a King and Queen."

"All of us here have been incredibly busy," Gabriel said. "But perhaps now is the time for us to discuss an important subject. Dominic the first time we spoke I told you that if we could liberate your people that we would have nothing to do with who assumed power after Teivel. Have you and your men thought about that issue at all?"

"Actually we have discussed that at length," Dominic said. "And it is not an easy answer. While many people would love to have King Nehmota rule, that is if he still lives; Nehmota may not be powerful enough to protect the kingdom. Nehmota as many of his predecessors have been mouth pieces for Teivel."

Dominic now looked around the room at the faces of the warriors. Gabriel told me that our people have been victimized for so long that even once they were freed they could easily fall victim to another tyrant. While these words greatly angered me, I now agree with what Gabriel said. We need a strong leader who cares about his people. My vote would be for High Priest Othnial."

"Is that something he would consider?" the Sanuri asked.

"I have no idea; it has never been discussed," Dominic said. "And if Prince Vincent and Prince Barid are alive the throne would be theirs.

"But aren't they children?" Bianca asked. "So someone would have to assume the throne until the children were old enough."

"Dominic have you considered it?" Rachel asked. "You are a strong leader who cares about the people."

"I am humbled by your suggestion. But I am a fighter and nothing more. I know nothing of politics and honestly I don't know if I want to." As Dominic spoke these words almost every warrior who was from Wetpr turned and looked at Michael.

"Michael do you want to explain why everyone is now looking at you?" the Sanuri asked.

Michael hesitated then he said. "I had been a prisoner my entire life. A few months ago I found out who my birth father was. I hunted him down with the intent of killing him for not saving me and my mother. My Father is King Sudfad who knew nothing of my existence. Instead of the battle I expected he and Renya claimed me and welcomed me into their family. Later the Sanuri told me I was the first born and heir to the throne. I was so scared of the idea that I almost left my new found family. When I spoke with Sudfad, Raul and Simon I said the exact same words you just said."

"So who will take the throne?" Dominic asked.

"Raul and Simon have trained their entire lives for that role; it should go to them. I now have what I always wanted."

Dominic stared at Michael for a few moments as he thought about Michael's words. Then Dominic turned to his left where Fennel and Asher were sitting. "You are both strong leaders would either of you consider such a role?" Both Fennel and Asher looked shocked at Dominic's question.

"I don't believe either of us have thought about it," Fennel said. "Dominic we have always followed you."

"I do not want the throne but I would support either of you if you make that decision."

"Dominic if you were a free man what would you choose for your life?" the Sanuri asked.

"Perhaps I have spent too much time with High Priest Othnial," Dominic said with a shy grin. "I would have liked to become a priest. Then as my life took its course I thought a warrior could not become a priest. That is until I met Gabriel."

Now it was Gabriel who got a shocked look on his face. "Would you like to become a Patronus Priest? I can help you."

"If we live through this," Dominic said. "That is a conversation I would like to have with you."

"Dominic if we cannot defeat Teivel, you and your men are welcomed to return to Wetpr with us," Gabriel said. "You can't live your lives hiding in caves."

"You are also welcome to return with us if we do defeat the tyrant," the Sanuri said.

Raphael and his men traveled without taking any breaks until late afternoon. While they did not encounter any more demonic traps the atmosphere around them was thick and acid smelling. No one had gotten sick or injured from this strange occurrence but the uneasiness that it caused kept everyone on edge.

"I know the horses and men need a break," Edward said to Raphael as they made camp. "But I would rather keep moving, maybe we can get away from this stuff."

"I'll be surprised if anyone gets any sleep," Raphael said and started preparing dinner. "I feel like we are surrounded by demons but we just can't see them."

"Let's talk about something more pleasant," Edward said. "Have you and Vivian decided on names for your baby?"

Raphael smiled, "I can't believe how much I miss her. I don't ever remember feeling lonely when I was single but now that I am married, I feel kind of empty without her."

Neither Raphael nor Edward spoke for a few moments as they were both lost in their thoughts. "My father's name was Robert. If we have a son he will be called Robert Joshua Gabriel. Iris' middle name is Crystal and my mother's name was Jillian. If we have a girl she will be named Crystal Jillian. I just hope I am back for the birth."

"Those are good names; you're set on them are you?"

Raphael laughed. "What's all of this interest in the names? Are you thinking about setting down?"

"No," Edward said with a hearty laugh. "But I was thinking about having something made for you. It wouldn't be good if I put the wrong names on it." Both Raphael and Edward laughed.

"Not that it is any of my business," Raphael said as he handed Edward a plate of food. "But can you see yourself getting serious with any of the four women you are dating?"

"Why?" Edward asked with a grin.

"Because Vivian and Diana have a friend they want to introduce to you but of course she lives in the Village of Gesmal."

"Really? Do you know anything about her?"

"Actually I've met her; she is really beautiful. She has auburn hair and green eyes. Her name is Kate. I don't really know her but the girls think you two would like each other."

"How can they say that, I hardly know Vivian and Diana?" Edward asked and laughed again. "But I would be up for meeting Kate. The women I am seeing now are beautiful and fun to be with but I can't really see myself settling down with any one of them."

"Are you looking to settle down?"

"I don't know. I was like you always working but now with this assignment I have more of a social life. And," Edward paused. "And all my friends here are married and really enjoying it; so I've thought about it."

"In a way that surprises me. You really seem to enjoy your single life."

"Oh, I do," Edward said with emphasis. "I said I am thinking about it not that I am desperate. Besides, I am going to need someone who can understand what we do. You know how that is. That's kind of what surprises me about your team. You all have wives who understand and work with you. That was a real shock to me when I first met all of you."

"You mean Queen Renya didn't shock you?"

"Actually King Tobias said his sister-in-law was trained with weapons but I don't believe he has any idea what Renya is really like. I have the ultimate respect for that woman and Emeral too. Did I tell you how I first met Emeral?" Edward stopped speaking as a flock of Enrops landed at their campsite carrying letters.

Raphael laughed when he saw all of the letters Edward received. "From your girl friends?"

"There is one here for both of us from Sudfad," Edward said with a smile as he opened that letter first. As Edward was reading, Raphael opened one of several letters he received from Vivian.

"This is interesting," Raphael said. "You know I told you that Vivian and some of the other team members searched Berta's house. Well, some of the Patronus priests have been tutoring Vivian and other members of the team so Vivian shows the priests the things they found at Berta's and Shanksaw's ledgers. The priests have been helping to decipher the coded ledgers and it sounds like they have made a lot of headway."

"Vivian said they have figured out how to decode the column of names and the column of payments but they are still working on the last two columns in the ledgers which they assume contain information about what jobs the people paid Shanksaw to do. She sent a list of the names to see if I recognized anyone."

Raphael quickly jumped up and ran to his saddlebags. He wrote a note and handed it to one of the Enrops. "Get this to High Priest Nicholas as soon as possible. Tell him it is urgent," Raphael said.

"What's the matter? You look like you've seen a ghost?" Edward asked. Raphael handed Edward Vivian's letter and pointed to a name. "You don't think that is High Priest Alfonso do you? I mean is that his full name?"

"That is his name. I am in shock I have known him for years," Raphael uttered. "I can't believe he is a terrorist."

Chapter XXIII
When Music Died

"Ratri really I am almost fine," Batina said as Ratri helped her to the breakfast table the morning after the battle with the army of demons. Once seated, Batina looked at others who were seated at the long table. "Every time I woke up last night I saw Ratri watching me. I don't think he slept at all."

"I know just how he feels," Calen said.

"Sanuri will I be healed in time for the Gefrey Games?" Batina asked. Calen laughed when he saw the look on Ratri's face.

"I expect that you will be healed long before the games," the Sanuri said with a smile.

All of the warriors who had been wounded in the previous day's battle were now seated in the banquet room. Gabriel stood up and addressed the group. "Thaos' group should be joining us today. While there is plenty of room in the castle and plenty of bedrooms there is only one cook because we did not want to bring outsiders in."

"The girls have been helping Zelda but they too must train for the games so I would like volunteers to help with the meals and that includes hunting. Diana I would like you to be in charge of organizing this help. Does anyone take issue with this request?"

"No," Jared said. "We all agree we need to eat but Zelda will have to tell us what she wants done."

"I don't think that will be a problem," Gabriel said. "Fortunately you brought enough supplies that we shouldn't have to go into the villages to purchase things. I don't think anyone here believes it is a good idea to bring people in to help with the work."

Raphael's troops resumed their journey to Fort Stanus well before daylight. While there had been no attacks, most of the men felt uneasy and couldn't sleep. With this new day the atmosphere around these troops was thicker and murkier than the previous day.

All of the men rode with their senses heightened as every one of them expected to be attacked. But no attack came. They arrived at Fort Stanus mid-morning.

"Thank you, Miranda and Daniel," Raphael said softly as the gates to the fort opened.

"You are welcome," Miranda's voice whispered in Raphael's ear.

Thaos and his warriors arrived at the castle of Erebus just before noon. Batina, Bianca, Jasmine and Darla were thrilled to be reunited with so many members of their tribe. Each of these four warriors kissed Sorren on his cheek which warmed his heart.

It took a little over an hour for this group to get settled into their rooms and to unload their supplies. Gabriel planned to have a huge meeting after the midday meal. Sorren and Joshua were the last two people to enter the banquet hall. These two men walked up to Gabriel and the Sanuri and whispered a few words then Sorren addressed the group in his loud and robust voice.

"I need everyone's attention," Sorren yelled and the room quickly became silent. "I believe everyone here understands how dangerous this mission is so I think we should have a little fun to give everyone a break from their work. Micha and Bianca will you please come up here."

Both Micha and Bianca were shocked to be called in front of the room. Although Micha started to smile when he saw the smiles on Joshua's and Sorren's faces.

Sorren continued to address the group. "For those of you who don't know, Micha son of Joshua and a Venator of the Clan of Gesmal has asked Bianca to be his wife. Bianca is a member of my tribe and our customs dictate that Micha must ask Bianca's father for her hand before a marriage can take place."

"Micha I don't know if you are aware that many letters have been sent between your parents and Bianca's parents. You have already met Bianca's family and all the families are warriors and understand the significance of this mission."

"So Bianca your father and mother asked me to represent them in this matter. If you choose to marry on this mission they will give you their blessing but they want a big celebration when we return home."

"Really?" Bianca asked; her eyes wide with amazement.

"Then I should ask you for Bianca's hand?" Micha asked with a broad smile.

"Yes and we can do that in private if you prefer," Sorren replied.

"Ask now," Joao yelled. And several warriors let out war cries. Everyone started to laugh.

"Sorren may I take Bianca for my wife?" Micha asked.

"Yes, you have her family's blessing. Now how soon do you want to marry?"

Bianca and Micha looked at each other then at Sorren and Joshua. "I don't know," Micha said.

"With all of us here we should be able to set up games and an altar pretty quickly. How about tomorrow morning," Sorren said and laughed.

"That's fine with us," Micha said with a grin.

"There is more," Sorren said and looked at Joshua.

"Your mothers have been writing to each other and Iris bought this ring. Now Bianca if you don't like it we can get something else," Joshua said and handed a small box to Bianca.

"Oh my! Look at this," Bianca said as she took the pink sapphire ring out of the box. Bianca's hands were shaking as she put the ring on her finger. "I can't believe it fits. Thank you so much. I love it." Bianca kissed Joshua then Sorren.

"Oh there is still more," Sorren said. "Hannah sent some instruments along so we could have music for the dance and your mothers sent a few other things which I will let you look through." Everyone in the banquet room started to clap.

"I believe this is just what we need," the Sanuri said to Gabriel.

"In light of the wedding," Gabriel said with a grin. "The work meeting will be postponed and a meeting to prepare for the celebration will be held after this meal." Some of the warriors started to whistle and clap.

Micha and Bianca now turned to face the room of warriors. "Ratri and Batina we want you to be the best man and maid of honor. Dack and Darla, Joao and Jasmine, Dagon and Rachel and Thor and Diana we would like you to be in the wedding."

"They have been thinking about this," Natasha said kiddingly.

"And we want to thank Diana," Micha said. "For bringing us together."

"I second that," Ratri said.

"No, don't encourage her," Thor said loudly as Diana gave him a proud smile. The room broke into laughter.

Preparing for the wedding of Micha and Batina allowed the many warriors at Erebus' castle to get to know each other in a different manner than preparing for war. Almost half of the warriors that accompanied Sorren were women which continually amazed Dominic and his men. Gabriel and Sorren hoped that featuring female warriors at the Gefrey Games would be a great distraction while the teams found and released the prisoners held in the arena.

Dagon's team of illustrators had made repeated trips to the City of Teivel where the games would be held. They drew pictures of the arena, the main and secondary roads in the city. They drew pictures of the soldier's barracks and all of the buildings immediately surrounding the arena. And they drew maps of the land between Erebus' castle and the City of Teivel.

Late that afternoon Dominic and Gabriel studied these illustrations. They were looking for both sites that would be advantageous to their warriors and sites that would be dangerous. "Sudfad has provided us with a great deal of money," Gabriel explained.

"I would like to purchase one of these buildings near the arena. Are you familiar with that immediate area?"

"It has been almost a year since I have walked those streets," "Dominic said. "So things could have changed greatly. But the streets immediately surrounding the arena were usually stores and taverns, there were a couple of small hotels. As you move farther from the arena are the nicer hotels and restaurants. The bars and streets closest to the arena are dangerous because they are frequented by criminals and demons."

"I would imagine the hotels will be filled for the games," Gabriel said more to himself. "I think it is time I took a trip to the city. I was thinking of asking Erebus to come with me because he might have more influence with the officials in Teivel."

"At least one of us should go with you," Dominic said. "It isn't safe."

"I think that is too dangerous for you and your men. I would prefer you keep distributing the weapons."

"I don't know if Rachel has told you that she has been to that city searching for her father. You should at least take her with you."

When High Priest Nicholas, the leader of the Patronus Priests at the monastery at Philiste, received Raphael's note that High Priest Alfonso was a terrorist. Nicholas wept at the betrayal of his loyal friend. But Nicholas' despair lasted moments and he organized a group of men to accompany him to Alfonso's chambers.

Alfonso was not in his room so larger search parties were organized to find him. Nicholas himself and a handful of men searched through Alfonso's rooms and belongings. They did not find anything incriminating. Alfonso's belongings were sparse, his personal letters detailed the man who Nicholas had believed Alfonso to be. Nicholas shook his head, never would he have imagined Alfonso to be a traitor to the church or to his men.

"We have something," one of the priest's said loudly as he tore the bedding from the mattress. The mattress was covered with blood stains that appeared old.

"Do you smell that?" another priest asked. The priests quickly lifted the mattress from the bedframe and found Alfonso's body. The gases that had built up in Alfonso's long dead body had already exploded through the skin, leaving little information about the manner of his death.

Nicholas and the other priests were greatly saddened by their discovery and yet relieved that the priest they loved and trusted was not a terrorist. "As Nicholas stared at the body he thought about the many recent encounters that had had with whoever assumed Alfonso's identity. "How could we not know?" Nicholas thought. "I felt no presence of demons. Is it a man or a demon walking our halls?"

High Priest Nicholas made arrangements for Alfonso's funeral then Nicholas went to his chambers and did something he had never before considered. He got on his knees and he called to the Angels who Raphael had told him about. And to the surprise of the priest it was not Miranda nor Daniel who answered his call but The Lion. Nicholas wept.

"Nicholas you are a faithful man and the leader of a powerful organization which serves The Great Ruler. Why have you never considered asking Him for help or insight?" The Lion asked.

High Priest Nicholas was shaking and trying to compose himself as the presence of the Angel was overwhelming his emotions. Nicholas thought about the question before he spoke. "I don't really know the answer to that question," he stammered. "I think I thought that somehow The Great Ruler would let me know if we were doing something that displeased him."

"Nicholas you know The Great Ruler created His children with freedom of choice. He is not going to compromise that. You are a wise man but you must realize that you are limited in many ways simply because you are human. You cannot assume that you know the will of The Great Ruler. He has been waiting for you to call upon Him as have I. In the role that you play in this world you must learn to call upon the heavens; for greater darkness has walked among you than you can realize."

The Sanuri performed the wedding ceremony for Micha and Bianca. Sorren proudly walked the bride down the aisle. Prior to the ceremony, friends of the young couple prepared a honeymoon suite. And among the flowers and fruit that decorated the room, there were a variety of gags and surprises.

Bianca's mother had made a wedding dress for Bianca and had sent many gifts for the newlyweds. After the ceremony Micha and Bianca decided they would renew their vows when they returned home so that their entire families could take part in the wedding.

Immediately after the wedding ceremony the games and competitions began. Pigs were being roasted and all manner of food prepared for the feast which would be served before the evening dance. "You look happy," the Sanuri said to Erebus as they walked among the competitions.

"Although most of these people are strangers to me, I find myself enjoying them. I have never had visitors here before."

"When this is all over Erebus, there really isn't anything holding you here."

"What do you mean?"

"Whether you want to admit it you have made many friends. Friends who I am sure would welcome you moving back to Wetpr." Erebus turned and looked at the Sanuri with shock. "You should think about it. You had such an isolated existence before."

"Are you insinuating that my isolation is what led me to dark magics?" Erebus asked sarcastically.

"I am just saying that new relationships have opened up for you and you might not want to let them go. And speaking of relationships you seem to becoming awfully attached to Zack."

"I will be honest, my one regret in life is that I never had children. When Sophie and I were young and in love we both wanted a big family. My life has been so consuming and I am suddenly realizing that I am old and will probably never have the family that I wanted."

297

"While I don't know if that is true, the people you are becoming attached to are not part of the world of dark magics. There might be a time when you have some serious choices to make."

Once Raphael and his men entered Fort Stanus they no longer experienced the thick murky atmosphere or any of the other sounds that had haunted them on their march to the fort. Immediately upon their arrival there was a meeting between Craven, Raul, Simon, Matthew, Edward and Raphael. Once these men shared their recent experiences with demonic entities they realized that Teivel or others from the dark worlds were aware of all of their movements.

"This could possibly have benefits," Raphael said. "If Teivel's eyes are upon us, hopefully he is unaware of Gabriel's group.

"While I agree," Simon said. "It is a slim chance now that we can make a surprise attack. I think we need to reevaluate our strategies."

"Are you going to call the Angels?" Edward asked.

"It is better if we have something to present them," Matthew said then he turned to Commanding General Craven. "We are going to need a large meeting room with tables. It would be best if this room was away from the eyes of others. And we are going to need maps."

"Are you talking a room large enough for all of us here or all of your men?" Craven asked.

"Us and maybe a few more. I would like the leaders of the Rualas to join us."

"Raphael and Edward why don't you stay in my home along with Raul, Simon and Matthew. We can use my study for these meetings. We can shutter the windows if you are concerned about spies."

After the feast and competitions, the banquet hall in the castle of Erebus was cleared out for the evening dance. There had been concerns that if the dance was held outside, the bonfires would bring attention to the group.

Dack and Joao were helping Sorren bring the instruments into the hall. Sorren felt that Hannah had entrusted him with the precious objects and he took his role seriously. "We have four guitars," Dack called out as the three men entered the hall which was already filled with people."

"Thor, Hannah sent our guitars," Diana said excitedly and started to move forward but stopped.

"What is the matter?" Asher asked, as he now was a constant companion of Thor, Diana and Misha.

"We are just learning how to play," Thor said with a laugh. "We don't really know any songs yet." Thor saw a strange look on Asher's face. A look of painful memories. "Are you alright?" Thor asked. Asher did not answer. "Do you know how to play?"

"When I was a child but music is forbidden here. I don't know if I would remember," Asher said with sadness in his voice. Misha walked forward and brought one of the guitars back to Asher, whose hands shook as he took the instrument. Hesitantly Asher started to strum the strings; after a few moments it was as if his fingers came alive and he played a song long forgotten.

"You're good," Diana said. "You have to play."

"Go on up there," Misha said as he saw a light return to Asher's eyes.

"Batina she sent your flute," Joao said loudly.

Ratri and Batina walked up to Joao. Her left side was bandaged and Batina was holding Ratri's hand with her right hand. "I don't think I am up to playing. Maybe we can find someone else."

"Does anyone know how to play a flute?" Ratri yelled as he took the flute from Joao. There was silence for a few moments then a husky male voice yelled through the crowd, "It's been a while but I do."

Brent was one of the soldiers from Lentz who Thaos and Stephan choose to fight in the Gefrey Games. Brent was a large and powerful man who bore the scares of his many battles. Brent walked up to Ratri and took the flute.

Brent handled the instrument clumsily at first and blew a few notes. Suddenly the room was filled with a melody that was so sweet and intense that it stirred the hearts of all. To see this mountain of a man play such beautiful music seemed ironic to some. When Brent finished the song, Batina realized she was crying.

"Would you teach me that song?" Batina asked. "It is so beautiful, what is it called?"

"Sure I'll teach you but I don't know the name. My mother taught it to me when I was a boy," Brent said.

"We have another guitar and a fiddle," Sorren called out. "Any players?"

"I play guitar," a female Ruala warrior called out and moved to the front of the room. Like most Rualas, Jana was tall, graceful and beautiful with dark hair and blue eyes.

Sorren handed Jana the fourth guitar, as he and Dack were also playing guitars. "Any fiddle players here?" Sorren yelled.

"We've got one," called out Martin who was one of Dominic's men. Martin pushed Seth forward. "Seth can play but he is shy." Seth was the young cousin of Dominic, Fennel and Asher.

"Come on up here Seth," Sorren called out and handed the young man Bekka's fiddle.

After a few practice songs this eclectic band filled the room with music. Soon people started to dance. Dominic's men watched from the side of the room. Noah, Martin, Oliver, Lawrence and Fennel had not seen people dance for so long it seemed like another life time ago.

Suddenly a group of Nordes female warriors came up to the freedom fighters. Even though the men tried to explain they couldn't dance the women pulled them onto the dance floor. Dominic smiled as he watched his men for it had been a long time since any of them enjoyed a celebration.

"You almost look sad," Gabriel said to Dominic as they stood with the Sanuri watching the band.

"I'm not really sure what I feel," Dominic said emotionally. "Music died here when Teivel banned it. Some people still play but they must do it in secret so Teivel's monsters don't arrest them. I had forgotten how beautiful music is."

"Why would Teivel ban music?" Gabriel asked incredulously.

"Because it stirs the hearts and souls of men and can help them break their bonds," the Sanuri said. "Teivel understands that."

"Erebus why don't you ask Zelda to dance; you both look like you would like to," Diana said as she and Misha walked up to the old sorcerer.

"Why aren't you two dancing?" Erebus asked with a grin.

"We're giving Misha's feet a rest; I always step on them," Diana said and laughed.

"She won't let me lead," Misha said and Erebus laughed loudly.

"Go ask her," Diana said. "What can it hurt? Some of the people here don't know how to dance but they are trying; if that concerns you."

"Oh, I know how to dance but I will admit it has been a while."

"One dance, Erebus," Diana cooed.

Erebus looked at Misha and grinned then Erebus bent down and kissed Diana on the head and walked across the room to Zelda.

"Now where is Thor?" Diana asked. Then she giggled loudly as Misha spun her around and ascended only a few inches in the air so they were dancing without touching the floor.

"You just can't stop playing matchmaker, can you?" Misha asked with a warm grin. "Thor can find his own girls."

"I just want everyone to be as happy as I am," Diana said as she lovingly looked up at Misha.

"This is so nice," Natasha said as she and Calen danced. "I'm glad that Hannah sent the instruments along."

"I know," Calen said and bent down and kissed Natasha on the lips.

"Calen don't get mad but I don't want Gabriel going into that city by himself, it's too dangerous I want to go with him."

"I thought as much," said Calen. "I was already planning on going with him."

"So you aren't mad at me?"

"No," Calen said and kissed Natasha again.

"I don't know what that Angel did to you but I like it," Natasha said and giggled.

Calen kissed Natasha again. "We might need to retire to our room soon," he said with a grin.

"Dagon, I don't know how to dance," Rachel said shyly.

"Is that why you have sent everyone away who has asked you?" Dagon asked. He was smiling but the intensity of his stare was making Rachel nervous.

"It's the truth, I am not lying," she said defensively. "Music has been banned here for centuries."

"Would you let me teach you?" Dagon asked. Rachel smiled and nodded. "I am going to hold you close so that you can feel the movement of my body. Just relax and let me lead." Dagon put his arm around Rachel's waist and pulled her close to him. She looked at the other dancers to see how they positioned their bodies. He took Rachel's hand and started to glide across the floor. "Don't look at your feet; look up at me."

After a few minutes Rachel smiled proudly. "I think I am getting it. This is fun."

"I am glad you like it," Dagon said. "When you get the basics down I will show you some other moves."

302

Dagon looked intensely into Rachel's eyes and asked. "Why are you always so quiet around me?"

Her eyes widened and she blushed. "I don't know," she said in a whisper. Dagon kept staring at her as if he was waiting for more of an answer. "Alright, you make me nervous," Rachel said defensively.

"Is that because you are promised to another and you are afraid he will get jealous?"

"I am not promised to anyone."

"Good," Dagon said with a grin.

"What do you mean?"

"I would like to get to know you better."

Rachel was silent for a few moments. "Dagon, I am not trying to hurt you or to make you angry but all I can think about is finding my father and protecting Mother and Zack. I don't think...oh I don't know what I am trying to say. But I can't seem to concentrate on anything else."

"Rachel, I know I would be crazy if my father was being held a captive. But you don't have to do all of this alone. I will help you as will others here."

Rachel looked at Dagon suspiciously. "Why would you do such a thing?"

Dagon got a sly smile, "Maybe you should get to know me better and find out. You are looking at me like you don't trust me."

"No one can trust in Ryed. We survive by not trusting."

"That is a very sad thing to say. I hope you learn to trust me and the others here."

"Dagon, this is how I grew up; I don't know if I can."

Chapter XXIV
Back at Home

Just as Hannah brought the last platter of pancakes to the breakfast table a small flock of Enrops scratched at the kitchen window. Hannah had been leaving all of the windows closed since baby Lily was routinely flying around the house.

"I am sorry I have to close the windows," Hannah said to the Enrops as she let them into the kitchen. "We have a Ruala baby who is flying around and we are afraid she will fly out of the house. Is there a type of latch I can put on the windows so you will be able to open them?"

"A pull latch with string on the end will allow us to enter," one of the birds said as others dropped envelopes onto the kitchen table.

"We have carpenters here now," Hannah said. "If I get one will you tell them what you need?"

"Certainly," the Enrop replied.

When the children heard Hannah talking in the kitchen they all ran in to pet the Enrops. Vivian walked into the kitchen to get the envelopes and to talk to the birds that she dearly loved. "I am getting one of the carpenters to put latches on the windows that the Enrops can open," Hannah said to Vivian and walked out of the kitchen.

"Good idea," Vivian said to Hannah then turned to the birds. "Have you seen Raphael?"

"No, we are bringing letters from Ryed," a bird replied as the children were feeding the birds cookies. A few moments later Hannah returned to the kitchen with two carpenters, who were more than amazed that the Enrops could explain the type of latch that needed to be installed on the windows.

Vivian returned to the breakfast table and handed out the envelopes. "These are from Ryed," she said with some sadness in her voice.

"Honey I am sure you will receive a letter from Raphael later today," Iris said. "He writes to you daily."

"I know; I just miss him so much," Vivian said and hugged her mother. "Look there are letters here for the children," Vivian said as she tried to sound cheerful.

"For us," Adrone repeated.

"Well, it looks like all of you got letters," Vivian said as she handed each child three envelopes.

"Children bring them here and Maxwell and I will help you read them," Emeral said as Christopher, Joey, Adrone, Paul, Nicholas, Cerey and Cecily quickly gathered around their adopted grandparents.

"Who are all of the letters from?" Hannah asked as she filled the coffee cups.

"So far it sounds like, Gabriel, Joshua and Micha, Natasha, Diana and Thor," Ella said as everyone listened to Emeral and Maxwell taking turns reading the letters out loud.

"Mama, Diana and Natasha drew us pictures of the castle," Nicholas said to Hannah who walked across the room and looked at the pictures.

"They did get married," Iris said as tears came to her eyes. She was reading a letter from Joshua. "And Bianca loved her ring."

"Mother why are you crying?" Paul asked and hugged Iris.

"Because I am happy."

Christopher got a curious look on his face as he stared at Iris then at Luca who was sitting next to her. "Luca why would she cry when she is happy?" Christopher asked loudly. "I thought we were supposed to smile."

"People have different types of emotions when they are happy," Luca replied with a grin. Christopher was going to ask another question when Bekka and Koby walked into the dining room carrying Ian and Emma.

"I am sorry we are late but both babies got hungry at the same time," Bekka said as she walked up to Luca and handed him his baby daughter. Christopher walked up to Luca and kissed Emma on the forehead.

"I think that is what Lila looked like when she was a baby," Christopher said and ran back to Emeral. Luca smiled and stared at Emma because he too thought she looked more like Lila with every passing day.

"Listen to this," Hannah said as she was reading a letter. "Gabriel thanked us for sending the instruments. He said that Teivel had banned music centuries ago as a means of controlling his people and some of the people at the castle got very emotional when they heard the music played. Have you ever heard of such a thing?"

"Unfortunately yes," Maxwell said. "That is the difference between dictators and kings. A good king leads and protects his people. A tyrant has to cripple and control his people to get them to submit to his will."

"If they can free the people of Ryed, I believe it will take them a long time to heal," Emeral said.

After much debate it was decided that Gabriel, Dominic, Natasha and Rachel would go into the City of Teivel to survey the area around the arena and to purchase a building. Gabriel and Dominic were playing the roles of brothers who owned gold mines in Nora. Rachel was pretending to be Gabriel's wife while Natasha pretended to be Dominic's wife.

Everyone at the castle was impressed with Dominic's transformation after Natasha put a black wig and a black goatee on him. And Rachel was transformed to a woman of means. Both Dominic and Rachel argued that anyone traveling inside of Ryed who had money hired body guards. Stephan, Thaos, Michael and Jared volunteered to act as the body guards. While Archetenus remained at the castle and led the training.

Gabriel's small group was flown to the City of Teivel by twenty Ruala warriors who were led by Lakin. Calen, Dagon, Joao and Dack were included in this group.

Teivel was the capital city of Ryed. It was large and greatly spread out. No one would notice that Gabriel and his small group suddenly appeared without a carriage.

While many of the men involved with this mission admired Rachel's beauty; she could only focus on finding her father and freeing him. Rachel did not trust easily but like Dominic and his handful of men they were now making friends with people who lived as free men and women. The freedom fighters of Ryed were experiencing many things with new eyes and for the very first time hope was igniting within them.

"I miss papa," Amy suddenly announced as the family of Claudius sat around the breakfast table.

"We all do Honey," Nikki said and leaned over and kissed Amy on top of her head.

Claudius looked at the sad faces of Ingr, Nikki and Bella because they all missed Stephan and Thaos. Ryan too looked at all of the women then at Claudius. "Ryan has been working on a surprise and although it isn't finished perhaps now would be a good time to show you," Claudius said and winked at Ryan.

"Where do you want me to put it?" Ryan said as he started to leave the table.

"In the parlor and have a couple of the men help you with it," Claudius said. As soon as Ryan left the room Claudius turned to Bella. "I am going to give you extra money today and I want you to take the girls and Ryan into the city. First it is time to find Ryan a store so he can sell his furniture and I am sure you will have to fix it up. Then I want all of you to have gowns made because we will be having a big celebration when everyone returns from Ryed. And leave the babies with the nurses so you can enjoy yourselves."

"That's a wonderful idea," Bella said with enthusiasm. "Does Ryan know?"

"No, I thought you could tell him," Claudius said then looked at Amy.

"Amy after Stephan and Thaos return we will be going to Salar for the wedding of Diana and Misha; so maybe you should look for some gifts for Christopher and the other children in Gabriel's house."

"Really," Amy said with a big smile that showed her dimples.

Ryan walked into the dining room and looked at Claudius. "Let's all go into the parlor now," Claudius said with a smile.

"Oh my god!" Ingr said with she saw the giant doll house. "Amy look at this."

"Why, Ryan this is wonderful," Bella said.

"Claudius asked me to make it," Ryan said. "I still need to paint it but now that it's not a surprise you can pick the colors.

Amy had been standing in front of the doll house and staring at it in awe. "Amy what do you say to Uncle Ryan," Nikki said with a big smile.

"Thank you Uncle Ryan," Amy said and ran to Ryan and hugged him.

"You will have to thank Grandpa too," Ryan said. "It's really a gift from him."

Amy ran to Claudius, who picked her up and the two hugged each other tightly. "Thank you Grandpa I love it."

"I'm making furniture but the paint isn't dry on anything yet," Ryan said then he turned to Claudius. "Do you think I should make one for Margarit too?"

"I very much like that idea," Claudius said proudly.

As Amy and the women all examined the doll house, Ryan looked at Claudius. "I have something to ask you but you might think, I don't know you might not like the idea." Ryan said hesitantly. Now Bella, Ingr and Nikki turned and looked at Ryan.

"I really didn't know Chaez very well before Tabeth was killed," Ryan said. "Now we write to each other often and have become good friends."

"Chaez is working real hard to become a Patronus priest because he wants to do good to make up for all the bad that Timothy did. And I have been thinking about that. I am not a fighter and the only thing I can do really well is to make things with wood." No one spoke as they listened to Ryan.

"When we were in Wetpr; so many of the children in Gabriel's house are adopted and they told me a little about the orphanage. Well, I was thinking that I could make a lot of toys and when we go to Wetpr we could take them to the orphanage. But that would mean we would have to pack them in a boca."

Nikki and Ingr both walked up to Ryan and kissed him on the cheek which made Ryan blush. "Why, Ryan I think that is an absolutely wonderful idea," Bella said and she too kissed Ryan on the cheek. "Claudius what do you think?" Bella asked.

"Ryan you make me proud," Claudius said. "And transporting the toys is no problem at all. I think now is a good time for Bella to tell you about a surprise we have for you."

"Ryan, I am taking you and the girls shopping today and one of the things we will be looking for is a building where you can sell your furniture."

"Really? Oh thank you that is the most wonderful thing," Ryan said and hugged Bella then to Claudius' surprise, Ryan hugged him too.

Gabriel, Dominic, Rachel, Natasha, Thaos, Stephan, Jared and Michael entered the City of Teivel just before dusk. Thanks to the drawings of Dagon's team, Gabriel knew where the hotels were located. While Ruala warriors watched Gabriel's small group from the rooftops of buildings, Gabriel registered for rooms in the most exclusive hotel in the city.

The Teivel Manor rivaled the Endleson Hotel in Nora with its extravagance. The chambers on the ground floor had stone patios while all of the rest of the chambers had balconies. Gabriel wanted to make his presence known so he rented the entire floor on the top of the hotel. Gabriel told the hotel manager that he wanted to maintain security for his group and the manager did not question Gabriel's request.

There were twenty rooms on the top floor with balconies that faced both the front and the rear of the building. As soon as Gabriel's group checked the rooms for intruders they opened the balcony doors that faced the rear of the building and their Ruala comrades entered.

It was decided that one of the body guards should be stationed at the top of the stairs that led to the top floor at all times. Thaos, Jared, Stephan and Michael worked out their own schedule. There was only one staircase that led to this floor. Although the Ruala warriors couldn't be seen by the public they volunteered to sit with the body guards.

Lakin and his warriors knew they could not yet be seen in the city so they brought their own provisions. Shortly after everyone was settled into their rooms, Gabriel's group walked down to the dining room for dinner. Gabriel wanted it known that wealthy investors were in the city. When they entered the main dining room, Gabriel requested that his group be seated in one of the smaller private dining rooms and he requested that the hotel manager join them.

The manager's name was Clay and he was honored to be requested as a guest. Gabriel realized that Rachel, Dominic and Michael had ever been in such an extravagant hotel, so Gabriel ordered the most expensive dishes and drinks for his group.

"Clay this is the first trip that Stone and I have made to Ryed," Gabriel explained. "After we read about the Gefrey Games that are to be held here; we wanted to see the city for ourselves. I am sure you are a shrewd businessman; tell me about the investment opportunities in this city."

This is a growing city and we are hopeful the Gefrey Games will greatly increase our business since they are now opened to other kingdoms. I would say, some businesses are ripe for the picking. What in particular are you looking for?"

"My brother and I have diverse interests. We have made our fortune from mining and am interested in the local prospects. But we also deal in weapons which is why the Gefrey Games peeked our interest."

"I would say you could do very well in both of those areas here," Clay said as he sipped his whiskey.

"That is exactly what we wanted to hear," Gabriel said. "Tomorrow we want to explore the city, especially the area surrounding the arena. I believe we could greatly profit by selling weapons near the arena. Do you know of any vacant buildings in that area?"

"While your men look more than capable of protecting you that area is very dangerous. You really shouldn't be walking those streets. I insist that you use my personal carriage it is large enough for your group and it has security features if you need them. Just tell me what time you want it ready?"

"That is very generous of you, I thank you," Gabriel said.

"Tell me were you planning on taking your beautiful wives with you?" Clay asked. "I am only asking because I want to emphasis that is a very dangerous area and your wives will be noticed."

"Thank you for that information," Gabriel said. "If we should find a suitable building, might I impose upon you to assist us with locating the owners?"

"Of course, I have lived in Teivel my entire life and I am not exaggerating when I say I know most of the land owners here," Clay said. Clay was a shrewd businessman and realized helping Gabriel could be profitable for him. "Please let me know of any way that I can be of assistance to you. Your food is being served I will leave you to enjoy your meal. Please tell me if anything in not to your liking." Clay left the small dining room.

"You know if you weren't a priest you would make a good con-artist," Stephan said to Gabriel in a low voice and everyone broke into laughter.

"You aren't leaving us behind," Natasha said as she sweetly smiled at her brother.

"Of course not," Gabriel said. "But we have learned a great deal tonight."

Even with a greatly altered appearance it was too dangerous for Dominic to use his real name in the City of Teivel. Natasha had forged paperwork for the entire group and she gave Dominic the alias of Stone.

Since Gabriel was the expert at this type of mission it was planned that he would do most of the talking and negotiating, at least in the beginning of the mission.

Rachel felt very much out of her element in both the role she was playing and the manner in which she was dressed. But she did have fun with Natasha as Natasha showed her many ways of concealing weapons. Rachel said little during dinner this first night in Teivel. It was obvious to all that she felt uncomfortable.

As Gabriel's group left the dining room, Gabriel asked Clay to have whiskey, wine, and a variety of trays of food delivered to the top floor. "Of course it will be our pleasure," Clay said. "And I got you a map of the city. We have copies available to our guests if you need more."

"Thank you, this will be very helpful," Gabriel said and the group returned to the top floor of the hotel. Both Jared and Michael sat at the top of the stairs and waited for the refreshments to be delivered. The food and drink was to be delivered to Gabriel's room only. The Rualas were to stay out of sight of the hotel staff.

"I already have our chambers prepared," Calen said when Natasha returned from dinner.

"Is there another bedroom in the one you chose?" Natasha asked.

"Yes," Calen replied. "Why?"

"Rachel you certainly can have your own room but you are welcomed to stay with us," Natasha said.

"Thank you; I believe I will," said Rachel. "This is just all so very new to me. I don't even know what some of the clothes are that you packed for me."

"Wow, I am sharing chambers with two beautiful women," Calen joked. Natasha rolled her eyes and playfully punched her husband.

"Dominic and Lakin, unless you have other preferences I thought we could take the master suite; it has four beds and we would be together to work," Gabriel said.

As Gabriel was talking some of the Rualas started to laugh and to hand money to Joao. "What's going on?" Natasha asked.

"While you were at dinner we pretty much divided up the rooms," Dagon said. "We had bets that Natasha would ask Rachel to join them and that Gabriel would ask Lakin and Dominic to join him."

"I can't believe you bet on that," Natasha said and laughed.

"We'll bet on anything," Dack said. "But Joao always seems to win."

"What else did you bet on?" Natasha asked with a grin.

"I don't think we should tell you," said Joao. "It could be dangerous for us."

"Oh, now I have to know," Natasha said.

"We bet on whether Rachel would want her own room or share a chambers with one of us. Then we bet on who she would share a chambers with," Dack said then he looked at Rachel who was blushing deeply. "Don't worry it is just all in fun."

"Rachel, you are going to have to get use to them," Natasha said. "Think of it as having a bunch of brothers. What you should do is learn to give it right back to them. They talk big but if you did choose to share a chambers with one of them, I'll bet they would be embarrassed." Both Dack and Joao laughed loudly.

"I don't think all of us would be embarrassed," Dagon said and winked at Rachel which made her blush a darker shade of red.

Rachel hesitated then said, "The three of you are very handsome and so nice. I am not a shy person and I don't know why I act like that around you but I have to be honest. Ever since my father was kidnapped all I can think about is finding him and getting him home; I don't mean to hurt anyone's feelings."

"We can understand that," Joao said. "We don't mean to make you feel bad."

"Rachel when all of this is over; is there any reason you and your family can't come back to Wetpr with us?" Dagon asked. "We can help you find a home. It is a much safer place to live."

All of Gabriel's group was in the hallway listening to the conversation between Rachel, Dack, Dagon and Joao. "You are always welcome to move to Lentz too and Dominic that goes for you and your men," Stephan said loudly. "Even if we overthrow Teivel this may be a war zone for a long time. Don't you think you have all suffered enough?"

Natasha knocked on the door to Rachel's bedroom. "Are you done putting your things away?" Natasha called through the door.

"Natasha you can come in; I just closed the door because I changed my clothes."

"Are you dressed because I have Dagon with me?"

Rachel opened the door and moved to the side so Natasha and Dagon could enter. "Rachel I need you to be honest with me and tell me if you are too tired for this tonight," Natasha said. "But I was just talking with Gabriel and you and I are going to have to be a distraction; probably more than once. I know that Dagon was teaching you how to dance but you have to improve at it since you are pretending to be a woman of means. I asked him here to give you a few more lessons. Are you up for it?"

"Sure, do I need to change my clothes?"

"Pull up your skirt a little so I can see your shoes," Natasha said. "Why don't you put on some of the really fancy shoes I bought for you because that is what you will be dancing in."

"I'll start moving some of the furniture in the parlor," Dagon said and left the room.

Natasha closed the door behind Dagon, "Rachel if you don't like Dagon I will find someone else."

"No, I like him; why did you ask that?"

314

"Because you act so differently around him," Natasha said with a grin. "I figured you either didn't like him or you are attracted to him."

Rachel blushed and didn't speak for a moment. "Natasha, I think Dagon is very handsome and really nice. But if we find Father alive, he may be seriously injured. I am the head of my family now; I can't think of, you know what I am trying to say."

Natasha put both of her hands on Rachel's shoulders. "Rachel you don't have to do this alone. Come back to Wetpr with us. We will help you start a new life and you will love that kingdom. And of course I am a little prejudice on the matter but Dagon is a really good man; think twice before you send him away."

"We are sorry to interrupt your breakfast," Emeral said as she and Hannah entered the dining room of the Royal Family of Wetpr. "But we wanted to talk to all of you together."

"You are always welcome here," Renya said. "Please join us."

"We've already eaten but we wanted to invite all of you to our home tomorrow for a picnic. We have all kinds of surprises for the children," Hannah said enthusiastically.

Emeral started talking before anyone could reply to Hannah's invitation. "Sam hasn't sat down since he and Ella got here. He and Koby extended the patio off from the kitchen and built outdoor tables for both adults and the children. Then they built a huge sandbox and swings and now they are working on something that the children can climb on."

"And, I am so excited about this," Hannah said. "Yesterday Vivian and Elan went shopping for a pony for the children and came home with six. They are buying the saddles today so we can have pony rides."

"Ponies!" Petra said. "Can we go?"

"Why I think that sounds like a wonderful idea," said Renya.

"And the nursery is finished so we have extra beds for your visiting babies," Emeral said as she looked at Delilah and Zoya.

"What time and what do you want us to bring?" Renya asked.

"We will have the picnic for the midday meal but please come over earlier so the children can play," Emeral said. "And you don't have to bring anything. We are fixing plenty of food and after the meal we will have cake and ice cream."

"Is Sam at the house now?" asked Alexander.

"Yes," Hannah replied. "Apparently he can envision a series of outdoor toys he wants to make for the children."

"I think I will go over and help him right after breakfast," Alexander said. "This will be fun."

"Can I bring Kyra and my pups?" Petra asked.

"Certainly," said Emeral.

"I am surprised he mentioned Kyra before the dogs," Annabelle said kiddingly.

"I love this idea and with all of our husbands gone maybe we should get together for things like this more often, so the children can play," Vitomas said. "We can host the next one."

Chapter XXV
Infiltrating

Immediately after breakfast the next morning, Clay the hotel manager had a luxurious carriage brought to the front of the hotel for Gabriel and his group. This specially designed carriage had seats on the outside for body guards. Jared road in front with the driver and Thaos rode on the rear exterior seat. Stephan and Michael rode inside with Gabriel, Dominic, Rachel and Natasha. Gabriel didn't want the Ruala warriors exposed so Enrops followed the carriage.

"I'm guessing we're near the arena," Jared said loud enough for his team to hear, as the driver maneuvered the carriage around a dead body in the street.

"Trust me," the driver said to Jared. "Don't ever get off your horse or carriage to check on the bodies cuz a lot of times its traps."

"You lived in the city long?" asked Jared.

"Most of my life," the driver said.

"My boss is looking for a large building to purchase near the arena. He sells weapons so back doors or tunnels are an added bonus. Now if you were to help him I'll bet he would pay you real good."

"Is that a sure thing?" the driver asked.

"As sure as I am missing an ear," Jared said and laughed.

"I know just the spot. It used to be used for selling slaves so it's big and got secret tunnels."

"Slaves! What kind of slaves are you talking about?"

"What do you think happens to the people who get taken from the villages?" the driver asked in a hushed voice.

"You mean to tell me that Teivel kidnaps his own people then turns around and sells them as slaves?"

"I can tell this is your first time in Ryed," the driver said. "I'm ok but be careful who you say things like that to or you'll end up on the block yourself."

As the driver spoke he turned the carriage off from a main road and drove down back alleys. Thaos had been listening to the conversation between Jared and the driver and was suspicious as to where the driver was taking them. About ten minutes later the driver stops the carriage in front of a large building. The sign on the building said auction house.

"Let me tell the boss what is going on," Jared said as he started to climb down from the carriage. "What's your name?" Jared yelled up to the driver.

"Tobey."

Jared opened the door to the carriage and said loud enough for the driver to hear, "Boss I told Tobey here that if he could find a place with everything you were looking for you would pay him. I'll tell you about this building when we get inside."

Everyone including the driver entered the building. "I'm surprised it's unlocked," Natasha said as several of the men started to light the torches on the walls.

"People think this place is cursed," Tobey said. "They don't want to come near here."

"Why is that?" asked Gabriel.

"Cuz they used to auction the people off that they stole from the villages here," the driver said. "There's tunnels underneath this building and one goes to the arena."

"How do you know about the tunnels?" Stephan asked.

"I've been a driver most of my life. People talk in front of me like they don't think I can hear and sometimes they want me to come in some place and wait for them."

"Tobey you said there were tunnels," Gabriel said. "How many?"

"That I don't know but you see they wouldn't walk the prisoners down the streets so they bring them in here from the dungeons I'm a guessing and the ones that don't sell get put in the arena."

Gabriel grabbed Rachel's hand and held it tightly so she wouldn't speak as they listened to the driver."

"Why is it empty now?" Dominic asked as he was trying to maintain a casual demeanor.

Tobey walked closer to Gabriel and Dominic. "I know you folks ain't from around here but you have got to be careful cuz the walls have ears." Then Tobey said in a loud whisper, "Teivel is cleaning things up for the big Gefrey Games cuz he wants to impress people. But don't you dare say I told you that."

As Gabriel and Dominic spoke with Tobey, Jared, Thaos, Stephan and Michael searched the building. "We found some cells back here and there's a door to a tunnel but don't know where it goes," Michael called out.

"Tobey you have done well and when we return to the hotel I will pay you handsomely for your service," Gabriel said. "By any chance do you know who owns this building?"

"Don't think anyone does but I can take you to the Land and Title place and you can find out for sure."

"We found a door to a second tunnel and the back door leads to an alley," Thaos said. "Jared and Stephan are upstairs looking round still."

"Don't take this the wrong way," Tobey said. "You folks seem awfully nice maybe too nice for these parts. You dress like you have money and your wives are real pretty. People are probably already watching you. Be careful."

"Why Tobey we haven't seen anyone who looks like a criminal yet," Natasha said sweetly.

"This is Ryed My Lady, some of the worse criminals dress like you do or are in the military. I'm trying to help you but if you tell anyone what I have been saying I could end up dead."

319

"Tobey we understand the seriousness of the situation," Gabriel said. "And we very much appreciate your help. Tell me do you have a family?"

"Yeah, why?" Tobey asked suspiciously.

"My brother and I have significant holdings in Nora. It is a much safer place to raise a family. If you would like we could help you," Gabriel said.

"Why would you do that?" asked Tobey.

"You seem like a good man and you have helped us more than you realize."

"I'll have to talk it over with the misses," Tobey said warily.

"We will be staying at the Teivel Manor. If you decide to take me up on the offer just come and see us."

Gabriel and his group returned to their hotel late in the afternoon. Gabriel held a meeting in his chambers to brief everyone about the building he had just purchased. Dagon walked up to Rachel when he saw that she was standing by herself near the front door of Gabriel's chambers.

"Are you alright?" Dagon asked as he saw tears in Rachel's eyes. She did not answer but shook her head from side to side to indicate 'no'. Dagon took Rachel's hand and walked out of Gabriel's chambers and into the chambers she shared with Calen and Natasha.

"We can go in my room," Rachel said and pointed towards a closed door. The two entered her room and sat down on the bed. Rachel immediately started crying.

"Do you want to talk about it?" Dagon asked as he put his arm around her shoulders.

It took several moments for Rachel to compose herself before she could speak. "The building Gabriel bought is an auction house where Teivel sells the people they kidnap from the villages. We were told that the people who aren't sold are forced into the arena. I may never find my father."

"You're not in this alone, we all will help you. So tell me about your father what does he look like?"

"His name is Horace, he's a big man almost as big as you both tall and muscular. He has black hair and brown eyes like the rest of our family."

"If he was a member of the Libertas I assume he is a fighter. You know he will hang on until he is freed."

"You don't understand what it is like here. In a fair fight my father could win but nothing is fair in Ryed. It is a kingdom of monsters."

There was a knock on the door. "Rachel are you alright?" Natasha called out.

"You can come in," said Dagon.

It was obvious to Natasha that Rachel had been crying. "Rachel we need to get dressed and go down stairs but first I want to tell you something," Natasha said as she sat down on the bed next to Rachel. "I can only imagine how difficult this is for you. But you are a fighter and you have to know that we are the only hope not only to save your father but many others. I know you aren't comfortable playing roles but the better we are at this the greater our chances of saving your people. Do you think you can focus and do this?"

"Yes," Rachel said as she wiped the tears from her cheeks. "But I need a few moments."

"Tonight Gabriel is going to introduce us to a lot of people and we need to act as distractions. I taught you how to flirt that is what tonight is going to be about. We are going to be talking with people and dancing and making sure they pay more attention to us then to the men. You are going to have to do this, it is important."

"I will Natasha."

Natasha stood up and walked over to the closet. She sorted through the different outfits that she had brought for Rachel. "Wear this and when you are ready come to my room and I will get you jewelry."

"Are you sure you can do this?" Dagon asked after Natasha left the room.

"I just have to remember how much I hate Teivel and I will be alright."

"Do you want me to help you with the buttons on the back of your dress?"

"Yes please," Rachel said and stood up with her back to Dagon.

Dagon unbuttoned Rachel's dress. "I can turn my back or leave the room."

"You're probably going to have to help me with the next dress. I have never worn clothes like this before; so you can just turn your back."

"You can turn around now," Rachel said as she stood with her back to Dagon a few moments later.

"Ok let's see what you look like," Dagon said after he finished buttoning her dress. When Rachel turned around, Dagon's eyes grew wide when he saw her in the form fitting black silk dress which exposed a great deal of her breasts. "Do you have a shawl to wear?"

"I don't know," Rachel said. "Why is something wrong?" Dagon did not answer her as he looked through her closet and brought her a shawl. "Dagon is something wrong? You are acting so strangely."

"You look beautiful and," he hesitated. "And you look very sexy in that dress." Dagon took Rachel's hand and led her into Natasha's room.

"Natasha are you sure this is what you want Rachel to wear?" asked Dagon.

"He thinks I look too sexy in it," Rachel said as she blushed.

"That is the very idea," Natasha said and laughed as she took the shawl off from Rachel's shoulders. "Rachel you look beautiful. Now let me find you some jewelry."

322

"And Dagon since you are so interested in what she wears why don't you pick out the perfume," Natasha said and nodded towards a dozen small bottles setting on one of the tables."

"I think he likes you," Natasha whispered to Rachel, who blushed and glanced at Dagon.

"You do know that I heard you," Dagon said and chuckled.

"Well am I wrong?"

Dagon turned around and looked at Rachel as he walked towards her with a bottle of perfume. "No," Dagon said and he watched Rachel blush. "What do you think about this?" Dagon asked as he held the open bottle for Rachel to smell.

"It's really nice," Rachel said shyly.

"Rachel can I visit you after all of you return? Perhaps we could have another dance up here," Dagon asked as he boldly stared at her.

Rachel smiled and nodded, "I would like that." Natasha looked back and forth between Rachel and Dagon and grinned.

"Dagon could you help me finish buttoning the back of my dress?" Natasha asked and turned her back to him.

"You look beautiful too," he said and kissed Natasha on top of her head as he was buttoning her gown, which was also black and form fitting."

"I don't think the two of you will have to flirt; the men won't be able to keep their eyes off from you," Dagon said and held out his arms for each woman to take.

"Wow!" Dack said loudly when Natasha, Dagon and Rachel walked into the hallway.

"You both look beautiful," Gabriel said and held his arm out for Rachel. "It is show time."

Dagon kissed Rachel on top of her head and said, "I will see you later."

Rachel smiled at Dagon even though she did not understand the significance of his action. But the other men now understood that there was something happening between Rachel and Dagon.

"I'm nervous," Rachel said as she walked down the stairs towards the dining room with Gabriel, Natasha, Dominic, Thaos, Stephan, Jared and Michael.

"Just remember why we are doing this," Natasha said.

"You will be just fine," said Gabriel.

Natasha now turned to Rachel, who was walking behind her. If anything happens and you want one of us to come to you, pretend that you lost your earring. I will do the same."

"Why would I need to do that?"

"You might not but we always have a plan," Natasha said.

"No I mean under what circumstances would I do that?"

"You realized the person you are talking with just caught you as an imposter or in a lie," Natasha replied.

"Or if someone gets fresh with you," said Thaos.

"Couldn't I just hit him?"

"We don't want anyone to know you two are warriors," Gabriel said. "If something like that happens drop your earring and one of us will come to your aid."

After Gabriel and his small group left the top floor of the hotel, Calen, Joao and Dack all walked up to Dagon and grinned. "So what is going on between you and Rachel?" Dack asked.

"I'm not telling my competition," Dagon joked.

"Well he is still calling us competition," Joao said. "That's good."

"We're going to have a dance up here when they are done downstairs," Dagon said.

"Actually that might have to wait," Lakin said. "You left the meeting early but we are going to explore those tunnels as soon as it gets dark."

Clay, the hotel manager approached Gabriel's group as they stepped onto the first floor of the hotel. "I must say you made an impression with your driver, he asked to work for just your party while you are here."

"He helped us find a suitable building; I just paid him for his services," Gabriel said.

"I took the liberty of asking some of the prominent businessmen in the city to a little gathering. I closed one of the dining rooms to walk-in guests."

"Thank you," Gabriel said. "I never expected people to be so accommodating."

Clay led Gabriel's group to a dining room which held around fifty guests, most of whom appeared to be couples. After Clay had introduced Gabriel's group to the other guests Gabriel turned to Rachel. "Dear why don't you and Natasha mingle; I am sure listening to us talk business will just bore you."

"You are right," Natasha said to Gabriel then smiled at Clay. "Will there be dancing? Rachel and I love to dance."

"The musicians should be arriving soon," Clay said and kissed the hands of both Natasha and Rachel then walked away.

"Go up to those two generals first," Gabriel said in a low voice to Natasha. Then Gabriel and Dominic walked up to a group of businessmen.

Thaos, Stephan, Michael and Jared were still playing their roles as body guards but they were dressed in suits to blend in with the guests. While the men mingled, Thaos and Stephan watched over Gabriel and Dominic and Michael and Jared watched over Natasha and Rachel.

Rachel let Natasha take the lead with introducing themselves to the guests. Rachel was impressed at what a great actress Natasha was. As Rachel started to feel more comfortable in her role she became more outgoing.

Earlier in the day, Michael unlocked all of the rear doors of the building that Gabriel bought. There was a door on the first level that led to an alley and three doors on the second floor. These doors appeared to once have opened to balconies in a time when the building was used for less heinous purposes.

When Gabriel paid for the building he received several keys, which Lakin now had in his possession. Since the Rualas did not know what to expect in the tunnels they brought extra torches, rope, chalk to mark the walls and paper and pen to draw maps.

Lakin divided his warriors into five groups initially. One group was to stay on the roof and watch for intruders. The other four groups entered by each of the four rear doors and systematically searched the building before they went into the tunnels. While nothing of interest was found inside of the building all of the warriors saw the blood stains that covered the wooden floors. After the building was searched the warriors divided into two groups and searched the tunnels.

The tunnels were large enough for the warriors to walk in without bending. Large boulders made up the walls of the tunnels. The floors were made of dirt and the ceilings made of wood with wooden support beams. Every five feet there was a metal torch holder anchored into the stone walls. The Ruala warriors lit these torches with the ones they carried. As the tunnels were illuminated, the horror of their purpose was exposed by the blood stains that seemed to cover everything.

Lakin led the team that searched the tunnel which ran to the arena. The arena was across the road from this building. The tunnel was deep into the earth which prevented the Rualas from hearing anything above them. This team walked for almost twenty minutes before they came to a large iron door. None of the keys that Lakin had would fit into the lock of this door. He and his men tried a variety of ways to open the door without success so they turned around and returned to the building.

Dagon led the second team. While the tunnels were identical in appearance this tunnel was significantly longer than the one that ran to the arena. This team walked in an easterly direction for almost forty minutes before they came upon a large iron door which they could not open.

"Voices," one of the Rualas whispered and the group became quiet. The voices of two men were heard on the opposite side of the door although the Rualas could not hear what the men were saying. Dagon and his team stayed by the door for a short while but heard no other voices so they turned around and walked back to the building.

Natasha and Rachel caught the attention of many men at the private gathering. Within the first hour of the party both women had a line of men waiting to dance with them. Six Ruala warriors had stayed at the hotel incase Gabriel and his group needed help. Among these warriors were Calen, Dack and Joao who were sneaking around the outside of the hotel looking in the windows of the gathering. Jared saw them and walked out of the gathering through a patio door.

"Is something wrong?" asked Jared.

"The cleaning women are in our rooms, so we grabbed everything that was important or valuable and left. I don't think they saw any of us," Calen said. "But maybe one of you can go upstairs and just stand around. I don't trust anyone here."

"I feel the same way," Jared said. "I'll grab one of the guys and go upstairs." As Jared was turning towards the door he saw the look on Calen's face as he watched Natasha dancing with an older man. "Now Calen don't get jealous the girls aren't doing anything wrong."

"I know but how would you like it if Zoya was flirting with other guys."

"But this is just pretend," Joao said. "You know she loves you."

"I was never a jealous guy until I fell in love. I know you think I am crazy but just wait your turns will come and you will see it isn't that easy."

"What isn't easy?" Dack asked.

"To be married to someone on the team," Calen replied.

"The only thing I am jealous of is those guys getting to dance with Rachel," Joao said with a mischievous grin.

Another two hours passed before Gabriel and Dominic returned to the gathering. Both men mingled with a few people then walked up to Natasha and Rachel. "I believe we can call it a night," Gabriel whispered to Natasha then to Rachel. The two couples joined up with Michael, Jared, Stephan and Thaos and they all walked up the several flights of stairs to the top floor.

Once they got to the top floor, Thaos started laughing. "Natasha I hope you can remember who all this stuff belongs to."

"What are you talking about?" asked Dominic.

"She was picking everyone's pockets then would drop her loot in my coat pockets.

"Natasha wasn't the only one," Michael said. "Rachel handed me a few things."

"I just taught her so not bad for her first night," Natasha said.

"But I almost got caught with that old general," Rachel said. "I was about ready to pretend I lost my earring."

As the others were laughing at Rachel's comment, Gabriel looked at Calen who was walking towards them. "Is Lakin back?" Gabriel asked.

"No, none of them. We really thought they would be back by now," Calen said. "Did you get what you wanted?"

"We made some good connections tonight. One of the men is going to get us and audience with Teivel."

"Why?" Rachel asked in shock.

"We told everyone that we are major dealers of weapons and explosives. And that we have some new weapons that are worth seeing. That was the bait. I want to meet Teivel so I can study him. A man like that you have to understand if you want to take him down."

As the group talked they walked into Gabriel's chambers. Thaos and Michael were taking the items from their pockets and putting them on a table, while Calen told Gabriel about the cleaning women.

"Stephan and me came up here and watched them," Jared said. "But they were up here alone for a little while."

"I find it suspicious that they were cleaning in the evening," Gabriel said. "I will speak with Clay tomorrow and arrange a specific time for them to come up here."

"This is interesting," Stephan said as he was sorting through the various items that Natasha and Rachel had stolen. "Do either of you remember who you got this from?"

"That is what I took off that old general, who almost caught me," Rachel said. "What is it?"

"A letter with Teivel's seal," Stephan explained. "It is telling the general how many people they should kidnap for the games. They want another three hundred."

"Do you think they are really going to put all of those people in the arena?" Natasha asked. "I am beginning to wonder if they are getting people to ..." Natasha stopped talking and glanced at Rachel.

"To what?" Rachel asked fearfully.

Natasha looked uneasily at Gabriel. "To sacrifice to demons. It is a common practice among the Insidiae," Gabriel said. Rachel did not speak but tears filled her eyes.

After a few moments Rachel said, "I would like to go to my room unless you need me here."

"No," Gabriel said. "Since Lakin and the others aren't back I will hold the meeting in the morning."

329

"I was going to ask her for a dance," Joao whispered to Dack. "But she looks too upset now."

Rachel had been in bed for almost an hour when there was a knock at her bedroom door. Rachel was tying her robe together when she opened the door and saw Dagon.

"I know it's late," Dagon said. "I just didn't want you to think I lied to you. We were on a mission. I'll see you in the morning."

"Dagon I wasn't sleeping and I would really like to know what you found. Do you want to come in?"

"It might be better if we sat in the parlor," he said and took Rachel's hand. No sooner had Dagon and Rachel sat down on a sofa when Calen opened his bedroom door.

"Dagon is everyone back now?" Calen asked.

"Yes, I was just going to tell Rachel about it; if you want to hear."

Calen closed his bedroom door and a few moments later he and Natasha joined Dagon and Rachel in the parlor. "There are two tunnels, the one to the west goes to the arena. My team searched the tunnel that leads to the east. Both tunnels are big enough for a man to walk in. The floors are dirt, the walls are stone and the ceilings are wood. There were blood stains everywhere, including in the building."

"It took about twenty minutes for Lakin's group to reach a locked iron door. They couldn't get it open and returned to the building. My team walked for about forty minutes before our way was blocked by a similar door. But we heard voices on the other side of that door. There was no writing or drawings in either of the tunnels. After our teams joined up we flew east of Gabriel's building trying to figure out which building that tunnel stopped at. We think we found it. There is a huge building with a sign that says 'Military of Ryed.' But it doesn't look anything like a fort."

"So you think that is where some of the captives are being held?" Rachel asked.

"Yes," Dagon replied. "Lakin is telling Gabriel about it now."

"We had a couple of old generals hanging all over us," Natasha said. "They asked us out for lunch but we declined. Perhaps Rachel and I should meet them and ask for a tour of their buildings." Then Natasha looked at Calen, "Don't you get mad about this; it is work."

"I'm not. I don't want you going out with those guys but it is a good idea."

"Actually we were wondering if Natasha could pick the locks on those doors," Dagon said then he looked at Rachel. "Natasha is great at picking locks and opening safes."

"I taught Rachel how to pick pockets tonight," Natasha said proudly as she watched Rachel and Dagon looking at each other. "But we can talk about all of this at the meeting in the morning. Calen and I are going back to bed," Natasha said with a grin and took her husband's hand, leading him out of the parlor.

"How are you doing?" Dagon asked Rachel.

"I stole a letter off from one of those generals. Teivel was telling him to kidnap three hundred more people. Natasha thinks they might be sacrificing people to demons. I have heard of such things but I didn't even consider it until now. I am so afraid I may never find my father." Rachel covered her face with her hands and started to cry.

"Come here," Dagon said and put his arms around Rachel pulling her close to him. "I've seen you with Zelda and Zach. I know you always act like the strong one. You don't cry in front of them do you?"

Rachel pulled away from Dagon so she could look in his face. "How do you know?" Dagon did not answer her question but kissed her on the forehead. "I'm alright," Rachel said as she wiped the tears from her cheeks.

"Would you like to have that dance now My Lady?" Dagon asked as he stood up and held his hand out to her.

Rachel laughed and took Dagon's hand. "This is the nicest dance I have had all night," she said then Dagon twirled her around.

Dagon and Rachel danced for over an hour before he said, "Perhaps I should go now; we have an early meeting in the morning." He took Rachel's hand and walked her to her bedroom door. "I would like to see you again," Dagon said. "How do you feel about that?"

"I would like that," Rachel said with a big smile.

"Good, but since we are on this mission we will be limited with what we can do."

"I understand."

Dagon bent down and gently kissed Rachel on the lips. She kissed him back and the two embraced for several minutes. "Like I said I better be going," he said with a large smile. Dagon found himself humming as he returned to his chambers. Rachel danced back to her bed.

Chapter XXVI
Reconnaissance

Gabriel was holding a meeting in his chambers before breakfast the following morning. Dagon met Calen, Natasha and Rachel in the hallway. Dagon took Rachel's hand and they walked into the meeting together. "Pay up," Jared said to Thaos with a smirk as they watched Dagon put his arm around Rachel after they sat down.

Lakin was the first to stand up and he briefed the group about the findings in the tunnels. Natasha followed Lakin and suggested that she and Rachel have lunch with the two generals then ask them for a tour of the military building.

"I like that idea," Stephan said. "But how are you going to contact them. And don't they realize you are saying you are married?"

"I don't think they care if we are married or not," Natasha said. "The one I danced with is named Boris and he certainly talks like he feels he is above all laws. He said we could leave a message with Clay and it would get to them. This comment also makes me more suspicious of Clay."

"Everyone has seen us as your body guards," Michael said. "What if you contact the generals then a couple of us tag along?"

"I really like that idea," said Calen.

Gabriel now stood in front of the room. "Rachel I want you to really think about this. If you go on that tour you might see someone in prison who you know. If you expose us, we won't be able to save anyone. No matter how painful this is; you will have to play your part or I can't let you go and comprise the mission."

"Honestly I have been thinking about that too," Rachel said. "But I believe that if my father or any others who I know see me walking around the cells dressed like this they will know something is up and it will give them hope. There are others who know I am a freedom fighter but I don't think they would expose me."

"I know exactly what we will do," Natasha said with a grin.

"I brought a couple of hats with veils. Rachel can cover her face or not depending on the situation."

"Then we have a plan," Gabriel said. "I will help you craft the note for the generals. Michael and Jared do you want to go with the girls and the rest of us will try to open those doors in the tunnels."

"I am pretty damn good at picking locks," Jared said. "And I have my tools here."

"I'll go with the girls," Stephan said. "It might help to have one of us with a lot of experience in military buildings in that group."

"If we can't get the doors unlocked today then Natasha will try tonight," Gabriel said.

"Rachel and I stole a lot of keys last night," Natasha said. "It is a long shot but maybe you should try some of them."

"Last night I asked Clay to set me up with some carpenters to remodel my building. The chances will be good that they cannot be trusted so everyone be mindful of that. I don't want them to start work until we have figured out how to unlock those tunnel doors. Also this morning I sent a note to the Sanuri. I briefed him on what is going on here and told him that I will need men to bring the weapons here from Erebus' castle. I want some of the soldiers to escort the bocas since we can't let the Rualas be seen yet."

"Last night I heard that men are already coming to the city for the games," Thaos said. "We might not have to keep them a secret much longer."

"But how are we going to explain the Rualas working with us?" Natasha asked.

"Sounds like we can move those plans up," Gabriel said to Lakin. Then Gabriel addressed the rest of the group. "Lakin will be registering in this hotel with his men. Since he is a prince I will be approaching him for a business deal. That will be our connection."

"I never realized how much you are like Calen," Natasha said jokingly as Dagon was helping Natasha and Rachel prepare for their luncheon date with the two generals.

"What do you mean?" Rachel asked.

Natasha glanced at Dagon who was buttoning the back of Rachel's dress. "I'll tell you later," Natasha said.

"You can tell her now," Dagon said and chuckled.

"Calen was attracted to me because I was a warrior then when we started dating he became really over protective," Natasha said.

"Are you becoming over protective?" Rachel asked Dagon in a joking manner.

"Apparently. I don't understand why they can't make these dresses with bigger buttons," Dagon said with frustration. "But the one good thing; as old as those two generals are they will never be able to get these dresses off you two."

"Dagon!" Rachel said as both women laughed.

"Well you know they want to get you two in bed," said Dagon.

"It's not going to happen," Rachel said.

Dagon leaned down and whispered into Rachel's ear, "They aren't the only ones."

Rachel quickly turned and looked at him. She smiled then asked, "So is that the reason you are becoming overprotective?"

"No. You mean you can't tell?" Dagon asked sincerely. "Perhaps we should have a talk tonight."

"I heard what Dagon said," Natasha said with a grin. "Rachel he is not a dirty old man like the generals."

"You know that's why Calen isn't in here helping you get ready. He really doesn't want the two of you going on this date," Dagon said.

"But Stephan and Michael will be with us," said Rachel.

"Doesn't matter," Dagon said. "Calen is still upset."

"I better go talk to him," Natasha said. "Dagon would you finish buttoning me up before I go into the hallway?"

Natasha, Rachel, Stephan and Michael met General Boris and General Clifford in the dining room of the Teivel Manor Hotel. Both generals stared at Stephan and Michael disapprovingly. "I don't know if you have met," Natasha said sweetly. "This is Stephan and Michael our body guards and this is General Boris and General Clifford."

"Do you really think body guards are necessary?" General Clifford asked in a harsh voice. Which made both Michael and Stephan grin.

"Oh, we don't go anywhere without our body guards," Natasha said as they all took their seats. "Here is a note from our husbands. As I told you in my note they wanted to join us but had a business meeting. But they want to meet with you also."

"Do you know why?" asked Boris.

"I image they want to talk about the new explosives they have."

"Explosives?" Boris repeated.

"Yes, our husbands sell weapons besides other things," Rachel said.

"What type of weapons?" Clifford asked with interest.

Natasha glanced at Stephan and Michael then looked at the generals. "Actually Michael and Stephan could probably answer your questions better than Rachel and I can. Our husbands don't really involve us in their work." Gabriel had previously told Michael and Stephan the information they should give to the generals.

The generals were intrigued with the explosives and weapons that Michael and Stephan described. While some of what Michael and Stephan were saying was fabricated, they were primarily describing weapons used by the Army of Wetpr.

Raul and Simon had previously designed a variety of tobisks, which were sphere shaped objects containing different chemicals that were made to be launched by trebuchets.

Stephan and Michael also described the explosives and smoke that Hannah had created which turned the tide in a battle in Nora between the Rualas and the Hutas. Stephan and Michael did not disclose the means by which Gabriel came in possession of these weapons, nor did they disclose the precise components of the weapons. But they did offer to set up demonstrations of the weapons for the generals.

Both Boris and Clifford came to the belief that Stephan and Michael played more significant roles in Gabriel's arms business than mere body guards. The four men actively engaged in conversation as the generals lost their resentment towards Michael and Stephan for intruding on their dates.

After a long lunch, General Boris and General Clifford offered to take Stephan, Michael, Natasha and Rachel on a tour of several facilities.

The first facility on the tour was a large military warehouse on the north end of the City of Teivel. Both Stephan and Michael were surprised at how antiquated the weapons appeared and wondered if the generals were not showing their complete arsenal.

"Are these actually the weapons you use?" Michael asked. "Because they look, well, they look past their prime."

"Our leader, that is Teivel," Boris explained. "Has such complete control over his people that we have not had a need to use these types of weapons for some time. And no one has dared to invade our kingdom for centuries. But as you know, Teivel is inviting the kingdoms here for the Gefrey Games and he wants to flex his muscles so to speak. We are extremely interested in your weapons."

"What do you mean by flex his muscles?" Natasha asked. "Are you going to attack the other kingdoms?"

"No," Clifford said with a grin. "Teivel wants to impress our visitors with his power. I believe he is more interested in putting on a show."

"Well we can certainly help with that," Stephan said. "Just out of curiosity do you have any explosives in your arsenals?"

"No the last time we used our trebuchets they launched boulders," Boris said. "Mind you, Clifford and I think Teivel is a wise leader but as military men we would prefer to have more up to date weapons. I am sure you can understand that; you both appear to be fighting men."

"We certainly can," Stephan said. "And I don't mean to insult you, but your kingdom is large. Certainly this isn't your only weapon's warehouse.'"

Neither general spoke for a moment then Clifford said, "Teivel has shall I say other things he prefers to use as weapons, so yes this is our only warehouse."

"You mean those gangs of demons we kept running into?" Michael asked. "Because we killed a few. Why the hell did they attack us?"

"You were attacked?" Boris asked.

"Yes and more than once," Stephan said. "We entered Ryed from Nora then turned north to travel here. We were attacked several times and saw that some of the demons were sporting tattoos. So we figured they were gang members."

"Yes, and it was just terrifying," Natasha said. "Certainly you don't employ those monsters, you seem like such nice men."

"There are many gangs in Ryed," Clifford explained. "But not all of them are employed by Teivel. In fact the gangs fight among themselves for territory. Do you remember what the tattoos looked like?"

Now Rachel stepped forward, "Those huge demons with the long hair had those strange tattoos by their ears. It looked like a curved knife surrounded with unusual symbols."

"Those are the ones that Teivel owns," Clifford said. "You say they attacked you, when and where?"

"About a week and a half ago," Michael said.

"We stopped the caravan for the midday meal and suddenly we were surrounded. We were five, six days south of here."

"And you survived?" Boris asked with surprise.

"We are very good at our jobs," Stephan said with a smirk. "And Gabriel and Stone are businessmen but you don't want to tangle with either of them."

"So why did they attack us?" Michael asked again.

"Perhaps you were just in the wrong place at the wrong time," Clifford said without convincing anyone of his sincerity.

"Then one morning these two ugly sons of bitches with horns jump out of a thicket," Michael said. "Their tattoos were four dots with swords underneath them. Three swords facing down and the last one facing up. I can tell from the looks on your faces you recognize the tattoos. Are they more of Teivel's demons?"

"We don't recognize those tattoos," Clifford said nervously. "Once again I am amazed that you survived."

"Hell the horned demons were a whole lot easier to kill," Stephan said. "We got rid of them right away. So all these demons; that's what this kingdom uses instead of a well-trained military? Not that it is my place to say anything but I would take a soldier any day over a demon."

While General Boris and General Clifford agreed with Stephan they dared not speak out against Teivel. "I can see from your eyes that you agree with me," Stephan said. "So is that why you don't have any forts around here?"

"You are an observant man," was all Clifford would say.

"Perhaps it is time to move on to another building," Boris suggested.

The next two stops on the tour were of no importance to Stephan, Michael, Natasha and Rachel. The stops were merely beautiful buildings that a tourist might be interested in seeing. The fourth stop proved more interesting for the members of Gabriel's team.

339

"This is our courthouse," Boris said as the small group entered a large marble building.

"I thought Teivel had supreme rule in this kingdom," Stephan said. "You mean there is a legal system here?"

"Teivel does rule this kingdom, he is the law," Clifford said. "This building has other purposes."

"Then why do you call it a courthouse?" asked Natasha.

"Teivel does not like to advertise his prisons," Boris said. "Some rulers have public executions and display their criminals by various means. Teivel believes that he creates more fear among his people by not letting them know what happens to their families and friends."

"I don't understand?" Rachel said with a little edge to her voice. Natasha quickly squeezed Rachel's hand.

"The peoples' imaginations create even bigger monsters than what Teivel employs," Boris said.

"So how many prisons does he have?" Natasha asked.

"Thirteen," said Clifford.

"Thirteen," Natasha gasped. "Are there that many criminals here?"

"Don't worry, it is safe to walk the streets here," Boris said. "Usually only one or two prisons are even full at any time."

"What do you mean usually?" Michael asked.

"The prisons are filled now so Teivel can put the prisoners in the games," Clifford said.

Natasha quickly spoke because she was afraid that Rachel would expose their roles. "Our husbands just bought a building near the arena; but if it is so dangerous here that you have thirteen prisons filled with criminals, I don't know if we want to start a business. I will speak with them when we return to the hotel."

340

"As Boris said it is safe to walk down the streets," Clifford said. "You need not worry."

"I am worried. If I show you where our building is can you tell me where the prisons are located near it? Do you have some paper and pen?" Natasha was acting anxious about the prisons; so Clifford ordered one of the soldiers, who was standing guard in the courthouse, to bring them paper and a pen.

Stephan and Michael tried very hard not to grin as Natasha charmed the generals into drawing the location of each of the prisons. "A couple of these are pretty close to our building; that scares me." Natasha said. "Your prisons are secure aren't they? I mean no one has ever escaped have they?"

"No my dear," Boris said. "Don't worry your pretty little head about such a thing. Actually Teivel was ingenious when he set up these prisons. Once a prisoner is put into prison they don't see the light of day again. They are transported in a series of underground tunnels."

"I don't understand where they would be transported to," Stephan asked as he looked at the drawing of prison locations. "Why do you need to move them?"

"Mostly they are transported to the arena but some go to auction houses to be sold for slaves," Boris said.

"You must have some damn long tunnels if you are transporting prisoners from some of these prisons to the arena or do you have more than one arena?" Stephan asked.

"Just the one arena and the tunnels run under the entire city," Clifford said. "They are really quite impressive."

"I am shocked that these people are sold for slaves," Natasha said. "I don't mean to insult your ways but I don't believe that is right. Just how many auction houses do you have here?"

"We had four but Teivel has shut them all down until after the games. He is afraid others will have the same reaction you do," Clifford said.

Rachel was now controlling her anger and realizing how much valuable information Natasha was getting.

341

"If the prisoners are transported through the tunnels does that mean the prisons are in the bottom of these buildings?" Rachel asked. "I mean are there actually prisoners underneath where we are standing now? I just had a chill go up my back."

"Yes, the entire cellar of this building is a prison," Boris said. "But that is two floors down, they can't get at you."

While Boris and Clifford gave a tour of the two above ground floors of the courthouse they did not offer a tour of the prison below. Late that afternoon, Stephan, Michael, Natasha and Rachel returned to their hotel. Gabriel had been waiting for the four to come back so he could hold a meeting.

The meeting was planned to start as soon as Michael, Stephan, Natasha and Rachel arrived at the top floor of the hotel. Calen and Dagon were waiting at the top of the staircase for Natasha and Rachel. "Everything went just fine," Natasha said as she tried to reassure Calen who was hugging and kissing her.

Dagon kissed Rachel, which surprised her since they were in front of the others. "We are having a talk after the meeting," Dagon said as he took her hand.

"Is anything wrong?" Rachel asked as she feared Dagon had information about her father.

Dagon heard the fear in Rachel's voice. "Nothing is wrong, I want to talk about us. What were you thinking?"

"I thought you heard some news about Father." Rachel and Dagon stopped talking as they took seats in Gabriel's chambers.

"Gabriel we got a lot of good information," Stephan said as soon as the group entered his chambers. "And now that I have seen Natasha at work I take my hat off to her. I'll let her tell you what she got."

"Why don't you four go first then," Gabriel said. Stephan and Michael started the meeting by telling of their conversations with the two generals and the tour.

"So Teivel has demons guarding the kingdom instead of a military; that is interesting, "Gabriel said.

"So did Boris and Clifford sound frustrated since they really don't have the power one would expect?"

"Yes they did but there is more going on here," Michael said. "We told them that our caravan was attacked by demons while we traveled here. We were trying to get information about the tattoos. The demons that attacked Rachel's family are Teivel's demons. He is stocking up on prisoners for the games. But when we described the tattoos with the dots and swords, both those old generals turned white and looked pretty damn scared to me. They said they didn't recognize the tattoo but we could tell they were lying."

Natasha stood up next. "I will make copies of this drawing," She said as she handed it to Gabriel. "There are thirteen prisons and four auction houses where prisoners are sold. The prisons usually aren't filled but they are now because of the games."

"The auction houses have been closed down until the games are over because Teivel wants to impress his visitors. All of the prisoners are transported by a series of underground tunnels which run under the entire city. The prisons are in the cellars of each building indicated on that map."

"I told them I was afraid for our safety with so many criminals here and that I was going to talk to you about this being a dangerous city to open a business in; so you might want to play that up when you talk to Boris and Clifford," Natasha said directly to Gabriel. "We didn't get a tour of the prisons."

"We only saw soldiers as guards, no demons on the tour," Stephan said.

"Jared was able to pick the locks on those doors in the tunnels," Gabriel explained to the group. "First we walked the tunnel that led to the arena. Once you are in a tunnel there isn't any place to hide; you are in the open until you enter the arena, which was empty and that surprised me. The lower floor of the arena is a series of cells. The prisoners have to be removed from the cells and taken to the doors that open into the battle floor of the arena. We need to spend more time in the arena to really understand the layout. Today we wanted to explore the tunnels."

"The second tunnel led to a prison and from looking at Natasha's map we found the building. The hinges of the door made a great deal of noise which caused a couple of guards to investigate. The guards are dead and we took their uniforms, weapons and keys. Their bodies are hidden in our building for now. Natasha you might need to help with some alterations on these uniforms until we can get our hands on others."

Chapter XXVII
Dagon

As soon as the meeting ended Dagon took Rachel's hand and they walked to her room. They entered the bedroom and Dagon closed the door then kissed her passionately. Rachel responded to Dagon's kisses and after a few moments he sat down on the bed and pulled her onto his lap.

"Rachel I really like you and I want to know how you feel about me."

"I really like you too. Dagon you look so serious what is this about?"

"I know everything is crazy with this mission and your father missing. And I know we haven't known each other long," Dagon said then paused. "Rachel I would like you to be my girl."

"What exactly are you asking?"

"That we have a serious relationship and we don't date other people."

"Is this because of Joao and Dack?"

"No. Do you want to date them too?"

"Dagon don't look like that. I am not interested in dating anyone else. But you are asking me for a commitment and I don't know if I can make one yet. If we live through this mission you will leave Ryed but I have my family to care for. And even if we find Father alive who knows what shape he will be in. I don't mean to hurt you I just don't think I am in a position to make a commitment."

"I keep telling you that you don't have to do all of this by yourself. I mean it when I say that I will help you with your family."

"You are such a sweet man," Rachel said and kissed Dagon on the cheek. "But there are just so many unknowns right now."

"So you are saying you won't be my girl?"

"I will be your girl until the mission is over then we will have to have this talk again. Is that fair?"

"I will agree to that," Dagon said and kissed Rachel. "I'll move my things in here tonight."

"What!"

"Don't you want me to?"

"It's not that. Dagon this is all so new to me and you have just taken me by surprise. Maybe I have been so focused on my father that, oh I don't know what I am saying."

"Rachel I can tell that you are overwhelmed and I am sorry for that. But you have to agree that the conditions we are under now aren't normal; who knows what will happen say a month from now. I have been on many missions and when they start moving everything goes really fast then it is all over. Which is why I am moving fast now; things could be different if we were in another place and time. Please just give us a chance and if it doesn't work out at least we will know and not spend the rest of our lives wondering what could have happened."

"Alright..." Rachel did not complete her sentence because Natasha knocked on the door.

"Can I come in?" Natasha asked.

"Yes," Dagon said.

"You both look so serious is this a bad time?" Natasha asked as she entered the room.

"I just asked Rachel to be my girl and things are moving too fast for her," Dagon said.

"Rachel all of Dagon's brothers and his father are the same way. Once they make their minds up they just jump in. While it is normal for him; be honest with your feelings."

"I am feeling overwhelmed but that may be because of my father too. We are going to give it a try and see if things work out," Rachel said.

"Good," Dagon said. "I will move my things in here tonight."

"Oh my god you are exactly like Calen," Natasha said to Dagon and laughed then Natasha looked at Rachel. "Calen moved in with me two days after we met then we married on the third day."

"Oh, I am not ready for that yet," Rachel said and looked at Dagon.

Dagon laughed. "I'll move in tonight and we will see where the relationship goes."

"I almost forgot why I came in here," Natasha said and laughed again. "Gabriel wants us to be ready to go downstairs for dinner in twenty minutes. Do you want me to pick out your dress?"

"Yes," Rachel said. "I can't think right now."

Gabriel, Dominic, Natasha, Rachel, Jared, Michael, Thaos and Stephan started to descend the five story staircase from the top floor of the Teivel Manor to the first floor. "I am going to ask Clay to join us for a drink," Gabriel said. "I suspect he has more involvement with Teivel than I first realized; I want to draw him out a little."

No one spoke for a moment then Thaos looked at Rachel and grinned. "You're awfully quiet," he said with a knowing look.

"Do you know?" Rachel asked with surprise.

"I know you look like you are trying to decide if you want to run out a door," Thaos said.

"What are you talking about?" asked Gabriel.

Rachel and Natasha looked at each other then Rachel said to Gabriel. "Dagon just asked me to be his girl and he is moving in with me tonight." She paused for a moment. "He is so sweet and I really like him but my head is spinning and I just don't know what to think."

"When I met my wife it was the same way," Thaos said. "I knew right away and Nikki was scared because everything was moving so fast."

"Wife," Rachel gasped. "I told Dagon that I can't make a commitment at least not past this mission. I have to find my father and I have Mother and Zack to take care of."

"What did Dagon say to that?" asked Natasha.

"He said he would help me with my family. And we will have that conversation again when the mission is over," Rachel said. "I know you are all Dagon's friends and I don't mean to say anything bad about him. I am, I don't know; scared I guess."

"Dagon has been my friend for many years," Gabriel said. "He is a really good man. And I am not saying he hasn't had girlfriends but he has pretty much dedicated his life to the missions. But you should know that once he makes his mind up about something he puts all of his energy towards it."

"That's what Natasha said too," Rachel said. "I don't know, maybe the timing is just wrong."

"How do you feel about him?" Natasha asked.

"I really like him but we haven't known each other very long."

"Rachel I don't know you or Dagon that well," Dominic said. "But take it from someone who has been alone for a long time. Timing is never good and don't use that as an excuse not to get into a relationship. If you feel there is something good between you and Dagon; really think things through before you give up on the relationship. Sometimes you only have one chance."

Rachel didn't say anything for a moment then she asked, "Is there something wrong with me. I mean wouldn't most girls just jump at this chance?"

"Rachel, your father has been kidnapped and your mother and brother are in hiding. You feel responsible for taking care of your family. You have a lot on your mind and you just sound overwhelmed," Gabriel said.

"There is nothing wrong with you. You are an incredibly strong women of integrity. But if I were to give you advice I would say, let Dagon help you with the load that you carry. He wants to take care of you and you don't have to shoulder everything alone."

Rachel wiped the tears from her cheeks as the group entered the main dining room of the hotel. Gabriel asked to have his party seated in a smaller private dining area. Then Gabriel asked the waiter to invite Clay to join them.

When Clay walked up to Gabriel's table he had two waiters following him. Each waiter carried a silver tray. One tray held bottles of fine wine and the other tray held bottles of fine whiskey.

Gabriel was spending a great deal of money at the Teivel Manor because he wanted to make his presence known in the city. Gabriel understood that money spoke loudly especially in such a corrupt city as Teivel. Gabriel was paying Clay to set up meetings with influential people in the city. Gabriel was sure that Clay was getting paid for many services that did not come under the title of hotel manager.

What Gabriel wanted to find out was who Clay really answered to. No one in Gabriel's group trusted Clay so it was a cat and mouse game when he joined the group for a few drinks. Clay was a shrewd man; little happened in the city that he did not know about. This night Gabriel planned to obtain some of Clay's knowledge.

As soon as the waiters left the small dining room, Jared closed the door while Natasha and Rachel walked up to Clay. The two women were distracting him as Gabriel poured a vial of truth potion into Clay's glass of whiskey. Clay spoke with the women for almost ten minutes then he turned his attention to Gabriel, who handed Clay a large pouch of gold coins. "I can't thank you enough for the introductions," Gabriel said. "I can see a lucrative future for us."

"So can I," Clay said and gulped his glass of whiskey down. Dominic poured more whiskey in the glasses of all the men. Gabriel's group were sipping their drinks. Within ten minutes Clay acted quite inebriated. Stephan and Thaos now stood by the door as Gabriel interrogated Clay.

The interrogation lasted twenty minutes. Afterwards Thaos opened the doors to the dining room and called one of the waiters over. Clay was acting very intoxicated. Everyone in Gabriel's group pretended to be drunk as they ordered their food. Gabriel wanted the hotel staff to see Clay laughing and joking with his group, so as not to draw suspicion if Clay became sick later.

Clay ate dinner with Gabriel's group and appeared not to remember being asked questions but Clay continued to drink whiskey; large quantities of whiskey. After the meal as Gabriel's group was leaving the dining room, Clay stumbled across the dining room floor and fell into a waiter who was carrying a large tray of food. Both men and the tray of food fell onto the floor and surrounding guests.

Gabriel called a meeting as soon as he reached the top floor of the hotel. Dagon arrived late for the meeting and found Rachel standing against one of the walls.

"I poured truth potion into Clay's whiskey. As much whiskey as he had tonight I doubt if he will even remember talking with us," Gabriel said. "Clay says he doesn't work directly for Teivel. Clay said that Teivel sends his men into all of the businesses to get information and if they don't get the information they want that people get hurt. Clay reports to one of Teivel's lieutenants named Saxton, who we met at the first party we attended."

"Saxton is a large burly man with a brown mustache. Clay did send his cleaning ladies to spy on us but they did not find anything unusual. Clay has been spying on us because we are rich strangers but he has not discovered anything that would compromise our roles."

"Clay said that many of the high ranking military officers are not happy with Teivel's regime because the military is merely a figurehead for the demonic activity in this kingdom. The military basically has no power. There are rumors that some of the generals are planning a coup but these rumors have been around for a while and none of the generals have disappeared so Clay thinks there is no substance to the rumors. So there may be several reasons that General Boris and General Clifford are so interested in our weapons. It would benefit us if this coup took place."

"Clay gave us the locations of the three other auction houses," Gabriel continued. "But Clay didn't really know any more information about the villagers who have been taken prisoner than we know."

"I asked him if Tobey our carriage driver works for Teivel and to Clay's knowledge Tobey is just a hardworking guy trying to support a family. Which means I may reach out to Tobey for information. I like Tobey and would like to help him and his family to relocate."

"So far Saxton and the generals want demonstrations of our weapons which we should do separately just in case the generals are part of a group planning a coup. The other three men who want demonstrations are actually arms dealers who sell to Teivel. That's Georganson, Ackly and Bremmer. We need to find out more about a possible coup. That would work greatly in our favor as a distraction."

"We also found out that a large number of people have entered Ryed for the games but most of them are staying in hotels that are less expensive than the Manor. So Lakin, tomorrow you check in here with your men and your presence will no longer be a secret."

"Are you thinking about giving those generals some of the truth potion?" Michael asked.

"First I would like to see how Clay comes out of this. Vivian is the only person we gave the potion to who wasn't killed afterwards but she became deathly sick. We don't want to harm them if they are planning a coup; at least not yet," Gabriel said. "Tomorrow we are going to investigate the other auction houses to see if we can determine where the tunnels lead. And I am going to set up a meeting with Boris and Clifford. Stephan and Michael I would like you to be part of that meeting since you have established a rapport with them."

After the meeting, Calen, Natasha, Rachel and Dagon walked back to their chambers. As soon as they entered the parlor, which was the first room, Natasha grabbed Rachel's hand and said. "I have to show you something." The two women disappeared into Calen's and Natasha's bedroom.

351

"Calen said that Dagon has a surprise for you," Natasha said as she looked through a dresser drawer. "Here take this," Natasha handed Rachel a black silk nightgown.

Rachel held up the nightgown to look at. "Natasha this is so beautiful; are you sure?"

"Yes and have fun."

"I am really nervous," Rachel said.

"Maybe you should tell Dagon how nervous you are," Natasha suggested.

"What are you two doing?" Calen called out then laughed. Both women walked out of the bedroom and into the parlor.

"What is that?" Dagon asked with a grin when he saw Rachel walking towards him with something in her hands.

"I'll show you later," she said and smiled.

Dagon took Rachel's had and opened the door to her bedroom. "Goodnight you two," Dagon said to Calen and Natasha.

"Oh Dagon this is so beautiful," Rachel said as she looked at the room which was filled with lit candles and bouquets of flowers. There was a small table with dishes of fruit, a bottle of wine and two glasses. "Can we show Natasha?"

Dagon started to laugh and opened the door. "Natasha, Rachel wants you to see the room."

"Dagon this is beautiful," Natasha said as she and Calen entered the bedroom. "You didn't go out and buy those flowers did you?"

"No, Thaos bought them for me," Dagon said. "But starting tomorrow it doesn't matter if we are seen."

"We will leave you two alone," Calen said with a grin and escorted Natasha out of the bedroom.

After Calen closed the door, Rachel looked at Dagon and said with a smile, "I didn't know you were so romantic."

"There's a lot you don't know about me," Dagon said and leaned down and kissed her. They kissed for several moments and when they stopped she put the palms of her hands on his cheeks and gazed into his eyes. Dagon was a large and powerfully built man with straight black hair and large hazel eyes.

"You are so tough looking yet your eyes are filled with kindness; that was one of the first things I noticed about you," Rachel said. "I love your eyes." Dagon leaned down and kissed Rachel with even more passion than their previous kiss.

"Do you want me to unbutton your dress so you can show me what Natasha gave you?"

"Yes," Rachel said with a shy smile and turned so her back was to Dagon. As Rachel was moving her long hair to the side she said, "Dagon, I have to tell you that I am really nervous and I don't really know why."

"I can tell," Dagon said as he was unbuttoning her dress. "It will be alright sweetheart."

"I know, I just don't know why I am nervous."

"Rachel have you slept with a man before?" She did not answer. So Dagon stopped working on her dress and gently turned her around. "Why aren't you answering me?"

"Dagon do you expect me to, well know a lot of things?"

"Why did you ask that?"

Rachel glanced around the room before answering. "You've slept with a lot of women haven't you?"

"If I tell you the truth are you going to get mad?"

"No, I just don't know what you expect and I don't really know why you want me?"

Dagon gently tilted Rachel's chin upwards so he could look into her eyes. "To answer your first question I only expect you to be yourself. I really like you Rachel and I think you are an incredibly beautiful woman. And yes, I have slept with a lot of women but I asked you to be my girl and that is different."

353

Rachel searched Dagon's eyes as he spoke. "This is all so new for me," she said. "I'll admit I really don't know what to do and I always know what to do."

"Is that what is scaring you?"

"I don't know."

"Why don't you change and we will have a dance," Dagon suggested. Rachel turned and walked into the closet to change. "Would you like a glass of wine?" Dagon called through the closed closet door.

"Yes please."

Dagon poured two glasses of wine and was putting one up to his lips when he stopped and stared at Rachel as she walked out of the closet. "You look so beautiful," he said and put down his wine. Rachel blushed at the intensity with which Dagon was staring at her.

He walked up to Rachel and took her hand, "May I have this dance My Lady?" Rachel giggled and the two danced around the bedroom furniture.

After several minutes, Rachel said, "Dagon I have to tell you something and you might get really mad at me but I want you to know."

They stopped dancing and Dagon said, "Go on."

"Right after you asked me to be your girl and we agreed to stay together I had to go downstairs with the others. Thaos asked me if I was alright because he said I looked like I was going to run out of the door. So I told the others what we said."

"Why would I get mad about that?"

"Because I asked them if there was something wrong with me because I was so scared."

"What did they say?"

"Well, first they all told me what a great person you are. Even Dominic said I shouldn't be scared off and he doesn't really know either of us. Gabriel said that I was overwhelmed. He said that I feel responsible for my family and since my father has been kidnapped and Mother and Zack are in hiding that I have more on my mind than I realized. He said that you wanted to take care of me and I should let you help me with my family."

"I agree with every word that Gabriel said but I still don't understand why you would think I would get mad."

"Because I was talking about you with the others."

"Rachel all of us on the team have become one large family. I would rather have you talk to them then to have you get scared and run out the door," Dagon said with a smile.

"There was something else," Rachel said hesitantly. "Thaos said that I reminded him of his wife because he knew he wanted to marry her right away and she was scared because things were moving so fast. And when he said that it kind of scared me more."

"Yes, Thaos and Nikki lived together for months. She was pregnant with their first child before she agreed to marry him. Are you afraid I am going to ask you to marry me?"

"In a way. I don't really know how to explain it. I need to get used to us living together and I have to find my father. I don't know if you are thinking of asking me but if you are I am not ready for a question like that now. Are you mad?"

"Have you ever seen me mad?" Dagon asked. "I can see us getting married but I agree with you that we need to get to know each other and to get used to living together. And I understand what you have going on with your family. So don't worry I won't ask you tonight," Dagon said and laughed.

"Well you two certainly look happy," Calen said with a grin as Dagon and Rachel walked out of their bedroom holding hands the following morning. Rachel blushed. "So how was your first night together?"

"Calen!" Natasha scolded. "You're embarrassing them."

"I'm not embarrassed," Dagon said and looked at Rachel.

"It was wonderful; I don't know why I was so nervous," Rachel said as she lovingly looked at Dagon.

"Good," Natasha said with a sweet smile. "Dagon you are going to have to make an entrance in the hotel with Lakin and the others. And Rachel I think you and I only need to make appearances for meals, so why don't you ask Gabriel if you can spend the day together."

Chapter XXVIII
Spies

Gabriel and his usual group walked into the main dining room of the Teivel Manor for breakfast. "We are waiting for some people, so we would like a table with a view of the lobby," Gabriel said to the waiter. "And can you ask Clay to join us?"

"Clay has not arrived yet," the waiter said. "But I will tell him as soon as I see him."

Gabriel's group was halfway through their meal when Prince Lakin led his group of Ruala warriors into the Teivel Manor. Rualas had never before been seen in Ryed and drew a great deal of attention. Lakin walked up to the desk and said loudly, "I am Prince Lakin of the Rualas. We are here for the Gefrey Games. I will be expecting more warriors so I want to rent an entire floor of the hotel. Is that possible?" As Lakin spoke he set several bags of gold coins on top of the desk.

"Yes My Lord," the clerk said. "Our manager is not here now but I can make the arrangements. Do you have a preference?"

"The top floor," Lakin said.

"That floor is already rented but the floor beneath that only has two guests who I can move."

"Very well we will rent that floor. I have both male and female warriors with me will that be an issue?"

"Female warriors! I have never heard of female warriors. No My Lord that is no problem at all."

As Lakin and his warriors were escorted to the fourth floor of the hotel, Gabriel called their waiter to the table. "Who is that?" Gabriel asked.

"Prince Lakin of the Rualas," the waiter said excitedly. "I have never seen a Ruala before and they even have female warriors. They are here for the games. They rented the entire fourth floor of the hotel. Wait until I tell my wife."

"Would you do me a service?" Gabriel asked as he wrote a few words on a piece of paper.

"Would you give this to Prince Lakin?" Gabriel handed the waiter the note and three gold coins.

"Yes, My Lord I would be happy to." The waiter said and quickly walked out of the dining room."

"I didn't realize how much attention they would draw," Thaos said in a low voice.

"That could be to our favor," Gabriel said and looked around the crowded dining room. Every person was watching the Rualas, some people even got out of their seats to get a better view.

"Have you ever seen such beautiful people," a woman gasped loudly.

"They look like Angels," another woman said.

"A man stood up in the dining room and said, "I travel for my work. Those Rualas saved the City of Nora from an army of Hutas. The people of Nora have dedicated their city to them because the Rualas were complete strangers and they saved everyone."

"Is that true?" Rachel asked in a whisper.

"Sure is," Jared said. "I was in Nora then. We can tell you about it when we get upstairs." Jared now looked at Gabriel. "I wish I would have known you then I would have loved to have been in that fight."

"You were there?" Rachel whispered to Gabriel.

"He led it," Natasha said proudly. "That was an incredible mission. I meet Calen on that mission and Gabriel met Hannah, who is his wife now. Dagon was there too. We will tell you all about it."

The waiter almost ran back to Gabriel's table and handed Gabriel a note. "He spoke to me just like a regular person," the waiter said. "He is a prince and he was really nice. Wait until I tell my wife she will never believe me." Gabriel and his group smiled at the excitement of the waiter.

Just as Gabriel was standing to leave the table, Clay walked up to the table. His gait was unsteady and his face was pasty white. Gabriel quickly held out a chair for Clay to sit in. "Clay you look awful are you sick?"

"How much whiskey did I drink last night?" Clay asked as he sat down at the table.

"Almost two bottles," Dominic said. "We were wondering if we should have told you to slow down but honestly you acted all right until the end of the night when it all must have hit you."

"Next time tell me to slow down. I can't remember when I have felt worse," Clay said as sweat started to run down his face. Natasha poured him a cup of coffee and set it down in front of him. "I came down because the staff told me about the Rualas. But I don't want to introduce myself to the prince until I have at least stopped shaking." Clay tried to smile at his remark.

"Everyone is so excited," Natasha said. "Did you see any of them they are absolutely beautiful. I'll bet you get a lot more guests just because the Rualas are here."

"You are probably right; I should tell the kitchen staff," Clay said then sipped his coffee. "I should arrange a gathering for them like I did for you," Clay said more to himself than to anyone at the table.

Natasha suddenly looked at Gabriel and winked, then she turned back to Clay who did not see what she had done. "Clay you have been ever so gracious to us. And honestly it pains me to see you look so ill. How about if I help you make the arrangements I just love doing things like that. You tell me who you want to invite and how I can contact them and I will do the rest."

"I couldn't ask you to do that," Clay said.

"You're not asking; I am volunteering. Besides Stone and Gabriel will be in business meetings all day."

"Normally I wouldn't impose but I am feeling awful. I would appreciate the help," Clay said.

Rachel looked at Gabriel, "Perhaps I should cancel my other arrangements and help Natasha."

"We can discuss that later," Gabriel said.

"The rest of you can go," Natasha said. "I will stay down here with Clay." Gabriel smiled at his sister's ingenuity.

As Gabriel, Michael, Thaos, Rachel, Dominic, Stephan and Jared walked up the stairs Gabriel said, "We don't want the hotel staff to see us on the floor of the Rualas yet so we will go to our rooms. Rachel I already told Dagon the two of you could spend the day together. If you want to help Natasha you will have to discuss that with him."

Stephan started to laugh loudly then said in a low voice, "By time Natasha is done she will have cleared out his desk and safe." The others laughed at this comment.

Raphael, Edward and their troops as well as Simon, Raul, Matthew and the armies they led remained at Fort Stanus. Everyday these men received messages from Gabriel and the new information that some of Teivel's military might be planning a coup put a new dimension on the plans of attack against Teivel.

The messages that Gabriel sent daily to Fort Stanus, King Sudfad and the troops hiding at Erebus' castle exposed the atrocities of the Teivel regime against its own people. King Sudfad forwarded these messages to King Mathas of Lentz, King Manu of the Rualas and King Neputa of the Shettees.

The primary focus of this mission had always been to eradicate Teivel and the Insidiae from Fort Polta and the Kingdom of Wetpr. But there wasn't a king, a prince or a high priest who wasn't touched by Gabriel's letters. While many people throughout the Continent of Opots thought only of Ryed as a kingdom of monsters, Gabriel's letters gave life to the everyday people of that kingdom. People who were trying to raise families. People who were trying to resist the darkness of a totalitarian regime. People who had no voice.

The family members of Gabriel's team who remained in Salar read their daily letters with mixtures of emotion.

Hannah and Vivian both wanted their husbands home for the birth of their babies but as these two women learned more of the mission their husbands where on; they wanted to join them. Maxwell, Luca, Emeral and Koby had responsibilities in Salar but they found their hearts spending more time in Ryed.

"We take so very much for granted," King Sudfad said as he passed one of Gabriel's letters to the family members seated around the breakfast table. "Reading letters like this makes us realize how much we have to be grateful for."

"I was so mad at Raul for leaving again," Vitomas said. "Now I just feel guilty."

"Sudfad isn't there something that we can do to help?" Annabelle said. "I too feel guilty. Those of us who lived under Roch's rule understand the horror the people of Ryed are living under. It seems like there should be something that we could do to help, although off the top of my head I don't know what."

"I have to be honest with you girls," Sudfad said. "Even if we topple Teivel, if the right people are not put in charge of rebuilding that kingdom it may fall victim to another tyrant."

"But the Angels wanted us to help," Annabelle said.

"They told us of this horror and gave us the choice as to what we would do. But the people of Ryed also have choices to make and if their choice has been to allow fear to govern their lives; they may choose fear again no matter what we do."

"You know we are still limited with what we can do," Dagon said to Rachel. "Even though I can be seen in public now; you are pretending to be Gabriel's wife."

"I know and I am fine with staying in the hotel. You said you wanted to take me different places but that really doesn't matter to me. I just enjoy being with you."

"I'm glad to hear that because we may be stuck in the hotel for a while."

"We can talk to each other at the party tonight can't we?"

"Yes, but remember we still have roles to play, so we have to be careful. And I mean we have to be conscious of how we look at each other, do you understand?"

"Yes," Rachel said as she sat down on the sofa in the parlor of their chambers. "So tell me about Nora. A man stood up in the dining room and said that your people saved the City of Nora from Hutas. Jared said it was a real battle that he wishes he would have joined. Natasha told me you were there."

"This is going to be a long story; perhaps I should pour us some wine," Dagon said.

Natasha had spent the morning sending messengers to every person who Clay wanted to invite to the evening's gathering. She worked quickly and efficiently as she wanted to gain Clay's trust.

Dominic, Gabriel, Stephan and Michael had a meeting with General Boris and General Clifford that started late morning but ran through the day so Rachel and Natasha did not eat lunch in the dining room. Since Clay was still quite ill in the afternoon, Natasha offered to help with the physical preparations for the gathering. To the surprise of the hotel staff, Clay allowed Natasha to supervise the room set up as well as the menu.

Although Natasha had ulterior motives for helping Clay; she found herself truly enjoying the work. Calen stopped into the dining room to visit Natasha but they pretended they were meeting for the first time. Calen gave Natasha advice on Ruala customs and she handed him papers she had stolen from Clay's office and the front desk.

Natasha took Calen into the kitchen and introduced him to the chef and the wait staff as the liaison for Prince Lakin. The employees were fascinated by the Rualas and Calen's easy going personality and sense of humor made the employees very comfortable around him. Soon Calen was surrounded with people who were asking him all variety of questions.

At the suggestion of General Boris, Gabriel, Dominic, Stephan and Michael met the generals for lunch at a restaurant called the Calla Lily. This restaurant was nothing fancy. It was small and crowded but it did offer private dining rooms.

This was not the type of establishment where one would expect to find Teivel or his leaders. As soon as Gabriel saw the restaurant he wondered if the two generals were indeed involved in planning a coup.

"Do not talk business in front of the wait staff," General Clifford warned as soon as the waiter left the small private dining room.

"Gentlemen," Gabriel said to the generals. "My brother and I make our money by keeping our ears to the ground. We have heard many rumors of a political nature regarding your kingdom. I want you to know that one of Teivel's lieutenants a man named Saxton has requested an audience with us. We decided to meet with you first. Now if you are interested in our weapons as representatives of Teivel or not that is not our business. But if you want to meet in a more private location we can meet in my hotel room."

Neither of the generals spoke for a few moments, then Clifford looked at Boris and turned back to Gabriel and said, "Perhaps that would be wise."

After a few more moments of hesitation Boris said. "Gabriel unless I misunderstood you I believe you said you were originally from Wetpr. I have heard that is a kingdom of freedoms. Ryed is not. Your thoughts can get you imprisoned here. There was a day when Ryed was a proud and grand kingdom, of course that was before our time. Our written history has been destroyed so the people will not question their lives. To question anything here is forbidden."

There was a knock on the door and a waiter entered with a tray containing glasses, a bottle of wine and a bottle of whiskey. Gabriel spoke about the building he had just purchased as the waiter poured drinks. When the waiter left the room, Michael stood up and held his hands up for the others not to speak. Michael was a giant of a man but he quickly and silently crossed the floor and pulled the door open. The waiter, who was leaning against the other side of the door almost fell onto Michael.

Michael grabbed the waiter by his collar and pulled him inside of the small dining room and closed the door. "What is the meaning of this?" Boris demanded.

The waiter was a middle aged man who looked terrified that he had been caught spying on this group of men. The waiter did not speak. Stephan stood up and checked the waiter for tattoos as Michael held him. "There are no tattoos," Stephan said to the group.

"Who do you work for?" Michael asked the waiter who was making no attempt to struggle with his captors.

"He is obviously afraid," Gabriel said.

"Then we will have to make him fear us more," Stephan said then he tore a piece of material off from the table cloth and was about to gag the waiter.

"No," the waiter said. "He will kill me if I tell."

"And we will kill you if you don't," Stephan said. "But your death with us will not be pretty. It is your choice."

The waiter looked at the men in the room fearfully then said. "After you walked in Lieutenant Saxton walked in and told me to listen to your conversation."

Clifford was about to speak but Gabriel held up his hand. "Is Saxton still here?"

"I saw him walk out of the door and he said he would return in two hours, but I did not watch him walk down the street."

"So you work for Saxton?" Gabriel asked.

"No, but Teivel's men are always asking people to spy on others and if we don't we disappear."

"What is your name?" Gabriel asked the waiter.

"Jonathon, My Lord."

"Jonathon you are in a bad situation here," Gabriel said. "I have a way you can get out of it but you will have to act a part. Do you think you can do that?"

"I don't understand My Lord."

"Michael why don't you and Jonathon leave the room for just a couple of minutes," Gabriel said. "Jonathon, he is not going to hurt you I need to do something."

"If you run from me I will hurt you," Michael whispered to the waiter as they walked out of the door."

Gabriel looked at both generals. "You don't really know us as we do not know you or any agendas you might have. But the fact that Saxton is spying on us makes me suspect that some of the rumors we have heard are true. Who is a rival of Saxton?"

"Why do you ask?" Boris asked suspiciously.

"You will find out. Now if you want to get out of this situation without suspicion I would suggest you give me a name," Gabriel said with authority.

"Leon, he is a captain in Teivel's inner circle. Saxton desires his positon."

"Stephan would you have Michael and Jonathon come in here?" Gabriel asked as he quickly wrote a note. Michael, Stephan and Jonathon entered the dining room and closed the door. "Jonathon you strike me as an innocent man who is caught in a bad situation. I have a way that your life can be spared and you can earn some money but you will have to lie convincingly. Do you think you can do that?"

"I don't know My Lord. What must I do?"

"We will be leaving now. You tell Saxton that you only heard us speak about properties that I was interested in purchasing. Then you tell him you found this on the floor after we left." Gabriel handed the note to Jonathon. Then Gabriel pulled five gold coins from his pocket and handed them to the waiter. "Jonathon, you do understand that if you betray us we will find out and return."

"Thank you My Lord. Is this all I have to do?"

"Yes, do you think you can do it?" Gabriel asked.

"Oh, yes My Lord. Thank you; I am in your debt," Jonathon said with such sincerity that he was almost crying.

After all the men were seated inside of the carriage and returning to the Teivel Manor Gabriel asked, "How long has Saxton been spying on you?"

"It is difficult to tell," Clifford said. "Everyone is spied on here."

"Now gentlemen do you mean to tell us that two astute and well trained officers such as yourselves don't know when you are being spied upon?"

"Gabriel we are beginning to realize there is more to you than you present," Boris said as he looked suspiciously at Gabriel.

"Isn't that true of all of us?" Gabriel asked. "We will separate once we reach the hotel. But Clay is hosting a gathering for the Ruala Prince and his men this evening. Plan to attend. Then if you choose to talk business with us it will not appear suspicious."

Little else was said inside of the carriage. Gabriel, Dominic, Michael and Stephan got out of the carriage at the front door to the Teivel Manor and the generals continued on to their offices. As Gabriel and the others were walking up the stairs to the top floor Gabriel said in a low voice, "Dominic I could tell you wanted to jump up and grab that waiter but you preserved your role that is good."

"It was difficult," Dominic said. "I am a fighter not a man of means. This is all very new to me."

"When you are in conflict, just think of the lives we are trying to save," Gabriel said.

"I'm not a normal member of this team," Stephan said to Dominic. "But the missions I have been on were incredible. Gabriel is very good at what he does. Trust him."

"This is my first mission," Michael said. "I will admit this cat and mouse game is not natural to me but I am learning a great deal and I can see how it is working."

"I don't know how your people can live like this," Stephan said to Dominic. "Always being in fear and being spied on. Being thrown into prison for your opinions. I would not believe such a world exists if I had not seen it with my own eyes."

"Teivel has been in power for centuries. This is the only life my people know. Sometimes I am afraid that as badly as the people want freedom they will submit again to another dictator."

"Dominic you and your brothers and your men should return to Wetpr with us," Gabriel said. "We can help you start new lives. Lives where you aren't living in caves. While I commend you for your integrity and resistance, you are like a group of ants trying to hold back an avalanche. And will your people betray you if their lives depend upon it?"

"Many have suffered to protect us," Dominic said with sadness. "And that weighs heavily upon my soul."

"Even if we lose this battle, that doesn't mean the war is lost," Gabriel said. "You can plan your battles from Wetpr."

"Or Lentz, I will make the same offer as Gabriel," Stephan said. "You are good men living in a kingdom that destroys good men. You might be able to do more good from outside of Ryed."

"While Teivel appears strong, ultimate control and domination are signs of the weak and the fearful. We need to find out Teivel's weaknesses and fears," Gabriel said.

Gabriel, Dominic, Stephan and Michael made an appearance in the main dining room of the Teivel Manor for a late lunch. Natasha walked up to their table to greet the men. "I am actually having fun," she said. "The gathering is scheduled to start at seven so that should give you time. And I already gave Calen a few things that I picked up." Natasha's comment made the men smile.

"How is Clay feeling?" Gabriel asked in a louder voice.

"He's walking around but he looks awful," Natasha replied. "If he continues to feel sick I may offer to help him some more."

"I think that would be fine, I hate to see him so under the weather," Gabriel said as the waiter approached the table.

"Well, I will leave you men to eat," Natasha said.

But before Natasha could leave the table Dominic said, "Honey I haven't seen you all day, give me a kiss before you leave. The waiter was standing at the table as Natasha leaned down and kissed Dominic on the cheek. He whispered into her ear, "Teivel's men routinely threaten the waiters to spy for them."

"I will save the first dance for you," Natasha said loud enough for the waiter to hear. She smiled and left the table.

After Gabriel ordered his food he walked out of the dining room and up to the desk clerk. "I would like a carriage in an hour. Tobey is our usual driver. Would you make the arrangements for me?"

"I would be happy to but Tobey hasn't been seen in a couple of days My Lord. I will get you another driver," the clerk replied.

"Has something happened to Tobey? I rather liked the fella."

"That I couldn't tell you," the clerk replied with sincerity. "Is there another driver you would request?"

Gabriel walked up very close to the clerk and pressed several gold coins into the palm of his hand. "What is your name?" Gabriel asked.

"Tom, My Lord."

"Tom, I need you to be honest with me. I offered Tobey a job to be my personal driver. Did he get into trouble for that?"

"I have no idea My Lord. All I know is that we have been short a driver for the last two days, then I heard that Tobey didn't show up for work."

"Is this normal for him; because I wouldn't want to hire someone so unreliable."

"My Lord I have known Tobey for five years and he has never missed a day of work."

"Tom, I know this is an unusual request but can you tell me where Tobey lives?"

"Yes My Lord, I will draw you a map." Tom took a piece of paper and drew a detailed map that showed both the location of the hotel and Tobey's home. "My Lord if Tobey is ill and needs something please let me know," Tom said as he handed the map to Gabriel. "Would you still like a carriage?

"Yes," Gabriel said and returned to his table in the dining room.

"Something is going on," Gabriel said in a low voice when he sat down at the table. "Tobey has been missing for two days and he hasn't missed a day of work in five years. I got a map to his house. I want to check on him then go to the other auction houses. Someone may have hurt Tobey so another driver can spy on us. We will bring Thaos and Jared too and when the carriage arrives I want one of you to replace the driver."

Gabriel stopped talking because the waiter walked up to the table. Dominic looked at the waiter and asked, "Would you be kind enough to ask my wife to come here? I assume she is still in the kitchen."

"Yes My Lord," the waiter said and returned to the kitchen.

A few minutes later Natasha walked up to the table and Gabriel told her about Tobey. Natasha got a look in her eyes that only Gabriel had seen before. "I liked that old man and if someone hurt him because he helped us there will be hell to pay. I'll bet Clay is behind this or at least knows what happened. Do you have any more of that truth potion on you?"

"Another dose might kill him," Gabriel said.

"The first dose might be killing him and if he dies we may never find out what happened to Tobey," Natasha said angrily.

"You stay close to Clay and we will go to Tobey's house if we don't find him we will return and deal with Clay," Gabriel said.

"Well don't be long because I might take matters into my own hands," Natasha said and stomped away from the table.

"Does she mean that?" Dominic asked.

369

"You have no idea," Gabriel said with a grin. "Is everyone done eating?"

"I'll go upstairs and get Thaos and Jared," Stephan said and left the table.

"Do you think Natasha will be alright?" Michael asked. "I mean I know she can handle herself but this entire hotel could be filled with spies. I think I will go upstairs and tell a couple of the others to watch over her."

Gabriel looked at Dominic and explained in a low voice, "I raised my sister and she has been helping me with these type of missions for years. She is smart and can think quickly on her feet. And she fights as well as any man I have ever worked with. But she looks so sweet and innocent that no one suspects what she is capable of."

"You know I didn't trust you at first," Dominic said. "But I must say all of you intrigue me. Perhaps when this is over I will take you up on your offer."

Thaos, Stephan and Jared walked up to the table. "Michael and the others are right behind us," Thaos said. Within moments, Michael and Rachel walked down the steps and behind them were Calen and Dagon. Rachel did not stop at the table but walked directly into the kitchen. Rachel had become very close to Natasha and did not want to lose another friend.

Gabriel quickly stood up and walked up to Calen and Dagon and acted like he was introducing himself to the two Rualas. Gabriel escorted Dagon and Calen to the table and all of the men sat down together. Gabriel knew that Michael had not been gone long enough to brief Calen and Dagon on the events of the morning so Gabriel did it now. Before Gabriel was done speaking Rachel and Natasha walked up to the table.

"Honey since you have plans is it alright if I help Natasha?" Rachel asked loudly as she looked at Gabriel. "I am getting rather bored sitting in the room."

"By all means dear. Natasha said she is having fun. I hope you both enjoy yourselves. But first let me introduce you to Calen and Dagon." Rachel walked up to both men who kissed her hand.

"Calen and I have already met," Natasha said. "He is the liaison for Prince Lakin and has been helping with arrangements. As Natasha spoke she walked up to Dagon and Calen and both men kissed her hand which made Natasha grin.

A waiter walked up to Natasha and said. "A carriage full of flowers just arrived My Lady."

"Good," Natasha said sweetly to the waiter then she turned to Rachel. "We have some work to do."

"I know you mean only the best," Calen said as he stood up. "But for formal events such as this we do have protocol. Perhaps we should join you."

"I am glad you said something," Natasha said. "We want everything perfect." Dagon and Calen left the dining room with Rachel and Natasha.

The desk clerk walked up to Gabriel, "Your carriage is here My Lord."

"Thank you Tom, I appreciate your service," Gabriel said and the men stood up from the table.

As the men were walking through the hotel towards the front entrance Michael laughed and said in a low voice, "I told Calen and Dagon that Natasha was mad and ready to take things into her own hands. Those two boys almost knocked me over running down the stairs."

When Gabriel and his group walked up to their carriage they saw that it was the specially designed carriage that Clay usually had for them but today there was a driver and an additional man riding in front. Gabriel walked up to the men and said with a voice of authority, "You can get down. My men will drive. I am learning that I cannot trust anyone in this city. I am sure you understand."

"But I must protest..." the driver didn't finish his sentence because Thaos pulled him out of the front seat and threw him to the ground. The second man climbed down from the front seat willingly when he saw the size of his opponents.

"I want to drive," Jared said and climbed into the front seat. Stephan sat next to Jared. Michael and Thaos took the rear security seats of the carriage while Dominic and Gabriel climbed inside.

"Do you have weapons on you?" Gabriel asked Dominic.

"Of course and I have a bad feeling about today."

Stephan had the map to Tobey's house and was telling Jared the directions. They drove through the city until they came to a street that was crowded with brick buildings that all looked the same. The buildings were dingy and there was trash everywhere on the street. When Jared stopped the carriage in front of Tobey's home they could see that the front door was open and hanging by only one hinge. All of the men dismounted the carriage and ran into the building.

They searched the three room home which was torn apart. "I found blood stains in the bedroom and children's toys," Stephan said angrily.

A small group of neighbors gathered around the front door of Tobey's home when they saw Gabriel and his men run inside. "What happened to these people?" Gabriel asked. But the neighbors looked fearful and no one spoke. "We mean you no harm," Gabriel said as he walked closer to the group of on-lookers. Gabriel did not see anyone in the small group who looked like one of Teivel's men.

"Did anyone hear or see anything?" Stephan asked. "We are here to help." Still the small crowd stood silent.

The people in the crowd started to move to allow and old woman to walk through. The woman was small with a black shawl covering her head and shoulders. She wore a black dress that was losing its color from age. The woman walked up to Gabriel and peered into his eyes. "Let me hold your hand," the woman said with a voice so powerful it did not seem to belong to such a fragile body.

Gabriel held out both of his hands and as the woman held them she continued to stare into his eyes. A smile came across her face and her demeanor relaxed. She turned back to the small crowd and said. "Tell this man what you saw."

Hesitantly a man in torn clothing came forward and stammered as he spoke. "The demons took them two nights ago."

"Can you describe the demons?" Gabriel asked. "Were they Teivel's or another group?"

"Teivel's," the man said fearfully. "They had the tattoos."

"Do you know where they were taken?" Gabriel asked.

"No one ever knows," the man replied fearfully.

The old woman looked at the crowd and said, "Leave us." Then she moved to the middle of the small house to a spot that could not be observed from the outside. Gabriel and the other warriors understood what she was doing.

"Are you a seer?" Gabriel asked as the men gathered around her.

"I am many things but I prefer to call myself a healer but the question is what are you?"

"What do you mean?" Gabriel asked. "What did you see?"

"When I took your hands I saw thick darkness then light exploded and the darkness was no more. Then I heard a voice that told me if I ever wanted to save my people I should work with you. I am at your service."

"What is your name?" Gabriel asked.

"Ruth."

"Ruth just out of curiosity was it a man's voice or a woman's voice that you heard?" Gabriel asked with a smile.

Ruth got a quizzical look on her face as she answered, "A woman's voice."

"Thank you Miranda," Gabriel said out loud.

"Who is Miranda?" Ruth asked.

"An Angel," Gabriel said with a warm smile. "Does that surprise you?"

"No," the old woman said with tears forming in her eyes. "I thought the Angels had forgotten us."

Gabriel grasped Ruth's hand and squeezed it. "You are not forgotten," he said. "But I fear that Tobey and his family were taken because he helped us. Are we putting your people in danger by being in this building?"

"We live in hell; we are always in danger," Ruth replied in a dry manner.

"Ruth we need to talk," Gabriel said as Stephan and the others were looking out the windows, expecting an attack. "Would I be putting you in danger if you returned to our hotel with us?"

"An Angel spoke to me today; I fear nothing." Ruth said with conviction.

Gabriel held out his arm for Ruth to take. "Ask her to bring the bag she has been protecting," Miranda's voice whispered into Gabriel's ear.

"Miranda just said I should ask you to bring the bag you have been protecting," Gabriel said.

Initially Ruth looked shocked then she said, "I guess I shouldn't be surprised. Gentlemen my home is across the street."

"Let me go out first," Michael said. Then Michael did something he had never done before, he called to the Angels. "Miranda I have a really bad feeling please protect these people."

"I was wondering what it would take for you to call upon us," Miranda said and her voice was heard by all in the house. Gabriel quickly put his arm around Ruth as he could feel her knees weaken when she heard the Angel's voice.

"Ruth pack a bag of belongings; you will be staying with Gabriel's team for a while," Miranda said.

Ruth looked around the room as she did not know where to direct her words. "My people, will you protect them while I am gone?"

"Yes but you should leave soon."

Michael was not the only member of Gabriel's group to have a feeling of foreboding. Jared climbed into the driver's seat of the carriage. Michael and Stephan stood on the street as Gabriel, Thaos and Dominic escorted Ruth inside of her small home.

"I am sorry I don't know all of your names yet," Ruth said. "But would you boys move this cupboard for me?" Dominic and Thaos moved the large and heavy piece of furniture. "Under that rug there is a loose floorboard," she explained. "Under the board is the bag the Angel spoke of. I will pack while you boys get that."

Thaos pulled the bag out of the hole in the floorboards and handed it to Gabriel who carefully placed it on a table. Gabriel took one of the linen wrapped objects out of the bag and said, "This is a Holy Scroll." Then Gabriel looked back into the bag and counted five more scrolls. Ruth entered the room with a cloth bag which Thaos took from her. "Ruth are these the scrolls that were originally given to your kingdom?" Gabriel asked as he held his arm out for her.

"Yes, my family has been protecting them for as long as I can remember. Will you take them someplace safe?"

"I will take them wherever Miranda tells me," Gabriel said. "Have you read them?"

"Of course," Ruth said with indignation. "Do you think I would endanger the lives of my people for nothing? When people come to me for healing, it is not just their bodies that I heal. I teach them about The Great Ruler."

"So all of the people in this community know of The Great Ruler?" Gabriel asked with surprise.

"Yes and to study the teachings of The Great Ruler is a death sentence here," Ruth said as Gabriel helped her inside of the carriage.

Dominic sat across from Ruth and asked, "So you have risked her life to teach of God?"

"My son, can you imagine any better reason to risk one's life?" Ruth paused as if she was studying Dominic. "Son let me hold her hand," Ruth said and leaned forward.

375

Ruth held Dominic's hand for several moments then let go and leaned back in the seat. "I thought you were a Libertas. It is no coincidence that we have all been brought together. I felt the loneliness and pain you have endured. And I saw a connection between you and Gabriel although I don't really understand what I saw. I believe your destiny has taken a change in course and you are now entwined with Gabriel. You are considering leaving here with Gabriel; the answer is yes, you should."

Gabriel looked across the seat at Dominic and smiled. "I will help you become a Patronus priest and I can always use a warrior on my team."

"You are a priest?" Ruth asked Gabriel.

"I am High Priest Gabriel of the Patronus and I serve The Great Ruler."

"What are you doing in this land that swears allegiance to all that is dark?" Ruth asked.

"I believe Miranda showed you when you took my hand," Gabriel said with a smile.

"I never thought I would live long enough to see my prayers answered," Ruth said emotionally. "There are so few of you; you must be very powerful men."

"I was just thinking the same about you My Lady," Gabriel said.

"We have company?" Stephan called down to the passengers in the carriage.

A dozen demons wearing the tattoo of a curved knife surrounded with demonic symbols stood in the roadway about one hundred feet in front of the carriage. "Do not stop there are more," Miranda's voice said to Jared.

"Hang on," Jared yelled. "Miranda said not to stop." Jared charged the horses towards the demons who did not move. The demons prepared for attack as the carriage drove towards them. Suddenly deafening screams were heard as the eighty demons hiding near the roadway burst into flames as did the demons that had been blocking the road. The horses and the carriage trampled over the smoldering ashes.

376

"Thank you Miranda," Thaos called out.

Tears ran down Ruth's face as she stared out the windows. "Is this really happening?" she asked in awe. Then Ruth looked upwards and said, "Thank you Miranda."

Chapter XXIX
Ruth

As Gabriel and his group entered the Teivel Manor Hotel they found chaos. The lobby and dining room were filled with Ruala and Shettee warriors and hotel staff appeared to be running in every direction. Gabriel was surprised because he did not know these warriors were coming to help with the mission. He stopped one of the frantic waiters.

"What is going on here?" Gabriel asked.

"All of these warriors are here for the games and we are trying to find enough rooms. There is even a king here, he is up at the desk," the young man said then hurried off.

"Michael, Jared would you please take Ruth upstairs and find her a room," Gabriel said then he pushed through the crowd until he reached the hotel desk. King Neputa and Thedes were standing in front of the group and both acted as if they did not know Gabriel.

"Tom," Gabriel said to the flustered desk clerk. "I am told there are not enough rooms for all of these warriors. They can stay on my floor." Now Gabriel turned to Neputa and Thedes and asked. "Which of you is King Neputa?"

"I am," Neputa replied in a dignified manner.

"I have rented the entire top floor of the hotel for security reasons. I have many empty rooms, please honor me with your presence." Before Neputa could speak Gabriel turned back to Tom and said. "Are there extra beds that your staff can bring up to my floor?"

"Yes My Lord," Tom said with relief.

Gabriel turned back to Neputa and said, "Each set of chambers is quite large, would your warriors mind sharing rooms?"

"Of course not and we thank you for your graciousness," Neputa said.

Thedes looked at Tom and asked "Would it help if our warriors also carried the beds upstairs?"

"Yes, My Lord it certainly would," Tom said.

Thedes turned to the army of warriors behind him. We will be going up to the top floor of the hotel but we will need to help carry extra beds," Thedes bellowed. "Half of you go upstairs now to make room down here." Thaos and Stephan were standing with Gabriel and grinning at their friend Thedes.

It took over two hours for the chaos to subside but all of the warriors were housed on the fourth and fifth floors of the hotel. Lakin had previously rented the fourth floor of the hotel. Staff from the hotel borrowed beds from other hotels to accommodate all of the warriors. Clay sent employees out to purchase more food, wine and whiskey.

As the warriors were settling in, Neputa and Thedes met with Gabriel and Lakin. "We were holding the weekly meeting of the Grand Council when Miranda and Daniel appeared to us," Thedes explained. "As you know we were all aware of your mission but Daniel said there had been some changes and that your group would need help very soon. He told us to come to this hotel and to pretend that we did not know you. Daniel said you would take care of the rest."

"I think we are under suspicion. We have been spied upon and Miranda just helped us as we were attacked by a group of demons," Gabriel explained. "First I want to have a meeting of the leaders and core group then we will meet with all the warriors. My chambers are straight ahead. Please make yourselves comfortable while I find a few others."

"Michael would you take Ruth to my chambers for a meeting, I have to find the others." Gabriel said as he worked his way through the crowd.

Michael escorted Ruth into Gabriel's chambers. The woman was excited to meet Rualas and Shettees. "Miranda just told us to bring Ruth here," Michael said to the group that was gathering in Gabriel's chambers. She was protecting a set of Holy Scrolls, she is a healer a teacher and a seer." Michael was about to introduce Ruth to Prince Lakin when Ruth walked closer to Lakin with a broad smile.

"My son the light surrounding you is almost blinding. May I take your hand?"

379

"Of course," Lakin said with a warm smile and reached out to Ruth.

"You are an incredibly powerful healer and warrior but you are yet at the beginning of your journey. You have sacrificed greatly for your work but you will not be able to imagine the rewards. Stay the course you are on. It is an honor to meet you."

"Perhaps after the meeting you would like to discuss healing," Lakin said.

"I would like that very much," Ruth said then suddenly turned to Thedes and Neputa as if she heard a voice. Both of the warriors stared at Ruth as she walked up to them and grasped each of their hands. Ruth closed her eyes and tears started to run down her cheeks.

"My sons you have seen such horror in your lives but the choices you have made are leading you on a much different path. A path of great honor and happiness. You both feared you were the last of your kind. Your people will once again flourish." Ruth opened her eyes then looked over at Lakin. "I see a connection between your two tribes. A very powerful connection as family but more. I am not sure I understand what I see."

"The Sanuri saved both of our tribes from extinction," Thedes said. "He gave us sanctuary in the Ice Caves of Mordv. Our tribes live there together."

"The Sanuri," Ruth gasped. "I didn't know if he really existed."

"He is here in Ryed with us," Thedes said. "Not in the city but close by."

Tears once again ran down Ruth's face. "Now I am beginning to understand. As I held your hands I saw your lives but I also saw two words over and over. The words were 'miracles' and 'hope'. I don't really know what to expect here but perhaps later you can tell me about your tribe. I would love to hear of your people."

"We would be honored," Neputa said as Gabriel entered the room with Natasha, Rachel, Dagon, Calen and Dominic.

Gabriel stood in front of the room and spoke. "First I wanted to have a meeting with all of you then later we will meet with the other warriors. Since our army here is so large now I will need you to delegate others to spread information from our meetings. Thedes said that the Angels Miranda and Daniel appeared at one of the Grand Council meetings in the Ice Caves and said that we would need help soon which is why so many more came today."

"Gabriel, Lakin and the others have to be downstairs at seven," Natasha said.

"I know dear, I plan to just quickly cover the bases here," Gabriel said. "This morning some of us had a meeting with two generals from the Ryed Military who we suspect are part of a group who are planning a coup. Our meeting was interrupted when Michael caught one of the waiters spying on us. The waiter did not seem like a terrorist and told us that Teivel's men often threaten employees like waiters to spy for them. So remember that."

"Previously we made contact with a carriage driver who not only helped us find the perfect building for our cover but gave us a great deal of information. I told him I would help him and his family to move to Nora. This morning we discovered that Teivel's demons kidnapped Tobey and his family two nights ago."

"What!" Natasha yelled and stood up. "I'm going to kill Clay. Tobey is such a nice old man."

Calen jumped up and grabbed his wife around the waist, lifting Natasha off the floor as she tried to leave the meeting. "Just hold on Natasha," Calen said. "At least let Gabriel finish talking." Calen sat down and pulled Natasha onto his lap. She was visibly angry.

"Ruth would you please come up here?" Gabriel asked. "As we were searching Tobey's home which had been torn apart a group of neighbors gathered. Ruth was the obvious leader and when she approached me Miranda spoke to her. Ruth is a healer, a seer, a teacher of The Holy Scrolls and I am sure I will find out more when we get a chance to talk. Ruth has been protecting the set of Holy Scrolls that was originally given to the Kingdom of Ryed. Miranda said that if Ruth wanted to save her people she should work with us."

381

Gabriel continued, "Miranda also said that Ruth should stay here with us for a while. Since we all just met there is much to discuss but we have a function to go to now. There is a party to honor the arrival of the Rualas in the main dining room in about twenty minutes. Everyone have fun but realize you are being spied upon. Natasha you and I will deal with Clay."

"Good!" Natasha said then looked at Calen. "You can let go of me now."

"I don't know when I've seen you this angry before," Calen said with a grin as he released his grasp on Natasha.

"Child please come here," Ruth said as she stared at Natasha who turned and walked up to Ruth. "Please let me take your hand." Ruth held Natasha's hand and stared at her for a few moments, then Ruth looked at Gabriel then looked at Calen and others in the room. "Are you and Gabriel related?" Ruth asked.

"Yes he is my brother."

"But there is another brother who also lives with you?"

"Raphael is like a brother and he is also a High Priest," Gabriel said. "My core team all lives together in one gigantic house."

"And Calen is your husband?" Ruth asked Natasha.

"Yes, why is something wrong?" Natasha asked.

"I also see another couple perhaps a brother of Calen's with a young wife with long blonde hair."

"Misha and Diana," Calen said. "They are in Ryed too."

"Gabriel, Raphael, Natasha and Calen, Misha and Diana you are all going to have baby boys in a short period of time and I cannot tell you why but that is significant."

"I'm pregnant?" Natasha gasped. Calen let out a war cry and many laughed.

"What do you mean it is significant?" Gabriel asked.

"I can't really explain it," Ruth said and paused as if she was listening to a voice. "I think it has something to do with a prophesy. But I am also seeing that many of you here are part of a different prophesy. You speak with Angels I believe this is a question you should ask of them."

"Gabriel does Ruth have to be in hiding?" Lakin asked.

"Miranda didn't say so."

Lakin walked up to Ruth, "Would you do me the honor of being my escort at this function. There is a great deal I would like to discuss with you."

"I would be honored," Ruth said with a huge smile. "But I am afraid I did not bring clothing for such an event.

"It doesn't matter," Lakin said. "Most of us are wearing our warrior robes." Lakin held out his arm for Ruth.

Calen walked up to Natasha and picked her up and held her high in the air. "I am so happy," he said.

"I am too Honey but I am still also worried about Tobey and his family. You know they took them because he helped us. We have to make this right," Natasha said.

"I'll go down with you and Gabriel," Calen said and kissed Natasha.

Rachel squeezed Dagon's hand and said with fear in her voice, "I want to ask Ruth about my father but I am afraid of hearing the answer. Is that awful of me?"

"I will walk up there with you if you like," Dagon said.

"I would like that," Rachel said and took a deep breath. She grasped Dagon's hand tightly and the two stood up.

Ruth and Lakin were walking out of the room when Dagon called to the woman, "Ruth would you talk to Rachel for a moment?" Lakin and Ruth stopped walking and faced Rachel and Dagon. Rachel was shaking as she approached Ruth. Dagon could feel Rachel shaking and saw the look of fear on her face so he spoke.

"Rachel's father is a freedom fighter and he was kidnapped by demons. The demons tried to take the rest of her family but we stopped them. Her mother and brother are in hiding and she is helping us to try and find her father."

Ruth did not speak but took Rachel's hand. The older woman was silent for several moments and Rachel started to cry. "What I am seeing is darkness," Ruth said. "I feel that your father is still alive but I don't know if the darkness is where he is being kept or a prediction of things to come. Child let go of Dagon's hand and let me hold both of yours."

Ruth's request scared Rachel more. "For such a young girl you carry a heavy burden. You have some important choices to make that partially involve that young man who loves you. Think wisely and do not let your fears dictate your future. You and your family have been exposed as Libertas although your identity here is not known. All of you are in great danger."

"But the Sanuri is with Rachel's mother and brother," Dagon said. "How can they be in danger?"

"But the Sanuri will be coming here soon." Ruth paused. "I see someone standing with the Sanuri but he is of great darkness."

"Erebus is a sorcerer who is helping us," Dagon said.

"A sorcerer!" Ruth gasped.

"It is a long story but he is an enemy of Teivel's also and is helping us for revenge," Dagon explained.

"The sorcerer is at a crossroads and has important choices to make. He is being pulled in great directions."

"Is he a danger to Mother and Zack," Rachel asked. "Because Erebus has been really good to us."

"He is not a direct danger but what haunts him is. I believe that is why the Sanuri is with him, although I don't really understand what I am seeing."

"I don't understand is Mother and Zack in danger of Erebus because he is hiding them?" Rachel asked.

"I would have faith that the Sanuri will make sure they are protected. You my child are in more danger than they are. The fears for your family overwhelm you; the decisions you make may cost your life as well as the lives of others. I can give you no more information than that for now."

Rachel was visibly upset so Dagon took her to their chambers. He poured two glasses of wine and they both sat down on the sofa in the parlor. "What Ruth said was vague but makes me believe that your father could be used in some kind of trap. I will speak about this with Gabriel as soon as we are done here. But I also agree with what Ruth said. Rachel you are a trained warrior but you have to admit you do not think clearly when it comes to your father."

"We promised to spend time together so we could get to know each other before all hell breaks loose here and I know that too has overwhelmed you."

"Dagon it did at first but it feels so good being with you that I am not afraid anymore. I really do care about you; it's just that with everything with my family, I am not sure I can really explain it," Rachel paused. "It's like my head and my heart just didn't have room for anything else but I am very happy that you talked me into a relationship."

"I am glad to hear your words. But I must talk to you seriously. I told you before that I have been on many missions and in the beginning they are usually like this in that we have time on our hands while Gabriel and the others find out information. But when things go bad that happens quickly. Once the battles begin it is like we are fighting then the next thing we know we are heading home."

"I have been thinking about some things and after hearing Ruth speak, well; Rachel I want to send you, Zelda and Zack to Wetpr. Most of my family as well as Gabriel's team lives together. I will find your father and bring him home to you. I will take care of you and your family even if you decide you don't want to be my girl."

"I feel both relieved and angry at your words," Rachel said as she stiffened up. "While I cannot image not wanting to be your girl; you are not my husband and you cannot control my life."

"I appreciate your offer but Mother will never leave until she finds out what happened to Father. And he is my Father I must find him."

"And if you get killed because you are too emotional who will take care of Zelda and Zack?" Dagon asked. "Rachel didn't you understand what Ruth was saying. You could get your entire family killed. I know I am not your husband, at least not yet, but I am going to tell you what to do in this situation. And you can just be mad at me but I like Zelda and Zack and I don't want to see them hurt because of your pride. I am sending Zelda a letter tonight telling her Ruth's words and making the same offer I am making you. She has a right to make her own choices."

Rachel stared angrily at Dagon. "Rachel we can always bring your family back here at a later time if they want to return. And I understand how your mother must feel but she is also protecting Zack. Give her the information and let Zelda make her own decisions. You would want that if the roles were reversed. My mother is one hell of a warrior and she will do whatever is necessary to protect her children and grandchildren. I would suspect Zelda is the same way."

"Alright we can both write her a letter tonight but I am staying here. And if Mother agrees to go to your home I will find a way to pay you back for their room and board."

"Oh I can think of plenty of ways you can pay me back," Dagon said with a mischievous grin. Rachel blushed then giggled then she playfully punched his arm. Dagon pulled her close to him and kissed Rachel on the lips. "So you like being my girl?" he asked.

"Yes, you make me happy but I am still staying here," Rachel said with a grin and kissed Dagon.

"Good then think about becoming my wife and tell Zelda I want to marry you."

"Are you serious?"

"Do you think I would joke about something like this?"

"I might just say yes," Rachel said with a big grin. "But you have to ask my father first."

386

"You aren't going to make it easy on me are you?" Dagon asked and kissed her again.

"You have no idea," Rachel said and laughed. "We should write a letter to your mother also tonight," Rachel said then paused. "Dagon I am going to ask you for a really big favor?"

"Ask," Dagon said and kissed the tip of Rachel's nose.

"If Father dies and if I am killed in battle will you take care of Mother and Zack? Mother is a great cook and seamstress. She could get a job some place but they will still need help; at least at first."

"I will make that promise but don't plan on getting killed," Dagon said. "I am serious I think you are just too emotional now to go into battle and I am going to tell Gabriel that. Now do you want to come with me when I talk to Gabriel or do you want to start the letters?"

"I'll come with you. You should also tell Gabriel what Ruth said about Erebus."

"I was planning to," Dagon said. "Rachel if we get married, Gabriel and the others will probably ask you to join the team as all of their wives also work with us. That is your decision to make but understand if you act in such a manner here that they lose trust in you; you will never be allowed on the team. Our team does a lot of good and we save lives; it is just something for you to think about."

When Dagon and Rachel walked out of their chambers they saw Gabriel, Natasha, Calen, Dominic, Thaos, Michael, Stephan and Jared just starting to descend the stairs from the fifth floor. "Gabriel," Dagon called. "Ruth talked to Rachel and there are some things I need to tell you. It will only take a few minutes."

"Can the others hear?" Gabriel asked.

"Yes," Rachel said.

Gabriel's small group now turned around and walked towards Gabriel's chambers.

Rachel let go of Dagon's hand and whispered into Natasha's ear. Natasha smiled and walked up to Dagon and kissed him on the cheek.

"What's going on?" Calen asked with a grin.

"I told Rachel I want to marry her and she is going to make me work for it," Dagon said happily.

"Good girl!" Calen said and kissed Rachel on the cheek. Everyone in the group smiled.

As soon as everyone was in Gabriel's chambers, Dagon told them word for word what Ruth had said to them. Then Dagon told them of the conversation that he and Rachel had after speaking with Ruth.

"This concerns me for several reasons," Gabriel said. "First the Sanuri was not supposed to expose his presence here for some time. I suspect something is going to happen soon since the Angels are sending us help. Also, if Rachel's family has been exposed others might also. Rachel I want to minimize your involvement for a while."

"What do you mean?" asked Rachel.

"I don't want you attending all of these gatherings in case you are recognized. We will say you are sick."

"I think we should say she is sick from pregnancy. Look how sick Vivian is one minute and the next she is better. That way we have a good explanation when Rachel does join us," Natasha said.

"I can do that," Rachel said. "But I would like other things to work on. I can make maps or write letters or draw?"

"Oh, I will put you to work," Gabriel said. "But you are going to get mad at me now. I agree with Dagon that you are over-whelmed by your emotions. Now don't get me wrong anyone would be in your place. But in our group when someone is like that we have them stand down for a while so they don't get others hurt. Rachel I do know you well enough that you would not want to expose the mission or get your friends hurt."

388

"I need to send a letter to the Sanuri about Erebus," Gabriel continued. "Rachel I don't know if you are aware that Erebus has turned against many in the dark worlds to enact his revenge. He has softened a great deal while working with us because he is being treated as one of the family. I cannot believe he would hurt Zelda or Zack, in fact I believe he is very attached to them. But if the Sanuri leaves the castle; as powerful as Erebus is he might not be able to protect your family."

"What do you mean he is attached to my family? Does he have feelings for Mother?" Rachel asked.

"I am going to tell you all something that you will not repeat," Gabriel said. "The Sanuri told me that for all of the wealth and power that Erebus has he greatly regrets that he never had children. He has no family of any kind and that is why he loves it that the younger members of our team in particular treat him like family."

"I can understand that," Thaos said. "I used to be the same way."

"I don't think everyone should leave Erebus alone at his castle," Jared said. "If Zelda and Zack don't want to leave Ryed, I say we take them to Vivian's village for protection and have the Sanuri bring Erebus here."

"I was thinking the same thing," Gabriel said. "I was also planning on speaking with Ruth later tonight; now I am convinced that I need to."

"Gabriel I have an idea that might be of use," Rachel said. "In our village when we have festivities artists will draw pictures of people, usually for money but sometimes not. But people really enjoy the pictures. I can draw well enough to do this. I know you want to keep me out of sight but people do know that I am here. Perhaps I can stay in the background and draw pictures of people you are interested in but I will also draw others so people don't become suspicious of me."

"It might be suspicious if Rachel suddenly disappears," Michael said. "I mean all of us are already under suspicion."

"I have paper, pen and charcoal," Natasha said.

"First Rachel and I have to write letters to Zelda, Emeral and Maxwell." Dagon said. "Do you want me to start a letter to the Sanuri then you can add what you want?" Dagon asked Gabriel."

"Yes in fact start letters to Sudfad and Raphael also. Tell them about everything that has happened today, the spies, the attacks and Ruth and I will finish them tonight. Also it is obvious to others that you two have feelings for each other. Unless you are really good actors you will need to stay away from each other in public."

"I thought as much," Dagon said.

"One of us will come up here in a couple of hours and if Rachel is done with the letters we will escort her to the gathering," Jared said.

"And Rachel I don't mean to be all business, welcome to the family," Gabriel said and kissed her on the cheek.

Chapter XXX
Clay

When Gabriel, Dominic, Natasha, Michael, Stephan, Jared and Thaos arrived on the first floor of the Teivel Manor Hotel they saw that all of the dining rooms and the lobby were filled with people for the gathering to honor Prince Lakin and the Rualas. Gabriel's group stopped for a moment and surveyed the crowd. "I have a bad feeling about this," Gabriel said. "There are so many people here; I will bet half of them are spies."

"Then let's give them a show," Jared said with a grin.

Natasha turned and handed Gabriel a metal ring that held two keys. "There is a large wine cellar below this dining room. No one has access to it without this set of keys which Clay believes he still possess. How much truth potion do you have on you?"

"A lot," Gabriel said with a broad grin. He always enjoyed his little sister's ingenuity. "So you want to take advantage of the spies being here?"

"Saves us time from hunting them down," Michael said with a grin. "I think it is time we went on the offensive."

"I can draw people out of the crowd," Natasha said. "But I want to start with Clay first. We have to find Tobey and his family."

"First, Natasha you distract Clay while the rest of us check out the cellar and set it up. We might need to bring Rachel down here too," Gabriel said. Before Gabriel finished speaking Joao and Dack walked up to the group.

"We have walked through all the rooms and while there are a lot of citizens here that are excited to meet Rualas there are a bunch of guys dressed in suits who look like hired fighters," Joao said. "I can just feel this is going to be trouble."

"We were just saying the same thing," Gabriel said. "Joao you and Dack go upstairs and get all the rope you can find. We will be taking prisoners and putting them into the cellar. Jared you run upstairs and tell Dagon and Rachel what we are doing, we will need her to help lure people. The rest of us will investigate the cellar."

391

"Where do you want us to meet you?" Dack asked.

"The door to the wine cellar is in Clay's office, which I find suspicious," Natasha said. "The larger key on that ring is to the office and the other one is to the cellar door. I am going to find Clay and introduce him to a few people to distract him. Let me know when you want me to bring him to his office."

"Thaos tell Thedes and Lakin what we are doing then meet us in Clay's office. The rest of you meet us there also," Gabriel said.

"I can't believe I am saying this but if you don't stop kissing me we will never get these letters written," Dagon said then laughed.

"So you are telling me the honeymoon is over already?" Rachel teased and feigned a pout.

"Just wait until we have a honeymoon," Dagon said and kissed Rachel on the lips. "But we need to get some work done."

"It's Jared," Jared called out as he knocked on the door to Dagon's and Rachel's chambers.

"Come in," Dagon yelled.

"You're gonna have to put that letter writing on hold," Jared said. "The place is packed and a lot of the guys look like hired fighters. Natasha stole keys to the wine cellar and Gabriel plans on removing people from the gathering and tying them up in the cellar then using the truth potion. Rachel he wants you and Natasha to lure people from the party."

"I'll get dressed," Rachel said and jumped up from the sofa and ran into her bedroom.

"Rachel I'll be back for you," Jared said. "Gabriel wants me to get some more vials of potion from his room."

"I'll help you," Dagon said to Jared. "What does Gabriel want me to do?"

"Join us in the cellar I am guessing. You will probably need to bring some paper if there are going to be interrogations," Jared said.

"Clay I have been looking all over for you," Natasha said sweetly as she took Clay's arm. "I know you were taking a nap so I wanted to introduce you to a few people who arrived earlier. Are you feeling any better?"

"No, I feel awful," Clay said. His face was pale and he was sweating profusely.

"Do you think you have something besides a hangover?" Natasha asked as she walked Clay towards Neputa, Thedes and Thaos.

"I am beginning to wonder that myself," Clay said. Then he smiled at Natasha. "I do appreciate your help. The rooms look beautiful."

By the time that Natasha approached Thedes, Neputa and Thaos; Thaos had briefed the two men on Gabriel's plan. Clay this is King Neputa of the Shettee Tribe and this is Prince Thedes he is married to Princess Ibula of the Ruala Tribe and you know Thaos. This is Clay he is the manager of this beautiful hotel and he has his finger on the pulse of everything that happens around here," Natasha said.

"It is an honor," Clay said as he shook hands with the Shettees. "I have never met any members of your tribe before. Please just let me know what I can do to make your stay more comfortable."

"Thank you," Neputa said as he stared at Clay suspiciously.

"Clay, tell me all of these thugs in suits are they your hired security?" Thaos asked.

"I don't know what you are talking about," Clay said with genuine surprise.

"You mean you haven't seen them?" Thaos asked suspiciously.

"I was in my room sleeping until ten minutes ago," Clay said. "Point these men out to me?"

As soon as Thaos and Clay disappeared into the crowd Thedes said. "We want to help you. What do you need?"

"First spread the word among our warriors about what is going on," Natasha said. "There are a lot of innocent citizens here so we don't want this turning into a blood bath. Rachel will be down soon and she and I will lure people from the gathering. I have to talk to Lakin. Gabriel is in the cellar now, when you see him ask him what he wants you to do."

When Natasha found Lakin he was sitting at a small table talking with Ruth. The two were so intent in their conversation that they were not initially aware of Natasha's presence. Natasha quickly sat down at the table and told Lakin and Ruth about Gabriel's plans and the possible threats. "Clay is with Thaos now. We are keeping him distracted," Natasha explained. "I was going to introduce him to you but I don't know if Clay should see Ruth."

"Why child?" Ruth asked.

"Because we want to protect you," said Natasha.

"I am always protected," Ruth said humbly. "Prince Lakin has been telling me about, well, what all of you are doing. I think you should bring Clay here and let me see if I can get a reading on him. All of you are from such different worlds that I don't know if you can really comprehend life here; and by no means do I mean to insult you. I mean that you are all such good people that you cannot understand the centuries of fear and tyranny of this land."

Ruth continued, "Think of an onion with all the layers of skin. That is what the underworld is like here. For as bad as Clay sounds he could be just one of the outer layers and have no idea of what the other layers are doing. There are no easy answers here. Your mission is immensely more dangerous and complicated than you understand. An Angel spoke to me today, never in my life..." Ruth stopped talking as she was becoming emotional.

"Never in my life did I believe I would be blessed in such a manner. Miranda told me to work with you if I truly wanted to save my people. Child, I will not hide in the shadows. You tell me what I need to do."

"I like you," Natasha said and leaned forward and kissed Ruth on the cheek. "First I think you need to tell Gabriel exactly what you just told us. Then come back here and I will introduce you to Clay."

Gabriel was just walking out of Clay's office when Lakin and Ruth approached him. As Ruth was repeating her words to Gabriel, Jared, Rachel and Dagon joined them. Everyone listened to what Ruth was saying. "Ruth while I appreciate what you have said I don't want you taking any unnecessary chances. You and I have not really had time to talk yet and I don't want to jeopardize anything the Angels may have put into motion," Gabriel said.

"Lakin why don't you and Ruth return to your table. Jared you go with them and bring Clay here as soon as you think it wise. Dagon go to the cellar and help the others. Joao and Dack brought ropes and Stephan, Dominic and Michael are searching the cellar and setting it up. We found a back door that appears to be an escape route but it just goes out onto the street. Rachel you come with me," Gabriel said.

Rachel took Gabriel's arm and they walked onto the dance floor. They glided through the dancing couples as they surveyed the room. Word of what was happening spread quickly through the Ruala and Shettee warriors who maintained their guise as party goers. Stephan and Michael walked out of Clay's office and started to walk through the crowd.

Dominic, Dagon, Dack and Joao were dividing the cellar into different areas where they could hold and interrogate prisoners. They cut rope into smaller lengths so they could quickly tie prisoner's hands and feet. They brought some chairs and a small table from Clay's office to the area that was set up for the interrogations. And they moved a heavy shelf in front of the rear door to prevent anyone from entering.

"Dominic you should probably return to the gathering," Dagon said. "We will stay down here. Tell Gabriel we are set up." After Dominic left Dagon turned to Joao and Dack. "I told Rachel that I want to marry her and I have been so focused on her that I haven't thought how you two might feel. I hope there aren't any hard feelings but if there are we should talk about them."

"Have us in the wedding and there won't be any hard feelings," Dack said with a grin.

"Both of us are attracted to Rachel but we aren't in love with her," Joao said. "There aren't any hard feelings."

"Good," Dagon said. "I was going to say that if you were mad you could punch me."

"We might want to do that just for the fun of it," Dack said and laughed.

When Dominic walked out of Clay's office he saw Thaos, Natasha and Clay walking towards the table where Lakin, Ruth and Jared were seated. Dominic walked up to Natasha and kissed her on the cheek. "I have seen so little of you today," Dominic said.

"Oh Honey I have had so much fun. Poor Clay is still ill so I am trying to introduce him to some of the guests that arrived while he was in his room," Natasha said and took Dominic's arm. Dominic positioned himself so he was on Clay's left side while Thaos was on Clay's right side.

Clay's eyes widened when he saw Ruth sitting with Prince Lakin and Jared. "Clay this is Prince Lakin of the Ruala Tribe and you know Jared. From the look on your face I believe you recognize Ruth," Natasha said. "Tell us how do you know her because you look as if you have seen a ghost."

"I know she is said to be a healer among the people, nothing more," Clay stammered. "I am just surprised to see her here with Prince Lakin."

"Why don't you have a seat," Thaos said and pushed Clay into a chair at the table. Thaos and Dominic stood behind Clay.

"I met these lovely people today when they were trying to find Tobey and his family," Ruth said as she coldly stared into Clay's eyes. "It is believed that you are the one who sent Teivel's monsters after that innocent family. What do you have to say to those allegations?"

"I don't know what you are talking about," Clay said.

"It doesn't take a seer to tell that you are lying," Ruth said. "Please hold out your hand."

"No," Clay said. Jared reached across the table and grabbed Clay's right hand and pulled if forward. As Ruth held Clay's hand Natasha mixed a vial of truth potion into a glass of whiskey.

"Thaos he lied to you," Ruth said. "He did not send for the thugs but he knows who sent them. Those generals are not who they act to be. Teivel has them pretend to be against the government to see if you would sell them weapons. Clay has made a great deal of money working for Teivel." Ruth paused. "It is time Gabriel spoke to Clay."

"Clay you look like you could use a drink," Natasha said sweetly and handed him a glass of whiskey which he swallowed in one gulp. Natasha put her right arm around Clay while she held a small knife in her left hand. "Clay I really like Tobey and I suspect that is the reason you had his family kidnapped. You have made me very angry and that is never a good idea." Thaos put his hand over Clay's mouth as Natasha plunged her knife into Clay's outstretched hand.

Natasha quickly pulled the knife out and covered the bloody hand with a napkin. "I will do that to your entire body if you do not tell us where Tobey and is family are." Natasha said sweetly as Thaos and Dominic pulled Clay to his feet.

"Natasha if we weren't both married, you would have my heart," Thaos said and laughed. Everyone from the table stood up and walked into Clay's office. Michael and Stephan now positioned themselves in front of the door to Clay's office so no one could enter.

Thaos removed his hand from Clay's mouth as soon as they entered his office. "What is the meaning of this?" Clay sputtered as tears ran down his cheeks from the pain in his hand."

"We know, you have been spying on us," Natasha said to Clay. "I put truth potion in that glass of whiskey he drank," Natasha said to her comrades. "I will search his office while you start and if he doesn't tell you where Tobey is I will finish the interrogation," Natasha said as she glared at Clay.

"Natasha I just realized you are the mean one in the family," Jared said and laughed. Natasha giggled and started to pull drawers out of Clay's desk as the others took Clay into the cellar. Gabriel and Rachel were in the cellar waiting for the group. Calen entered the office and started to help Natasha with her search.

While Joao and Dack tied Clay to a chair, Ruth and Lakin pulled Gabriel aside and talked.

"That is very interesting," Gabriel said and turned to Clay who was showing the effects of the potion. "Clay, Ruth tells me that Teivel is afraid of a coup and has been using us to try and expose anyone thinking of overthrowing the government. So you set us up with those two generals to trap us?" As Gabriel spoke he poured blessed water onto Clay's arm but there was no reaction. "I can see you aren't a demon or dark lord; you are just a man. A devious and treacherous man."

"Did you suspect us from the beginning?" Gabriel asked. Dagon was taking notes of the interrogation.

"No."

"Then why did you set us up with the generals?"

"Because no one knew you here so no one would believe you worked for Teivel. He thought that anyone involved with a coup would reach out to you. All of the other arms dealers in the kingdom work for Teivel."

"What do you know of us?"

"Me, I believed who you were until they brought me to Ruth and Natasha stabbed me."

"Who do you think we are now?"

"Are you the coup?" Gabriel did not answer.

"Why did you have Tobey's family kidnapped?"

"I didn't. I just told Teivel that Tobey asked to be your personal driver because you paid so well."

"Are you saying Teivel had Tobey's family taken?"

"Yes."

"Why?"

"For some reason he felt that Tobey might be loyal to you and he wanted his own men driving you."

"Where is Tobey and his family?"

"I don't know."

Thaos laughed. "Natasha will cut you to shreds if you don't tell us."

"I really don't know. I would assume they are in one of his prisons like everyone else that he takes."

Suddenly Gabriel realized that the information the generals had given them about the prisons was possibly false. "How many prisons does Teivel have?"

"Four."

"We heard thirteen."

"Thirteen! Who would tell you that?" Clay asked and scoffed.

Gabriel pulled a map out of his pocket and showed it to Clay. These buildings with stars are supposed to be the prisons. And the buildings with squares are the auction houses. Tell me what is wrong with this map."

Clay looked at the map for a few moments. "I don't know where you got this information. Every prison is attached to an auction house. They are connected by tunnels. Those other buildings are Teivel's."

"What do you mean they are Teivel's?"

"That's where he houses his men, like the ones at this gathering."

"Show me which buildings are the prisons."

"Well they aren't really hidden. Have you seen them?"

"I don't know," Gabriel said. "Tell me what you are talking about."

"Each building has a statue of a man and a woman, each holding a small child. The statues are in front of the buildings."

"We have seen that image; what does it mean?"

"The futility of trying to escape the Insidiae."

"Are you a member of the Insidiae?"

"No, only the most powerful and wealthy are allowed to join."

"Why did Teivel send an army of demons after us today?"

"And you live?" Clay asked in astonishment. "I don't know. I serve Teivel I am not his confident. In fact I have never spoken to him directly. I give information to Boris and Clifford and they give me my orders."

"Who is Saxton?"

"A lieutenant of Teivel's."

"Who is Leon?"

"A captain of Teivel's."

"Do they work with the generals?"

"I don't understand the question."

"The generals said that Saxton was a threat to them."

"Perhaps they think he is involved with planning a coup."

"Does Teivel suspect us of anything other than possibly selling arms to his enemies?"

"Not that I am aware of but I told you I am merely a servant."

Natasha walked up to Gabriel and handed him some papers. "Then why did you look so shocked when you saw Ruth?" Natasha asked Clay.

"Because she is a peasant, why would a prince of another kingdom be associating with a peasant?"

"Is that the only reason?" Natasha asked.

"I have heard she has special powers. Powers she has used to protect her people from the demons."

Natasha pulled a knife out of a sheath inside of her dress and held it menacingly in front of Clay. "How do we break into the prisons?"

"I have no idea, really. Why would you want to break into a prison?" Natasha pressed the tip of the knife near Clay's eye. "Natasha really if you want to know about the prisons, ask Boris and Clifford, that's their assignment. Have Ruth touch me she will say I am telling the truth."

"Natasha cut him loose," Gabriel said.

As Natasha cut the ropes that bound Clay's wrists, Gabriel handed Clay a pen and the papers that Natasha had given him. "Sign these." Gabriel ordered.

"What are they?" Clay asked as he read the papers. "Where did you get these?"

"I just drew them up," Natasha said. "Now sign them."

"But these were in my safe. How did you get these?" Clay asked.

"I hope you didn't spend a lot of money on that safe," Natasha said and laughed. "Sign them."

"But these are all of my properties," Clay protested.

"Yes," Gabriel said. "Turns out that Clay owns this hotel and several other buildings."

"But why should I turn them over to you?"

"Because I will let Natasha have you if you don't," Gabriel said although he had no intention of letting Natasha hurt Clay. Natasha took a step closer to Clay and he quickly signed all the deeds over to Gabriel.

"If you are still alive you might get these back," Gabriel said.

"What are you going to do with me?" Clay asked.

"Clay is there any reason that we should keep you alive?" Gabriel asked. Clay sat in silence. "Is there anything you can offer us?"

Thaos started to pull Clay out of his chair. "No wait," Clay said. "Have you not wondered how a regular person, who is not a member of the Insidiae can own this grand hotel? I started here as a clerk when I was a boy. I kept my eyes and ears open and I saved everything that could be used against the powerful and rich. Go into my bedroom chambers and move the dresser that has a vase of flowers on it. Lift the rug and under the floorboards you will find my files."

"So you are saying you have blackmailed your way to a position of wealth." Gabriel said.

"I prefer to call it protection," Clay said. "It is the only thing that keeps me out of the prisons like the rest of the poor fools."

"He might be of some use to us," Jared said. "But I don't know how we could trust him."

"Just keep me alive until you read my files," Clay said. "Giving you those files puts a price on my head. I will work with you if you can protect me."

Jared and Thaos left the cellar to find Clay's files. "Clay you seem like a man who is motivated by money," Gabriel said. "I am not going to give you details but if you work with us you could possibly have more wealth than you can imagine."

"You are planning a coup!" Clay gasped.

"No, we are not from Ryed and only heard the rumors about a coup from you the other evening when you got so drunk."

"I told you. I must have been really drunk," Clay said in amazement. I will listen to your proposition. I serve Teivel as we all are forced to but I have no love for him. My parents died in his prisons."

402

Gabriel stared at Clay for several moments as he was trying to determine Clay's intention. "Natasha go to my room and get that jar of Aplewort."

Ruth stepped forward and asked, "Why are you giving him that herb?"

"To cleanse the truth potion from his body, we really don't know how dangerous it is," Gabriel said.

"That will take a couple of days," Ruth said. "I can help." The elderly woman walked up to Clay and put her hands on his shoulders. Ruth started to hum and everyone in the room watched her with amazement. A light started to emit from Ruth's body. Clay slumped forward in his chair, Gabriel and Natasha grabbed Clay to prevent him from falling onto the floor.

"Is he alright?" Natasha asked Ruth.

"Yes, he passed out, when he wakes his health will be restored," Ruth said. "He will help you but he will sell you out to the highest bidder. Do not reveal much to him. While he is not in Teivel's circles, Clay is not the servant he would have everyone believe."

"Did he lie under the potion?" Gabriel asked with concern.

"Not lie as much as he believes his own stories," Ruth said.

"Ruth we have all seen the Sanuri work miracles," Lakin said. "I have seen no other human do something like you just did. Are you like the Sanuri?"

"I have never met him but to be compared to him is a great honor. My children I have been teaching The Holy Scrolls for a life time and I will admit every day I understand something in a new way. But you must understand that man brings this darkness upon himself. The Great Ruler never abandons those who call out to Him. No matter how thick the darkness there will be a flicker of His Light."

"When I first started to teach The Holy Scrolls I had three students. I have over six hundred now. Don't you think that in itself is a miracle in this dark kingdom?"

"Ruth how old are you?" Lakin asked.

"My child, you know you never ask a woman that question," Ruth said with a smile.

"Ruth are you an Angel?" Natasha asked.

"Now wouldn't Miranda have told you that?" Ruth asked. Her evasiveness was raising everyone's curiosity. The room was silent for a moment then Rachel spoke.

"If Boris and Clifford are in charge of the prisons then they know where my father and Tobey are. Natasha you and I should find them. I am sure they are here."

"Stay here until Thaos and Jared return," Gabriel said. "Then the generals will be next." Gabriel turned back to Ruth. "Why did you heal Clay?"

"I was waiting until you made a choice to rise above the darkness we are wallowing in here. Gabriel you and your team are good and faithful people who work on behalf of The Great Ruler. You often have to do unsavory things but don't forget who you are or your purpose here. For a moment I thought you would lower yourself to Clay's level."

"I shouldn't have stabbed him," Natasha said guiltily.

"Look at his hand it is healed," Ruth said.

"Ruth I think you might be an Angel..." Natasha did not finish her sentence because Thaos and Jared entered the cellar. Thaos handed Gabriel a box that was the size of a large book.

"Is he dead?" Jared asked and nodded towards Clay.

"No, Ruth healed him," Lakin said. "Now we are all wondering if she is an Angel in disguise."

Gabriel quickly scanned the contents in the box. "It is going to take me a while to read all of this but I don't see anything with either Boris' or Clifford's name on it. It's time to get the generals."

Clay moaned loudly then suddenly stood up and stared at everyone as he tried to collect his thoughts. "Do you remember our conversation?" Gabriel asked.

"Yes," Clay said as he saw that Gabriel held the box of files. "I am not sick anymore, how can that be?"

"Ruth healed you," Gabriel said. "Clay I believe you have trampled on and betrayed everyone you could to become a man of wealth and means. I have no idea if you have a conscious but if you do I am going to give you a chance to lighten your burden. I want you to go upstairs and tell a waiter to have Boris and Clifford come to your office. Give no reason and you do not leave your office."

"I'll go up with him," Thaos said.

"No, please let me and Natasha go," Rachel said.

"Oh, we all will be in Clay's office when the generals arrive," Gabriel said.

Chapter XXXI
Clarity

General Boris and General Clifford both stopped in front of the door to Clay's office and looked at Stephan and Michael with disdain. "I suppose if you are out here that means Gabriel and Stone are in the office," Clifford said.

"What's your second guess?" Stephan asked with a smirk.

Both of the old generals now grinned as they believed that Rachel and Natasha had set up a meeting with them. When Boris opened the door he saw Natasha, Rachel and Clay sitting in the room. Boris and Clifford entered but as soon as they got through the doorway they were grabbed from behind. Stephan reached over and grabbed the door knob and pulled the door closed.

Michael nodded to King Neputa who now walked up to the musicians and asked them to stop playing. Neputa spoke to the group at the gathering. Neputa thanked everyone for the wonderful reception then went into a lengthy history of his people. As Neputa distracted the audience. The Ruala and Shettee warriors quietly attacked Teivel's hired fighters and dragged them out of the reception.

"What is the meaning of this?" Boris barked as Dagon and Joao were tying Boris' hands behind his back.

"I believe we have a great deal to talk about," Gabriel said. "Which of you will speak with me first?"

"Neither of us are going to tell you shit," Clifford spat.

"I think that is a vote for Clifford," Jared said with a grin and dragged Clifford into the cellar.

"Don't think your hired thugs out there are going to help you," Gabriel said to Boris. "By now they are our prisoners too."

"Who the hell are you people?" Boris asked as he looked at Gabriel and Dominic with new eyes.

"Who do you want us to be?" Gabriel asked sarcastically.

"Are you that special unit that works for...?" Boris didn't complete his sentence.

"That works for who?" Gabriel asked with a grin.

"The Grand Masters," Boris said in a whisper.

"You really aren't as stupid as you look Boris," Gabriel said. "Now you can make this easy on yourself or not; it is your choice."

"But we have done nothing wrong?" Boris stammered. "We have followed every order we have been given." Everyone in the room stared at Boris and grinned. No one spoke because they realized that Boris' fears would loosen his tongue. "Wait you don't think we are part of that coup do you? We were just supposed to pretend we were to see if you were part of it."

"I see," Gabriel said then he looked at Dagon and Joao and said. "Tie Boris to a chair while I interrogate Clifford."

"Wait," Boris said fearfully. "If you think we are members of a coup then we have been set up. We suspect Saxton that is why we wanted to know if you had talked to him." Gabriel did not respond for a few moments.

"Just say I would believe you. Who are you going to tell me gave you the orders to pretend you were members of a coup?" Gabriel asked. "Are you going to say Teivel gave you the orders?"

"No of course not," Boris said. "You know that Teivel doesn't communicate with any of us directly. Captain Shard is our contact. But you probably already know that."

"You are telling me that Shard actually gave you orders to pretend you were in a coup?" Gabriel asked skeptically. Boris looked around the room nervously. "Yes, I am telling you the truth."

Natasha had previously followed Jared and Clifford into the cellar; she now entered the office and whispered into Gabriel's ear. Then Natasha walked up to Boris and poured blessed water on his arm; there was no reaction. "What is that all about?" Boris demanded.

"There are some who believe you have consorted with powerful demons to, shall I say improve your position," Gabriel said.

"That's a lie," Boris yelled. "I can't stand those stinking things."

"And yet you have compromised the prisons so that Teivel will be humiliated at the games," Gabriel said.

"I don't know what the hell you are talking about," Boris said. "What are you saying?"

"I am saying that not all of the prisoners are who we think they are but you already know that."

"I don't know who the hell you think those prisoners are," Boris' voice was rising with his anger and fear. "You know as well as I that Clifford and I only maintain the prisons we aren't responsible for the kidnappings. That comes from a lot higher than us. So if someone put demons or who the hell knows what with the prisoners it was someone within Teivel's inner circles. Clifford and me just have to make sure the prisoners don't escape."

"And just how many inner circles do you think Teivel has?" Gabriel asked sarcastically.

"I think we have all heard that he has four, but who really knows?" Boris again looked at all of the faces in the room. "Wait if you work for the Grand Masters why are Rualas working with you?"

"I didn't say we work for the Grand Masters; you did," Gabriel replied with a grin.

"Well who the hell are you? Do you work for the Grand Masters or not?" Boris yelled as Gabriel turned his back and walked into the cellar. "What the hell is going on here?" Now Boris looked at Clay accusingly. "Clay are you part of this?"

"I know as much as you do," Clay said with a smirk. "But I am enjoying watching you squirm. You have always been such a pompous ass."

"I'll burn your hotel to the ground when I get out of here," Boris yelled.

"It's Gabriel's hotel now and I have a feeling you aren't getting out of here," Clay said and laughed because Boris and Clifford had intimidated him for decades.

"He's already been given the potion and we have started the questions," Calen said as Gabriel looked over the notes that Dominic was writing.

Gabriel looked up from the notes and asked Clifford, "So you have had men watching the building I bought for a store. Why is that?"

"To see if we can find out who the traitors are?" Clifford said.

"Traitors to who?" Gabriel asked.

"To Teivel of course."

"So you believe the stories about a coup?"

"They are more than just stories?"

"How do you know this?" Gabriel asked.

"Teivel's home and office were attacked in Wetpr, then he comes home and finds that his castle has been attacked."

"What do you mean?" Gabriel asked. "Who attacked it?"

"We don't know. Teivel's soldiers said they never saw anyone approach the gates but I heard that everything Teivel owned was destroyed. All of his black magic stuff. I don't understand how it works but apparently Teivel lost some of his power."

"Don't the Grand Masters protect Teivel?" Gabriel asked.

"We have always believed that, so I don't know if all the stories are accurate. I mean how could someone get past the Grand Masters. Unless perhaps it was other Grand Masters."

Gabriel looked at Ruth and asked, "Do you know anything about these attacks on Teivel?" Ruth merely shook her head from side to side; she did not speak.

Jared and Thaos stepped out of Clay's office and into the gathering. The citizen's and hotel staff acted as if they were unaware of anything besides the celebration. Thaos and Jared relieved Stephan and Michael as door guards. Stephan and Michael walked around the gathering until they found Thedes.

"Five were killed as they fought with us," Thedes said. "We have them all in one of the barns. They aren't telling us who sent them or why they are here. Ask Gabriel what he wants us to do with them."

"See if you can figure out who might be a leader among them," Stephan said. "We will be back." Michael and Stephan entered Clay's office. Dagon, Clay, Joao, Boris, and Natasha were in the office; the others were in the cellar with Gabriel.

"Natasha these two old goats got real excited when they thought you and Rachel were meeting them," Stephan said and laughed.

"Oh shut the hell up," Boris said with disgust.

Stephan laughed again and walked into the cellar where he spoke with Gabriel. "Come on Michael, we're going to do a little interrogating," Stephan said as he returned to the office. "Hey Boris what do you think your men will tell us?"

Now Boris laughed. "You damn fools, we didn't bring those guys. Someone else is watching you and when they realize their men are gone they will send more."

"Actually we are counting on that," Michael said. "Do you think anyone is going to fight to get you and your buddy back?" Boris stopped laughing. "That's what I thought," Michael said. "I'll bet you two aren't even missed."

Thedes, Stephan and Michael interrogated the men in the barn while Gabriel and some of his team interrogated Boris and Clifford. The interrogations lasted for hours. Lakin returned to the gathering several times so as not to draw suspicion. Natasha and Rachel also returned to the gathering mainly to watch the hotel staff. Every time the women returned to Clay's office they brought trays of food and beverages.

"Why don't you two get something to eat?" Natasha said to Jared and Thaos. "Rachel and I will watch the door."

"Thanks," Jared said. "I am kind of hungry."

"Go on in," Thaos said to Jared. "I think I will take a walk."

Thaos walked into the kitchen and filled a plate with food. He stared at the staff as he ate. No one seemed to pay much attention to Thaos because they were used to seeing him around the hotel.

"You got another cellar here where you keep all the meat and such?" Thaos asked one of the cooks.

"Yeah through that door," the man said and nodded to a door at the far end of the kitchen. "You hungry for anything in particular?"

"No, just looking," Thaos said. "Would there be another entrance to that cellar?"

"Yeah, that's where all the deliveries come," the cook said. "If you're still hungry there are some pies that just came out of the oven on the table near the cellar door."

"Thanks, the food is great," Thaos said and walked across the kitchen. He ate two pieces of pie while he watched the staff then he opened the cellar door. There were lit torches on the walls; Thaos grabbed one and walked down the stairs. The cellar was filled with food; enough to feed their little army for about a week, Thaos thought. He found the delivery door and walked out into the back alley. Thaos walked up and down the alley without seeing anything suspicious.

He heard the flapping of wings just before two Enrops flew down to him. "Part of our flock landed in Gabriel's chambers with mail about an hour ago," one of the birds said. "Then another group came about half an hour later with messages from the Sanuri and those with him. Those birds fought with a flock of ravens and killed them. They said the ravens were flying around the hotel."

"Thanks, wait here and I will bring out some baskets of food," Thaos said and walked back into the food cellar.

411

Thaos carried out several large baskets of fruits, vegetables, grains and bread. "Will this be enough?"

"Yes," replied one of the birds. "We will tell the others."

Thaos walked back inside of the food cellar and up the stairs to the kitchen. The hair on the back of his neck was standing on end. He knew something was wrong but he couldn't figure out what it was. Everything in the kitchen seemed normal. It was very late in the evening and many of the guests were leaving the hotel although the dance floor was still filled with dancers. Thaos walked up to Natasha and Rachel who were standing guard outside of Clay's office.

"I found a food cellar that goes out to the alley. Everything looked alright but some Enrops said that two flocks are in Gabriel's chambers. The second flock fought with a flock of ravens that was circling the hotel. I didn't see anything suspicious but the hair on the back of my neck is standing on end," Thaos said.

"I know; Natasha and I were saying the same thing," Rachel said. "We are wondering if we will be attacked when everyone leaves."

"Teivel has a reputation for slaughtering innocent people," Thaos said. "I don't think the guests would stop his attack." Thaos walked back into Clay's office and found Clifford in the office acting drunk from the truth potion while Boris was being interrogated in the wine cellar.

Thaos walked into the wine cellar and interrupted the interrogation to tell Gabriel about the food cellar, Enrops and ravens. While Lakin had been leaving the wine cellar to make appearances at the gathering, Ruth stayed in the cellar to watch the interrogations. Gabriel noticed that both General Boris and General Clifford got the same shocked looks on their faces when they saw Ruth as Clay had. And both generals gave a similar explanation for their reactions as Clay had. Gabriel wondered if these three men could see something about Ruth that he could not.

Another hour passed and Natasha walked into the wine cellar. "The guests are gone," she said.

412

"We rather expect an attack but so far no one has seen anything suspicious. Stephan wants to know what they should do with the men in the barn."

Gabriel handed Natasha a large ring of keys. "Our friends," Gabriel was sarcastically referring to the two generals. "Tell us that the prison on Mound Street is empty. Lock them up in there."

"Which keys?" Natasha asked.

"Apparently all the locks to the cells are the same. It's the locks to the front doors of the buildings that are different. Key number four is for Mound Street," Gabriel explained.

"Do you want the generals in there too?" Natasha asked.

"Not yet, we will keep them down here," Gabriel said. "Boris here, has said that Teivel is the only dark lord that he knows of so Teivel probably sent the ravens and the demons we encountered earlier."

By dawn the interrogations had been completed. The hired fighters were locked in the Mound Street prison and Boris and Clifford were tied up in the wine cellar. Clay was allowed to resume his normal duties but someone from Gabriel's small army was with Clay at all times.

As exhausted as everyone was they all gathered around Gabriel's chambers where two flocks of Enrops had mail.

"Michael there are some here for you too," Jared said as he handed Michael several thick envelopes.

"Who would write to me?" Michael asked then smiled as he pulled childish paintings out of one of the envelopes. "Vitomas and Annabelle had the children make these for me," Michael said with an emotion that was heard in his voice.

Stephan and Thaos sat down next to each other as they opened their small stacks of envelopes. "Thaos open that thick one first," Stephan said with a grin and held up a leather bracelet.

"What is that?" Thaos asked as he tore his envelope open.

413

"Ingr said that Amy runs around the house saying how much she misses us," Stephan said. "So the girls talked to her and since then Amy has been training really hard so she could earn a bracelet for each of us. The girls helped Amy make the bracelets bigger so they would fit us." Stephan put his bracelet on as he spoke.

Thaos read his letter in silence as his emotions were surging within him. Then he proudly put his bracelet on. "I really miss them too," Thaos said. "It keeps getting harder to leave them."

"Jared this envelope has your name on it," Michael said as he took one of the envelopes from his pile and handed it to his friend. "Renya, Sudfad, Laurel, Vitomas and Annabelle all sent me letters," Michael said with disbelief.

"Well they are your family now," Jared said with a grin. Jared became silent for a moment then he showed his gift to Michael. Zoya had a locket made for me and it has her hair and William's hair in it." Michael could hear the emotion in Jared's voice. "Michael I think you and I are in the same boat. We have been alone so long that it is hard to think that anyone cares about us." Both men read the rest of their letters in silence.

Gabriel stood up and announced, "All of the warriors that were at Erebus' castle are traveling here. They left two days ago. Daniel and Miranda told them to start out. The Sanuri and Erebus are with them."

"Where are Mother and Zack?" Rachel asked loudly as she quickly opened an envelope.

"They were taken to the Village of the Clan of Gesmal," Gabriel said to Rachel. "They will be protected there." Gabriel spoke to the group, "Everyone get a few hours of sleep then I want to look at the various buildings that Clay signed over to us. I don't want all of our people in one building in case we are attacked."

Ruth had been sitting in Gabriel's chambers watching all of the warriors opening their letters. "Gabriel you are in my city and you don't think to ask me for help," Ruth said and stood up slowly. "What would you desire for a building?"

"Something that we could defend and large enough to hide the people that we free. I don't want to endanger the innocent citizens."

"Would a castle fit your needs?" Ruth asked with a bright smile. Everyone in the room was now looking at Ruth. "Our King and Queen sent their small sons from this dark kingdom and for that Teivel had them murdered. But, Teivel likes to keep up appearances. The castle of King Nehmota is being cared for as if the Royal Family still lived there. The staff are students of mine. There are only a few soldiers stationed there for show. But those soldiers as the staff were very loyal to the King and Queen. The castle is just southeast of this city."

"Ruth you truly are a gift to us," Gabriel said warmly. "Since you know the area, when would you suggest we look at it without causing suspicion?"

"I believe the storm that is brewing will prevent anyone from seeing all of you leave this hotel and move into the castle," Ruth said.

"I told you she is an Angel," Natasha said with a smile.

"And when is this storm expected to hit the city?" Gabriel asked.

"I guess that depends on whether you want to get a couple hours of sleep before the move," Ruth said with a grin. "Understand your group is not safe in this building."

"We should move now then?" Gabriel asked.

"That would be wise," Ruth said. "But first send a message to your troops who are traveling here. Tell them not to enter the city but to go straight to the castle. The storm will strike as soon as the Enrops are safely from here. Dominic and Gabriel you must understand that while fear would grip the hearts of many; hope is a great gift. There will be others standing with you; you are not alone in this battle."

"Ruth are you actually Miranda in disguise?" Natasha asked.

415

"No my child," Ruth said with a warm smile. "Now hurry you must prepare to leave here."

Gabriel, Calen, Dagon, Joao and Dack quickly ran down to Clay's office while Natasha wrote a note for the Sanuri. The Rualas ran into the wine cellar and stripped the uniforms and papers from Boris and Clifford. "Your deeds are signed back into your name," Gabriel said to Clay. "We will be leaving tonight; Gabriel deliberately gave Clay false information. I would appreciate it if you fed Boris and Clifford for a few days then let them go."

"I didn't think you were telling me the truth that I would get these back," Clay said as he looked at his deeds. "Just so you know I don't like those generals. I will feed them but I will keep them here for longer than a few days. I don't know what you are up to but a voice in my head says you are the first good men I have met in a long time. Those generals are a threat to you. Please let me know how else I can be of service and I really mean that. Have Ruth look into my mind again if you want."

Gabriel stared at Clay while Miranda's voice rang inside of Gabriel's head. "He is telling you the truth, say it."

"Clay if I tell you I will be putting you in grave danger. I do not need your help but your own people will. Do you want me to say more?"

"Yes," Clay said and Gabriel was confused because Clay's voice carried emotion.

"You said your parents died in the prisons. If all goes well we will be freeing the prisoners. I am sure many will need food and medical care. They may not have homes or families to return to. You have beds and food here. Just think about the good you could do?"

"I knew it," Clay gasped. "Every time I looked at Ruth all I saw was brilliant light. You are Angels. I will help however I can."

Gabriel laughed, "Ruth might be an Angel the rest of us are merely men. And your help is appreciated."

"I will send staff out today to purchase more food and medical supplies," Clay said more to himself than to Gabriel. "And I will need to hire men to protect everyone."

"You can't tell anyone what I have told you," Gabriel said. "And be discreet; you never know who is watching you."

"Oh believe me I know," Clay said enthusiastically.

Gabriel turned and started to walk out of the office. "Gabriel," Clay called. Gabriel turned around. "Thank you and I really mean that," Clay said.

The Rualas had already left the wine cellar and were back on the fifth floor of the hotel when Gabriel reached his chambers. Many people were still sitting in Gabriel's chambers including Ruth. Gabriel walked directly up to Ruth. "You obviously saw something in Clay that I couldn't see," Gabriel said.

"Imagine that," Ruth said with a grin.

"Is he really going to help the prisoners?"

"That and more." Ruth said. "Gabriel, Miranda and Daniel told you this would be a very difficult assignment for you. In the past most of your assignments have been rather black and white in that your enemies were well defined and very evil. This assignment exposes you to fear. Centuries of fear have disfigured many of the people of this kingdom. It is not as easy to tell if the mask a person wears is a result of evil darkness or darkness caused by their fears."

"But isn't fear a choice?"

"Yes, but few realize that when they are afraid."

"Ruth, our warriors will be risking their lives to free these people and understand that is a goal we all want. But do the people of this kingdom really want freedom? Are we trying to impose our beliefs onto them?"

"You are feeling that many of your warriors will die and the people of Ryed will just submit to another dictator. You are feeling guilty that you may be leading many to their deaths."

"Exactly," Gabriel said solemnly.

"It is their choice to be slaves to another dictator just as it is your choice to try and help these people. But remember the battle of Ogg and the battle in Nora. Over and over you heard people say that just having a glimmer of hope changed their lives. If you accomplish nothing more than to give these people hope then you have given them a great gift. Don't you see that?"

"It just doesn't seem like enough."

"Gabriel you sound as if you have lost hope. You don't know the outcome of this mission. Hope, like faith can start out as a tiny flame. And sometimes that little flame exists on the verge of extinction and sometimes it grows into a raging fire."

"I know you are right. Maybe I just feel like this because I am exhausted."

"Gabriel you carry a great weight on your shoulders which causes your knees to weaken once in a while; that is all. At times like this you should call to the heavens and ask for help with that load you carry."

"Ruth I don't understand how an Angel can live a lifetime in this darkness like you have. I know you have the power to get rid of Teivel and all these demons."

"I too, have my assignment Gabriel. And my assignment was not to take away the free choice of the people."

"But they have willingly let Teivel take their freedom of choice."

"Have they?"

Gabriel was silent for several moments. "I am feeling even more confused."

"We have a little time before our departure. Perhaps you should go to your room and pray for clarity. I will stay out here and help the others."

Chapter XXXII
Shelter from the Storm

A storm of great proportions hit the City of Teivel. Blinding rain and strong winds made people scurry for shelter. The roar of thunder and the intense lighting strikes prevented even the Grand Masters from realizing that Gabriel's army left the hotel and was traveling to the castle of King Nehmota.

To the surprise of all, the Rualas and Enrops appeared to be flying under some type of umbrella in that the elements were not affecting them. The Rualas carried the humans and Shettees from the hotel. Lakin carried Ruth as the soldiers and servants at the castle were not aware of her true identity.

The handful of soldiers that guarded Nehmota's castle had taken shelter from the storm and did not realize a small army had landed within the castle walls until Ruth had the doors to the castle open. She led Gabriel's troops inside of the castle. They were initially met by a maid named Mable. Ruth told Mable to gather all of the servants and soldiers and to bring everyone into the Great Hall of the castle.

It took Mable almost twenty minutes to gather the staff and soldiers as the castle was expansive. Ruth stood in the doorway of the Great Hall to quell the fears of the soldiers who were seeing the visiting army for the first time. When everyone had gathered in the Great Hall, Ruth moved to the front of the room and spoke with a voice of such strength and authority that it did not seen to come from the frail body presented to the group.

"Do not fear. You all know me and you know I would never bring harm to you. But this day I am asking you to make choices that will change your lives. Before you is but a small army of humans, Rualas and Shettees. These brave men and women have left their homes and their families behind to come to Ryed. Teivel's poison is expanding into other kingdoms and while many will stand by until the threat is at their door, these warriors before you will not."

"More of their comrades will be arriving here in two days," Ruth continued. "But even with reinforcements their army is small compared to that of the dictator who has taken so much from all of you."

419

"These brave warriors have left behind, husbands, wives and children to free the people of Ryed. Many of these warriors will die in their efforts. The choice you have to make this day is whether you will allow their sacrifices to be in vain."

"For those of you who will stand with these warriors go now and bring your families here for protection. Gather your comrades who will stand with us and tell them my words. You will be protected from the storm. Leave as soon as your choices have been made." With Ruth's words all of the staff and soldiers ran out of the castle except for three women who approached Ruth.

"We will stand with you but we no longer have families, what would you have us do?" asked an elderly cook.

"Go into the chambers that once belonged to your beloved King and Queen. In the parlor is a painting of their family. Behind the painting is a safe which will open for you. Take some of the money and purchase food and medical supplies. You will be protected from the storm. As the others return I will send them to help you."

Ruth now turned to Gabriel and his warriors. "Do not fear, these people will not betray you. The storm will last until all have taken shelter here and the supplies have been purchased. Feel free to explore the castle for I have unlocked all of the locks. Gabriel the King's study would be a suitable place for you to make your headquarters. There is plenty of lodging here, choose your rooms. It will take a while for Teivel and the Grand Masters to turn their eyes upon this fortress."

"When the storm subsides it will not take long for Teivel's men to realize you are no longer at the hotel. Clay will not betray you. The generals on the other hand have made poor choices. They are bartering with demons for their release. As soon as that cellar fills with demons, lightening will strike it. But the rest of the hotel will remain undamaged."

"Ruth, our original plans were to cause a distraction during the Gefrey Games that would allow Raphael and the others to attack Fort Polta. Has that changed?" Gabriel asked.

"The eyes of the dark worlds have noticed the movement of The Seven Sons and you and Raphael."

"There are now many more players in this scenario than you originally expected. We said we would help you and we will not allow you to be massacred. Miranda and Daniel will primarily be working with Raphael, Raul, Simon and Matthew. I will be with you."

Ruth now looked at Michael. "Michael I know that you are barely understanding your destiny but you too are one of The Seven Sons. You have to understand that as a group The Seven Sons wield great power. There will be a time when you must join the others."

"There is a large weapon's room here. I would suggest that you store the weapons that Sudfad purchased in the castle as your building is under constant surveillance. The King's treasury is also in the castle. We will go there and I want the leaders to delegate warriors to distribute the wealth to the citizens of Ryed. You will start with those who take shelter within our walls."

"Ruth, are the two young princes still alive?" Dominic asked.

"Yes, but they are too young to rule. Even after these battles it will not be safe to return them to Ryed for a while."

"Ruth if we succeed in toppling Teivel; who should run the kingdom?" Dominic asked.

"Many believe that you should."

"But I don't want to be a king."

"What do you want?"

"To become a Patronus priest."

Ruth smiled, "You would give up such power and wealth to become a warrior priest?"

"Yes unless you tell me I have to rule this kingdom."

"I would never tell you that but the choice that you have made actually makes you an even better candidate for the role of king. I told you when we first met that your destiny was entwined with Gabriel's. Your choices are worthy, follow them."

"Thaos stepped forward. "Ruth we haven't really spoken yet and you probably are reading my thoughts. But in my life I have seen others ruled as the people here are. How do we get them to choose freedom from their demons? Because it has been my experience that as soon at the top man falls others come out of the woodwork to take his place."

Ruth looked at Gabriel, "Perhaps you can answer his question."

"I was basically asking Ruth the same questions and she told me to pray for clarification. That is not our role here. Those of us who live through this will return to our homes and the people of Ryed will have choices to make. I was not told how this mission would end, only that our presence here is already changing lives. And that our actions will affect the people of this kingdom for generations."

"And these changes are for the better?" Jared asked.

Gabriel looked at Ruth who said. "Most." Ruth paused and looked at the faces before her. "I want every one of you to know you can come to me with any questions and concerns and I will answer them as I can. But Gabriel is still in charge of this mission. I am here to help. But now you must learn the layout of this castle because you will be in battle sooner that you thought. And you all are in great need of sleep. Take advantage of the storm and get some rest. I will watch over you."

The gigantic rock wall that surrounded Nehmota's castle protected dozens of small cottages, barns and gardens besides the castle itself. The outside of the wall was surrounded by a centuries old moat that was thirty feet wide and almost fifty feet deep.

King Nehmota as his predecessors had been powerless figureheads for the Teivel regime. A once peaceful kingdom of farmers and fishermen; Ryed was defenseless against the demonic armies that conquered them.

First came the Grand Masters and Teivel's demons, then came the witches, sorcerers and criminals as Teivel proclaimed Ryed a home for darkness. The people rebelled and were murdered. Time passed and the people of Ryed rebelled again and again they were murdered.

As the centuries marched on Teivel spent less time terrorizing his people because they built their own prisons with their fears. Teivel conditioned the people and they reacted accordingly.

Over time Teivel believed the people would never rise against him. It was the leaders of his regime that he continuously suspected of treason. Teivel saw enemies everywhere and trusted no one. He limited the number of people who could join the Insidiae in his kingdom for he feared the power the people would gain by their allegiance to the demonic organization. No other Master of the Insidiae in any world took such measures.

Cedrick Teivel was actually a distant cousin of the Grand Masters Emeric and Banaka. Teivel was unaware of his family's history until Emeric and Banaka paid him a visit. At the beginning of time in the World of Nunc, the original people who called for demons to enter their world, lived in a region now called the Kingdom of Marba. As with all the kingdoms, the original tribes of Marba migrated to other regions within the Continent of Opots. Over time some of these tribes traveled to other continents and brought their worship of demons with them.

Teivel was originally the name of Emeric's and Banaka's father. The original Teivel was horrified at the plague his children had brought upon the World of Nunc. This man became filled with fear and hopelessness as he watched his only two children transform into monsters. Teivel killed his wife and then himself not only as a means to escape his children but also because of the shame they brought him.

Prior to becoming the tools of demons, Emeric and Banaka loved their parents. Their father's suicide filled them with a range of emotions. As the evil grew within Emeric and Banaka they no longer felt guilt about the deaths of their parents. Emeric and Banaka's pain turned into hatred and loathing. This brother and sister sought out Cedrick and turned him into a monster as a means of revenge against their father. And to add to the insult they had Cedrick take Teivel as a name and to call his clan Teivel.

Cedrick Teivel was a cruel warlord when Emeric and Banaka found him. He had always been driven by a need for ultimate power and control. It took little persuading by Emeric and Banaka to get Cedrick to join them.

So dark was Cedrick's soul that he noticed little change when he sold it to the demon Ahriman. When Ahriman was defeated by The Lion of The Great Ruler and imprisoned in The Abyss, the children of Ahriman felt the loss of power. When King Roch was allowed to transform into a demon, then defeated by three of The Seven Sons; shock waves of holy energy shot through the connective veins of the Insidiae and their demon masters. These shock waves greatly weakened the worlds of darkness.

Then in the following months as many of the Old Ones, the most powerful demons in the World of Nunc, fell to the Angels the underworlds knew they were under attack.

The Great Ruler and the Angels always had the power to destroy the demons and dark lords. But the World of Nunc belonged to mankind. It was mankind who brought the demons into their lives and it was mankind who continuously fed and worshipped them. It would have to be mankind to denounce their dark masters and to call the heaven's in. For the heavens would not overrule the freedom of choice of mankind.

The severe storm that attacked the City of Teivel lasted two days. In that time, farmers, fishermen, freedom fighters and citizens from all walks of life found their way to the castle of King Nehmota. The Ruala and Shettee warriors immediately started to train this contingent of people to use weapons and to fight.

Gabriel and his team held meetings with the people who were flocking to the castle. Many citizens had maps or valuable information that aided Gabriel with his strategies.

Natasha set up medical area's as Hannah had taught her. Natasha divided the volunteers into groups to prepare food, to make medicines and to provide care to the wounded when the battles began. Rachel never left Natasha's side. The two women had developed a strong bond and Rachel was eagerly learning all that Natasha could teach her.

As the sun rose on the morning of the third day, no signs of the treacherous storm remained. Immediately guards were stationed on top of the walls of Nehmota's castle.

"An army rides from the south," a freedom fighter yelled down from the wall. All of the citizens of Ryed who responded to Ruth's call now called themselves freedom fighters.

"It is the Sanuri," a Ruala warrior called out. "Lower the bridge and open the gates."

The Sanuri did not drive his boca but rode a horse at the front of the procession. To the Sanuri's right rode Chief Sorren and to the Sanuri's left rode Archetenus. Joshua and Erebus rode in the second line with Asher, Fennel and the higher ranking officers of the Army of Lentz. Although the freedom fighters within the walls of the castle did not know the Sanuri or the army he led, they cheered, clapped and cried at the reinforcements.

Misha led the company of Ruala warriors who flew over the castle walls and landed in the courtyard; while the other warriors crossed the castle bridge on horseback. As friends and family members greeted each other, Ruth walked up to the Sanuri, who dismounted in her presence.

"I have heard a great deal about you," Ruth said and extended her hand.

"As I have you," the Sanuri said and kissed Ruth's hand. "Tell me how long did it take for them to figure it out?"

"Oh these children are smart," Ruth said with a wink. "They knew who I was by the end of the first day."

Gabriel walked up to the Sanuri, "We have a meal prepared. After everyone is settled we will hold a meeting."

"Erebus you may come forward," Ruth said as she saw him standing behind the Sanuri, staring at her.

"Your light is so bright that I couldn't see your human form," Erebus said and bowed before Ruth. "I am at your service."

"I will say I have never had a sorcerer say that to me before," Ruth said with a warm smile. "You have been making very good choices of late. And the motivations for your choices have changed greatly."

"That is what he keeps telling me," Erebus said and nodded towards the Sanuri.

"You cannot see that in yourself?" asked Ruth.

"I don't really know," Erebus said seriously. "But for me to help you I need to retain my dark powers, you do understand that?"

"Actually I don't understand that at all," Ruth said. "We will talk later. You should find Rachel she is worried about Zelda and Zack. And she too has news."

"Why do I have a feeling there is more to what you just said?" Erebus asked skeptically then laughed. At that moment Erebus heard Rachel calling his name. He smiled and walked towards Rachel.

It was almost noon before a small army of Teivel's hired fighters stormed into the Teivel Manor Hotel. Clay had expected such action and had removed any evidence that General Boris or General Clifford had recently been in the hotel.

"May I help you?" Clay asked the man who appeared to be in charge but did not identify himself.

"That arms dealer and the group of Rualas where are they?" the man asked gruffly.

"I don't know," Clay replied. "They had paid in advance for several weeks but left the first night of the storm."

"So they may return?"

"I don't know but as I said they did pay in advance for all those rooms. You are free to search them. They paid for all of the rooms on the fourth and fifth floors."

The man nodded towards the men behind him and they proceeded to run up the staircase. "Also," said Teivel's man. "Have you seen either General Boris or General Clifford?"

"They were here two nights ago for that large gathering we had," Clay said. "And as usual they were drunk and holding their private little meetings."

426

"Private meetings?"

"Well yes, that is why they come here. Our rooms are very private."

"Who did they meet with?" the man asked.

"Well, no one ever told me a name but the generals met with all manner of men and even some demons."

"Demons, they met with demons?"

"Yes, and I had to talk to them about that because the demons scared our guests. So many times the demons would enter by the back doors."

"This is all very interesting," the man said. "Do they have chambers here?"

"No they only used our small private dining rooms. But..." Clay did not finish his sentence.

"But what?"

"Well I don't want to get them into trouble and I don't even know if it is important."

"Tell me."

"Well that last gathering we had here was for the Prince of the Rualas and at the beginning of the night a group of men who looked like hired fighters joined the celebration. But all these men were doing was watching what was going on. The only people who seemed concerned that the hired fighters were here were Boris and Clifford. In fact they seemed rather nervous about it."

"How so?"

"Well, I have had a great deal of interaction with those generals over the years and I have never before seen them act scared. They also asked me about ways they could leave the hotel without being seen."

"This is very interesting," the man said again. "Is there anything else that seemed unusual to you?"

427

"The arms dealers and their wives are the most gracious people and asked me to join them for drinks several times. On one such occasion they said they were having second thoughts about opening a business here because the generals were hounding them for weapons and fighters. Gabriel and Stone said they did not want to get involved with local politics and felt that Boris and Clifford were up to no good."

"So do you think that is why they left?"

"As I said before I don't know, but they were wonderful guests. Wait now that I remember, the night of the gathering I overheard Boris asking Prince Lakin if he could hire some of the Ruala warriors?"

"Really! What did the Prince say?"

"Oh, I could tell the Prince was quite disgusted with Boris and Clifford. Prince Lakin told the generals it was out of the question and walked away. Clifford saw me looking at them so I walked away."

"You have been very helpful and I thank you," the man said then looked up as some of his men were returning from searching the rooms on the fourth and fifth floors."

"There's all kinds of things in those rooms," one of the men said. "Looks like they are all coming back."

"Anything suspicious?" the leader asked.

"No, what you would expect to see. Suitcases, clothes, hair brushes and things."

The leader of the men looked at Clay and said. "I thank you again. We will take leave of you now." Clay walked the men to the front door of the hotel and watched as they mounted their horses and rode away. He knew he was bringing more attention to the hotel by setting up the rooms to make it look like Gabriel's army would return. But, Clay wanted to draw attention away from wherever Gabriel's army was really staying. Clay found himself humming as he returned to his office.

428

Chapter XXXIII
Perceptions

"Is it true?" Jasmine asked as she, Darla, Joao and Dack walked up to Dagon, Rachel and Erebus. "Are you really getting married?"

Dagon, Rachel and even Erebus were grinning. "Well, I haven't officially proposed but yes," Dagon said happily.

Jasmine let out a squeal and jumped into Dagon's arms and hugged and kissed him. Then Jasmine hugged Rachel and said, "Dagon is just like my brother. I am so happy for you."

Darla hugged both Dagon and Rachel then Joao and Dack shook hands with Dagon and both kissed Rachel on the cheek. "I hope there aren't any awkward feelings with us," Joao said.

"No, I like both you and Dack very much but Dagon had my eye from the very beginning," Rachel said.

Dagon, Joao and Dack all looked at each other then back at Rachel. "None of us realized that," Dagon said. "Why is that?"

"Because with everything going on with my family I would never have acted on my feelings."

"Boy, I'm glad I talked you into giving us a chance," Dagon said. "Look what we would have missed out on."

By time the small army that the Sanuri led, ate a meal, got rooms, took care of their horses and unloaded supplies it was mid-afternoon. Gabriel initially called a meeting of his team and the leaders of the group. He wasn't sure if the newly acquired freedom fighters were ready to hear all of the information.

The single significant issue they all discussed was that although three Angels had told the group to meet at the castle of Nehmota and had protected them; the Angels had told no one why there was a change in plans. Ruth was in this meeting and sat quietly as the warriors talked.

"Ruth is this some kind of test of faith?" Gabriel asked. "Normally we have to figure things out and when we get the right answers Miranda and Daniel help us."

Ruth laughed. "Perhaps the Angels are being tested here." Everyone in the room sat in silence as they waited for her to say something else but she did not.

The Sanuri looked at Gabriel, who spoke again. "Should I be asking the questions differently?"

"Miranda and Daniel have taught you well," said Ruth.

"What would you have us do now?" Gabriel asked.

In that instant Miranda and Daniel appeared in the room next to Ruth. "Three Angels," Sorren said loudly. "Is all of hell coming for us?"

"Sorren you always see the big picture," Daniel said with a warm smile. "Gone are the days when warriors as powerful as you can travel without garnering attention. Emeric and Banaka have been doing business with demons from other worlds. Now those demons are also paying close attention to you. I can see that many of you are automatically thinking Hecate is behind this. For now she is no threat to you. She is in hiding with her new husband and baby son."

"Sampson's son?" Joshua asked loudly.

"Yes, Hecate's new husband is a demon but he is tempering her greatly. While this demon is powerful he wants a family before war," Daniel said.

"I can't believe that," said Joshua.

"Stranger things have happened," Daniel said with a grin. "But their benefactor is a demon named Samael. He is as powerful in the world of Orantho as Ahriman was here. Samael is watching you. But the Old Ones are taking a back seat now. They have not only lost too many battles with us but they are consumed with the battles over the hell regions in this world. Many demons from other worlds are launching attacks trying to claim territory in the World of Nunc. Emeric and Banaka are behind some of these attacks."

430

"This battle in Ryed has taken on a different course. The Grand Masters are watching you and trying to protect the Old Ones. None of the Grand Masters are aware of Emeric's and Banaka's treachery at this point. Your battle will be with men but the layers of darkness that exist in this kingdom will make it difficult for you to recognize friend from foe."

Miranda now spoke, "Clay a man who you would have killed has caused a great distraction to give you time to perform your mission. He does not know what you are doing but he is spending his fortune preparing to care for and protect the victims of Teivel."

"Now I feel really guilty," Natasha said. "I stabbed him and was going to kill him."

"This is not a mission where you will easily recognize your enemies. Raphael found out that two men he believed to be terrorists where actually victims who were unaware of the evil they carried. You too will have such encounters. Darkness has no integrity. They will use the weak and the innocent as weapons and as shields."

"That is why we are taking a more active role to help you," Miranda continued. "The goodness in you is not prepared for the darkness you face. A bad decision on your part can cause the death of many innocent people. Do not take anything for granted in this kingdom."

"Those you may trust wear the masks of deception. Which is why Ruth had to introduce herself before you became too involved with Boris and Clifford. Now I want you to think about who you may have trusted since you arrived here," Miranda said.

The room was quiet for a few moments, "Not Tobey," Gabriel said.

"Yes, he works for men who are part of Teivel's inner circle," Miranda explained. "Boris and Clifford feared that Tobey would take their prize, which of course was you. The generals started a false rumor and Tobey was removed to a prison. Ruth protected the people in Tobey's neighborhood from him. You would have killed Clay and gotten others hurt trying to save Tobey. Gabriel you should never have offered Tobey a new life in Nora; you exposed yourself and your team."

431

"You are good people who want badly to help the people of this kingdom; your desire to save others is in a way blinding you to the reality of this land," Daniel said. "You are not the first army to face these challenges nor will you be the last. We cannot make your decisions for you. We are suggesting you call upon us more in this mission than you normally would feel comfortable doing. We will help you understand what you are seeing."

Gabriel now stood up and faced the group. "I pride myself on my ability to read others and I read every single person wrong that the Angels are talking about. I could have gotten everyone killed. I am so sorry."

"You weren't the only one," Natasha said. "We all did." Then Natasha turned to the Angels. "Do something to us to help us see clearly."

"For that my dear you each need to pray to The Great Ruler," Ruth said warmly. "And it is a great gift to ask for."

"Well are we still going to be fighting in the Gefrey Games?" Archetenus asked. "Have all of us been exposed?"

"Tell us again what you had planned," Miranda said.

"A bunch of us would pay to fight in the games," Archetenus explained. "Sorren and Lakin brought extra female warriors as a distraction. While the crowds were watching us the Venatores were going to unlock the prison doors of the arena and lead the prisoners to Gabriel's building. We were going to care for and give weapons to the prisoners."

"That is a good plan," Daniel said. "Except that Gabriel's building is being watched night and day. And some of Teivel's men have walked through the tunnel from the prison and tried to gain access to that building."

"In addition, it is known that the Rualas disappeared when Gabriel's group did so the Rualas are under suspicion now," Miranda said. "Clay filled your rooms in his hotel with belongings. When Teivel's men searched those rooms, Clay said you had paid in advance for several weeks and were returning."

432

"Clay also incriminated Boris and Clifford as traitors against Teivel. Clay said that Gabriel and Lakin were both uncomfortable because the generals were demanding you provide them with weapons and warriors. I am telling you this to help you in planning your next moves."

"What are you not telling us?" Archetenus asked.

"Ask your questions specifically," Miranda said.

"The original plan that we discussed with you," Gabriel said to Miranda and Daniel. "Was that my team would cause a diversion that would allow Raphael and the others to attack Fort Polta. Then as a secondary mission if we could get the Libertas and the people to work with us we would try to overthrow Teivel's hold on Ryed."

"Gabriel I am not admonishing you but review what has taken place since you arrived in this kingdom. All of you have become so emotionally involved with the plight of these people that your secondary mission has actually become your first. Do you see that?"

Before Gabriel could speak Misha asked, "Are Raphael and the others still at Fort Stanus? If we are being watched they must be also. What about the element of surprise for that attack?"

"I find it curious that no one has mentioned that three of The Seven Sons are at Fort Stanus and two are here," Daniel said. "I bring this up because none of you really seem to understand the power these men possess when they are together."

"Are you telling us to rethink this entire mission?" Sorren asked. "Because isn't it a little late in the game?"

"You are all still alive and you are getting reinforcements," Daniel said. "I would not say it is too late in the game."

"Joshua would you please tell the group one of the main rules when training Venatores?" Ruth asked.

"Demon's at least in Ryed are well known for setting up ambushes. That is how Thor and Diana lost their parents and also how Thor and Diana were injured."

"We train our warriors never to trust what their senses are telling them. If they see one demon, they should expect five. If something appears safe it is not. We train Venatores to make multiple strategies so they can change plans quickly as their threat level changes."

Thor now stood up. "And you have just told us that we have more enemies than we originally anticipated. That we all are being watched which means ambushes will be in play and that we have more obstacles because we cannot go by our senses of who to trust here."

"You are all battle savvy warriors. You understand that this will not just be a battle but a rescue mission," Daniel said. "Learn from the Venatores and prepare yourselves for events and your environments to change quickly."

"Just so you know, we had this same meeting with Raul, Simon, Matthew, Raphael and Edward. They have been briefed about your concerns here and will be communicating with you about various strategies," Miranda said. "Now just to make a point I am going to ask the Venatores to come forward and show you some of their training to enhance their senses."

"Can I be the one blindfolded?" Diana asked enthusiastically as she jumped out of her chair."

"I didn't know you liked that," Misha said kiddingly.

"Misha there are Angels here," Diana scolded which made everyone laugh.

Thor tied a bandana around Diana's head that covered her eyes. Micha tied a second bandana that covered Diana's ears. Joshua walked up to Sorren and whispered into his ear while Thor and Micha were preparing Diana. Once the bandanas were secured, Thor and Micha moved her to the front of the room. They moved furniture around as a means to confuse Diana. Joshua put a shield in her left hand and a sword in her right hand."

Silently the three men walked around Diana and would randomly lunge at her.

434

Diana either held up her shield or thrust her sword as she felt appropriate but the crowd was amazed that she could sense where her attackers were in relation to her.

Joshua looked at Sorren and nodded. Sorren was already standing and reluctantly threw a knife at Diana who immediately swung around and held up her shield. The knife impaled the shield.

"My heart stopped beating," Misha said as he quickly walked up to his wife and hugged her tightly. Thor was untying the bandanas as everyone in the room applauded and yelled war cries.

"When you work on your strategies I want you to realize you are as blindfolded as Diana was; when you entered this kingdom. You are used to battles where you have some idea of where your enemy is coming from. Ryed is a different world; you would be wise to learn from the Venatores," Miranda explained.

"Tell us how you did that," Jared said. "That was the damndest thing I ever saw. I want you to train me."

"Everything living or not gives off energy. Most people feel the energy but aren't really aware of it," Joshua explained. "We train long and hard before a warrior can perform as Diana just did. From childhood our warriors are taught to train themselves to be sensitive to the energy levels."

"I can understand that with the three of you around Diana but how did she know Sorren was going to throw that knife?" Archetenus asked.

Diana looked at Sorren and smiled sweetly. "I don't know how to explain it but I could feel his fear that he was going to hurt me."

"Misha remember when Nada threw dirt in Diana's eyes during that competition? I didn't let them call off the competition because of the way we are trained. I knew my little sister would still win," Thor said with a grin.

"Everyone notice how nice Thor is being to me since he found out we are naming one of the babies after him," Diana teased with a mischievous grin. Her comment again brought laughter to the room.

"There is something that we aren't seeing here," Matthew said with frustration during a meeting with Raul, Simon, Raphael and Edward. "I keep feeling like we are missing the obvious."

"What bothers me," Simon said as he poured coffee into everyone's cups. "Is that no matter how well we plan, Teivel always seems one step ahead of us. I wonder if we have more spies or if Teivel is somehow listening to us talk."

"Or if we are just that damn predictable," Edward said. "We are all strategists how can we not figure this out."

"I think you just did," Raul said. "We are too predictable. We see the enemy, we go to them and we fight. That is why they know we are coming."

"Do you remember Gabriel telling all of you about his encounter with The Lion before we left Wetpr?" Raphael asked. "It still brings me great shame to admit this. But The Lion asked why Gabriel and I had not given comfort or offered confession to Misha after we found out that he had been molested and tortured by Nada and her boyfriends. Misha never appears as a victim and Gabriel and I didn't want to embarrass him. And in our hearts we didn't want to know that darkness."

"The Lion said that we had to understand the mindset of the demons in order to complete this mission or we would all be killed. The Lion said he wanted us to talk with Misha. But it wasn't the demons from hell that Misha told us about it was the personal demons of Nada and her men. I will tell you that Gabriel and I wept with Misha as he spoke. We, I mean me and Gabriel are not naïve men but we could not comprehend what those people did to Nada's children. The Lion healed Misha during that confession and taught us a lesson but I am just realizing that Gabriel and I did not understand the lesson."

"What do you mean?" Raul asked.

"We expect any type of cruelty or devious behavior from the true demons. But for some reason it is difficult for us to realize that humans can be just as evil as the real demons. The Angels said that we have never before been to a place like Ryed where there are layers of evil that have been created by men over the centuries. We truly are not seeing our enemies before us. I think our people in Ryed are in grave danger. Perhaps we attack Teivel on his home front first then clean out Fort Polta."

"Teivel would expect that we attack Polta, if for no other reason than the man who killed the Patronus priests took refuge there," Simon said.

"Ambush number one," Edward said.

"Gabriel told us that the generals said that Teivel doesn't have much of a military. We need to find out if that is true," Simon said.

"Ambush number two," Edward said. "This is becoming clear to me."

"I think we should expect to be fighting an army of demons and an army of men," Matthew said. "And the men at Fort Polta will be wearing Wetprian uniforms."

"The Angels said that Teivel was a flamboyant man who craved attention and wanted to prove his power," Raphael said. "Did the Angels tell us that is why he is holding the games or did we just assume that was the reason. Because this entire thing could be an ambush."

"I am writing down every question we have so far and sending it to Gabriel's group," Raul said. "Even if we are wrong, they are in hostile territory and should be considering these things."

"Do you think it is possible that Teivel set this entire thing up to lure us into a trap?" Simon asked. "If so I actually give him credit. But why and why now? He has been pretending to be a general of ours for decades. Do you think this has anything to do with Michael's appearance?"

"What do you mean?" asked Edward.

"Well we know the Insidiae and dark lords have been watching us for a long time. Maybe with Michael they are counting sons or something else. I mean we were told they have their own prophesies," Simon said. "There is just more to all of this and I know it. I agree with Matthew, no matter how much we discuss all of this we are missing something really important."

Miranda and Daniel had left Gabriel's group at Nehmota's castle but Ruth stayed behind. She walked around the Great Hall and listened as Gabriel's core team and the leaders discussed various strategies.

"I find it interesting," Ruth said loudly. "That you have been discussing your blindness to the evil within men and no one has thought to ask Erebus to join this group. That is his expertise. How many times has the Sanuri told you there are no coincidences in this world? You have identified a weakness and there is an expert among you. Why do you not call him in?"

"Because we don't trust him," Sorren said.

"Erebus is changing," Diana said. "I spend a lot of time talking to him and, well there is still evil in him and maybe there aren't things I am seeing. But I see good in him too."

"Sanuri, you have been unusually quiet during all of this," Gabriel said. "Why is that?"

"Before I answer that let me ask all of you a question," the Sanuri said. "While it is not unwise to mistrust Erebus is that the real reason you don't include him in the meetings?"

"I don't understand what you are asking?" Soren said.

"What do you think he will do?" the Sanuri asked.

The room was quiet for a few moments then Michael spoke. "Actually I think many of us have come to like Erebus but we don't know really were is allegiance lies. He could work for a demon."

"He has been very forthcoming about his darkness and his motives," the Sanuri said. "The point being that this is still the same issue that the Angels were talking about earlier."

"You see him and identify him with evil. And don't get me wrong he was very evil but I agree with Diana. Your real enemies are not the ones who tell you who they are. Erebus wears his identity like a badge. Has anyone actually felt threatened by him?"

"Where are you going?" Ruth asked Archetenus as he stood up.

"To get Erebus and I am getting a little frustrated. Obviously we are missing something really important. Can't you just tell us what the hell it is?" Archetenus paused. "Sorry Ruth I didn't mean to say hell in front of you."

Ruth smiled. "First of all hell is a place, I was not offended. Secondly if we have made you pause in your mission it is to save your lives and to save the mission. And thirdly I believe you, especially Archetenus already knows the answer to your question."

"Because the answers will change our choices," Gabriel said. "I am beginning to realize something during this meeting. I believe I speak for everyone in this room when I say we all believe in The Great Ruler yet we have never seen Him. We all believed in Angels before we met any. Why is it that we can't seem to grasp the concept of such powerful evil hidden within men?"

"Fear," the Sanuri said. "I am not talking about any of you feeling personally attacked. I am talking about the way you look at your world. Sorren do you remember when we were going to attack Ogg and you asked me if there had always been all of these demons in the world because you were not aware of them before?"

"Yes," Sorren said. "And the ones we were talking about were the easy ones to identify. You are saying that none of us want to go through this life not trusting anyone or anything we see."

"There are some of us in this room who lived lives like that," Thaos said. "And I think all of us have happy lives now but we never really drop our guards."

"The answer to your question Gabriel is that I have to let you figure this out," the Sanuri said.

"Archetenus why don't you get Erebus now," Ruth said. "We will take a break because several flocks of Enrops are headed here with letters. Gabriel one letter is from Raphael's group. Miranda helped hasten the journey of the birds bringing that note. I will want you to read it out loud."

Archetenus and Erebus returned to the meeting and both men were laughing. "Do you really want me to explain the darkness of men to you?" Erebus asked. "I would say you already understand that."

"Erebus I consider myself an expert at what I do," Gabriel said. "Yet since we have arrived in Teivel I have trusted and condemned all the wrong people; that is why the Angels are intervening."

"It wasn't just Gabriel, we all did," Natasha said. "We got played like fiddles."

"So what is it you need me to do?" Erebus asked with a confused look on his face.

"Jared you are closest to the door would you please open it?" Ruth asked. "Erebus, Gabriel and his team so dearly want to help the people in Ryed, that their sight may have become a little clouded." The room filled with Enrops that were delivering mail from Wetpr and Lentz. "Gabriel please read out loud the letter that Raul just sent you. Erebus please wait until Gabriel is done reading then you take the floor."

Gabriel stood up and read the notes from the meeting between Raphael, Edward, Simon, Raul and Matthew. While Gabriel's group had discussed many of the same issues that were mentioned in the letter some new questions were raised.

"Natasha I see that you are taking notes," Ruth said. "You will need to send the notes from this meeting to Raphael and the others. Erebus you have the floor."

"First who told you that Teivel doesn't have an army?" Erebus asked.

"The generals," Stephan said.

440

"Well he has a vast army and if he is hiding it from you that means the he suspects all of you." Erebus said. "And I think I am beginning to understand the problem. I have been alive for a very long time and it has opened my eyes to spend time with people like you again. I do not mean to insult anyone here but even the worst of you are good men and women. Thaos look at the reputation you had as a mercenary and yet you are a man of great integrity and loyalty. Jared and Archetenus you were created to become demons; look at the love and loyalty you have for others."

"Many of you wear your hearts on your sleeves for everyone to see and that includes the dark lords and demons. This is Ryed, there is no sense of loyalty here. Well, with possibly a few exceptions. While every person in this room would die to save the person sitting next to them, that mindset is not even known among Teivel's men. The soldiers, the demons, the dark lords here have no allegiance or loyalty to anyone but their private agendas. And they have many private agendas."

"Anyone who wants to gain power and wealth in this kingdom will sell out their family, their friends and their kingdom and Teivel has nourished this environment. While I know little of your plans I agree with what Edward said in that letter; all kinds of ambushes have been set for you. You are shall I say heroes. You see someone in need and you run to their assistance. Do not think that Teivel plays by the same rules that you do." Erebus paused.

"Erebus say what you are thinking," said Ruth.

"If Teivel doesn't know where you are he will start setting up situations like executing innocent people to draw you out of the shadows because he knows you cannot stand by and watch."

"Have we done more harm here?" Gabriel gasped.

"No, not yet and that is why we intervened," Ruth said. "Erebus you will now be a part of all of these meetings. And the others can fill you in later. But first I want Jared to open the letter he just received from Zoya."

"There are a couple," said Jared.

"Open the thickest one," Ruth said.

441

Jared quickly looked over the letter, "Do you mean the message for Michael?"

"Yes. Please hand that part of the letter to Michael and Michael read it out loud," Ruth requested. Michael took the letter and stood up. "Please read exactly as Zoya wrote it," Ruth said.

"*Jared the next part is for Michael and I feel it is very important so please show it to him right away. Michael the spirit of your mother Nadia has come to me several times since you left Wetpr. I can see her presence and she is acting scared but most of the time she does not speak to me. Last night Nadia woke me from my sleep and she was not alone. Your grandmother Fiona was with her. Both women acted frightened.*"

"*Michael, Fiona said that Nadia's linage goes back to a tribe call the Epocos. They are one of the original tribes of Ryed. Centuries ago much of Ryed was conquered by Stordt so some of your ancestors lived in both kingdoms. As Fiona was telling me this, both spirits became very frightened and started to fade away. I yelled to them and then I saw the words Prophesy of Izera.*"

"I have no idea what that means," Michael said as he handed the letter back to Jared.

"I have a copy of that at my castle," Erebus said as he stared at Michael. "It has been a very long time since I read it but..." Erebus paused and looked at Ruth.

"Tell him," Ruth said. "Some of the Rualas will take you home to retrieve it."

"It is written in a very old language that is very descriptive in nature. It talks about Ryed being a beautiful garden and then the demons plant a dark seed. The seed grows into an incredible tree. And everything living thing around the tree dies. But the tree bears fruit, although not a lot. There is a lot more to the writing but the end of the prophesy is something like the fruit of the tree returns and cuts the tree down," Erebus explained.

"I have not read that prophesy," the Sanuri said. "But that answers Simon's questions about why is Teivel doing all of this now. I think Teivel believes you are the fruit of the tree, Michael."

442

"There is more to the prophesy which is why you must read it," Ruth said. Prince Lakin would you be kind enough to have Erebus flown to his castle to retrieve this scroll? Your way will be made clear." Ruth turned to Erebus. "I believe you have some more scrolls about the history of this kingdom, I would bring everything you have."

"Now wait; are you telling me I am Teivel's long lost something?" Michael asked.

"Fruit," Jared said with a grin. "You're his fruit and apparently his undoing."

"Michael remember what you told me about your stepfather; this is starting to make sense," Gabriel said to Michael then he turned to Ruth. "Have the Angels been protecting Michael so Teivel and Karzman couldn't kill him?"

"What do you think?" Ruth asked with a warm smile.

"That's why Teivel has been in Wetpr, to keep an eye on Michael. I am sure Teivel or the Grand Masters know about The Prophesy of The Seven Sons. But maybe Teivel didn't know that Michael was written about in both prophesies. Now that Teivel realizes what a force Michael is; he is trying to stop him," Gabriel said.

Ruth smiled at Gabriel then turned to Jared. "Jared what is the date on that letter?"

"Zoya wrote it this morning. But how can that be?"

"Gabriel you need to ask me a question," Ruth said.

Gabriel grinned, "Ruth please help us in every way possible with this mission."

"Time is very important if we want to save the lives of many innocent people," Ruth said. "Erebus you and the warriors who escort you will be aided by the heavens. You will return here before nightfall and you must become heavily involved with the planning. Perhaps Prince Lakin can carry you and fill you in on all that has been planned to this point."

443

"Natasha write down everything you just heard and I will assist an Enrop in getting that letter to Raul and the others very quickly," Ruth said then she turned to Archetenus. "Archetenus you grew up in Roch's army. Roch has many similarities to Teivel. Use your knowledge of that man to help lead the discussions that will take place after Lakin and Erebus leave."

"Now I hope you understand the layers of ambushes that have been set and the desperation of a tyrant to kill his biggest threat. Teivel will stop at nothing to destroy you. Now my brave warriors, now you make your plans. And you will understand how this knowledge changes your choices. Sanuri you no longer have to remain silent; your assistance is greatly needed here for there are foes these humans cannot conquer."

"Wait, why all these cat and mouse games?" Michael asked angrily. "Why am I just hearing about this now?"

"Michael you made the choice to find your father but you did not make a commitment to that family," Ruth explained. "The scars around your heart would not let them in. Tell me my child, when did you make that commitment?"

Michael's anger started to pass as he thought about Ruth's question. "When I got the drawings from my nephews and the letters from the rest of the family."

"Miranda did whisper into Thaos' ear so he would speak with you the night you were planning on leaving the castle of Sudfad but that was not enough," Ruth said.

"I didn't realize Miranda talked to me," Thaos said.

"Sometimes that is the way Angels work," Ruth said. "Now I am going to share something with you. All of you here are under the assignment of The Lion, Miranda and Daniel. My assignment has been to keep the tiny flicker of faith and hope alive in the City of Teivel. Now that our assignments are combining I do not want to see any of you hurt nor do I want to see my tiny flames extinguished. But this is your world. You must make the choices. The lives of a kingdom lay upon your shoulders. You would be wise to pray for guidance and for clarity. I will leave this meeting now but I will remain in the castle."

Chapter XXXIV
Fruit of the Tree

"The Angel Ruth helped us to fly faster one of the Enrops explained as a small flock flew into the room where Raphael, Edward, Raul, Simon and Matthew were still working on battle strategies. "You are to read this right away," the bird continued.

Raphael read Natasha's letter out loud. "So this is about Michael?" Raul asked.

"It's about all of us," Simon said. "But now instead of us being ambushed we know what Teivel wants."

"Miranda, Daniel," Matthew called out. The two Angels appeared in the meeting room. "Is Michael the fruit of the tree?"

"Yes," Miranda said.

"Then shouldn't we go to that castle in Ryed and protect him?" Matthew asked. "Then five of The Seven Sons will be together."

"I am pleased that is the first time any of you have thought about bringing The Seven Sons together. That is how you must think always."

"I think we should go to Ryed first then clean out Fort Polta afterwards," Raul said.

"You know bringing an Army of this size into Ryed is an act of war," Daniel said.

"Maybe it's time we declared war on Ryed," Simon said.

"It is not all of Ryed you should declare war against," Daniel said. "You are on the right path but think this through."

Michael was asked to stand up and talk about his stepfather Karzman and his life. Michael did not feel comfortable but he understood the others needed this information. After he finished speaking, Archetenus stood in front of the group and talked about King Roch. Gabriel had studied Roch for a long time before the mission in Stordt, so Gabriel also addressed the group.

After the Sanuri spoke, the group divided into smaller groups to work on strategies. "I think it is time we set up a few ambushes of our own," Sorren said with a hearty laugh. For the first time all day the group felt that it heading in the right direction.

Chaez the son of Fahron had begged Thaos and Stephan to allow him to accompany them to Ryed. Chaez thought he would greatly improve his fighting skills so he could pass the training to become a Patronus priest.

Chaez had remained at Erebus' castle when Thaos and Stephan went to the City of Teivel with Gabriel. Chaez had learned a great deal but he also felt shy and somewhat intimidated by the warriors and soldiers who had volunteered for the mission. When others of the group socialized, he trained and studied.

Chaez did not attend any of the planning meetings for the mission. This afternoon he was practicing shooting arrows from a moving horse in one of the arenas of Nehmota's castle. Chaez stopped and jumped off from his horse when he saw Ruth walking across the courtyard.

"My Lady," Chaez called and ran up to Ruth, who turned and smiled. "Excuse me My Lady but are you really an Angel? That is what the others are saying."

"Do you need an Angel? Ruth asked.

"Oh yes My Lady."

"And why would the son of one of the ruling families of Lentz need an Angel?"

"You know who I am, you must be an Angel," Chaez said happily then his demeanor suddenly changed. "Then you know about my brother Timothy?"

"I know that you are killing yourself because you feel so full of guilt over what your brother had done."

"Oh no My Lady, that is not why I am killing myself. I mean I am not really killing myself. Well maybe some of what you said is true but now that I understand that people like my brother exist in this world I want to stop them."

"And I want to protect other people and to help them heal. I am working really hard because I want to become a Patronus priest."

"My child you are covered with bruises. You have given up the life of a young nobleman because you want to become a priest?"

"Yes, My Lady. But that is why I wanted to ask you well, will I be able to do it?"

"Tell me Chaez what have you been doing?"

"I have been learning all manner of fighting and horse riding. I am learning how to use different weapons and how to read people."

"That is all very good training to become a warrior. What are you doing to become a priest?"

"The Sanuri has been teaching me The Holy Scrolls," Chaez said enthusiastically.

"And do you understand what you have been learning?"

"I think so."

"You understand that the Patronus priests are warriors but they also teach people and comfort them. They listen to people and help them to unburden their souls. Would you like some lessons in how to become a priest?"

"Oh yes My Lady."

"You may call me Ruth. Come let me introduce you to some of the citizens of Ryed."

Ruth and Chaez walked around the castle courtyard until they came upon a group of people. Dominic, Asher, Fennel and Rachel as well as other freedom fighters were talking with the citizens of Ryed and helping them to train for battle. "Dominic it is time for you and your brothers to join that meeting," Ruth said. "Rachel you come with Chaez and me."

When Prince Lakin, Erebus and thirty-five Ruala warriors landed in the courtyard of Erebus' castle they could tell something was wrong. A gray mist shrouded the castle although no other area.

"Stay here," Erebus said to Lakin. "If something happens to me the scrolls you want are on the two shelves in the far left of my library."

"Wait, what are you going to do?" Lakin asked.

"That cloud is not only a warning it is an alarm. If we were to walk through it; you would not notice anything but an army of demons would be tipped off that we are here. And there may be other traps." Erebus started to walk closer to his castle then he turned back to Lakin. "Prepare your warriors to fly. Once I start using my powers others in the dark worlds will be able to locate us."

Anger filled Erebus as he once again found his home violated by others. Erebus had deliberately given up performing any kind of spells for months so as not to alert the dark world as to the location of Gabriel's team. Now Erebus felt as if he was going to burst from the pent up energies mounting within him.

Erebus slowly and deliberately walked towards the castle, softly mumbling incantations. Soon loud noises and screams were being emitted from the ominous cloud. Then lightning strikes were seen within the cloud only.

"Is he doing that?" Ratri asked Lakin.

"I am not sure," Lakin replied. "But I think that cloud was more than an alarm."

"Look at Erebus," Ratri said in amazement.

As Erebus attacked the cloud a dark aura surrounded the sorcerer. Suddenly there was the sound of an explosion and the cloud burst into flames. "Stay out here until I tell you it is safe," Erebus yelled to the Rualas then he disappeared inside of the castle. Most of the Ruala warriors were in the air watching for intruders, Lakin and Ratri walked closer to the castle.

448

Fifteen minutes passed without any sign of Erebus. Lakin and Ratri walked up to the closed front door when it opened. "There were a few other surprises," Erebus said. "We must get those manuscripts now."

Lakin motioned for some other warriors to follow them into the castle. They all walked quickly to the library, where Erebus pointed out the things they would need. "I sent a message back to the underworlds, "Erebus said with a grin. "So I want to take more manuscripts than we originally planned in case Gabriel needs them. Who knows what will happen to this place the next time they attack."

"Are all these books and scrolls about dark magics?" Lakin asked as he looked at the massive library.

"No, those shelves you are emptying are all about the histories of different kingdoms. There are quite a few written by Shamans, I find the early medicines fascinating. In fact..." Erebus quickly ran to a large book case and looked through a shelf of scrolls. "Oh lets, just take all of these." Erebus said as he emptied the shelf. "I thought you and Hannah might find these interesting."

"We should take these too," Erebus said as he carried two huge scrolls and three large bound books. "They are prophesies of the dark worlds."

"No Ratri!" Erebus yelled as the young Ruala warrior walked towards a bookshelf on the opposite side of the room. "Those books contain such darkness that it could damage you."

"I don't know why I was walking over there," Ratri said with a rather shocked look on his face.

"The books were calling to you," Erebus said.

"Calling to him!" Lakin said.

"Yes, some of these books have an essence of their own. Even we cannot read them without preforming protection spells first," Erebus said then he grabbed a piece of paper and quickly wrote down a few words. Erebus handed the paper to Lakin. "As soon as you have the manuscripts take your men back to the court-yard. I am going to put some protection spells on the castle."

"But if I am killed and any of you need to get back in here, well, show this to the Angels. None of you will have the power to remove the spells."

"The Angels probably don't need this," Lakin said as he put the paper inside of his pocket.

"I realize that but just in case." Erebus said. "We need to leave. I do believe we will have company soon."

The Ruala warriors put the last of the manuscripts into their backpacks and everyone quickly ran out of the castle. Erebus remained inside for five minutes then walked out to the court-yard. The earth started to shake as Lakin grabbed Erebus and ascended into the sky."

"The word 'Betrayer' was written on the walls," Erebus said. "I removed it before you came in. I don't believe Hecate has any-thing to do with this. Others know I am working with you."

"After this mission it may not be safe for you to return to your castle," Lakin said. "You should probably consider moving to Wetpr or Lentz. I would have to speak with the Sanuri before I could make such an offer in the Ice Caves."

"You would offer me a home?" Erebus asked in disbelief.

"Why did you say it like that?"

"I guess I still believe many of you look upon me as your enemy."

"Perhaps that is a wall you have put up," Lakin said and flew higher into the clouds. Loud rumbling sounds as if thunder now came from Erebus' castle.

"Chaez until Timothy destroyed your family you have never known want or tragedy," Ruth said. "For you to truly help people heal the wounds of their lives you have to be able to really understand what they are saying. If you merely do lip service they will know it and stop talking to you."

"While I agree with what you are saying, I cannot change my life. Are you suggesting that I postpone my studies as a priest?"

"You want to become a priest?" Rachel asked with surprise.

"Yes, why did you ask it like that?" Chaez asked.

"I didn't mean to insult you, I guess I don't really know," Rachel said.

"Tell her about Timothy," Ruth said.

Chaez hesitated. "My parents are wonderful. My father is a great warrior and wanted to protect all of his children from the horrors he had seen. I had an older brother named Timothy and a younger sister named Tabeth. Timothy was always difficult and drew a great deal of my parent's attention." Chaez hesitated again.

"We didn't know he was a rapist until he attacked the wife of Prince Simon. He was put into prison and later told my parents he had raped other women. When my parents refused to ask for his release Timothy swore to kill them. He made contracts with demons who helped Timothy and others escape prison. Timothy and the others did not just kill they butchered and raped everyone they came across even little children."

"In an attempt to weaken Father so he would be easier to kill, Timothy raped and butchered Tabeth. Timothy was killed but the harm that he did still sits upon us all."

"Go on," Ruth said.

"I lived a pampered life. Don't get me wrong I had my studies and my responsibilities but I never knew that people like Timothy existed in this world. And when I saw what he did and the effect it had on those that survived I swore to stop that evil. Gabriel and Raphael are getting me into the training to become a Patronus priest but I had never even been in a fight before so I am greatly behind the other applicants."

"As you can see from looking at the boy he has concentrated his efforts on learning how to become a warrior. But he must also learn of the people he will nourish and protect," Ruth said to Rachel. "Rachel, Chaez has told you of the horrors of his life I would like you to tell him of yours. He must know how you felt and what you thought. Then I would like you to introduce him to others." Ruth turned to Chaez.

451

"This is not like your other training. You do not have to preform or know the answers but you must listen and I mean really listen to what the others are telling you. Open up your heart, The Great Ruler will do the rest."

Erebus, Lakin and the other Rualas suddenly appeared inside of the meeting room in less than an hour after they had left. Ruth had just entered the room before this group arrived. "Did you do that?" Erebus asked in amazement.

Ruth smiled. "Time is very important now. Erebus and Lakin please tell the group what you found as the others pile the books and scrolls on those tables."

"A dark cloud surrounded the castle only," Erebus said. "It was a warning and would tell others of our arrival if I would have let the warriors walk through it. I destroyed it and entered the castle because I knew there would be more traps. The word 'Betrayer' was written on many walls in what appeared to be blood. When it was safe the others entered then I put a protection spell on the castle before we left. If I die and you need to get into the castle Lakin has the words."

"You left out a great deal," Ruth said. "Tell them everything."

"Before Erebus could speak again Lakin looked at Gabriel and said. "That cloud reminded me of the ring that surrounded the Patronus Headquarters in Nora when Ahriman was trying to get the prisoner Meekos. And when Erebus attacked the cloud we saw creatures within it and heard screams."

"Alright, it was a little more than a warning but I didn't want to scare everyone," Erebus said. "Only a very powerful demon could do something like that or perhaps a Grand Master could pay an Old One for such a favor."

"Erebus I know you are powerful but are you that powerful?" Gabriel asked in amazement.

"When Erebus attacked the cloud, a darkness appeared around him," Ratri said.

"Erebus why don't you tell them why you seemed to have more power," Ruth said.

452

"I really don't think that is important," Erebus said with a hint of indignation.

"Actually it is more important than you realize," she said. "And start from the beginning."

Erebus stared at Ruth stubbornly because he did not want to explain himself. "Alright, many of you know that I have not been practicing any dark magics because I was afraid the dark worlds would locate me. For those of you who know me you know I didn't care for myself but I did not want to give away the location of all of you. When I saw my castle I was angry that my home had been violated again and..."Erebus paused.

"And what Erebus?" Diana asked.

"And I started to think about all of you who have been staying with me and my anger was out of control. I sent the demons back to those who sent them with such force that whoever sent then would feel the impact."

The room was quiet and Thor could see that Erebus was embarrassed. "Erebus are you really saying you've adopted all of us as your grandchildren and you're telling the demons not to go after your family?" Thor asked with a grin. "Because it sounds like it was that kind of anger."

Erebus laughed, "You might be right."

"Alright," Diana said with frustration. "Maybe I am just stupid but I don't understand how any of that works. Erebus did you call on demons to help you?"

"No, I called upon the darkness within me."

"What darkness, even the trees started growing around your castle again," Diana said. "Erebus I talk with you every day. I just don't see it anymore."

"I have never tried to hide who or what I am," Erebus said. "And while everyone keeps telling me I am changing you just saw that I am still a sorcerer. Does that make a difference to anyone?"

"Actually I think I trust you more now," Sorren said.

453

"If time is important we should move on. I thought you were just going to get a couple of scrolls and those tables are filled."

Erebus was relieved that Sorren had changed the subject. "Give me a moment and I will find the ones containing the Prophesy of Izera. Most of the rest of these manuscripts contain information about the histories of the kingdoms and I brought some about ancient medicines for Lakin and Hannah."

"Before we get into that, I want to finish talking about the castle," Gabriel said. "So possibly an Old One knows Erebus is helping us. If Hecate is not responsible for that, then we have more spies than I thought."

"And now you are beginning to understand why we made you pause in the mission," Ruth said to Gabriel then turned to Michael. "Michael the scroll that contains the prophesy of Izera is written in Cerfic, perhaps you would translate for us."

As Erebus looked for the scroll, Michael walked to the front of the room. "I'm not really looking forward to this," Michael said as he left his chair.

"What, you mean about you being a piece of fruit?" Jared asked kiddingly.

Michael unrolled part of the scroll and read in silence for several moments. "This language is written as if they draw pictures but with words. The beginning is talking about what a beautiful and wonderful place Ryed is." Michael looked at Gabriel. "That was the same with that scroll I read at your house." Michael read farther in the scroll. "Unless anyone wants to hear about the beautiful plants, birds and animals I am going to just read the parts that pertain to Teivel."

No one in the room responded so Michael read more of the scroll in silence. Erebus walked next to Michael and helped him find the area of interest. "Now we have something," Michael said. "This talks about two children who come to Ryed. They appear to be innocent and lost but that is a disguise because they are the children of Ahriman."

"For those of you unfamiliar with that term it means they worship the demons, Ahriman in particular," Gabriel explained.

"Remember most people did not know the true identities or even numbers of the Old Ones. So it appears the phrase the children of Ahriman is similar to saying the children of a devil."

"Gabriel, this scroll also talks about the craziness and plagues that were inflicted upon the people of Ryed," Michael said. "It says that the children who are brother and sister went from village to village telling the people to worship them in order to be healed. Many people died because they would not bow before Emeric and Banka." Michael now looked at the audience. "This scroll hasn't used their names yet but that is who they are talking about."

"This said that when Emeric and Banaka went to the village of the Epocos which was then in the northeastern corner of Ryed they found another of their kind. It says the man's name was Morton and he eagerly bowed before the children of Ahriman. This says they blew into Morton's face and when he turned towards the other villagers they no longer saw the face of a human but that of a monster. Morton then tore apart everyone from his village who would not bow before Emeric and Banaka."

"This says Emeric and Banaka were pleased with the way Morton slaughtered his friends and family and they gave him a new name, that name was Teivel. Whoever wrote this said that Teivel became like an animal with rabies and savagely killed anyone who would not bow before Emeric and Banaka." Michael read in silence again. "This is going into detail of all the people Teivel slaughtered. He traveled the kingdom killing and raping."

Michael got a shocked look on his face and looked up from the scroll. "Joshua did you know this?" Michael asked. "This says that Teivel gathered demons around him and they terrorized every village and city until they came to the village of the Venatores. The Venatores where children of one god, a very powerful god. The Venatores would not bow before Teivel and his demons. The Venatores were the only village to fight Teivel and the battle lasted for twelve days."

"The Venatores won the battle and as Teivel's army was riding away in defeat..." Michael stopped reading and looked at Ruth. "An old and frail woman with a dark shawl covering her head suddenly appeared on the battlefield."

"She told Teivel that the village of the Venatores was protected by their god and that Teivel had no power against them. She warned Teivel to change his ways. When Teivel mocked the woman she told him that one would be born from the seed of Teivel's loin and that child would destroy him."

Now the entire room was looking at Ruth who said, "Teivel never raped anyone after that." Many in the room laughed and many stared in awe. "Michael keep reading," Ruth said.

"It says that Teivel started to scream as if he was in great pain and he fell from his horse. The demons surrounding Teivel moved towards the old woman but soon they too screamed and turned into piles of ashes on the ground. The woman again told Teivel to change his ways. He cursed the old woman. Soon Teivel's skin started to smoke and he rolled around the ground screaming. The old woman walked up to Teivel and whispered into his ear then she was gone. Teivel looked terrified. He got off the ground and mounted his horse and never returned to the village of the Venatores."

"Ruth is that true?" Diana asked emotionally.

"Yes."

"I am so proud of our people," Diana said and Misha put his arm around her.

"Finish the scroll," Ruth said to Michael.

"It says that Teivel was so fearful of the prophesy of the old woman that he never took a wife. And that he tried to find all of the women he had raped to kill any of his offspring. But he never found any offspring because the women were protected."

"Michael your mother's linage is from the loin of Teivel and your father's linage fulfills the prophesy of The Seven Sons. You have had an awful and painful life. But you have learned more about how to take down Teivel than anyone in this room. I know you try to block your memories but the answers are in your dreams."

Michael suddenly looked overwhelmed so Gabriel stood up and spoke.

"Ruth, Teivel must have sent Karzman to threaten Nadia's clan. Nadia was going to marry Sudfad and didn't to save the lives of her people. How did Teivel know about Michael?"

"You already know that the demons and dark lords have been trying to figure out for centuries who would become The Seven Sons. That was not the only prophesy they are worried about. The darkness pays great attention to any threat against them. The Royal Families of Wetpr have been watched for generations. As soon as it came to Teivel's attention that Prince Sudfad had fallen in love with a woman whose linage traced back to the origins of Ryed he became terrified. Karzman still is one of Teivel's lieutenants."

"Michael you have met Teivel. He came to see you. Karzman is a monster but he was becoming fearful because no matter what he did to you he could not kill you. Teivel came to your home and he tried to kill you but his sword melted in his hands then he was inflicted with great pain. Karzman made you cage fight because he thought he would have you killed that way. My child the life you have endured here brings tears to my eyes but you have been protected more than you will ever understand," Ruth said.

"I think Michael needs some air," Natasha said and quickly jumped out of her seat and took Michael's hand and led him out of the Great Hall.

"I think we are all wondering the same thing," Gabriel asked. "Why?"

"Is there a man or woman in this room who has not endured great hardship?" Ruth asked. No one answered. "Thaos your early life was very similar to that of Michael's. Everyone in this room is stronger because of their trials and tests and look at the men and women you are now."

"I hear the questions in your hearts but remember this is your world, you have freedom of choice. Many in this world want the demon's here. Nadia and Michael never called to us. We do not force our way in."

Chapter XXXV
In Your Dreams

"Michael do you want to take a walk or find some place to sit?" Natasha asked sweetly as she could see how distressed her friend was.

"Let's walk," Michael said in a voice that was barely audible. Natasha took Michael's arm and led him towards one of the large gardens that surrounded the castle. They walked in silence for several minutes before Michael said. "I don't know what happened to me I could barely breathe."

"Michael, your life has been a nightmare; it is understandable;" Natasha paused. "Please don't take this the wrong way because none of us on the team really know everything you went through. But of what we do know, well, we all agree you must be a very special person to have come out of it the way you did."

"What do you mean?"

"I am sure you carry a lot of pain and anger but honestly on the outside you seem like a wonderful person. You are strong and caring. For myself I wouldn't expect you to be so open and friendly. You are just a really nice person. It shows how strong you must be to not have let Karzman turn you into a monster."

"I am not sure there isn't some monster in me," Michael said after a pause.

"I think there is some monster in all of us. I stabbed an innocent man and was ready to kill him. I will never live that down."

"You didn't know; you were trying to save Tobey."

"You know the Angels always talk to us in a way that, well they never give you the complete answers because they seem to want us to really think about their words. But we have Angels that come the second we call to them. I think Ruth wants us to remember that before we act hastily. I knew that and I never asked if Clay was a good or bad person. I would have murdered one of the only people in this kingdom who is helping us."

"If the Angels knew what was happening to me and my mother and sisters why didn't they help us?" Michael asked as anger rose within him.

"It sounds like they did."

"Natasha you have no idea what was done to us," Michael said angrily. "I need to talk to Ruth." Michael left Natasha and ran into the castle. Natasha ran behind him.

"Ruth!" Michael bellowed as he barged into the Great Hall. "I want to talk to you."

"And it is about time," Ruth said as she walked towards him. The room fell silent.

"About time!" Michael screamed as his anger consumed him. "You all saw what they did to us. You were watching and you didn't help us! Now you tell me why?"

"Michael would you like to speak in private?" asked Ruth.

"We do everything you ask; perhaps none of you are who we think you are. Maybe everyone needs to know why you let a monster rape and beat his own daughters and wife and torture me. Tell me, tell me! What kind of Angels are you?"

"Michael do you remember that dream you used to have? The one where you were in a loving home. You were eating at a table in front of a hearth and your mother would hug you tightly and you felt loved and warm."

Michael stared at Ruth without speaking. He started to shake so badly that others in the room could see. "Yes, I had that dream all of the time."

"What face did your mother have, was it Nadia or Renya?"

"No. Now that you say that, I don't know whose face it was."

Batina gasped loudly as she saw Ruth transform from a fragile old woman into a beautiful young woman; who was radiant."

"You! You came to me in my dreams. Why?"

"Do you remember what I would say to you in that dream? I would tuck you in bed and whisper in your ear. Do you remember my words?"

Tears started to run down Michael's face. "You told me to pray," he said haltingly.

"Michael I was not the only Angel who came to you. We whispered into your head and your heart. We came to you in your dreams and we did the same with your mother and sisters. Why my child did none of you ever call us in?"

Michael's knees became weak and he staggered to a chair. "You mean I could have stopped all of it?"

"You had a destiny that needed to be played out but we certainly could have made your lives easier. We intervened more than you realized but you still have freedom of choice. We kept dropping breadcrumbs but you wouldn't follow the path. Michael that love you felt in the dreams was real. It was my love for you, it was the love of The Great Ruler and other Angels. Don't you think we wept? When you don't call to us it is like you bind us."

"Michael in the last few months you have met three Angels. Do you realize the miracle that is? And still you do not call to us, you do not ask us, you do not pray. Others pray for you now. Your newly found family. Even the children pray for you at night. Michael you are such a special person. Don't let the darkness you have fought your entire life cripple you. As powerful as you are you will be even stronger when you let us in."

In the instant that Ruth stopped talking she and Michael disappeared from the room. No one spoke in the room. The only sound was the soft crying of several of the women. Gabriel stood up and addressed the group, "I think we could all use a break. Everyone come back in an hour."

Dagon left the Great Hall and walked around the courtyard looking for Rachel. Ruth had previously told him that Rachel was introducing Chaez to some of the freedom fighters.

"Dagon," Rachel called when she saw him. She left the group of six people she was sitting with and walked up to him.

"Honey are you alright?" Dagon asked as he saw that Rachel had been crying. Dagon put his arms around Rachel and hugged her tightly.

"Oh, I am alright," Rachel said. "Ruth wants me to introduce Chaez to people so he can learn to talk to them and listen; you know for when he becomes a priest. And we have just heard so many sad stories; that is why I am crying. Chaez is crying too."

"You could use a break," Dagon said and took Rachel's hand. "Let's go for a walk."

They walked in silence for a few moments then Rachel said, "Dagon, Ruth wanted me to tell Chaez about my life first. I have never told you about my life. It is not fair that he should know and not you. You have told me about everyone in your family and on your team; didn't you question that I didn't share anything with you?"

"Of course but I thought you were so overwhelmed about your family that I didn't want to push it."

"As Chaez and I have been talking to these people I realized one thing we all have in common is that none of us trust anyone. All of you are so different. You all trust each other. Here everyone sells out their families and friends either for profit or to save themselves. If we are to be married, I need to trust you. I mean I do trust you but I haven't been acting like it."

"I am glad to hear you say that."

"Dagon my father is a lot older than my mother. She is his second wife. His first wife was killed when a band of men raided the village they lived in. She risked her life to save their only child. His name was Giovani and he was just a baby when his mother was raped and murdered."

"Father married my mother a few years later. Giovani was six years older than me and I absolutely adored him. I would follow him everywhere. Now that I think about it Giovani always seemed older than his age. He was so handsome and funny and smart and he had a way of making everyone feel good."

"One day when Giovani was twelve, father was hunting and a group of Teivel's soldiers rode up to our house."

461

"Zack wasn't born yet. Mother hid me and Giovani in the cellar and walked out onto the porch. One of the soldiers demanded to know where Father was because they said that someone in the village said that Father was a freedom fighter. Father wasn't then, he became one later."

"Mother told the soldiers that Father wasn't a freedom fighter. The soldiers got off their horses and one of the men slapped her. Giovani and I were on the ladder going into the cellar and we had the door propped open so we could listen." Rachel started to weep. "The men grabbed mother and started tearing her clothes off. We heard her screaming. Giovani jumped off the ladder into the kitchen and put a chair on top of the cellar door so I couldn't get out. After that all I heard was screams and crying. The soldiers raped mother and killed Giovani."

"Father found us all when he returned to the house. He is the one who let me out of the cellar. Those men hurt my Mother badly. Dagon I heard it all and I have never felt so helpless. I swore that day that I would never let anyone hurt my family again. And I told The Great Ruler that I would never feel that helpless again. But I have felt helpless since Father was taken."

Dagon hugged Rachel tightly, "I am glad you told me. Rachel I will help you find your father no matter what. But I am even more convinced that you have to let me move your family to Wetpr. Why would any of you want to live here? This is like a hell dimension. Has your mother returned our letter about her and Zack moving to Wetpr?"

"No, I will let you know as soon as we get it."

"Do you mind if I tell my mother what you just told me?"

"Not really but why?"

"Emeral just has a way with people, you will see when you meet her. Your mother could use a friend who she can trust. Perhaps the two can write to each other."

When the meeting in the Great Hall resumed Michael and Ruth were noticeably absent. During the hour break, Erebus had been sorting through the various scrolls and books that he had brought from his castle.

Sorren and the Sanuri were the first two to enter the Great Hall after the break and they saw Erebus busily organizing the tables of manuscripts. "Sanuri can I ask you a question?" Sorren asked in a whisper.

"Of course."

"Don't get me wrong, I am alright with Erebus but I don't understand the way the Angels have been treating him. It confuses me."

"How have they been treating him?"

"Well, like he is one of us."

"He is a member of this team."

"But the Angels work for The Great Ruler and Erebus is a sorcerer. Doesn't that mean he worships the demons?"

"He doesn't worship demons. But he doesn't worship The Great Ruler either. Angels aren't as judgmental as humans; perhaps they see something in him that others do not."

"I still think it is strange."

"Erebus has been changing because he is responding to the kindness and respect he has been shown. He may not even realize it but he has. Everyone wants to be loved and accepted and Erebus has been leading a very lonely life."

"You are probably right but it still seems strange to me."

The meeting had been going on for almost two hours when Michael and Ruth returned to the Great Hall. It was obvious to everyone that Michael had been crying but both Lakin and the Sanuri noticed a great difference in him; Michael no longer had a dark stormy aura around him.

"Michael sit with us," Diana said. Michael stood motionless.

"We need help with this translation," Joshua said and Michael joined the small group at their table. Joshua handed Michael a scroll.

"What is this?" Michael asked as he scanned the page in front of him.

"Well, we think it is a history of the Epocos Tribe," Joshua said. "I can't read Cerfic like you can. It started out talking about that tribe then it was like the scroll was talking about something else completely and I got lost."

Michael went to the beginning of the scroll and started reading after a few minutes he asked, "Does anyone have a map that at least shows Ryed, western Stordt and western Wetpr?"

"I have several maps," Gabriel said and brought them to the table where Joshua, Thor, Micha, Bianca, Diana, Misha and Michael were sitting. Gabriel spread out the maps and Michael looked back and forth between the ancient scroll and the maps several times.

"I believe this is saying that the Epocos Tribe lived near the caves of Muldun. They must have lived very close because it is talking about the foothills that now separate Stordt and Wetpr. It is describing the Gants that live in the caves. Ruth can this be right?" Michael asked. "Did that tribe live peacefully near the Gants?"

"In the early days yes, both tribes respected each other and their boundaries," Ruth replied as she walked closer to the table.

"So is that the word for Gant?" Joshua asked as he pointed to the scroll. Because I got confused about who was attacking who?"

"Teivel led men into the caves and they fought with the Gants," Michael said. "Teivel battled the Gants several times and never got the holy scroll that the Gants protect," Michael read out loud.

"The Scroll of Imari," Gabriel said. "Teivel knows about it?"

"Many know about it," Ruth said. "And many armies have tried to take it over the centuries."

Now others in the room walked over to the table to look at the maps. "Is that why King Sharonne kept attacking Ryed to acquire the caves?" the Sanuri asked Ruth.

"Yes and he too tried to obtain that gift," Ruth replied.

"Michael, Sharonne is the great, great, great grandfather of all you boys. He is the one who sold his soul so he could start the seed that would produce Roch as a vessel for the demon Omnibus," the Sanuri explained. "Sharonne greatly expanded the boundaries of Stordt during his reign. I am surprised that Sharonne beat Teivel in battle since Emeric and Banaka were helping Teivel."

"But some of the Old Ones were helping Sharonne," Ruth explained. "Why do you think all of this is important now?"

"I am surprised that Teivel hasn't gone after the scroll again," Gabriel said without answering Ruth's question.

"Oh he has," Ruth said. "You know a demon now sits on the throne of Stordt. That is not by chance. Roch was a demonic human who was controlled by the dark lords and demons. All of the underworlds would have The Scroll of Imari. The Old Ones had to put a demon in Stordt that was powerful enough to prevent Emeric and Banaka as well as others from trying to steal the scroll."

"Zieman is the name of the demon who controls Stordt. Karzman is still a lieutenant of Teivel's the two have been battling and Karzman has sustained some heavy losses. This war consumes Karzman and turns his attention away from finding Michael and brutalizing his daughters. The war also distracts Teivel who believes it was Zieman that attacked Fort Polta."

"How could we know nothing of this?" the Sanuri asked.

"You do now and it is just another way that your paths are being cleared for you," Ruth said.

"Is that why Zieman put bounties on my team?" Gabriel asked.

"There are several reasons," Ruth explained. "Ahriman was the benefactor of Zieman. There is a loyalty among the demons."

465

"Now my children I will ask you again why do you think this is important? I have told you time is precious now and yet we are reviewing this."

"Are we supposed to get the scroll?" Lakin asked.

"Not you my friend," Ruth said warmly. "Michael you have the blood of the Epocos in your veins; the Gants will recognize it. You and the Sanuri must make that journey but it will not be easy."

"Is that how I will have the power to destroy Teivel?" Michael asked. "You said the information was in my dreams but I don't remember."

Ruth walked up to Michael and placed the palm of her right hand on his head. Suddenly everyone in the room was viewing Michael's dream.

"Are we seeing a hell world?" Sorren asked as the group watched monstrous creatures walking, swimming and flying in a desolate world riddled with fires.

"No you are seeing the future of Ryed if you do not succeed in this mission," Ruth explained. "Do you understand now why it is so very important that you make the right choices?"

"Explain what we are seeing," said the Sanuri.

"Teivel made a covenant with Emeric and Banaka centuries ago. Teivel has held up his part of the commitment which comes to fruition soon. Energies have already been put into motion," Ruth explained but was interrupted by Sorren.

"Are you saying his payment is hell?" Sorren asked.

"A hell domain on the surface of Nunc. Such things have happened in other worlds. Teivel will be the equivalent of an Old One and this will be his kingdom that you see before you. You know none of Opots will be safe if this occurs."

"If time is so important why are we just hearing about this now?" Archetenus asked with frustration.

"Because choices had to be made and I am not just talking about the people in this room," Ruth said. "You will need The Scroll of Imari to stop this."

"When do we leave?" Michael asked. "And how much time do we have?"

"When are the Gefrey Games scheduled?" Ruth asked.

"Less than three weeks," said Jared.

"Teivel had hoped that leaders of the kingdoms would attend. He wanted to display his power. This will take place on the thirteenth day of the games. He wants the world to see him transform into an Old One."

"Michael you have made your choice?" Ruth asked. "You are going to protect others when no one would protect you?"

"Yes."

"And you Sanuri?"

"You know my answer, of course."

"You two will leave tonight."

"Ok I don't mean to be disrespectful," Archetenus said with frustration. "We made some mistakes but it seems like you and the other Angels have been playing with us. Are the games over? Just tell us what you need us to do. You know we will do it."

"I can see that all of the time that Miranda spent with you paid off," Ruth said to Archetenus with a smile. Then she looked at the faces in the room. "Is there anyone who does not want to be part of this? Be honest there is no shame."

"Why are you looking at me?" Erebus asked. "Do you think I am going to run from this?"

"It is not your fight why would you risk everything?" Ruth asked. "And don't say revenge, this is far beyond your revenge."

Erebus stared stubbornly at Ruth. "He's part of the team," Thor yelled out.

"I am part of the team," Erebus repeated then he looked at Dagon and said. "We have to get Zelda and Zack out of here. Will they go to Wetpr?"

"I was thinking the same thing." Dagon said then turned to Ruth. "Ruth we have to tell the Venatores about this; can we send some of our warriors to the village then have them take Zelda and Zack to Wetpr?"

"Yes. You also need to write letters explaining all of this to your Kings and whoever else you want. Do that now, I will make sure the messages are received quickly," Ruth said. "Miranda and Daniel have been with Raphael and the others. They now possess the same information that you do. They have made the same choices that you have and will arrive at the castle soon."

"How soon?" Gabriel asked.

"You better start those letters now," Ruth said. "We will meet again when the others arrive."

"You and Natasha are going home," Misha said to Diana.

"No we aren't," Diana said angrily. "We are warriors too."

"Ruth," Misha said.

"I am not telling them to go home," Ruth said. "They have made their choices. You would be wise to put your energies towards the problem at hand and not fight with each other."

Chapter XXXVI
Changing Time

Dagon ran outside and brought Rachel and Chaez back to the Great Hall. As Dagon talked with Rachel, Thaos and Stephan talked with Chaez.

"We are sending you home kid," Thaos said. "This is getting real ugly. Maybe none of us are making it back and we promised your father we would protect you."

"I'm not going," Chaez said. "I can fight now, not as well as you but I am getting good."

"You don't understand," Stephan said. "We just found out that Teivel is turning into a demon and wants to turn this kingdom into a hell world above ground. We haven't faced anything like this before. Thaos and I might not be able to watch over you."

"Then I will die fighting at your side," Chaez said. "I am not afraid."

"Then you are a fool kid, because we are," Thaos said. "You better write a quick letter to your parents."

"Rachel do you understand why you and your family have to leave?" Dagon asked after he told her of the new information they had received.

"I understand why Mother and Zack must leave but I am staying with you. And I need to find my father."

"Rachel I want you to go to Wetpr," Dagon said angrily.

"No and you can't make me."

"See what it's like being married," Calen said jokingly as he listened to Rachel and Dagon.

"Rachel if you stay then we are getting married today."

"Why? What is the hurry?"

"I don't know I just feel like we need to. We can have another ceremony later with our families."

"Alright but I don't understand this at all."

"Rachel," Erebus said as he walked up to Rachel and Dagon. "Are you going to Wetpr with Zelda and Zack?"

"No I am staying here."

"Will they go?" asked Erebus.

"I am your husband now and the head of this family until we find your father. We will explain to Zelda what is happening and I will tell her she has to leave," Dagon said.

"Here, have the Rualas give this to Zelda," Erebus said as he handed Dagon a large pouch of gold. "They will need to find a home and food and things."

"Erebus why would you do this?" asked Rachel.

"I have more money than I will ever use and your family has nothing. Maybe one day we will meet again and your mother can make me one of her great pies."

"Gabriel," Dagon called out. "Will you marry Rachel and me as soon as we finish the letters?"

"Sure," Gabriel said with a grin. "But I have a few to write also."

The doors to the Great Hall were left open as Enrops and Ruala warriors hurried in and out carrying messages. An hour later Dagon and Rachel walked up to Gabriel. "We will have another wedding later. I just feel like we need to get married now," Dagon said. "Nothing fancy." Then Dagon looked at Rachel. "I don't have a ring yet."

"That doesn't matter," Rachel said. "But you know my parents are going to be mad."

"I'll make it up to them," he said.

"We can take a few minutes out and have a proper ceremony," Ruth said smiling. "Batina and Bianca why don't you pick some flowers from the garden. Some of you clear and aisle. Lakin you were put in charge of dispersing Nehmota's treasures among the people. I am sure you can find a couple of rings in that vault."

Dagon and Rachel whispered to each other for a few moments. "Calen and Natasha will you stand up with us?" Dagon asked.

"Yes," Natasha said and hugged both Rachel and Dagon.

"Erebus will you walk me down the aisle?" asked Rachel.

"Me? Why I would be honored," Erebus said with shocked surprise.

Dagon turned to the group, "We will have another wedding and everyone who lives through this is invited."

"I thought we were going to be in the wedding?" Dack joked.

"You two will be in the next one I promise; besides then girls from the house will want to be in it. Unless you want to walk down the aisle with each other," Dagon said and laughed.

"No, we can wait," Joao said.

Lakin returned with a hand full of rings. Dagon and Rachel picked out two that fit them. "I will buy you another one later," Dagon promised.

"Why?" Rachel said. "These are just fine."

Batina and Bianca returned with flowers for Rachel and Natasha to carry. The room became quiet as Gabriel started the ceremony. Loud voices were heard and many turned to see Raphael, Edward, Raul, Simon and Matthew stop in the doorway as they realized a wedding was taking place. Miranda and Daniel materialized next to Ruth and they watched the ceremony.

After the ceremony Dagon and Rachel did not walk down the aisle and out of the room because they had to return to business. Rachel turned her back to the group and threw her bouquet into the air. There was laughter and war cries when Joao caught the bouquet.

"I don't like it," Raul said. "The Gants have killed entire armies and you are saying there will be those trying to stop Michael and the Sanuri from getting to the caves."

"What is it specifically that you don't like?" asked Ruth.

"The Sanuri is part of our family and Michael is my brother. I haven't even gotten to know him yet and I don't want to see him killed."

"So what are you suggesting?" Ruth asked.

"I will go with them," Raul said. "Simon and Matthew are both Seven Sons they can stay with the rest of you."

"Of your entire family it has been the hardest for the two of you to accept each other," Ruth said. "This is an important mission. Do you think you can set your petty jealousies aside and work together?" Simon grinned as he listened to Ruth speak. Raul and Michael looked at each other as they were both insulted by Ruth's words.

"Well I wouldn't call them jealousies," said Raul.

"Me neither," Michael said. Now others in the group were grinning at the two young princes.

"We will work together," Raul said.

"If you can't I will have to spank you both," the Sanuri said with a solemn look and the room broke into laughter.

"I thought Michael and I were getting along," Raul said defensively.

"Are you kidding me," Simon said. "You two will probably fight with each other more than the demons. This will be good for you."

Raul looked at Michael, "I didn't think we were that bad."

"Me neither," said Michael.

"You two sound like little kids," Matthew said with a grin.

"Changing the subject," Daniel said and stepped forward. "We have a gift for you." Suddenly the Great Hall filled with Enrops. "Your families and friends received their letters the instant that you sent them out. And every letter they have written has been sent here instantly."

"But it has only been a couple of hours," Thaos said. "Did you tell them in advance?"

"Sudfad was told in advance that this mission was going to take on incredible proportions. He passed the news to the other kings and families. The meeting is over. Enjoy your letters and gifts. The Sanuri, Michael and Raul need to prepare because they will be leaving tonight," Daniel explained.

Chaez was surprised that he received letters from his parents, Sally, April, Ryan and Bella. "I don't understand, how did they know I was staying?" Chaez asked out loud.

"They know their son," Miranda said with a smile.

"Are you alright?" Stephan asked Thaos as he saw the look on Thaos' face as he read a letter. "Is anything wrong?"

"Amy could hardly read or write when we found her," Thaos said. "The girls have been teaching her because she wanted to write us letters. You must have one too." Thaos handed his letter to Stephan. In a childish scrawl were the words *Papa I love you and I miss you. When are you coming home?* "It's amazing I never realized a child could have such a hold on your heart."

Neputa and Thedes always sat together; both men were so in awe of the Angels that they rarely spoke in the presence of the holy messengers. "Ibula is pregnant again!" Thedes shouted as he jumped out of his seat. Several people said congratulations and clapped.

"Thedes you already look nervous," Simon said with a huge grin.

"We just had a baby and I left her with the three boys; now she is pregnant," Thedes was speaking very fast.

Lakin stood up and put his hand on Thedes' shoulder. "Mother and Father are helping her, she will be alright."

473

"No, I know you are right," Thedes said as he started to calm down. Then Thedes turned to Neputa with an almost shocked look on his face. "Neputa I am going to be a father again." Neputa laughed and shook Thedes' hand.

"You think he is bad now," Raul said. "Wait until the baby comes. It took three of us to hold him back when Tamas was born."

Raphael and Gabriel sat together as they opened their letters. These two longtime friends sat in silence as they looked at all of the pictures the children had sent to them and read the letters from their wives and others. Both of these brave warriors now realized they would not make it home in time for the births of their sons; they only hoped they would make it home at all.

Raul and Michael finished their letters to their family then packed their gear and food. The Sanuri was waiting in the courtyard when the two princes walked out of the castle. The Sanuri was on horseback; he was leaving his boca at the castle. Others were gathering outside of the castle to see the three warriors off. In this crowd were Ruth, Miranda and Daniel.

"So how close is Michael going to have to get to the Gants before they realize his bloodline?" Raul asked as he looked at the Angels who did not answer but smiled. Now Raul looked at Michael, "That may not be a good sign."

A flock of Enrops flew over the Sanuri, Raul and Michael as they rode out of the castle gates.

"This is the first night that we have made love as man and wife," Dagon said and kissed Rachel again. "I am sorry that nothing has been romantic. If we weren't going to war I would be doing all of this very differently."

"Dagon I don't need all of the fancy trimmings. We are together and that is all that matters. But I would like another ceremony when our parents can join us."

"We'll have another ceremony I promise," Dagon paused and got out of bed. "I was saving this for a surprise but why don't you read it now." He handed Rachel a letter from Emeral.

474

Rachel moved closer to the lit candle that was on the small table next to the bed. "I am so confused with what the Angels did with the letters, it's like they changed time. Did you get this today? How did they know?"

"Yes I got it today. Emeral told each of us that she and Maxwell would fix up a home for us when we married. Our new home is luxurious chambers in the house we all live in."

"Wait I haven't read that far yet," Rachel said excitedly. "I couldn't get past the part about Emeral knowing we are married." Rachel read the letter in silence for a few moments. "They fixed up rooms for Mother and Zack in our chambers but want to know if they will need their own chambers when we find father." Rachel put the letter down and had tears in her eyes. "They want us to live with you?"

"Wait until you see this house. It's not the size of a castle but it is always under construction. Vivian's parents have a home there and it sounds like Sam and Ella will be there for quite a while. But it is Gabriel's home so he and Hannah have been involved in this also. You should thank him in the morning."

"I just can't believe how good everyone has been to us," Rachel said emotionally. Your family and Erebus. Even when the crops were good we always struggled." Rachel paused. "Dagon do you think that Erebus has feelings for my mother?"

"I certainly think that is a possibility," Dagon said. "But he knows your father is probably alive. I think Gabriel is right, that Erebus is a lonely man. He seems to really like you and Zack. I think the death of his wife made him reevaluate his life. He has so much money and no one to share anything with. Are you afraid that he will expect something in return?"

"Oh no. I actually like him and I know Mother and Zack do also. It is just strange to see someone interested in your parent. Don't you dare tell anyone what I am going to say. If father is dead and if Mother refuses to stay in Wetpr with us; well I kind of hope that Erebus will watch over them. I don't want Mother living in Ryed by herself."

"Do you think she would do that? After all of this?"

"You don't know my mother well. She is very strong willed and as bad as this place is it is the only home she has ever known. Right now I don't know what she will decide to do."

Dagon kissed Rachel on the forehead. "We should probably get some sleep."

"No, let's write a letter to your family and Hannah first. I want to thank them."

Raul, the Sanuri and Michael traveled under the cloak of darkness. They crossed the border between the Kingdoms of Ryed and Stordt just after midnight. They were riding northeast towards the Caves of Muldun.

"I have never actually seen a Gant," Raul said as they rode. "But Simon and I have heard them screaming as they hunt, it is enough to chill your blood."

"It has been a very long time since I have laid eyes upon a Gant," the Sanuri said.

"Do you think they will recognize you?" Raul asked the Sanuri.

"I certainly hope so," the Sanuri said with a smirk then he turned to Michael and said, "You are awfully quiet."

"I am just thinking about everything that happened," Michael said. "And no I have never seen a Gant or heard them but I have heard of them."

"Michael it is your business but since Raul is risking his life to help us; you might want to share some of the things that Ruth told you," the Sanuri said.

"You mean about the Epocos Tribe?" Michael asked.

"You know what I mean."

Michael hesitated. "Nothing personal Raul, I am not sure I am ready yet."

"That's fine," Raul said. "I haven't shared anything personal with you."

"Well perhaps this trip would be a good time for you two to start talking," the Sanuri said with a smile. "It's not like Vitomas and Annabelle haven't said that enough."

"What?" asked Michael.

"Vitomas and Annabelle really like you and they tell Simon and me to get to know you better," Raul said then laughed. "Yes and they pretty much tell us every day."

"I like them very much also," Michael said. "Vitomas, Annabelle and I have a great deal in common; I think we just understand each other better."

"That is exactly what Vitomas says," Raul said. "Michael I am not making excuses and this is not anything against you but my, I mean our father is the most perfect man I know. And to find out he had another family and then you and I are identical. I don't know it is just taking some time to sink in."

"Well that is one thing that you and I have in common," Michael said. "That day I barged into the castle I was expecting anything except for absolutely everything I found. I didn't even look at all of you at first because I couldn't take my eyes off Sudfad. My mother never told me what he looked like. Then I see you and I swear my heart stopped beating. I came there to kill Sudfad and as I looked around the table I thought I couldn't fight him in front of all those babies."

Michael paused before continuing. "Then when Sudfad claimed me and Renya said I was home." Michael paused again. "You and I are both warriors. We anticipate every scenario before we go into battle. For all the years I thought about the different ways I would meet my father I was not prepared for anything that happened. I don't even know how to explain it. Suddenly it was like everything that had been driving me was gone; I felt like I could collapse."

"Renya saw that," the Sanuri said. "That is why she had Marie take you to your chambers right away."

"I was angry at you," said Raul. "Then I was angry at Father and now I think I am just plain angry and I am not even sure why."

477

"Because you had to see your father with a new set of eyes," the Sanuri said. "Both you boys did and it was very unsettling for you. Raul remember what a shock it was to you and Simon when you found out that Renya was not only your mother but a fierce warrior, a military strategist and a Keeper of the Scrolls?"

Raul started to laugh and turned to Michael, "You could have knocked Simon and me over with a feather; we were so in shock. Then shortly after we learn this, Mother and the girls kill Hutas together when the castle is attacked. You think you know someone your whole life and they aren't anything like you think."

"You have accepted that in Renya but you have not been as gracious with Sudfad. Why is that?" the Sanuri asked.

"Is that what you think it is?" Raul asked. "Maybe you are right but I don't have an answer."

"Let's try a different direction," the Sanuri said. "Raul how many girlfriends do you think that you and Simon have had in your lifetimes?"

"Now you sound like our wives," Raul said and laughed. "I don't think Simon and I could even remember. We got interested in girls when we were pretty young."

"And yet you don't think Sudfad should have had any girl-friends or have ever fallen in love?" the Sanuri asked.

"Well no," Raul said. "He should have and he did. It isn't that."

"Then what is it?" the Sanuri asked.

"I don't know, he has always been so adoring of Mother maybe I can't think of him loving someone else."

"You are adoring of Vitomas," the Sanuri said. "Do you want your sons to distance themselves from you when they find out you had girlfriends before you married?"

"This is different," Raul said defensively.

"Tell me how?" the Sanuri said. "Raul some day you or Simon may discover you have a child you were unaware of."

478

Raul looked over at the Sanuri. "Then what is my problem?" Raul asked with frustration.

"You are disappointed that your father isn't perfect and no man is. And Ruth was right. Whether you two realize it, you are both a little jealous of each other. You both look exactly like Sudfad and like each other and on some level that makes a difference to each of you. Michael what do you think?"

"I don't know what to think. Honestly I can understand what you both are saying. If I was Raul I would be mad about me. I never expected any of them to claim me or to welcome me into the family. That is more surprising to me than any tension between us."

"I hope you two boys are realizing just how much you are alike," the Sanuri said.

"So was this trip set up so we would have to talk this out?" Raul asked with a grin.

"No, but I am taking advantage of the situation," the Sanuri said. "Your entire family can feel the tension between you and Sudfad and if that isn't a good enough reason to work this out; you both have important destinies that are entwined. Today Michael finally broke the chains that bound his heart and really accepted his new family and his destiny. You are both smart and responsible men. Work this out."

"You sound like our father," Michael said with a grin.

"I was thinking the same thing," said Raul.

Chapter XXXVII
Tunnels of Doom

The army at the castle of Nehmota rose early the next morning. Since they now realized this would not be a battle but a war, Simon and Matthew directed work crews in the building of trebuchets.

Natasha, Rachel, Bianca and Jasmine, disguised themselves as peasants and accompanied some of the castle staff into the city to buy supplies that would be needed for the tobisks that would be launched from the trebuchets. The castle staff as well as many of the new freedom fighters were taking turns going into the City of Teivel to purchase food. Gabriel wanted the supplies to be bought in small quantities so as not to raise suspicions.

Batina and Darla were in charge of organizing and distributing the weapons that Sudfad had sent to Ryed. The warriors and soldiers who had arrived with Raphael had to familiarize themselves with the castle so they could defend it. Every day more citizens of Ryed came to the castle to fight with the freedom fighters. No one really understood how these farmers and villagers received word that they were needed. But they came, men, women and children.

Since most of the citizens that were volunteering their services were not trained fighters, Dominic and his brothers organized training sessions that would be taught multiple times a day until the war started.

Archetenus, Jared, Thaos and Thedes were training with the warriors who would fight in the Gefrey Games.

Raphael and Sorren dressed as businessmen and went into the city to the Teivel Manor Hotel. Two Wetprian soldiers were disguised as the driver and guard.

"The hair on the back of my neck is standing on end," Sorren said as he and Raphael walked from their carriage and through the front door of the hotel.

"I know," Raphael whispered. "I feel it too."

These two men were seated in the main dining room for lunch. It was still early and only half of the tables were filled. As Sorren and Raphael surveyed the customers in the dining room they did not see anyone who looked suspicious but they both felt as if they were being watched.

"Is Clay working today?" Raphael asked the waiter as he approached the table with a pot of coffee.

"Yes, he is in his office, who shall I say is here to see him, My Lord?" Raphael did not want to use the names of Gabriel or any of his team. "Actually it is my mother who Clay knows, I promised her I would visit him. Would you tell him that Ruth's son is here?"

"Yes My Lord," the waiter said without suspicion and walked out of the dining room. A few moments later, Clay accompanied the waiter to the table of Raphael and Sorren. Clay played his part and greeted the men and loudly asked about Ruth.

"I know it is early but please come to my office and we will have a drink. We have much to catch up on," Clay said and escorted Raphael and Sorren through the dining room. As soon as Clay closed the door to his office he said, "It is safe to talk in here."

"We came on behalf of Gabriel. I am High Priest Raphael and this is Chief Sorren of the Nordes Tribe from Lentz. The Angels told us that you can be trusted and that you are prepared to help but we have now found out the enormity of the problem here and came to warn you."

As Raphael spoke, Sorren was looking out the windows of Clay's office. "Someone is watching us I can feel it."

"You must be new here," Clay said. "Everyone spies on everyone else. It is a way of life. But I am sure that Teivel's men are still watching the hotel waiting for Gabriel and the Rualas to return. How can I be of help?"

"Actually you might want to leave Ryed," Raphael said. "I am not going to mince my words. Teivel is a dark lord and has made a covenant with demons. He will be rewarded for his work soon and his reward is that he will become a very powerful demon and Ryed will become a hell world."

481

"You mean more than it is now?" asked Clay.

"Son, he means the real hell," Sorren said. "That is why we came to warn you."

"We know you helped Gabriel and plan on helping the prisoners we release but now this is so much bigger than all of that," Raphael said.

"Are you leaving?" Clay asked.

"No we are going to try and stop it," said Raphael.

"Why do you risk your lives?" Clay asked.

"Your people have been brutalized by Teivel as a man," Raphael said. "As a demon he will try to spread his darkness across the continent. We are not waiting until this is on our doorstep."

Clay turned and poured three glasses of whiskey, "I believe these are appropriate now," Clay said and handed glasses to Sorren and Raphael. "So let me understand this," Clay said and sat down behind his desk. "You are strangers who plan to free our political prisoners. Stop Teivel from turning into a demon and killing or enslaving the people left here?"

"That pretty much sums it up," Sorren said sarcastically.

"You are either fools or very brave men, which is it?" asked Clay.

"After seeing what the Angels showed us I would go with fools," Sorren said. "But that doesn't mean everyone needs to die. Pack your things and get the hell out of here."

"If you call to Ruth would she come here?" Clay asked.

"I believe so," said Raphael.

"Please do so."

"Ruth would you please join us in Clay's office?" Raphael called softly. Clay stood up from his desk in anticipation. Ruth appeared in the room in her guise as a frail old woman. Clay quickly walked up to Ruth and bowed before her.

482

"My Lady, I am at your service. I am wealthy and well connected in this city. Just tell me how I can be of service," Clay said emotionally.

"My son you might lose your life and all you possess if you stay here," Ruth said.

"Are you saying I cannot be of service?" Clay asked sadly.

"No I want you to understand the situation," she said. "This kingdom will be filled with monsters from hell if Teivel is not stopped."

"Then please allow me to help you stop him," said Clay.

"Chalk up another fool," Sorren said jokingly.

"Now my children we need to talk," Ruth said.

Raul, Michael and the Sanuri rode through the night and took shelter in a thick grove of trees when the sun came up. Enrops watched over the men as they slept.

The Sanuri was the first to wake in the afternoon and saw that the number of Enrops in the trees had greatly increased. The Sanuri called to one of the birds. "Uri has something happened?"

"We killed a flock of ravens while you were sleeping. You were not seen. We called to others to join us."

"Tell me about the flock of ravens were they searching the area or carrying a message?"

"It was a small flock of nine; we found no messages," Uri said.

"Uri if we are being watched I don't want your flock seen so I am going to call to others," the Sanuri said and softly started to chant. Within twenty minutes the Sanuri was surrounded by dozens of species of birds. He spoke to the birds who then flew towards the Caves of Muldun.

Several of the Enrops landed near the Sanuri as he started to prepare a meal. The conversations between the birds and the Sanuri woke Raul and Michael.

483

"Where did all the Enrops come from?" Michael asked as he looked around.

"They killed a small flock of ravens that were probably searching the area. Our friends here called for reinforcements. Dark lords and demons will recognize the Enrops so I called to other species to fly to the caves and to tell us what they see."

"If they don't see any ravens can we start back up or do you want to wait until dark," Michael asked as he poured himself a cup of coffee.

"Let's wait until the birds return before we make plans," the Sanuri said and handed plates of food to Raul and Michael.

"Do you think Teivel knows we are headed for the caves?" Raul asked.

"No, I think he would be sending armies after us if he knew for sure," the Sanuri said. "He is close to his transformation and is probably not taking any chances that something could go wrong. But remember there are others beside us who seek the scroll. We may have company that has nothing to do with Teivel."

Simon and Matthew set up an assembly line to make the parts of the trebuchets. Different groups were responsible for making specific pieces; the final group assembled the weapons themselves.

"I want to learn how to make that," Diana said enthusiastically as she found Misha, Calen and Dagon setting up an area where they were going to make the same explosives that Hannah had made in the battle of Nora.

"You aren't learning to do this when you are pregnant or ever," Misha said.

"Well do you know how to do it?" Diana challenged.

"Actually Hannah and Natasha showed us," Gabriel said as he set down a small table. "And Hannah said that anyone who is pregnant shouldn't even smell the chemicals once they start cooking."

484

"Well what can I do to help?" Diana asked.

"In Nora, Natasha found all kinds of nails in a wood shed," Calen said. "We put them in the jars of explosives."

"Ok I will look for the wood shed," Diana said and started to turn around.

"Talk to Simon and Matthew before you take anything," Gabriel said. "Actually why don't you get a few others and search the cellar of the castle and the sheds. We need more tables, jars or crocks and crates to put them in. That would help a lot."

Diana walked around the courtyard and saw Chaez taking a break from training. Chaez had his shirt off and Diana stared at his body as she approached him. "Chaez you don't even have any more room for cuts and bruises. Take a break. Gabriel gave me an assignment and I need help. And we need to get some more people."

"Ok," Chaez said and started to put on his shirt.

"I really hope you feel better than you look," Diana said. "I think you should ask Lakin for some medicine. You aren't going to be in any shape to fight when we really need you."

"Diana you grew up learning all of these skills, I have a lot to catch up on."

"But Chaez, seriously. Every warrior tries to rest up before a big battle. You are so beat up now, just heal and save your energy, because you are going to need it. There's Ratri."

Diana and Chaez walked up to Ratri and asked him to join them. Ratri turned around and yelled for help and eight more Ruala warriors joined the small group. They walked into the castle and Ratri asked one of the staff for directions to the cellar. Two Ruala warriors carried lit torches and used them to light other torches attached to the stone walls as the group descended a long staircase.

"I don't think I have ever been in a cellar in a castle before," Diana said in awe. "This is huge."

"There is a lot of stuff down here," Ratri said then turned to one of the Ruala warriors. "Cleta get some more people down here to help." The young female warrior ran up the staircase.

"This is going to be fun," Diana said as several other warriors gave her disapproving looks. "Oh come on, we'll have fun. We need tables, crates, jars, crocks, nails and if we find any weapons let's take them too."

Fifty people spent over four hours in the cellar of the castle sorting through things. Natasha joined the group when she returned from the city and was the only one who understood the strange markings on the walls. "Stop! Stop!" Natasha screamed everyone out of here now."

"Natasha what is it?" Ratri asked as others ran towards her. "Get Gabriel and Simon and get these people out of here."

"I'm staying with Natasha," Diana said and drew her sword.

"I am too," said Chaez."

"You two stay behind me," Natasha said and grabbed a torch out of a holder on the wall.

Within minutes Gabriel, Calen, Misha, Simon, Matthew and Ratri ran into the cellar. "Grab some torches," Natasha said and come to me."

"Gabriel, Simon remember when we got pulled into hell when we were on that mission in Nora? Remember what we saw? Follow me. Once people started clearing all this stuff out we found these tunnels and look." Natasha held up her torch and exposed various symbols written on the walls all of the symbols made up the number thirteen."

"Natasha stop," Gabriel said. "Let me look at these."

"What are you talking about?" asked Diana.

"Natasha and I were poisoned by dark magic and pulled into some kind of hell world," Simon explained. "We weren't together but we basically saw the same things. There were stone tunnels like this with the number thirteen everywhere. We heard people screaming for help and were trying to get to them."

"A demon spoke to me and said he knew who The Seven Sons were and was going to kill them. Then he said thirteen levels, thirteen doors."

"I put blessed water on this writing and it did not smoke," Gabriel said. "It appears to be very old. We need to explore these tunnels but I don't want us dividing into small groups in case it is a trap. One of you run outside and get Lakin. Tell him what we have and that we need warriors to help search these tunnels."

"I will," Chaez said and ran up the stairs.

"Gabriel this is just like what I saw only without all the furniture and stuff," Natasha said. "Diana said that she has been down her the entire four hours and nothing unusual has happened.

"I have too and we haven't heard any strange sounds," Ratri said.

Within minutes dozens of warriors were running down the stairs, Lakin, Thedes, Jared, Archetenus, Thaos, Stephan, Thor and Joshua were included in the group. Gabriel quickly explained about the significance of the tunnels and the markings on the walls. "This can't be a coincidence," Gabriel said. "We need to explore these tunnels but I want us to do it in large groups. No one wanders off by themselves."

"How many tunnels are there?" Jared asked as he grabbed a torch.

"So far we have found four. But apparently these four were hidden by all of the piles of things down here; so there may be more," Gabriel explained.

Gabriel led one group, Lakin the second, Thedes the third group and Thaos the fourth. Each group consisted of at least a dozen warriors. Another eighteen warriors searched the giant cellar for more tunnels and more writing on the walls.

"Chaez you stay with Thor and me," Diana said.

"I can fight," Chaez said defiantly.

"But you don't know anything about demons," Thor said. "Diana is right stay close to us."

Every time the groups turned a corner or walked through an archway they would see thirteen symbols written on the walls. "This is exactly how it was," Natasha whispered to Calen.

"I think we are going down," Gabriel said to his group as he led the way through the dank darkness. They walked for thirty minutes when the tunnel suddenly ended at a huge wooden door. Calen and Misha broke the lock on the door as Gabriel held the torch for them. It took two men to push the door open. The hinges screamed and the smell of death filled everyone's nostrils.

Rats ran as Gabriel's group intruded in their territory. Those holding torches walked around the walls of the room so the skeletons could be exposed. "Look at these jewels," Gabriel said at the extravagant jewelry that was on the skeletons. "I'll bet this was one of the royal families."

"No one is chained or even tied up," Dagon said as he was examining some of the skeletons. "I wonder if they were put in here to starve to death."

"Search the area, there has to be more to this," said Gabriel.

"Gabriel that ring," Chaez said as he pointed to a skeleton. "I saw it in one of the paintings I moved."

"Take the jewelry maybe it will help identify who the bodies are," Gabriel said as he searched the walls. "Look at these," Gabriel said and pointed to huge claw marks that started well above his head. "These people didn't make these."

"There's more over here," said Ratri. "Do you think these people were fed to a monster because some of these skeletons are pretty broken up?"

"We've been walking for almost an hour," Dominic said to Lakin. "Where can this lead to?"

"That is the question," Lakin said as he led the way. "Something doesn't seem right here. The next time we come up to symbols we are going to stop and study them."

"What do you mean?" asked Fennel.

"Can't explain it," Lakin said. "I feel like we are in a labyrinth instead of a tunnel."

"Thedes do you smell that?" Jasmine asked as she was walking directly behind their leader.

"No," whispered Thedes.

"Stop! Seriously," said Jasmine. "I know that smell."

"I smell it too," Darla said. "That was the same smell from when Raphael threw that demon book into the fire and all the demons started screaming."

"Thedes I think we are walking into a trap," Jasmine said.

"Jared stick your hand in the water and see what happens," Thaos said jokingly as his group stood around a pool that was in the end of the tunnel they were searching."

"No way in hell," Jared said. "Look at the size of some of these bones, what the hell do you think they were?"

The entire group was looking at piles of dried bones that surrounded the pond. "Do you think this pond goes out to the moat?" Stephan asked. "Because we really don't know what is swimming around in there."

"This doesn't make any damn sense," Archetenus said. "Why would the Angels have us take refuge in a castle that has demons or something in it? Doesn't make no sense at all. Search the walls maybe there is some kind of clue."

"Gabriel, look there is an opening to the left," said Calen. "That wasn't there the first time we walked down this tunnel."

"I don't like this," Natasha said.

Gabriel's group had been returning to the main area of the cellar and now stood before an archway which suddenly appeared on the left wall of the tunnel. Misha picked up a rock and threw it into the opening. They all heard the rock hit the ground in what seemed like a distance.

"I don't think we should go in," said Natasha. "That could close back up."

"It was either opened by dark magics or the Angels," Gabriel said as he held up his torch and examined the wall around the opening.

"There might be a third option," Dagon said as he was examining the right wall of the tunnel, there is a sort of lever here. Everyone stand away from that opening and I am going to move the lever." Dagon pushed the lever into a downward position and a section of stone wall moved to the right, closing off the new opening. Dagon moved the lever back to a forty-five degree position and the wall moved again exposing the opening."

"How could we not have heard that?" asked Thor.

"This lever is tight, you have to really work it. One of us didn't just bump into it," Dagon said.

"Miranda is this you doing this?" Diana asked with a tinge of fear in her voice.

"Prepare for attack," Thedes whispered and moved forward in the tunnel.

"The smell is gone," Jasmine whispered. The group continued to move forward.

"Is it my imagination or did we stop seeing symbols?" Fennel asked.

"The air is getting thicker," said Asher. "I think we are going lower into the earth."

Suddenly Lakin stopped.

"If those bones belong to animals how the hell did they get in here?" Thaos asked as he and the others were searching the cave that contained the pool.

"If the kings of Ryed were good, why would they have demons or whatever down here?" asked Dack.

"Were the kings good?" Joao asked. "I don't think we know about any of that."

"Ok, since we haven't found anything; everyone stand back by the tunnel," Thaos said. "I am going to threw a couple of these bones in the water and let's see what happens."

"Miranda," Diana whispered again. "Are you doing this or is it a trap?"

"What is that?" Dominic asked Lakin as they looked at a huge statue that was blocking the tunnel.

"I think a better question is why is it here?" Lakin said. "Everyone stay back." Lakin said a quick prayer and walked towards the enormous marble statue of a monster."

"Why isn't she answering?" asked Thor.

Gabriel prayed to The Great Ruler for guidance and his group stood in silence.

Thedes turned a sharp corner in the dark tunnel and suddenly stopped. Before him loamed an enormous marble statue of a monster.

"I smell that smell again," Jasmine said and picked up a rock and threw it at the statue; nothing happened.

"Stay back," Thedes said and approached the statue.

Thaos threw two huge bones into the pool and was picking up a third bone when the water started to ripple. The ripples became intense until waves formed on top of the pool. The group stood silently and waited for attack.

"What the hell is that?" Jared asked as they watched as a huge marble statue of a monster ascended from the pool.

Miranda's scolding voice resounded throughout the tunnels and the cellar. "All of you have disappointed me greatly. Have we not spent a great deal of time telling you that on this mission in particular you need to ask us for guidance? Then you believe you might be entering a hell world and you all just charge in! Do you want to die and cause the death of so many others or are you just apathetic because I know you are not ignorant?"

"Gabriel your group may move forward study what you see and return to the cellar. Lakin, Thedes and Thaos study the objects before you and return to the cellar."

"I have never heard Miranda yell before," Stephan said as he moved closer to the statue.

"Oh, I have," Archetenus said. "You would think I would learn by now."

It took an hour for all four groups to return to the cellar. The warriors who had remained in the cellar were directed to bring more torches, paper and pens back to the cellar by Miranda. Lakin's group was the last to return. When the last warrior from his group entered the large room, Miranda, Daniel and Ruth appeared.

"Tell me Simon and Matthew where would this mission be if two of The Seven Sons were killed or imprisoned?" Miranda asked sharply.

"Miranda you are right," Simon said. "We are sorry."

"Sorry! Simon do you understand how frustrating this is for us. We will not overrule your freedom of choice."

"You are an exceptionally bright group of people who have been given many blessings to say nothing of an enormous amount of information. Is it that you don't really listen to our words?"

"You give us lip service then the first sign of a trap you run right into the fire like fools. Archetenus you were so frustrated with Ruth because she was making all of you work to figure things out. This is why we do that; so you learn. But apparently you have learned nothing here."

"I have two questions for you and this will be the last time they are asked," Miranda continued. "First, do you want to continue on this mission and secondly if you do; think honestly if you will be able to do it? Because if you continue to behave as you just did this mission is already lost and you should just leave Ryed quickly."

The group stood in shameful silence for a few moments then Gabriel drew his sword and thrust it into the dirt floor of the cellar. Gabriel was quickly followed by every warrior in the room.

"We sincerely hope you mean that," Miranda said. "On that table is paper and pen. In every group was at least one person with artistic skills please draw the statues you saw."

"Gabriel please tell the group a brief synopsis of your mission in Nora," Miranda asked.

"I know what you are getting at," Gabriel said to Miranda.

"And what is that?"

"In Nora we were trying to stop the transformation of Roch into a vessel for the demon Omnibus. We had to find the locations set up for the transformation. And Natasha, Simon and I would recognize the symbols of thirteen because of our experiences. Teivel is transforming will he need a chamber?"

"Yes," Daniel said. "If you haven't figured it out by now we were protecting you in those tunnels. Are the drawings completed?"

"Yes," Natasha said as she, Joao, Lakin and Jasmine all stood at a table near their drawings.

"Everyone will be able to see those drawings," Daniel said but you four tell us what you see."

"All of the statues are large and appear to be made of marble," Lakin said. "They appear identical except for what they hold in their hands. Each statue is holding a vessel with a different symbol on it. I don't know what the symbols mean."

Gabriel walked over to the table and looked at all of the drawings. "Fire, water, air and earth," Gabriel said. "That's what the symbols mean."

"Very good," Daniel said. "And what do you think the significance is?"

"It has to do with Teivel's transformation," Gabriel said. "Tell me is there anything behind those statues?"

"Yes, they block tunnels that run under the City of Teivel and to the lower levels of the castle of Teivel. That is how Teivel breached the walls of the first king of Ryed and that is how he will attack you, when he realizes where you are."

"And the pool?" asked Thaos.

"That would lead to the moat around Teivel's castle," Daniel said.

"And that moat is filled with monsters?" Archetenus asked.

"Yes," Daniel replied.

"We can use these tunnels to attack Teivel," Simon said. "How do we destroy the statues? Are they protected by dark magics?"

"Yes, they are protected and we would destroy them for you," said Daniel.

"Is Teivel's transformation chamber similar to what Roch needed?" Gabriel asked.

"The specifications are contained within one of the scrolls that Erebus brought from his castle. Erebus has read the scroll but is unaware of what it is referring to," Ruth said.

"Where in Teivel's castle is the transformation area?" Matthew asked.

"That information is also in that scroll," said Ruth.

"I know you are all mad at us, but was this some sort of test?" Archetenus asked.

"Disappointed is a more appropriate word," Daniel said. "And yes."

"Did you put the thirteen symbols on the walls as clues?" asked Natasha.

"Yes and we disabled the many traps," Daniel said. "We also opened the side door in the tunnel Gabriel's group searched. Take your drawings and return to the Great Hall. Find the scroll about the transformation. Not all of you are needed to read the scroll, your warriors should continue with the construction of the weapons."

Chapter XXXVIII
One More Day

Erebus looked up from the manuscript he was reading. He was sitting at a table in the Great Hall when Gabriel, Simon, Matthew, Thaos, Stephan, Calen, Archetenus, Jared and Lakin entered. "Is something wrong?" Erebus asked. "Did someone get hurt?"

"No, we were tested," Archetenus said. "And let's just say the Angels are mad at us."

"Erebus laughed. "You all look like kids who got caught stealing from the cookie jar."

"I'll tell you about it," Gabriel said. "But first; you brought a scroll that tells of a transformation. It is talking about Teivel."

"Actually several manuscripts talk about transformations," Erebus said as he stood up and started to sort through the table of scrolls.

"Are they all about Teivel?" Simon asked.

"I don't know but understand there are people who desire to become demons."

"Can't understand that," Jared said. "Sounds like we will be here a while, I am getting us some coffee."

"Erebus we found four tunnels in the cellar. Each was blocked by a giant marble statue. All the statues were the same except for the vessels they held and each vessel had a different marking. They said fire, water, earth and air. When you get done there, would you look at these drawings," Lakin asked.

"On the other side of the statues are tunnels that lead under the city and to Teivel's castle," Gabriel said.

"Here are some scrolls," Erebus said and handed three to Gabriel. "Let me look at those drawings." Erebus looked at all four drawings. "The elements are for power for the transformation. And I have seen this image before. I'll bet it is a demon common to this area from ancient times. Let me do some research."

It was late afternoon before Raphael and Sorren returned to the castle of Nehmota. Enrops flew over the carriage to make sure it was not being followed. "We have a great deal to tell you," Raphael said when he and Sorren walked into the Great Hall of the castle.

"We have a lot to tell you too," Gabriel said. "You go first."

"Well your friend Clay wasn't anything that we expected," Sorren said as he poured himself a cup of coffee.

"What do you mean?" Gabriel asked. "Was he difficult?"

"No, he refused to leave and asked me to call to Ruth," Raphael said with a grin. "When she arrived he pretty much swore allegiance and demanded to help."

Gabriel smiled, "So why did it take you so long?"

"Ruth had a plan," Sorren said and chuckled. "And there is a lot to it. Turns out Clay owns more businesses than the hotel. One of his businesses is a laundry that just happens to wash the uniforms of Teivel's army. And he owns some hot springs where only the wealthy and elite go to bath in the waters. It is very secluded so we would have access to those men."

"Before I forget," Sorren continued. "Clay has some more papers for you and a couple of maps."

"Give the papers to Edward," Gabriel said as he took the map.

"Where is Edward?" Archetenus asked. "I haven't seen him since he arrived."

"Clay took meticulous notes on many people of importance. The kind of notes you use to black mail people," Gabriel explained. "It was his insurance policy. He gave me all of the notes and Edward is sorting them out to see if there is anything we can use. He is in his room."

"Back to Ruth's plan," Raphael said. "We need to get to the prisoners before the transformation. Ruth wants us to get uniforms and have our men walk into the prisons as guards."

"We can find the men with the papers and keys we will need at the hot springs. Of course there is a little more to it but you get the idea."

"And when are we to do this?" Gabriel asked.

"She didn't tell us that," Raphael said. "Do any of you have a feeling that there is more to this than the Angels have told us?"

"I think we all do," Stephan said. "And I am not sure why everything is such a secret."

"We know they have their reasons," Gabriel said. "And maybe part of that is because of our behavior."

The following morning as everyone was being seated in the Great Hall of the castle of King Nehmota for breakfast, Natasha, Calen, Diana, Misha and Thor walked up to Gabriel. It was apparent that Diana had been crying.

"Gabriel, Diana and I are going home," Natasha said.

Before Gabriel could speak Diana blurted out, "Misha, Thor and Calen talked to us last night and said that we had to start thinking about the welfare of the babies. And they are right but we really don't want to leave all of you either."

"I know you don't want to hear it but I think the wisest thing is for you to go home," Gabriel said. "There are always missions."

"I agree," Joshua said as he was taking a seat at the table with Raphael, Edward, Lakin and Gabriel.

"I'll get some warriors," Lakin said. "Unless you want to take your wives home."

"No, if we go home we won't want to come back," Calen said and you need your regular team here."

Gabriel stood up and said in a loud voice, "Everyone, Natasha and Diana are going home today. Anyone who has letters or gifts for your families can send them with the girls. They will make sure everything is delivered."

"You're going to Wetpr," Rachel said and jumped out of her chair. "Will you watch over Mother and Zack?"

"Rachel go home with them and take care of your family. Zelda and Zach are in a new kingdom with strangers; they need you," Dagon said.

"I agree," Erebus said as he was sitting with Dagon and Rachel.

"But I have to find father."

"I will find him and if he is alive I will bring him home then he and Zelda can decide what they want to do."

"But you don't know what he looks like," said Rachel.

"You are a good artist draw a picture and write him a letter so he knows that I am telling him the truth," Dagon said.

Rachel looked at Natasha who said, "Dagon is right, come with us."

"Gabriel can some of us go into the city and buy gifts?" Thaos asked.

"I can disguise them," Natasha said.

"Yes, just be careful," Gabriel said.

"Thaos if I give you money will you buy some jewelry for Ibula," Thedes asked. "Natasha can't disguise a Shettee."

"Sure and anyone else," Thaos said. "We will make a list."

"I am going with you," Archetenus said.

"So am I," Sorren said with a big grin that made others wonder what he was thinking.

"Natasha I took some of my mother's things from storage when we were in Philiste, would you give them to Vivian?" Raphael asked.

"Of course."

"Well I might as well give you my surprise," Edward said with a grin. "When Raphael and I were looking for his mother's things I found some of Natasha's toys. Thought you might want them for Lily."

"Oh Edward that is so sweet of you," Natasha said and walked around the table and kissed Edward on the cheek.

"Calen you certainly could tell the boxes I opened belonged to Natasha. Dolls that looked like they had never been played with and bullwhips," Edward said with a grin which made many people laugh. "Hope you don't mind I took a few bullwhips."

"No I have plenty at home," Natasha said with a big smile.

As soon as everyone had eaten breakfast, a large group of people left for the City of Teivel. And each member of this group had lists of items they would buy for the warriors staying behind. Every member of this small army wondered if they would see their loved ones again after this war and they wanted to take this opportunity to buy gifts. It was decided that Gabriel should not go into the city so Raphael was going to purchase the things that Gabriel wanted for Hannah and the children at their home.

Archetenus joined Raphael and Sorren as they went to the Teivel Manor Hotel to meet with Clay. "I always feel like we are being watched when I come here," Sorren said as they entered the hotel. "Problem is I don't know who is watching us."

The men met in Clay's office for almost an hour discussing the logistics of various ideas. "There was a loud knock on the door and one of the waiters yelled frantically "Clay you need to come out here."

Clay opened the door and saw that the lobby of the hotel was filled with Teivel's men. The same man was leading them as had come to the hotel a view days earlier. "It's Teivel's men," Clay whispered to Raphael, Sorren and Archetenus. "You might want to leave through the back door."

"No, invite the leader in," Raphael said. "I want to size him up."

Clay walked into the lobby and smiled a gracious and welcoming smile, "Can I help you?"

The leader of the men, who had never revealed his name spoke loudly. "Have you heard from the arms dealer or the Rualas?"

"I haven't," Clay said. "I can ask my staff if they have. Why has something happened?"

"I would prefer not to talk about it out here," the man said. "We need to search their rooms again."

"Of course," Clay said. Then he turned to the clerk standing behind the desk. "Please make sure our staff unlocks all of the rooms these gentlemen want to see." Clay turned back to the leader of Teivel's men. "I am meeting with some men in my office, you might say old family friends, would you care to join us for a glass of whiskey?" Clay had spoken loud enough for the men in his office to hear.

"Yes I believe I will," the man said more out of curiosity at who Clay was meeting with.

"I am sorry I never got your name," Clay said to the man as the two entered his office.

"My name is Schuester."

Raphael quickly stood up and shook hands with Schuester, "Hello my name is Bartholomew and these are my business associates Cates, Raphael pointed out Sorren and Carlton, Archetenus nodded at the mention of this name. Raphael, Sorren and Archetenus all had forged paperwork with these names. Sorren and Archetenus also shook hands with Schuester.

Clay poured Schuester a glass of whiskey while the men were shaking hands. "Please gentlemen have seats," Clay said. "Bartholomew and I are rather informal cousins, might be a way of explaining it," Clay said. "Our families were close when we were children."

"So you are from Ryed?" Schuester asked.

"Born here but my family moved to Stordt when I was a child," Raphael said as he studied Schuester. "I travel for my job and when I am in the area I visit Clay."

"What sort of work do you do?" asked Schuester.

501

Raphael gave Schuester a wryly smile. "Mainly I am in mining but shall I say we do an assortment of things." Schuester noticed that all three men visiting Clay looked like hired fighters. "What sort of work do you do?"

"You might say I am in security," Schuester replied.

"That is right up our alley," Archetenus said with a grin. "Do you own a security business?"

"No I work for the government," Schuester said as he held his glass out for Clay to fill again.

"I am confused are you in the military?" Raphael asked. "Because we heard that Teivel didn't hire private security businesses." Raphael smiled. "Believe me I have already inquired."

"Really, who did you ask?" Schuester asked suspiciously.

"Well that is an interesting story," Raphael said. "I was in Nora inspecting some mines and the word was out that some men in Ryed were paying top dollar for shall I say security men. I got the names and came here about eight weeks ago. Two of the generals from your military were the men who wanted to hire men."

"Give me their names," Schuester said anxiously.

"Generals Clifford and Boris," Raphael said. "They wanted to hire an army and needed additional weapons. We had several meetings then one day they tell me that Teivel said he didn't want to hire a private army and I never heard from them again. They were acting very strange so I didn't ask any questions."

"How were they acting strange and did they tell you it was Teivel who wanted the army?

"They said your government wanted it; I guess we assumed that was Teivel," Raphael said. "And at our last meeting they were acting nervous and paranoid. Which gave us all a bad feeling so I wasn't upset that the deal fell through."

"You might as well tell him all of it," Sorren said as he watched Schuester.

"I don't think we want to get involved in all that," Raphael said to Sorren. "For all we know those generals were lying. And Schuester could be one of the men they spoke of."

"Tell me," Schuester said with such a look of anticipation that it almost made Archetenus laugh out loud.

"During our first couple of meetings," Raphael explained. "The generals mentioned several times that they would have to get final approval for the deal with their bosses. They never named their bosses but one time Clifford said, 'the lieutenants'. Which we found curious since the generals were higher ranking officers."

"And they were in a big hurry at first because they wanted the army and weapons available before the Gefrey Games," Sorren said. "You know the big ones coming up."

"Did they say anything else?" Schuester asked as Clay poured more whiskey into his glass.

"No and we didn't ask. I am sure you understand the necessity of privacy in a business like ours," Raphael said. "So from the look on your face should we assume that it wasn't Teivel who wanted to hire the army?"

"No it wasn't," Schuester said as he was now rather intoxicated. "I am the commander of a special group of the government. Our responsibility is to track down those who would betray our leader, Teivel. So as you can understand all matters of security interest me. I have heard some other stories about Boris and Clifford but I can't find them to question them."

"What do you mean you can't find them?" Clay asked.

"They seem to have disappeared," Schuester said. "The last time anyone saw them was at that gathering here for the Rualas. I had a group of my men here also, just watching and they disappeared too," Schuester said suspiciously.

"You do know that we weren't the only business those generals were negotiating with don't you?" Archetenus asked. "And I don't mean any disrespect but those generals had their offers circulating in several kingdoms; how could you not be aware of that?"

503

Schuester looked embarrassed, "I didn't say that I wasn't."

"I am not as accommodating as my two partners here," Archetenus said. "Those two generals like to drink and they talk a lot when they are drunk. The first time I saw that; I didn't want to do business with them. They kept bragging basically about their importance and the ring of spies they have working right under everyone's noses. We all thought it was bullshit but if you guys didn't even know about the offers that were circulating, well I guess anything is possible."

Schuester stared intently at Archetenus because Archetenus' words both insulted and scared him. "I believe I need to go," Schuester said. "If Boris and Clifford contact you again, let me know."

"How do we contact you?" Raphael asked.

Schuester walked over to Clay's desk and wrote a few words on a piece of paper and handed it to Raphael. This is the building I work in. I am the fourth office on the first floor."

"Write down the directions," Raphael said. "Schuester I don't know if anything that Boris and Clifford told us was true but I did ask them if they wanted the army to guard the Gefrey Games and they said they needed it for something else that was happening."

After Schuester left Clay's office, Archetenus laughed. "That guys knows he is dead if any of the stuff we said is true. I'll bet the wheels start churning now."

"We may have bought a little time," Raphael said. "Let's finish shopping and leave."

"You know he will be watching you," Clay said.

"Yeah, we will give him a show," Sorren said with a chuckle and the three men left Clay's office.

"I think we bought the city out," Thaos said as the group that went shopping returned to Nehmota's castle and entered the Great Hall. "Lakin you may have to send some extra warriors along to carry this stuff."

"I will say that is the first time Thaos and I ever went shopping for dolls," Stephan said. "Of course Sicily is still pretty little but we found one that actually looks like Amy."

"What is the matter?" Thaos asked as he looked at the serious faces of the men in the Great Hall.

"We think Teivel suspects us and is trying to draw us out into the open," Gabriel said. "Dominic's men went into the city and people are saying that Teivel is going to start executing prisoners."

"He has never made such an announcement before," Fennel said. "This is very suspicious."

"We haven't called to the Angels yet because we are waiting for everyone to return so we can compare stories," Gabriel said. "Another thing that is suspicious is that Teivel is always afraid of rebellion by his men more than the freedom fighters and why would his men care about the fates of the prisoners."

"So either he knows something about us or he has heard about activity among the freedom fighters," Thedes said as Thaos handed Thedes the items he wanted. "Thank you for doing this; these are perfect." Thedes said as he examined the toys and jewelry.

"I don't want to leave you," Rachel whispered as she and Dagon cuddled together in their bed. I don't have a good feeling about this. I should fight at your side."

"You know Zelda and Zack need you and honestly I will be able to focus better on the battle if I am not worrying about you. Now listen because there are some things that I want you to do when you get home. Emeral and Hannah have prepared a home for us but my things are probably still in my old room. Move them to our new home. In my old bedroom there is a large chest at the foot of the bed, it contains weapons and a great deal of money."

"I want you to get to know my family; well it is like we are all one big family there. First take some of that money and buy clothes for yourself and things for our home. Second tell Emeral and Zelda that we will have another wedding ceremony as soon as I get back and ask them to plan it."

"That should please them and help them to get to know each other. Now Emeral kind of takes things over so don't be afraid to tell her what you want. But know that if you don't want to help with the planning that Emeral always does a great job. She's been planning a lot of weddings lately."

"Then I want you to tell the other women that we want all of them in the wedding and take them shopping. This will help get everyone's minds off this war and give you all a chance to get to know each other. You will like them. All of the women are warriors and they are all good people. There are a lot of children in the house and most of them are adopted. They are already training to be warriors and you might want to help Vivian with that training."

"Do something for the children, have a party or take them all shopping and tell them that everyone here misses them a lot."

Rachel was staring into Dagon's eyes as he spoke, "You are such a good man; you just made my heart jump." Rachel put her arms around Dagon's neck and kissed him passionately. "You will be a wonderful father."

"Do you think you are pregnant?" Dagon asked with excitement in his voice.

Rachel laughed, "Not yet."

"We can work on that when I get home," he said and kissed her. "I have told you about everyone at the house. But know they may act strong but they all have been on missions and in battles and they know what we are facing here. Whatever you can do to ease their worry is a good thing."

"Now you two take care of each other," Diana said to Misha and Thor. "Golly I don't know why I can't stop crying. And you better be home for when the babies are born."

"We have a lot of time yet," Misha said and laughed as he hugged Diana. "Keep yourself busy getting things prepared for the babies and if you run out of things to do have Emeral help you plan the christenings."

"You can move my things into your chambers," Thor said. "Although that won't keep you busy for long."

"Give Thor that really big room with the balcony and buy him some more furniture. You never know when he will get a girlfriend," Misha said with a wink.

"Thor, Misha is right. I will fix that up real nice for you," then Diana got a mischievous look on her face. "Maybe I should ask Melinda to help me."

"She's not my girlfriend," Thor said and laughed

"Thor, she is pretty and nice and everyone knows you both like each other," Diana said. "Take the next step. I mean what can it hurt?"

"Did you ever play with any of these?" Calen asked as Natasha had lined up all of her childhood dolls. "They look new."

"No, I was too busy following Gabriel around. That was so sweet of Edward to get these things. I really like him," Natasha said and paused. "You know I don't want to leave you and Gabriel but I really miss Lily. I am glad to go home."

"I miss her too and I am glad you are going home. Now start thinking of some boys names," Calen said and hugged Natasha. Then he laughed. "You might not be able to get Lily back from Elan and Cassandra. I hope they can have a baby soon, they want one so badly."

"What is all of this?" Gabriel asked when Raphael, Sorren and Archetenus returned to the Great Hall.

"Everyone has such damn long faces around here. It's like they all think that we are going to die," Sorren said. "We have to change that attitude. The Sanuri gave us his boca and it is filled with things for a feast. Tell the girls to stay one more day and we will have a great celebration. And we still have the instruments with us."

"We will unpack everything," Archetenus said to Raphael. "Why don't you tell them about our meeting with Schuester?"

While a great many people were preparing the feast, many people were inside of the Great Hall. Tables were filled with gifts and letters for loved ones. People were organizing and packing the gifts. Many people were drinking wine and ale and a joyous atmosphere developed.

"This is the first time we have seen most of these people laugh since we got here," Gabriel said to Raphael. "Sorren was right we have to change the attitude but I am just as guilty as everyone else."

"You have faced horrors and incredible odds before," Raphael said. "I think being away from Hannah when she is so close to giving birth is affecting you more than you realize."

"I hope that is just it," Gabriel said. "I don't want to spoil anyone's evening. I was going to call to the Angels in private, would you like to join me?"

Gabriel and Raphael walked into a small room near the Great Hall. Gabriel got on his knees and prayed for guidance. To Gabriel's surprise it was The Lion who appeared in the room.

"You always act so surprised to see me; that will change some day," The Lion said.

"I am sure you know that I've made a number of mistakes that could have cost lives," Gabriel said. "And I rarely make mistakes so I am not feeling secure in my decision making. The last of our people just returned from the city. Some were followed, although not to the castle and several heard a rumor that Teivel will execute prisoners. Please don't let innocent people die because of my decisions."

"You believe this is a trap and you are correct. Your armies have been watched by many and they know that you, Raphael and some of The Seven Sons were seen near Ryed. But Ruth, Miranda and Daniel have been protecting you and the dark worlds do no know exactly where you are or why you are here. Teivel had set a trap at Fort Polta. He ordered the murders of the Patronus priests and had the murder flee to the fort."

"So those priests were killed as a trap for us?" Gabriel asked sadly.

"Gabriel their bodies were hidden in the room with your belongings. Of course this was a trap. You are letting fear consume you. You have never doubted yourself before and now you doubt every thought you have. Pray to The Great Ruler to remove your fear for you only have one more day before the battles begin."

"I feel like this mission is a maze and I have been getting lost," said Gabriel.

"Then what should you be praying for?"

"Guidance; that is why I called to you."

"Pray that The Great Ruler will give you clear vision in this web of darkness. You have many enemies here with numerous agendas do not get bogged down with all of them. Know they all want power and control of this kingdom. Few in the dark worlds know about Teivel's covenant with Emeric and Banaka. If they did; some would try to stop him because he is competition. Gabriel the Prophesy of The Seven Sons tells of all varieties of people joining together against darkness. You have a wealth of resources available to you. Look at those who surround you and use them. You are not in this alone."

"You said we have one more day until the battles begin; what are you talking about?" Gabriel asked.

"Although Teivel threatens to execute the prisoners tomorrow morning it will be postponed for one day. Because you would be wise to have Erebus send messages to the dark worlds about Teivel's transformation. Erebus's location will not be revealed. That will give you one day to get the uniforms and your warriors in place. I believe the Sanuri can provide the distraction you need. Bring the prisoners here initially. Let them make their own choices."

"But the Sanuri is traveling to the Caves of Muldun," Raphael said. "How will we coordinate the distraction?"

"When the sun rises your warriors must be in place," The Lion said.

"Also you should know that a very powerful demon named Visterle owns the souls of Morgan and Bruno as well as Nada. This demon has taken Nada for his wife and shows no mercy to her former lovers. Visterle has sold Morgan's and Bruno's services to Dael."

"Dael is one of the Old Ones. He has not been taking part in any of the attacks against you. He has been watching and studying everything and everyone for a very long time. While many demons are consumed with the wars of the underworld Dael has been making plans to greatly increase his power. He knows that Rualas have been sighted in Ryed and he is sending Morgan and Bruno here to be spies. There is a likely hood that Morgan and Bruno will encounter the group that is returning your family to Wetpr before they reach Ryed."

"Should I tell the girls to stay here?" Gabriel asked.

"That is up to you," The Lion said. "You could also prepare them for a possible attack. Morgan and Bruno can still be killed like any other men. There is one more thing before I go. Visterle stole Sampson, the son of Chief Duncan. Visterle was a loyal lieutenant to Molach, who as you know is now imprisoned in The Abyss. Visterle blames Hecate and stole Nada and Sampson hoping that Hecate would try and retrieve them. She has not."

"Hecate's antics has made her many enemies. Ale, another of the Old Ones also believes Hecate was behind the fall of so many of his peers. Sampson's body was still in transition from his attempt to become a demon. Ale completed that transition but turned Sampson into the demonic version of an attack dog. Sampson has no mind of his own and both Ale and Visterle have programed Sampson to find and to kill Hecate. Sampson was released from his cell this morning."

"Is Sampson a threat to others?" asked Raphael.

"Yes and Miranda and Daniel warned not only the Clan of Gesmal but Sudfad and those in your home. Sampson was not being held in the World of Nunc do not worry about his presence here for some time."

Chapter XXXIX
Family Matters

After the meeting with The Lion, Raphael urged Gabriel to call a meeting of his core group immediately. Gabriel wanted to let his people enjoy the celebration but eventually agreed with Raphael.

Thaos, Stephan, Sorren, Archetenus, Thedes, Simon, Matthew, Neputa, Joshua, Edward, Lakin, Erebus and Jared had all been present at the competition when Diana exposed Nada's crimes against her children. All these men now sat in silence and watched Misha and his brothers as Gabriel explained that it was very likely that Morgan and Bruno would cross paths with the warriors assigned to take Natasha, Diana and Rachel to Wetpr.

Diana jumped out of her chair before Gabriel finished speaking. "You are making this sound like a trap for us but we can trap them," Diana said. "This is our chance to stop at least two of them."

"What is she talking about?" Rachel whispered into Dagon's ear.

"I will tell you later," Dagon whispered. "But this is important."

"Diana you are not getting involved," Misha said.

Thor now stood up, "Misha this is a family matter; you don't think you are going to fight them alone?"

"Gabriel can you spare some of us for a few days to take care of this?" Calen asked. "Because it is our family that is threatened by these men."

"Not to get picky here," Thaos said. "But all of us in this room have become family and I think we all would like a piece of Morgan and Bruno."

"This is my fight," Misha said angrily.

"No it isn't," Dagon said. "My question is do Morgan and Bruno have any special powers because they are owned by a demon?"

Erebus stood up, "This is my area of expertise. If they sold their souls and are not transforming into a demon they are mere men. But at any time the demon who owns them can control them and thus give them special powers. This situation is a little sticky because Visterle owns them but he basically rented them out to Dael, which means that either or both demons could control the actions of those two. I can severe the connections but I must be with you to do this. And of course I can help with other threats that come at you."

"I agree that this must be a team effort and not Misha going on his own," Gabriel said. "But there is more. Teivel is planning to start killing prisoners tomorrow morning as a way to draw us out. But before the executions The Lion wants Erebus to send messages to the underworlds about Teivel's transformation. The Lion said there will be many in the dark worlds who will try to stop the transformation and this will give us time to rescue the prisoners. The Lion said that Erebus' location will not be exposed. Erebus can you do this?"

"Of course. I have the things I will need with me."

"The Lion said that Teivel will postpone the executions for one day," Raphael said. That will give us time to get the uniforms and to get our people in place. He said the Sanuri will cause a distraction and that everyone is to be brought back to this castle."

"I have to stay here in case we find father," Rachel said to Dagon as she tightly held his hand.

"Dagon stay here with your wife," Calen said. "We will take care of Morgan and Bruno."

"Now just hold on a minute," Sorren said to Calen then he looked at Gabriel. "Have you already determined who you are going to put on each mission or are you taking volunteers?"

Both Gabriel and Raphael smiled. "We had a rough idea who we were going to put on each mission but let's hear your suggestions."

"You know you are going to have to use some of the girls as bait," Sorren said.

"I volunteer," Batina yelled and jumped out of her chair. "They have an axe to grind with me. And honestly they have hurt a lot of people because I didn't stop them."

"Batina and I will go on that mission," Ratri said.

"And so are Natasha and I," Diana said. "They want me in particular."

"I think we all want to go after those two child molesters," Simon said. "But we can't. Matthew and I should release the prisoners. I think Archetenus, Edward and Jared should be with us also. Thaos and Stephan, I would really like you here but I won't stop you from going with Sorren and the others."

"Just how did you know I wanted to go after the Rualas?" Sorren said with a chuckle.

"The tone of your voice," Simon said and grinned.

"I am torn on this but I believe I should stay here also," Prince Lakin said.

"Misha is family," Joshua said. "I am sure that Micha and Bianca feel the same way."

"Thaos and I will stay here," Stephan said. "But give those two perverts something from us."

"Unless someone else wants to speak, the twelve of you will leave tomorrow morning. Of course additional Ruala warriors will go. Because this is such an emotional issue for our family and team members, I am putting Sorren in charge of this mission," Gabriel said.

"My question is how do we determine which route to take?" Calen asked.

"Let me work on that," Erebus said.

"They're here," Christopher yelled as he, Nicholas, Joey, Paul and Adrone ran into the kitchen.

"Mama, they are landing," Nicholas said and grabbed Hannah's hand."

"They're early," Hannah said to Ella then she turned back to the children. "Boys run upstairs and get Emeral and Iris."

"We heard," Cassandra yelled from the playroom.

"I'll get Koby and Sam," Elan called out as he ran out of the house.

Hannah and Ella walked out of the house to the front lawn where six Ruala warriors were landing with Zelda and Zack. Both Zelda and Zack looked uncomfortable as they looked at the beautiful mansion before them.

"Please come in everyone," Hannah said to the group. "I am Hannah, wife of Gabriel and this is Ella she is the mother of one of our team members. The group had not taken two steps towards the house before Emeral, Iris and the boys came out.

"I am Emeral, Dagon's mother," Emeral said and hugged Zelda. "We are so glad you came. There are a lot of us here, we can make all the introductions over some refreshments."

"I am very grateful to be here," Zelda said shyly. "But I have to admit this is all very new to us."

"Can we show Zack the fort?" Paul asked as Zack was petting Jasper the dog.

"Yes, but don't knock over the girls," Hannah said as the boys all ran inside the house. Cassandra, Vivian, Bekka and Melinda came out of the house with Lily, Ian, Emma, Cerey and Cecily.

"Oh my, look at all the babies," Zelda said with a big smile.

"Yes, we have a house full and more on the way," Hannah said and laughed as both she and Vivian had large protruding stomachs.

"Zelda, you look overwhelmed," Emeral said sweetly. "You are family now. Please come in."

Then Emeral looked at the Ruala warriors. "We have rooms prepared for you also. Come in and you don't have to act so formal we are all family here."

"Did you see anything?" Michael asked as Raul walked into the cave with an armload of wood.

"No and that in itself makes me uneasy. We haven't been attacked or even seen anything suspicious since we started out. Something is going on, I can feel it."

"I think we all feel it," the Sanuri said as he was preparing the evening meal. "But traveling at night has protected us greatly."

"Can't demons see in the darkness?" asked Michael.

"That depends on the demon," the Sanuri replied. "But remember the heavens are watching us also."

"So you don't think we are going to be attacked?" Raul asked.

"Oh I certainly did not say that," the Sanuri said and laughed. "These old bones just feel there is a lot more going on here than any of us are aware of."

"Michael, I was thinking that after this mission is over," Raul said as he filled his cup with coffee. "We should pay your stepfather a visit."

Before Michael could speak the Sanuri said, "Raul that won't be a visit that will be a war."

"Then war it is. Besides what he did to Michael and his family, Karzman works for Teivel."

"Here's to war," Michael said with a grin and held up his cup of coffee as a sort of toast.

"Understand I am not against what you boys are saying," the Sanuri said. "Karzman has caused great darkness in this world and needs to be stopped. But I would not be surprised if your father doesn't feel that this is his fight."

515

"What do you mean?" Michael asked.

"Remember Sudfad was in love with your mother and Karzman not only ruined that but tortured both of you. I know your father and he will want to be the one who calls Karzman out. Why do you look so surprised Michael?"

"I don't know, I just am."

"I know your world has changed completely in the last few months," the Sanuri said. "But understand that your new family loves you."

"They don't really know me."

"We know you well enough," Raul said with a grin. "If there is going to be a problem it is because you, Simon and me are very much alike. Vitomas told me that but I didn't realize it until this trip."

"Well it's about time," the Sanuri said with a grin.

Gabriel's core group spent little time at the celebration that evening. They divided into groups to work on the plans for their missions. Erebus had not been seen for hours and late into the night he walked into the Great Hall. People stopped talking and stared at Erebus.

"Were you successful?" Gabriel asked. "Because you rather look like you have been in a fight."

"Let me pour a glass of whiskey and I will tell you," Erebus said. "Actually I feel rather exhilarated. I haven't practiced magic in a while and it felt good but I took advantage of the fact that the Angels were protecting us."

"First, I spent several hours spreading rumors through the dark worlds by a variety of means," Erebus said. "And I did this so it would appear that the rumors came from various sources. When I did as much as I could I turned my attention to Morgan and Bruno." As Erebus spoke he walked up to the table where Sorren's group was sitting and placed six large necklaces on the table.

The necklaces were large metal medallions that hung from chains made of metal and leather. In the center of each medallion was an amber colored stone.

"Sorry I don't have enough medallions for everyone," Erebus explained. "When a person sells their soul to a demon it is like they open their souls to all forms of darkness. So while only that one demon may own that person, it is almost like every other source of darkness can have a connection."

"I was able to make a sort of connection with Morgan and Bruno. It's complicated to try and explain but the bottom line is the stones on those medallions will glow red when Morgan or Bruno are near."

"Well this is something," Sorren said with a grin as he picked up one of the necklaces.

"Is there anything in that necklace that can harm Natasha or Diana since they are pregnant?" Calen asked.

"No, no one can be harmed by them. But you won't feel or hear anything when they start to glow so you will have to wear them on the outside of your clothing."

"How close can they get before we get a warning?" Misha asked.

"Normally I would say within a couple of hundred feet," Erebus said. "But since two powerful demons are controlling those Rualas, the power might be projected farther out."

"Will they be able to detect us by any unnatural means?" Joshua asked.

"I don't know if their masters gave them some kind of gift but from what Gabriel said it sounds like they are simply supposed to spy on you," Erebus said. "I also have one of those medallions. I need for you to show me the various routes you might take on a map. Then I will take a pendulum and see if I can figure out the routes Morgan and Bruno might take."

"Here, I have extra maps," said Gabriel.

"I will need to draw on one," Erebus said.

"That is fine," Gabriel said. "Mind if I watch?"

"I think we would all like to watch," Archetenus said.

After the children were put to bed, Maxwell, Emeral and all of the other adult members of the household sat up late into the night talking with their guests.

"Maybe I shouldn't have told you some of that," Zelda said when she saw the looks on the faces of Vivian and Hannah.

"No we want to hear it," Vivian said. "It is just more difficult because we aren't with our husbands. They wouldn't let us go because we are pregnant."

"I know you are warriors but that is no place for you," Zelda said. "I did not meet Raphael but those who stayed at the castle of Erebus were wonderful people. And they spoke of their families often. Iris, I was there when Micha and Bianca married. It was very nice and she loved the ring you bought. And we celebrated when Misha and Diana announced the names of their babies. Everyone was like a family. And to think they all came to Ryed to save my people is unimaginable."

"Oh my, I am not thinking clearly with everything going on," Zelda said as she jumped out of her chair. "Zack and I stayed with the Venatores and I have a bundle of letters for all of you. I will be right back."

As soon as Zelda left the parlor, one of the Ruala warriors named Curtis said, "Ryed is a horrible place to live. Everyone is so afraid. They don't trust their neighbors. Gangs of demons roam freely and terrorize everyone. The Clan of Gesmal were the only normal people we met. You must be exceptional warriors to live in such a place."

"I will take that as a great compliment to my people," Vivian said. "I miss our village but I am just so happy to have my family here."

Zelda quickly walked back into the parlor carrying a large stack of papers. "I think there are letters for almost every one of you," Zelda said and started to sort the letters into small piles.

"I will help you," Iris said. "This is exciting."

"I heard so many stories," Zelda said. "They talk about all of you like you are heroes of old. I heard about you freeing the captives of Ogg and how the earth opened up around the village and you battled demons. And I heard about how you cared for the sick and injured. I will admit I didn't know if people were exaggerating at first."

"They were not exaggerating," Maxwell said as he poured more wine into everyone's glasses. "Zelda, I don't know if Emeral told you that Rachel and Dagon write to us almost every day. They are dedicated to finding Horace and hope that when the family is reunited you will stay in Wetpr."

Zelda was quiet for a moment. "Ryed is the only home I have ever known. But, I don't know how to explain it. When I met your warriors and then the Venatores you are all so different. You are so warm and friendly and now coming here. I think it would be good for us not to return. But I will have to see what Horace says. He has been a captive for many months; I don't know what to expect if he is alive. He might be very injured."

"You are welcome to stay with us," Hannah said. "But if you want your own home we can help you find one."

"Thank you, all of you are so kind. I have to tell you something which shocks me. When these wonderful men came to get me and Zack," Zelda smiled at the Ruala warriors, "Why, Harris hands me a large bag of gold coins that Erebus sent along for Zack and me. Can you believe that? I never met a sorcerer before; I thought they were all evil."

"I am not sure Erebus is a true sorcerer anymore," Luca said with a grin. "From the letters we get it sounds like he has changed a great deal."

"He must have," Emeral said. "Calen wrote the Angels have appeared before him too."

"Perhaps," Koby said skeptically. "I have never had an issue with him but I don't know if I would ever completely trust him."

"Well that is my cue," Bekka said with a laugh as baby Ian started to cry. Bekka walked out of the room with her son.

Koby turned to the six Ruala warriors, "Curtis when are you returning to Ryed?"

"Tomorrow morning, why?"

"Wait a little, I might go with you," Koby said.

"But what about Bekka and the babies?" Emeral asked.

"Sam and I have already talked about this," Koby said. "He and Ella will help Bekka. I am feeling guilty staying behind."

Well before dawn the next morning, Raphael, Archetenus and Sorren went to the Teivel Manor Hotel and woke Clay. Under the cloak of darkness the four men went to the laundry that Clay owned. Lakin and dozens of Ruala warriors were hiding near the laundry, when the four arrived.

Clay opened the back door of the business and assisted the Rualas in taking every military uniform out of the building. When the last Ruala was in flight, Clay set fire to his building to cover the theft. Raphael, Archetenus and Sorren escorted Clay back to his hotel as they were concerned for his safety.

By the time the four men returned to the hotel, the dining room was opened for breakfast. Clay went to his office while Raphael, Sorren and Archetenus sat at a dining room table that gave them the best view of the front lobby of the hotel. Not twenty minutes had passed before two men ran into the hotel to tell Clay that his laundry was on fire. Clay acted surprised and ran out of the building with the men.

"One down," Sorren said as he took a sip of his coffee.

The hot springs that Clay said he owned was actually an elaborate lodge located some thirty miles north of the City of Teivel in a hilly region. The lodge was extremely secluded and built close to a series of natural hot water springs.

The lodge had seventeen rooms for guests, a large kitchen and dining room and an equally large bar room. Clay bought the lodge when it was in disrepair. Almost as soon as Clay finished the remolding of the building it became the play spot for the rich and connected in the City of Teivel. Rarely was there a vacant room at the lodge which became a place of secret meetings and private affairs.

Simon and Matthew led the warriors who attacked the lodge before sunrise. The attack was swift and well planned. Because of the desire for privacy few of the guests ever had body guards stay at the lodge. The body guards usually transported their clients back and forth from the lodge.

The employees were gathered and taken to one of the barns on the property where they were tied up but not harmed. Clay had already given Gabriel's people the keys to enter all of the rooms at the lodge. The rooms were entered simultaneously but the warriors kept the guests in their rooms until it was time for interrogations.

Simon, Matthew, Thaos, Stephan and Edward all led interrogations in separate areas and each guest was given a vial of truth potion. Jared led a group of warriors who searched the inside of the lodge, while Dominic was in charge of the security outside of the lodge. Joao and Dack each led details of Rualas who watched the road and surrounding areas.

On this night all of the guests in the lodge were high ranking men in Teivel's military and inner circles. Clay had previously informed Gabriel of the clandestine three day meeting that was to be held in the lodge. Gabriel's team had already planned to attack the lodge on this night; before word came of Teivel's threats against his political prisoners.

The military leaders who were renting the lodge had ordered Clay not to open the lodge to others during the three day meeting and to minimize the number of staff. In the twenty years that the lodge had been open under Clay's management no crimes against guests had ever been committed. On this night the guests were shocked and enraged as their rooms filled with Ruala warriors and soldiers from the kingdoms of Wetpr and Lentz.

Raphael, Archetenus and Sorren dragged out their breakfast as they waited for Clay to return to the hotel. When he returned he spoke with several people before acting as he had just seen Raphael and the others in the dining room. Clay joined the three men at their table.

"The laundry is destroyed and no one acted suspicious," Clay said in a low voice. "I have not heard any word of the lodge."

"We are sorry for your loss," Raphael said.

"It is a small sacrifice," Clay said. "I am already making plans to have it rebuilt." The men stopped talking as a waiter came to the table with a cup of coffee for Clay.

"I know you are a shrewd man," Raphael said to Clay. "But we are worrying about you. If you need help; know you can call to Ruth because it is difficult for you to contact us."

"And you think she would come?" Clay asked in amazement.

"The Angels don't always answer us in the ways we expect," Raphael explained. "But I am sure she would help you."

"I need to leave soon," Sorren said to Raphael.

"Clay be careful and remember what I said," Raphael said as he, Archetenus and Sorren stood up from the table.

Calen, Misha and the members who were going to find Morgan and Bruno were waiting for Sorren when he returned to the castle.

"Everything is packed and ready to go," Misha said as Sorren entered the Great Hall.

Erebus had determined what he believed to be the most likely route that Morgan and Bruno would be flying and Sorren's group planned to intercept the two Rualas. Erebus had also determined two secondary routes. Flocks of Enrops were already flying along these routes.

The two dozen Ruala warriors who were flying with Sorren's group carried gifts and letters for the families of the warriors as well as important papers for King Sudfad and King Mathas.

"Rachel, after they find Morgan and Bruno, Calen and Misha are taking the girls home. You really should go with them," Dagon said.

"Honey we discussed this all night, I am staying. With all that is going on if we find father he may not believe you. I need to do this; surely you can understand that," Rachel said.

"I just want you safe too," Dagon said and kissed Rachel on the forehead. "We need to go downstairs I want to see them off."

The Sanuri, Raul and Michael rode all night then took shelter in an abandoned farmhouse they found just after sunrise. Michael was taking care of the horses as Raul gathered wood and water and the Sanuri prepared food.

"I found old blood stains in the barn," Michael said as he entered the farmhouse.

"I found some in here also," the Sanuri said. "Who knows what fate befell these people."

Raul entered the house with an armful of wood. "Am I the only one who feels, I don't know how to explain it, evil?"

"No, the feeling of malevolence is growing stronger as we near the caves. And in all the many times I have traveled this way I have never felt it before," the Sanuri said. "While I do not want to expose us I also do not want to go to the caves at night when the Gants are hunting. We should get a couple of hours of sleep then start out again."

"If we leave here around noon, we should get to the caves before dusk," Michael said as he looked at a map. "So how am I supposed to communicate with the Gants to tell them of the history of our tribes?"

"I will try to communicate with them," the Sanuri said. "If that doesn't work then speak to them in Cerfic and if that doesn't work; may The Great Ruler be with us."

Chapter XXXL
Monsters of Ryed

Even with five interrogators it took most of the day to question the sixteen guests at the hot springs lodge. This group of sixteen men were part of an elite group within Teivel's first inner circle. They were some of the few military officers who had direct contact with Teivel.

None of these sixteen men were dark lords but they all worshiped Emeric and Banaka and paid homage to Cedrick Teivel. These men were responsible for keeping the masses in perpetual horror by organizing the terror raids and creating and circulating false rumors. And it was this group of sixteen men who were responsible for hunting and trying to destroy the freedom fighters. When this information was revealed, Dominic, Fennel and Asher were brought into the interrogations.

When Dominic started to interrogate one of the generals the horror of life in Ryed started to unfold before those observing the interrogations. General Madix gave the locations of mass graves that were so large they held thousands of bodies. Bodies that would never be identified because Teivel's men kept no records of names.

Dominic's questions all related to the people of Ryed who had been taken in the terror raids. Madix explained that the young girls and woman were usually forced to be prostitutes but that men, women and children were also sold as slaves. Madix told the interrogators that Emeric, Banaka and Teivel would sacrifice some of the prisoners to demons. Emeric and Banaka in particular liked to sacrifice children.

Madix explained that the strongest captives would be forced to fight in the Gefrey Games for the entertainment of the elite in Ryed. While many of Madix's statements horrified his listeners they were all shocked when he said that Teivel had twenty thousand prisoners in the dungeons. Most of these captives were supposed to fight in the games but that Teivel wanted a great number for some kind of secret he had planned on the thirteenth day of the games. None of these sixteen men knew of Teivel's transformation.

Madix also said that Teivel had ordered five hundred prisoners executed every morning until the freedom fighters surrendered. After the interrogations were completed the sixteen men were turned over to Dominic and his men who executed the monsters of Ryed.

The uniforms, papers and possessions of the sixteen men were taken for use in the mission to free the prisoners. Dominic and his men talked with the few staff members at the lodge. Each of these people were given money and told to return to their homes and not to speak of the events of the day. It was dusk before Simon and the small army he led returned to the castle of Nehmota.

It was dusk as Michael, Raul and the Sanuri dismounted their horses and crept towards the Caves of Muldun. They were a few hundred feet from the opening of a cave and all they heard was the wind and their own hearts beating. All three men were aware of an overpowering sense of evil that increased as they neared the caves.

"This evil we are feeling is something I have never before experienced here," the Sanuri whispered. "It is not caused by the Gants."

"Then we face more enemies?" Michael asked.

"As terrifying as the Gants are they may not be our enemies," the Sanuri said.

"So the Gants are keeping demons from the scroll which means the demons will attack us if we get it," Raul said. "I really hope one of you can communicate with those monsters."

"We might need some help down here," the Sanuri whispered under his breath; then he said to Raul and Michael, "Let me go first, then Michael come when I motion for you."

"What about me?" Raul asked.

"If we are killed; run like hell," Michael said.

The Sanuri stood up and walked towards the opening of the cave; he carried only his staff in his right hand. He stopped about one hundred yards from the entrance and began to hum. Soon a white light encircled him like a huge aura. The Sanuri started to speak loudly in a language that Raul and Michael had never heard before. Barely had he started to speak when four huge male Gants charged out of the cave. Raul jumped up to run to the Sanuri but Michael pulled his brother back down to the ground.

As the Gants aggressively lunged towards the Sanuri, he pointed his staff and shot lightning bolts into the ground near the feet of the creatures. The Gants stopped and the Sanuri continued to speak loudly in the language of the Gants.

Soon a fifth Gant walked out of the cave. This Gant was larger than the others with a large silver stripe down his back. The four younger Gants moved to either side and allowed their leader to approach the Sanuri. Raul and Michael both held their breath as the King of the Gants walked within several feet of the Sanuri. The older Gant spoke to the Sanuri and even though Michael and Raul could not understand the words they could hear the tone of authority in his voice.

The Sanuri and the King of the Gants spoke for almost ten minutes before the Sanuri turned and motioned for Michael to approach.

"Where do you think you are going?" Michael asked Raul as the brothers stood side by side.

"With you," Raul said. "Let's not keep them waiting."

By the time that Michael and Raul walked up to the Sanuri's side, dozens of Gants had walked out of the cave and were watching this most unusual meeting before them. "This is Manutu, the King of the Gants," the Sanuri said to the two young princes in their language. Then the Sanuri introduced Michael and Raul to Manutu in the language of the Gants.

"Manutu says that all members of the Epocos Clan have a birthmark on their left forearm," the Sanuri said. "Do you have such a mark?"

Michael rolled up his shirt sleeve and walked up to Manutu, who towered over him. Michael held out his arm which was covered with scars. Manutu gently touched Michael's arm and nodded when he saw the mark that resembled double triangles.

When Simon and the others returned to the castle of Nehmota they found it bustling with activity. Almost every woman on the property was working on altering the newly confiscated uniforms to fit the soldiers from Lentz and Wetpr. Teivel demanded that his soldiers appear in perfect attire and to do otherwise would expose these men as imposters.

The men who were not being fitted for uniforms were building beds and tables to prepare for the arrival of the prisoners. Lakin had previously given the cooks recipes for medicines and those women worked diligently all day to prepare the concoctions.

The older children at the castle were tearing up sheets to use for bandages and helping to set up medical stations. Gabriel and Raphael were organizing and directing the operations. As soon as Simon's group arrived at the castle a meeting was held in the Great Hall.

"Twenty thousand prisoners!" Raphael said in a voice that was clearly overwhelmed by the horror of the statement."

"Our problem is going to be finding all of these people," Matthew said. "We know that the executions are planned to be held in the large park in the center of the city. The auction house that we call number three is the closest to that park and the building the prisoners will be moved to tonight. Teivel gave orders to execute five hundred prisoners every morning until the freedom fighters surrendered. After our first attack it may be harder to locate the prisoners."

"I was waiting until your return before I called to the Angels for more guidance," Gabriel said. "But let's hear the rest of your information first."

"Those sixteen men were about half of Teivel's first inner circle," Simon explained. "Teivel has four inner circles and none of the men in these circles trust each other. And they are all competing for Teivel's favor."

"The group at the lodge were meeting so they could figure out what big secret Teivel has planned for the thirteenth day of the games. And all of the men were paranoid because Teivel had not shared his secret with them. Some of the men feared that Teivel was going to purge his own leaders."

"Normally a leader has one inner circle," Gabriel said. "I wonder why Teivel has four; he is not an ignorant man so there must be a reason."

"A lot of what we heard about Teivel reminded me of Roch," Archetenus said. "Roch pitted his leaders against each other because he liked people fighting for his attention. It made him feel more important. If Teivel and Roch are alike that means that Teivel has an enormous ego also. Which is something we could possibly play upon."

"Oh, I am sure he has a huge ego," Gabriel said. "I just wish we could find a weakness besides his paranoia."

"While I believe you," Manutu said to the Sanuri. "Our tribe made a covenant with The Great Ruler to protect The Scroll of Imari. We will not break that covenant, so I will need a sign from The Great Ruler that He wants us to relinquish this precious gift. And if He does, will you return it to us after you use it?"

Suddenly The Lion, the most powerful warrior Angel in the heavens appeared next to the Sanuri. Manutu recognized the messenger of The Great Ruler and instantly bowed before him, as did the tribe of Gants.

"Manutu please rise," The Lion said warmly. "The Great Ruler is pleased with your dedication but you have protected the scroll for centuries so that it could be used at this time by these men. It will be returned to you as you have proven yourselves again and again."

Then The Lion turned to the Sanuri, Michael and Raul. "And the three of you have overcome great fears to do as I requested; you have done well. But you know that your journey back to Ryed will be much more difficult when you are carrying the scroll. Perhaps it is time to learn of its powers."

"Do you think Visterle can tell what we are thinking?" Bruno asked Morgan as they prepared their campsite.

"No, because the Sanuri once said that demons don't have that power," Morgan replied as he put more wood on the campfire. "But I will bet he has some way of tracking us." Morgan was quiet for a few moments. "I've been thinking that Visterle could make a lot of money off us by renting us out to demons in this world because we are more use in this world."

"What the hell are you talking about?" Bruno asked with agitation.

"Well on Sidus the demons are exposed and some of them fly. In the World of Nunc we are a rare item. I think we should try to get another demon to buy us from Visterle."

"Buy us! I'm getting damn sick of being a bitch to these demons," Bruno yelled. "We've got to find a way to kill them then kill Nada for betraying us."

"I don't think Nada had a lot of choice in the matter," Morgan said.

"You always defend that whore," Bruno spat. "She married that demon!"

"Have you or I been able to stand up against Visterle?" Morgan asked. "Hell if he wanted one of us for his wife you know we would be." Morgan and Bruno stared at each other then they both laughed hysterically.

"Erebus," Sorren asked as the group ate around their campfire. "I watched you basically mark the trail of Morgan and Bruno but why do you think they are going to Nora before Ryed?"

"If I had to guess I would imagine they have a treasure hidden somewhere around Nora," Erebus said.

"A treasure," Calen repeated. "Just how many people did they rob?"

"It is more than likely they earned the money from working for the demons," Erebus said.

"And Hecate has a reputation for paying her underlings very well."

"The demons pay them?" Joshua asked in shock.

"Demons base their loyalty on who pays the most," Erebus said. "Not unlike some humans."

"So they are living a good life?" Thor asked incredulously.

"Just because they are paid for their work does not mean that their masters treat them well. For myself I find it curious that Visterle takes Nada as a wife then saves her two long time lovers."

"What do you mean?" asked Misha.

"Visterle is not an Old One but he is almost as powerful. He has been around since time untold and has a vicious reputation which is how he became so powerful. Misha please don't be insulted," Erebus said. "I know Nada is an incredibly beautiful woman but I would really doubt that she has Visterle wrapped around her finger. I'll bet he saved those two Rualas so he could torture them."

"Why do you say that?" Batina asked.

"Well Visterle certainly didn't do it as an act of mercy or out of any sense of goodness; as I said he is very powerful. A demon doesn't become that powerful for being a good guy," Erebus explained.

"Why even bother then?" Ratri asked. "I mean what are Morgan and Bruno to him?"

"Demons are made up of jealousies and hatred. I am sure he wanted to show Nada's boyfriends who was boss," Erebus said.

"So what kind of life do you think Nada is living?" Diana asked. "You would think she would be punished in hell."

"She is not in the type of hell world you are thinking and if Visterle made her his queen she might have a very good life."

531

"Never before has a demon taken a Ruala in such a manner and such a beautiful woman; Nada is likely a show piece for Visterle," Erebus explained.

"She is a monster and should be punished," Diana said angrily.

"Visterle might be treating her well but he is a very powerful monster himself. Nada will have to act carefully not to get on his bad side."

The Lion led the Gants and the humans into the large cave then he took a tunnel to the right. Everyone followed The Lion as he walked deeper into the bowels of the earth. The air became thick and dank which affected the breathing of the humans.

The light that surrounded The Lion illuminated the way until he stopped in a small cavern. Suddenly this stone room filled with light. A loud grating sound was heard as part of the floor started to move to the left. A stone pedestal ascended from the darkness underneath the floor. The pedestal was made of marble and was ten feet in height. The King of the Gants picked up the scroll from the top of the pedestal and handed it to the Sanuri.

The scroll was encased in a golden tube which also gave off great light. Small precious stones where embedded in the golden tube and formed a code.

"As with all gifts from The Great Ruler, The Scroll of Imari can be used in many ways. It contains powers beyond your imaginations and there will be a time when this gift will not need to be hidden from the darkness that men call to," The Lion said. "The Great Ruler has blessed many different species of His children with the responsibilities of protecting certain gifts. The Gants have done well in their role. While many would think of the Gants as monsters it is the true monsters of this world who seek to misuse the power of this gift."

The Lion now turned to Michael, Raul and the Sanuri. "You will use this gift for one purpose alone then you will return it to the Gants for protection. A few days ago, Daniel, Miranda and Ruth gave you a small preview of what this scroll can do. They did this to prepare your minds to comprehend the task ahead of you."

"The mail," Raul gasped. "The Angels somehow changed time."

532

"Emeric and Banaka have made covenants with some very powerful demons from other worlds. These two Grand Masters plan to use Teivel's transformation as a diversion. By the time the transformation is complete the World of Nunc will be invaded by demons from other worlds. The demons and Grand Masters have combined their powers to alter time. Something that has never before been done in this world by darkness. Basically neither the humans nor the demons of this world will be aware of the invasion until after it has taken place. It actually is a very ingenious plan."

"What is it you need us to do?" the Sanuri asked.

"The three of you will have to use the scroll to counter balance the energies that Emeric and Banaka have put into motion. This will allow the hell regions to be aware of the invasion. They are better prepared to fight the invading demons than mankind."

"Are you going to let the hell worlds know about the invasion?" the Sanuri asked.

"Of course, but as usual they will not know the information came from us," The Lion said. "But if you fail the demons of this world will not be aware of the invasion as it happens."

"I don't understand," Michael said. "Why don't you just stop them?"

"Because Emeric and Banaka are not the only humans to invite the invaders in. These people are selling out this world and have been promised new lives in other worlds for their service. For you to complete your task you must be inside of the temple of Emeric and Banaka on the twelfth day of the Gefrey Games."

Chapter XLI
War Begins

Michael, Raul and the Sanuri left the Caves of Muldun shortly after receiving The Scroll of Imari. Manutu still felt it was his responsibility to protect the holy gift so he sent fifty Gants to escort the three men. The Gants also were aware of the ominous atmosphere which had developed around the caves and were preparing for an attack.

While the men and the Gants were concealed by the darkness of the night, the scroll's light shown through the saddlebag in which it was carried.

"What is that buzzing sound?" asked Michael.

"The scroll is not of this world," the Sanuri explained. "It pulsates at a different speed."

"I don't understand at all what that means," Raul said.

"Everything is made up of energy, my sons," the Sanuri said. "The energies of the heavens are lighter and faster than the energies here; that is why you notice the difference."

"Why is that?" Michael asked.

"Because the energies here are weighed down by the darkness. The energies in the hell worlds is slower and heavier."

"Well, I feel like we are sitting ducks with that scroll glowing like it is," Michael said as he looked around uneasily. "The hair on the back..." Michael did not complete his sentence as a shrill scream pierced the darkness.

The three men grabbed their swords and stopped their horses. They could hear the sounds of battle around them. "What is happening?" Raul yelled. "I can't see anything. Is this some type of demonic fog?"

"Raul above you!" Michael screamed as a flying beast from hell suddenly appeared above Raul's head. Raul ducked and his horse lunged forward.

A beam of light shot out of the Sanuri's saddlebag which contained The Scroll of Imari; the beam did not strike the hell beast but engulfed it with light. The beast instantly turned into ashes. Soon the demonic fog was dispersed by the light of the scroll, thus exposing the army of beasts that surrounded the men and the Gants.

Thousands of monsters of every horror were suddenly frozen in time for a few seconds before they disintegrated into ashes. "Sanuri are you doing that?" Raul yelled.

"No, I think the scroll is acting on its own," the Sanuri responded as he too was perplexed.

"Is it supposed to do that?" asked Michael.

"I am guessing it is," the Sanuri said. "We need to keep riding, I have a feeling this is long from over."

"They are moving prisoners," screeched an Enrop as a small flock burst into the Great Hall of the castle of Nehmota. It was two hours before dawn and everyone in the castle had been up all night preparing for the rescue mission.

"Where?" yelled Gabriel as he jumped out of his chair.

"We were watching auction house three," an Enrop said. "The rest of our flock is still there."

"How many prisoners?" Gabriel asked.

"Nine hundred to a thousand," a bird said as another small flock entered the Great Hall.

"There are prisoners in Auction house four," the Enrops said. "And many of them look hurt."

"How many?" Raphael asked as everyone in the Great Hall realized there would be a change of plans.

"Five or six hundred," an Enrop said.

"Auction house two has prisoners," a third flock of Enrops announced. "And there are many soldiers with them."

535

"They are expecting attacks," Gabriel said. "This is a trap."

"Miranda," Matthew yelled.

Miranda, Daniel and Ruth instantly appeared in the Great Hall. "How can we save all of these people?" Gabriel asked. "What is the best way?"

"You made three plans did you not?" Miranda asked; but before anyone could answer she said. "I would use plan number two." And the three Angels disappeared.

"Well that was a lot of help," Jared said sarcastically. The Great Hall emptied as men ran to change into the stolen military uniforms of the Army of Ryed.

Waves of attacks were launched against the Sanuri, Michael, Raul and their band of Gants. The assailants seemed to appear out of the air as armies of demons and men tried to take The Scroll of Imari from this small group.

"Where the hell did they all come from?" Michael yelled as they sped through the night.

"Only the most powerful demons can transport armies like that," the Sanuri said.

"Are we leading them all to the castle?" Raul yelled.

"I certainly hope not," the Sanuri yelled but his voice was obliterated by loud war cries.

An army of men wearing the uniforms of the Taperian military were traveling quickly. In the darkness they did not see the Gants that they were closing up on. They only saw three men who were illuminated by the light of the scroll. Michael felt a searing pain in his left shoulder as an arrow lodged itself deeply into his body.

Raul saw his brother fall forward on his horse. "Sanuri, Michael is hit," Raul yelled as he grabbed the battle axe that was slung across his back and struck a man who quickly rode up to Raul's right side and tried to stab him with a sword.

"I'm alright," Michael yelled as he drew a machete from a sheath on his saddle and stabbed a Taperian soldier who was trying to push Michael from his horse.

"Where are the Gants?" Raul yelled as an arrow narrowly missed his left ear.

"Circling," the Sanuri said.

"Do we stop and fight?" Michael yelled as he sliced open the forearm of Taperian soldier who was riding next to him.

"No, we keep moving," the Sanuri yelled.

Suddenly the screams of the Taperia Army pierced the night air as did the screams of the Gants. The horses of the soldiers had tried to warn their riders of the presence of the Gants but the men did not listen. This was the last ill-fated decision these soldiers would make.

Auction house one was owned by Gabriel and did not contain prisoners selected for execution but it was filled with soldiers from the Army of Ryed. A flock of Enrops hovered over this building to watch this army. Enrops, like most creatures had eyes that were attuned to see in the darkness better than the eyes of men. Flocks of Enrops peered through the windows of all of the auction houses.

The prisoners had been transported to the auction houses through underground tunnels but they would have to be moved to the execution locations by walking out in the open. The prisoners were not chained to each other but they all had their hands bound. The sheer number of prisoners made it impractical for the military to bind their legs and be forced to help some of the prisoners walk.

The Enrops and the Rualas that were flying over the city did not see any troop movement but they knew it would come. Since Teivel was using the executions as a trap he would have his army in place to destroy the freedom fighters. Dominic's men were divided into three groups so they could accompany each attack on an auction house. It was believed that the prisoners would recognize the freedom fighters and follow them.

Forty-five minutes before sunrise the City of Teivel shook violently as Ruala warriors dropped crocks of explosives on Teivel's castle, three buildings which housed demons and soldiers and auction house number one.

Simultaneously with the explosions members of Gabriel's army threw crocks of chemical smoke through the windows of the three auction houses that contained political prisoners. The war had begun.

Enrops attacked the soldiers who were escaping the flames of auction house number one. Simon led the attack on auction house three, Matthew on auction house four and Gabriel on auction house two. Raphael was preparing the defenses at the castle of Nehmota.

The first soldiers from Lentz and Wetpr to run through the smoke into the auction houses to do battle were not wearing the uniforms of the Army of Ryed so as not to add to the confusion. Many of the citizens of Ryed who had been training with Gabriel's army ran into the auction houses to free their country-men and to give them weapons. These new freedom fighters were to take the freed prisoners to the castle of Nehmota while Gabriel's army fought with the soldiers.

"Something isn't right here," Simon yelled to Dominic and Jared. "There are too few soldiers here." Then they felt the earth shake.

The rescuers ran into horror

To save the victims there

But they cannot escape the darkness

The terror that they share

Horrified by the carnage

That the demons leave in their wake

They strive to control the darkness

For all creations sake

Souls On Fire © 2008

By

Sandra J Yearman

Glossary of Characters

Aaron: an escaped prisoner from Wetpr

Aaryan: a male Grand Master of the Insidiae

Abaddon: an ancient demon/one of the Old Ones

Abella: daughter of Prince Lakin and Princess Zada/Ruala

Abigail: sister of Marie/ nurse for grandchildren of King Sudfad

Ackly: an arms dealer in Ryed

Adi: son of Elen and Batya/ Ruala

Adrone: youngest son of Joshua and Iris/younger brother of Vivian/Clan of Gesmal

Adwell: Prince/ son of King Zachariah and Queen Noella of New Samona/husband of Nada/father of Misha/ Adwell was killed in battle leaving Nada to raise ten children/Ruala/

Ael: an ancient demon/ one of the Old Ones

Aetes: Shettee warrior

Ahriman: an ancient demon/ one of the Old Ones

Aiden: five year old Ruala boy/son of Artis and Jenna/nephew of Ratri

Akasha: former king of Ryed/grandfather of Nehmota

Alexander: former servant of King Roch's parents/ father of Annabelle

Alexander: one of the twin sons of Simon and Annabelle

Alexandras: King of Wetpr/brother of Jaretta/uncle of Sudfad and Roch

Alexas Rose: daughter of Matthew and Angelina

Alexis: son of Usman, the leader of the Valdore Tribe

Alice: and her husband find Jorge near death in Nora

Aloeus: Shettee warrior

Amiee: sister of Marie/ nurse for grandchildren of King Sudfad

Amundsen: Commanding General of Fort Friada in the Kingdom of Ganz

Amy: a young girl who was kidnapped by Sal

Ana: eleven year old Nordes girl/daughter of Edgar and Cora/younger sister of Batina

Ana: Princess/daughter of Zeman and Oda/niece of King Manu of New Samona/Ruala

Anda: one of Chief Romogi's three wives/Huta

Andrea: female Ruala warrior/ sister of Bekka

Andres: Princess of Ryed/daughter of Oren and Astrel/ has twin sister Jorga

Andrew: jeweler in Salar

Andrus: father of Rabi/Ruala

Angelina: daughter of Sorren, Chief of the Nordes Tribe/female warrior

Annabar: daughter of King Sharonne

Annabelle: handmaid and best friend to Queen Vitomas of the Kingdom of Stordt

Anthony: one of the twin sons of Simon and Annabelle

April: a young girl who was kidnapped by Sal

Arca: Enrop leader who protects King Mathas' family

Arches: a Patronus priest

Archetenus The Brave: Captain in the Taperian Army

Arianna: daughter of Simon and Annabelle

Ariel: daughter of Raul and Vitomas

Arlene: housekeeper and cook for Erebus/wife of Theodore

Armstrong: soldier and scout in the army of Wetpr

Arthur Marcus: father of Hannah

Artis: male Ruala warrior/oldest brother of Ratri/husband of Jenna

Asher: male Ruala warrior

Asher: youngest of three brothers who formed the Libertas in Ryed

Asmodeus: an ancient demon/ one of the Old Ones

Astrel: former princess of Ryed/daughter of Akasha and Norah

Atomos: Elder of the Centras and Keeper of The Box of Itifer

Augustus Endleson: a wealthy businessman who owned part of the City of Nora

Ava: twin of Benjamin/daughter of Archetenus and Delilah

Baal: an ancient demon/ one of the Old Ones

Babu: Enrop

Bac: male Ruala warrior

Bachnenus: warrior guarding refugees/Shettee

Bali: Enrop leader of the flock that does battle at Juleta's castle

Balin: Prince of Norkv/son of Thaddius and Omara/grandson of Benjeman and Esther

Balius: Shettee warrior/brother of King Neputa

Banacus: General in the army of King Tobias of Puntd

Banaka: a female Grand Master of the Insidiae

Barak: Prince of Norkv/grandson of Benjeman and Esther

Barak: Prince/son of King Neputa and Queen Tiara/Shettee

Barid: Prince of Ogg

Barid: Prince of Ryed/son of Nehmota and Vasart

Bart: male Ruala warrior/ married to Bekka's sister Andrea

Bartholomew: alias used by Raphael in Ryed

Bastra: Huta captain

Batina: young female Nordes warrior

Batya: wife of Elen/Ruala

Beatrice Endleson: wife of Augustus

Becca: Princess of Norkv/daughter of Thaddius and Omara/granddaughter of Benjeman and Esther

Behtay: Princess/daughter of Segal and Cahina/niece of King Manu of New Samona/Ruala

Bekka: female Ruala warrior

Bella: wife of Claudius and mother of Stephan

Benedict: Prince of Norkv/son of Benjeman and Esther

Benjamin: twin of Ava/son of Archetenus and Delilah

Benjeman: vicious rebel leader who overthrew the government of Samona

Benson: a Private in the Wetprian military

Bentra: an ancient demon/ one of the Old Ones

Berta: cook at Racing Horse Tavern

Berta: Queen of Stordt/wife of Micha/grandmother of Roch and Sudfad

Bertha: an elderly woman from Nora

Betty: a woman from Nora

Betu: male Ruala warrior

Bianca: young female Nordes warrior

Black Jack: a regular patron at the Ghost Ship Tavern in Port Friada

Bode: Shettee warrior

Boris: a general in the Military of Ryed

Botis: a demon

Bremmer: an arms dealer in Ryed

Brent: a soldier from Lentz who fights in the Gefrey Games in Ryed

Brik: son of Prince Lakin and Princess Zada /Ruala

Brina: Princess of Norkv/daughter of Valor and Cai/granddaughter of Benjeman and Esther

Bruce: male Nordes warrior/eldest son of Edgar and Cora/older brother of Batina

Cabal: son of Karzman and Nadia

Cacu: Enrop leader that joined Raul and Simon on a mission

Cade: son of King Pergo and Queen Vinus/ Kingdom of Gandt

Cadi: daughter of Prince Hadar and Princess Paj/ granddaughter of Manu/Ruala

Cael: Shettee boy who is adopted by Thedes and Ibula

Cage: male Ruala warrior

Cahina: Princess/ married to Segal son of King Zachariah and Queen Noella of New Samona/Ruala

Cai: Princess of Norkv/wife of Valor who was the son of Benjeman and Esther

Calen: male Ruala warrior/cousin of Luca/son of Maxwell and Emeral

Calla: female Ruala warrior

Calvin: a desk clerk at The Captain's Retreat Hotel in Port Friada

Campbell: one of the spies at the Castle at Wetpr

Canton: Cisero's second in command

Cara: Princess of Ogg

Carlsman: a Lieutenant in the Army of Lentz

Carlton: alias used by Archetenus in Ryed

Carson Dormors: a wealthy landowner in the Kingdom of Ganz

Carston: member of the governing body of Nora

Casey: male Ruala warrior/father of Melanie/husband of Tasha

Cassandra: female Ruala warrior

Cassandra: daughter of King Friada and Queen Marla of the Kingdom of Ganz

Cates: alias used by Sorren in Ryed

Cedrick Teivel: a ruthless, powerful man in the Kingdom of Ryed

Celo: Prince of Ryed/son of Oren and Astrel

Cere: daughter of Tristt/Shettee

Cerephus: General in the Taperian Army

Cerey: orphan girl/sister of Nicholas/adopted daughter of Gabriel and Hannah

Ceria: Princess/daughter of Gunnel and Uma/niece of King Manu of New Samona/ sister of Elan/Ruala

Chaez: son of Fahron

Chaladrone: an ancient demon/ one of the Old Ones

Chalice: hired fighter for Dieter

Chalta: daughter of King Pergo and Queen Vinus/ Kingdom of Gandt

Chance: works with the Patronus

Chara: three year old Ruala girl/ daughter of Orin and Rene/niece of Ratri

Charlene: a woman from Nora

Charles: Father of Cassandra, Joao and Melinda

Charles: hired farmhand of Arthur Marcus

Chief Romogi: leader of the Hutas/ Kingdom of Marba

Christopher: six year old boy who Luca saves from the Hutas/brother of Lila

Ciao: female Ruala warrior

Cicely: adopted daughter of Elan and Cassandra

Cisero: a member of the Insidiae

Clair: a woman from Nora

Clair: female Ruala warrior/mother of Ratri/wife of Joseph

Claudius: General in the Army of Lentz

Clay: the manager of the Teivel Manor Hotel in Ryed

Cleo: a man who works for Cicero/a vessel

Cleta: female Ruala warrior who fought in Ryed

Clifford: a general in the Military of Ryed

Cobren: Prince of Norkv/son of Grace and Makalo/Grandson of Benjeman and Esther

Compro: Taperian soldier injured at Wall of Dorath

Cora: mother of Batina/wife of Edgar/Nordes warrior

Corina: young female Nordes warrior

Corwin: son of King Fahra and Queen Sitha of Zorta

Crater: a Sergeant in the Wetprian army

Crater: a soldier in the army of Wetpr

Crispus: a guard at King Roch's castle

Crocell: a demon

Cronn: a demon

Cronos: Shettee warrior

Curtis: male Ruala warrior who fought in Ryed

Dack: male Ruala warrior

Dacron: former prince of Ryed/is murdered by his younger brother Nehmota for the throne

Dael: an ancient demon/ one of the Old Ones

Dagon: a male Ruala warrior

Dagor: son of King Fahra and Queen Sitha of Zorta

Dai: son of Gael, grandson of Manu/Ruala

Daisy: nine year old Nordes girl/ daughter of Edgar and Cora/younger sister of Batina

Damas: an ancient demon/ one of the Old Ones

Danar: a man created to be a vessel for demons

Daniel: an emissary of The Great Ruler who takes on the disguise of a human man

Danilla: mother of King Mathas

Dano: seven year old Nordes boy/son of Edgar and Cora/youngest brother of Batina

Darius: Prince of Samona/son of Thomas and Rewel/brother of Varden

Darla: young female Nordes warrior

Darlah: sister of Marie/ nurse for grandchildren of King Sudfad

Delilah: wife of Dieter

Delilia: Queen of New Samona/mother of Ibula, Lakin, Gael and Hadar/ wife of King Manu/Ruala

Demanko: a demon

Demetries: a demon

Denise Froush: wife of Martin who is a wealthy ship builder in Port Friada

Denks: a soldier in the army of Wetpr

Denton: one of the spies at the Castle in Wetpr

Derek: friend of Thaos

Derlock: Huta warrior

Diana: a Venator/sister of Thor

Dieter: member of the Insidiae

Dion: Princess of Samona/wife of Yorggi who was the son of Thomas and Rewel/brother of Varden

Dixon: a Taperian soldier

Dominic Petlov: was the senior High Priest at the monastery at Malga before he was murdered

Dominic: oldest of three brothers who formed the Libertas in Ryed

Dorme: Prince of Ogg

Doros: works for High Priest Meekos

Douma: King of Ogg

Dresden: a Sergeant in the Wetprian army

Duncan: Chief of the Clan of Gesmal in Ryed/ husband of Liza

Duran: father of Nikki/Nordes Tribe

Dymas: Shettee warrior

Eachann: Shettee warrior

Edgar: father of Batina/husband of Cora/Nordes warrior

Edith: wife of Lloyd a banker in Nora

Eilig: male Ruala warrior

Elan: male Ruala warrior/son of Gunnel and Uma/

Eldridge: works with the Patronus

Elen: son of Andrus and Naomi/ brother of Rabi/ Ruala

Elexas: a female Nordes warrior

Ella: female Ruala warrior/mother of Bekka/wife of Sam

Eloise: female Ruala warrior/oldest sister of Bekka/wife of Tony

Elsa: female Ruala warrior/mother of Mia/wife of Tyron

Emeral: mother of Calen/Ruala

Emeric: a male Grand Master of the Insidiae

Emma: daughter of Luca and Lila

Emmet: worker for Gabriel

Emon: a male Grand Master of the Insidiae

Erebus: sorcerer from Ryed

Erwat: a member of the Half-Man's Tribe who helps the Clan of Gesmal

Esser: Prince/son of Segal and Cahina/nephew of King Manu of New Samona/Ruala

Esteban: a member of the Insidiae

Esther: Queen of New Norkv/wife of rebel leader Benjeman

Fabron: Prince of Ogg

Fadil: a male Grand Master of the Insidiae

Fahra: King of Zorta

Fahron: General in the Army of Lentz

Fairoot: demon/ lieutenant for Salzar

Fala: female Ruala warrior

Farnsworth: General in charge of building Fort Serpha in Wetpr

Fatima: Prince of Ryed/ son of Oren and Astrel

Fatronas: an ancient demon/one of the Old Ones

Fengu: Enrop leader who helps Gabriel and his group against Omnibus

Fennel: one of three brothers who formed the Libertas in Ryed

Ferguson: a Sergeant in the Army of Lentz

Fiona: mother of Nadia/grandmother of Michael

Fraisier: a businessman and member of the Insidiae in Nora

Frank: a villager in Telmark

Fred Stapleton: a farmer in Wetpr

Friada: King of the Kingdom of Ganz

Gabriella: sister of Marie/nurse to grandchildren of King Sudfad

Gad: male Ruala warrior

Gael: Prince/son of King Manu and Queen Delilia/Ruala

Gala: a healer from the Kingdom of Stordt

Galen: male Nordes warrior

Geoff: Prince of Lentz/son of Princess Isabella and Captain Josef

Geoff: Prince of Norkv/son of Benedict and Sasaha/grandson of Benjeman and Esther

Georganson: an arms dealer in Ryed

George: an advisor for King Fahra of Zorta

George: middle son of Chief Duncan and Liza of the Clan of Gesmal in Ryed

Giovani: Rachel's older half-brother

Gita: wife of Hadi/ Ruala

Gladys: member of Nordes Tribe/ mother of Nikki

Glenda: great, great, great grandmother of Gala/ a healer from the Kingdom of Stordt

Grace: Princess of New Norkv/daughter of Benjeman and Esther

Gracie: cook for the Arthur Marcus family

Grady: worker for Gabriel

Great Ruler: God

Gregory Bancar: a wealthy landowner in the Kingdom of Wetpr and member of the Insidiae

Greta: older Ruala woman/friend of Emeral's

Greta: wife of Hugo/mother of Sasha/ sister-in-law of Sorren

Gunnel: Prince/ son of King Zachariah and Queen Noella of New Samona/husband of Uma/father of Elan/Ruala

Gus: owner of Racing Horse Tavern

Haas: a Lieutenant in the Wetprian military

Hadar: Prince/son of King Manu and Queen Delilia/Ruala

Hadi: son of Andrus and Naomi/brother of Rabi/Ruala

Hadu: female Ruala warrior

Hamon: one of the members of the Nordes Tribe who was injured in an attack at Snakes Crossing

Hamond: General of the Taperian Army who declares himself king

Hanger: one of the spies at the Castle at Wetpr

Hangered: Wetprian soldier

Hannah: physician in Nora/ Roch murdered her sister

Harold: husband of Berta/part owner of the Racing Horse Tavern

Harold: owner of the general store in Nora

Harriet Marcus: mother of Hannah and Laurabelle/wife of Arthur

Harris: male Ruala warrior who fought in Ryed

Hatus: General in the Army of Lentz/on loan to Sudfad

Hector: fighter hired by Juleta

Hector: Prince of Samona/son of Varden

Henry: and his wife Alice find Jorge in Nora

Henry: husband of Noreen/father of Jacob

Hermanas: second in command to Archetenus at Wall of Dorath

High Priest Aaron: member of the Patronus

High Priest Alfonso: a member of the Patronus

High Priest Amos: a member of the Patronus

High Priest Barnabas: most Senior High Priest of the monastery at Leven

High Priest Caleb: member of the Patronus

High Priest Ephraim: a member of the Patronus

High Priest Gabriel: member of the Patronus/demon hunter

High Priest Gideon: a member of the Patronus

High Priest Gregory: member of the Patronus

High Priest Joseph: member of the Patronus, in charge of the Cicero Headquarters

High Priest Josiah: member of the Patronus

High Priest Meekos: priest at the monastery at Malga

High Priest Nicholas: most Senior High Priest of the monastery at Philiste and most Senior High Priest of the Patronus

High Priest Othnial: Senior High Priest of the monastery in Rubar in the Kingdom of Ryed

High Priest Paulas: member of the Patronus

High Priest Phanuel: member of the Patronus

High Priest Philetus: member of the Patronus in charge of Malga Headquarters

High Priest Pravis: priest at the monastery at Malga

High Priest Raphael: a leader of the Patronus

High Priest Rueben: member of the Patronus in charge of Nora Headquarters

High Priest Silas: a member of the Patronus

High Priest Tenebrae: priest at the monastery at Malga

High Priest Timothy: was murdered by Meekos, Pravis and Tenebrae

High Priest Tyrus: a member of the Patronus

High Priest Uriel: member of the Patronus

High Priest Vincent: assigned to the monastery at Malga before he was murdered

High Priest Zophar: priest at monastery at Malga/ trained as a healer

Hobart: a man who works for demons

Horace: father of Rachel and Zach/husband of Zelda/freedom fighter in Ryed

Hores: son of Chief Romogi and Anda, Kingdom of Marba/Huta

Horta: Prince/son of Gunnel and Uma/nephew of King Manu of New Samona/brother of Elan/Ruala

Hugo: younger brother of Sorren/father of Sasha/husband of Greta

Hunter: Prince of Samona/son of Varden

Ian Maxwell Luca: son of Koby and Bekka

Ian: husband of Mia/ brother in law of Calen/ Ruala

Ibula: warrior princess and healer of the Ruala Tribe/daughter of King Manu and Queen Delilia/

Iden: warrior guarding refugees/Shettee

Igor: brother of King Sharonne

Imad: a male Grand Master of the Insidiae

Ina: daughter of Mia and Ian/ Ruala

Ingr: female warrior of Nordes Tribe

Inon: one of Cisero's men/a vessel

Ipos: an ancient demon/ one of the Old Ones

Iris: mother of Vivian/wife of Joshua/Clan of Gesmal in Ryed

Irit: daughter of Hadi and Gita/ Ruala

Isabella: Princes of Lentz, sister of Mathas, Renya and Tasha, married to Captain Josef

Isadore: wife of Fahron

Isla: daughter of Prince Lakin and Princess Zada/Ruala

Isla: female warrior of Nordes Tribe

Ivan: youngest son of Chief Duncan and Liza of the Clan of Gesmal in Ryed

Jace: husband of Oda/ brother in law of Calen/Ruala

Jack: member of governing body of Nora

Jackson: a private in the Army of Lentz

Jackson: an escaped prisoner from Wetpr

Jacob: boy who Angelina found in the woods

Jacot: son of Prince Lakin and Princess Zada/ grandson of King Manu/Ruala

Jaden: Sergeant in the Army of Lentz

Jago: son of Elen and Batya/ Ruala

Jake: works for Talverson Transport Company in Port Friada

Jakiv: Prince/son of Segal and Cahina/nephew of King Manu of New Samona/Ruala

Jama: Enrop leader who protects Chief Sorren's family

James: Taperian soldier

Jana: female Ruala warrior

Janja: Princess/daughter of Gunnel and Uma/niece of King Manu of New Samona/ sister of Elan/Ruala

Janson: Wetprian soldier

Jared: hired fighter

Jaretta: King of Stordt/husband of Queen Lillian/ father of Roch and Sudfad

Jarrod: works for Pravis/leads attack on castle in Wetpr

Jarvis: a farmer who is killed by escaped prisoners

Jasmine: young female Nordes warrior

Jasper: a large white dog that Gabriel brings home

Jasper: Prince of Lentz/son of Princess Isabella and Captain Josef

Jatu: Enrop leader who protects Fahron's family

Jeb: friend of Thaos

Jeb: one of Cisero's men

Jela: Queen of Samona/wife of Varden

Jenna: female Ruala warrior/married to Ratri's oldest brother Artis

Jeremy: cousin of Andrew the jeweler in Salar

Jerik: a male Grand Master of the Insidiae

Jess: a soldier of Wetpr

Jillian: Queen of Ogg/wife of King Douma

Jinn: an ancient demon/ one of the Old Ones

Joao: male Ruala warrior

Joey: adopted son of Elan and Cassandra

Jonas: Captain in the Taperian Army

Jonathon: a waiter at the Calla Lily Restaurant in Teivel Ryed

Jorga: Princess of Ryed/daughter of Oren and Astrel/ has twin sister Andres

Jorge: a cook who is kidnapped from Endleson Hotel in Nora

Josef: Captain in the Lentz military/ married to Princess Isabella, sister of King Mathas

Joseph: male Ruala warrior/father of Ratri/husband of Clair

Joseph: nine year old Ruala boy/son of Artis and Jenna/nephew of Ratri

Joshua: father of Vivian/husband of Iris/Clan of Gesmal in Ryed

Josie: an escaped prisoner from Wetpr

Juleta: cousin to Raul and Simon/daughter and oldest child of King Mathas and Queen Rosa

Kadin: a member of Valdore Tribe

Kagen: a man who kidnaps and exploits children

Kalee: female Ruala warrior/married to Ratri's older brother Quinn

Karl: two year old Ruala boy/son of Artis and Jenna/nephew of Ratri

Karta: male Ruala warrior

Karzman: leader of Kozach Tribe/ stepfather of Michael

Kasper: Prince/son of Zeman and Oda/nephew of King Manu of New Samona/Ruala

Kata: Princess/daughter of Gunnel and Uma/niece of King Manu of New Samona/ sister of Elan/Ruala

Kate: a Venator from the Clan of Gesmal

Khryriss: an ancient demon/ one of the Old Ones

Kiana: Princess/daughter of Gunnel and Uma/niece of King Manu of New Samona/ sister of Elan/Ruala

Klass: Lieutenant in the Wetprian Army

Koby: male Ruala warrior

Koh: son of Prince Gael and Princess Mada/grandson of King Manu/Ruala

Kora: Princess/ married to Raphael son of King Zachariah and Queen Noella of New Samona/ mother of Luca/ Raphael and Kora were killed in battle when Luca was a small boy/Ruala

Korth: son of Tristt/Shettee

Kraus: hired fighter and intended vessel, works for Dieter

Kretcher: Commanding General of Fort Polta in Wetpr

Krister: Princess of Samoan/daughter of Thomas and Rewel

Kyra: young sister of Marie/ friend of Petra

Laban: Prince of Samona/son of Yorggi and Dion/grandson of Thomas and Rewel

Lael: daughter of Nina and Rhea/ Ruala

Lakin: Prince/son of King Manu and Queen Delilia/husband of Zada/Ruala

Lala: Princess/daughter of Adwell and Nada/niece of King Manu of New Samona/ sister of Misha/Ruala

Lana: female warrior of the Nordes Tribe

Lana: Princess/daughter of Segal and Cahina/niece of King Manu of New Samona/Ruala

Lani: daughter of Mia and Ian/Ruala

Lara: one of Usman's wives

Larson: a fighter hired by Juleta

Laurabelle: Hannah's sister who was murdered by Roch

Laurel: Annabelle's mother and former servant of King Roch's parents

Lawrence: a member of the Libertas

Lazo: fighter hired by Juleta

Lea: Princess/daughter of Adwell and Nada/niece of King Manu of New Samona/ sister of Misha/Ruala

Leith: four year old Ruala boy/son of Quin and Kalee/nephew of Ratri

Leo: Prince of Samona/son of Darius and Rebek/grandson of Thomas and Rewel

Leon: Captain in the Military of Ryed/ a member of Teivel's inner circle

Lieutenant Tarp: Lieutenant in the Wetprian Army

Lila: seventeen year old girl who Luca saves from the Hutas/sister of Christopher

Lilian: female warrior of the Nordes Tribe

Lillian: Queen of Stordt/wife of Jaretta/ mother of Roch and Sudfad

Lily: daughter of Calen and Natasha/Ruala and human

Liza: wife of Duncan the Chief of the Clan of Gesmal in Ryed

Lloyd: banker in Nora

Loftus: Commanding General of Fort Styls

Loni: daughter of King Friada and Queen Marla of the Kingdom of Ganz

Louie: works for Talverson Transport Company in Port Friada

Luca: male Ruala warrior

Lucene: male Nordes warrior/oldest son of Hugo and Greta/older brother of Sasha

Lucifer: an ancient demon/ one of the Old Ones

Luque: Prince/son of Segal and Cahina/nephew of King Manu of New Samona/Ruala

Mab: a female Grand Master of the Insidiae

Mable: a servant in the castle of King Nehmota of Ryed

Mabon: warrior guarding refugees/Shettee

Mada: Princess /wife of Prince Gael/Ruala

Madam Bular: owner of a dress shop in Port Friada

Madix: General in the Army of Ryed/member of Teivel's first inner circle

Maggie: elderly store owner in Salar

Mahon: son of King Neputa

Makalo: Prince of Norkv/husband of Grace who was the daughter of Benjeman and Esther

Malana: daughter of King Neputa

Mali: Princess of Norkv/daughter of Makalo and Grace/granddaughter of Benjeman and Esther

Maligma: an ancient demon/ one of the Old Ones

Malik: member of the Insidiae

Malus: sorcerer from Ryed

Mandrake: Taperian soldier

Manu: King of New Samona/The Chief of the Grand Council made up of Rualas and Shettees/ father of Ibula, Lakin, Gael and Hadar/husband of Delilia

Manutu: King of the Gants

Marcia: friend of Hannah's/ Roch's men murdered her family

Marcus Stephan: son of Stephan and Ingr

Margarit: daughter of King Mathas and Queen Rosa of the Kingdom of Lentz/ cousin of Raul and Simon

Margo: a young girl who was kidnapped by Sal

Margolia: girl from Nora who was sacrificed to a demon

Marie: a cook for King Sudfad and Queen Renya

Markus: a soldier in the Army of Wetpr

Marla: High Priest Meekos' housekeeper

Marla: Queen of the Kingdom of Ganz

Marsha Jarvis: a sixteen year old girl who is raped and killed by Timothy

Martha: a cook for Cerephus

Martha: hotel owner in Telmark

Martin Froush: wealthy ship builder in Port Friada/husband of Denise

Martin: a member of the Libertas

Mary: Jared's young wife who was brutally murdered by Hutas

Mata: Igor's wife

561

Mateo: Chief Healer of the Ruala Tribe

Mathas: King of Lentz/ brother to Queen Renya

Matilda: one of Usman's wives

Matthew: son of King Mathas and Queen Rosa of the Kingdom of Lentz/ cousin of Raul and Simon

Maximus Bartholomew Joshua: twin son of Misha and Diana/brother of Thor Adwell Gabriel

Maxwell: father of Calen/ Ruala

Maxwell: infant son of Nina and Rhea/grandson of elder Maxwell/Ruala

Melanie: female Ruala warrior/daughter of Casey and Tasha

Melina: mother of Thaos

Melinda: grandmother of Misha

Melinda: older sister of Cassandra and Joao

Mia: daughter of Maxwell and Emeral/ Ruala

Mia: female Ruala warrior/daughter of Tyron and Elsa

Mica: Princess of Norkv/daughter of Benedict and Sasaha/granddaughter of Benjeman and Esther

Micha: oldest son of Joshua and Iris/older brother of Vivian/Clan of Gesmal

Micha: son of King Sharonne/ grandfather of Sudfad and Roch

Michael: ancient king of Wetpr/father of Queen Sumona

Michael: son of Sudfad and Nadia

Milo: male Ruala warrior

Miranda: daughter of Raul and Vitomas

Miranda: emissary of The Great Ruler who takes on the disguise of a human seer

Miriam: a friend of Hannah's/works at Endleson Hotel in Nora

Misha: male Ruala warrior/lieutenant

Molach: a member of the Insidiae

Moloch: an ancient demon/one of the Old Ones

Morris: member of governing body of Nora

Morton: Cedrick Teivel's original name

Muhar: Shettee warrior

Myla: wife of the owner of the Dragons Inn in Salar

Naal: warrior guarding refugees/Shettee

Nabi: male Ruala warrior

Nada: Princess/ married to Adwell son of King Zachariah and Queen Noella of New Samona/ mother of Misha/ Adwell was killed in battle leaving Nada to raise ten children/Ruala

Nadia: wife of Karzman/mother of Michael

Naomi: mother of Rabi/ Ruala

Napo: Enrop leader who protects Claudius' family

Natasha: sister of High Priest Gabriel

Nathaniel: Sorren's oldest son/ Nordes Tribe

Nebula: son of Chief Romogi and Anda/ Kingdom of Marba/Huta

Nehmota: King of Ryed

Nelpus: Shettee warrior

Neputa: leader of the Shettee Tribe when it was conquered by the Hutas

Nestor: a demon that specializes in procuring things for a price

Nica: Enrop leader who protects Sudfad's family

Nicholas: orphan boy /brother of Cerey

Nicolas: Prince of Puntd/son of King Tobias and Queen Tasha

Nieatzae: an ancient demon/ one of the Old Ones

Nikki: female warrior of Nordes Tribe

Nina: daughter of Maxwell and Emeral/Ruala

Nina: youngest daughter of Karzman and Nadia

Nita: Princess/daughter of Adwell and Nada/niece of King Manu of New Samona/ sister of Misha/has twin brother Waed/Ruala

Noah: a member of the Libertas

Nobel: former prince of Ryed/son of Akasha and Norah/father of Nehmota

Noella: the first Queen of New Samona/wife of King Zachariah/mother of seven sons/Ruala

Norah: former queen of Ryed/grandmother of Nehmota

Noreen: mother of Jacob/ wife of Henry

Norris: hired fighter and intended vessel, works for Dieter

Nyla: oldest daughter of Karzman and Nadia

Oda: daughter of Maxwell and Emeral/ Ruala

Oda: Princess/ married to Zeman son of King Zachariah and Queen Noella of New Samona/Ruala

Odam: male Ruala warrior

Odell: one of the spies at the Castle at Wetpr

Oliver: a member of the Libertas

Omar: Prince/son of Zeman and Oda/nephew of King Manu of New Samona/Ruala

Omara: Queen of Norkv/wife of Thaddius who was son of Benjeman and Esther

Omnibus: an ancient demon/ one of the Old Ones

Omoria: former queen of Ryed/wife of Nobel/mother of Nehmota

Opago: an ancient demon/ one of the Old Ones

Orbus: a powerful demon and former lover of the demon Hecate

Orcus: Shettee warrior/brother of King Neputa

Oren: former prince of Gandt who marries princess Astrel of Ryed

Oriah: name used by the Grand Master Banaka

Orin: male Ruala warrior/older brother of Ratri/husband of Rene

Ottillia: Princess of Lenz/daughter of Princess Isabella and Captain Josef

Otu: son of Hecate and Sampson

Padre Augustus: a member of the Patronus

Padre Bartholomew: survives the massacre at the monastery at Avaide

Padre Cornelius: a member of the Patronus

Padre Darius: a member of the Patronus

Padre Dibon: a priest at the monastery at Malga

Padre Dominick: priest at monastery at Malga

Padre Edgar: member of the Patronus

Padre Edward: a member of the Patronus

Padre Finn: Patronus priest assigned to the Cicero HQ

Padre Francis: priest at monastery at Malga

Padre Joram: member of the Patronus

Padre Lucas: a member of the Patronus

Padre Markle: a Patronus priest

Padre Nebat: alias for Dominic leader of the Libertas

Padre Octavos: runs orphanage in Salar

Padre Philip: a member of the Patronus

Padre Philip: a priest at the monastery at Malga

Padre Simpson: priest at the monastery at Malga

Padre Sorben: a member of the Patronus

Padre Sornce: Patronus priest assigned to the Cicero HQ

Padre Stephens: priest at monastery at Malga

Padre Thomas: priest at the monastery at Malga

Padre Tobias: a member of the Patronus

Padre Xavier: priest at monastery at Malga

Paj: Princess/wife of Prince Hadar/Ruala

Pallas: Shettee warrior

Pata: daughter of Chief Romogi and Trina/Huta

Paterson: a Private in the Wetprian military

Patris: six year old Nordes girl/daughter of Hugo and Greta/younger sister of Sasha

Paul: third son of Joshua and Iris/younger brother of Vivian/Clan of Gesmal

Paulas: a man who works for Cicero/a vessel

Paulas: Sergeant under Archetenus in Taperian Army

Paullo: works for High Priest Meekos

Pearl: eldest daughter of King Tobias and Queen Tasha of Puntd

Pergo: King of the Kingdom of Gandt

Peter: Sorren's second son/Nordes Tribe

Peters: member of the governing body of Nora

Petorus: an ancient demon/one of the Old Ones

Petra: peasant boy from Ort who saves Padre Bartholomew

Phifer: nine year old Nordes boy/ son of Hugo and Greta/younger brother of Sasha

Philip: Prince of Puntd/ son of King Tobias and Queen Tasha

Phillip: Court Physician to the Royal Family of Wetpr

Polgate: one of the men who kidnapped Petra

Potomas: warrior guarding refugees/Shettee

Powell: a lieutenant in the Military of Lentz/stationed at Fahron's castle

Prescott: a hired killer

Quin: male Ruala warrior/older brother of Ratri/husband of Kalee

Rabi: male Ruala warrior

Rachel: member of the freedom fighters in Ryed

Radnor: a male Grand Master of the Insidiae

Rael: Prince of old Samona/husband of Krister who was the daughter of Thomas and Rewel

Rahi: a female Grand Master of the Insidiae

Rakio: Prince/son of Adwell and Nada/nephew of King Manu of New Samona/brother of Misha/Ruala

Rako: a male Ruala warrior

Raphael: Prince/ son of King Zachariah and Queen Noella of New Samona/husband of Kora/Ruala/father of Luca/ Raphael and Kora were killed in battle when Luca was a small boy/Ruala

Ratri: male Ruala warrior

Raul: Prince/son of King Sudfad and Queen Renya of the Kingdom of Wetpr

Raum: an ancient demon/ one of the Old Ones

Rebek: Princess of Samona/wife of Darius, who was the son of Thomas and Rewel

Rebke: six year old Ruala girl/ daughter of Orin and Rene/niece of Ratri

Rene: female Ruala warrior/married to Ratri's older brother Orin

Renya: Queen of Wetpr/ wife of Sudfad

Rewel: Queen of Samona/wife of Thomas/mother of Varden

Rex: a notorious pick pocket in Port Friada

Rhea: husband of Nina/ brother in law of Calen/ Ruala

Riftca: male Ruala warrior

Riker: a scout in the Wetprian military

Risha: a witch who deals with potions

Roch: King of the Kingdom of Stordt/brother of King Sudfad

Rogers: one of the men who kidnapped Petra

Rolif: son of Chief Romogi and Silva/ Kingdom of Marba/Huta

Romale: member of the Insidiae

Romos: an elder of the Centras

Rosa: Queen of Lentz/wife of King Mathas

Rosalie: a dressmaker in Nora/wife of Peters

Ruth: emissary of The Great Ruler who takes on the guise of a frail old woman

Ryan: grandson of Jeb/friend of Thaos

Sabot: member of the Insidiae

Sahil: a male Ruala warrior

Sal: a murderous pedophile/also goes by the name Tyrone

Sally: a young girl who was kidnapped by Sal

Salzar: powerful demon on Sidus

Sam: male Ruala warrior/father of Bekka/husband of Ella

Samael: a demon as powerful as Ahriman who rules the hell world Xibalba

Samara: wife of Tristt/Shettee

Samat: son of Chief Romogi and Silva/ Kingdom of Marba/Huta

Samos: Prince of Norkv/son of Thaddius

Sampson: oldest son of Chief Duncan and Liza of the Clan of Gesmal in Ryed

Sampson: Sergeant in the Taperian Army

Samuel: a high priest at the monastery at Malga who was murdered

Samuel: Prince of the original Samona/grandson of Thomas and Rewel

Samuel: second son of Raul and Vitomas

Sanuri: a holy man/emissary of The Great Ruler/warrior

Sar: an Enrop

Sar: male Ruala warrior

Sara: daughter of Usman

Sarah: baby granddaughter of Mathas and Rosa

Sarah: housekeeper for Claudius and Bella

Saran: daughter of Karzman and Nadia

Sasaha: Princess of the original Samona/granddaughter of Thomas and Rewel

Sasha: young female Nordes warrior

Sasha: female warrior of the Nordes Tribe/wife of Galen

Satan: an ancient demon/ one of the Old Ones

Satter: male Ruala warrior

Sattleman: a Sergeant in the Wetprian army

Sauer: male Ruala warrior

Saunders: a Taperian soldier

Saxton: powerful lieutenant who works for Teivel the dictator of Ryed

Schroeder: man who works for Insidiae leader Dieter

Schuester: Commander of a special unit of Teivel's government/identifies betrayers

Segal: Prince/ son of King Zachariah and Queen Noella of New Samona/husband of Cahina/Ruala

Seguna: former princess of Ryed/daughter of Akasha and Norah/ committed suicide

Selen: house keeper for Juleta

Seth: a member of the Libertas

Shanksaw: mercenary

Shara: wife of Sorren/Nordes Tribe

Shard: Captain in the Military of Ryed/ a member of Teivel's inner circle

Sharonne: King of Stordt; great, great, grandfather of King Roch and King Sudfad

Shon: son of King Fahra and Queen Sitha

Shone: Princess/daughter of Zeman and Oda/niece of King Manu of New Samona/Ruala

Sicily Bella: daughter of Stephan and Ingr

Sila: Princess of Ogg

Silva: one of Chief Romogi's three wives/Huta

Simmons: Commanding General of Fort Nir

Simon: adopted son of King Sudfad and Queen Renya of the Kingdom of Wetpr

Sinclair: King of Lentz/father of King Mathas

Sirius: works for High Priest Meekos

Sitha: Queen of Zorta

Smoking Joe: a regular patron at the Ghost Ship Tavern

Sonja: female warrior of the Nordes Tribe

Sophie: cook and servant of King Roch

Sorren: leader of the Nordes Tribe

Soto: male Ruala warrior who leads first death squad for criminals

Sporos: priest turned demon

Stephan: Captain in Army of Lentz/son of Claudius and Bella

Stiller: a fighter hired by Juleta

Stolas: an ancient demon/one of the Old Ones

Stone: an alias used by Dominic during the mission in Ryed with Gabriel's team

Stone: hired fighter and intended vessel, works for Dieter

Sudfad: King of the Kingdom of Wetpr and brother to King Roch of Stordt

Sudfad: little Sudfad is grandson of King Sudfad

Sumona: Queen of Wetpr/wife of Alexandras/aunt of Roch and Sudfad

Swenson: one of Shanksaw's hired men

Syrius: a Bakken hired by Juleta

Tabeth: daughter of Fahron

Tabith: son of Tristt/Shettee

Tabitha: Princess of Lentz/daughter of Princess Isabella and Captain Josef of Lentz

Tadeo: Prince/son of Adwell and Nada/nephew of King Manu of New Samona/brother of Misha/Ruala

Tafer: a warlord who drove the Hutas out of the Kingdom of Norkv after years of wars and rebellions

Tahira: a female Grand Master of the Insidiae

Tahira: Princess of Samona/granddaughter of Thomas and Rewel

Tal: son of Oda and Jace/ Ruala

Talmai: Shettee boy who Thedes and Ibula adopt

Tambor: male Ruala warrior

Tamour: General in the Army of Lentz/on loan to Sudfad

Tanner: a Lieutenant in the Wetprian army

Tanner: a Sergeant in the Army of Lentz

Tapster: a demon who works for Meekos

Tarig: a lieutenant in the Huta army

Tarin: son of King Neputa and Queen Tiara/Shettee

Taron: Prince/son of Adwell and Nada/nephew of King Manu of New Samona/brother of Misha/Ruala

Tasha: female Ruala warrior/mother of Melanie/wife of Casey

Tasha: Queen of Puntd/ married to Tobias/ sister of Renya and Mathas

Tate: a Lieutenant in the Wetprian Army

Tatterd: a Sergeant in the Wetprian military

Tavin: son of Prince Lakin and Princess Zada/Ruala

Teddy: male Nordes warrior/son of Edgar and Cora/ older brother of Batina

Tega: housekeeper for the cabins of the captains of the Taperian Army

Tegman: soldier of Wetpr

Tehtfote: a Lieutenant for Dieter

Temark: villager of Neva

Tetro: Huta warrior who was a captive in Ogg

Thadddius: Prince of the new Kingdom of Norkv/son of Benjeman

Thaddies: member of Nordes Tribe/ father of Ingr

Thanatoes: an ancient demon/ one of the Old Ones

Thaos: a hired fighter

Thatcher: Prince/son of Zeman and Oda/nephew of King Manu of New Samona/Ruala

Thatus: Taperian soldier

The Lion: emissary of The Great Ruler who takes on the appearance of a lion when he is in the world of man

Thedes: warrior guarding refugees/Shettee

Theodore: handyman for Erebus/husband of Arlene

Theodore: the physician at Fort Stanus in the Kingdom of Wetpr

Thomas: King of the original Kingdom of Samona/father of Varden

Thomas: second son of Joshua and Iris/older brother of Vivian/Clan of Gesmal

Thomas: the young husband of Zoya who was murdered in Taperia

Thompson: Wetprian soldier

Thor Adwell Gabriel: twin son of Misha and Diana/brother of Maximus Bartholomew Joshua

Thor: a Venator/brother of Diana

Thronson: one of Meekos hired killers

Tiara: Queen of Shettee Tribe when it was conquered by Hutas/wife of Neputa

Timothy: son of Fahron

Tina: Mother of Cassandra, Joao and Melinda

Tito: member of Valdore Tribe

Titus Derek: son of Thaos and Nikki

Titus: a lieutenant in the Taperian Army

Tobart: a member of the Nordes Tribe

Tobey: a carriage driver in Ryed who helps Gabriel's team

Tobias: King of Puntd.

Tomas: works for High Priest Pravis

Tome: a businessman and member of the Insidiae in Nora

Tomi: son of Usman the leader of the Valdore Tribe

Toni: young female Nordes warrior

Tony: male Ruala warrior/ married to Bekka's oldest sister Eloise

Toomback: Huta warrior

Torance: father of Thaos

Torin: oldest son of Karzman and Nadia

Trace: male Ruala warrior

Tratz: one of the men who kidnapped Petra

Travor: Taperian warrior who was injured at the Wall of Dorath

Tresdore: son of King Sharonne

Trevor: Prince/son of Zeman and Oda/nephew of King Manu of New Samona/Ruala

Tria: daughter of Oda and Jace/Ruala

Trina: one of Chief Romogi's three wives/Huta

Trina: Princess/daughter of Zeman and Oda/niece of King Manu of New Samona/Ruala

Trist: a male Ruala warrior

Tristt the Horrible: Shettee warrior

Tritor: a powerful demon of Sidus and ex-lover of Hecate

Tye: Prince of Norkv/son of Princess Grace and Prince Makalo

Tyron: male Ruala warrior/father of Mia/husband of Elsa

Tyson: Wetprian soldier

Ulger: a demon

Uma: Princess/ married to Gunnel son of King Zachariah and Queen Noella of New Samona/mother of Elan/Ruala

Umar: Prince/son of Adwell and Nada/nephew of King Manu of New Samona/brother of Misha/Ruala

Uri: an Enrop

Uri: son of Nina and Rhea/ Ruala

Usman: leader of the Valdore Tribe

Valdus: name used by the Grand Master Emeric

Valerie: young female Nordes warrior

Valor: Prince of the new Kingdom of Norkv/son of Benjeman and Esther

Vandrew: Petra's male tutor

Vania: Princess of Samona/daughter of Yorggi and Dion/granddaughter of Thomas and Rewel

Varden: last king of Samona/he and his family were murdered by rebels

Vardin: one of the men who kidnapped Petra

Vasart: Queen of Ryed/ wife of Nehmota

Viktor: an ancient priest in Ryed who tried to stop the Insidiae

Vinca: Queen of Stordt, wife of Sharonne

Vincent: Prince of Ryed/son of Nehmota and Vasart

Vinus: Queen of the Kingdom of Gandt

Visterle: a powerful demon

Vitomas: Queen of Stordt

Vivian: a demon hunter from the Clan of Gesmal

Voltar: Prince of Samona/son of Darius and Rebek/grandson of Thomas and Rewel/later becomes King of Wetpr

Vuall: a demon

Waed: Prince/son of Adwell and Nada/nephew of King Manu of New Samona/brother of Misha/has twin sister Nita/Ruala

Wallis: member of governing body of Nora

Wilard: Captain at Fort Polta

William: son of Jared and Zoya

Willis: son of King Pergo and Queen Vinus/ Kingdom of Gandt

Xeni: a female Grand Master of the Insidiae

Yara: daughter of Nina and Rhea/Ruala

Yorggi: Prince of Samona/son of Thomas and Rewel/brother of Varden

Yori: son of Usman the leader of the Valdore Tribe

Yuri: Prince/son of Adwell and Nada/nephew of King Manu of New Samona/brother of Misha/Ruala

Zac: one of the men who kidnapped Petra

Zachariah: first King of New Samona/husband of Queen Noella/father of seven sons/Ruala

Zack: eight year old brother of Rachel

Zada: Princess/wife of Prince Lakin/Ruala

Zadok: a male Grand Master of the Insidiae

Zede: an ancient demon/ one of the Old Ones

Zehmann: an ancient demon/ one of the Old Ones

Zelda: mother of Rachel and Zack

Zeman: Prince/ son of King Zachariah and Queen Noella of New Samona/husband of Oda/Ruala

Zieman: a demon

Zorda: Taperian soldier injured in battle at the Wall of Dorath

Zortus: demon/lieutenant of Visterle

Zoya: a seer from Taperia

Glossary of Terms

Aboultis: the calling cards of demons

Abrax: the planet that orbits closest to the three suns/ uninhabited

Abyss: a vast void used to imprison demons

Acura: the whispering shadows/are in the inner circle of demons that directly serve the Old Ones

Alferto: a type of grain that is common in Opots

Amark: ancient language of The Great Ruler

Amulth: means filth in the language of demons/these monsters are made out of the waste of tortured souls from the hell dimensions

Anewa: one of seven continents in the World of Nunc

Aplewort: an herb when mixed with water purges poisons from a body

Asherane: ancient tribe that lived in the northern regions of the Kingdom of Lentz

Ashta: a common herb/when the dried leaves are boiled they give off a pleasant scent

Astras: the ancient underground city of the Centras

Astrum: the solar system that consists of three suns that form a triangle and seven planets

Beltrad: a species of lower level demons

Blood rings: Large red rubies set in silver with markings of the Old Ones

Boca: a covered wagon pulled by horses

Box of Itifer: a gift to the world of man from The Great Ruler; this gift affects the balance of creation

Bozie: a game of skill played by the Nordes Tribe

Cava plant: a poisonous plant that grows freely near bodies of water

Centras: ancient race of creatures who have the responsibility of protecting the Holy Box of Itifer

Cerfic: an ancient language widely spoken among many kingdoms/a language of the masses not royalty

Chalice of Ascension: a gift from The Great Ruler, this gift contains unimaginable powers

Cicero College: in Wetpr, outside of Salar, where Raul, Simon and Hannah attended college

Clan of Gesmal: a tribe of demon hunters who live in the southern region of the Kingdom of Ryed

Crystal pillars: in the Ice Caves of Mordv/are blessed by The Great Ruler and filled with spiritual life force

Czarsta: one of seven continents in the World of Nunc

Demalogs: an inferior species of demons

Demosa: a slow acting poison from the cava plant

Diamond of Cazo: a gift from The Great Ruler, this gift can unleash powers from the center of the world

Durisks: large demonic birds/their elongated beaks contain rows of fangs

Ekel Beast: similar to a deer

Engas: a wild cat that inhabits the Vandrew Mountains

Engor: a small pack animal that lives in trees

Enrop: a large species of bird that can speak many human languages

Epocos: one of the original tribes in the Kingdom of Ryed

Farduth: a Shettee necklace that symbolizes a male has completed his rite of passage to become a warrior

Filsum: the sixth planet in the Astrum Solar System/ two moons

Gafet: an ancient Shettee weapon

Gants: large apelike creatures/Watchers of the Caves of Muldun

Gate of Isula: the only opening in the great Wall of Dorath

Gefrey Games: games of sport where men fight each other and great beasts to the death

Grand Masters: the first people to call to the demons and invite them into this world

Great Ruler: God

Half-Mans: a tribe of creatures that are partially human and partially nature. They are three feet tall and walk on two legs but can change their coloring to match their environment.

Hall of Antiquities: a giant hall located in the monastery at Malga/ a sanctuary for holy items and manuscripts

Hall of Light: the Great Hall in the Ice Caves of Mordv

Hengers: giant blue eagles/ birds of war

Highland Pass: the only passage through the Rosu Mountain Range

Holy Scrolls: gifts given to each kingdom by The Great Ruler, these gifts contain powers, wisdom and immortality

Holy Vault: a secret vault under the King's study in the castle in Wetpr designed to protect holy objects

Horn of Asher: a horn used by the Patronus warrior priests to signal each other

Horn of Cass: a horn used by the Wetprian soldiers to signal each other

Horn of Cornwell: a horn used by Dieter's men to signal each other

Horn of Eel: a horn used by the Ruala warriors to communicate with each other

Horn of Esker: a horn used by the Valdore Tribe to communicate with each other

Horn of Ire: a horn carried by the Taperian soldiers to communicate with each other

Horn of Shana: a horn carried by the soldiers of Lentz to communicate with each other

Horn of Tula: a horn used by the members of the Nordes Tribe for communication

Horn of Vamont: a horn used by the Kozach Tribe for communication

Horn of Xepoltr: a horn used by the Shettee warriors to communicate

Huta: a race of humans that is driven by hatred and ideas of racial superiority who live in the Kingdom of Marba

Insidiae: means conspirators/a highly organized secret group of humans who have sold their souls to demons

Jacar: giant leech-like creatures

Jacept Plant: a plant that a powerful poison is made from

Kafer: a small crescent shaped knife carried by the Beltrad

Keepers of the Scrolls: the Royal Family of the Kingdom of Wetpr entered into a covenant with The Great Ruler to protect his gifts until a time when they can be safely given back to the world of man

Kozach: a tribe that lives in the far north central regions of the Kingdom of Wetpr

Lamsman: an ankle bracelet worn by Venatores/stones in the bracelet signify great feats they had to accomplish to become a demon hunter

Learning Center: the first of its kind/a complex educational facility that is open to multiple peoples and guards the students and staff from terrorists

Libertas: the name of a group of freedom fighters in northern Ryed

Linges plant: a plant that grows in damp, swampy regions in Opots/the white berries are used to make the drug Melanwhop

Lynswood: an herb that reveals tracks that are concealed by black magic

Mark of Satan: a coiled red snake with green eyes and a yellow tongue

Matu potage: a food staple of the Shettee Tribe

Mayka: one of seven continents in the World of Nunc

Melanwhop: a drug made from the linges plant, causes lethargy and apathy

Mordov: the special place in hell for hypocrites

Motfer: the land of the dead

Nefandus: a secret sect within the Insidiae

Nordes: a tribe of fiercely trained warriors who live in the northern region of the Kingdom of Lentz

Nunc: the world where this story takes place/third planet from the three suns

Old Ones: the original demons that came to the World of Nunc

Opatu bread: a food staple of the Shettee Tribe

Opots: one of seven continents in the World of Nunc/the continent where this story takes place

Oran: a tobisk that is filled with a mixture of ramni oil, buruto powder and meno salts, designed to explode on impact

Orantho: the seventh planet in the Astrum Solar System/inhabited/four moons/ large planet/many hell worlds

Patronus: an elite group of men who serve as the protectors of the church

Pfison screen: a type of demonic cloaking devise/it is sensitive and has to be calibrated for the specific individuals it is intended for

Planteen: the fourth planet in the Astrum Solar System/inhabited/two moons

Porto: one of seven continents in the World of Nunc

Prophesy of the Blood Moon: a demonic prophesy that predicts the doors to hell being opened.

Prophesy of Izera: Predicts the downfall of the Teivel regime

Propilatry: a powerful form of demonic curse

Prostras: an ancient tribe that once inhabited the Ice Caves of Mordv

Raftifa: ancient bat-like creatures that devour human flesh

Ravens: messengers used by the dark lords

Recupero: a sect within the Insidiae that worships the demon Omnibus

Rogetts: a tribe of humans that have digressed into murderous mutant monsters

Rualas: an ancient tribe of warriors said to be half human and half bird

Salszar: one of seven continents in the World of Nunc

Salts of Envoy: a sleeping potion

Scio: a crystal ball

Scroll of Imari: a gift of The Great Ruler, a scroll that unleashes the power of The Box of Itifer

Seal of Natun: a gift from the Holy Ruler that can open doors to other worlds

Serpents of Satan: can only be called forth by dark lords and demons, large red snakes with green eyes and yellow tongues

Seven Sons Prophesy: an ancient prophesy about seven sons who stand up against the demons and dark lords

Shesone: an ancient fighting style of the Shettee Tribe

Shettee: an ancient tribe of warriors said to be half human and half lion

Sidus: the fifth planet in the Astrum Solar System/inhabited/red fog surrounds the planet

Solv: a specific prison within the Abyss

Song of the Second Son: an ancient prophesy about an evil that is passed between second sons of a family resulting in a monster that brings terror and darkness to the world of man

Sundra Templer: a gift from The Great Ruler that was stolen by dark lords/an orb with extraordinary powers that can be used in multiple ways such as transporting humans through other worlds

Tabutu: an ancient form of fighting developed by the Asherane Tribe of the Kingdom of Lentz

Talisman: an object with magical or supernatural meaning

Talmuth: giant red dragon-like creatures

Taluth: a light weight metal used to make the ancient Shettee weapons called the Gafets

Tameric: the place where Karzman claims he came from although it does not exist on any map of Opots

Tangers: large wild, grazing animals that travel in herds

Tansof: one of seven continents in the World of Nunc

Tarus demon: huge, power creatures that walk on two legs but have the head, neck and shoulders of an ox

Telgras: a hell beast that looks like it is half wolf and half panther

Teragon: death terror/a monster created as a result of diabolical acts

585

Terbot bear: a bear that roams in the northern regions of the continent of Opots

Tervator: fourteen foot monster that walks like a man with long dark hair over its entire body and bull- like horns protruding from its head

Texts of Semalia: ancient texts about demonic language and rituals

The Book of Horror: a book that is worshipped by demons/contains prophesies

The Celebration of Days: an annual celebration of the Centras

The Hall of Understanding: the building in Astras where the history of the Centras is documented in drawings

The Hunters: another name for the Shettee Tribe

The Lion: a very powerful messenger of The Great Ruler assumes the form of a lion when he walks in the worlds of man

The Thirteenth Color: not seen in the world of man it is the color of horror/hell

Timbar: ghost dragons/ demons that can fly

Tinchure water: an herbal pain remedy used by the Nordes Tribe

Tincture of the Redeti Plant: Hutas dip the tips of their weapons in this insect infested liquid. The insects lay eggs inside of the victim. When the eggs are mature and hatch, two inch worm-like creatures are produced and will eat the organs of the victim causing a long and painful death

Tobisks: sphere shaped objects, metal and hollow inside that are designed to be launched from a Trebuchet

Traxsor: the second planet in the Astrum Solar System

Trebuchets: wooden machines used to catapult objects

Trimoth: a game of skill, strength and speed

Triolie: a Nordes gambling game

Tygrus: a ship that docked in Port Friada

Unholy altar: altar used to worship demons

Valdees: the tribe that lives in the underwater Kingdom of Ogg

Valdore: a tribe of merciless separatists who live in the extreme northern regions of the Kingdom of Lentz

Venator: means hunter in the old language

Venom of the Atha serpent: one of the poisons that Hutas put on their arrows

Vessel of Darkness: a human created from darkness to hold the essence of a powerful demon

Wall of Dorath: a giant wall that separates the Kingdoms of Norkv and Xepoltr from the Kingdom of Marba

Willimonns: small furry creatures that are hunted for food and sport

Xelope: the oneness of spirit with all that lives

Yellow Jay: a bird native to Opots

Yellow Mandeze: a song bird common to Opots

Zehno demon: thin, creature with long red and blue plumes on the back of its head with large eyes and round mouths

Zendoti: demons that are distinguished by the geometrically shaped tuffs of hair that protrude from their heads

Glossary of Maps

The maps are displayed in order of relevance

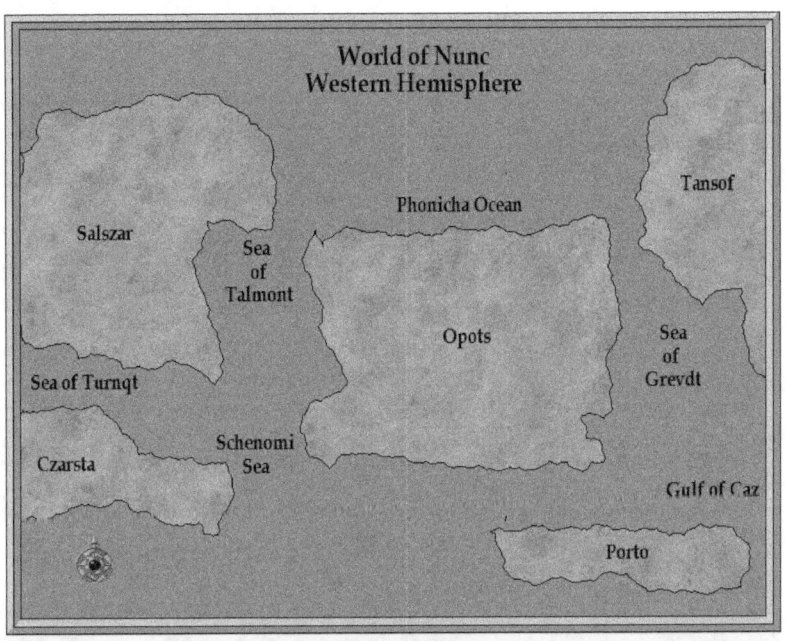

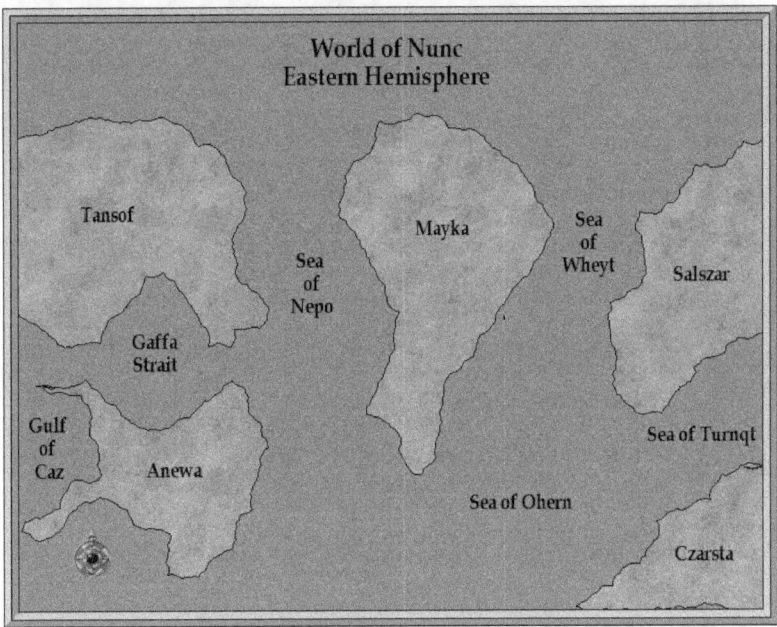

Continent of Opots
With new forts

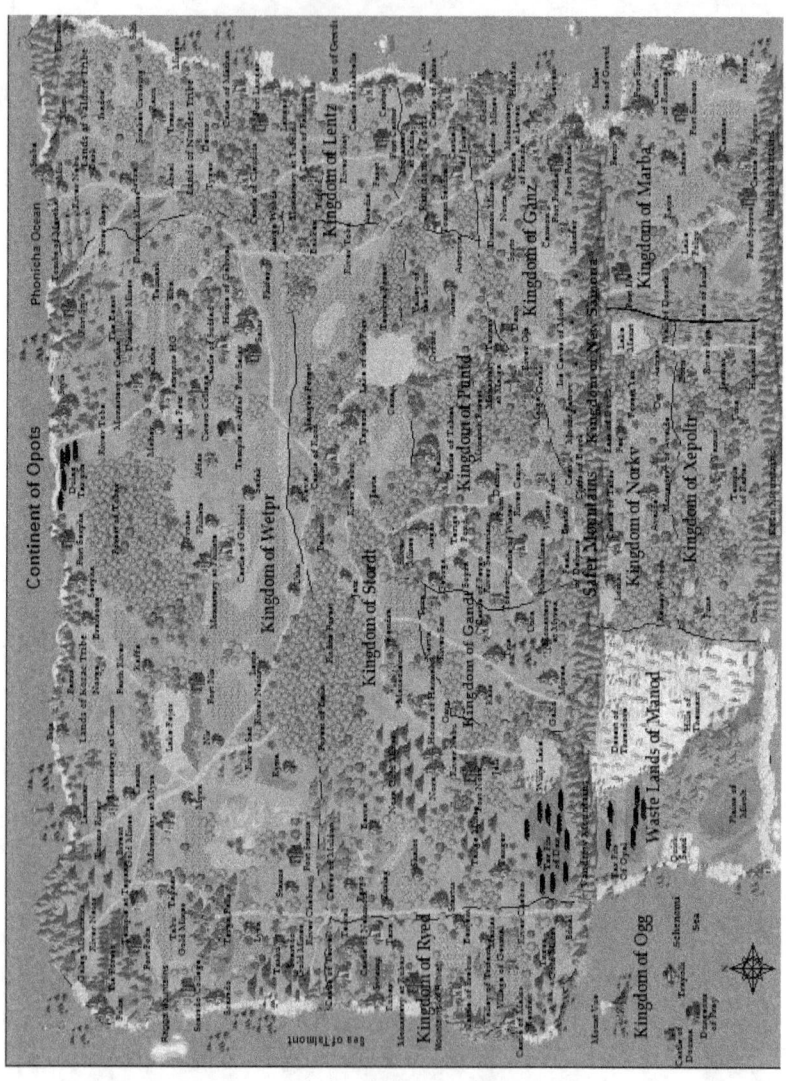

590

Western Stordt
With Fort Nora

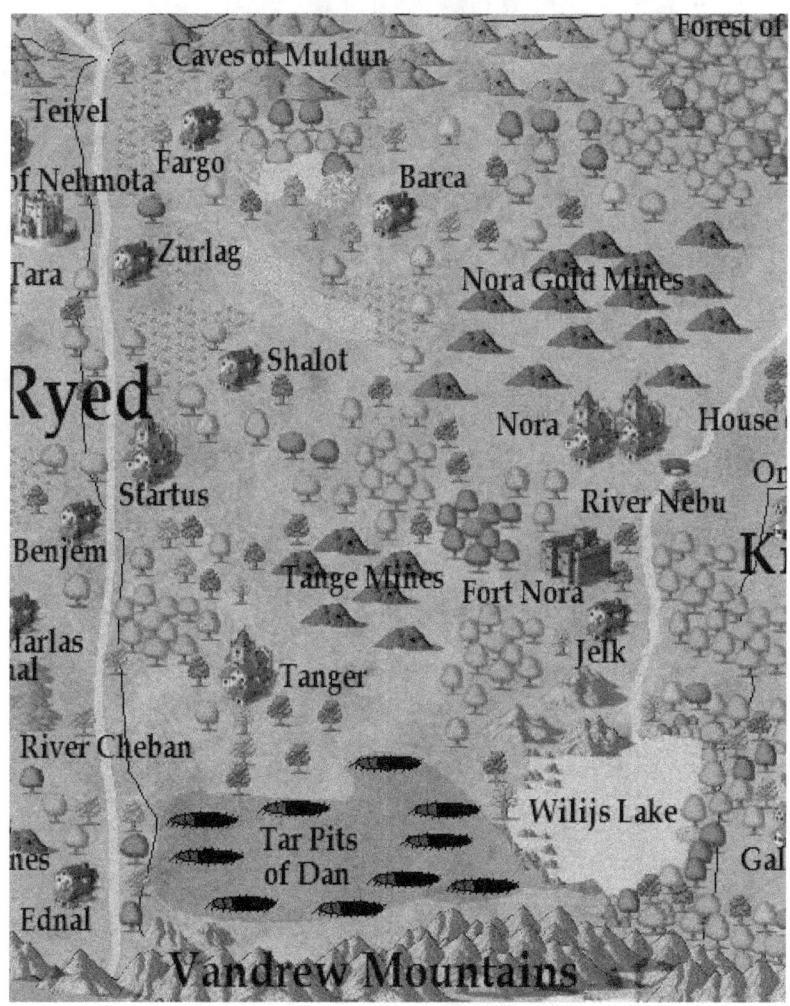

Forest of

Caves of Muldun

Teivel

f Nehmota Fargo

Barca

Tara

Zurlag

Nora Gold Mines

Ryed

Shalot

Nora

House

Or

Startus

River Nebu

Ki

Benjem

Tange Mines

Fort Nora

larlas
al

Tanger

Jelk

River Cheban

nes

Tar Pits
of Dan

Wilijs Lake

Gal

Ednal

Vandrew Mountains

Northern Stordt

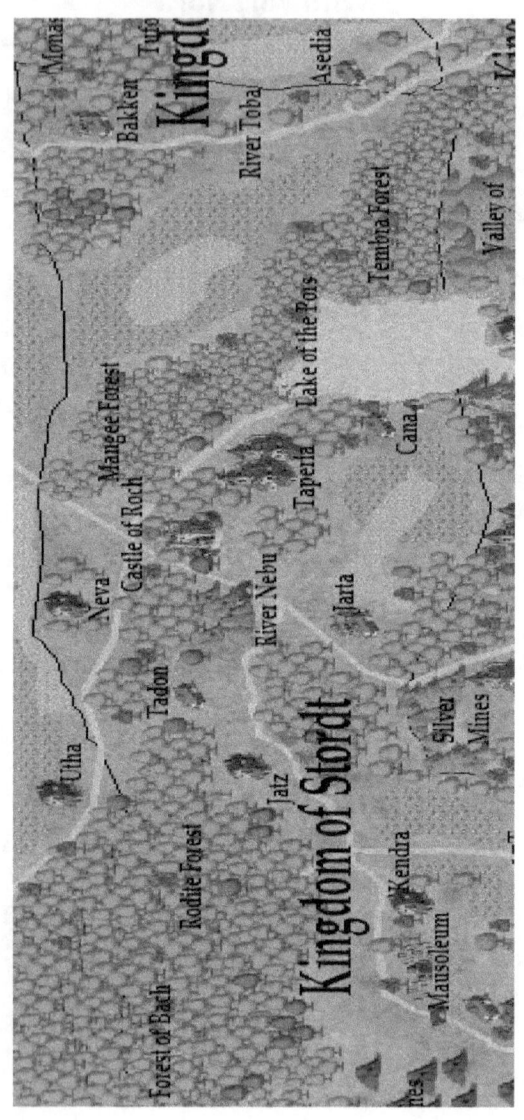

Western Wetpr
With Fort Stanus

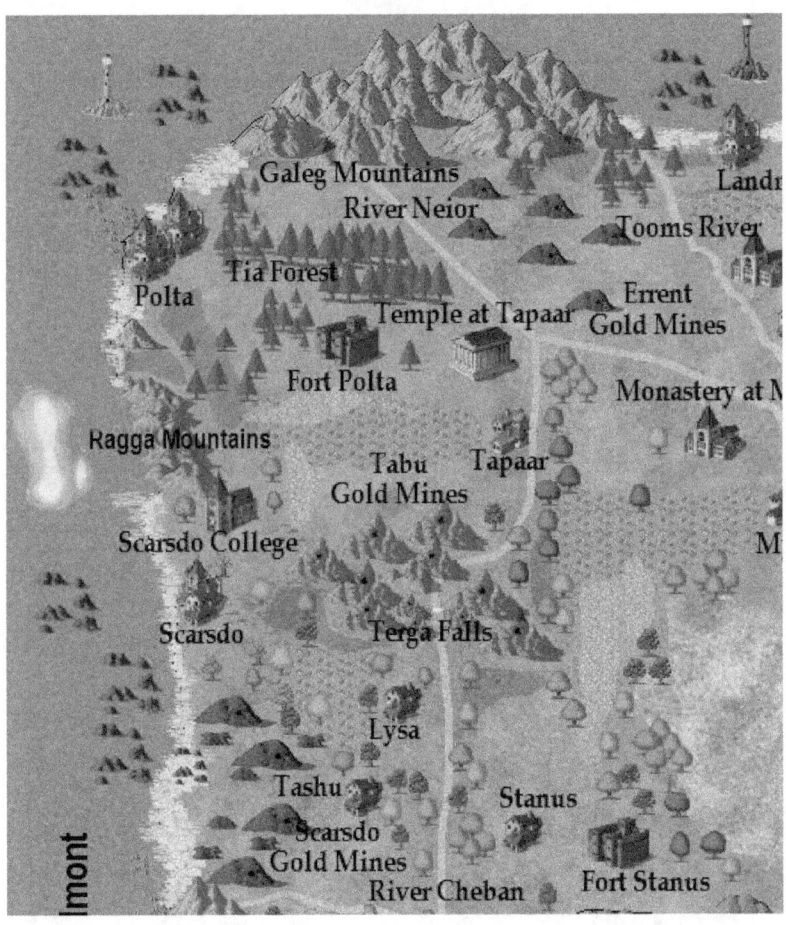

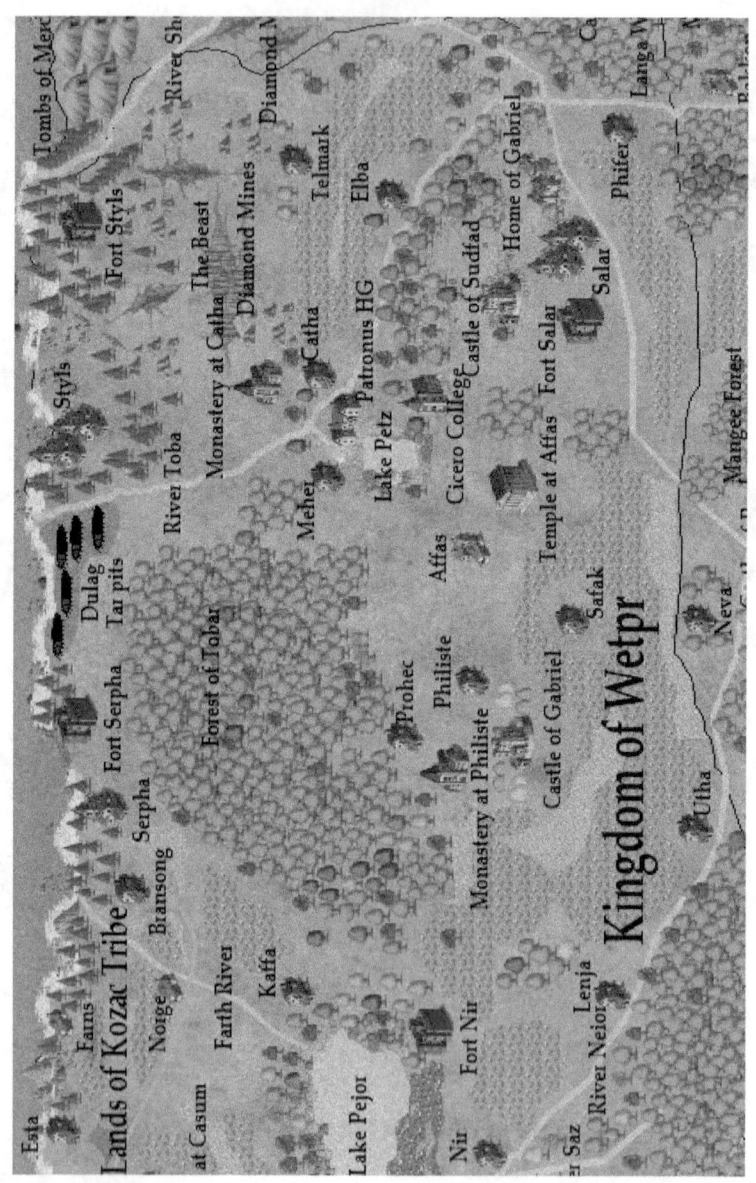

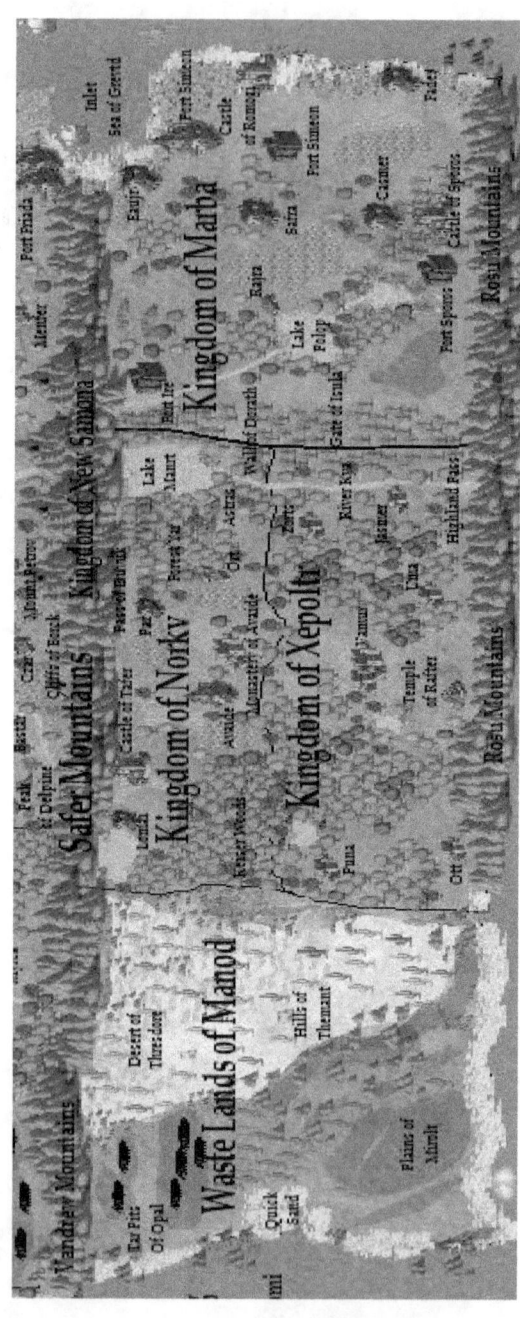

605

606

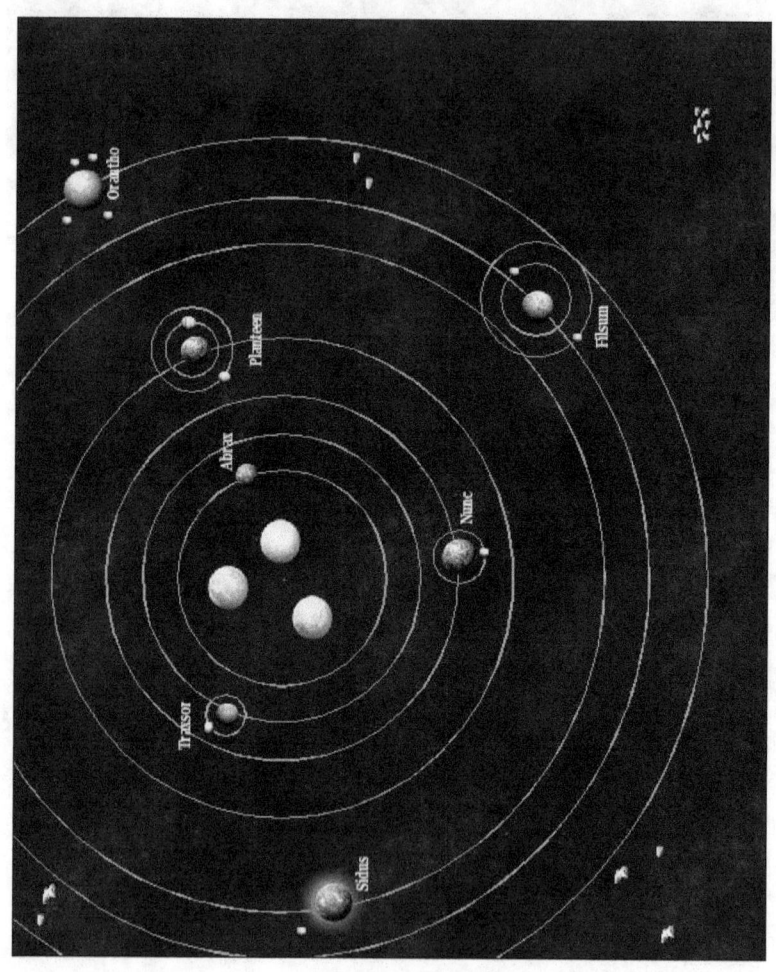